The Uncivil War of 2020

By Dr. Patrick Johnston

The Uncivil War of 2020
by Dr. Patrick Johnston

Published by
Right Remedy Publishing
5063 Dresden Court
Zanesville, Ohio 43701

ISBN: 978-1-4675-1159-9
First printing – November 6, 2012

Printed in the United States of America

To purchase the author's novels in bulk quantities, contact author through his website www.RightRemedy.org.

Special Thanks

Thank you, my dear editors: Cal Zastrow, Shirley and Tenney Fuller, Matt Byers, Cynthia Manion, Norman Myers, and my lovely daughters Charity and Anna.

As I wrote this final novel in the Trilogy, and came to grips with the necessity of godly leadership to avert divine judgment and preserve God's blessing of freedom for our posterity, I realize just how I have taken for granted those leaders who have impacted me over the years. My father, who prodded me onto a love of Scriptures and study; Chip Bueller and Ed, who introduced me to the fullness of the Holy Spirit; Cindy Wilkens, whose prophetic impact on me at Florida State University cannot be understated; Dan Young, who pastored me during my formative years in college and gave me a vision for a restored body of Christ; Jed Smock, whose theology and example equipped me to proclaim God's law and Gospel on the streets and on campus in the open-air; Pastor Bob Enyart, whose teaching on theonomy invited a transformation of my entire worldview; Pastor Matt Trewhella and Flip Benham, who provoked me to be God's prophetic oracle the nation; and Cal Zastrow, who helped me prioritize the discipleship of my children and imparted to me a vision for victory. Thank you.

Part I

The Red Carpet of Anarchy

1

Helena, Montana

Governor Benjamin Boswell huddled in the security of a secret underground bunker just northwest of Helena in a valley between two mountains. The stress of the direst straits of his life had thinned him down to his high school physique.

"They intend to destroy us," Guard General Bryan commented, his eyes fixed on the screen where they observed the images of federal fighters and bombers crossing the southern and eastern Coalition borders. He turned to a computer monitor to discover the vectors of the bombers' courses. "It looks like they're targeting our underground nuclear facilities, our Guard facilities, and our capitol buildings," he predicted, tapping on the screen with one hand and massaging his thick goatee with the other.

All eyes were fixed on the Coalition chairman, Ben Boswell, as if expecting him to snap his fingers and keep them safe from the predictable consequences of seceding from the United States.

The Texas Guard General who had fled to Montana, Alan MacIntosh, placed his hand over his sat phone's receiver and turned to Boswell. "We should have the missiles armed and ready any minute now, Governor."

Boswell sighed deeply and turned to his chief of staff. "Call her."

The buzz on the speakerphone was initially unwelcomed. "Madam President, it's Ben Boswell on a scrambled sat line."

The president was in a meeting with her Joint Chiefs, mulling over the evolving military scenarios. She was in her classic red dress, her shoulder-length blond hair sprayed as stiff as her plastic-surgeon-carved facial features. She nodded and smirked at the secretary's announcement, as if anticipating the interruption. "There he is now."

She picked up the phone enthusiastically, pleased to finally have the upper hand with the incorrigible Montana governor. She imagined her high heel shoe pressed over his lumpy neck as his face reddened and he gasped for mercy. The corners of her mouth rose involuntarily. "What a pleasant surprise, Governor Boswell," she said mockingly. The joint chiefs tapped earpieces over their ears to listen in to the conversation.

"Call off your bombers or we will fire on you."

She raised her eyebrows, surprised at his stubborn resilience. "*You* will fire on *me*?"

"You've got bombers striking at underground nuclear facilities in Salt Lake City and Boise, and you have others headed for Billings, Seattle, Spokane, Denver, Omaha – all of our capital cities…"

The president jolted. These were the targets of their stealth bombers. How did he discover the targets of their stealth bombers? Her brow wrinkled and her eyes darted to the Air Force general, who suddenly looked like a deer in the road hypnotized by approaching headlights.

Boswell read her thoughts. "Yes, we can see them. Call them off or we will fire one nuclear-warhead-armed ballistic missile at Washington, D.C. and another at Edwards in California…" Boswell kept his gaze fixed upon the satellite images projected on the white wall in their underground bunker. Governor Littman's former NASA engineer filtered the hijacked satellite imagery through experimental magnetic imaging technology, which allowed them to detect all flying metallic objects in CFCS air space.

President Brighton suspected he was bluffing. She glanced at the joint chiefs, most of whom shook their heads side to side, reinforcing to her their belief that it was impossible for the Coalition to arm and launch the stolen warheads so quickly. One of the generals shrugged, precipitating a hushed argument with another.

"Shhh!" the Air Force general ordered them.

The president's tone with Boswell was condescending. Trembling, she pressed the phone tight against her cheek. "Those warheads belong to the United States government!"

Boswell spoke calmly, "You've committed acts of aggression and war against this Coalition of sovereign Christian states."

"Trying to secede *is* an act of war!"

"We did not *try* to secede. We seceded, and we did so peacefully," he stated matter-of-factly, poking his index finger at where he imagined her face to be if he were face to face with her. "You have violently attacked us without provocation."

"What!" the president shouted. "There's violence against abortion providers and federal agents all across this nation because of–"

"Therefore–"

"... Because of you and your freakish Coalition!"

"Therefore," Boswell raised his voice over her interruption, "we are confiscating your weapons within our sovereign borders for our self-defense." Governor Boswell took a deep breath, trying to resist the urge to lash out angrily. "The burglarized have no duty to let lawless assailants use weapons in their own home against them."

"You have stolen at least *two*" – spite flew out of the corners of her mouth – "of America's nuclear warheads and you are about to face the most bitter of consequences!" she belted.

"No," – he shook his head – "they're still America's, they just belong to the *free* states of America now."

"Don't you think that we will retaliate?!" Her shrill, unpresidential tone frustrated the chiefs who sat around her, who paused their vigorous conspiring to cast a disapproving glance down their long noses at her.

"Just leave us alone, Madam President, and we'll leave you alone and have peace," Boswell assured her. "It's that simple."

"Have you lost your mind?" she screeched.

Boswell read a hand-written note that a Guard general handed him. "At least 100 Coalition citizens have been killed by your bombers thus far, not to mention the thousands slaughtered at your U.S. Marshall-guarded abortion clinics and your physician-assisted suicide mills masquerading as medical clinics. Didn't you expect us to defend the innocent?"

"I expected you to come to your senses and submit!"

"To a tyrant who attempts to disarm us and murder us?" He puffed out his cheeks. "Think again! I am willing to die for my cause – are you?" he challenged her. "You can't bluff me. The playing field's level now." He held the phone like a microphone and raised his voice directly into the receiver. "Call off your invasion force or I'm firing my missiles at you and destroying Washington, D.C.! End of debate!" He stood up as he continued, "If you think you can survive in your Pentagon bunker, you need to think again."

"You're crazy, Mr. Boswell! You say you want to protect the innocent unborn and the elderly – how many innocent Americans will perish if you launch a nuclear weapon?!" she screamed, her eyes darting from general to general in the underground war room. "You're freaking out the whole civilized world!"

"The choice is yours." He slammed the phone upon the cradle with a crash, startling the state leaders around him.

Boswell took a deep, uneasy breath. He glanced at General MacIntosh. "I'm sorry. I tried not to yell."

MacIntosh grinned and put a reassuring hand on the governor's shoulder. "You were calmer than I expected."

"God help us," Boswell mumbled, leaning over the desk toward the satellite imaging.

Moments passed and the fighter jets and bombers continued their present vector against their targets. On the screen, they saw some objects enter the western edge of the Coalition border. "General Bryan!" Boswell pointed at the screen. "What are those, coming from the ocean?"

Bryan put his intelligence officer in Washington State on hold. "That's what I'm on the phone about. Those are missiles coming from aircraft carriers in the Pacific."

The room full of state leaders gasped as Boswell's face reddened. "You tell them to get that warhead ready now! We have a cause worth dying for, gentlemen. They" – he extended his index finger toward the screen of red and white dots over a green outline of the Coalition's border – "do not."

"Yes sir." MacIntosh nodded.

"Tim?" Boswell called out to a communications officer.

"Yes sir?"

"Get David Jameson on the ringer and tell them to get everybody up and praying, now. Tell him we're in the midst of a crisis and we need every believer in the Coalition pounding heaven now for victory."

"Should I fill him in on the details?"

"No. Just let him know that this is ***the*** crisis for which we have been preparing, and without divine aid, the Coalition will not survive till morning."

"Oh God, hear our prayer!" David Jameson knelt, still in the sweat pants in which he slept, earnestly praying at the first stair of the altar of the largest church in Helena where they had been holding nightly meetings for Minutemen leadership training. Thousands of believers surrounded him, praying to be free, praying for protection, praying that the Coalition would survive the night. "Plead our cause with those who rise up against us," David pleaded fervently with his God, clasping his hands tightly together. "Defend us against those who seek to slay the innocent and enslave your people. Rise to help, for the sake of our children and our children's children…"

His mind rushed to thoughts of his wife and children as tears spilled down his cheeks and onto his beard. "Oh God, keep them safe, wherever they are."

He reached down beside him to pick up his black Bible so he could pray the words of Psalm 91 when a mini-DVD fell out of the pages. *What's this?* he wondered. He picked it up and flipped it over. The black words on the plastic yellow DVD jacket read, "It's about Darlene."

Darlene, my wife?

He put it in his pocket and reminded himself to look at it later, but the mysterious DVD occupied his mind for most of the night.

The faithful trickled into the church until there was no more room to kneel. They made their way into the Sunday School rooms and hallways, the nursery and the gymnasium. Phones rang and woke people up all night, and they got their coffee brewing and joined together to pray. The churches were soon filled with those who prayed as if their lives and their freedom depended on it. It certainly did.

"Do you realize how many will die if we fire nuclear warheads at D.C. and at Edwards?" General MacIntosh gently protested.

"If we lose tonight, the tyranny and the bloodshed will commence afresh in our states," Boswell reminded him. "They've slaughtered more Americans every year in the Abortion Holocaust than our bomb will slay to stop their Holocaust. Tonight, our faith puts God on the spot, and I believe He *will* show Himself strong on our behalf." He stood erect behind his desk, confidence emanating from his tone and demeanor. "If we're defeated in the end, at least D.C.'s destruction will give the next state who wants to secede a fightin' chance." His gaze shifted around the room, from state leader to state leader, searching their eyes for doubt or fear. When he saw the A.G. from the state of Utah trembling in his chair, Boswell clenched his fists and passionately pounded them against his wooden desk. "It's liberty or death, but either way, the blessing of God."

"Amen." General MacIntosh nodded, encouraged by the Coalition chairman's commitment to his mission.

General MacIntosh's aid handed him a satellite phone and he held it up to his ear. At the other end of the phone a guardsman lieutenant carefully observed six nuclear specialists as they meticulously unlocked, armed, and inserted a nuclear warhead into an intercontinental ballistic missile. Surrounding them were dozens of scientists and computer technicians offering assistance at a table full of manuals and laptop computers.

"How long, Lieutenant?"

"They say 20 minutes at the soonest."

MacIntosh turned to face Governor Boswell and spoke into the phone. "We don't have 20 minutes, Lieutenant."

Boswell overheard that estimate and told MacIntosh, "Tell them I need that ballistic missile armed and programmed for D.C. right now. Now!" As Boswell spoke, MacIntosh extended the phone toward him so that the Guard lieutenant could hear it straight from the Coalition chairman's mouth. "And I need a second one for Edwards Air Force Base in California right after it!"

MacIntosh put the phone back to his ear. "Did you hear that?"

"I heard it. We're going as fast as we can."

"I'm keeping this line open. You let me know when you're ready to fire."

General MacIntosh turned toward Governor Boswell and was taken aback at what he saw. The governor was on his knees in the middle of the room, hands clasped, and face grimaced in intense, silent prayer. They all stood and watched him for an uncomfortable moment. Then, one by one, the statesmen and Guard leaders walked over to him, got on their knees around him and joined him in prayer for victory.

Four months earlier…

The governors of Washington, Idaho, Montana, Utah, Wyoming, Nebraska, Arizona, and both Dakotas were discussing their options through a secure internet connection. A few trustworthy cabinet members and U.S. congressmen and women from those states were also represented, invited to participate on condition of maintaining absolute secrecy. Each governor's computer monitor showed all of the faces of the other leaders. With the relentless FBI and ATF firearm confiscation raids and with the credible Bureau agent leaking that the explosion at the

Reproductive Rights Convention in Ohio was an accident, tempers were high. They were fed up with Margaret Brighton's usurpations and Congress' cowardice. But fear of the repercussions kept them from unanimity.

"We're crazy if we think that the federal government is just going to let us leave. Shouldn't Texas and South Carolina have taught us something?" Governor MacKenzie of Nebraska, the most cautious of the Coalition's governors, was not so easily swayed by the Montana governor's arguments.

"There's power in numbers, gentlemen," responded Governor Boswell soberly. "Of the 37 states in the country that have passed sovereignty resolutions since 2009, 26 have added teeth to them. We have a block of nine adjoining states here that have laws in our legislatures to resist the federal government in many areas. That alone will give us major bartering power with them. They're not going to make war against nine sovereign states. Texas and South Carolina were acting unilaterally."

"Why did you call us a Coalition of Free ***Christian*** States? Why Christian? I thought we agreed to the title, Coalition of Free States?" complained Governor Jungling, the six and a half foot tall former reverend who was governor of Wyoming.

"Call it a divinely-inspired mistake," Boswell responded with a smile. "According to several large polls, most of our people – including your constituents in Wyoming – love the title." A few of the government leaders frowned.

"I love it!" James Knight exclaimed. The Wyoming governor turned his attention to his state's favorite statesman and his protest was silenced. "The charters of the 13 colonies, the Mayflower compact, the founding documents of this nation – all confirm that we, at least at one time, were a Christian nation. In 1892, the Supreme Court said, 'This *is* a Christian nation.' Let us not forget that in the past six months a major spiritual awakening has swept our people off their feet in love with the Savior, and our Coalition is the fruit of that work of God's Spirit. The Lord deserves the honor and glory for what He's done here."

"He's right," said the governor of North Dakota. "We need to build upon the proper foundation from the start. 'Blessed is the nation whose God is the Lord.'"

The governor of Idaho, usually reserved, was enthusiastic. "My people love the title."

"All right." Governor Jungling of Wyoming found the Idaho governor's broad grin contagious.

"The threat alone," Boswell asserted, "of a block of nine sovereign states seceding will be as far as we have to go." After a pause, he cautiously added, "Probably."

"Make that ten." Montana's attorney general, Chad Dreifuss, leaned against the wall across Boswell's office with a Bluetooth in his ear.

"Make that ten!" Governor Boswell repeated, smiling into the camera affixed to the top of his monitor.

"Who?" asked several governors simultaneously.

Boswell glanced over at his A.G., one of the most respected men in his cabinet, awaiting the answer to that question. Dreifuss stepped a few strides closer to Boswell. "I'm on hold with Colorado's A.G., who just informed me that Governor Gary Wilson will be joining you momentarily. Their legislature passed a resolution today that they are to cooperate with the Coalition in asserting their state's sovereign rights."

"Governor Wilson will be joining us momentarily," Governor Boswell informed the others with a smile that revealed his gold-capped molars.

"Great!"

"Praise God!"

"We can learn from Henry Adams' mistakes," Boswell assured them. "We know the damage a single non-allegiant informant can do. We must make sure that those in our inner circle agree with our vision of a sovereign state that respects the laws of God. We know the importance of a well trained, complicit State Guard and Highway Patrol, should any conflict arise. We must also make it plain to the feds that we are perfectly content to stay in the United States if we are allowed to outlaw abortion and physician-assisted suicide within our borders."

"They gotta let us keep our arms, too," someone added.

"…And ban gay marriage."

"…And have free speech…"

"…And get the U.S. out of the UN…"

"…And have sound money…"

The governor of Nebraska laughed. "There goes your dream of makin' peace with the Union."

Boswell heaved a weary sigh. "Some issues justify secession, some may not. The shedding of innocent blood is one sin that will bring God's wrath against us, so that's priority. Remember, as long as innocent children are killed in our state, we don't deserve liberty. Protecting the innocent within our lawful jurisdiction is a priority."

Governor Pollock of Idaho leaned into the microphone on his desk. "Do you think Margaret Brighton would ever let a state leave without unleashing all of the might of the United States military on them, as she has done in Texas and South Carolina?"

James Knight chimed in: "Win or lose, it is better to walk in Henry Adams' footsteps for the right cause than to lose for lack of trying because of fear and unbelief."

"I agree," said Boswell. "If God is for us, then who can be against us? Let us remember that the measure of success is not victory and independence; it's God being for us. It is better to have the blessing of God in defeat than *not* have the blessing of God in peace."

Those eloquent words were hard words to hear, but several of the governors exhaled "Amen" nonetheless.

"If we do secede and employ force," Boswell said, "it will only be done defensively to protect the innocent. That was Henry Adams' strategy, and I agree with it. The president has been aggressive with Texas and South Carolina because she wants to set a precedent that would frighten off other states tempted to resist. If we allow ourselves to be intimidated, then Henry Adams has suffered for nothing."

The silence that followed that comment was telling. Those men respected and admired the Texas governor, the famed Henry Adams. His bravery had been a reproof to their cowardice, and they were different men: confident, determined, and prayerful.

"A seed provides very little benefit on its own, but if it falls into the ground and dies, it brings forth much fruit." They all understood the relevance of Boswell's paraphrase of Jesus' words. They and their brave constituents were the fruit of Henry Adams's labors.

"The president has postponed her disarmament deadline to August 1st in the Coalition states," Governor Jungling of Wyoming reminded them. "That's just one week away. If the feds take away the right to keep and bear arms, then we ultimately lose every other right worth defending because we lose the ability to defend it."

The live video feed of the governor of Colorado popped up on their computer screens, and Boswell welcomed him. "Good to have you with us, Governor Wilson."

"Thank you." He briefly removed the half-burnt cigar from between his lips so he could speak his gratitude without his characteristic mumble. "It's an honor." He never inhaled it, but when the federal government banned smoking in state government buildings and his legislature defied the feds in allowing it, he was proud to display his iconic political incorrectness as a celebration of "states' rights." "Mr. Dreifuss has briefed me on your discussion to this point. Please continue where you were."

"Has it occurred to anyone here that our armed forces do not even comprise a fraction of the size of the federal military?" said the governor of Nebraska. "The number of federal military personnel is greater than the entire population of Montana and North Dakota combined. The armed forces of the United States receive over half of the military expenditure of the whole world…"

"And they are spread all over the world in over 130 countries," the governor of Idaho reminded them.

"We need to bring our state guards together for cooperative training," Boswell proposed. "We each have to implement a careful inventory of our resources to precisely determine our capabilities."

"I'm sure my state's on the federal government's high value list," Governor Wilson of Colorado admitted. "We have the most critical defense installations in the country."

"Yes, you're vulnerable." Boswell nodded.

The Colorado governor removed his half-burnt cigar momentarily. "We were the first state to de-criminalize abortion in 1967, and so it'd be an honor to be the state that sacrifices the most to re-criminalize it."

"Washington State's participation in the Coalition may be brief," admitted Governor Frank Littman. He wanted to prepare them for the potential that they would have to withdraw from the Coalition. "I'm under vigorous scrutiny and opposition whatever I do as a Christian conservative, but my involvement in the Coalition riles up the hornet's nest unlike anything I have ever seen. I have a very strong backing from the Christian community and have a slim majority in the House who are supportive, but not the state Senate, where there has been serious attempts to impeach me. Even if I remain in power, it wouldn't surprise me a bit if our entire Guard force has to spend most of its time in Seattle just trying to stop riots."

"Riots are the least of our worries," the pessimistic governor from Nebraska responded. "We could be hiding from stealth bombers by the end of the month. We could be brought up on crimes of treason."

"So could have George Washington and Patrick Henry," Congressman Knight reminded them. "Liberty requires the brave to risk much to preserve. Tyrants do not surrender God-given liberties to their subjects easily."

"I'm having a list of grievances against the federal government faxed to each of your offices as we speak," said Boswell. "Please give them careful consideration. Make a list of non-negotiable priorities, as not all of our grievances justify secession, and it may weaken our moral authority if we dilute our strongest objections with weaker grievances. Discuss these with your cabinets and your legislatures. Jot down any changes you would like to make. We will discuss this again tomorrow evening. We can't do this on our own strength, so implore your legislatures and our citizens to pray fervently for God's assistance. The battle belongs to the Lord."

Austin, Texas

"Who took it? Tell me now!" The German-accented English perfectly accentuated the fear that the guard's voice shot out like shrapnel at the rows of prisoners that stood in front of her. The UN guard, trembling with rage, grasped her short leather strap as if it were a snake that would bite her if she loosened her grip. Before her stood 50 female recalcitrant hate-speech offenders, who cowered for fear of the threatened abuse.

Darlene Jameson stood on the end of the third row, stiff as a board, careful not to swat at the mosquitoes that lazily sucked the blood from her arms and legs. Any extraneous movement during 6 a.m. morning roll call was harshly punished with a vicious lash across the back or a loss of a meal.

The guard began to thrash her whip through the air in front of her, as if warming up for the 25 lashes she was about to deliver to the soft-skinned American woman whose hunger pains had tempted her to steal. "We know that one of you took from the kitchen! We are reviewing the videos and we will discover who did it. Admit your crime now, and you will receive the mandated penalty. Come on! I'm tired of waiting. Let's get this over with."

The guard stopped in front of a frail African American woman at the front of Darlene's line. The guard pointed the stiff belt at her face. "If you do not confess, and we are forced to discover your identity through the security footage, then we will *double* your punishment!"

The horrified gasps rose from the crowd and made the guard grin mischievously. She thrived off of her power to make these proud

American traitors tremble. When she was done with them, these religious fanatics would worship at her feet for a crumb of bread.

"It wasn't me!" The African American woman in front of the guard began to weep for fear. "It wasn't me!"

The guard snarled, and delivered a swift swing of her leather belt against the side of the woman. The belt wrapped around her side and smacked against her lower back, causing her to scream and lurch to the side. "I'm sorry, I'm sorry!" the woman wailed as she tried to step back into line.

The guard screamed in her face, "Did I give you permission to speak? No! Now, tell me," – the guard began to pace back and forth again in front of the crowd – "who took the food?!"

After her first several weeks of constant hellish interrogations, Darlene Jameson had been sent to this outdoor detention facility south of Austin. The consensus of her inquisitors was that she had been telling the truth. She beat all their expectations in holding up under intense physical and mental pressure. She knew the only way she would ever see her children again was if she followed her husband's instructions and repudiated his views. It was extremely difficult, but through every scream, every water-board drowning, every electric shock and psychological torture, she held out, clinging to Jesus with all her heart.

The five-acre outdoor detention facility was built like a concentration camp – recalcitrant hate-speech violators, traitors, and gun criminals packed into bunks like sardines, guarded by foreigners donning baby blue UN helmets. An hour of NEA-directed tolerance and sensitivity seminars followed roll call, and then the criminals were filed into various work details to help defer the cost of their re-education and incarceration. Unbeknownst to most of the staff and all of the inmates, the entire facility was designed to find a way to coerce Darlene Jameson into telling the interrogators where to find her husband. Well-concealed video cameras and microphones were set up all around the camp. A whole team of federal investigators scoured every aspect of Darlene's conversations to try to discover any clue as to her husband's whereabouts. If the investigators discovered that Darlene befriended one prisoner more than the others, they would torture that prisoner if necessary to force them to cooperate to make Darlene talk. The president wanted daily updates on any intelligence gained; their federal jobs and generous benefits packages were on the line.

Darlene was assigned the duty of using a sewing machine to sew loops onto camouflage pants for military personnel. Compared to weeks of constant interrogation, life at this outdoor detention facility was country-club living. However, this morning's routine was interrupted with the theft of food, and tensions were high while everyone waited for the unfortunate thief to confess.

"Have you made any headway?" The FBI investigator stepped into the dark room at the crack of dawn, sipping his first cup of coffee. He leaned against the table upon which six flat screens were erected.

The subordinate in the swivel chair removed his headset. He took a deep breath, weary from his night watch. "I'm sorry, sir?"

"I asked if you made any headway with her through the night?"

The junior agent sighed and kept his gaze fixed on the screens. "She's befriended a couple of prisoners, but she's keeping quiet about anything worth listening to."

The senior investigator saw the screen where the 50 female prisoners were lined up for roll call. "What's Sergeant Hitler there blarin' about?" He motioned to the German guard with the whip in front of the prisoners.

"Someone took some food." The junior agent leaned forward and rubbed his eyes. "No!" He quickly brought one of the earmuffs up to his right ear. "Oh, good grief. What is she doing?"

Darlene raised her hand on the edge of her row. "I took it." She stepped out of line, walked up to the guard and admitted, "I took the food. I'm sorry."

Two UN guards marched up to Darlene, dutifully grabbed her wrists, and led her to the post directly in front of the rows of inmates.

The German guard did not look pleased with Darlene's confession. The guard rolled her eyes and cursed under her breath. This was one of the few UN guards who knew that this entire work camp was set up to try to discover ways to make Darlene spill what she knew. She knew Darlene like the back of her hand. Darlene's shirt was pulled down to her waist and her hands were bound to a metal hook on the backside of the post. The German guard handed her stiff leather belt to a tall, lanky guard. Darlene would be this week's second object lesson on stealing. "This is the punishment," she told the crowd, "for theft."

As the tall guard rolled up her sleeves, Darlene took a deep breath and turned her gaze to heaven. Her lips mumbled a quiet prayer for strength. For her babies. For her husband. Her back was already criss-crossed with scabby strips and long pink scars.

* * * * *

"There comes a time in societies when peaceable means fail that violent democratic upheaval becomes necessary to assert the rights of the people." Professor Paine paced across the front of his 20th century history class, smacking a ruler against his palm. As a leader of the "Occupy" movement and a public defender of the more radical elements of the environmental, pro-choice, and pro-gay agenda, this was a topic near and dear to him. "When the establishment fights progress because it wants business as usual, someone has to stand for the people. The people." He paused and started his way down the aisle toward the rear of the building. "They have the interests of the democracy, the poor, and the powerless at the forefront of their thoughts. The establishment only sees money." He rubbed his thumb and index finger together. "The people want peace; the establishment wants wars because it sells the weapons. The people want education, but the establishment thrives on the ignorance of the masses to supply the work force for their sweatshops. The people want better pay and better benefits, but the establishment wants more work from their employees for less money." He sneered as he turned in the aisle and made his way back toward the front. "The people want freedom, but the establishment wants slavery, business as usual.

"But how can the people compete with their bosses and their bosses' bosses? They lack the influence to promote a massive boycott. They lack the funds to buy them out. They lack the power to make the bosses of the bosses relinquish the love of the billion-dollar-bill for the good of the people. What do they have?" He continued to smugly smack the wooden ruler against the palm of his hand. "How can the people compete with the CEO's, their attorneys, accountants, and the whole army of capitalist exploiters?" No one ventured to propose an answer to the rhetorical question.

His cell phone vibrated and he unlatched it. Glancing at the caller ID, he noticed that it had a Washington, D.C. area code. He handed it to a flamboyant grad student in a colorful rainbow-dyed shirt who sat in the front row. "Find out what they want." The young man took the phone from him and walked from the room.

"Take the ruler company." Professor Paine raised his ruler into the air. "The ruler company doesn't care about trees, because it is cheaper to exploit another third-world forest than it is to replenish the one they just devastated. The ruler company doesn't care about child labor laws, they don't care about sex discrimination, and they don't care about safe workplaces. They only care about the dollar. What power do you have to change them? Who can afford the mercenaries that could compete with theirs? They have the governments fighting their wars – the little man doesn't stand a chance. But if one of you took a ruler, and" – he raised his ruler into the air with both hands, and then snapped the ruler in half – "a few others liked the sound, and they snapped a few more, and then hundreds, even thousands of Americans walked into the Walmart and K-Mart and University Bookstore and snapped a ruler or two, that kind of thing could really catch on." He picked up half of his broken ruler and held it with both hands. "The people might not dig a boycott, but" – snap! – "it sure can be fun to snap a few rulers." The class was pleasantly amused with their professor's creativity.

"Sometimes, when peaceful means fail to produce a successful change, violent means become necessary. That's what we've seen in 'the Arab spring.' That's what we've seen time and time again when third world nations evolved away from their religious traditions to become more progressive. It often took raw democratic violence."

The professor raised half of his ruler and studied it for a moment. "When a Christian sees a hippy snap a ruler in the bookstore, he says, 'Thou shalt not steal.' When a Taliban imam sees a ruler, he says, 'I'm going to hit my wife with that ruler.'" The class chuckled in spite of his political incorrectness. "When a Buddhist sees a ruler, he says, 'There is no ruler!'" Again, they laughed. "When I see a ruler," – he paused and then repeated slowly and purposefully – "when I see a ruler, I see a broken ruler." He tossed one half of the ruler over his shoulder. "A broken *rule*." Then, pointing the other half of the fractured ruler heavenward, he said with drama, "A broken *Ruler*." Students throughout the auditorium applauded to express their approval of their beloved professor's irreverent poetry.

He clenched his fingers around his fractured ruler and passionately raised his fist into the air. "I see the people's power, the people's influence, and the people's progress. When I see a broken ruler, I see the rule of the people. Raw democratic violence can be a legitimate steppingstone for the people's progress." He paused to glance at his watch. "Well, I'm going to let you out a little bit early today. About half of you still need to make an appointment with me to discuss the topic of your term paper." The students began to gather their books in preparation to leave. "I want some imaginative topics, all right? Expand your mind. *Gaia* will help you," he remarked slyly, gaining the flirtatious grin of a curvy brunette in the front of the class.

"Professor Paine?" The grad student who took the professor's phone call tapped him on the shoulder.

"What?" The professor seemed irritated with the distraction.

"You're going to want to call them back right away." The student's mischievous grin sparked his curiosity.

"Who was it?"

"You wouldn't believe me if I told you."

Aurora, Illinois

The media hype about the formation of the Coalition of Free Christian States had fascinated Arnie York, but he still judged them to be cowards. Why all this dancing about the main issue? Why ignore the elephant in the room? Babies are dying every day at the hands of bloodthirsty doctors and the tyrants who defend them, and we want to debate constitutional law and federal jurisdiction? Where's our sense of urgency about the Abortion Holocaust? Where's our pity for the 3,500 babies that are ripped to pieces every day while we debate the legalese on a piece of paper? What if it were our child on the abortionist's chopping block? Would we then be inclined to stop debating and start acting in their defense?

The 24-year-old, 155-pound dirty blond hoped that Governor Boswell would win, but in the big scheme of things, he and all those big mouth cowboys in the statehouses out west were part of the problem. They claimed that abortion is murder, but they wouldn't act like it. Compassion provoked this young man to what he considered a more appropriate response.

Three weeks ago, when he shot the abortionist in between the eyes as he blew out his birthday candles, the media labeled him the Chicago Sniper. He was amazed at how easy it was to do and get away with it. He'd only read a few books about sniping and had seen a few movies. One thing he learned was the necessity of being discrete. Be a master of camouflage. Move slowly. Don't attract attention to yourself. Be patient. Wait for the perfect opportunity. Don't pull the trigger for anything less than a sure kill. And do not pull the trigger unless you are sure that you can get away to kill another day. Don't give away your secrets to anybody. And never, ever strike twice from the same position. Be unpredictable.

The past year, he had carefully prepared for this role. He quit protesting abortion clinics and was careful to diligently defend unconditional pacifism among his friends. Suspecting that at least one of his acquaintances must be one of the ubiquitous FBI informers that he just knew filled the ranks of pro-life activists, he even risked fierce arguments to defend pacifist submission to judicial tyranny. He even took some of his friends with him to sell his prized possessions at a gun show, keeping only what was absolutely necessary for his mission. He intended to be the last person to ever be suspected of shooting abortion doctors.

For many weeks, Arnie followed a gray-haired gynecologist from Rockford, Illinois, who was traveling around to different women's health clinics performing about 150 abortions weekly. He had gotten a good grasp on the doctor's predictable pattern. Then Arnie took six weeks off. He knew that when the physician was eliminated, the FBI investigators would want all the surveillance videos that captured images of the abortionist's trips to and from clinics. They would pour over those videos looking for someone stalking him.

It was 7:05 p.m. – the sun had just set and darkness was falling quickly. The abortionist walked out of the Aurora Women's Clinic and shook the hand of the U.S. Marshall that was assigned to him. The Marshall stepped into his unmarked car and drove off as the physician waved. "See you tomorrow."

"No, you won't," mumbled the self-proclaimed baby-defender under his breath. The doctor was 50 yards away, but the powerful binoculars brought him up close. To this young man, the dilemma had a clear-cut solution. The strong should defend the weak. He was the defender of the slaughtered children – a freedom fighter. The death of one baby-butcher meant hundreds, or maybe even a thousand babies would live who would otherwise have died. At least they lived longer anyway. The killing of one baby-butcher meant dozens, or maybe even hundreds retired from the baby-killing business, and even more refused to consider going into the abortion industry. The riskier the baby-killing business becomes, the less likely that people would be willing to take the risk. It was a statistical fact, and perfectly reasonable in light of human nature. The love of money was the root of all evil, and what good was money if you weren't around to spend it? To keep the baby-butchers in business, the demand side would have to cough up more money to compensate for the increased risk for the supply side. Making abortion more costly saved lives.

He thought for a moment about that big target – the one for which all lesser targets were simply training. He fantasized of taking out one of the Supreme Court justices who had perpetuated *Roe vs. Wade*. He had memorized the names and faces of those murderers, just in case fate would ever allow him to see one through a crowded restaurant, or find one pumping gas at a fuel station.

Who was it that said, "Forceful means become necessary once peaceful means become illegal?" Was it John Kennedy? I think it was.

Arnie shook his head to try to focus. His thoughts were taking over again. He was so scatter-brained. He hated that about himself. Maybe he should have stayed on that medicine the psychiatrist prescribed for him.

He took a deep breath and gripped his rifle tightly as he peered through the scope in a murky ditch between the highway and the entrance ramp.

For years, he only dreamed of fighting abortion with violence. He thought that he would never actually be able to pull the trigger. Was he ever wrong. He couldn't wait to pull that trigger and see the baby-killer's head explode in a cloud of blood and tissue. *I'm pro-choice when it comes to aborting abortion doctors,* he thought to himself with a crooked grin. *Keep your laws off my body.* He chuckled at his own sadistic humor.

He watched the doctor pull out of the parking lot onto the four-lane highway. He set his gun down on its bipod and followed the physician with his binoculars. The doctor would go out of his field of vision for about 20 seconds, during which time he would take two lefts, and then take the on-ramp to the interstate. It was there that the physician was most vulnerable. It was there that the baby-defender was best camouflaged and an escape route most accessible.

The young man was using his .22 magnum for this mission. The smaller caliber was all that was necessary from this distance through an open window – the doctor always drove with his window open if the weather was mild. It also made a softer sound, which would attract less attention. He put the crosshairs exactly where he expected the physician's forehead to appear directly under the streetlamp, as he would slow down for the sharp turn of the on-ramp. He took a deep breath, and went through the calculations again. *Sixty-five feet away, eight feet of elevation, the target will be about four feet off the ground...*

He grinned excitedly and whispered to himself, “If you think it’s wrong, then don’t do it. There’s no such thing as absolute truth.”

Ten seconds later, the despised face came into view. He double-checked to confirm that no cars were following. “The question is not whether aborting abortionists is right or wrong, but who decides?” he mumbled. His countenance became more sober as the much-anticipated moment approached.

“We don’t really know when life begins anyway, do we?”

A steady hand, an unblinking eye, a soft trigger collapses, a faint thump in the distance, and the car careens off the road through a shallow ditch and comes to a stop about 40 feet from him.

Bingo! That’s 100 appointments cancelled and 100 babies saved.

The 24-year-old then quickly took two more shots to put out the headlights. He stretched a gloved fist over the ground and opened his palm, and three Scrabble pieces dropped haphazardly onto the damp grass. Three letters, scrubbed of fingerprints – A, O, and Y – were the initials of his name, Arnie Oswald York. He found it humorous that the media would be so quick to consider those letters evidence of a grand, nationwide conspiracy of violence against abortionists. They would never even consider that those were the initials of the avenger of innocent blood. *How amusing!* It must have been fate, thought Arnie, that his initials were identical with the acronym of the name of the infamous “Army of Yahweh.” The group was thought to be a well-organized underground of violent anti-abortionists, but in fact was just a website managed by a few disgruntled abortion clinic bombers on parole too cowardly to practice what they preach. They were useful, he thought. He’d do the exploits and they’d defend it on the news, much to the chagrin of hordes of pro-life leaders and their army of activists and donors.

It’d be morning before the abortionist’s wife would find him missing. And from what Arnie learned of the couple, she’d probably blame his mistress. There would be plenty of time for him to wipe his tracks and make his get-a-way. He’d be stalking his next target by the time it hit the papers.

Austin, Texas

"Oh, Darlene. Why did you do it?" Janet, a pastor's wife that Darlene befriended, dabbed Darlene's bloody stripes in the dark after the day's labor ended. "Your skin's as soft as paper tissue," she whispered. "Everyone knows you didn't steal any food."

"Jesus suffered for my sin," Darlene responded softly. "I am honored to suffer for someone else's sin. Honored."

The pastor's wife protested Darlene's implication. "Sin? Do you really think it's a sin to steal food from foreign soldiers? We're starving to death."

"Shhh. You'll wake the others."

"What they are doing to us is wrong, Darlene. They have stolen your children. They have tortured you. You don't owe them anything."

"I'd gladly give my life if just one of them would turn to God, Janet. If I save my life, I lose it; but if I lose my life for the Gospel, I save it. Maybe the salvation of just one of these guards is why God put us here, Janet."

"What?" Janet dropped her bloody rag into the bowl of water on the floor beside the bed. "You're confusing God and the devil, Darlene. It's the devil that conspires to inflict pain on innocent people. God is a God of love. At least, I always thought so. I'm beginning to doubt that."

"Oh, Janet, don't say such a thing." Darlene sat up and grasped Janet's wet hands. "If you lose faith in God's love, then you will lose

God's blessing. Nothing can separate us from the love of God – nothing."

Janet shook her head, aghast at how this woman could speak of love while saturated in cruelty behind this barbed wire.

"The Lord loves these women, Janet, and we must always pray for them. Love your enemies, Jesus said." Janet searched the shadowy figures of Darlene's face in the darkening room as the emotion in Darlene's voice strung a chord in her own heart. "I feel sorry for these UN, Janet. So many of them are suffering so much. They may have never even heard the Gospel. They don't have husbands that love them like our husbands love us…"

"*They're* suffering?" Janet couldn't believe her ears. "What about us? What about you? They've made our lives a living hell!"

"Shhh. Keep your voice down."

They watched the shadow of a fellow prisoner step away from a bunk across the room, and make her way toward them. "I'm sorry," Darlene said, worried that their chatter had awakened a fellow inmate. She put her shirt back on with a painful grunt.

The approaching prisoner tiptoed to Darlene's bed and fell to her knees beside it. She was sobbing. "I'm the one that should be sorry." She wept bitter tears as she buried her face in Darlene's sheets to try to quiet her sobs.

"Is that you, Wilma?"

Darlene placed a palm on her head and felt her head nod. Darlene reached for the frail woman with both hands. "Oh, dear, why? What happened?" She lifted her face with her hands.

"*I* took the food," the woman confessed. "They beat you for what *I* did. I was just so, so hungry…"

"Shhh." Janet urged Wilma to whisper quietly.

Darlene smiled and wrapped her arms around Wilma's frail shoulders. "Oh Wilma, you just made me feel so much better," Darlene exclaimed with a joyful tone.

"Feel better?" The woman stopped her weeping and drew nearer to Darlene's face to try to make out her facial cues. "How did I do that?"

"By letting me know whose back was spared the whip because I offered mine. Oh, if you only knew, you have thrilled my soul so much." Darlene's voice choked with emotion as she knelt beside Wilma.

The woman wept afresh, and Darlene began to pray. "Oh, Lord, bless Wilma. Let her feel your arms of love about her. Fill her with faith for her family. Let her fear be replaced with confidence in Your love.

When the devil tries to seduce her into sin and unbelief, let her remember so vividly the stripes your Son endured for our healing and forgiveness…" Janet just sat on the edge of the bed in silence, awed by Darlene's magnetism.

Darlene finished her prayer, hugged Wilma once more, and the woman hobbled across the room back to her bunk. As Darlene got back into her bed, she mumbled, "Lord, bless her." She looked at Janet. "Now, that was worth 25 stripes, wouldn't you say?"

An uneasy silence punctuated Darlene's piercing words. Janet sighed heavily in the darkness. "If you say so," she mumbled.

Darlene could sense her conflicting emotions. "Janet, I want you to listen to me. I have never felt closer to the Lord since I have been separated from my family and made to suffer so much. His love fills me to overflowing sometimes, so much that I feel like I just can't stand it."

Janet was silent.

"Janet, I want you to pray with me, and confess any bitterness that you have in your heart. If God takes something away from us and it makes us angry toward Him, then that thing was an idol, whether it be our husbands, our children, our health, our ministries, or our houses and wealth. Let's ask the Lord to take away our fear and bitterness and give us the peace that passes understanding and the joy of our salvation. Let's commit our families to the Lord, and He will take care of them. Oh, can't you sense God's smile on us right now?" Darlene reached for her hands and squeezed them gently in her own, as tears of gratitude began to flow down Darlene's cheeks.

Janet was reluctant to fully engage in the conversation. The sacrifice appeared too costly. She closed her eyes tightly and forced her thoughts to other things as Darlene began to pour her heart out before the Lord. Momentarily, Janet found herself unable to maintain her emotional distance from her friend. She took a deep breath and began to soak in Darlene's spirit, feeling like she was being ushered into a king's feast hand-in-hand with the king's daughter.

* * * * *

The three Jameson girls had been sent to bed early. Their foster parents were out of town for the evening and the hired baby-sitter was reclining on the couch with her new boyfriend. The foul words and the violent screaming that they could overhear on the television were as foreign to the Jameson girls as fornicating baby-sitters.

"Mommy," the youngest child began to cry out fearfully. "Mommy…"

The eldest, five-year-old Charlotte crawled down the ladder out of the top bunk and walked over to the crib where her baby sister tried to rest. She leaned over it and put her finger in Johanna's palm. "I'm here, Johanna." Mary had crawled out of the lower bunk bed and hobbled over to her big sister. Mary wrapped her right arm around Char's waist.

"I want Mommy," Mary mumbled. "Why won't Mommy and Daddy come get us?" Mary and Johanna began to cry with longing.

"Shhh. Keep quiet," Charlotte said as she stroked Mary's head with one hand and squeezed Johanna's fingers gently with the other. She cast a glance over the shoulder at the sliver of evil light and noise that emanated underneath their bedroom door.

Char got on her knees and wrapped her arms around Mary. "Shhh. It's okay."

Johanna grew envious of the attention Mary was receiving, so she stood up and reached over the top of the crib with both arms, begging to be held. Charlotte picked her up and they all climbed into Mary's bottom bunk together. They pulled a blanket over their heads, and Char sang "Jesus Loves Me" until the others slept peacefully.

Now that Char was the only child awake, the sounds of the climax of the horror movie outside her door made her more frightful. She began to cry pitifully, turning her head and burying her sobs in her pillow to keep from waking her sisters. "Oh Jesus," she prayed through the tears, "help Mommy and Daddy to find us."

Great Falls, Montana

"Jesus would never employ violence to start his own nation!" The pacifist pastor of First Community Church in Great Falls was the most vocal opponent of the Coalition. This was a conference of church officials from every Christian denomination in Montana. A panel of leaders gathered around several large tables on a stage, before which thousands of Christian pastors and elders sat, prayerfully weighing the arguments their denominational leaders and bishops presented, preparing for the Q & A that would follow the discussion. "You're no better than those crazies who are murdering abortionists for whom Christ died!" The ad hominem rebuke provoked moans of disapproval throughout the auditorium.

"Not so fast, Pastor Dustin–"

"What would Jesus do?" The aging, well-respected pastor of the largest church in town tapped his finger on the table in front of him. "That's the question on the table."

"Listen, Pastor Dustin." Chad Dreifuss, the Montana Attorney General, was present to represent the views of Governor Ben Boswell and the state legislature. As a former pastor who knew many of the denominational leaders personally, he felt right at home. "We're not going to be able to communicate effectively if we continue to misunderstand each other. No one's talking about using violence to start a new nation. We are pursuing a peaceful resolution to protect the innocent preborn."

"You know your so-called peaceful resolution may mean invasion and war."

"If so, that's not of our doing."

"And you know that Montana will defend itself if war is waged on us."

Dreifuss nodded. "Only to protect the innocent and defend God-given rights. That's a lawful and biblical use of force."

Pastor Dustin waved his hands at the mass of pastors and elders who sat on the edge of their seats before them. "How can we, as people of God, defend violence even as a last resort? We need to stick with preaching the Gospel and stay out of political matters. Jesus is coming very soon – I'm sure of it! We need to just stick with converting sinners and get out of the politicians' squabbles. The Bible says Satan's the god of this world. Let's keep our eyes on heaven…"

"False god," another pastor on the stage rebutted. "Satan's the *false* god of this world. Jesus is King of kings and Lord of lords, and thou shalt have no other gods before Him." That comment unleashed a roar of vigorous applause that would not subside for several minutes.

The vice president of a charismatic denomination sympathetic to Dreifuss' arguments leaned into the microphone. Dreifuss held his peace and nodded at him. "Where in the Bible, Brother Dustin, does it speak of the soon coming Savior as an excuse for tolerating injustice and mass murder? Does the nearness of Christ's coming mitigate our obligation to protect and defend the innocent, to be Good Samaritans to the preborn? If we have all knowledge but not love for our preborn brothers and sisters, then we are as a sounding brass and tinkling cymbal." The room full of church leaders on stage shuffled uneasily at hearing those conscience-pricking words. "Amens" filled the auditorium, as the raindrops on a tin roof before a coming squall.

Pastor Dustin wagged his head and grunted disapprovingly. “The Bible speaks about the Christian’s duty to suffer patiently and not take up the sword for the kingdom’s cause. God’s kingdom is not of this world, else would His servants fight. Recall how King David was disallowed from building God’s temple because his hands were stained with blood from war.” Pastor Dustin pointed his arthritic hands heavenward. “We can’t support violence, in *any* circumstance,” he insisted, thumping the table with his lumpy knuckles. “Vengeance belongs to the Lord.”

The charismatic denomination’s V.P. responded, “And it says in the next chapter, chapter 13 of Romans, that God delegates the sword of vengeance to civil authorities, who are to be a terror to evil works and a friend to the good. It says that they are to be ministers of God to us to execute wrath upon those that do evil – like those that murder babies and the sick and handicapped. Benjamin Boswell is that man. Shouldn’t we respect the higher powers like the Scripture says?”

Another pastor at the table leaned into the microphone in front of him to rebut. “But Margaret Brighton is *his* higher power, and she’s resisting.”

Dreifuss grabbed the microphone from its stand and stood to his feet. “The Constitution is *her* higher power, and *she* is resisting! God is *the* highest power and the federal government is resisting Him and Montana is submitting to Him – finally!” Again, the rustle of affirmations stirred, leaving Pastor Dustin breathless with concern. “Listen,” Dreifuss continued, “when it comes between an anti-Christ higher power and a Christian higher power, who should we choose? The anti-christ or a Christ-follower? The devil or Jesus? This is the choice that we are presently facing. I’ll support the civil magistrate that’s standing for righteousness. I’ll take the guillotine before I idolize human rulers over God and take the government’s mark.” A hail of applause rippled across the room.

“The government’s mark?” Pastor Dustin took offense. “Are you accusing me of taking the apocalyptic ‘mark of the beast’ mentioned in the book of Revelation?”

“I use the term metaphorically, my friend, and it applies. To take the mark in the book of Revelation, someone had to submit to an evil government and defy God’s authority. That’s quite similar to the issue we are facing today with your urging us to submit to the federal government and let innocent children be slaughtered. Montana is obligated by God to defend these children! It’s better to obey God than man!" The thunderous applause that followed was interspersed with strong shouts of affirmation. Dreifuss nodded gratefully and took a seat.

"Listen, Pastor Dustin." A leader on the platform waved his hand to gain the attention of the one who had come to be the vocal leader of the minority pacifist movement in Great Falls. "It's hypocritical of you to condemn *all* violence and yet offer support of Margaret Brighton, the most unlawful and violent of them all." Here, the "Amens" grew more robust. "If Governor Boswell resists the federal government with violence, it will be for one reason and for one reason only: because Margaret Brighton first employed unlawful violence to assault a sovereign people and commit mass murder. The 'lesser magistrate doctrine' is an orthodox Christian doctrine throughout church history, and allows lesser magistrates to interpose themselves between the tyrant and the people they took an oath to protect. Like Jehoida in First Chronicles 23, who united the people to arm themselves and resist Athalia."

"I agree." A regional council member of a large denomination nodded. "The Bible clearly justifies force in self-defense and in defense of others – can you deny this, Pastor Dustin? Would you condemn someone who used force to defend themselves from assault, or someone who would resist a terrorist who had slaughtered our leaders and usurped power that was not lawfully his?"

"Some would," Pastor Dustin reluctantly admitted. There were many strict pacifists in the audience who would not justify force under any circumstances. "Jesus said to turn the other cheek."

"That may be the higher way when *your* cheek is slapped, but would you, Pastor Dustin, condemn someone that struck at an intruder to protect a baby from an assault?"

When Pastor Dustin was hesitant to answer, the elder answered for him: "No, you wouldn't!" Pastor Dustin hung his head, finding it difficult to reconcile his conscience and his doctrine. "You know that the Bible and conscience justifies such defensive force. Well, Montana's our house and Governor Boswell's doing his best to protect Montanans from an invading burglar who wants to kill our unborn children and our handicapped grandparents. How many good Christians must be persecuted? How many Downs syndrome children must die? How many home-schooled kids must be kidnapped from their homes before you will defend them? They've been citing the UN Convention on the Rights of the Child to justify taking our kids and putting them under the care of godless social service agencies. Our fuse is too long…"

The debate went on late into the night. The final vote of the Montana church leadership was 998 to 419 in support of the state government joining the CFC States. Hundreds of church leaders who were strict pacifists went so far as to announce that they were fleeing the state to other parts of the country. It was better to tolerate a tyrannical secular government, according to them, than to live under a heretical Christian one.

Washington, D.C.

"But Speaker–"

"I'm sorry, James, I'm sorry. This issue is just too divisive. It's not worth the contention."

"But our silence on this issue is tearing the country apart – you said so yourself!" James Knight leaned over the desk of the new Speaker of the House and rapped his knuckles against the polished wood.

"Listen, James. We've got terrorists taking over the friendly skies with empty briefcases. We've got armed citizens shooting government agents. We've got martial law in Texas and South Carolina. We've got anti-abortionists burning down clinics and murdering doctors. We've got the largest crime-fighting package in our history going into effect this week with the repossession of illegal guns. Don't you think it's high time for some good ole' fashion reachin' across the aisle? Don't you think it's time for the United States of America to be united for once?"

"Don't kid yourself, Rich. That package doesn't fight crime – it fights freedom."

The Speaker flinched. "Huh?"

"There's no punishment for crime in that piece of legislation, just punishment of innocent, law-abiding citizens who want to exercise their second amendment rights. Will you trade in the Constitution for a fascist police state?"

Rich Faulkner shook his head and rolled his eyes in frustration. "I can't even hold a level-headed conversation with you filtering my words through your grid of radicalism."

James Knight tensed, stood erect, and shook his head. "Radicalism?!"

"Peace is more important than your precious second amendment liberties when liberty comes at the cost of terror and violence."

"Apathy is consent, Rich!" Knight again leaned over the Speaker's desk, stretching his index finger toward Faulkner's face, getting into his personal space and prompting him to roll his chair back six inches. "Congress must not consent to her unconstitutional usurpations!"

"Well, *quit then!*" shouted Faulkner. "I hear the NRA's looking for a new director, or the Gun Owners of America if the NRA's too liberal for ya'."

"Please! Rich!" James interrupted him, took a deep breath and sat back down. "All I'm asking is that we debate the cause of the states that are beginning to buck Brighton's executive orders." Faulkner glanced at a text message on his phone as Knight pleaded with him. "States are actually discussing *seceding* from the United States! Why? Because *this Congress* won't do its duty and address Brighton's abuses!"

Faulkner studied Knight for a moment, and then shook his head side to side. "I cannot allow the debate on the subject now. It's too divisive and contentious at such a volatile juncture. Not on my watch, Jim."

Knight opened his mouth to speak again, but he clearly saw that it was no use and held his peace. The Speaker of the House had made up his mind. A familiar *déjà vu* sensation overcame Knight, giving him chills. His thoughts moved to the previous Speaker, Jerry McAvery, and the pressure the White House had put on him to silence the dissent in Congress.

"Do you remember what happened to McAvery when he succumbed to pressure from this president?" Knight reached down to pick up his briefcase, hoping that his implications would intimidate the Speaker, but when Knight looked into his eyes, the Speaker appeared more bored than fearful. "Rich, this nation is supposed to have a system of checks and balances that prevents the executive branch from controlling the legislative branch, and that system of checks and balances has failed again because of *you!* If states secede and people die, their blood rests on your hands."

"Oh, I see." Faulkner raised his voice as Knight turned to leave. "That's a classic blame-shift, Jim! It's your contentious rhetoric on the airwaves that has raised up an army of assault-weapon-totin' political dissenters in the first place."

"*My* contentious rhetoric?" Knight stopped half way to the door and turned around. "Would you like the phone number of the parents of the 14-year-old that was killed by the BATF squad in Montana? How'd you like a face-to-face meeting with the parents in my district whose four children have been kidnapped by government social workers because their parents refused to give them a vaccine made from aborted baby tissue? How about the phone number of Henry Adams' distressed wife who still doesn't know if her husband's even alive? Who needs an arrest warrant, after all," he said with his arms outstretched, "if you can just shoot 'em or threaten to poison their kid?"

"That's enough!" Frustrated, the ex-marine dropped his cell phone onto his desk and bellowed, "I've had enough of your conspiracy theories, Jim. Get outta here!"

"I'll be speaking with the other representatives about your impertinence." Knight headed for the door. "It seems to me like trading an adulterer for a coward wasn't a good move, even if he did *used to be* a brave Marine. We need a Speaker who won't be beholden to the White House's agenda..."

"Jim!" Faulkner stood and shouted as Knight continued to walk away. "Why do you leave a graveyard of contention and division behind you whenever you open your mouth?"

Knight opened the door then turned to face the Speaker of the House once more. "I just put the tombstones on the dead bodies, Rich. Dead to duty and honor. Dead to God. I leave your judgment in His hands." Knight stomped through the door and slammed it behind him.

Faulkner sat back in his chair, red-faced, twiddling his pen anxiously. He picked up the phone and speed-dialed a number. "Knight was just here. He's not giving up."

* * * * *

"I called you here this evening for an urgent announcement." Knight projected his voice into the room full of fidgety journalists and television cameras. Behind him stood almost all of the representatives of every one of the Coalition states, a large showing of political power for this late evening press conference. Once they realized that they would lose their positions in Congress if their states seceded, the in-betweeners easily found the courage to join Knight in a public appeal for more aggressive measures to alleviate the escalating political conflict. "Many Americans will find this announcement to be quite startling, but I believe the astonishing historical circumstances in which we presently find ourselves demand such measures."

Jaws dropped and journalists held their breath as James Knight made the unexpected announcement. "In order to avert a broadening conflict between a tyrannical federal government and freedom-loving Americans and sovereign states, I am calling for a convention of states to convene to petition the federal government for a redress of grievances and lay down an ultimatum." Knight paused until the rumble of murmuring calmed down. "If the federal government does not soon relent from its present tyrannical course, more states will and should follow the example of the Coalition of Free Christian States and resist."

He raised his voice to be heard over the roar of dissent. "Can it be any clearer that our government has grievously and repeatedly trespassed the boundaries of the Constitution? The president's armed squads leave footprints of blood wherever they tread, carrying confiscated weapons and captured slaves on their way. More and more good men and women – your representatives, neighbors, and pastors – are locked away without a formal charge and without a trial. We are more like the Great Britain of 1776 than we are like the nation our forefathers founded. The federal government has failed us, and may be broken beyond repair. The legislative branch of this government refuses to do its duty and halt the judicial and executive infringements on the rights of the people. The federal government is in complete defiance to the Constitution, the will of the people, and the will of the Almighty God.

"We, the people, must hold our government to the contract that was the foundation of our Union. We must emasculate the gigantic federal monster of all of its unconstitutional usurpations and make it the servant and protector of the people, as the founders intended, and not our master and abuser.

"We," he said, glancing at the brave congressmen and Senators who stood on the platform behind him, "fully support the Coalition of Free Christian States. We endorse the Coalition's resistance to the federal government and their long-overdue attempts to protect the right to life and the other God-given rights secured in the Bill of Rights."

James Knight paused, and studied the shocked countenances of his disbelieving audience. Then, solemnly and respectfully, he said, "'We hold these truths to be self-evident, that all men are created equal, that they are endowed by their Creator with certain unalienable rights, that among these are life, liberty and the pursuit of happiness. That to secure these rights, governments are instituted among men, deriving their just powers from the consent of the governed. That whenever any form of government becomes destructive of these ends, it is the right of the people to alter or to abolish it, and to institute new government, laying its foundation on such principles and organizing its powers in such form, as to them shall seem most likely to affect their safety and happiness. When a long train of abuses and usurpations, pursuing invariably the same object, evinces a design to reduce them under absolute despotism, it is their right, it is their duty, to throw off such government, and to provide new guards for their future security.'

He paused to let the room grow quiet again. "Sound familiar, Americans? If the uniting of our states was justified in the 18th century, then the *dissolution* of it is justified today for precisely the same reasons." Audible gasps resounded throughout the pressroom. "I prefer the *dis*united States under God than the United States under God's wrath. Lovers of God and liberty should courageously resist the godless, unconstitutional dictates of this federal government, in submission to the King of kings and Lord of lords. If state secession is the only way we can restore lost liberties and stop the slaughter of the innocent, then we urge the American people to resort to this remedy as an unfortunate but necessary final option."

* * * * *

As James Knight pulled past the security gate into the driveway leading to his condominium in the shadows of a setting sun, he remembered that his wife and children would not be waiting for him. Ever since the threat had been made against his daughter at her school, his wife and children had been staying with his mother several hours away. He suddenly felt so very lonely, as empty as a bus running on fumes. He had moved out of his house and into a condominium closer to work because he hated living in such a large residence alone, but the smaller residence did not satisfy his deep down desire to be with his wife and children.

Feeling a sudden urge to speak to his wife, he touched a button on his dashboard. "Phone. 608, 555, 9373," he enunciated clearly as the voice-technology-equipped cell phone affixed to his car's dashboard dialed the number.

An elderly woman picked up on the third ring.

"Hello, Momma. Is Nancy there?"

"Oh, hey Jim. Just a moment," the familiar voice replied as Knight pulled to a stop in front of his condominium.

"Hi, honey. Is it true?"

"Is what true?"

"Is Wyoming seceding with Montana and those other states?"

"Nobody's seceding yet, honey. We're just expressing our willingness to secede to protect our rights. Enough of that, dear. How are you? I miss you so much. How's my little Cynthia?"

"She's great. She's in the bath now, or I'd let her talk to you. She misses you."

"And my little boy?"

"Asleep already, in spite of a bad bout of poison ivy…"

As Nancy spoke, Knight's attention turned to the U-Haul truck next to his vehicle. *Is somebody moving out or moving in?*

Knight saw his neighbor, Ross, a red-haired State Department attorney in his early thirties, walk out with a chair in his arms. When Ross' eyes met his, Ross smiled, set down the chair, and walked toward Knight's car.

"…He's made some new friends in the neighborhood. We all miss home though. How long do you think this will last?"

"Oh, I have no idea, honey." Knight's neighbor knocked on his window. "Hold on, dear." James put his palm over the phone and rolled the window down. "Hey Ross, what can I do for you?"

"Just ten seconds of your time, Jim. I need help carrying a couch into the U-Haul."

James nodded and then spoke into the phone. "Honey, I'll call you tonight. Give my love to the kids. Love you."

"I love you, too. Goodbye."

James stepped out of the car and followed Ross up the stairs toward his front door. "I only have a minute, Ross." James smiled and nodded at Ross' wife, who walked past them, down the stairs, and onto the U-Haul ramp with a box in her arms. "Where are you moving?"

"Texas."

That was an answer Knight did not expect. "Why in the world are you going to Texas? It's practically a police state."

Ross snickered as he reached down to pick up the old couch at the far end of the living room. Knight picked it up at the near end. "You wouldn't believe how cheap property is there. It's a buyers' market."

"I'll bet. It's because the government confiscates the property of everybody they're arresting." Knight backed the couch through the living room and onto the front porch. "I pray God keeps you safe. A lot of social conservatives are either incarcerated, have disappeared, or are exchanging fire with soldiers."

"Conservative means resistant to change, Jim. It's a subjective term."

"What kind of conservative are you, then?" James backed down the wooden stairs and into the dark U-Haul.

"I want things to stay the way they are. With one exception." They set down the couch simultaneously inside the U-Haul.

"What's that?"

"I want you to disappear."

At hearing those words, Knight felt a sharp stab behind his neck. He squinted in pain and reached back to feel the hand of Ross' wife squeezing a hypodermic syringe into the right side of his neck. The pain quickly turned into numbness. The silhouette of Ross at the precipice of the U-Haul truck faded to a blur, and then the bright front porch light shining through the rear door of the truck faded to darkness.

* * * * *

"Ladies and gentlemen, the President of the United States." Dena Halluci, sporting her new auburn-dyed hairdo, introduced Brighton to the packed White House press conference room.

Margaret Brighton stepped into the limelight of camera flashes in her characteristic classy red dress, long red fingernails, and fashionable neck-length hair. The wrinkles of her years were well camouflaged in a layer of make-up, and the diamonds of her jewelry were shimmering in the flashing bulbs of the nation's most expensive cameras.

"Good evening, my fellow Americans. At a time when we should be pulling together to fight the common enemies of foreign and domestic terrorism, anti-choice violence, anti-gay hate-speech, child abuse, and racial and gender inequality – we have found that our most dangerous enemies are the ones that we trusted the most. These traitorous wolves in sheep's clothing have deceived many into thinking that America's government is the enemy. Their conspiracy for an independent theocracy has widened the gulf that divides our country. These rebels have become our greatest national security threat." She paused for a moment to absorb the admiration in the room that was radiating toward her.

"There has been a concerted effort on the part of many states to undermine the system of checks and balances that have made this nation one of the greatest in the history of the world. These insubordinate states have spurned the decisions of the Supreme Court, Congress, and the executive branch regarding reproductive choice and the right-to-die with dignity. They have disregarded federal laws designed to give equal rights to gays and to fight crime and terrorism." She paused, reminding herself to restrain her tone. "The states of Washington, Colorado, Montana, Nebraska, Idaho, Utah, Wyoming, North and South Dakota, and

Nebraska are treading the treacherous paths paved by the states of Texas and South Carolina. Mississippi, Alabama, and Georgia are on the precipice of the same insane decisions. These states are actually threatening armed revolt against the United States of America!"

She paused and took a deep breath, finding the national situation incredulous. Gazing into the camera, she continued, "I am here to tell you, my fellow Americans, that we will *not* let this country be torn apart." Her volume increased and her expressions grew more flamboyant as her thin arms began to flail. "The United States of America *will* remain united, and we will *not* fail to conquer our enemies!" It felt good to raise her voice and her audience of admirers applauded her zeal.

"No single person has been more responsible for encouraging the anarchy and treason in the incorrigible states than James Knight." She paused, swallowed hard, and feigned to be personally offended. "The congressman from Wyoming committed a plethora of hate crimes and grievous acts of treason against the country he was elected to serve. He has encouraged the governors of the so-called Coalition of Free Christian States **to secede and even fire on American troops!**" A collective gasp filled the room. She took a deep breath and furrowed her brow, forming her most confident presidential grimace. "It is for this reason he has been arrested and charged with federal crimes." Two journalists had a difficult time concealing their glee at hearing of Knight's arrest. They slapped a high-five on the front row.

"I am warning the legislatures and governors of the states aforementioned. We will not tolerate treason. If citizens commit violence against your government's agents or troops, the United States of America *will* send forces in as we have done heretofore. We will keep the United States united." She brought her right fist down into her left palm. "We will not let this anarchy and lawlessness continue. We will prevail against all enemies, foreign and domestic."

* * * * *

"What?" The announcement stunned Nancy Knight. She dropped the iced tea she held in her hands and it shattered on the living room floor.

Her mother heard the glass shatter on the wood floor of her old house, and she hollered from the kitchen. "Everythin' all right?"

"James, oh no," Nancy quietly muttered, her hands covering her mouth as a wave of horror flowed over her body.

Her mother-in-law came running into the living room. “Jimmy? What happened to Jimmy?” Her gaze shifted from Nancy to the television screen, back to Nancy.

“They’ve arrested him.” Tears filled her eyes and her hands became as cold as the cubes of ice scattered amongst the shards of broken glass at her feet.

Part II

The Unseen War

3

Olympia, Washington

Most of the Coalition leaders taking part in the decision-making process did not appear to have the anxiety one would expect of those involved in such a historic, dangerous meeting. The governors and their cabinet members sat on swivel leather chairs in a room with a large ceiling in Washington State's elegant statehouse. Monitors were fixed to the walls and cameras scanned the scene from the far end of the room.

Dark circles under their eyes revealed the sleepless nights that haunted many of them the past few days leading up to the final decision. David Jameson, who was personally invited to be present by Governor Boswell, was the only one who looked like he'd had a wink of sleep.

"Keep your eyes on the prize – the blessing of God," Jameson counseled them. "Securing liberty and justice for all in your state is the key to God's blessing. If you don't protect the least among you – the preborn and handicapped – you *deserve* judgment."

Governor Littman took a deep breath and fixed his gaze on his fists, clenched on the table in front of him. "What do you say, Mr. Jamestown," he asked, articulating his words thoughtfully, "to the question that abortion is necessary only in extreme crises, such as in rape?"

David Jameson jolted when Littman called him by the alias he had used among the Coalition leadership – Jamestown. He still hadn't gotten used to his new name. "Abortion for rape?" David stuttered.

"Yeah. What if your underage daughter was raped and couldn't carry to term? I mean, what if the baby couldn't survive outside the womb anyway?"

Others at the table nodded, as if they were struggling with whether to allow the same seductive exceptions. All eyes fastened on Jameson, as if expecting him to answer a question that they were all thinking.

"Shouldn't we at least make exceptions for the life of the mother?" Littman asked, his eyes roaming around the room, searching for sympathetic countenances. "Maybe for rape and incest?"

"That's barbaric! Kill an innocent human being because they were conceived in rape?! Kill an innocent human being to improve another's health?!" David's volume was excessive and his tone critical. He paused and reminded himself to be patient. Just because he had answered this question thousands of times in the course of his ministry, that didn't mean that these leaders had ever heard satisfactory answers. He sighed heavily. "I thought you all were beyond this."

"I thought we were, too," said Boswell with a demeaning smirk aimed at Littman.

"I am committed to the life principle," Governor Littman assured them. "I just want to know how to answer that question. I hear it constantly. I know it's my weak link."

"Answer with the sixth commandment: 'Do no murder.' It's that simple," said David. "It's *always* wrong to intentionally kill an innocent person. A premature delivery may rarely be necessary to save the mother's life, but the physician must do everything in his power to save both lives."

"What if it was your underage daughter that was raped, Mr. Jameson?" Littman asked.

David responded without missing a beat. "Rape is a violent crime against an innocent person. How can a violent crime against an innocent person remedy a violent crime against an innocent person? The preborn child's innocent. The baby doesn't deserve to die for the crime of his father. The mother can place the child up for adoption…"

"You honestly would force your daughter to carry a rapist's baby for nine months, even if it was a threat to her health?"

Governor Boswell inhaled deeply. "It's a baby, not an 'it.'"

"No, I want to hear him say it!" Littman aimed an index finger at David. "Mr. Jamestown, if it were your wife or daughter, you would force them to carry a rapist's baby that they didn't want? Would you endorse the death penalty for them if they got an abortion?"

David's eyes fastened on the Washington governor. "I pray the Lord never tests me on this, but yes, aborting a rapist's preborn baby is murder, a capital offense. It's always wrong to kill an innocent person. Always."

Governor Littman sat back in his chair and nodded, deep in thought.

"It's not even a sincere argument, Governor." David leaned forward and stretched out his hands. "If I held an infant and said that this infant was conceived in rape, mentally handicapped, and just the thought of this child made the mother suicidal, would you justify killing the baby?"

"An infant?" Littman shook his head. "Of course not."

"Which goes to show that the circumstances surrounding conception are irrelevant. It's a person, Governor. The government shouldn't deprive a person of life or liberty without due process. Intentionally killing an innocent person is murder. Period. We must never waver on the law of God."

"I gotcha," Littman responded with a wink, hoping to distract from the embarrassment that reddened his cheeks. "I should've figured that out on my own."

With David's wise counsel, a consensus soon formed that the divine gavel of judgment was falling upon the nation, and they wanted to separate themselves if for no other reason than to safeguard their people from the wrath of God. After the repeated failure of impeachment efforts in Congress, secession was the only way to free themselves of the bloodguilt of abortion and physician-assisted suicide. They had exhausted lesser means to have their grievances addressed; the arrest of the Wyoming congressman James Knight settled all doubts. The level of oppression and tyranny had become intolerable. They feared not seceding more than they feared the consequences of seceding.

"Secession," David assured them, "was the lesser of two horrors."

They discussed and debated the proposed list of grievances and demands until they practically had the letter memorized. They argued over the wording and each was influential in the formation of the final draft. Ben Boswell, since he initially drafted the letter, was very gracious in deferring to the other governors and the trusted members of their respective cabinets in determining the final version. They had each met with the leadership of their respective legislatures to acquire their input. Unanimity of opinion was finally achieved in the wording of the letter that formalized their secession from the United States. They were also unanimous in electing Ben Boswell to be the chairman of the Coalition of Free Christian States. He reluctantly accepted.

At last, there was a moment of silence. There was nothing left to discuss. There comes a time when the words come to an end and men must act on principle.

"Are we ready?" Ben Boswell was as somber as a man preaching at his best friend's funeral.

Governor Littman's A.G. tapped some numbers into the computer that was installed in a recess in the table, preparing to send their ultimatum electronically to the leaders of the three branches of the federal government and the mainstream press.

"Let's do it." Governor Wilson of Colorado emanated confidence.

"It is time for you to work, O God," David quoted a passage from the Psalms, "for they have made void Your law."

"Send the letter. Then make the call." Washington Governor Littman nodded at his A.G.

They all listened intently to the plinking of the plastic keys of the keyboard against the sensors, knowing full well the magnitude of what they were at that moment doing. The A.G. looked up. "It's done."

"Let's give it a minute. Then confirm that it has been received," said Littman.

"Yes sir."

Ben Boswell bowed his head and prayed silently as the most ground-breaking document since the Declaration of Independence was transmitted via satellite uplink across the nation into Margaret Brighton's private E-mail inbox, CC-ed to the FBI director, the State Department, the CIA, the Supreme Court, Homeland Security, every congressman and woman and the mainstream media outlets. Their signature at the end of that document could result in their imprisonment, infinite libel, or even their death. It could thrust the entire nation into a bloody war.

David's eyes met Boswell's and David nodded and smiled at the C.F.C. chairman, as if to let him know that he was proud of him. Ben Boswell took a deep breath.

"Dear God," Boswell uttered softly, "we need you now…"

Washington, D.C.

"Madam President?" Dena Halluci's voice over the president's desk phone was urgent and demanded the president's attention.

"What is it, Dena?" She turned her attention away from some DHS briefs.

"I just received notification from Governor Littman's office that an urgent E-mail has just been sent to your personal inbox. My cell phone's buzzing constantly with calls from the media. Whatever he sent you, it's big, and the press knows about it."

The president tapped a few keys on her computer. Her eyes grew stern and her brow furrowed as she read the two-page document. A moment later, she printed the document and re-read it. Then she dropped the papers and they floated gently to her desk. She put her head in her hands for a moment, awestruck at the implications of this pivotal moment in American history.

The president tapped a button on her desk phone.

Dena stopped reading a text message on her cell. "Yes, Madam President?"

"Convene the Joint Chiefs immediately."

"I thought you'd say that."

Brighton sighed and for a brief, unexpected moment, she missed her husband. The thought, like a sniper's bullet through the Oval Office window, was uninvited. An unwelcomed recollection of the last, well-publicized, terrifying moment of her husband's euthanasia pierced her mind like an electric shock, causing her to blink hard, as if to keep some grains of sand in the throes of a stiff wind from getting into her eyes. She mumbled, grieving, "I'm so sorry, dear."

Her brief lapse of sorrow made her heart feel like it just dropped into her stomach. She took a deep breath and clenched her fists to fight the urge to cry. She turned her thoughts to the leaders of the Coalition, reviving her hate and bitterness. She cursed the Coalition and found the foul words energizing. Suddenly, like a grenade with the pin pulled, she exploded in a rage. She picked up the stapler on her desk and threw it across the room, colliding with and breaking a two-hundred-year-old lamp. She kicked her chair onto the ground and swept all of the papers off her desk with a quick brush of her thin forearms. She slammed her fists against the desk and screamed a high-pitch squeal that sent every Secret Service agent within earshot sprinting to her aid.

Olympia, Washington

After a long, silent moment, Littman's A.G. tapped some numbers into the computer that was installed in a recess in the table. He nodded at Governor Littman.

"Oval Office. May I help you?"

"I dialed the president's direct line," said Governor Littman toward the sensitive microphone that was in the center of the oval-shaped wooden table.

"She's not taking calls. I have been told to hold all of her–"

"This is urgent," Benjamin Boswell interrupted. "Please tell her that the leaders of the Coalition of Free Christian States need to speak with her."

"Just a moment. I'll get her for you right away." The secretary spoke more courteously than they expected. She placed them on hold as the president's insignia with a royal blue background flashed on their monitors.

The sound of a two Coalition fighter jets patrolling the skies overhead made their hearts skip a beat. Their worried countenances looked heavenward, as if expecting to hear the whistle of a missile headed toward them. Littman pointed toward the sky and reminded them, "It's ours, remember?"

They recalled that they had ordered Guard fighters to scour the skies for any signs of attack or invasion, preparing for the worst.

Benjamin Boswell's mouth went dry and sweat beaded on his brow. He lifted a glass to his lips and drew in the cool spring water. He took a deep, cleansing breath, preparing for the inevitable confrontation with Margaret Brighton, who was everyday appearing more emotionally labile and unpredictable. It was clear God had ordained him to be the leader of this historical revolution of righteousness in government, this defiance of federal tyranny, this political extension of the spiritual awakening that had rocked rural America the past six months. He was the primary target of the most powerful tyrant of this century, and he wasn't sure if he liked it. But he had long ago surrendered any self-will for God's will.

David began to feel uneasy. He felt like *he* was the primary target of the most powerful tyrant this century, and he began to doubt the wisdom of accepting Governor Boswell's invitation to this meeting. For him to influence these leaders, he knew that he had to keep his true identity concealed, but there were so many politicians and bureaucrats present in this large statehouse room that he felt exposed.

After a few minutes passed, the Coalition leaders began to shift uneasily in their chairs, trying to be patient.

The Idaho governor broke the uneasy silence, "It's sure taking long enough."

"You'd think that something of this magnitude would have high priority on the president's list of things to do," said Governor Reynolds of Utah.

"You'd think she'd put her medium on hold to take our phone call," someone opined, prompting nervous chuckles around the room.

"Oh, she's probably tidying her make-up behind her desk just trying to irritate us," Boswell guessed. "Her power's being threatened and she doesn't like it."

"I suspect she'll have nothing but contempt for our demands," said the always-pessimistic elderly Governor MacKenzie of Nebraska. "She's probably on the phone with the Air Force calling in our coordinates for a carpet bombing."

"She's wetting her pants, fellas." Boswell glanced at Littman's state attorney. "How do you put this on hold? Is this the button?" He turned the face of the remote controller device toward him.

"Yes sir, that's it."

David discerned what Boswell was thinking, and asked, "Does our new CFCS insignia flash up on the screen when you place an online caller on hold?"

"Yes."

"Governor Boswell?" The White House secretary finally returned.

"That's me," he responded with a warm smile.

"The president will speak with you now."

The president's face shone up on the screen, but as she opened her mouth to speak, Boswell interrupted her. "Excuse me, Madam President, we'll be with you in just a moment." Boswell then tapped the button and placed her on hold.

"What are you doing?!" three or four governors simultaneously wondered aloud. David crossed his arms over his chest and laughed.

"I'm giving her a dose of her own medicine," Boswell said, imitating David's confidence. "I'm also giving us time for a quick word of prayer. David?"

"Sure," said David. He prayed for a long five minutes and tensions eased, in spite of the phone that buzzed incessantly on the table. You could see the sincerity in their faces and hear the passion in their exclaimed affirmations of "Amen" and "Yes, Lord." It became palpably plain through his prayer that for success to be possible, the God that created the heavens and the earth, that sustained Joseph through slavery and prison, that led Daniel through the lions' den, and that delivered Israel out of Egyptian bondage must once again show Himself strong on behalf of His people. Through David Jameson's passionate prayer, their faith was stirred. They had no choice but to do right and trust in God for victory.

When the prayer concluded, Boswell hit the proper button on the remote and the president's face flashed up on the monitors. Beside her stood Dena Halluci. A facelift and her new auburn-dyed hairdo made them wonder who she was for a moment, but her flashy pink top and artificial tan helped them identify her as the president's chief of staff. On screens beside hers were the images of the U.S. Attorney Victor Meyers, the Secretary of Defense General Green, and FBI Director Todd Hamilton. An empty screen labeled "Department of Homeland Security" informed them that the DHS director would join them momentarily.

"Excuse me," David said, before standing and exiting the room without another word.

"What?" Boswell turned to protest his untimely exit, but he was already out the door.

"Good afternoon." The president released a smile that didn't seem to fit the mood. "So," she said, holding the infamous letter out in front of her, "since when did insanity become a trait for state governors in the Rocky Mountains?"

Boswell wagged his head as a collective wave of nausea rolled through the room like stench from a nearby landfill.

Without warning, her eyes bulged with the veins in her neck as she crumbled up the printed E-mail and threw it at the camera on top of the monitor, causing the refined Dena Halluci to jolt. The president leaned into the camera: "Just who do you morons think you are!" Even the sober Vic Meyers, rarely riled under the most intense stress, developed a squint, a furrowed brow, and appeared irritated at the president's temper.

"We represent the people of our states," said Ben Boswell calmly, "and Jesus Christ, the King of nations. These grievances are legitimate and our demands are non-negotiable."

"Demands?" She clenched her fists as her fury poured upon them like water from a breaking dam. "Demands?! Your demands?!"

"Yes, demands." Boswell's demeanor and tone exhibited confidence and peace.

"Your pathetic demands are as worthless as your pathetic abortion bans and your gay marriage bans and your euthanasia bans! *My* judiciary will rule your bans and your infantile attempt to secede unconstitutional by the end of next month!"

Boswell took a deep breath and sat back in his chair, careful to remain calm and not be provoked by the president's spiteful words. "As we said in our Declaration of Independence, from now, we're ignoring every unconstitutional and immoral dictate coming out of Washington, D.C. The Coalition has a new king." The other CFC state leaders nodded, adopting their chairman's fortitude.

"How'd you like to rot in military prison the rest of your miserable lives? All of you! You, you traitors!"

"Madam President," Boswell said calmly, "if this is difficult for you due to your emotional instability, perhaps you would like to have someone else on your staff be your liaison between–"

"How'd you like to be locked away as an enemy combatant, Mr. Boswell! How'd you like an expensive vacation with James Knight in Guantanamo for 20 years?"

"This does not have to end with *a conflict of violence*." He wanted to insert that in the conversation early so as to let her know that they meant business. "This can end peacefully, but we are immovable on our priorities."

"I've got a mind to have you shot for treason for just *mentioning* a conflict of arms with the United States! How dare you, you *extremist, Jesus-buffoons, how dare you?!"*

The CFC state leaders sighed heavily and wagged their heads. This was turning into a big joke. They could see it in the eyes of the president's cabinet. "We will not let innocent people be murdered in our borders," Boswell said, ignoring her insults and continuing his short list of non-negotiable demands. "Neither will we let you trample our first, second, fourth, or fifth amendment rights underfoot. We are holding you down with the chains of the Constitution. Short of *immediate* concession to these *non-negotiable* demands, we *will* take this document to our state legislatures and preside over an emergency vote to secede. Then we will peacefully secede and govern ourselves independent of federal tyranny."

"I'm the one that's going to be giving demands in this scenario. Here are ***my*** demands." She pointed at the screen as she scolded them. "Comply with federal law – the supreme law of the land – and maybe – *maybe* – I'll forget you wrote this *worthless* piece of rhetoric and *maybe* I won't have you and the instigators of this Confederate-nonsense shot for treason and your families arrested!" Todd Hamilton and General Green almost jumped out of their skin when she said that. "If you make any moves toward armed conflict, we will turn your Guard bases and your capital cities into huge craters," – she spread her hands as she spoke

– "huge craters so deep that you won't even be able to see the bottom from the edge! Do you want that? You have 24 hours to recant this, this nonsense!" She cursed as she railed, visibly jolting the bureaucrats around her with her utter contempt for the Coalition's threat.

Boswell witnessed the scowls of disapproval from Hamilton, Meyers, Halluci, and General Green, as she behaved in a manner unfit for the head of state. "Madam President, please don't underestimate our resolve."

The DHS director's red face shone up on the screen just as the president spoke her final words. "I'm done – those are ***my*** demands." Then their screens went blank.

The governors and others who attended the meeting were unabashedly angry.

Boswell breathed deeply and grit his teeth as he tried to resist the urge to throw the remote control at the nearest monitor.

Chicago, Illinois

Arnie Oswald York heard from a friend at church that a 14-year-old daughter of the pastor of the Metropolitan Church had conceived, and that the girl's mother had scheduled an appointment with an abortionist without her husband's knowledge. The 14-year-old was reluctant to go through with it, but she consented at her mother's persistence, and the unwanted child was killed.

This jarred his memory. He recalled the exchange in front of the abortion clinic in downtown Rockford, Illinois. He remembered the African American woman, with straight black hair and pointed glasses, telling him to "Shut up!" when he called out to them not to murder their baby.

"My husband's a pastor!" she squealed.

"Sure he is," Arnie replied mockingly.

"He is! At Metropolitan downtown! And my 14-year-old cannot carry a child!"

"But ma'am," he beckoned, "she's already carrying a child." The abortion clinic volunteers rushed the two into the clinic and he never saw them again.

York searched the church online and recognized the woman by her photograph on the church website. Jessica Taylor's husband was the senior pastor. She held the title of "Women's and Children's Pastor" and was responsible for managing Sunday School volunteers and leading women's Bible study on Thursdays at noon.

This made Arnie's blood boil. Abortionists aren't the only ones doing the killing. They have accomplices. Mrs. Taylor was an accomplice in her own grandchild's death, much more so than her easily manipulated 14-year-old daughter. Although the grandparents of the aborted babies don't do the dirty work, they make the appointment, hire the assassin, trudge their way through a flock of pro-life protesters at a distant clinic where they are unlikely to be recognized, sign the consent form, coax the teenager's conscience to sleep with lies and threats, and murder the inconvenient baby. York felt the tug of destiny on his heart: Mrs. Taylor's date with justice had come.

Up to this point, Arnie had always targeted abortionists. Their hands were directly stained with innocent blood, and every slain abortionist motivated others to abandon the child-killing business. He had always claimed that his motive was defensive, not retributive. He wasn't punishing the abortionist for past crime, but rather, trying to prevent inevitable future crimes. But with this news, he sensed the door opening to a different calling. This wasn't a defensive act of killing to stop a serial killer. Not at all. This was an act of vengeance. This was justice. Vigilante justice, he reasoned, was better than no justice at all. The government was bequeathed the sword of vengeance, but instead of executing justice to protect the innocent, they became the perpetrators. At such times, a Phinehas must rise to the occasion to make atonement and win God's mercy.

What was God's plan for justice? In the Bible, executions had to take place publicly. This was an important aspect of God's criminal justice system, to offer a disincentive to on-lookers. The execution was also to take place quickly, without delay. Moreover, he reasoned, the witnesses were to be the first to throw the stones. He was a witness; he saw the woman grasp tightly to that tearful teenager's arm, and lead her into that abortion mill. Since Mrs. Taylor was an accomplice and more accessible than the baby butcher, he would take up the mantle of what the Bible called "the avenger of innocent blood" and execute justice upon her.

Of course, another qualification for justice according to the biblical system was that a judge rule on the case after a fair trial. Arnie would have to forego that little detail because of the circumstances. There were simply no judges who executed justice. The judges, he reasoned, were accomplices and would be next in line. True justice would have to accommodate for this godless society. What he lacked in elected or appointed authority, he made up for with courage.

Arnie York did his homework. He carefully scoped out Mrs. Taylor's every move for a month. He studied her as she dropped her three children off at the Christian school. He observed her get a manicure every other Monday, drop off and pick up her pressed laundry at the laundry mat on Wednesday mornings, and he followed her to Wednesday morning prayer meetings at a neighbor's home. He watched her shop at Krogers on Thursdays and then fuel her Hummer at the BP across the street. He followed her and her husband when they hired a baby-sitter and went on their date night every other Friday to dinner and a movie, or when they visited the sick in the hospital together on Saturdays. He studied every corner where there may be a surveillance camera, making mental notes. Stealth and an escape plan were critical to his success.

After much preparation, he picked his spot and prepared his trap.

"Hello Abby."

"Good morning, Pastor Jess." The laundry mat owner reached and took the dresses and pants from her friend and pastor. "Press only?"

"Of course."

"How's them babies?"

"Aw, growing up faster than you realize," Pastor Jess responded with a warm smile. "Della turns 15 tomorrow. Oh, she's growing up into such a beautiful lady."

"That she is. Pick up the clothes tomorrow?"

"You betcha. Have a nice day."

Mrs. Taylor exited the store and went back to her Hummer. She entered the car, buckled herself, and then started it. A black-hooded face in her rear-view mirror caused her to scream.

"Turn left." Arnie pointed a gun in her ribs. "I just want a ride. Keep your hands on the wheel at all times."

Jessica Taylor was stripped to her underwear and strapped to a table. Her hands and legs were tightly bound. She was gagged with a Confederate flag bandana. He hoped that this would throw off the investigation by leading authorities to investigate known racists. Pastor Jessica's eyes were wide with fear and she struggled in vain against the duct tape that held her fast.

Arnie set up a video camera ten feet away. He had tacked tarps and sheets up on the walls of his basement behind Mrs. Taylor to conceal any evidence of the location of this project.

He had coarsened his voice to make it unrecognizable to voice recognition software by screaming The Best of Skillet songs for two hours. He watched one of his favorite Hollywood movies, *Frailty*, to gather up the courage. Seeing Matthew McConaughey play a character executing vigilante vengeance on unconvicted capital criminals encouraged him.

Then he walked over to a CD player and hit *Play,* and a faint recording of highway traffic began to play in the background – just enough to throw off the investigation. Then he walked to the camera, pushed the *Record* button, covered his face with a desert cam handkerchief, and stepped in front of the camera.

"Hello." He waved his right hand in the air briefly. "Jessica Taylor, date of birth December 21, 1974. One of the pastors of the Metropolitan Church in downtown Chicago. Her home address is 1454 Lane Way, Chicago. I am an eyewitness to her murder of her unnamed grandchild, the daughter of her 14-year-old girl Della Shae Taylor. They marched into the child-killing facility, Rockford Choice Center, in Rockford, Illinois, on February 28, 2020, and paid Dr. Emilio Vanderville to kill their preborn child. I, well, I represent justice denied, and today justice is going to be restored. Ideally, a civil authority should be doing this, but vigilante justice is better than no justice at all."

As he recited the indictment, Mrs. Taylor's eyes flooded with tears. This was the first time she learned of the reason for her abduction. She struggled against the silver duct tape to no avail. This wasn't a money-hungry criminal planning to ransom her – this was a religious fanatic on a mission from God to murder her on film.

"Exodus 21 says, 'life for life.' Genesis 9:6 says, 'If a man sheds man's blood,'" – he stepped out of view of the camera momentarily to reach for a three-foot long Pakistani-sword purchased at a pawn-shop a decade earlier – "'by man shall his blood be shed." He stepped back into view of the camera with his weapon held up for all to see. "'For in the image of God made He man.'"

Arnie York turned to his trembling, fear-stricken victim. He stood at her feet with his back to the camera. "From the looks of your daughter Della's belly, your grandchild was less than two months gestation. So that child must have received a D & C abortion."

Arnie then calmly and methodically described the procedure as he demonstrated it on Pastor Jessica Taylor.

When he was done, he went back to the front of the camera, wiped his bloody gloved hands with a white towel, and bowed low. "Stop killing people or you might be next. Thank you for watching. This is A – O – Y, signing off."

He burned the body in a bonfire at night at a secluded area of a national forest just north of the Michigan border. When the ashes cooled, he pulled out the bones, encased them in cement along with the weapon, and rolled the hardened bucket of cement off a precipice into a nearby river.

To add another element of mystery to his plan and send investigators onto a dead end road, he drove to the Taylor's residence when her husband was at the police department filing a missing person report. He hacked into their computer and uploaded the video to dozens of public websites from their home P.C.

Helena, Montana

It was the day before August 1, the president's final deadline to turn in all weapons in the CFC States. The other 40 states had already passed their deadline and the feds had gained a lot of experience in confiscating illegal weapons from stubborn citizens. They were prepared to disarm the Coalition.

Ben Boswell received intel updates that FBI and ATF personnel were amassing in several government buildings in Montana cities. FBI agents in SWAT gear guarded federal buildings. Although most abortion clinics had voluntarily closed their doors, federal Marshalls armed with fully automatic machine guns guarded the one in Missoula that dared to remain open. The opportunity for peaceful reconciliation between the federal government and the Coalition was coming to a close.

Governor Boswell stood on the floor of the state legislature and passionately pleaded the case of the Coalition of Free Christian States to the state's representatives in order to win their vote for the bill that would bring about Montana's formal secession. He updated them on the alliance with the nine other Rocky Mountain states to re-criminalize abortion and physician-assisted suicide. That was the first priority for each of the Coalition states.

Montana's bill of secession had several amendments that went further than the general document. They disallowed same-sex marriage, protected the first amendment right to free speech, the second amendment right to keep and bear arms, the fourth amendment right to be free from unreasonable search and seizure, and the fifth amendment right to a trial by jury. Their document prescribed severe penalties for federal agents who dared to violate these rights of Montana citizens, as well as for anyone who dared to assist federal agents in violating the rights of Montana citizens.

"We will," Boswell assured the enthusiastic statehouse full of state reps and senators, "not submit to the federal government's unlawful, unconstitutional, and immoral orders. What this state has become under the federal government's rule is not what our forefathers sacrificed to create. If George Washington, Samuel Adams, and Thomas Jefferson were alive today, they would do more than defend our cause against tyranny, they'd be rebuking us for taking so long to finally do it! We walk in their footsteps today, and we are willing to sacrifice our lives, our fortunes, and our sacred honor to restore freedom to our people." A rustle of applause spread through the chamber.

"One of my aids told me just yesterday that it was hard to imagine Old Glory with only 40 stars. I corrected him: there would be ten stars. It is the other 40 that have fallen."

The whole building seemed to shake with thunderous applause, and Boswell paused until it subsided. "We are the ones holding to the tried and true principles of liberty that God Almighty has ordained. Other states may bow the knee to tyranny and risk the judgment of God, but the bearers of this ten-starred, red, white, and blue flag will stand fast therefore in the liberty wherewith Christ has made us free."

Boswell stepped away from the microphone and stood at attention as a line of Montana state guardsmen marched in procession to the sound of drums down the center aisle of the chamber with the ten-starred flag in the lead. Many legislators stood, clapped, and cheered.

When the soldiers had lined up in the front of the statehouse, the entire room had stood to their feet to salute the Coalition flag. Tears were flowing down many cheeks. Television cameras zoomed in to catch ever ounce of emotion for the nation's viewers.

Boswell continued. "Short of violating our consciences, the leaders of the Coalition of Free Christian States have done *everything in our power* to maintain our union. In response to our grievances, lawfully and patiently delivered, the federal government has continued to kill babies, the elderly, and the handicapped. They have continued to harass and arrest Christians for their faith without charge or jury trial. They conspire to disarm us on the morrow. Tell me, should we surrender to tyranny or to God?"

"To God!" came the unified reply.

Boswell fought off the urge to grin at the enthusiastic response. "We have tried to secede peacefully and avoid an armed confrontation, but if this president insists on keeping her promise to violently deprive you of your God-given rights, then an armed confrontation we will have!" The applause progressed to a roar. Shouts, cheers, loud "Amens" and clapping became so vigorous that Governor Boswell had to raise his voice directly into the microphone to be heard.

"I call this legislature to vote to formally declare our independence from the United States. I call all the citizens of Montana to prayer and fasting for peace and justice in the Coalition of Free Christian States, that we might be blessed by God. Pray for our brothers and sisters in Texas and South Carolina, who suffer under martial law. Pray for the other nine Coalition states to be true to God, come what may. Pray for the other states to follow our example and resist tyranny. Without Jesus," he said, pointing heavenward, "we can do nothing, but with God, all things are possible. Thank you." The forthcoming applause thundered around the state.

In Montana, the vote to secede was almost unanimous. The other Coalition states voted to secede by a wide margin, with the exception of Washington State, where the vote was close.

The United States was formally disunited.

Washington, D.C.

It was 5 o'clock p.m. on August 1. Bill Erdman clasped his hands over his cramped, ulcerated stomach behind his desk at the Bureau of Alcohol, Tobacco, and Firearms. After weeks of managing gunfights and sieges in the rural neighborhoods of Texas and South Carolina, where martial law granted them an opportunity to commence disarmament earlier in those states, he was longing for some good news in the gun confiscation campaign. After gathering up the numbers in the eastern districts, he discovered that the failure was grander than he imagined. Brighton would take credit for all the successes and he for all of the failures, and at this stage of the game, Brighton was as intolerant of failures as a Superbowl coach is of fumbles in overtime.

Finally, Erdman received some good news. An ATF subordinate stationed in Atlanta informed him that the confiscation campaigns had gone very well in the southeast. As expected, thousands waited until the last minute, hoping that somehow the political environment would shift and they would be allowed to keep their guns. But with the government in possession of the FFL records, most felt that they had no choice but to give up their guns on the appointed day. It was a matter of self-preservation. Hunters and gun enthusiasts lined up for miles in some areas to turn in their now-illegal guns for the promised 25% of their market value. Many states matched that and the owners of the guns were recompensed 50% of their market value.

"Did that sheriff in Charlotte give you any problems?"

"They were first in line, sir. I told you that guy was all mouth. After what we did in South Carolina, he has been careful to go out of his way to encourage submission to the federal laws."

"Good."

An hour later, Erdman was on the phone with a senior ATF agent in the Midwest. "How's the confiscation going in Illinois?"

"All who bucked the executive orders initially are now cooperating fully. There was a rally in a rural area of southern Illinois where thousands planned to show up for a shooting contest with their illegal firearms this morning in defiance of the confiscation program, but when we threatened the governor and the legislators that we would withhold Medicaid and Medicare funds, they fell right in line. To avoid federal intervention, the governor sent the Guard and the police down there to take the guns and knock some heads."

"Welfare saved us again! Thank you, FDR," Erdman exclaimed gleefully as he tapped some keys on his laptop.

As he feared, the news was dismal in the Rocky Mountain states.

"Not one gun?" Erdman said, surprised.

"Not even a B-B gun." The regional ATF director sat behind the former desk of the now deceased Ernie Harris. "Governor Boswell promises a ten thousand dollar fine for anyone who turns in a gun…"

"Ten thousand dollar fine?"

"Yes, *per gun!* Some cowards have sold them, but not to us."

"Aw, he's not going to enforce that fine."

"The bumpkins buyin' up the guns are exactly the kind of folks we don't want to have guns, people who'd use them against us."

Erdman hung his head in disappointment and sighed heavily.

"It's the churches, sir. Down south, those churches want to stay in the good graces of the IRS, so they're complicit. But in the Rockies, they act like the second amendment is one of the Ten Commandments." The Bozeman director laughed at his own comment, but Erdman did not find that humorous.

"Unbelievable!" Erdman exclaimed, distraught over the update, and filled with trepidation over having to share this with the president. "We're gonna have to start knocking on doors where we know they have guns."

"Door to door?" The senior ATF agent stood up out of his chair, disbelieving his ears. "Remember what happened when they raided the militia here? If you think the guerilla battles you have in the Texas suburbs are bad–"

"I know, I know." Erdman shook his head back and forth. "I don't have another option. The president has personally delegated these duties to us and failure is not an option. We *have* to go after the guns in Montana."

"You'll have an all-out war on your hands if you come in here door to door and try to take their guns." The ATF agent stood before the window where the bullet entered the room and slew Ernie Harris. He fingered the hole in the glass, which was now covered with duct tape. "You'll have to find someone else besides me to manage that nightmare."

August 1st came and went without a hitch in the Coalition of Free Christian States. Many communities held "Gun Shoots" where locals competed for prizes. The streets of Montana became a huge gun show where, for the first time in half a century, a background check was no longer necessary to buy or sell a gun.

The few remaining abortion clinics cancelled appointments for a couple of weeks and the abortionists fled the state for vacation, or worked temp jobs in safer places to kill. Physicians who practiced euthanasia procedures returned to their former practice of healthcare.

Federal buildings were strikingly silent, as most personnel called off work. The weather – dark and cloudy in the east, colorful in the west, with a chilly, gusty westward wind – seemed to reflect the strange uneasiness of the city streets. Big changes were coming, and only the naïve expected comfort and ease. The price for their freedom had not yet been paid.

Helena, Montana

"All right, General Bryan, summarize our combined military capabilities." Boswell motioned to his adjutant general in the presence of his cabinet in a stately room beside the governor's office. The leaders of the other Coalition states were present by way of their encrypted internet connection.

Bob Bryan introduced himself as the senior adjutant general of the Montana State Guard, and then he introduced Colonel Rod Sanders. "Rod Sanders led the Montana Guard's charge up the hill past ATF and FBI forces during Barry Friar's siege," he told them as the governors and their cabinets recollected and nodded. "I've asked him to report to you on the inventory we have taken of our military capabilities."

"Thanks you, sir," Sanders replied through a bushy blond mustache and redder goatee. He cleared his throat as he dropped the papers he held in his well-calloused hands to the finely polished table.

Sanders then recited from memory the extensive inventory of each the State Guards of the CFC States, the fighter jets, the bombers, the tanks, the helicopters, the Bradley fighting vehicles, and their fuel and ammunition capacity. He concluded, "Our combined Guard force is 12,500 men and women, a number that I suspect we could roughly double in the coming months with the influx of so many people from other states sympathetic with the Coalition. Thanks to hordes of Texas guardsmen who've immigrated here, we'll have approximately twice as many pilots as we have birds to fly. Most of the guard forces of the Coalition states have been integrating for training for decades."

General Bryan nodded at Sanders. "If we are invaded, the one capability that is perhaps most critical to our survival is control over at least one of the nuclear arsenals within the Coalition boundaries. Each of our states has nuclear weapons, but if Montana seceded all by itself, we would be the third largest nuclear power in the world, second only to the United States and Russia." That comment greatly encouraged the hearers, as evidenced by their nods and smiles. "The federal government secures those facilities and has control of the codes that are necessary to fire or transport the missiles. But, as for Montana, we have men that work in those facilities that are willing to aid us in gaining possession of those weapons if the federal government invades and violent self-defense becomes necessary. I cannot stress enough the importance of gaining control over at least one of those weapons. Just one weapon levels the playing field. It would give us a seat at the table of nations. If we lose that capacity, we will probably quickly lose any conflict of arms because they will have the only trump card."

"Would you," Governor Littman asked the question they all were thinking, "ever seriously consider firing them?"

Sanders and Bryan nodded at Boswell, as if expecting him to answer. All eyes fastened on the Montana governor. Boswell pursed his lips and crossed his hands over his chest. "It is a bluffing tool. We don't want to beat the bully on the block, we want to bluff them into a stalemate for fear of us. We want them to leave us alone. With a nuclear weapon, we'll have *less* violence and bloodshed in the streets."

"But taking control of a nuclear weapon belonging to the federal government…"

"Belonging to the people," Boswell corrected him. "It belongs to the taxpayers who paid for it."

"Operated by the federal government then," Governor Pollock asserted matter-of-factly. "You must know that confiscating a nuke would be considered an act of war. Our peaceful secession ceases to be peaceful when we confiscate a nuclear weapon within our borders. It escalates the conflict. The civilized nations of the world will unite against us."

"But they'll also leave us alone. Nuclear powers aren't invaded. Hasn't history shown us that? We would only confiscate one if invaded, or if invasion appeared inevitable."

"They would destroy us, Ben, if we moved on a nuke," someone added.

You could see the wheels in Ben Boswell's mind begin to turn. You could cut the tension in the room with a knife as the Coalition leaders began to count the cost once again. "That is our dilemma," Boswell admitted. "The best chance of preventing an invasion and winning our freedom may also be the quickest way to get invaded and annihilated. We need to give careful prayer to this, and at the very least monitor the nuclear arsenals within our borders."

* * * * *

"So you think Louis is going to do something to try to stop us?"

Governor Boswell grilled his chief of security, Isaiah Knabb, about a potential threat in the statehouse.

Isaiah Knabb was a short, balding man with thick arms and shoulders. He had managed the security for the governor and the statehouse for nine years. He stood in his beige suit in front of the governor's desk. "We know he's been talking to the FBI behind our backs. He's a fan of Margaret Brighton. He was on the list I gave you of employees whose loyalty to our independence was shaky."

"Being an unbeliever doesn't get you fired from employment in the state government, Isaiah." Governor Boswell rocked silently in his leather swivel chair for a moment. "I want to see the evidence that he's actually planned something."

"It's all circumstantial, sir. We've been watching him closely as you requested, and he spoke to the FBI district office in Billings for an hour yesterday. In the past week, he's made four phone calls to two different unregistered, untraceable numbers. Furthermore, we have just learned that he has a one-way plane ticket to Baltimore tomorrow. It leaves from Idaho."

Boswell raised one eyebrow and leaned forward on his elbows. "From Idaho?"

"And he's scheduled to work and hasn't requested time off. I don't know what he's planning, but the worst case scenario is that the feds will use him to do here what they did to Governor Adams in Austin."

Boswell appeared deep in thought. "Now'd be the time to do it, on the eve of their attempt to disarm us."

"Those who don't learn from history are bound to repeat it."

Boswell nodded soberly. "Do you have the perimeter secure?"

“Absolutely. There are no FBI personnel, as far as I know, in the vicinity. We have undercover personnel closely watching the FBI district office.”

Governor Boswell stood up from behind his chair, walked around and leaned against the front of the desk. “What do you propose we do?”

“I have no idea what Louis is planning, sir. He could be planning to shoot you as soon as you walk out that door, sir.” He pointed at the door to Boswell’s office.

“Where is he now?”

“I just put a lot of this information together in the past ten minutes, sir, and so he’s still on the job. He’s downstairs with the out-of-towners you planned to meet with five minutes ago.”

“I see.” Boswell rubbed the stubble on his chin and paced toward the mirror on the wall. *What could he be planning?*

“I guess the good news is that he has probably not planted the building with bombs, because he’s still in it.”

Boswell chuckled at Knabb’s attempt to look on the bright side. “I feel better already,” the governor muttered as he walked back around his desk and took his seat.

“We could apprehend him in the next 20 seconds, sir.”

“For what? He hasn’t done anything illegal.”

“Not yet, sir. He hasn’t done anything illegal yet. But he might break under interrogation. Our evidence against, although circumstantial, could provoke a confession. Give me a loose rope with him for 20 minutes in a sound-proof room, and he’ll be silly putty in our hands.”

Boswell shook his head, appearing disappointed with Isaiah Knabb’s proposal. “I know your resume, Isaiah. I know your experience as an Army interrogator. If he attempts to assassinate me, we’ll shoot him dead or put him on trial. But if there’s even a slim chance that he’s innocent, our interrogation will not involve torture in any way. Is that understood?”

Isaiah Knabb shrugged. “Even if it could save lives? Even if it could save our Coalition and our liberties?”

The governor spoke emphatically: “What if someone is setting him up, Isaiah? Circumstantial evidence is not sufficient to confirm guilt for a capital crime. He could just be a distraction that the feds are setting up to keep our sites on the wrong person. All the evidence against him could be fabricated.”

"I don't understand, sir. You're willing to fire a nuke at Washington, D.C. to save the Coalition, but not willing to torture one man in order to do so?"

"I can biblically justify annihilating the enemy, even with a significant amount of unintentional collateral damage, but I cannot biblically justify torturing this man if there's a chance he is innocent. We will not sacrifice our principles to torture him even for the chance that it will save our lives or our liberties. Our souls aren't expendable." Boswell shook his head vigorously back and forth. "We'll wage a justifiable war if we must, but we will not torture a potentially innocent man."

"Yes sir." Knabb nodded dutifully.

"How can God bless us with victory and liberty if we abuse an innocent man? Even if he confesses, how can we trust that confession and act on it with confidence if it was obtained by coercion?"

Knabb took a deep breath, and Boswell discerned that he still had something on his mind that he was reluctant to say. "Speak up, man. I know you want to say something."

"If we act on this intel and interrogate him, and he confesses guilt, then we could save lives and save our cause with minimal collateral damage."

"Almost anyone will reach the point of confessing a lie in order to stop pain."

Knabb raised his eyebrows and leaned into the governor. "I've been there, sir. Terrorists will confess the truth to stop the pain. I have proven it."

Boswell shook his head. "Possibly, but how could we use that confession in his trial?"

"We don't have to use it at his trial, or even have a trial. We just want to survive whatever he's conspiring to do."

"But how can God bless the devil's methods?" Boswell sighed. "Better to perish with the blessing of God than survive without it. Is that understood?"

Knabb heaved half a smile, wondering if the governor was being naïve.

"Don't be my Joab." Boswell thrust a stiff index finger at his chief of security. "You do not have permission to do something in your position that my conscience forbids. I'll stand before God and give an account for what you do under my authority."

"The call's yours, sir. We can still use this in our favor."

"What do you mean?"

"P.R., sir. If we catch this guy trying to do something to you and he confesses, we can make the case that Margaret Brighton conspired to overthrow our state government and our democratic Coalition with violence. That would do much to encourage public sympathy and expose her tyranny."

Boswell nodded. "Yes, it would."

"But we have to catch him in the act. It's risky because we don't know what he's going to do. We do have an advantage in that he doesn't suspect we're on to him, so I think we can trap him into making a move."

"Spring that trap with your finger on the trigger, Isaiah, or our foreknowledge won't help us at all. And keep your eyes in the shadows across from him. He could be a decoy to distract us."

* * * * *

David Jameson was the first in a line of 33 immigrants preparing to enter Governor Boswell's office. When a security guard opened the door and invited them in, David held the door for the men behind him. They trickled in, awestruck and honored to be in the presence of the Chairman of the Coalition of Free Christian States, who stood up from behind his stately desk. David was the last to enter. He removed his cap, sporting his recently shaved head. His leadership skills were self-evident among the caravan of Christians who joined him on their way to Montana. They impacted city after city with revival meetings. David's thin goatee had evolved into a light brown beard. He wore a white T-shirt, dark green carpenter pants and sandals. He was surprised to find the governor to be thinner and taller in person than he appeared on television. He hoped that it was because the governor was fasting. David imagined the many snares that the enemy must be setting up before this great statesman. David couldn't imagine such a man holding true without continual prayer and fasting.

"Why don't you each have a seat?" Governor Boswell motioned to the men and women that trickled into his office. He shook the hand of the first uniformed Texas Guard officer to get within reach. "Honored to have you join us."

"Thank you." The Texas Guard Major grabbed Governor Boswell's outstretched hand with both of his. "If you're honored to have me, then surely you will want to meet Alan MacIntosh, the Adjutant General of the Texas State Guard." He glanced toward the door. "General MacIntosh," the Guard officer called out to him, "meet Governor Benjamin Boswell." General MacIntosh, sporting a black cowboy hat, approached the governor with his wild-west swagger. He had a small black Bible in the top pocket of his khaki shirt and donned well-worn Ariat boots.

"How did you come to be the only one in Governor Adams' cabinet not to get arrested by the FBI?" Governor Boswell asked as they shook hands.

"When they barged in with their guns, I made a break for a closet door and locked it behind me. I got away through a tile in the ceiling before they could get the door open."

Governor Boswell put his head back and laughed. "Thank the Lord! We sure could use you up here."

The security officer that Knabb suspected had turned against them approached from the corner of the office toward the semi-circle of 35 chairs that were in front of the governor's broad desk. He came to a standstill behind David Jameson's chair, which was the third chair away from the desk. He rested his hands on the back of the chair.

When Boswell saw the suspicious security guard draw near, he went and sat behind his desk. "Let's take turns introducing–"

"Excuse me for a sec." Isaiah Knabb interrupted the governor. With his eyes fixed on his cell phone, he said, "I need to speak to you for a moment about a matter of some urgency."

Boswell appeared frustrated at the unwelcomed interruption. He clasped his hands on his desk and cocked his head to the side. "What is it?"

Isaiah Knabb stepped between the governor and the suspicious security guard, the stout-faced Louis Derry. He leaned close to the governor's cheek and whispered loud enough for Louis to hear, "We suspect that one of your employees is participating in a plot to take you down today."

"Today?"

Knabb nodded. "Soon."

"Why am I just learning about this?" The governor stretched out his hands in frustration. "Why now?"

Knabb turned his cell phone briefly toward the governor, as if blaming his technology for the inconvenient timing of the warning.

David overheard the chief of security's comments, and had a strange *deja vu* sensation. The whole scenario reminded him of how he envisioned the governor of Texas going down. He began to pray silently and recalled a vivid dream that placed him in a similar scenario. He knew that this was not a coincidence. He was here by God's design.

Boswell looked surprised at the warning from his chief of security. It took a lot of effort to keep him from glancing at Louis to see the grimace on his face when he overheard Isaiah's warning.

General MacIntosh of the Texas Guard, who sat next to David, also overheard the comment. "We've got your back, Governor."

Governor Boswell inquired of Knabb, "Who is it?"

"We've got an insider at the Bureau's office in Billings who's going to call me in a few minutes with a name," he whispered, again loud enough to be heard by those nearby. "I've got the exits covered. We'll catch him."

Boswell finally turned his gaze to the suspicious guard. His eyes locked with Louis Derry's. The guard's shifting stance and sweaty forehead declared his guilt. The governor was careful to glance at the other security guards, but then his eyes turned back to Louis.

Isaiah Knabb's cell phone rang. "There he is now. Just a minute and I'll have a name for you." He flipped open his folded cell phone and brought it to his face. He turned his back to Louis and reached for his taser gun inside his sports coat. The two security guards behind Louis also reached inside their shoulder holsters and rested their hands on their weapons.

General Macintosh leaned toward Governor Boswell and rested his left elbow on the arm of his chair. "Maybe you shouldn't have had us declare our handguns downstairs," he complained. "Then we could defend you."

Ben Boswell did not make eye contact with the Texas Guard general, as greater concerns held his attention. "Maybe you're right," he mumbled.

Most in the room were too distant to make sense of the worried whispers, and they chatted with each other softly, oblivious to the contention. Isaiah Knabb heard a snap coming from the security guard behind David Jameson – it was Louis Derry, inconspicuously unsnapping his under-the-jacket holster. Knabb's hair stood up on end. The guards reached for their handguns and began to close in.

David's eyes were closed as he prayed silently in his seat, when suddenly Louis grabbed David by the arm. "This fellow's suspicious. I'm taking him out of here." He lifted David out of his seat and began to pull him toward the door.

"What? What did I do?" David pleaded for an explanation of the security guard's treatment of him as he was pulled toward the door.

Isaiah Knabb knew immediately that Louis was taking a hostage. "Now!" he shouted as he drew his taser weapon. The two other security guards that were aware of Knabb's plan to try to trap Louis finally drew their handguns. Governor Boswell instinctively dropped under his desk and most of the men in the room, having risked so much to even be there that day, stood to their feet, preparing to come to the Coalition leader's aid.

David felt the guard's arm around his neck squeeze tightly, making his eyes feel like they were going to bulge out of his head. Before he even caught a glimpse of the traitor's handgun, he saw the other security guards raise their weapons and scream out incoherent threats. When he sensed the handgun move past his ear and level out toward the governor's desk, David jerked his head to the right to disturb the traitor's aim. The bullet went high and right, piercing the window behind the desk. The window cracks expanded outward from the bullet hole as fast as lightening, brightening the room with reflected sunlight.

The other security guards were prepared for Louis to make his move, but they were not prepared for a stranger to be used as a shield. To those who stood around the room in front of their chairs, seconds seemed like minutes.

Screaming in pain from the loud blast of the gun right next to his ear, David reached up and grabbed the traitor's wrist. He pulled it down and sunk his teeth into it.

The assassin fired again and his bullet struck the front leg of the governor's desk. It came crashing to the floor. Isaiah hit the traitor in the left shoulder with a taser, which sent him to his back, seizing from the burst of electricity. David, whose left arm was still in the grip of the traitor and whose teeth were still clenched to the man's wrist, received a burst of voltage and rolled off the traitor.

The security guards rushed to subdue the semi-conscious traitor and place him under arrest. The room went black to David for a moment, and then he felt hands under his arms pull him to his feet.

"Are you all right?" Governor Boswell studied David's glazed-over eyes, tempted to call for paramedics.

David shook off his shock, and asked Governor Boswell with a trembling voice, "Are you?"

"Yes." The governor smiled and patted David on a shoulder. "He missed."

"The Lord has protected us." David's entire body was covered with goose bumps. The whole room unleashed a gasp of relief and David, still dizzy with adrenaline, fell to his knees. He bowed his body to the ground in reverent worship. "Praise the Lord Jesus Christ."

The meeting continued in the governor's office as Isaiah Knabb questioned the handcuffed traitor in an adjacent room.

As everyone settled into the seats around the governor's office, they chatted excitedly. Two security guards kindly brought bottles of water, hot coffee, and platters of donuts, and the men were helping themselves.

David spoke with Governor Boswell in the corner of the room as the Montana attorney general and two security guards stood beside them. "The greatest threat to the Coalition comes not from traitors," David ventured to say. "It comes from your own heart."

"My own heart?" Boswell glanced at his A.G., Chad Dreifuss, who shrugged. He had expected David to say that the greatest threat comes from those in your inner circle, given how the governor of Texas was brought down by a cabinet member and how Louis Derry just made an attempt on Boswell's life. "From *my* heart?"

David nodded.

Governor Boswell moved in closer to David. "Why would you say that?" He expected like-minded Christians emigrating from military-occupied Texas to be awed in the presence of CFCS leadership, not critical.

"I believe the Lord would say to you that traitors are manageable, but there are moral pitfalls nearby which you may have not foreseen and which have felled leaders much greater than you. King David's secret sin of numbering Israel brought a plague upon the whole nation." David paused to ascertain whether the governor was following him.

Boswell looked at his A.G., then glanced back at David, cockeyed. "You're worried that I'm going to number Montana?"

David smiled warmly, disarming the governor. “No sir, but there are moral pitfalls that you may not have considered and the whole Coalition will suffer for it should you stumble into ‘em.”

“And what are these moral pitfalls, sir, that may bring suffering upon the Coalition?” Boswell’s tone was skeptical and untrusting. He was unaccustomed to being addressed in such a condescending fashion by unemployed lay pastors, and there were a lot of fruitcakes out there.

David’s gaze penetrated deep into the eyes of the Montana governor. He spoke firmly, with confidence. “Faith in the flesh. The Bible tells us not to trust in chariots and horses but in the Lord. It is He” – David pointed heavenward – “that tears down one king and sets up another, and it is He that gives victory or defeat. The battle belongs to the Lord.” The governor nodded, agreeing. “Do not make King Saul’s mistake and become great in your own eyes. Do not place your faith in guns, good legislation, and popularity. We don’t war against flesh and blood, but against principalities and spiritual wickedness in high places. The weapons that will win this war are heavenly. Just as Moses raised his hands toward heaven and Israel experienced victory in the valley below, and when Moses lowered his hands, the enemy encroached upon them, so you must keep your eyes on Jesus and your prayers fervent for victory to be assured. The Coalition needs an army of Christian evangelists and prayer warriors much more than we need an army of skilled M-16-toting soldiers, Apache helicopters, and a nuclear weapon.”

The reference to a nuclear weapon startled the governor, as if he was stunned that David had read his mind. The concern that he gain control of at least one nuke had possessed his mind, and his conscience nodded at this reminder from the strange bald man with the brown beard that had saved his life. Victory was more contingent on the favor of God Almighty than it was on becoming a nuclear power.

“God might wish to whittle our little army down as he did Gideon’s army. The Coalition forces might go from tens of thousands to hundreds. Don’t lose faith when that happens. *Faith* is the victory that overcomes the world, and faith is the evidence of things *not* seen with the natural eyes.”

David paused. The Coalition chairman seemed deeply introspective. David noticed the security personnel that stood beside them shift uneasily. He had delivered the mail that he believed God wanted him to deliver.

Governor Boswell squinted, and then nodded soberly. He turned to Chad Dreifuss. “Did you write that down?”

Dreifuss' countenance changed. "Uh, not yet." Dreifuss fumbled for a pen in his coat pocket.

"I have it in writing." David reached into his pants pocket and handed Boswell a folded piece of paper. "Everything I told you has been bathed in prayer."

Boswell glanced at the folded paper, opened it, and looked at Jameson again. *Who was this strange man with a shaved head and scraggly brown beard who dressed like a bum but spoke like a prophet?* "Thank you, Mr., uh," – he looked at the name tag adhered to David's white T-shirt, which only had David's first name on it. "Mr. David…?" He paused to let David finish his sentence by giving him his last name.

"Jameson – uh, Jamestown, sir. David Jamestown. From Texas. I've been pastoring about a dozen Coalition-bound families."

"You look vaguely familiar to me. Have we met before?"

"No sir," David responded instinctively. Then he began to wonder if the governor recognized him as the suspect of the terrorist bombing in Ohio. His picture was on the FBI's ten most wanted list and was in every post office and federal building in the nation. His beard, after all, was not that thick, but his face had developed a darker complexion with all the sun exposure he received on the road. He was also quite a bit thinner at 150 pounds. Perhaps the governor had seen him between Robert Boniface and Governor Adams before Adams' famous speech on the floor of the Texas legislature. He further wondered if the governor would turn him in if he figured it out. But when Governor Boswell shook his hand firmly, he saw trust in those eyes. Governor Boswell's warm smile calmed David's fears as quickly as they came.

A security guard made an announcement. "Everybody, please be seated." More leaders from out-of-state had arrived and chairs had to be set up two rows thick in a semi-circle in front of the governor's desk.

When they all quieted down, Boswell sat back down behind his desk. Several books had been propped under the front part of the desk where the leg was shot out from underneath it by Derry. Two strips of gray duct tape were spread across the bullet hole in the glass behind the governor, artfully forming the shape of a cross. "I invited you all here because you want to serve the cause of liberty. You're pastors, mayors, engineers, electricians, carpenters, and military officers." He paused, and then glanced at David with pursed lips. "But there are also evil men among you." Everyone looked startled and began to look around at the others around him. "Not necessarily in this room, but among your acquaintances, among the people you have brought to the Coalition. Like the Apostle Paul said, there are false brethren creeping in, sent here to spy and hinder your liberty. The Lord has taught us a very important lesson today, and we must learn it well. It's the lesson that Henry Adams had to learn the hard way. It's the sinners closest to you that will betray you for the federal government's silver pieces. Like Jesus said, it's the wolf in sheep's clothing that destroys the flock. It's the little foxes that spoil the vine. A little leaven leavens the whole loaf of bread." He paused, looked down at his hands, and sighed deeply.

"The most devious of the little foxes is the sin in our own lives, gentlemen. We need to get the sin out of our lives before we'll ever be able to keep the federal government out of our states, for tyranny always enters a vacuum of righteousness. We don't want to learn the hard way what Israel learned with their first defeat in their Promised Land through the sin of Achan. If there is sin in our camp, we will suffer defeat. Our God shows Himself strong on behalf of the pure in heart." The men in the room did not expect such words from the governor of Montana. As honorable a man as he was, he was still a politician, not a preacher. Even his A.G. Chad Dreifuss simply stood in awe, completely stunned with the spiritual depth of his understanding, fixed on his every word.

"I was going to ask you each to join the Guard, but," – the governor paused and looked at David – "I stand corrected. Those of you with military experience would do well to join the Guard, but that is not our greatest need right now. I'm going to ask you each to fast, pray, and prepare the people for liberty."

Most of the men present seemed surprised at the comment, but David smiled.

"There is an incredible enthusiasm in the people of the Coalition states to be free from the tyranny. To desire to be liberated from tyranny is one thing, but to want to submit to godly government is quite another. We have had a spiritual revolution in our states, no doubt about it, but do we have the character necessary to secure victory all the way to the next generation? It is one thing to cross the Red Sea to leave Egypt and enter the desert, but it is quite another to cross the Jordan to leave the desert and enter the Promised Land. Not all who came out of Egypt made it. Do you understand?" The room full of men nodded soberly.

"General MacIntosh, I see you have a Bible in your top pocket. Will you read Jeremiah 18, verses 7 through 10?"

"Sure." The general opened up his small black Bible. "At what instant I shall speak concerning a nation and a kingdom, to pluck up, to pull down, and to destroy it, if that nation against whom I have pronounced turn from their evil, I will repent of the evil that I thought to do unto them. And at what instant I shall speak concerning a nation and concerning a kingdom, to build and to plant it, if it does evil in My sight, that it obeys not My voice, then I will repent of the good wherewith I said I would benefit them."

Boswell began to elaborate on the passage, "You see, defeat under a tyrant and victory over a tyrant are simply two different consequences of following two different paths. I'm not convinced that the people of the Coalition are fit for the path of liberty. Not yet. I want each of you to discover how many mature saints you have among you who are willing to be the prayer warriors and prophets of the Coalition. I've got a meeting this evening with about 700 pastors representing 50 thousand Christians, and we're going to raise a new kind of spiritual army. Before we can repel the gates of hell outside our borders, we need to tear them down within our borders. We need to prepare the people for freedom. I envision conferences and lectures all over the Coalition that will instruct the people on the role of the law and the Gospel, of the role and limitations of godly government. We need to learn how to be free again." Many of the men nodded enthusiastically and exhaled "amens" at the governor's thoughtful words.

"So we're gonna have a state-sponsored church?" someone ventured to ask.

Boswell shook his head. "No. The church of Jesus Christ," he spoke deliberately and circumspectly, "is the salt of the earth, not the state. The gates of hell will not prevail against *the church.* If our liberties are to be preserved, it will not be because of our state government. It will be because the church has risen against the moral corruption in our land that would usher up in defeat." He turned to David.

"David Jamestown?" Governor Boswell's eyes studied him carefully for a moment. "Is your family in order?"

David was surprised that he was being singled out for questioning in front of everybody. His mouth suddenly became as dry as a desert. "As much as is possible now that they are behind enemy lines in Texas. Yes sir, we're in order."

Suddenly, Isaiah Knabb barged into the room. "Governor Boswell! I'm sorry to interrupt, but I must have a moment with you."

Governor Boswell stood up from his chair. "Of course. I'll be right back."

The governor followed his chief of security from the room, down the hall, and into an adjacent room. "Did Louis confess anything?"

Knabb sighed and turned on his heels in the hallway, his shifting eyes searching the shadows for eavesdroppers. "He claims he's acting independently. I know you didn't want me to get aggressive with him, but I have another plan you might appreciate."

"What's that?"

"Let's make the president think he's talked," Knabb proposed. "Or else, let's get her to fear that he might."

Boswell grimaced and leaned against the wall. "We're not going to make the president think that we are willing to torture her spy, anymore than I'm going to try to make her think that I'm going to commit adultery or do anything else immoral. We don't defeat the enemy by imitating their immorality."

"No, no, no. Let's barter with her for him." Knabb grinned widely and shoved his hands deep into his pockets. "We can even send her the footage of the attack that we retrieved from the cameras we installed in your office."

"Barter for what? If she won't give in to our demands to prevent ten states from seceding, what makes you think she'll give in to keep a spy from talking?"

"What does she have that you could use, something that isn't very valuable to her?"

Twenty minutes later, Governor Boswell re-entered his office. "I apologize for the interruption." The governor took his seat as the men quieted down their chatting. "Where were we? Oh yes, David Jamestown."

David set down his coffee and nodded at the governor. "Yes sir?"

"David Jamestown will be training all our prayer warriors and speakers for, oh, let's say four weeks. During that time of prayer and preparation, we'll be scheduling conferences all over the Coalition, in auditoriums, large churches, colleges and universities. We'll get as much air and radio time as possible."

David was stunned at the honor just bestowed upon him. The governor didn't ask if David would lead, he just stated that he would.

"We've had a great revival in Montana, but the churches generally don't address what God's Word says about civil government, probably for fear of losing their 501c3 IRS status. Well, thank God that chapter of our state's history is coming to a close." He lifted an envelope on his desk into the air. "Just in time, too, for I just received a letter from the IRS that I've been audited." Laughs broke out throughout the room. "David Jamestown will be responsible for training the army of Christian warriors who will secure the hearts of our people for God and prepare us for the Promised Land of liberty and justice for all."

"I love the idea, Governor," said David, "but–"

"You're also going with me to the pastor's conference in a few hours, if that's okay with you. We've got to sell the local spiritual leadership on our vision."

"But you already have local leadership. If you place new captains on old ships, you'll have a mutiny on your hands. I'm an outsider, but I've been here long enough to discover that Montanans are naturally distrusting of outsiders."

"You'll have a local leader to help," the governor added with a broad smile. "I just spoke with President Brighton, and she's agreed to trade Louis Derry, the security guard who attempted to kill me an hour ago, for Barry Friar."

The men in the room gasped. Even the security guards were taken aback. "Barry Friar?" said three or four people simultaneously with their eyebrows raised.

"How is that possible?" a security guard blurted out.

"But he's been in federal custody ever since he was acquitted in his state trial," someone else said.

"Well, turns out that the president wants her spy more than she wants Barry Friar, and has agreed to a prisoner exchange. I'd trust Barry with my life. He's earned the respect of every patriot in the nation. He'll have to stay in the Coalition to remain free, and it would be in our best interest to keep it from the media as long as possible, but free he will be. He'll be assisting David Jamestown in this endeavor. Chad?" The governor turned his attention to the attorney general. "Get some of my speech-writers to make some television and radio ads. Address it to the church in the CFC States. Inform them of our mission and call for volunteers. We've got an army of godly freedom-lovers immigrating from all over the country into the Coalition, and I want to give them something to do as soon as they arrive. I want a website on this, too."

"Yes sir," Dreifuss said, tapping on his miniature laptop.

"In the first American revolution, the Minutemen were the heart and soul of the resistance, prepared to defend their liberties with just a minute's notice. Priority number one is calling God's people to prevailing prayer. The weapons of our warfare are not carnal, but mighty through God to the pulling down of strongholds and every high thing that exalts itself against the knowledge of Christ."

Chief of Security Knabb leaned over with a doubtful grimace and asked Attorney General Dreifuss, "Do you think the governors will go along with this idea?"

"Of course. We're a Coalition of Free *Christian* States, are we not?"

* * * * *

"This is the *craziest* thing I have ever heard," blurted out Governor Pollock from Idaho, flanked by his cabinet and his Guard generals. The entire Coalition leadership, with the cabinets and Guard generals, were present via their encrypted internet connections.

Boswell was adamant with his plan. He wasn't budging. Beside the governor sat David Jameson, whom Boswell had just introduced to the Coalition's leadership as "David Jamestown, a pastor from Texas."

"You can't have freedom without morality and you can't have morality without God!" Boswell asserted. "It's the *Christian* Bible our presidents place their right hand upon when they take their oath. It was the *Christian* Bible that George Washington and Thomas Jefferson said was indispensable to good government." Most of the governors were speechless, listening intently.

"How is this compatible with the first amendment?" the elderly Nebraska governor asked. "Our federal Constitution forbids a state establishment of religion?"

"*Congress* shall make no law respecting an establishment of religion," said Boswell. "Is Montana Congress?" He paused and no one responded. "At the time the first amendment was penned, almost every state had a tax-subsidized Christian denomination. That did not violate the first amendment. When the American forefathers forbade an establishment of religion in the Constitution, they were forbidding a federally authorized church like the Church of England. Our Minutemen are diverse, from many different Christian denominations and persuasions." The CFCS leaders appeared remarkably subdued in spite of the political incorrectness of Boswell's impromptu history lesson.

"One of the *first acts* of the original Congress," Boswell continued, "was to spend taxpayer dollars to purchase Bibles for distribution throughout the nation. They knew that the religion of Christianity must flourish in the hearts of Americans in order for our nation to remain free. Without a thorough saturation of *our* people with the teachings of God's

Word on law, liberty, and justice, we will not remain steadfast when the times get tough. Oh, our people might be cheering us on now, but when their stomachs growl and when the caskets of their sons and husbands start piling up, will we keep firm in purpose then? This notion that we can be neutral with regard to Jesus Christ is a lie straight from the pit of hell. Jesus said that we're either for Him or against Him. We're either gathering for Him or scattering abroad. We must build the Coalition upon the religion of Jesus Christ, or we will fail."

The governors were silent as they measured all their beliefs about duty and government in light of the standard of righteousness that Boswell proposed. The supreme lordship of Christ over their land and their people was a truth that they all intellectually embraced, but had not yet applied to every aspect of their state governments.

"Our states are still in the danger zone," Boswell said. "Our freedom is only as secure as our virtue. 'Righteousness exalts a nation,' it says in Psalms, 'but sin is a reproach for any people.' We still have sin – *a lot* of sin – in our states: sodomy, adultery, drunkenness, pornography, divorce, casinos full of prostitution. I've read that a sect of anarchists has grown so large in Seattle that the downtown auditorium isn't large enough to seat them all. Is that right, Governor Littman?" Littman nodded.

"We have followed a secular, pagan model for government for so long that most of us don't even know what a godly government would look like. The success of the Coalition may depend more on our ability to move heaven through our prayers and capture the hearts and minds of our citizens than it does upon our armed forces."

David just couldn't control his glee anymore. In the midst of the zeal of the chairman and the silence of his listeners, his laugh seemed quite out of place. This was a dream come true, and joy bubbled in his bosom like a lively spring. He exclaimed, "Praise God!" and laughed again.

In response to David's spontaneous release of joy, all eyes were on him. So Governor Boswell offered him an opportunity to address the Coalition's leadership. "David, would you like to say something?"

"I am so thrilled with what I'm hearing," he said with a wide smile. "To think that ten states are daring to build their government on the shoulders of the Most High is evidence of a powerful move of God here. We *will* tread Satan under our feet shortly, if we will trust God and be obedient. I do have some concern." He adopted a sober countenance, "that many of you are not strong enough in your commitment. If you object to Governor Boswell's rhetoric, what are you going to do when it's practiced?" After a pause, he asked, "Have you each banned the shedding of innocent blood?" The governors were silent. David asked again, "Have you each banned abortion in your states?"

Governor Boswell was the first to respond. "Well, I don't know about you all, but Montana's still working things out with prosecutors. How do you punish people for a crime for which a judge will not convict them because of Supreme Court precedent? How do you arrest an abortionist when he has armed Marshalls as bodyguards? Passing our Life Bill did shut down almost all of the abortion clinics as far as I know, but we haven't worked out the kinks in the system to prosecute the law's violators yet."

"Until we do," David said matter-of-factly, shaking his head, "then we're wasting our time. An abortion ban is just hypocritical rhetoric until we disseminate justice. Shouldn't the Confederate states' resistance to federal usurpations have taught us something? The Confederates wanted to protest D.C.'s tyranny against them while justifying their tyranny over the slaves. As long as we have the log in our own eye in allowing the killing of innocent children in our state, we have no business trying to get the mote out of the federal government's eye. Until we end abortion in our lawful and constitutional jurisdiction, our attempts to secede will not have the blessing of God."

"But how will they be judged?" Governor Pollock of Idaho asked. "How can we judge abortionists if the judges adhere to precedent and submit to the High Court's lawless decisions?"

David grinned. "I'll be glad to be a judge, if you lack any who know what justice looks like. Give us one month to train volunteers, and if you're content to have the Bible as your rulebook for criminal justice, I'll get you 1,000 righteous judges."

"Are you an attorney?" someone asked.

David laughed and shook his head. "God's law doesn't require you to be in order to do justice. Only when justice has been done will we finally cleanse the Coalition of the guilt of innocent blood and win our liberty."

Ben Boswell smiled as he nodded at David, and then his A.G. "Yes sir."

Billings, Montana

"Uh, Dr. Terrence?" The nurse poked her head in the door and interrupted the abortionist.

"Can it wait?" he barked as he crouched between the legs of his sedated patient.

"No."

Her urgent tone concerned him, and so he turned away from the patient to see a guardsman in uniform with a hand on a holstered handgun. A police officer with his pistol drawn followed the guardsman into the room.

The physician covered the patient's privates with a sterile green towel and pulled his surgical mask off of his face. "I'm in the middle of a life-saving procedure," the physician breathed nervously.

"Have you killed the baby yet?" Colonel Rod Sanders asked as he moved to the side of the young lady. When the abortionist was hesitant to answer, he repeated a little louder, "Have you killed the baby yet?!"

The abortionist was as speechless as the patient's volleyball coach, who sat in a chair in the corner of the room. "Uh, yes," the physician said, carefully setting down the bloody suction tube and pointing at the half-filled plastic container on the side of the suction machine. "This is a therapeutic abortion, medically-necessary. I'm almost done, sir. I need you to step outside and give the patient her privacy."

"You're under arrest," Sanders informed him. He glanced at the man with the cap in the corner of the room. "Are you her father?"

The man swallowed hard. "No."

Sanders turned to the officer that stood behind him. "Call 911. Have the county coroner examine this," he said, pointing at the jar on the machine. "We'll need an autopsy of the victim for evidence."

"Autopsy of the victim?"

"Yeah, of the dead baby if the baby's dead." Sanders turned to the chief of police that was just entering the room. "We need to get your best investigators in here and document this evidence."

"This is absurd!" the abortionist blurted out.

"This is a legal procedure," the man with the cap insisted, standing to his feet.

Sanders placed his hand on top of his unsnapped holster and shouted, "Sit down!" The man's face grew redder by the minute. Trembling, he complied with the feisty guardsman.

"We have U.S. Marshalls here," the abortionist said, his gaze shifting back and forth from guardsman to guardsman. "Where are they?"

"Oh, we've got 'em down the hall. They're under arrest as well as the other accomplices. And if we catch the janitor and the guy who mows the lawn out front, they'll be arrested, too, if they know what goes on inside this building."

"I want to speak to my lawyer," the man with the cap adamantly demanded.

"All in due time," Sanders said as he grabbed the abortionist by the sleeve, twisted him around, and thrust his wide frame against the wall. "I'd like to meet the guy who's got the guts to defend you in Montana. If he justifies the killing of innocent children, we might charge him as an accomplice too. Up against the wall!" he ordered the reluctant abortionist. A police officer entered the room and began to pat him down for weapons.

Sanders walked closer to the sedated girl. "She doesn't look a day over 15!" He grabbed the chart and exclaimed. "She's 14 years old!" Sander's gaze shifted to the man in the ball cap. "Are you her father?"

He shook his head side to side. "I'm her coach, volleyball coach. Just doin' a favor for my star player."

Sanders' gaze turned to the abortionist. "Even when abortion was legal in Montana, you know state law mandated that health professionals must inform the authorities if they suspect the sexual abuse of a minor?"

"This pregnancy is a threat to the patient's psychological health according to her psychiatrist," the abortionist responded. With his hands cuffed behind his back, he motioned with his head to the patient's chart on the counter, which Sanders snatched up. "It's medically necessary!"

"Is this the psych's name?" Sanders pointed at a name on the chart. "Dr. Tom Donald?"

The abortionist nodded.

Sanders handed the chart to an officer in the doorway. "Put a warrant out for the psychiatrist's arrest."

"Yes sir!"

Sanders turned to the red-faced man with the black ball cap. "Is the baby yours?" The man did not answer, so Sanders speculated, "You got her pregnant and are trying to cover your crime, huh?" When the man did not defend himself, Sanders unholstered his weapon, keeping it at the ready. "You're under arrest for raping a minor, an accomplice to murder if the baby's dead, and accomplice to attempted murder if the baby lives. Cuff him!" The coach's red face turned even redder as the deputy walked over to him, stood him up to face the wall, roughly frisked him, and began to cuff his hands tightly behind his back.

"Aren't you gonna read me my rights?" the coach mumbled.

"You have the right to a fair and speedy trial," the officer replied.

Sanders handed the chart to an officer. "Notify her parents immediately."

The coach spoke up. "We have a court order to get the abortion without notifying the parents. Please!"

"Who? Which Judge?" Sanders asked. When the coach was reluctant to answer, Sanders said, "We're going to find out and arrest him as an accomplice, too."

"We're going to sue you in federal court for everything you have, you know that?" the physician threatened as he was being led from the room.

"You'll have to file that suit in another state, and you'll have to survive your own jury trial here first."

"You're not going to get away with this!" the physician hollered frantically as an officer pushed him down the hallway.

Sanders handcuffed the girl's coach, and then the nurse. He marched his prisoners, including the two U.S. Marshalls, out the front door in a single file line as two paramedics rushed into the building with a stretcher to carry one live patient and one dead baby to the emergency room. As he walked his prisoners toward the police vehicles, the twelve pro-life protesters on the sidewalk vigorously clapped and cheered. One of the young men walked onto the property and began to wave a large flag that read "Personhood now!"

Colonel Rod Sanders stopped the line and had his prisoners turn toward the protesters. "Smile!" he told them as the camera flashes overwhelmed the light of the morning sun. "Got to look good for tomorrow's front page."

The crowd cheered and praised God as the Guard colonel assisted the abortionist into one squad car, and the chief of police directed the two Marshalls and the other accomplices into a police van. Sanders slammed the door of the car and turned to the protesters. The words he spoke would be the next day's headline of every newspaper in the entire nation.

"You win!"

Washington, D.C.

"Montana has begun to arrest abortionists, Madam President," Hamilton informed her over the secure internet connection as she sat at her office desk writing a letter. "A physician named Dr. Al Terrence and his entire nursing and secretarial staff have been arrested at the last standing abortion clinic in Montana. Even a 14-year-old patient who was undergoing an abortion was charged with murder."

"Murder?" The president looked up from the letter she was writing to the family of an Army private that was killed by Texas citizens during a raid. She took a deep breath. "Where were our Marshalls?"

"Arrested as accomplices, Madam President. Montana's abortion ban isn't just rhetoric anymore."

The president appeared stunned by the announcement, and Hamilton judged that naïve. After the failure of Louis Derry, he thought this outcome was predictable.

"Do we have anybody else inside besides Derry?" the president asked.

"We did, but they won't cooperate with us anymore."

"Is Louis Derry back yet?"

"He's being debriefed. We'll keep you up to date on any intel gained."

"I want you to take Ben Boswell out of the equation, Todd. We'll get the judiciary to release those people as soon as possible."

"The Coalition won't respect any federal court's decision – they've already made that plain. And state judges that side with the reproductive health providers have been threatened with arrest."

"How are we going to fix this, Todd? How are we going to keep the clinics open in the Coalition states?"

"I was speaking with Cameron Weaver about it. He thinks we should take advantage of the tremendous negative publicity regarding the killings of abortion providers. You've heard about the Chicago abortion sniper? He's struck again."

The president nodded and turned her attention to the letter she was writing. "They are beyond the point of being intimidated by the media, Todd. It will certainly affect Boswell's popularity here, but not in Montana."

The FBI director shrugged. "Short of invasion, I don't know. They're not letting our jailed agents go. It's time for you to meet with the Joint Chiefs. The National Guards in the northwestern states aren't national anymore. They are allegiant to their governors. We need the armed forces."

She had drained her FBI director of all his best answers, and so now he would not protest as much when she proposed hers. "I'm not gonna let you knock the ball into somebody else's court, Todd. I have been in contact with some friends who have another plan to go in and turn the tables on those Confederate trouble-makers."

"Really? Who?"

"They're on their way here now."

In a room full of slang chatter, Mitch Paine could barely make out the familiar voice that called out his name from the other end of the room: “Professor Paine?” Paine wore his classic silk button-up T-shirt with flower embroidery, khaki slacks and shiny maroon dress shoes. As always, his shoulder length hair was pulled back to a ponytail. “Professor?” Paine turned and saw a face approaching that looked familiar.

“Will Overall, remember me?”

The clean-cut 30-year-old college dropout extended a fist, which Paine tapped with his own. “Oh yes. White Overalls.” The White Overalls were a group of Marxist social activists.

“Hi Mitch!” someone called out beside him.

This was a former student of Paine’s and the present national director of Act Out, a homosexual activist organization. “Good to see you again.” Paine shook his sweaty hand gently, careful not to wince at the sight of his long, pink-painted fingernails. The man tried to look like a princess, but still shook hands like a sumo wrestler.

Behind him, were the leaders of the Sienna Club, Anti-Fascist Action, and the Abortion Rights Action League.

Dozens of some of the most famous and infamous liberals and social activists in the nation began to trickle into the large waiting room of the federal government building in downtown Washington, D.C. Several anti-gun groups were present as well. There were a few leaders from “Enough Already” and other environmental organizations. There were also some anarchists and anti-capitalists that, as far as Paine was aware, were wanted by the United States for terrorist activities. Mitch was surprised that they appeared fearless in the presence of the federal agents at the door. He recognized one anarchist who he thought had a 20-year prison sentence for killing a police officer with a Molotov cocktail at the last G-20 conference. *What are they doing here?*

Introductions were warm and cordial between all, but Paine clearly was the most recognizable and most admired personality in the room. His books, his motivating speeches, and his televised debates with right-wing religious leaders won him many admirers on the left.

The group gradually grew to 40 until several government agents in dark suits joined the two at the door and they entered the room together, silencing the whispering throughout the room. "Can I have your attention, please?" one of them shouted louder than necessary.

"It's Agent Smith." The comment from one of the hippies nearest the door sparked light-hearted laughter among the others.

"Take the blue pill, Neo," a thoroughly tattooed young man near Paine humored the guests.

"Let's get out of the matrix and back into reality," the agent responded without smiling. "Please line up in a single file line for a brisk search. Thank you for your cooperation."

Some of the social activists complained. "Search us? Why? We had to go through a metal-detector downstairs."

"If you want to meet with the president, you must consent to be searched. No exceptions."

Mitch Paine was the first in line. As one of the agents began to search him, he said, "It's a small price to pay to get on board with President Brighton's fundie eradication project." Dozens of progressives chuckled in response and reluctantly began to line up for the search.

Mitch Paine led the way down the hall and into a room where 40 elegant chairs were set in rows in front of a large wooden desk. He took the seat nearest the desk, and the others followed his lead.

When President Brighton walked into the room five minutes later, flanked by Secret Servicemen, all of the progressive activists spontaneously stood to their feet out of reverence.

"Thank you," she said, handing her briefcase to one of her guards and marching right up to Mitch Paine. She took his right hand in both of hers.

"I appreciate what you've done in Texas, Mitch. You're important to me."

He gave her a half bow. "Whatever you want, Madam President, whatever you need, I'm your man." She walked around the room, shaking hands and expressing her gratitude while the Secret Service agents against the walls shifted nervously.

The president took a half an hour to explain to them her whole-hearted commitment to their agenda. She promised them full implementation of the environmental proposals of both Kyoto Treaties, stronger hate-crime laws, stronger anti-corporation legislation, broader gun control measures, and gay and transgender rights legislation that went even further to promote the gay lifestyle than the legislation that she had already pioneered under former President Ray Fitzgerald. The occasional applause failed to slow her speech. Lastly, she promised broad monetary support for their organizations, which absolutely stunned them. These were fringe leftists that professional politicians were unlikely to publicly support, even if they secretly agreed with their agenda.

"And I will give you the glory of helping me to rid our nation of the fascist social poison that's taken root in the northwest." One cursed joyfully. Many grunted in ecstasy at the thought. "All I ask from each of you is to give me your best within the problem states." The following pause raised the suspense. What exactly did she want of them?

"Best of what?" someone asked.

The president ignored the question and turned to the famous U.T. professor. "I want you, Professor Paine," – he jolted with surprise that she was singling him out – "to kindle a grassroots fire in Montana and in those other states that'll smoke those pigs out of their holes in the capitol buildings. I want riots, massive, dangerous, expensive riots in the occupied northwest." The activists at first gasped that she was asking such a thing of them, and then they mumbled their approval. "I want abortions to be available in those states, and whatever means you employ that will secure that goal is fine with me." Mitch Paine smiled broadly. "Now, hear me out." She paused for a moment until the room faded to silence again. "Some of the state governments in the so-called Coalition states have already arrested abortionists and their staff, effectively shutting down reproductive health clinics within their borders. Most of them have already passed legislation to secede from the United States. I suspect they will try to repel you and prosecute you to the fullest extent possible. You have to play hardball with 'em," she said with clenched fists. "You have to get the common people on your side."

"We can do it," someone blurted out with a contagious enthusiasm.

"Yeah!" others agreed.

"Strictly speaking, this is a war measure and perfectly legal. However, for political reasons, I will deny encouraging this if I am ever cited. Do you understand?" Heads nodded. "I also promise to have each of your criminal records cleared *if* you keep our agreement private."

That comment caused an ecstatic eruption of glee among the typically glum progressive activists. "But any snitching from any one of you and all crimes for *each* of you previous to this date and henceforth will be prosecuted to the fullest extent of the law. I wouldn't inform those within your groups and organizations of my connection with your plans, as they might turn on you and expose us. I'm sure the opposition will have some insiders among you, so you must maintain a strict control of all communication. If you or any of those among you get arrested by the rebels and confess, it will not go well for you. You will have made enemies on both sides of the border. Do we understand each other?"

Heads nodded.

"You tell your followers that you're going to the insubordinate states to protest their fascism. Not because I asked you to, but because it's best for the cause."

A bearded, thoroughly pierced and tattooed member of the Sienna Club raised his voice. "Anybody who busts up my chance for a clean record gets *whacked!*"

The president was wondering what it meant to get "whacked" when Mitch Paine stood to his feet and addressed the crowd.

"I will personally cut the throat of the man or woman in this room who tries to violate your confidentiality, Madam President." His brazen comment surprised many and earned wild-eyed cheers from more than a few. Many of the president's Secret Service personnel in the room gasped in amazement at the professor's fearlessness among such people. The president was entertained at the extent of Mitch Paine's devotion. Whatever it meant to get "whacked," it couldn't be any worse than that.

"That would be a justified measure in a time of war, and that, professor, is exactly why you are the *perfect* leader of this unofficial mission." She stood from her desk, walked around it and stood in front of him. She placed a hand on his shoulder and looked around at the others. "Listen to me, all of you. You are all strong, independent leaders, but I'm going to ask you to unify and follow this man. Do what he says without question or hesitation. That's the best way to be devoted to our cause. Especially you fundie-whackers." She glanced at the tattooed Sienna Club devotee as a few grins and laughs broke out. "If Mitch says to whack 'em, you whack 'em'!"

"Gotcha," the hippy responded.

"Can I trust you?"

Heads nodded. "Yes," many responded simultaneously.

"Very well." She looked into the professor's cool blue eyes. "You have the power to prevent a full blown war, now do it. I want results."

"We'll be starting on the college campuses." Paine glowed with confidence as his gaze drifted around the room, finding admiring smiles and thumbs raised. "Anarchy – creating chaos from within – is the key to the overthrow of the Confederate West."

Austin, Texas

"It is a time of unprecedented national crisis." Professor Mitchell Paine began to pace across the room as he pronounced his indictment of the radical right in his sociology class at the University of Texas. "The ideology of religious totalitarianism that is sweeping this nation will take us back to the dark ages, back to the Crusades, back to the Salem witch trials, to a place where Americans are burned at the stake for heretical beliefs, for being gay, for taking contraceptives, or for honoring Mother Earth. This ideology will take us back to the patriarchal age when women were sub-human and were forced to conceive and bear children contrary to their will. 'Suffer not a woman to speak,' Ben Boswell's King James Version reads in First Corinthians 14. Women will be enslaved by the chauvinist perversion of marriage that the Christian church founded and promoted. This ideology will take us back to the days when one class of people can enslave another class of people because of God told 'em to. Where equality is only granted to those who meet the subjective criteria of the religious totalitarians in power. This ideology will move radical, violent abortionist-killers up to hero status. Gays will be stoned by mobs of snake-handling fanatics in a stuporous trance. This ideology is worse than Nazism, because it justifies the annihilation of Jew *and* Gentile. It's worse than fascism, because the adherents don't even tolerate each other!"

He stopped his pacing, turned and faced his students. "These abuses are perpetrated not in the name of government, not in the name of a man, not even in the name of an ideology, but in the name" – he paused and pointed to the sky – "of God Almighty! This poisonous philosophy is the enemy of freedom, equality, justice, and peace – it is the enemy of America and it is its greatest threat since the Confederate uprising in the slave states of the Bible belt!"

The auditorium full of U.T. students began to applaud vigorously. News cameras had been set up in the rear of the room in expectation of the international peace award the professor was about to receive. No one expected, however, the announcement that he was about to deliver.

"The cause needs our help, and I am answering the call. Hordes of restless, freedom-loving college students are just the army that our country needs right now to brush the fanatical patriarchal vermin out of the way of our nation's progress, and I'm going to lead them. I am retiring from my tenured position at U.T.," he said as the student body gasped, "and I plan to go on the road from campus to campus to rally the troops."

"I'm going with him," Nick Crowder, the president of Students for Social Action, whispered to his friend, Damon, who sat next to him on the back row.

"What? And quit school?" Damon whispered back.

"You heard him," Nick whispered. "We're in a crisis. What good is an education degree in a country without free choice? All the religious totalitarians want school choice anyway, and you know what that'll do to teachers' salaries. It's self-preservation, man."

"Yeah," Damon mumbled.

"Why don't you come? It's with Mitch Paine. He'll probably give us credit toward our degrees."

Berkeley, California

"Can you believe it?!" Nick exclaimed from the back of the stage. His friend Damon stood beside him, awed at the size of the crowd. Their hero Mitch Paine was behind the microphone, rallying the crowd to a fever-pitched frenzy. Paine raised his half-drunk pint of vodka into the air and howled giddily. The crowd cheered wildly.

Damon turned to Nick. "They love him!" Nick nodded, wide-eyed.

Mitch Paine was the middle act of a rock band concert on the huge lawn in the center of the University of California's Berkeley campus. It was standing room only. He stood behind the microphone on a stand, rallying the crowd of admiring progressives and intoxicated students to vigorous applause over and over again. He began with a lesson in world history: "Whenever fundamentalist Christianity flourishes, slavery, racism, sexism, child abuse, ignorance, poverty, homophobia, and fascism prosper!" he screamed. "The God of the fundamentalists leaves a graveyard of suffering in his wake, which is about as good of an argument against the existence of God as I've ever heard! To believe God's good takes faith, but to see that the right-wing Christian's God is a sick sadist is empirically verifiable fact. They say revival's made them ban gays and abortion, criminalize euthanasia, spread hate, and arm themselves to the teeth, but if that's true then we need a new kind of revival – a revival of the people's power! The pillars of fascism will collapse in a tidal wave of the people's power!"

"Yeah!" screamed Nick and Damon from the back of the stage as the crowd was whipped to an inebriated cheer once again.

"Are you ready to rock the nation back to its senses?!" The professor practically screamed into the mic, thrusting his audience into a prolonged period of shouting and applause.

"We," – he thrust his right fist in the air – "the people, *we* control our destiny and the future of America, not some invisible 'Magical Sky Gawd'. There's no compromise with these religious fanatics. There are no peace treaties with them. These bigots can understand only one tone of voice, only one means of communication – the language of their God *–fire and brimstone! Violent force! Coercion.* If that's their language, then *we*" – he thumbed his chest with his fist – "must learn to speak it! If they don't relent, we'll make their lives a living hell! And you know what?" He paused to take a deep breath and belted out, "We will win!" He thrust his fist into the air again in a victory shout.

The applause grew vigorous, and when it died down again a moment later, he continued. "And here comes the fun part." He lowered his voice to a whisper. "We have a part to play – emphasis on that word *play*." Laughs followed as the crowd caught on to his implications. "*We*" – his index finger scanned the width of the massive crowd – "are more critical to the success of the cause of choice, world peace, and social justice than any politician in D.C. *We are the people!* Can you drink to that?" More applause commenced as Nick and Damon on the back of the stage took turns taking swigs from their pint of vodka.

"It'd be so easy to stop here. I see the smiles on everybody's faces. Y'all are slapping high-fives, cheerin' me on. You'll text your friends about what a wonderful speech that was. You'll go on planning your parties tonight, hopin' that drunk chick on the front row shows up." The crowd laughed and the young woman, clenching a tall can of beer in front of the crowd, turned and waved at the audience, prompting more cheers.

"Amen!" Nick shouted from the back of the stage, provoking laughter across the field.

"But how many of you will actually do anything to resolve the crisis?" the professor continued. "You'll end up going back to your career, back to the comfortable bed in your parents' house, back to your dorm to get your degree and join the capitalistic, sexist, third-world-exploiting, mainstream workforce. But I have a dream for you so much grander than your parents' dreams for you. I'm going further than vague third-person admonitions to stop the fanatics and promote choice. I have a dream" – he pointed at the students – "*for you!* Are you feeling me? There are times when chanting 'Stop the hate' just isn't enough. There are times when we go and 'Stop the **haters!**' Now is one of those times. We gotta take our parties on the road. Know what I mean? I am calling for volunteers..."

Thousands of hands shot up into the air.

Langley, Virginia

"I want out of here!"

James Knight shouted at the top of his voice as he slapped the cold, steel door with the palms of his hands. "Somebody help me! I want a lawyer! I want to speak to my wife! Somebody!" He stopped slapping and listened for a response, but heard nothing but the sound of his own breathing. His palms were beet-red from slapping the metal door. "Please!" His echoes faded to silence and his mind was gripped by silent fears.

He plopped down on the cement floor and moaned. He had awakened from his drug-induced stupor in this chilly windowless cell. He had spent several weeks without any contact with anybody save a psychiatrist on the first day and a mute fellow who slid his meals under the door. Only the dimming of the 120-volt light bulb in the center of his small cell told him that it was nighttime.

If his circumstances didn't change, James Knight thought that he very well might end up with a psychological problem. What torment solitary confinement brings upon the mind in just a few weeks. Demons seemed to swirl in chaotic fits around his head throwing fiery darts of doubt, fear, lust, and hopelessness upon him. It was all he could do to raise his shield of faith to quench them.

He laid his arms across his bent knees, closed his eyes, and dropped his head onto his forearms.

A poem he memorized in college came to his mind:

No one's safe when freedom fails,
And good men rot in filthy jails,
And those who cried, "Appease, appease!"
Are hung by those they tried to please.

Near his cell at the maximum security federal prison in Langley were dozens of "copperheads" being held under the president's executive orders: Texas Governor Henry Adams and his press secretary Robert Boniface, Bozeman Sheriff Randall Woods, South Carolina Governor Ted Cropp, and many others. All waiting for something – anything – to happen, praying diligently, fighting fear and loneliness, wondering if their families were still free.

The orders to have them held in solitude were for an indefinite period of time: "Until I tell you otherwise," the president personally told the director of the CIA-managed cells. "These are enemy combatants of the worst kind, the most dangerous fanatics in America. They could destroy our Union if we don't put them in a soundproof box and seal the lid. They must not be allowed to mingle with other prisoners, for they will rally them to their cause and propagate insubordination. They must not be allowed to even speak to each other, for they will encourage each other in their anarchy. These men and women must be broken down to their lowest common denominator. Only then will they be beneficial to us. They must be rehabilitated into submissive allies."

Helena, Montana

Barry Friar and David Jameson met for the first time in the front of the Helena Civic Center, which Governor Boswell had reserved for this historic conference. Barry Friar, his beard thick and graying and his body thin from fasting as frequently as his captors would let him, walked up to David and extended his right hand for a handshake. David, however, would have none of that. He grabbed the hand of the man he had only seen on television and heard on the radio, and he pulled him close and gave him a bear hug, causing Barry to drop his briefcase.

"It's so good to meet you, Brother Barry!"

Barry laughed. "Thank you, thank you." He reached down and scooped up his briefcase. "We have two hours to prepare, David," said Barry as he opened the front door for David and then followed him into the unlit foyer.

"Let's sit down in here." David led Barry into an unoccupied office.

Once seated, they small-talked for a few minutes, familiarizing themselves with each other. Barry briefed him on the raid on his home, the killing of his wife and son, and the intervention of Ben Boswell and the Montana Guard that saved his life. They praised the Lord together about the state trial that resulted in all charges being dropped, then his arrest and incarceration for federal offenses. David learned of his subsequent solitary confinement at a maximum-security federal prison. Since Governor Boswell had negotiated his release, he had been reunited with his daughter Teresa and his youngest son Timmy, but he was unable to ascertain the whereabouts of his son Marion.

"So tell me about yourself," Barry asked him. "The article I read went on and on about the mysterious David Jamestown – the Texas pastor who came out of nowhere to save Governor Boswell's life and lead this spiritual army of prayer warriors and freedom fighters. Where's your family?"

That question struck David like a 50-pound brick of ice in the chest. "My family?"

"Yeah. I read in the newspaper that you were separated from your family." Barry could tell by the change in David's countenance that the question did not settle well with him. "Are they all right?"

"I, I don't know," David stuttered, turning his gaze from the cold blue eyes of Barry Friar to the beige tile under their feet. "We got separated in Texas and they're supposed to be in Ohio by now, but they never arrived."

Barry sighed deeply, and leaned forward to put a comforting hand on David's shoulder. "Your patient suffering of wrong-doing at the hands of evil men is the sweetest sacrifice of praise to your Lord."

Those words warmed David to the core. "Thank you. I'll fetch them once I find them, but until then, I've got a vision for the Minutemen."

"Tell me about it."

"I think we should start with prayer and fasting – perhaps the entire first week, along with some foundation in basic Christian theology, just to make sure we're all on the same page and there aren't any heretics or theological nit-picks among us."

Barry laughed. "I know what you mean. Gotta have unity on the essentials and tolerance with everything else."

"Then we'll train them to defend the faith well and defend what the Coalition states are doing. When you and I aren't teaching, we will be meeting with established church leaders to get them on board with our vision and to console any fears they might have."

"Oh yes," said Barry, massaging his beard. "I am sure that the Lord definitely wants us to mend the nets, not make new ones."

"What do you think about organizing the religious conferences while I manage the outreaches to the secular audience?" David proposed.

Barry clasped his hands behind his head and grinned mischievously. "Ah, please don't throw me in the briar patch."

* * * * *

As Elijah, Cal, and Jared left their tents for the large auditorium, they merged with hundreds of other men and women.

"God's raising up quite an army," Elijah said to Jared. "Wonder where He's takin' us."

Jared wasn't amused with the crowds. "We'll all be dead in six months, bro."

Elijah winced at Jared's persistent pessimism.

One of their new friends, a young tanned carpenter from California, frowned at Jared's negative comment. "Ah, where's your faith, Jared?"

"That's a good question, Carson." Elijah nodded at the new acquaintance as he glanced inquisitively at Jared.

"The Coalition exists because the globalists want it to," Jared responded. "It's all part of their plan. I think they just want to get all of the Christians in one corner of the country so they can blow us all to smithereens."

"How can you not realize that God is doing something great here?" Carson said, following behind his elders in the faith on a narrow trail through a plot of woods between the campground and the auditorium.

Cal was quietly contemplative as he walked with his wife, Sabina, and three daughters in tow: "I've read the end of the book, friends," he finally spoke up. "The saints end up dead or in prison at the hands of an evil world dictatorship. I don't expect many earthly victories in this apostate nation. I'm here because I want to go down fightin'."

Elijah glanced back at Cal. "Remember King Josiah. God postpones judgment when His people repent. As long as the salt's salty, then we're not going to get tread underfoot."

Cal nodded hopefully. "That'd be fine with me. I hope you're right."

"Heaven won't come to earth till Jesus comes back," said Jared. "You've got to lower your expectations, Elijah, or you're setting yourself up for disappointment."

"We're to pray 'Thy kingdom come, Thy will be done,' right?" said Elijah. "Must I pray only in disbelief? I think God's found a people in whom He can show Himself strong, fellows, and He's answering their prayers and helping us beat on the devil." Elijah grinned ear to ear and acted as if he were wielding punches at a threatening menace in his path.

"A remnant of the American church is putting off the spots and wrinkles," Carson added, "and has not yet seen her best days. Jesus is at the Father's right hand *until* the Father makes His enemies the Son's footstool."

Jared grunted and shook his head. "The only way to beat the New World Order is to destroy its advocates. They'll not accept peaceful co-existence. Prayer meetings only go so far."

They arrived at the door of the auditorium, and Elijah opened it for Carson, Cal and his family, and Jared. "Can you pray for the restoration of godly government, Jared?"

"Sure!"

"Can you pray in faith, believing that you have received it?"

Jared winced, seeing where Elijah was going with this line of questioning. "If you can't pray in faith," said Elijah as he followed Jared in, "then don't waste your time praying, because your praying in disbelief makes the miracle we need even less likely."

Ft. Peck, Montana

Jack Handel was *en route* from a grocery store in Brockton at the edge of the Ft. Peck Indian Reservation in Montana. He and Dixie had been staying with some Native American friends hoping to ride out the storm until things calmed down.

He pulled into a one-pump station to fill up, and the headline of the local newspaper caught his eye. "Gun Confiscation a Failure in CFC States." The title didn't catch him by surprise, but his heart throbbed in his chest nonetheless. He purchased the newspaper and headed home. A strange euphoria flooded his senses. Things were coming down to the wire in the country of his forefathers, and the leaders of ten states were defying all of his pessimistic expectations. What calamity the federal government schemed for them, he could only imagine. He suddenly had a great feeling of abhorrence for everything that the United States of America had come to represent.

At a stop sign one block from where he was staying, he glanced at the paper in the passenger seat, and the headline of another front-page article caught his eye: "Governor Boswell Calls for Volunteers." He picked up the paper and read the first paragraph. "At a press conference late last night, Governor Ben Boswell urged all freedom-loving patriots to join the State Guard, the civilian militia, or the new Minutemen group he has formed to prepare the hearts of the people for freedom."

He gasped, disbelieving his own eyes. He began to quickly peruse the article. The heaviness that had settled upon him seemed to lift off of his shoulders in an instant. He continued to read until the driver of the pick-up truck behind him beeped his horn. Jack dropped the newspaper in his lap and hit the gas.

Dixie met him at the front door of the trailer where they were staying with a curious smile. Her hands were on her hips, her lips puckered as if she had a surprise for him.

Jack showed her the front page of the newspaper. "You'll never guess what the governor's doing?" Dixie gave no response. He stopped in the doorway and looked up at her. Her curious snicker appeared strangely out of place.

He kissed her and said, "You look happy today."

"I am." Her grin was so broad he grew suspicious.

"What?"

"Guess."

"What? I don't know. You pregnant?" he said, half jokingly.

"He guessed it!" Dixie shouted through the open door as two elderly Native American ladies squealed with glee inside. She threw herself into his arms, knocking the newspaper to the ground, and hugged his neck tightly.

Jack was in a state of shock, and didn't hug back.

"You're not happy?" She withdrew from his embrace and stared into his eyes.

"You're pregnant?"

She held her grin, nodding timidly. "Uh huh."

"How?"

"If you don't know, we are in trouble!" She joined her friends in a full laugh. "I thought you'd be happy."

He smiled briefly as he reached down and picked up the paper. "Of course I'm happy. I'm just shocked. I didn't think you could get pregnant at 43 years of age with three grown kids."

She laughed and patted his cheeks. "Oh, God, sanctify my husband. I'm 44, dear."

"Oh."

"Well, the Lord surprised us both, Jack. Life comes from God." She paused to kiss him on the lips. "I am so grateful." Her joyful grin warmed his heart.

Jack hugged his wife, and then pulled back and looked into her eyes, which welled with happy tears.

He hugged her again and whispered his love for her into her ear. But deep inside, his heart ached. As the nation drifted further into the unknown territory of tyranny and communism, and the conflict between the state and federal governments grew more heated, his responsibilities were increasing. Now, it was not only his wife he had to worry about, but a baby as well. He had a sudden urge to go clean the few guns he still had and take an inventory of his ammunition. To this point, Jack just wanted to get in the fight to fight, with no hope of ever winning. Freedom was a pair of fading jeans, more likely to be discarded than repaired. Better to fight for freedom and lose than not fight at all, but was victory over tyranny even possible? Jack felt a palpitation in his chest at the fleeting thought, and he felt just for a moment that he had the faith to believe God for that which he had always thought impossible to achieve: to actually win freedom for his new baby's generation.

Helena, Montana

"The State Guards are integrating nicely," General Bob Bryan informed the governor of Montana with a grin of pride at the cabinet meeting. "They've all been moved up to full time for more intensive training, and we're becoming a finely tuned fighting machine."

"And your birds?" Boswell asked.

"We're working overtime training for various contingencies. Wanting to conserve fuel as much as possible, we are training mostly in flight simulation."

"Speaking of fuel, we've begun drilling for our own with a measure of success," the energy secretary announced enthusiastically. "Since we've begun to spurn federal regulation, it's been easy and will be quite profitable. In three months, the partial fuel blockade may not have any impact on us at all. Americans and businesses will soon want to move here just for the price of gas."

"That is good to know." The governor paused to look at his agenda. "Gilman?" He glanced at his treasurer. "Go ahead."

The treasurer clasped his hands in front of him and took a deep breath. "As of this morning, the feds have begun to withhold the disbursements as expected for infrastructure, Medicaid, Medicare, education and a host of other funds, as we worried that they would," he glumly told them. "They're giving ultimatums regarding abortion, physician-assisted suicide, and gun control, as you would expect."

With these words, the bureaucrats in the room began to taste the bitter consequences of state secession and decentralization of power. You could see the tension rise among the cabinet members. Boswell had prepared them that this could be the outcome of the Coalition's formal secession, but many of them had still not come to grips with the fact that they would lose federal funding for the state bureaucracies and programs they managed.

Boswell interjected, "We – the Coalition governors – have agreed to respond to this by letting all of our citizens know that they are free to withhold all of the income taxes owed to the IRS, as well as the funds allocated for Medicare…"

The rise of complaints in the room was simultaneous and incoherent.

"Hold up!" Boswell stretched out his palms to slow down the flood of criticism. "This is where the rubber hits the road with bucking tyranny, friends. If they are going to block our ports, blockade our oil, withhold our Medicaid and Medicare funds even though we pay taxes into those programs, then it is *they* who have seceded from *us*. We're not going to keep sending them our money."

"If we let Montanans keep that much more of their own money," the treasurer added with a smile, "I predict that our economic boom will overwhelm negative effects of losing our federal safety nets. It's like giving everyone a 30% to 40% raise. Also, remember that the debt load of the federal government is unfathomable, amounting to a half a million dollars per family the last time I counted. Having seceded, our citizens won't be forced to repay it. The crushing weight of federal regulations will vanish. No more unfunded federal mandates. The sizeable amount of land that the federal government owns inside our border will go up for sale and be open for industry and drilling." He grinned wildly. "We'll have an economic boom you can't imagine! Instead of businesses flowing from the U.S. to Mexico to lower their overhead, they'll be coming here!"

"The feds'll make up the difference with tariffs they'll collect on goods leaving the Coalition's border," someone argued.

"That argument is significant if we were just one state, but we're not," Boswell responded. "Taken all together, we're larger than most European countries. Financially, we'll do better after seceding, especially since the feds are bankrupting this country right now. Once we finally move to the gold standard," he said, glancing at his treasurer, "our currency will do *better* than the dollar."

"And with the exponential rate of hyperinflation right now, we're going to have to go to the gold standard soon," the assistant to the state treasurer asserted.

The treasurer nodded. "We've prepared for the feds withholding finances. In two weeks I can have our interstate toll booths built and manned to pay for infrastructure."

"Good job." The governor looked around the room at the members of the cabinet. "I see those of you whose departments are most dependent on federal funds are all looking like your doc just told you you've got cancer. Our state must learn to survive without federal funds and we'll have to get skinny – real skinny."

"What about education, sir?" asked the Secretary of Education, the only female in the room. "A third of Montana sends their kids to private school or home-educates them, but the rest cannot afford to do that." The first complaint was a crack in the dam.

"The convalescent homes are dependent on those funds, sir," said the jittery director of the Department of Aging, as the director of the Department of Mental and Developmental Disabilities nodded.

"And the prisons and jails," said the director of the Department of Rehabilitation and Correction.

"And what about the reservations?" said the only Native American in the room, the Health Secretary.

"Hold on, hold on," the governor raised his voice and waved his hands horizontally to quiet the noise. "You look like a nest of hungry chicks squawking with your jaws open because momma-bird's late with the worm. My goodness!"

"One at a time," said Dreifuss as he pointed to one of the cabinet members. "You first."

"No!" shouted Boswell, "not, 'you first'! Listen to me. We counted the cost before we drew a line in the sand. We knew we could lose millions in federal funds, but it was worth it. I know most of you are lovers of God and liberty first. Would you," he said, pointing at his health secretary, "kill or allow to be killed one baby just so you could keep your federal funds?" She reluctantly shook her head from side to side.

"But sir," said the labor secretary, "I would never have thought in a million years that you would have just *abandoned* the elderly and the poor. This is just what the federal government wants! We have to raise state taxes to care for the poor and elderly."

The governor sighed and folded his hands in front of him on the table. "I knew we were going to have to have this conversation some day, but I thought it would be easier."

"What?" the labor secretary snapped, piping up at the governor's mumbling in response to his objection.

"No," Boswell coldly responded, "the government does *not* have to feed the poor and the elderly. The Bible says that if a man doesn't work, he shouldn't eat. Wealth redistribution is sinful, sir. There's a reason that socialist nations become communist and communist nations fail. Stealing is an addictive habit of tyrants that can never be quenched. We're going to be governed by the law of God supremely, and that law forbids stealing."

"Using tax money to provide for the poor is stealing?" The labor secretary couldn't believe his ears.

"Of course, it's stealing! It's not our money! The government has got no business feeding kids with money it's coerced from taxpayers, or caring for the elderly, or bailing out failing companies, or any of these things. The government's obligation, as delineated in our nation's founding documents, in our state's constitution, and in the Bible is to protect God-given rights and provide for infrastructure and defense. That's it! We have an all-powerful, monstrous, intrusive federal government, and we've sacrificed our freedoms to feed this beast for most of a century. Montana's been using even state funds for unconstitutional programs for decades and–"

"Let me get this right," the labor secretary interrupted with an irritated tone, "you don't think the government should be involved in caring for the poor and the elderly? In healthcare? In economics? In public education?"

"The state should care about the poor and elderly by punishing crime against the poor and elderly. But we don't care so much for them that we are willing to steal from others for them. And let me tell you why… Hold on, hold on," he tried to calm the labor secretary's protest, "let me finish. Socialism makes men less free. The best thing the government can do in behalf of freedom is to let the free man alone and make others leave him alone."

"And how does the government take away one's freedom by providing food stamps to an 85-year-old widow?" the labor sec asked. "Maybe some government housing so she doesn't have to live out her days in a nursing home?"

"Because if the taxpayer withholds the money that the government demands for the government's charity, he goes to jail! I'd say that's an affront to his freedom, don't you? The poor *should* be cared for, and Jesus condemned the rich for not caring for the poor…"

"Then what's the problem?" The labor sec shrugged, perplexed.

"It's not the government's job," Boswell insisted. "According to Jesus in Matthew 15, it's the job of the children to care for their elderly parents. It's the job of the church. The same God that says we should feed the poor also condemns theft and injustice. Socialism is legalized plunder." The labor sec shook his head, downright angry at the governor's politically incorrect notions. "It's an affront to the God-given right to property. The government has no business plundering the taxpayers for charitable causes. Government leaders are bound to the same moral law to which citizens are bound. 'Thou shalt not steal' applies to politicians and voters alike."

"There are economic and social injustices that only the government can remedy, Governor Boswell. We are obligated to spend the taxpayers' treasury in ways that will better our society."

"Theft may benefit the thieves and plunderers, but what about those whose wealth we exploit? It's their money. What about their freedom?"

"It's how we've *always* run the government." The labor sec's eyes shifted around the room, searching for and finding sympathetic countenances.

"That's a logical fallacy called the 'is/ought fallacy,'" Boswell responded. "Just because something is a certain way, that doesn't mean it should be. Tyranny exists because the government does what it should *not* do in aiding some at the expense of others, or because the government does *not* do what it *should* do in enforcing laws against theft. We've elevated the state to the status of deity as it declares its right to all property and wealth at a rate the politicians decide, and too many of us have clamored for our portion of the stolen booty. This is idolatry and state worship, and we've got to stop it."

The labor secretary absorbed the reproof without response, and stared straight ahead as the governor continued.

"Aside from constitutionally justified obligations, you aren't going to be dependent on the feds or the state to steal money from hard-working citizens to get the funds you want. Instead, we're going to have to be dependent on voluntary charity for all of our obligations except providing for the Guard forces, the prisons, and critical infrastructure, each of which are authorized by the state constitution. We're cutting the pork out of government. Many of your employees will be heading into the private sector. It'll be good for our economy and good for our liberty. Montana needs to become accustomed once again to living free of slavery chains and silver spoons. Understand?"

Heads nodded reluctantly, though the governor could see that many of them were not happy at all.

"And what about the reservations, sir?" asked the director of Health and Human Services. "America owes it to the native Americans to–"

"Tell them that they can join the Guard or get a job. No more sucking on the taxpayers' nipple." The governor's cross words stunned the HHS director. Countenances frowned painfully at the governor's insensitive words. "Please don't take offense, Gary. It's the whole self-serving, socialistic mindset I despise, not the Native Americans. Good grief, I'm married to one!"

"Yes sir."

"My wife has told me repeatedly that the worst thing that has ever happened to the Native Americans is welfare, and given all that community has endured, that's saying a lot. State subsidies have freed men of responsibility to their families, made fornication profitable, and subsidized substance abuse. We've made laziness and malingering profitable. I don't know what the other Coalition states are going to do, but Montana's not going to be using taxpayer money to turn good men into slaves, and we're freeing the ones we've made."

Dreifuss was not convinced that the cabinet members were embracing the governor's hard-line philosophy of government. "I hope you each get the take-home message and learn to defend it, because you are going to have to in dealing with your subordinates. I'd encourage you to tune in to hear Pastor David Jamestown on the radio over the next couple of days, because I know he's teaching on this subject."

The governor nodded at the attorney general, who he was growing to appreciate more and more by the day. "It all comes back down to this: according to what standard should we live? If we stick with God's Word, then we'll be free. Every other standard is a counterfeit. Now Montanans are going to be keeping more of their own money. They'll be able to afford charity now."

The governor stopped talking while the labor secretary began to gather his things together and put them in his briefcase. Every eye stared at him uneasily for a moment until he stood and headed for the door. Governor Boswell didn't try to stop him.

"It's obvious I'm not needed here anymore," the labor sec said as he opened the door.

"It's been a pleasure working with you." The governor turned in his chair to face him. "I wish you all the best in the free market." He turned back toward the others as the labor sec shut the door behind him. "If any of you want to make the best of it in the private industry, you are welcome to do so. If the statehouse passes my economic plan, all state salaries will be cut 10% as of next fiscal year. Those who have duties without constitutional authorization will be released into the private sector. I just wanted you to be warned."

A knock on the door interrupted their conversation. The Chief of Security Isaiah Knabb did not wait for the expected invitation to enter. He opened the door and the look of urgency on his face concerned the governor.

"You all are dismissed," Boswell said. As his cabinet members left the room, he waved Knabb toward his desk. "What's the problem?"

"I have just been informed of a potential security breach."

Part III

Conquering the Evil Within

The Oregon-Washington border

"Now, we are crossing into the land of the religious totalitarians, the Confederacy of Enslaved Christian States!" Mitch Paine stood in the front of the yellow school bus as he rallied the troops to a frenzy once again. The bus, packed with college students, hippies, gothics, socialists, environmentalists, and gay activists, rocked with the cheers, clapping, and stomping of the motley crew.

Paine turned to the bus driver and raised his voice in order to be heard over the shouting of the students. "How long until we get into Denver?"

"We'll meet up with the others in about three hours."

"Three hours until it's time to rock!" Mitch shouted to his youth with his right fist thrust into the air.

The students replied in like manner, chanting and shouting with their clenched fists thrust into the air. Twenty-four other buses and hundreds of vans, cars, and motorcycles followed Paine's bus. They were on a mission to liberate the Coalition citizens from the vice grip of religious tyranny.

Denver, Colorado

"Do it! Do it!" shouted Professor Paine through a loud speaker from the safety of a Volkswagen as 40 college students sent chairs and couches through cracked and broken windows onto the streets below. Others were torching cars parked in the streets, the subsequent explosions catching many shops on fire. Others were sitting Indian-style five rows thick across the four roads that led to this part of downtown Denver, arms linked as they chanted memorable slogans. When officers and fire trucks rushed toward the melee, these students obstructed their progress, refusing to move. Other young people rushed into stores, terrifying employees, and stole whatever they could carry out the broken doors and windows. The rioting had gone on for 20 minutes when finally, police in riot gear broke through the lines, dodging rocks and beer bottles thrown from shadows in the alleys and from behind cars. The officers began making arrests of rioters too intoxicated to flee, and opened the way for fire trucks that rushed to the scene with sirens screaming.

"Fourth and Commons," the bandana-wearing anarchist ordered the bus driver. "Drop us off right there." He turned to the crowd of excited students and activists. "Ready to rock'n'roll!?"

"Yeah!" they shouted unanimously. Most of them were dressed similarly with black bandanas to make it more difficult to distinguish them for identification purposes should any of them get arrested. It would be impossible to identify which of those arrested were responsible for the most violent criminal acts.

"It's time! Go, go, go!" The leader of Paine's second group shouted as the students rushed from the buses, vans, and cars, into the malls and shopping centers of another part of downtown Denver. He picked up his walkie-talkie and gave a similar order to the ones who followed them in vans and cars. Then he clicked a different channel. "Mikey? Mitch here. Your turn." He handed the radio to the bus driver and was the last one to leave the bus.

A third group in Paine's entourage consisted of the felons and wanted criminals who had more to lose from being arrested because they would face longer prison sentences. They would riot in the areas where the police would be scarce.

"Tenth and Tailor," the blond felon with a purple-dyed goatee, wearing a black shirt and jeans, told the similarly attired bus driver.

"One block away," the bus driver informed them.

The leader of the third team turned to the group of ex-cons and drug-abusers, raised a satanic hand-symbol into the air, and shouted, "Payback time!"

Paine's strategy maximized damage and minimized the arrests of the most violent activists who were most important to him. Correction: it wasn't *his* strategy, though he did take credit for it. Unbeknownst to Paine, the plan was developed by undercover agents posing as grad students. They were very helpful at maximizing the effectiveness of the rioting and preventing capture, as well as orchestrating sympathetic journalism on the front pages and on prime-time television.

Once the officers broke through the lines, Mitch Paine put his escape plan into action. "Salisbury! Whistler! Chance! Cops! Cops!" he shouted into the microphone in his vehicle. The one in 20 students with communication devices inside their ears – provided courtesy of the undercover FBI agents – echoed the code word and hundreds of students who were in an area designated by those code words rushed into the stores and made their way to the back doors and then into the parking lots behind the stores. Since they were tremendously outnumbered, most of the officers dared not follow hordes of enraged, intoxicated students down dark alleys, but rested content with clearing the streets, making a few arrests, and helping the fire trucks put out the fires.

Before Denver, Professor Paine had been in Seattle, Spokane, Tacoma, Boise, Idaho Falls, and Salt Lake City. He had delivered dozens of well-attended speeches on large university campuses along the way, filling the ranks of the hundreds of his followers who had been arrested during the rioting.

Only one student was killed in Salt Lake City – hit in the back of the head by another student who swung a golf club against a window and missed. Of course, witnesses testified that the 20-year-old's head injury was due to police brutality. Mitch Paine went to great lengths to promote this story in the media, and many outlets sympathetic with his cause – CNN, ABC, NBC, and CBS – carried it prime time for days.

"This young, bright college student gave up his life to liberate the northwest from the religious totalitarians," Paine mourned into the television camera one evening in front of hundreds of his admirers and students who sat peacefully across the full length of a four lane road behind him. "Some of the students take the protesting to unlawful extremes, and although I contest their extremes, I can't really blame them. The religious extremists in your statehouse have silenced all dissent in Utah, and democracy has no other recourse. The question I want to ask is: Where are the sensible liberty-loving American patriots of

Utah?" He gazed passionately into the camera, sweat beading on his furrowed brow. "When will they rise to the occasion of democracy and free thought and overthrow these Taliban-like religious fanatics and traitors?"

The buses had begun to attract too much police attention and they were thenceforth abandoned for rented cars and vans. The crowds continued to swell with every campus rally and positive news story.

After Denver, Mitch Paine planned to take his entourage south to Wyoming, then Nebraska, north to the Dakotas, and then, last but not least, westward to the finale in Montana, which all the rioters anticipated with great enthusiasm.

A path of unexpected destruction had driven fear into law enforcement and their governors. Most Coalition governors were unable to call the State Guards out to assist the police in halting the mayhem because they were training in the state of Montana. Governor Pollock in Idaho finally did call his Guard home, but by the time they arrived, the students had vacated the state. But this was President Brighton's *modus operandi*: she had secretly caused a problem for which she was prepared to offer a solution. She had started an epidemic for which she was prepared to offer a cure. The pretext was laid for her seductive proposal.

"Governor Wilson." The governor's secretary called out to him on the intercom.

"I told you no calls," the Colorado governor snapped as he sat down with the director of the Highway Patrol and several sheriffs from large counties in the state, many of whom were present via the internet.

"It's the president."

"The president? The president of what?" His eyes widened as he sat chewing on an unlit two-day-old cigar.

"The United States, sir. I assumed you would allow this exception."

"You assumed correctly, Minnie." He turned nervously to the law enforcement personnel. "You must excuse me, gentlemen, for just a moment." They stood up and walked out of the room and Governor Wilson put his internet subordinates on hold. "Put her through, Min."

The president set down the letter from the Coalition governors declaring their sovereignty and she touched a few keys on her keyboard. Her face popped up on Governor Wilson's screen.

"Hello, Madam President." The governor tried to sound calm and collected.

"I hear you're having some problems with rioting." The president smiled smugly over the internet connection, sending a cold chill up the elderly Colorado governor's spine.

"What do you want?" Governor Wilson assumed that this woman was up to no good. Surely she didn't mean to call just to gloat in their miseries.

"How bad is it, Gary?"

The governor clenched his teeth as he stared into the monitor. "Dozens of civilians have been killed in the past two days of rioting. Local jails are overcrowded with hundreds of arrestees – we're just leavin' them handcuffed in the paddy wagons at this point. I've got several officers charged with police brutality of suspects after a mad 48-hour shift. Hospitals overwhelmed with the injured…"

The president chuckled, much to the governor's dismay. His ears reddened as his blood pressure rose. The president saw Wilson's disapproving smirk, and said, "I don't mean to laugh, but I find it sadly amusing that your people are so bursting with discontent that they are rioting in the streets. Perhaps the unconstitutional measures passed of late do not bring as much holy joy to the hearts of your citizens as you supposed."

"Don't feign ignorance to me, Madam President," he barked, clamping down on his cigar. "You know who's fanning the flames of these riots. It's *not* the people of Colorado. It's Mitch Paine and his army of Marxists and anarchists!"

"I have heard this rumor, but am unaware of any evidence that this is indeed the case." Brighton shook her head and shrugged.

"He's *boasted* for weeks on college campuses all over the nation that he was going to wreak havoc in the Coalition states."

"My intel informs me that the students under his charge are peaceful."

"Sure they are," he said, rolling his eyes.

"It's locals that are going to extremes, Governor Wilson. There isn't any evidence that Professor Paine has done anything violent or illegal."

"Of course not, Madam President. And of course his speech would not qualify as *hate-speech* either, would it?"

The president sighed. "I called to offer my condolences, Gary. And much-needed financial aid."

Wilson cocked his head to the side, surprised. "Financial aid?"

"I want to help. I disagree with your state's hollow unconstitutional attempt to outlaw abortion and euthanasia and declare your independence."

"What do you care about the Constitution? I don't watch *your* mainstream media – I know what's going on here."

She took a deep breath. "I still would like to help you in your predicament."

"How?"

"I'd like to send you the manpower, the funding, and the supplies you need to get this anarchy under control."

"I'm sure you would," he responded sarcastically. "That manpower wouldn't happen to be the ATF, FBI, and Army infantry, would it?"

"*For God's sake*, Gary, I'm trying to help you!" she snapped, her face glowing with poorly restrained intemperance. "Can you cut out the paranoia and the sarcasm for the sake of your constituents? You're state's coming to pieces, your streets are on fire, and your law enforcement has miserably failed to curb the violence! You're so consumed with the religious fanaticism of Ben Boswell, that you can't even see it. We can help you."

"I really don't wish to have this conversation right now, Madam President." He acted as if he was going to disconnect the line.

"There's more, Gary. I'm not done."

He sighed and leaned back into his chair. "What?"

"I have a position in the Department of Faith and Family Services, and would like to rethink a conservative trend to the department's services. It's part of my cabinet."

His jaw dropped. His cigar fell onto his lap, and he picked it up without looking at it. "What?" After a failed run for Congress and the Senate, he managed to make it to the governor's mansion, but he always had his sights set on D.C.

"I know it's your dream, Gary. There are many more qualified, but I'm giving *you* a chance to step out of the political nightmare you might find yourself in with this so-called Coalition of Free Christian States. Yet you can keep your conservative reputation. You won't have many more chances like this, so you'd better think seriously about taking it. Let me send some troops in to restore order, then you can quietly resign as governor, take the position in Washington for a $350,000 salary, and save yourself a lot of heartache and jail-time. Move up, not down…"

Governor Wilson listened in stunned silence, his mind was buzzing under the temptation. The spirit is so willing, yet the flesh is still so weak. The flesh pulls so persuasively to comfort and peace, whereas the spirit pulls to the conflict and crucifixion. The flesh's hope is in keeping your stuff and your pleasures. The spirit's hope is in the resurrection. Governor Wilson felt like he was getting dizzy with the contrasts that so vividly played in his mind, with two different spirits tearing him between two different destinations. He slumped into his leather seat as the president continued to lay the perks of surrender before him. He felt so old right at that moment. Maybe he should give up. He fought the good fight. He did the best he could. Wasn't defeat inevitable anyway?

Governor Wilson put up a palm to stop the president mid-sentence. He looked down and took a deep breath. He knew what was happening. He was Adam before the forbidden tree, Israel before the Jordan River, the Savior in the Gethsemane garden savoring the thought of gaining paradise without pain, treasure without atonement, and deliverance from divine destiny through a spectacularly convenient detour. The governor recognized the perfumed scent of the spirit who was behind this seductive offer. He squinted away his doubt, fearful of how close he came to betraying the Master for some easy change. "Not my will," he mumbled, "but Thine be done."

The president leaned her ear closer to the monitor, unable to make out the governor's incoherent mumbling. "Excuse me?"

When Governor Wilson spoke those words, a surge of strength filled him at that moment, and he felt like Sampson before the Philistine army. He felt like nothing could conquer him if he could only conquer himself.

Brighton saw his change in demeanor, and grew concerned. "Think of Marsha and your kids," she said, referring to his wife and six children. "Your statehouse's Speaker will assume your responsibilities until–"

"What!?" The governor clenched his fists, enraged. "The Speaker's in on this?"

"You know he's been sympathetic with the democrats' attempts to have you removed from office. Why are you so surprised? Mr. Traviston has already agreed–"

A holy boldness filled Governor Wilson's bosom. "This is treason! Treason against the people of Colorado!" He leaned into the camera as if he were prepared to punch the screen in rage.

The president smirked as the governor's face reddened. "You've got no business lecturing me on treason, Gary."

He aimed an index finger at her forehead on his screen. "We seceded peacefully to govern ourselves, but you want to overthrow our democratically elected leadership and take over, without so much as the pretext of law! That's treason!"

"Would you relax?" the president beckoned calmly. "Calm down or you're gonna have a stroke! Now, be reasonable. I'm giving you the opportunity to successfully affect the cultural landscape of the entire nation for the good of your religion in a cabinet position, Gary. You can work within the system, within the constitutional boundaries. You might even be able to convince me to temper my hate-speech laws in order to safeguard your precious fellow religious provocateurs."

The governor appeared deep in thought, and so she continued, leaning into the camera on top of her monitor. "I'll raise it to $395,000 dollars annually, Gary. Regular promotions. Plus the opportunity to promote your conservative ideals from the District of Columbia as part of *my* cabinet!"

He stared into her eyes. *$395,000 dollars! I can't believe they pay those worthless bureaucrats that much money!*

His gaze shifted to a portrait of him with the CFCS governors on the wall. He massaged the back of his neck with his right hand.

"Don't throw this opportunity away," she pleaded with him. "There will be no second chances. I'll have a ten million dollar grant for your local law enforcement distributed to you tomorrow. I'll give you all the resources you need to help your people recover from the riots and rebuild. Save the day in Colorado, then triple your income in Washington. Let someone else absorb the headache in the Colorado statehouse. It's a deal for you! Take it!"

He took a deep breath. "Colorado isn't for sale, Madam President, and neither is my conscience. Our liberties will not be bartered away for political trophies."

"Name your price, Governor! How much will it take to—"

"Excuse me, I have an urgent phone call to make. I think I've finally found the Achilles heel for my thorn in the flesh in the statehouse, Mr. Traviston."

"Wha–?"

Click!

Washington, D.C.

The president cursed. "That son of a gun!" (That is the gravest of insults that this president could give anybody, based on her hatred of guns.)

Before she was finished slapping her desk, grinding her teeth, and cursing the God of the religious totalitarians, the secretary buzzed.

"Madam President?"

"What?!" She was perturbed by the unwelcomed interruption of her string of curses.

"Governor Ben Boswell's on line one for you."

The president quickly regained her composure. She punched a few keys on her computer. "Well, well. Benjamin Boswell." She smiled broadly into the screen when Boswell's stern face shined up on her monitor.

Boswell's face had broken out in a sweat. He raised his voice, "The Coalition of Free Christian States won't give in to your bribery and intimidation, Madam President." David Jameson was the only person in the Montana governor's office, sitting quietly in a chair next to his desk, out of range of the governor's computer camera. He felt out of his league before the governor of Montana and the Coalition leadership, but Governor Boswell dragged him everywhere with him as a personal assistant. But David especially felt out of his league as the governor raised his voice on the phone with the president of the United States.

"We're not going to give in to your scheming!" Boswell shouted over the phone, causing David to flinch with his caustic tone.

The president pretended ignorance. "I haven't the faintest idea of what you are talking about, Governor."

Boswell raised his voice, fuming. "You've spoken with Governors Littman, Pollock, and probably Governor Wilson by this point now that your brigade of vandalizing rioters has arrived." David caught the governor's eye and with both hands, palms down, he urged him to be calm.

"What?" President Brighton pretended to be insulted at the derogatory implications. "They're not *my* rioters!"

"They're working for you, whether you want them to or not! They're assaulting people and destroying property in the name of *your* agenda. And you've exploited the crisis to try to subjugate us and expand your unconstitutional power."

She swallowed hard. "Listen, Ben. I called the governors to offer my help. I was prepared to–"

"You called to *bribe* them!"

"Listen! Unlike you, I care!"

"There are strings attached to your aid and your promotions, Madam President. We've counted the cost, and we're unified against you. Cease from your attempt to shed innocent blood in our land."

"Innocent blood?" Her rage began to stir and it showed in her grimace and could be heard in the raspy quality of her voice.

"That's right!" he said before she could complete her thought. "The Psalms says that God ***hates*** the hands that shed innocent blood! And we aren't so fond of them either!" He pointed at the screen as he barked his reproof. "We still put murderers to death in Montana, and we'll do so more frequently with your wicked judges out of the equation. And we don't grant clemency to the agents of the federal government."

"You don't know who you're messin' with!" she shouted. "You've resisted the Supreme Court, Congress, the president of the United States, and–"

He raised his tone to match hers. "It's you who have resisted the Lawgiver of the Universe! You've defied His commandments and persecuted His children!" David gave up trying to motion for the governor to calm down. He turned and knelt in front of his seat, praying fervently for a good outcome to the explosive conversation between two of the most powerful leaders in the nation.

The president's mood swung erratically from angry to mildly humored. She chuckled mischievously. "Spare me your sermonizing, Mr. Boswell."

Boswell pointed at the screen. "I warn you not to underestimate us! The Bible says that Israel sinned against the Lord in submitting to the statutes of the heathen. We will not sin against Him in submitting to your heathen statutes that legalize suicide and abortion and celebrate sodomy and fornication."

Brighton's bottom lip began to tremble involuntarily with anger. She swallowed hard and took a deep breath, deciding to take the moral high ground. "I'm going to pray for you, Governor Boswell. You are so full of hate! You have no tolerance at all for those of differing opinions."

"God doesn't hear your prayers anyway, Madam President," Boswell snapped.

"What?"

"The Bible says that God turns His ears away from the prayers of those who turn their ears away from His law. Go ahead and send your army of rioters to Montana, and see what wrath we don't unleash against them. I won't be as passive as the other governors, I promise you that!

I'm extending immunity to any armed citizen who shoots one of your burglars or rioters."

Brighton laughed mockingly, and stuttered in her search for words to accurately express her disgust at the Coalition chairman's statement. "Uh, I, well, that makes perfect sense, doesn't it? Kill 'em all and let God sort them out. Is that Montana's policy now? I still don't know what you mean by 'my rioters'. They're not *my* rioters–"

"It is I who have a proposal for you, Madam President."

She raised her eyebrows. "Really?"

"Repent for euthanizing your husband, for murdering the preborn, and for promoting sodomy, and then call on the name of Jesus so that God's wrath against you will be abated!"

"You're delusional, Governor Boswell! You need a psychiatrist! It's you who needs to worry about *my* wrath!" The veins in her neck were bulging and her bony finger was aimed at Boswell's image on her screen.

"Well, you do your worst, Madam President, and we'll see whom God defends."

With those words – "do your worst" – David Jameson's thoughts went to his wife. For all he knew, Darlene was in the custody of federal agents, being tortured for information to his whereabouts. Still on his knees, he clenched his fists and passionately prayed for her, "God, save her. Bring us together again. Please…"

* * * * *

"I want you to take him down, Mr. Hamilton, *now*!" Everyone in the president's cabinet was on edge, bracing for their Jekyll-Hyde president at her worst.

"Madam President, these plans take time. We need intelligence–"

"If you had a teaspoon of intelligence in between your ears, Mr. Hamilton, you'd know what's best for you and invade Helena and arrest Governor Benjamin Boswell. You read their little secession letter. They said that this is their declaration of independence! Can you believe that? You know that they've arrested abortionists *and* their patients. They've shot at and killed federal agents. What more do you want, Todd?"

"We had a man on the inside," the director of the FBI explained, "but they caught him trying to take pictures, and now he's scared. He won't help us."

"You don't need a man on the inside, Mr. Hamilton. You just invade and kill the rebel!"

"We just can't kill him, Madam President. All of our intelligence leaders agree."

"And why not?"

"Removing Boswell with force will only worsen the problem," Hamilton responded coolly. "The civilians are armed and prepared for combat. Unless you want to endure a decade of guerilla warfare or commit genocide against civilians and turn the media against you" – Cameron Weaver snorted at the notion, evoking a disapproving glare from the austere FBI director – "killing Boswell or invading the Coalition, Madam President, will only exasperate your problems."

"And make your PR problems ten times worse," Halluci added.

"They have contingencies for continuity of leadership should Boswell be killed or removed by force. If we kill him, our problems will get worse, not better."

"You can arrest this dangerous religious fanatic tomorrow morning," the president snapped, "or you can step down!" She flung her arms like a pentecostal preacher. "You know he is raising a so-called army of Minutemen for His God? *Please!* What are these Confederate fear-mongers going to do, go around the nation trying to browbeat Americans into submission?" Spit flew out of the corners of her mouth as she ranted. "How can we tolerate this, this, this... ***traitor one more minute!?"***

"Calm down, Madam President."

"Arrest him, or resign and I'll find someone else to do it. Those are your choices."

The ultimatum had been issued, and they all knew that the president would not retract it. "Yes ma'am," he said, swallowing his pride and jotting down some notes. "By next week, we'll either have captured Boswell, or we'll have 100 coffins full of agents who died trying. He's beefed up security around him, you know. We don't have a Terry Markison within a block of him."

"Just do it!"

Hamilton nodded. "Consider it done."

Halluci and General Green shook their heads in disapproval, yet were too intimidated to speak their minds.

"If you fail, Todd, it'll be time for General Green to move into action. Are you up to the task, General?"

The Army general appeared downcast and didn't answer right away.

"General?"

"Whatever it takes, Madam President," he responded. "I must inform you, however, that we are having more resistance in Texas since our last briefing. We've stirred up the hornet's nest down there. Knocking on doors in rural Texas is bloody business."

"Well, make sure it's their blood."

"We are running out of prison space," Tom Davis, Homeland Security director stated. "We have to move to some detention facilities we have prepared for such circumstances."

"What detention facilities?" Danny Connor wondered out loud.

"FEMA detention facilities."

Danny turned to the president. "Bad idea."

"We've got to put them somewhere," Davis complained.

"We've been denying for decades that these facilities would ever be used for such purposes. The media will hurt us with this."

"Don't you worry about the media." Cameron tried to console the fears of Danny Connor and the chief of Homeland Security.

"Would you quit with the 'don't worry about the media' speech?'" General Green was overtly irritated with Cameron's attempt to comfort their reasonable fears. "People are going to see Americans interned behind barb wire and they're going to think 'Red Dawn' and call them concentration camps."

"Hold on, General," the president raised a palm to silence his critique. "We've got to get things under control in Texas, and letting incorrigible hate-speech criminals and gun criminals go free because we've run out of space is going to hurt us."

"We have 21 sieges in homes or neighborhoods right now in Texas," General Green announced painfully.

"Twenty-one?" someone mumbled, disturbed by the news.

"And for every conflict we resolve we create two new ones. And to compound the problem, some of our boys in the infantry are having a problem with raiding the homes of citizens and shooting at them. When our ground forces get cornered in a gunfight and call in air support, some of our pilots are reluctant to shoot their machine guns and mortars into American homes. The problem is systemic. We—" The general paused and appeared uneasy for a moment, and the president was disturbed by his tone and his reluctance to conclude his sentence.

"Do I sense some disapproval from you, General Green, of the firearm repossession plans of Mr. Erdman?" The president cast a suspicious glance at the general.

"Not me, Madam President," Green said shaking his head. "My boys."

"Well, get rid of them. Punish them. Your men reflect on you."

"Well, Madam President…" He stopped to scratch his balding scalp, leaving his hair disheveled. "It's not that easy when its 15% of your infantry, and another 20% are sympathetic with them."

The president cursed, and then threw her pen on the table in front of her, causing some to jolt. "What in the world is going on here, gentlemen?"

No one responded to the rhetorical question.

After an uneasy pause, the president mumbled, "Well, it may be time to wag the dog."

"Excuse me?" said General Green.

The president turned to the director of the CIA. "You've informed us that the cooperative Arab troop movements in the Middle East on the border of Israel were only exercises, is that correct?"

He nodded, unsure of this question's relevance. "Yes, that's correct."

"Are you absolutely sure that it's only an exercise?"

"Absolutely," he said, with a furrowed brow that exposed his curiosity as to the point the president was trying to make. "It's a business of best guesses and cleaning up messes."

"So there is the possibility, albeit faint, that the Arab nations are conspiring to cooperate for an assault upon Israel?"

The aging CIA director laughed, then quickly regained a serious countenance and rubbed his chin soberly. "Very faint, Madam President. Israel would nuke 'em if they thought that they were about to be assaulted. Israeli intelligence agrees with our men on the inside, who–"

"That's all I need to know." The president cut the CIA director off, showing him the palm of her right hand. Her gaze darted to General Green, whose countenance also relayed his confusion as to the president's line of questioning.

"General Green? What do you think of this? Let's transfer the most uncooperative quarter of our troops in Texas and as much as you can spare in the other U.S. bases to our bases in the Middle East under pretense of protecting our allies from the imminent threat of attack from terrorist-sponsoring nations. I will call General Petri Urlich at the UN after our meeting and approve the use of UN troops in the troubled areas in Texas…"

"What?"

“You really want UN troops policing on American soil?” Halluci blurted out.

General Green leaned forward in his chair and thumped his elbows against the table. “You must be out of…” General Green stopped himself, and leaned on his elbows. “You cannot be serious, Madam President.”

“This administration isn’t a democracy, gentleman!” she interrupted curtly. “We already have UN forces managing detention facilities in Texas and South Carolina, which harbor hardened traitors and hate criminals. Get your emotions under control.” That comment almost brought a mocking laugh from Danny, but he held it in.

The president’s chief of staff was apoplectic, but spoke as softly as her adrenaline would allow her. “This is an extremely unwise move on your part, politically and militarily.”

“It’s political suicide,” added Representative McGinnis.

The president casually waved off their criticism. “The United States should have made this military move decades ago. We’ve accepted the global economy, but resisted the inevitable political unity that follows. Much of the rest of the civilized world has accepted the UN as the primary legitimate military force in the world, and it’s time that the United States awakens to that reality. It’s been two decades since Kofi Annan admitted that ‘The UN Security Council is the sole source of legitimacy for the use of force in the world,’ and the more I think about it, the more I kind of like the idea.”

General Green cleared his throat. “Are you *daring* to imply that the Army, Navy, Air Force, and Marines of the United States should be subjugated to a foreign military power that has no respect for our constitutional separation of powers?”

“Hello?” she snapped her fingers sarcastically. “Last time I checked, the UN’s headquarters are in New York City.”

“Headed by those terrorist-sponsoring nations we have been railing against the past month,” General Green complained.

“Where we have only one vote among hundreds of dictatorships,” McGinnis added. “The UN is only as useful inasmuch as it propels *our* agenda.”

“And in this mission,” the president said with a nod, “it would be more useful than ever.”

Though he was filled with glee at the president’s willingness to employ UN forces in the U.S., the CIA director could sense the resistance in the room. He interjected with a quote from former Secretary of State Strobe Talbot. "All nations, no matter how permanent or sacred they may seem, are in fact artificial and temporary. Within the next 100 years, nationhood as we know it will be obsolete; all states will recognize a single global authority.'" He cleared his throat. "All of our colleagues in the CFR have admitted this for generations."

"Well said." The president nodded at the aging CIA director's quote. "This is a golden opportunity to cover more ground for global unity and peace than any opportunity we've had in hundreds of years. Unity's the future, gentlemen – economically, politically, and" – she glanced at General Green – "militarily. America, with all her stubborn nationalist pride, needs a baptism of globalism consciousness, and I'm pushing them to the bottom of the pool."

"We cannot take America there until she's willing to go." Senator Tindale's voice quivered, which the president found unbecoming for the stalwart liberal icon. He was foreseeing the watershed replacement of incumbents in Congress if the president's plan materialized.

"You're welcome to issue condemnations of it in the Senate and the House if you must to protect your re-election campaigns, but I'm not a finger-in-the-wind type of leader. I don't have anyone near me in the polls, so I have room to wiggle. We cannot let this crisis pass unexploited. You're blind if you don't see it! It's time we join the world community of enlightened democratic governments."

General Green's medals clanged as he leaned back in his chair and leaned forward on his elbows again. "But Madam President…" He looked down at his hands, calloused and scarred from 30 years in the trenches of warfare, and sought for the right words that would turn the tide of this meeting.

"General Green." The president waited until he looked up at her. "You've admitted that a quarter of your troops in Texas are at best quietly critical of our disarmament plans and sympathetic with the gun-owning law-breakers, and at worst, are traitors to our cause. How are those thousands of troops going to respond when we have to attack the Confederate rebels in Montana and Wyoming? How's your Navy going to feel about bombing the ports of Washington State? How are they going to feel dropping bombs on American airfields in Seattle, on laying siege to Denver, and hitting the nuclear silos in Montana?" That spun a few heads and they were now listened intently. "I cannot afford – *we* cannot afford to allow sentimental American troops to ruin this for us. This conflict is escalating every day. The self-proclaimed leader of this movement, Ben Boswell, has resisted every effort to settle our disputes peacefully, and has repeatedly admitted he will use what means he has at his disposal to defend his religious totalitarianism. That's the combined forces of ten State Guards – including considerable airpower – with almost as many nuclear warheads as the rest of the continental United States. We will *not* win this conflict against these insubordinate states with insubordinate American troops who are sympathetic with them. We need warriors who will not hesitate to follow orders and who are absolutely dedicated to our cause. Inevitably, we will have to *crush the rebels!*" She thrust her fist into her palm for emphasis.

Danny wanted to stand up and scream, but pragmatism tied him to his chair. *Just when you thought it couldn't get any worse, it does.*

"With the UN's assistance, Texas will be more easily subdued. Then when armed conflict arises in the northwest, they'll be in an ideal position to help us. We already have some UN troops here in the U.S. training. They don't have the hang-ups of traditions, misplaced moral judgments, and the sympathy for guns in the hands of the general population. They aren't bound to our Constitution. It's that simple."

"Madam President?" said General Green.

"Yes."

"Just give us a chance first. That's all I ask. You're turning your back on your armed forces too easily."

"Would you be willing to fire on American citizens, sir?"

"Fire when fired upon? Absolutely!"

The president leaned forward in her chair and clasped her hands in front of her. "How about fire when *not* fired upon?"

General Green took a quick, nervous breath. "But the rules of engagement—"

"For the United States of America," the president interjected. "You see, that's part of the problem. The United Nations doesn't have the inalienable-constitutional-rights hang-ups that our troops do. They understand that the circumstances may arise in which the rights of the individual may be safely violated for the greater good. The rules of engagement for the United Nations are unrestrained by such religious traditions."

"Madam President, if you want me to fire on American citizens who aren't firing at me, fine! I'll do it. Just don't give my job to a South African general. Please!"

"He's right," said Congressman McGinnis. "This is premature. You want the common American to be sympathetic for the Coalition's cause? This is how to do it."

“It’s a bad move, Madam President.” Dena Halluci patted the bangs of her newly dyed yellow hairdo. “Very bad move.”

“You need to listen to your cabinet on this one, Madam President,” said Senator Tindale.

President Brighton shook her head and glanced down at her notes. A moment later, she looked up. “Okay, General Green. I’m not going to beg and I’m not going to step on the toes of everyone in my cabinet. We’ll leave the UN out of it right now, but I will speak to UN Security General Petri Urlich about possible intervention in the future.”

“Thank you, Madam President. We won’t let you down.”

“Wise move, Madam President,” added Chief of Homeland Security, Tom Davis.

Danny sat as quietly as he could for the remainder of the staff meeting, and only spoke when he was addressed. He had been giving information to Josh less frequently in the past few weeks because he suspected that the president knew he was the rat in the bunch. He could only play this game for so much longer. Then it would be time for him to make his move. But he had to move before she did, or it would all be in vain. If she bombed Montana or if she brought the UN forces into the United States to subjugate American citizens, he will know that she had crossed the line.

Helena, Montana

“These are our orders, men.” Adjutant General Bryan of the Montana State Guard briefed a select force of 5,000 guardsmen comprised of troopers from each of the ten Coalition states. General Macintosh of Texas flanked him at the front of the large auditorium. General Bryan aimed his laser-pointer to a projected image of a map of downtown Lincoln, Nebraska. “We inserted a spy into Paine’s entourage in Boulder, and this is what we’ve learned so far. The rioters will begin here.” He pointed to an area that was highlighted red on his map. “We will be concealed in these six buildings downtown.” He pointed at the yellow highlighted areas. “They’re storage areas that have been quietly evacuated for our purpose. Once the rioters arrive and begin wreaking havoc, we let the police do their duty. We suspect that a large portion of the more violent rioters will then be unleashed upon the areas where the police are less concentrated – that appears to be how the rioters are operating to maximize the damage done and minimize the capture rate of the most violent and experienced criminals.”

He clicked off his laser pointer and turned to face his men. “When the major rioting begins, we will be in an ideal position to surround the rioters and make our arrests. Our mission is three-fold: protect the innocent, apprehend and arrest as many of these rioters as possible, preferably without lethal force.” He took a deep breath. “And catch Mitch Paine.”

“How many do they have right now?” someone asked.

"About twelve thousand, and growing." Gasps all over the auditorium informed Bryan that the 5,000 guardsmen weren't looking forward to this mission.

"If there aren't any further questions," said Texas General MacIntosh as he glanced at his watch, "we need to hit the road." Bryan nodded as MacIntosh stepped toward the edge of a platform. "If the rioting starts tomorrow evening as we have been told it will, we will still only get there four hours before the rioters. Then we need to get out of sight as soon as possible. We'll be taking buses that will be driving different routes to minimize exposure of our plans to the general public. That's one of the reasons you've all been ordered to wear civilian clothes here today."

"I have a question," someone asked with a raised hand in the front row. "You said that you'd prefer that we not use lethal force. My question is, if we do need to use lethal force to protect people, are we gonna be scrutinized and put on trial for it?" Thousands of guardsmen grunted and shifted in their chairs, as if the question was one that they all pondered.

Bryan nodded. "This is not just an ordinary civilian riot. This is an act of war. Most of the civilians will be unarmed, but that in and of itself is a weapon, for it keeps us from exercising the force that we must employ in order to halt this overwhelming invasion force. We must stop these rioters not just to protect life and property, but to protect freedom. We have no doubt that Mitch Paine's mission is to totally destroy the Coalition from within. He wants our leadership dead. He wants our pastors imprisoned without charge or trial. He wants judicial tyranny to trump our democratic vote. He wants Children Services to kidnap our kids and he wants our babies to die in abortion clinics. Understand? That's what is at stake." The men were quiet and sober as they realized the seriousness of the day's conflict. "Let's close in a word of prayer."

* * * * *

General MacIntosh got a call on his cell phone on the way to the bus. He read the caller identification number. It was Governor Boswell. He tapped the phone icon and brought the phone to his ear. "MacIntosh here."

"Hello, General. Change of plans."

"Change of plans? This late in the game?"

"Lieutenant Dantin has given me credible intel of a sudden, hurried increase in FBI personnel in Billings overnight. Also, federal agents are secretly heading west as we speak, toward Helena."

"You think they're planning an attack?"

"Possibly."

"That'd be crazy. If they wanted to take you out, they'd kidnap you in the middle of the night, not in your office with guards all over the place."

"They probably want to take the whole cabinet down like they did in Texas. They want to hinder our plans for continuity of leadership. We need you to come back and mount a defense for what may be a coordinated assault on Montana's leadership. Lieutenant Dantin apparently took the liberty to have a few hundred Montanan guardsmen under Rod Sanders briefed on the situation."

"Oh, yes! Isn't Rod Sanders the Guard captain who rescued Barry Friar during the siege on his home?"

"He's a colonel now. He's adequate to the task, but you were present when they arrested Henry Adams, and the feds will probably be following the same playbook. I want your leadership to manage our defense."

"Yes sir. I'll reassign the command of my unit and be in your office in an hour."

Boswell hung up the phone and his chief of security, Isaiah Knabb, raised his voice, "I don't like this. Why can't we cancel the cabinet meeting and use a decoy?"

"No. If they are going to launch an attack" – Boswell aimed an index finger at Knabb and leaned into him – "and you know they will! – then I *want* them to do it when we're ready for it. And I want to repel it. The footage we obtain will be a powerful tool to turn the other states to our side. If just a few more states turn, I think the feds will be forced to accept peaceful secession. If this spy catches wind that I'm not in my office, the opportunity's gone. We don't even know who this rat is, so we can't take a chance of sending a decoy in my place."

Boswell expected his chief of security to be more sympathetic when he understood his reasoning, but Isaiah Knabb looked down at his calloused knuckles, his lips pressed tightly against each other. "So we're using the leader of the Coalition as bait so that we can get some video footage?"

Boswell grunted. "We've no king but King Jesus, and we're all expendable for His glory and posterity's freedom."

Billings, Montana

FBI Sergeant Roger Hammel had very little time to digest the assault plan that was handed him on a silver platter. It was clear that personnel much higher on the totem pole had decided this, and he was simply to follow orders. It would be a simple attack. Communications would be jammed. The building would be surrounded, the guards neutralized, and then his team would charge the stairs and the elevators. Very simple. They had obtained the layout of the building and had plans to seal every possible route of escape. The feds had an insider offering assistance – a telephone operator in the basement of the governor's office building. Their insider would confirm Boswell's presence before the attack.

One of Hammel's subordinates, who rode in the same vehicle, got Hammel's attention. "You know, Sergeant, we're staking a lot on this intelligence about Boswell's staff meeting at 4 p.m."

"It's solid intel," Hammel responded.

"You think it'll be that easy, huh?"

"The rebellion'll end today." Hammel's confident demeanor did not reflect what he felt in his gut. Being back in Montana revived the painfully embarrassing memories of the siege he managed at the Friar's compound. Hammel had been temporarily demoted as a result of the Montana Guard's success in getting past the barricades and into the Friar's house. But when the Bureau became unimpressed with his replacement, he was placed back in command of his men.

It was Roger Hammel's second lap around the capitol in Helena. He was in a white van with ten other men. His hands were beginning to tremble.

An agent beside Hammel read a text message on his cell, slapped it shut, and then tapped Hammel on the arm. "It's confirmed, sir. Our inside man in the basement has confirmed the 4 p.m. staff meeting and it looks like a lot of important suits are here. He doesn't recognize some of them so he thinks that they must be from the other Coalition states."

"And security?"

"Nothing's changed. They're right where he told us they'd be."

Hammel smiled and tapped his earpiece-mic. "We're live. Drivers, get to your positions. Mission Honest Abe underway in 60 seconds, on my mark." The SWAT agents loaded full magazines into their automatic weapons, and adjusted their ammo belts as their commander counted down.

* * * * *

"Hey, excuse me." Elijah Slate rang the bell on the desk in the foyer of the entrance to the state administration building.

The security guard who sat watching the monitors was unfriendly. "What is it?" he snapped, keeping his gaze fixed on the monitors.

Elijah smirked. "Having a bad day?"

"What do you want?" The guard cast a critical glance at the African American man who stood before him. He snarled when he saw one of the two glass doors had been propped open, which allowed the stranger to sneak up on him. When Elijah did not respond quickly, the guard ordered sternly, "Come back later, sir."

"Is everything okay?"

The guard kept his gaze fixed on the screen. "It's just bad timing. Real quick, tell me what you want?"

"Can I give this to Governor Boswell?" Elijah held out a black, leather-bound Bible. "It's been signed by all of the Minutemen. I'm one of the leaders…"

"Not today," the guard responded. "Try tomorrow."

A female guard stepped out of the hallway with a cup of coffee. "Oh, that's nice," she said, leaning forward to look more carefully at the large black Bible.

"We signed on the back pages," Elijah said, opening to the back of the Bible. "The Acts of the apostles are still being written, and we just want to thank Governor Boswell for his leadership in this God-glorifying chapter of history."

The guard turned from the monitor to glance briefly at the signatures. "That's a big book."

"My friend, David Jameson, said the governor prefers large print." Elijah shuffled through the pages to show the guard that there was nothing worthy of his suspicion.

"David who?"

"Jameson."

The guard's brow furrowed. "David Jameson? I know that name. *The* David Jameson?"

Elijah winced. "No, I mean, Jamestown. David Jamestown."

The guard's eyes widened. Elijah's sudden nervousness piqued his suspicions. The muscular guard studied Elijah for a moment. "Is David Jamestown his real name?"

Elijah frowned and hesitated. His reluctance to forthrightly answer the question irritated the guard.

The security guard stood up and leaned toward Elijah. "Is David Jamestown's real name David Jameson?" he asked more firmly, his hand on his unsnapped holster.

Elijah glanced at him cock-eyed for a moment. "David Jameson is a pale fellow with brown hair – at least he was on the picture I saw on the news – not my bald, brown-faced, blond, goatee-wearing friend who saved Governor Boswell's life." Elijah faked a light-hearted laugh. "It was a slip of the tongue, friend."

"I hope so." The guard stood upright and made a mental note to inform Isaiah Knabb later of his suspicion that a wanted terrorist was close to Governor Boswell. "I'll see that Governor Boswell gets your gift." The guard stretched his arm to take the black Bible but Elijah pulled it away.

"I'd like to give it to him in person, if I may."

"No. You…"

Another guard stepped out of an adjacent room and interrupted. "There they are." He motioned at the white van that was driving past them the second time.

The guard's head snapped back to the monitor. "I see them. Several vans." A half dozen vans and SUVs suddenly pulled into the road around the administration building from various side roads and alleys.

"What's going on?" Elijah asked, concerned with the guards' obsession with the monitor and the sudden traffic in front of the building.

"Should have left when I told you to, bud. Now get in there and sit down against the wall." The muscular security guard motioned toward a doorway beside them.

Elijah looked over his shoulder through the glass walls at the green lawn in front of the building, wondering what so worried the two starched guards.

"Now!" the guard reiterated, pointing into the adjacent room.

Through his scrambled radio, Isaiah Knabb tried to comfort the agents stationed outside the entrance. "Keep cool. Keep your hands off your weapons. Look calm. You'll have a few seconds to get inside when they make for the building..."

Three blocks away, two semi-trucks pulled off the interstate, their cabins teeming with FBI SWAT. On Hammel's order, the vans and SUVs screeched to a halt all around the administration building that housed the governor's office. Suddenly, the doors of the vans and SUVs swung wide open and agents in plainclothes, bulky with bullet-proof vests, converged on the building like water, screaming orders to security to lay down their weapons.

The muscular security guard at the front entrance quickly tried to shut and lock the two glass doors, but not before a gas canister made it through an open door and began to fill the foyer with a potent tear gas. He held his breath, bolting the door shut. The other guard tossed him a gas mask from behind the desk. A secretary that was coming down the hall dodged into a side room and let out a scream, slamming the door behind her. The skin of the two agents in the foyer began to burn, but the adrenaline kept it tolerable.

Elijah heard the distinctive hiss of the gas canister and the blast of gunfire from outside the building, and tried to calm the hysterical secretary, whose eyes began to tear and face began reddened. Elijah hugged the large black Bible against his chest as if it were a life raft on a hurricane-ravaged ocean. He unholstered his behind-the-belt .45 caliber Glock with the other. There was a pause in the firing; Elijah put his ear to the door to try to understand the conversation on the other side.

Suddenly, a .223 caliber bullet penetrated the wall and struck the Bible that he pressed against his chest. It penetrated it and thrust Elijah against the wall with a thud.

When Hammel and his team of agents reached the front entrance, he rattled the locked glass doors with his large hands. He raised his weapon to shoot through the glass when he heard the automatic gunfire from behind him. He looked back, stunned when he saw them coming from all directions. At least 100 guardsmen in camouflage gear sprinted toward his position with automatic weapons, some of them affixed with grenade launchers.

He tapped his radio: "Roberts! Falwell! Where are you?"

The drivers of the two semis full of SWAT troopers plowed through Guard vehicles obstructing their path down an ally. "The Guard's onto us! Trying to pull us over!" one of the drivers shouted as the agent beside him returned fire out the window at guardsmen pursuing in a Hummer.

Hammel cursed. "I hate Montana."

"Drop your weapons and put your hands in the air!" General MacIntosh gave the order over a loud speaker from an unseen location.

A federal agent shouted frantically at Hammel. "What do we do?"

Sergeant Hammel turned toward the locked front entrance, pointed his machine gun at the glass door and let out a volley of bullets that shattered it. He then crashed through the door, followed by his men who were quickly overwhelmed by gunfire from security guards hiding inside the foyer. The Bureau agents braved the hail of bullets and the toxic mist fuming from the gas canister they had shot into the foyer, and they took cover behind couches and chairs in the waiting room, pulling their masks over their heads. A bitter, close-range firefight broke out between Hammel's men and the security guards shooting from behind the security of steel doors and concealed locations. Some of Hammel's men took cover under the bushes beside the doors.

More gunfire was heard outside, except this time those bullets were not fired into the sky but at their feet. "Drop your weapons and surrender. Now!"

The firefight dwindled in the foyer as the guardsmen quickly came within 20 feet of the front entrance, surrounding Hammel's team. Most of Hammel's men dropped their guns and placed their hands in the air.

The two semis full of SWAT were disabled a half a block away and surrounded by several dozen heavily armed guardsmen. The overwhelming force quickly disarmed the cabin full of FBI agents, unloaded them from the cabin of the semi, handcuffed them, and put them in vans with bars on the windows.

One of the federal agents in front of Hammel raised his hands and shouted frantically, "I surrender! Don't shoot."

"No, you don't," the surrendering agent heard Hammel say from inside the building. "You're K.I.A."

The agent turned toward Hammel with his hands still raised, his eyes wide with fear.

Blam! Blam! Blam!

Hammel's first three bullets riddled the torso of the surrendering subordinate and hit one of the charging guardsmen. The other guardsmen halted, fell to the ground, and prepared to fire back, but could not identify a target inside the gas-filled foyer. The other surrendering agents flung themselves to the ground as bullets whizzed over their heads. The security guards in the foyer kept concealed for fear of being struck by incoming fire from the approaching Guard.

Hammel paused and all was quiet for an eerie second. Hammel looked behind him just in time to see the barrel flash that discharged a .45-caliber bullet through his head, splattering his brains across the broken glass. Elijah's Glock ended the life of the murderous senior federal agent. An agent beside Hammel turned to fire at Elijah, and Elijah killed him as well with two quick shots through his skull.

"Freeze! Drop your weapons!" Elijah screamed, inviting the other agents to surrender and live or retaliate and die. He pressed his left hand against the pain over the left side of his chest, suspecting several broken ribs from the severe, sharp pain he experienced with every breath. Even though the black Bible had prevented the bullet from killing him, it still struck him with a lot of force. "Now! Drop 'em!"

With Hammel's caved-in skull in clear view, the other agents were quite susceptible to Elijah's hollow-pointed persuasion. They dropped their weapons and prostrated themselves face down on the ground with their hands behind their heads.

Reinforcements tripled the number of security guards in the hallway that led to the elevator and stairwell. When they reached the foyer they expected a firefight, but instead found Elijah Slate holding five frazzled federal agents at gunpoint in the middle of a puddle of blood from several dead ones.

"That guard has been shot!" Elijah motioned toward the guard who had been monitoring the security monitor, who had suffered several gunshot wounds in the firefight.

One of the agents checked on him. "He's already dead."

"Clear in the northeast!" one of the guards shouted.

The FBI troops at the side exits surrendered quickly. The agents had applied the C-4 explosive over the door bolts, but were unable to detonate it before Guard forces overwhelmed them.

"Clear on the northwest exit."

"Clear on the southwest side."

After a moment's pause, Knabb asked into his headset microphone, "And the southeast?" His gaze darted to the security camera's view of the rear southeast entrance.

Things were not as quick in the rear of the building, where large glass doors led into a large foyer. One of the FBI agents had heard Hammel's first shot on the opposite side of the building, and he assumed falsely that he was being fired upon from inside the building. So he shot his M-16 through the locked glass door with a wide circumference and launched a mortar from his grenade launcher. The blast killed three security guards who crouched behind the secretary's desk. A half dozen security personnel in a room down the hall were wounded with shrapnel from the grenade. The other security personnel in the room stayed low, hoping that the approaching guardsmen would distract the federal attackers and give them a chance to get between the invaders and the elevator and the stairwell.

Holding his hands over his ringing ears, one of the trapped security guards asked at the senior guard beside him, "Should we get out?"

"What?"

He motioned to the side door that led away from the foyer. "We need to retreat!"

The senior security guard was appalled at the thought. "Retreat? This is *our* capitol!" He snatched the grenade launcher out of the hands of one of the other security personnel, jumped into the hallway, and launched two grenades before taking two bullets in the chest. The high-octane bullets of the FBI easily penetrated his bulletproof vest.

"Everybody down!" The security guard closest to the door shouted and ducked for cover in the office room. Seconds later, two explosions decimated the foyer, dicing the torsos, limbs, and faces of the federal invaders with careening shrapnel. Glass, drywall, and mutilated body parts scattered across the yard.

The guardsmen approached cautiously, crouching as they fired at surviving federal agents in the windows and in the foyer. When they secured the first floor, they began to aid the wounded and took a census of the casualties.

"Clear on the southeast front," the senior guardsman reported into his headset. "Finally."

Unbeknownst to Security Director Isaiah Knabb, the telephone operator had a Plan B. This tall, thick man with short, blond-dyed hair was not going to let a failed raid affect his chances for fame and fortune with the promised tax-free million dollars for the capture or death of Benjamin Boswell. He planned to shoot him, surrender, and then let himself be taken into custody until the feds restored order. Then, he predicted, he would be elevated to hero status. As long as he surrendered before being shot, he was sure to succeed. Realizing that the federal agents were being overwhelmed, he snuck up the internal stairwell and pulled a .38-caliber revolver from a concealed holster on his calf. Just as the door to the internal stairway shut behind him, the security guard assigned the duty of watching the basement offices for potential moles grew suspicious. He entered the stairwell and followed at a distance.

Four flights of stairs led the phone operator to a side door to Boswell's office. He put his ear to the door as sweat dripped from his furrowed brow. He listened intently to try to decipher what the whispering voices behind the door were saying. He thought he recognized the voice of Governor Boswell, so he reached for the doorknob and slowly wiggled it to see if the door was locked. It was.

He stepped back, preparing to shoot the doorknob and kick the wooden door open. Just before he pulled the trigger, a shotgun blast tore the door in half and sprayed speeding pellets into the unsuspecting man's chest and abdomen.

The blast knocked him down several stairs before his heavy body got hung up in the handrail. General Alan MacIntosh stuck the shotgun barrel and then his face through the hole in the door as the wide-eyed telephone operator heaved gargled breaths.

"I sure hope that's the bad guy," said MacIntosh.

Isaiah Knabb followed MacIntosh through the shattered door. The security agent that was following the mole up the stairwell reached down to pick up the man's revolver just as the man's consciousness returned. With a trembling hand, he raised his .38 caliber at the security guard and received two quick bullets in the chest for it.

Fully armed Guard jets paroled the skies overhead as Governor Boswell immediately ordered the public relations machine into full swing. The 60 seconds of video surveillance footage most likely to gain sympathy for the Coalition was compiled. The footage was then distributed to the national media and U.S. congressional offices, with an official statement of condemnation for the raid. The final numbers: 44 federal agents dead, 35 wounded, and 85 captured and held without bail, to be tried on aggravated assault and murder charges. Eleven security employees and eight guardsmen were killed and five were wounded.

Most importantly, the Coalition of Free Christian States was still alive. They were overcome with a renewed confidence that the King of kings was taking their side in the conflict.

Washington, D.C.

"The raid failed, Madam President." Todd Hamilton thought it best to inform the president face-to-face.

"Failed?" Her shocked countenance appeared like the calm before the storm. Hamilton let the moment come and go without an answer. "How? What happened?" She sat behind her desk with a look of confusion on her taut countenance, her wiry body as rigid as an ice cube.

Todd Hamilton sighed and looked down. "I don't know, Madam President." He lied to her, not having the courage to tell her that Montana leadership must have known they were coming. He then gave her the numbers and handed her Boswell's press release. She read it silently and grew more furious with every sentence.

"They're trying our agents for *murder*?"

"Keep reading. You were indicted as well. There is a warrant out for your arrest."

"My arrest?!" She put her head back and laughed again. Her countenance shifted so quickly from violently angry to hysterically laughing that Hamilton wondered if she had multiple personalities.

"Governor Boswell and the other CFCS governors are ordering you to be in court in Helena in two weeks for your arraignment."

The president laughed the hardest that Hamilton had ever seen. "Oh my, oh my!" she exclaimed between fits of hysterical laughter as she heaved and smacked the table in jest.

Hamilton grinned, more from the president's outburst of laughter than from finding any humor in the situation. "He's released footage of the assault to the national media, including footage of one of our own FBI sergeants apparently shooting a surrendering subordinate. Cameron Weaver's already instructing them not to run it, but it'll carry to the public on the net."

That comment put a halt to the sarcastic jab she was going to make about the Coalition, and her countenance grew more serious. Her tongue mumbled several curses, forging through the banks of political correctness that less and less often restrained her. "Is the footage bad for us, Todd?"

Hamilton nodded. "We were clearly the aggressors. From a PR standpoint, it doesn't get much worse. Your ratings will certainly take a dive. Even the media may turn on you temporarily just to feign objectivity."

"We cannot afford a dip, much less a dive." The thought of the American people obsessed with even more video footage that embarrassed her and threatened to slow the progress of her agenda nauseated her. "Maybe we can blame the Bureau man in charge of the raid for this – the middle man."

"I thought you would entertain the thought." Hamilton shifted weight uneasily from one leg to the other as he mulled over the arguments in his mind.

"They didn't follow orders precisely." The president began to bite a fingernail as she sat back down, her eyes focused on a point in mid-air. "They were excessive in their use of force. They'd take the fall to save the administration?"

Todd Hamilton leaned in closer. "Captured agents are being tried for murder, Madam President, and with Congress having a predictable short fuse to launch a full-scale investigation, I suspect they'll find no shortage of agents who will turn on you for leniency."

Brighton reluctantly nodded with a labored sigh.

"Senior Bureau agents would gladly defy Montana law to protect you, Madam President, but would they risk contempt of Congress to lie for you? I wouldn't bet on it."

"Would you?"

"Of course," Hamilton responded without thinking. "The cause merits any cost."

Without acknowledging Hamilton's loyal response, the president tapped a button on her phone. "Get me Cameron and Dena on the phone," she ordered the secretary.

The secretary responded, "Cameron's on line two for you now."

The president pushed another button and her press secretary's image shone up on her computer screen. "Cameron!"

"I know about the failed raid and the footage."

"You have to stop them from showing it."

"Some of them are not making promises over the phone. I'm meeting with two CEO's in the next hour."

"Threaten them with audits, boycotts on the White House – do whatever you have to do."

"The net will still carry it, along with talk radio," Cameron Weaver warned her. "I think the best the media can do is not be silent, but rather propagate contradictory versions of the story to make Montana's version less believable."

Todd Hamilton sat down and Brighton told him, "Don't get too comfortable."

"What?" asked Cameron, thinking she was talking to him.

"Not you, I was talking to Todd. Tell the media, Cameron, that we'll be appointing another FBI director."

Hamilton's face paled. "Wha…"

She hung up on her press secretary, and without looking at Hamilton, said, "You're going to have to take a long vacation, sir."

"This wasn't my fault, Madam President!" He stood from his chair, his pale face reddening with his adrenaline rush. "A failed raid was among our contingencies. You *need* me. I've proven my loyalty."

"Get out of my office," she snapped without looking at him, pointing her bony finger at the door. "I don't ever want to see you again except on C-Span when you're before the congressional committee that investigates this raid, admitting how badly you screwed this up. Flub that up, and I'll see to it that you never get a job anywhere else in the United States either. And if you speak one word of criticism to the media, I'll make your life hell for the rest of your days. Got that?"

Todd Hamilton reluctantly accepted her decision and nodded. He could see that argument was fruitless.

"In the meantime," she said, trying to lighten her tone, "go skiing in the Swiss Alps. When we get over this crisis, maybe we could put you back to good use." She didn't want to make an embittered enemy out of him, at least not before she could have him killed by one of her CIA assassins in Europe.

"Yes ma'am." He turned to the door and pondered whether he should just purchase a one-way ticket.

President Brighton immediately got on the phone and invited Bill Erdman, the Director of the Bureau of Alcohol, Tobacco, and Firearms, to come up and be the Interim Director of the FBI. He was more in tune with her social flavor anyway, a die-hard liberal in social matters – unlike a lot of the Bureau staff who sympathized with fiscal conservatism. Erdman, fed up with the gun confiscation campaigns in Texas and South Carolina that felt like endless quicksand, enthusiastically accepted the promotion.

10

Lincoln, Nebraska

Adjutant General Bob Bryan smiled. “Thanks for letting me know.” He slapped his cell phone shut and relayed the information to his six squad leaders. “Good news, men,” Bryan reported through a desk-mounted microphone in the rear of a black van. “General MacIntosh and the governor’s security team just successfully repelled a massive federal raid on Montana’s capitol building.” The men in riot gear in basements and vacated offices let out a muffled cheer and talked excitedly amongst each other while those who chatted and shopped throughout the downtown area’s stores tried to be more subdued.

That was just the news they needed to stir their spirits in time for the evening’s work. The thought of trying to stop over 12,000 intoxicated college students from rioting and vandalizing the downtown of one of the largest cities of one of the most liberal Coalition states tested their nerves, and after an hour of waiting, they were getting anxious. The streets were so calm and the shops and customers appeared so ordinary, that General Bryan wondered whether his intel was wrong. He tapped a button on the radio affixed to his belt, connecting his Bluetooth with the communication line of the local police.

“Captain Gilles?”

“The rioting just began at Fortieth and Main,” Gilles informed him through the motorcycle helmet’s communication device. He idled his motorbike on the sidewalk about 50 yards away from the growing mayhem. “I was just about to call you. It’s light. Looks like some locals are challenging them.”

"Has your police force arrived yet?"

"Not yet. I've notified them."

"Get out of there, Gilles. We need your eyes and ears. Don't get stuck in the rioting."

"I'm leaving now. Traffic is slowing." Gilles winced as three bricks suddenly crashed into the hood of the pick-up truck in front of him. He looked up and saw students breaking glass windows in the second story of a department store, throwing bricks and goods onto the vehicles below. The driver of the pick-up, unable to move his vehicle in the traffic, abandoned his truck and rushed for cover.

The police captain sent smoke rising from the spinning tires of his motorcycle as he did a quick 90-degree turn and sped down an alley between two buildings.

It was ten minutes before Gilles called again. His voice trembled as he updated General Bryan. "Lots of vans and packed cars just got off the interstate, heading east down Seventh, right toward you. It looks like there's a convergence of rioters right to your block."

"We expected that." Bryan spoke calmly to try and settle the nerves of the one who was his primary source of intelligence.

"Rioting's bad on Main. Churches and stores burning."

A subordinate beside General Bryan was listening into the police line. He frantically tapped Bryan on the arm and hurriedly informed him, "We've got gunfights between rioters and policemen on Westwood Avenue."

"Gunfights?" Bryan was surprised.

"Yes. Police are retreating."

Bryan turned his attention back to Gilles on his Bluetooth. "Keep your distance, Gilles."

"Yes sir. I'm out."

Bryan leaned into the microphone affixed to the narrow table in front of him, tapped a button on its base, and addressed the squad leaders. "Squad leaders, get ready. The rioting will begin at your block any minute. Don't exit until I give the command. Be forewarned, some of the rioters are armed."

Four and a half minutes later, all hell, figuratively speaking, broke loose.

A squad leader ducked in a real estate office to keep from being seen by the hordes of students outside the window. "General Bryan? Now?" he asked through his headset.

"Not yet!" Bryan responded. "They're still unloading. We have to have all of them unloaded off their vehicles. Hold your positions."

"People are getting assaulted, sir, within 30 feet of us," another squad leader spoke hurriedly from where he and his 50 men hid concealed in an empty storefront building. "They have Molotovs. If they throw them in here before we can evacuate, we might have to retreat out of the rear of the building."

"Try to hold your positions until I give the word!"

Gilles tapped back in. "General Bryan? This is Gilles."

"I'm here." General Bryan leaned closer to a map of downtown Lincoln on a computer screen affixed to the wall of the van as a subordinate tapped it with a pen to highlight areas where the rioting had begun.

"Hundreds, maybe thousands of young people unloaded from vans and autos all over downtown, sir. Rioters are assaulting shoppers. Unleash the force now!"

It happened just as expected. There was light rioting in three spots around town that suddenly grew in intensity just as the police forces were exhausted in those areas. Then heavier rioting from the more violent protesters began right on the very block around which the combined Guard forces were stationed. General Bryan's plan was working.

Bryan leaned into his microphone and flipped all of the switches on his controller to relay the message to every guardsman with a communication device. "Unleash Justice! I repeat, Unleash Justice! We're live!"

Bryan turned and ordered the driver of the van, "Let's move, or we're going to get surrounded." He ordered the subordinate beside him who was listening to the police line, "Tell Wingate at the highway patrol to cordon off the perimeter. No one leaves the area except locals with local ID."

"What perimeter?"

"This perimeter!" He pointed out the pink highlighted area on the map. "Wingate knows about it."

As they moved into traffic, the driver immediately began to try to persuade the general that they needed to move back into the garage. Students were trashing the streets, breaking the windows out of parked cars, burglarizing stores, and fighting with one another over booty. Someone was throwing furniture out of a department store onto the streets. "It's out of control, sir! We need to get you to a safe location…"

"There is no safe location in downtown Lincoln," someone from the back of the van mumbled as he unholstered his handgun.

"We need to be outside of the garage if it is surrounded," General Bryan told them. "Just keep moving!"

The driver pulled their van out of the three-story parking garage and into the congested streets. "This is crazy!" a guardsman exclaimed, aghast at the mayhem everywhere.

"Shh!" Bryan ordered. He thought he heard a voice outside that he vaguely recognized, a voice on the loudspeaker. The voice was in front of them and then behind them, so he knew it had to be coming from inside a vehicle that passed them on the two-lane road. The voice was giving orders to the rioters and encouraging them. "I know that voice! That's Mitch Paine!"

General Bryan instructed the driver to do a 180 and go the opposite direction.

At once, thousands of guardsmen burst into the street with automatic weapon fire into the air, stunning the rioting anarchists and students. Some of the more sober rioters dropped their tire irons and put out their Molotov cocktails, and fell submissively to the ground when ordered to do so. The students were prepared for arrest for their cause, but they were not prepared to die for their cause. Many students fled and guardsmen gave chase. A few attacked the guardsmen and those were destroyed with overwhelming force. Lethal force was justified against anyone who attacked civilians or guardsmen with weapons, regardless of the weapon used – a brick, a tire iron, a torch or Molotov cocktail, a knife, or even a rock. The guard snipers that were stationed on the roofs of the buildings took their aim at those who refused to put out their Molotovs or who assaulted civilians.

The Guard chased about 100 drug-crazed rioters down an alley toward a dead-end street. The students were trapped – they couldn't squeeze into the alleys as fast as they were pressed against the walls that surrounded them. Some of the students started getting trampled. In desperation, some of them fired handguns toward the guardsmen from the center of the crowd of rioters. Unable to locate the shooters, the squad leader at this location was hesitant to fire into a crowd. He shouted for the students to lie down prostrate, but they would not respond, even when he intermittently fired rubber bullets among them. After four of his men were shot down from the unseen sniper in the crowd, the squad leader ordered the unleashing of a barrage of rubber bullets at the lawless crowd. They fired until every one of the rioters was flat on the ground from injuries or from fear and the ones who possessed firearms had been exposed and eliminated.

General Bryan again heard Mitch Paine's voice coming from ahead of him, down the congested road. He saw a speaker affixed to the top of a Yellow Volkswagen bug about a dozen cars ahead of their van.

Bryan moved up beside the driver of his van and knelt between the front two seats. "Pass 'em. Catch up to that yellow car!" The general pointed ahead at the VW, urging the driver to bypass the car in front of them.

The driver screeched to a halt as the mobs swarmed around them on both sides of the van with reflective tinted windows. "How, sir? I can't move!"

Bryan stepped out of the side door of the van. Mitch Paine's voice continued to ring out, echoing off the buildings all around them. General Bryan climbed onto the hood of the van and then onto the roof. He saw the yellow VW bug prepare to turn down an alley. He jumped off the van and opened a door.

Addressing the driver, he ordered, "Roll up your windows and stay in the van. It's safer unless you're set on fire." He pointed at two guardsmen assigned to protect him, "You two! Grab extra clips of ammo and come with me."

Professor Paine hesitated when he saw the soldiers converging on the thousands of rioters who were wreaking havoc on the capital city of Nebraska. Then he remembered his numbers. He was invincible.

"Fight 'em!" Paine shouted into his microphone. "Fight 'em! The Confederates have arrived! Give 'em hell! Make 'em pay!"

As he ordered the students to repel the Guard, the driver of the vehicle, the SSA leader from the University of Texas, urged him to give up the microphone. "The Guard had to have been waiting for us, Prof! We need to give up the microphone or they're going to catch us."

"Try to get down one of the alleys between the buildings."

Nick's friend Damon sat in the back seat of the two-door car. He pleaded with Nick to let him out. "Open your door! Let me out! I'll clear the way for ya."

Nick opened the door and pulled his seat forward so Damon could exit.

"Come on!" The professor turned to Damon. "Quickly!"

Damon squeezed out of the car and Paine pointed. “There! Down that alley!”

“Out of the way!” Nick waved an arm out the window, motioning for the rioters to move.

“Hurry!” Paine was growing anxious.

Damon cleared the path for the VW, and then he saw the three guardsmen sprinting right toward him. He saw that the yellow VW was trapped in the throng of people. He pretended as if he didn’t see the guardsmen as they sprinted past him and then he turned and caught one of the guardsmen with a left hook that struck his jaw and knocked his feet out from underneath him! The guardsman’s head smacked the cement hard with a nauseating thud. General Bryan and the second guardsman came to a quick stop just as the bushy-headed young man took a swing at the general. General Bryan ducked just as the second guardsman hit the student with a rubber bullet in the center of his abdomen. The student fell to the ground, breathless.

The general turned his attention down the road.

The guardsman bent down to check on his fellow soldier. “Are you all right?”

The felled guardsman’s consciousness returned, and he rose to his knees and put his hand on the back of his head. He removed his hand and saw blood covering it.

“We need to get you to a hospital.”

“Go!” the injured guardsman shouted. “I’ll make it back to the van. Get Mitch Paine!”

Mitch Paine looked out of his window and saw the fight between Damon and the guardsmen. Then two of the three guardsmen began to charge his vehicle on foot again, with their guns at the ready. “The Guard found me. They’re coming!”

“Out of the way!” Nick stuck his head out of the window and shouted at the rioters who obstructed their path down the alley. “Move!”

“Go! Go!” Mitch Paine yelled as he stepped over and put his foot on top of Nick’s foot on the gas pedal. The vehicle jerked into the narrow alley, colliding with a young woman in black. The rioter was struck in the hip by the vehicle and thrown onto the hood, cracking the windshield.

“Are you crazy!” Nick’s eyes were wide and his face flush with trepidation as the injured rioter flipped over the hood of the car. He glanced into the rearview mirror to see that the young woman collapsed to the cement, motionless. “That was Serena! She’s one of us!”

"Go! Go!" Paine was more attentive to the soldiers chasing them than to Nick's pangs of conscience. "If they catch me, then we're ruined." He caught a glimpse of the shock in Nick's face. "She's expendable for the cause, Nick, just like you, just like me. You can't be soft in this business..." As the professor lectured, Nick wasn't paying attention to the road. Paine looked ahead and his eyes widened. "Whoa!"

Nick slammed on the breaks as they skidded into a dumpster that had been set on fire and moved partially into the alley.

Mitch Paine's seatbelt was not fastened, so his body flew forward with the collision and his forehead hit the windshield. He blasphemed God angrily as he checked for blood in the overhead mirror. "Come on Nick! Get with the program!"

Nick cursed his inattentiveness as he tried to reverse back. Burning trash rolled off the dumpster onto the hood of the car.

General Bryan and his subordinate followed the yellow VW bug down an alley when the general collided with an intoxicated student who was carrying a red brick. The student cursed and re-directed his aim toward the guardsmen. The general's companion fired three rubber bullets from his M-16 and laid the student out just as the heaved brick connected with the general's forehead. Bryan fell to one knee holding his rapidly swelling brow.

"Are you okay?"

General Bryan looked up, the white of his right eye turning red with blood.

"You need to be directing this mission from the cover of the van, not out on the street where you can get–"

"Look out!" General Bryan pushed the private out of the way of a Molotov cocktail at the last moment. The flaming glass struck the ground at the general's feet, and caught the lower part of his pants leg on fire. Fortunately, the glass did not break. The perpetrator fled and they kicked away the bottle of fuel and patted out the flame.

General Bryan turned to an elderly lady ducking in the front seat of her locked vehicle as six students jumped up and down on the hood and trunk, crumpling the hood and denting the ceiling of the red two-door Ford Escort. The general aimed his gun at the students and fired two shots just over their heads, quickly wiping the intoxicated smiles off their faces.

"Off the vehicle! Now!"

The students fled, blending with dozens who exited through the broken glass windows of an electronic store, carrying stereos, televisions, iPods, laptops, and hand-held video games.

General Bryan went to the side window of the Escort and knocked on it three times. “Ma’am?”

The elderly lady cowered with her face in her palms for fear. “Ma’am, I am General Bryan with the Coalition Guard.”

She peeked through her fingers to judge his sincerity and his uniform, and then slowly rolled down the window. “Thank you.”

“I need your vehicle to chase the leader of this riot. Will you–”

“I ain’t getting’ out!” she heaved, short of breath with anxiety. “It’s too dangerous!”

“If you won’t get out, will you scoot over then? We got to catch the guy that’s responsible for all this!”

She reluctantly unlocked her doors and scooted her thin frame over into the front passenger seat.

“Where are your keys?” General Bryan asked her.

“I, I don’t know,” she stuttered, her fearful gaze observing the melee outside her passenger window. Bryan found the car keys on the floor of the car where the elderly lady had dropped them in her nervous frenzy. He started the vehicle, thrust it into drive, and steered the small car onto the sidewalk, intermittently firing his handgun out the window into the air to scatter the students who obstructed his path. With every bullet fired, the elderly woman squealed, “Oh! Oh dear! Oh!”

The general caught a glimpse of Paine’s bright yellow VW bug turn right down another alley about 100 yards ahead past a torrent of fleeing rioters.

He smacked the car’s horn on the center of the steering wheel and swerved to avoid some booty-burdened hippies. The frail elderly lady beside him squealed, her hands pressing against the roof to steady herself. “Oh dear!” She wailed and gasped as he swerved back and forth down the wide alley.

“I’m sorry ma’am.” He steadied his Bluetooth over his ear. “What’s your name, ma’am?”

“Gracie. My name’s Gracieeee!” she squealed as the general spun the tires and launched the Escort onto the sidewalk, sending a wave of sparks in their wake.

“Buckle up, Gracie.” He activated his Bluetooth. “Call Gilles.”

“Gilles here,” Gilles responded to General Bryan through his voice-activated microphone in his motorcycle helmet.

"I'm chasing Mitchell Paine, and need your help. He's in a yellow VW bug, and just turned east down an alley behind Foresters Hardware on Seventh. I need you and your men to try to cut him off."

"Now that's a prize!" Gilles turned around his motorcycle and sped toward the area.

"Hurry! Paine's moving fast and I don't think this civilian's car'll survive the trip." The ancient vehicle knocked and sputtered at the high speeds.

"Oh! Oh my! Careful, careful…" The elderly woman, with hairspray-stiffened silvery white hair and a pale face covered with smeared make-up and streaking mascara, braced herself with her hands on the ceiling. "Please! Oh!" she squealed.

"Please buckle up." Her hands were shaking too much to respond quickly, and just when she almost had the buckle inserted, another quick turn sent her reeling against the door.

"Oh my!"

Bryan couldn't help but grin at the sight of this 80-year-old bundle of skin, bones, mascara, and anxious exclamations. "Gracie, please, buckle up," he urged her as he fired another round outside the window to scatter those who obstructed his way.

"I'm trying! I'm trying!"

"Right! Right! Turn right!" When he saw that they were being pursued, Mitch Paine began to micromanage Nick's driving. "Toward the interstate!"

Nick turned and saw the red Ford Escort closing on them rapidly from behind. Paine cursed and slapped the dashboard in anger. "Left here!"

"Alright! Alright!" Nick scraped the fender against a brick wall as he made the sharp turn.

"Come on, Nick! We have to lose them on the interstate!"

"I see him, General!" Gilles said. "He's heading right toward me." He skidded his motorcycle to a halt in the middle of the narrow one-way street. They were now blocks away from the rioting.

"Stop him!" Bryan responded. "We can't let him get on the interstate!"

"I thought the Highway Patrol sealed all exits."

"Not this one. It's been left open for quick interstate access for the police and the Guard. Paine must have his own intel."

Gilles saw the entrance to the interstate halfway between him and Paine, who was racing toward the on-ramp down the one-lane road. Gilles accelerated toward the yellow Volkswagen, trying to get in front of Paine before he turned onto the interstate ramp.

Gilles converged on the Volkswagen just as Nick prepared to turn it on to the ramp that led to the interstate. Gilles raised his handgun just as the driver of the vehicle put an arm out the window and aimed a handgun at him.

Blam! Blam! Blam!

The motorbike slid onto its side and Gilles went rolling onto the sidewalk heels over head. One bullet struck the gasoline tank of the motorcycle, which exploded in a ball of flame that went 30 feet into the air. The motorcycle spun around on its side still speeding toward the Volkswagen, when Nick, unable to avoid the flaming motorcycle spinning toward him, slammed on his brakes. The motorcycle collided with the Volkswagen, catching it on fire, and the vehicle then collided with a telephone pole, which fell onto the front of the car, sending electrical sparks flying in all directions.

Paine was dizzy and disoriented from the collision. When he gained his bearings, he saw the flames rolling over the front bumper and he smelled gasoline. He heard the chaotic zapping of the live electrical wires on the ground beside their car. "Nick! Get out! It's going to blow!"

Nick didn't move. Nick, who didn't have his seatbelt on, leaned against the bent steering wheel, breathing heavily while a head laceration spurted blood rhythmically onto the dashboard monitors. "Nick!" Paine grabbed the young man's arm and shook him. He stared at him for a second as he wiped the blood from his own brow and then he turned and saw the general's red Escort skid to a stop behind his vehicle. *Where's Nick's gun?* Paine wondered. He saw Nick's stainless .45-caliber handgun under the steering wheel, and he retrieved it and quickly fired through the VW's rear windshield at the Ford Escort.

"Duck!" The general grabbed Gracie's gray-white head and pushed it down, away from the shattering glass and speeding bullets. He was surprised to find his fingers wrapped around a silvery wig.

"Oh my!" she squealed, reaching up and feeling her mostly bald scalp.

"Down!" He dropped the wig and so reached up and tried to push her head down again.

The elderly lady turned to see the fear in the general's eyes and she mumbled with a wit-under-fire that surprised the general: "I thought that liberals are supposed to be against ownin' guns." The general managed to grin at the comment as bullets whizzed over their heads and shards of glass collapsed on their backs.

The professor emptied his clip into the Escort and then attempted to retrieve another clip out of the glove compartment.

The general winked at the elderly lady as she reached down, picked up her wig, and tried to put it back onto her head. "Stay here." She peeked above the dashboard as he opened his door and quickly stepped out of the car, leveling his weapon at the yellow Volkswagen. He glanced into the backseat to see the guardsman that was with him was dead, his face pressed against the window. A bullet had penetrated his forehead.

Mitch Paine cursed when he could not open the jammed glove compartment to fetch another clip of ammo. He opened his door and, avoiding the live electrical wires in the road, began to run with a limp in the direction of the downed motorcycle rider, Gilles. He looked back and exclaimed another foul curse when he saw the general take aim. He hoped that the downed motorcycle rider would have a weapon he could retrieve to defend himself. His leg was hurting badly, but he picked up his pace nonetheless.

"Stop! Get down on the ground!" General Bryan yelled while taking aim.

The professor turned to look back at the general when he received a hard whack across the chest that knocked the breath out of him. His feet flew out from underneath him and he landed on his back on the curb. He suddenly became frantically breathless as he struggled to remain conscious. Gilles stood over the conquered professor, massaging the forearm he had swung against the upper chest of the liberal icon. Gilles was also breathing heavily and bleeding from skinned knees, elbows, and shoulders. A bullet streak on top of his helmet was evidence of the bullet that just missed his face shield, the jolt of which temporarily knocked him unconscious.

"Are you shot?" General Bryan asked Gilles.

"I'm okay. Better than him." Gilles removed his helmet to examine the damage to it. He dropped it on the ground, breathing heavily. He leaned over and placed his hands on his knees. Gilles saw the empty gun that Paine dropped and he slowly reached down and picked it up. *What do ya know? Smith and Wesson .45.* Gilles had lost his Smith .45 in the wreck and the professor had run out of ammo. Gilles removed an extra clip from his belt and inserted it into the handgun. He motioned to the professor. "His head hit the ground pretty hard."

General Bryan felt over his ear and realized that he had lost his Bluetooth in the commotion. Gilles tucked the handgun under his belt as Bryan felt for his cell phone.

A loud voice from the direction of the Volkswagen gave them both a nauseous chill.

"Get away from him!" came the hoarse, garbled scream. "Move away!"

It was the driver, a college-age young man with bushy, shoulder-length hair and multiple facial piercings. His voice was barely comprehensible due to the streams of blood that dripped from a severe head laceration into his left eye and the left side of his mouth. He held a cocked pistol in one of his trembling hands. He limped pitifully toward them, away from the burning motorcycle that was blackening the yellow bumper of the Volkswagen. His left arm hung limp by his side, with a shard of bone protruding from his forearm.

"Get on the ground!" When the guardsmen did not quickly back away from Mitch Paine, he shot a round in the air. "Now!"

Startled at the blast of the gun, the general immediately did as the student demanded but Gilles left the professor's gun under his belt. He laid down flat on his belly with his hands behind his head so as to conceal the weapon from the student.

"Put that gun down, boy," Bryan ordered, "and we'll get you a doctor. You don't want to–"

"Shut your mouth!" Nick screamed. "Face down on the ground!"

Bryan and Gilles complied and laid flat on the ground.

Nick looked and saw the professor. He gasped. "Prof! Professor Paine!" The professor's moans softened, his eyes rolled back into his head, and he began to hyperventilate.

"If you want him to live," Bryan pleaded, "we need to get you both to a doctor. You broke your arm and it's bleeding–"

"What did you do to him?" Nick shouted in a high-pitch tone as he looked down at the heaving chest and pale face of his fallen hero.

"He fell down and hit his head." Gilles began to rise up on his elbows to make eye contact with the student.

Nick responded with a point blank gun shot to the cement right next to Gilles' head. Shards of cement embedded into Gilles' scalp, and Gilles was temporarily deafened by the blast.

Bryan shouted for fear that Gilles had been shot. "No! Don't shoot!"

"Shut your trap!" Nick spit out the blood that had accumulated in his mouth from his lacerated tongue and he aimed his weapon at the general.

"We've got people on the way, son," said General Bryan. "Drop your gun. There are video surveillance cameras all around here. Just take off and things'll go better for you."

Nick rebutted with a loud curse as he watched Professor Paine's respirations slow to an ineffective gasp. The professor then began to seize. Nick cursed again and began to despair as he held his head with both hands, his finger still on the trigger. The professor looked as if he would die any moment, and Nick's headache made it difficult to decide what to do.

"His head did hit the ground pretty hard," said General Bryan calmly. "We can get him to a doctor. You can't. Take off and we'll get an ambulance–"

Nick was furious. He pressed his gun against the top of the general's head. "I'm going to blow your brains out!"

Suddenly, the VW bug exploded, sending fiberglass-tipped flames high into the air. Nick ducked but regained his composure quick enough to see the motorcyclist reach for something under his stomach.

Nick aimed his gun at Gilles just as Gilles fired a round, striking his left shoulder. Nick's bullet struck the police officer in the face, snapping his neck back and spraying blood several feet past his falling body.

"No!" General Bryan shouted.

Nick turned his weapon toward the general. "You killed the professor!" he screamed in anger. Although he had never killed anyone before, Nick's adrenaline gave him the composure of a man who was accustomed to killing. "I'm going to blow your head off!" Nick pressed the hot barrel of the smoking gun into the side of the general's head, pressing his face hard against the hot asphalt.

Nick screamed God's name in vain at the top of his lungs and Bryan closed his eyes and called upon the Lord in prayer. "Oh God," he prayed. "Help, Lord…" He thought that this would be the end for him.

Blam!

Bryan surely thought the gun blast was the one that had killed him, but it was the student that was hit. General Bryan gasped and grabbed the back of his own head, relieved when he discovered he was still alive. The student had been struck with a 12-gauge shotgun load in the back of his neck. The force of the blast knocked him ten feet over and almost severed his head, killing him instantly. When General Bryan saw the lifeless corpse of the student, he remained in a state of shock for a moment.

He rose to his knees and saw the elderly woman whose red Ford Escort they had borrowed, standing erect with her thin green dress waving haphazardly in the warm Nebraska breeze. Her wig laid behind her on the ground, knocked off her head with the force of the shotgun blast. She had quietly retrieved her husband's old double-barrel shotgun from the trunk of her car, a weapon she had been intending to drop off at her son's house ever since her husband passed away last year. She grasped it proudly with both hands, grateful for the mild case of dementia that kept that gun in her trunk much longer than it should have been.

"That boy ain't going to take God's name in vain anymore now, is he?"

She tried to raise the double-barrel shotgun into the cloudy city sky to let out a victory yelp, but the yelp became a yelp of pain instead. "Ow!" She lowered the shotgun and grabbed her right shoulder with her left hand. "I think I broke my collarbone pullin' both triggers at the same time, though."

Helena, Montana

The civilian riots and federal raids were easy victories for the Coalition compared to the internal strife and division that daily threatened to unravel their fragile unity.

"How can we be assured that your Christian government won't discriminate against us in the same way that you're discriminating against atheists and humanists in your endorsement of the orthodox Christian religion?" Two Mormon elders from Salt Lake City, two Catholic bishops, and a Unitarian denominational leader were sitting with Governor Boswell and Barry Friar, objecting to the religious philosophy of the new state government. They were seriously considering issuing binding resolutions to order the faithful in their churches to abandon the Coalition and pursue reconciliation with the federal government on their own.

"Would you rather have an atheistic government?" Governor Boswell inquired.

Barry Friar added, "Do you think that pleases God more than a sect of Christianity with which you disagree?"

"Our tax money," the eldest Catholic bishop said, leaning into the governor and raising his voice, "will be used to fund this army of so-called Minutemen who will be proselytizing Catholics all over the Coalition states."

"And Mormons," one of the Mormon elders added.

The younger Catholic bishop nodded. "Our tax money will be used to fund the teaching of un-Catholic doctrine in public schools!"

"Some of your Minutemen think we're heretics!" one of the two Mormon elders complained, his gaze darting back and forth from Governor Boswell to Barry Friar. "Our theology allows exceptions for abortion in cases of rape, incest, maternal life and health, and fetal handicap. How can we sit by and let our tax money and our state government endorse a theology which contradicts our religion and violates our lawful rights?"

"Hold on, hold on!" Barry Friar protested, putting up his palms. "Your tax money's been used to fund the slaughter of millions of children – including healthy babies, not just the sick ones your dogma lets you kill." He pointed at the Mormon elder. "Your tax money's been exploited to euthanize the elderly and infirmed, to perform grisly experiments on children who survive abortions. The federal government's been propagating an anti-Christian education in public schools and institutions for decades. Have you met with the previous state leaders to protest that with threats to leave?" The four religious leaders appeared speechless. Friar's gaze darted back and forth between them. "Would you rather have atheists teach the Big Bang theory and pass out contraceptives to your kids without your consent? If you don't prefer Montana's schools, gentlemen, you don't have to pay for them. They'll be privatized."

"Privatized?" The two Catholic bishops exchanged a curious glance. "You mean, not taxpayer funded?"

Governor Boswell nodded. "That's right. We're embracing a free market educational system that puts parents in charge of the cost and the curriculum of their own child's education. You are now free to spend your own money on your own religious schools. You are now free to claim the name of God in your local government. You are free to govern yourselves without being forced to pay for humanistic curricula and murder. Now," he said, tapping his desk, "I'd say that's a step in the right direction for any sect of the Christian religion, whether heretical or orthodox. And a step up for freedom."

After a pause, Barry Friar pointed at the elder Mormon leader. "You are, however, not free to kill your handicapped preborn children. If you're caught taking someone to any back-alley abortion clinic here or an abortion clinic in another state, you will be arrested and tried for murder. And you." He pointed at the Unitarian leader and the Catholic bishops. "For decades, you have consistently opposed personhood legislation that protects the right to life of preborn babies..."

"We agree with it in principle," a bishop interrupted, "but disagree with the strategy. We were worried the Supreme Court would overturn the abortion ban and that would make it more difficult to protect the preborn later on, whenever we do have a pro-life majority on the High Court."

"Well, now that we've seceded, that's no longer an excuse now, is it? We've exercised our sovereignty and protected the innocent within our jurisdiction."

The Catholic bishops crossed their arms over their robes, deep in thought.

"The Coalition of Free Christian States will protect your freedom to disagree with strategy," Friar asserted, "but we will not allow speech that promotes the genocide of innocent children anymore."

"That's right." Boswell nodded, affirming Friar's statement. "Do you understand?" The religious leaders reluctantly nodded.

There was a hurried knock on the door. The governor told the religious leaders, "Hold on a minute. Come on in."

"Good news, Governor," Knabb said as he poked his head in the door. When he saw Barry Friar and the religious leaders, he cleared his throat. "Can I have a word with the governor in private?"

"Excuse me a minute, fellas. Just wait outside."

Barry Friar stood to his feet. "May we continue the conversation in the room next door?"

"Very well."

The religious leaders followed Barry Friar out of the governor's office, with much less angst than with which they came.

"Well, good and bad news." Knabb walked toward the governor's desk. "I'll give you the good news first. We've got Mitch Paine."

The governor leapt to his feet, and shouted, "Praise the Lord!" He enthusiastically shook the hand of his chief of security.

"Only four Guard casualties, 79 casualties among rioters, 15 civilian casualties, hundreds wounded and over 5,000 arrested. We basically cut their numbers in half, but it was bloody."

The governor's smile faded to a frown when he learned the cost of their victory. "God, have mercy."

"Mitch Paine's injured, unconscious, and headed to the University of Lincoln Medical Center in an ambulance."

"I want him interrogated, Isaiah." Boswell pointed at him. "If he's mentally or physically weak, he might confess to acting under the authority of the president."

"I've spoken with General Bryan about that already," Knabb said, nodding. "He's getting a team on it."

"Schedule a conference with the governors in an hour. We need to plan a public statement."

"One more thing. We have two Minutemen who have accepted the invitation to represent our cause at a National Council of Evangelical Churches in Los Angeles."

The governor frowned, massaging his chin. "Don't they know that we can't protect them?"

"Of course. David Jamestown and Barry Friar offered no strong opposition as long as the men were confident that God was leading them there, but I thought you should know, since they will reflect on the Coalition and California has been particularly venomous against our mission."

"They must know that the National Council of Evangelical Churches is not friendly to our cause."

"Well, they're giving them an hour to speak, plus extensive time for Q & A. The conference leadership has promised them safety and the university where they are speaking has promised them free speech. The two missionaries have an impressive presentation that is very persuasive and defends our cause well."

"I see. Who is it?"

"Cal Manning and Carson Jensen. They should be crossing the border into California right now."

Part IV

Lions' Dens and Fiery Furnaces

11

Northeast California

Cal Manning surprised his young companion Carson the morning of their departure for California. He had taken a lesson from Jared and disguised himself in the most interesting way. He had tanned his skin with a cream product and dyed his hair and eyebrows dark brown.

Carson had one look at him, and was stunned. "What in the world?"

"Let me just say that I don't want to be recognized," Cal responded with a cheesy grin.

"You know they're gonna look at your ID."

"So what if they do?" Cal held up in the air between two fingers his new driver's license.

Carson grabbed it and read the name. "Cal Alexander Buckner? Where'd you get that?"

Cal smiled. "One of the Minutemen who worked in the DMV made it for me."

"You've got to be kidding me!"

"Mr. Buckner died in a car accident a few weeks ago. He's got a clean record."

"Why didn't I get one of these?"

"You don't need one. You're not a wanted man across the border. I am."

They channel-surfed all the way into California, listening to news stories about the FBI's raid on the capitol building in Helena and the rioting in Lincoln. They were aghast to learn how many had been involved in the rioting in Lincoln.

"Praise the Lord!" Cal exclaimed. "God's blessed us with victory."

After a timid pause, Carson spoke up. "These talkin' heads are giving me second thoughts about this conference."

Cal looked at him with bewilderment. "It's a little late for that. What's on your mind?"

"You know, it's just…" Carson paused and looked out the window, his young face wincing with secret fear as he watched the sun beyond the hills. "With the raid on Helena, and with the rioting, there's just so much violence, Cal. We could get arrested. We could get charged with treason." He cast a quick glance at Cal, as if to measure the confidence in his body language. "This could mean our death."

"They've been killing a million and a half people a year since *Roe v. Wade*, Carson. Wouldn't you be willing to die just for a chance to defend those children?" Carson nodded. "The Bible says we can only defeat the enemy if we love not our lives unto death."

"Wait, wait!" Carson hastily turned the radio back up. "It's the president."

…Footage may have been doctored and is not trustworthy. Nevertheless, my administration wholeheartedly supports the congressional investigation into the failed raid. The FBI has commenced an investigation of their own, and we are taking steps to see that those responsible for this embarrassment – on both sides of the border – come to justice.

Todd Hamilton has been replaced as director of the FBI with Bill Erdman, who has successfully directed the Bureau of Alcohol, Tobacco, and Firearms the past three years. Mr. Erdman's stamina and leadership in the arms repossession phase of my anti-terrorism, crime-fighting package was unparalleled. He is the leader we need for this fragile time.

Your nation's armed forces are being placed on high alert. We are extending the reach of the cooperative United States and Canada embargo on all goods going into and out of the Coalition States, effective immediately. The FAA, the Coast Guard, and the Navy will cooperate to blockade all Coalition ports and cease all flights into the insubordinate states. We encourage all faithful citizens of the United States to abandon the Coalition territories and to refrain from excursions into the Coalition at this time, now that we have entered a violent phase of our political disunity. We apologize for the inconvenience, but we have to respond to the violent attacks against your government. Be assured that we will not allow these fanatical leaders of the so-called Coalition Free Christian States to kill federal agents and get away with it. It is our hope and prayer that the dissenting states will come to their senses and turn over those responsible for the bloodshed of the federal agents, that they will respect the laws of our land and bring an end to this madness and anarchy without further violence. Thank you, and as always, God bless America.

"She's blaming the Coalition's leadership for having the audacity to fend off the federal assault!" Carson couldn't believe his ears.

"Nothing would surprise me anymore."

"Cal, do you think that secession will succeed?"

"Honestly?" Cal paused. "Short of a miracle from heaven, no." He shook his head and shrugged. "And I'm not convinced God wants to give us that miracle. We may not be worthy of it. But it doesn't matter. We all die, friend. We just have to make our death, like our life, count."

Lincoln, Nebraska

"No way! This is Mitchell Paine!" The younger paramedic's eyebrows were raised in awe, and a faint smile shone upon his thin face. He pointed at the unconscious but stable patient. "Dan, he was my sociology professor at U.T. when I was a sophomore!"

"Mitch Paine?" The senior paramedic pulled the chain on the steel handcuffs that locked his patient to the gurney. "Where do I know that name?"

"He's the leader of the protests," the younger paramedic responded, surprised that his colleague didn't recognize the professor's name. "He's famous! He's leading the people's fight against the Coalition."

The older paramedic's eyes brightened. "I knew it had to be somebody important." He cast a wary glance through the window at the Guard general in the front seat.

"He's somebody important all right. Man! This is one of the most powerful men in America. There's probably a reward if we can free him. We can't let them take him down. This guy's a freedom fighter."

"But what can we do?"

At this moment, Mitch Paine jerked, and his eyes opened slightly. He had a neck brace in place to keep his cervical spine stationary in case he had a fracture.

"Mr. Paine?" The younger paramedic looked into the professor's eyes with a penlight.

"Oh," Paine moaned. "Oh, my head!"

"Can you move your hands and feet? How many fingers do I have up?"

"Yeah," Paine stammered. "Yeah, I can see you."

"You've got a bad concussion at least, a bleed on the brain at worst. You've been unconscious for about 20 minutes."

Paine jerked his hands against the handcuffs. "Oh, oh my head."

"Let's break him out, man! What an opportunity, Dan."

"He could have a cerebral hemorrhage or fracture." The senior paramedic leaned over the professor. "Any problems with your vision, Mr. Paine? Any numbness in your hands or fingers? Neck pain?"

"No, no. Just a headache," Paine responded. "I'm all right."

"We're gonna break you out of here," the former U.T. student said. "How are we gonna get these cuffs off?"

"You think Drake's going to let us get away with this?" The older paramedic, Dan, motioned to the driver, who, fortunately for them, couldn't hear their chatter thanks to the blaring ambulance siren. "You know, they'll be after us after this."

"We've been talking about joining the students at the University of Nebraska anyway," the younger paramedic said. "We'll hit the road and campaign for free thought! Man! This is our opportunity to get famous quick."

"The bolt-cutter!" Dan reached under the cabinet and pulled out a heavy, red bolt-cutter. He quickly snipped the handcuffs off the professor.

"Oh, my head." The professor writhed as he moaned.

"We're going to give you something for pain, and then try to break you out, Mr. Paine, but you have to follow our instructions exactly."

"He started seizing and the I.V. blew!" The young paramedic appeared panic-stricken as he pushed the gurney through the rear door with the patient motionless upon it. "We couldn't get it under control with IM medication and had to intubate."

"Why didn't you inform me?" The driver hurriedly grabbed the end of the gurney and pulled it out, extending the wheels to meet the ground. "Hey, Dan," the younger paramedic said as he looked back at his partner in the ambulance, "clean up the mess. We'll have to go right back out. Drake and I'll roll him in."

General Bryan rushed to the side of the gurney, disappointed in the change in Mitch Paine's status. "What happened?"

"He's crashing!"

"Will he make it?" Bryan inquired, grabbing the paramedic's arm. Bryan looked down at the professor, who began to tremble slightly. The intubation tube was taped to his face and the paramedic squeezed the bag that fed his lungs with oxygen.

"Could have an intra-cerebral bleed. Needs a scan of his brain." The paramedic pushed the patient into the Emergency Department entrance with the general following close behind.

"Why don't you stay in the waiting room?" the paramedic told the general.

"No. I need to stay with him," Bryan insisted.

"Doctor! Doctor!" the paramedic shouted. "Need a central line! Stat!"

"I'm not leaving his side," General Bryan insisted, grabbing onto the side of the gurney as they rolled it into the trauma room.

"Well, stay outside the room." A physician rushed to the side of the gurney for the paramedic's update. "We'll have a lot of people working on him for a while."

"Fine, I'll be just outside the room." The paramedic swung the curtain shut and began to hurriedly relay info to the physician.

Meanwhile, the real Professor Paine, wearing green scrubs, was pretending to clean the ambulance. When it quieted down outside, he jumped out of the vehicle and headed for the parking lot, rubbing his dizzy head as he briskly walked away, a free man.

San Antonio, Texas

Darlene was thrilled to find herself stationed next to her best friend Janet in the un-air-conditioned facility that was basically a large green tarp stretched over their heads by poles and ropes. They busied themselves sewing belt loops onto drab green and brown pants. Their sewing machines were powered with a generator that made the air stink of fumes in the afternoon heat.

"Where do you think he could be? He was your husband – you have to have some idea." Janet spoke in a soft, fragile voice. She was careful not to look up from her sewing machine to keep from attracting attention.

Darlene paused her sewing momentarily, and wondered whether she should trust this stranger whose company she had come to enjoy. "I know he's helping people, wherever he is. I, I don't believe what they're telling me about him. He's not a traitor to his–"

"Wilma Cowers!" The bellowing female voice with the German accent immediately halted all the whirring of all the machines and everyone stood at attention. "Raise your hand!" A woman on Darlene's aisle timidly raised her hand, her gaze fastened passively on her sewing machine. "Come with me!" the German guard barked.

Darlene glanced over at her with pity and prayed a silent prayer for her safety and strength. Everyone feared being ratted on by others and being dragged back into the interrogation cells. A removal of one such person caused dozens of others to tremble and fear because of the likely chance that the person being interrogated would tattle on them or even lie about them stealing food or violating a camp rule in exchange for repose from their suffering. It would not be uncommon for the interrogators to come and remove another person every ten or 20 minutes for further interrogation. New guards freshly rotated into the camp needed practice with torture techniques. The UN interrogators did not harbor a fond sentiment of American Christians, and they enjoyed engineering their suffering.

Wilma Cowers was led from the room and the whirring of the sewing machines commenced.

"She won't be able to handle it," Janet worried. "She's ill."

"Pray for her." Darlene encouraged those around her in a voice as loud as she dared without looking away from her duties. "Do not fear. God goes with her."

Janet wagged her head and fought the urge to cry.

Ten minutes later, the German female guard returned. "Janet Raleigh!" Immediately, Darlene's friend began to cry. "Oh no!"

Darlene gasped. Her friend was next. "Be strong in Jesus, Janet." Darlene mumbled encouragement to her. "Fear not." Her face flushed with fear for her dearest friend.

Janet fell to her knees and cried, "No! I won't go!"

"No, Janet," Darlene whispered inconspicuously. "Fear not…"

Two guards hastened down the aisle, grabbed Janet by the arms, and dragged her from the facility through a storm of dramatic wails and screams.

When she had disappeared from the room, Darlene began to weep. She sewed as she prayed, and did not so much as wipe her tears.

Janet was half carried, half dragged over the red desert sand to a military tent where interrogations occurred. Inside the facility, she regained her composure, and began to walk with the guards. She passed an open door where Wilma had been tied to a table face up and was being alternatively water-boarded and shocked with electric cattle prods.

Janet was led to the room at the far end of the hall. The German guard unzipped two heavy cloth doors in the tent and Janet entered to see a thick-bodied female Russian captain with a baby blue UN beret. The German guard was told to stand guard outside, and the Russian zipped the door shut. A thick plastic square window in the roof and on one side of the room provided the only light into the otherwise drab green room. When the door was shut, Janet and the Russian guard stood face to face.

Suddenly, Janet's face became harsh and she slapped the guard across the face! The baby blue UN beret tilted to the side and the Russian appeared stunned at the outburst and took a step back.

"What in the world do you think you are doing?" Janet scolded her in a heretofore well-concealed British accent. "Do you realize you have put everything I've done at risk? I've earned this woman's trust and she was talking!"

"I'm sorry, I'm sorry…" The Russian captain cowered at the disapproval of the superior officer.

"Why did you do it?"

"I have orders from the president."

"The president? What orders?" she barked, her hands on her hips.

The Russian guard wiped her bleeding nose on her sleeve and reached into her front jacket pocket to remove a folded white piece of paper. She handed it to her superior, and Janet Boltere snatched it out of her hand.

As Agent Boltere read it, the Russian captain said, "The FBI has been kept up-to-date on the interrogation of Mrs. Jameson, and they want results. Even the president has a keen personal interest in knowing what she knows."

"We probably already know what she knows!" Agent Boltere handed the brief letter back to the subordinate. "If the Bureau would only re-consider my plan to set both of us free simultaneously, she'd probably lead me straight to her husband!"

"The Bureau wants Darlene Jameson in custody and wants you to work harder to find her husband and his accomplices."

"Darlene's not responded to the most intense interrogation methods we have applied. This undercover approach is more effective, but it takes time to build trust."

"I'm sorry, Mrs. Boltere. I'm just the messenger."

"I know, I know." She swatted away the guard's attempt at humility and walked to the plastic window to gaze at the contour of the desert sands, interrupted intermittently only by the erratically sprouting cacti. "But now that Darlene thinks I'm being interrogated right now, what do you think is going on in her mind?" She turned back to face the Russian. "She's back there thinking, boy, I'm sure glad I didn't tell Janet anything!"

"I'm sorry. What do you want me to tell the White House?"

Agent Boltere sighed and paced toward the wall and back. "I need you to help me earn her trust quickly. She needs to know that I'm not going to break under pressure."

"How?"

Agent Boltere reached down and unlatched the three-feet-long stiff leather whip that hung on the Russian captain's belt. She held it up at her.

"Twenty lashes. You're going to give me 20 lashes in front of the camp at the end of the day. Say I confessed to stealing food."

"You want me to do what?" She shook her head vigorously, "I can't do that."

"I'm ordering it!" she barked. "You will do it, or I'll do it to you!"

Helena, Montana

"I'll miss you, Elijah." Elijah set down his duffel bag, teeming with laundry, as David reached for him with both arms. David gave a back-slapping hug to the friend he had come to love through the most trying times of his life. "Heard you survived a shot in the chest during the raid."

"Yeah." Elijah rubbed the spot over his heart, which was still paining him with deep breathing. "I was clutching a Bible that had been signed by the Minutemen. It was going to be our gift to him. It saved my life."

"Unbelievable," David exclaimed with a grin.

"Yeah. It knocked me out and cracked some ribs, but saved my life."

"Praise God!"

Elijah grinned. "I'm glad it was large print, not one of those skinny ones. Your tip that Governor Boswell preferred large print Bibles was life-saving."

David patted his friend on the shoulder. "God never ceases to amaze me."

"I've got an interesting fact for you." Elijah leaned against the RV where he had been staying with some other Minutemen. The landscape was speckled with tents and RVs. "I opened the Bible to see just how far the bullet penetrated before it came to a halt. The bullet mushroomed to a stop and made just a small dent at the beginning of Revelation 12:11."

"Whoa! Went through all sixty-six books, huh? That was close."

"Yeah. But do you know what Revelation 12:11 says?"

David's eyes lit up. "I think so. Remind me."

"They overcame the devil by the blood of the Lamb, and by the word of their testimony; and they loved not their lives unto death."

David's eyes widened. A grin shone upon his face as he said, "That's providence."

Elijah put both hands on David's shoulders. "We've got to be willing to sacrifice our lives to win this thing, David. Don't be ashamed of your testimony in the heat of battle. Don't hold back for fear of death. On the edge of our lives, our celebration of the power of Jesus' blood to save us sinners is what clenches the victory."

David nodded. "Yep."

"Any word on your Darlene?"

David took a deep, tremulous breath, his eyes downcast. "She never arrived, Elijah. Brother Boswell's been pulling some strings inside the prison system to try to discover her whereabouts, but Texas is still a battle zone. Intel's hard to come by. The UN's taken over many of the detention facilities where they're keeping hate criminals. I'm going to get her as soon as I find out where she is."

"You'll face life in solitary confinement if you get captured leaving the Coalition."

"So, I'm not supposed to fear death, but I should fear solitary confinement?"

"Just count the cost, David. Stay in Montana and you're safe. Well," – he shrugged – "relatively safe."

"It was a mistake, Elijah." David fixed his eyes on the rays of sunlight that shone through the leaves of the dogwood tree overshadowing them. "I never should have left her."

"The feds were listening in – you know that. They would have captured both of you and she'd be in the same situation except with no one to rescue her. You need to quit second-guessing yourself. Every decision you've made has been the right one. The steps of a good man are–"

"Ordered by the Lord." David finished the Bible verse. He sighed and looked away, squinting away one of the many tears he had shed since he learned Darlene and his family had disappeared. "Well, until rescuing my wife and kids becomes possible, I'm committed to train the Coalition's Minutemen."

"Is it true you've got a body guard now?"

David nodded. "With all of the threats on my life, Governor Boswell insisted. I don't like it."

"Why?"

David shook his head and shoved his hands into his front jeans' pockets. "That's not the way God works. No flesh will glory in His sight. We are told to trust in the Lord, not in men and horses."

"Even King David had his mighty men around him."

"Yet he confessed that his faith was in God to defend him."

Elijah tapped his index finger on David's chest. "And you do the same, bro." They shared a warm smile. "Who is your bodyguard anyway?"

David's grin widened. "Do you remember Matt Wellington?"

"Yeah, the sheriff that arrested the abortionist at the Austin Women's Clinic. Ain't he a little out of shape for body-guarding? I mean, I know he used to box, but could he go three rounds without passin' out?"

David laughed. "You should see him now. He's lost about 75 pounds. He's a lean, mean, fightin' machine. And he can pray the paint off the walls."

Elijah's sober countenance evolved to a toothy laugh. "Unbelievable! Just like the David of the Bible: a harp-playing shepherd boy chosen to be slayer of giants and King of Israel. Here you are, a sign-wielding pro-life missionary with an arrest record as long as your arm, falsely accused by the federal government for a terrorist act that killed the president, now side by side with seceding sheriffs and governors of the Coalition of Free Christian States!"

Elijah's praise lifted David's spirits. He grinned sheepishly and waved off the compliment. "Don't set me up for trials by flattering me, Elijah. You know that doesn't help."

"Oh, spare me your false humility. The Bible says those who labor with doctrine are worthy of a double honor."

"The Bible also says he that flatters a man lays a net before his feet," David rebutted. "As long as I'm dung in my own sight, like Paul said, it's easier to resist the temptation to think that by my own strength I've done anything. One second without God's mercy and I'm roasting in hell forever." He pointed at Elijah's chest. "Don't you forget that. Judas was closer to Jesus than you. He healed the sick and cast out devils. He was trusted to keep the money, yet look where his pride got him."

"I'll not leave my first love," Elijah assured him, putting a hand on his shoulder. "Don't you either. Do they still think you're David Jamestown?"

David nodded. "I've been able to keep my photo out of the papers, so they have no idea who I really am." David laughed. "It's kind of funny. Matt had to pass a criminal background check to be my bodyguard, yet I didn't have to pass one to carry Brother Boswell's briefcase for hours a day. You're going to Seattle, right?"

"Yeah. I'm leading a team of about 150. We've got three conferences and dozens of church meetings scheduled. We're going to be doing some street ministry in downtown Seattle. Pray for us. There's a lot of rioting and vandalism still going on."

"Ships weren't made for the harbor, Elijah. The best place to be is in the center of God's will, whether it's on the hottest battle line, in the darkest dungeon, or preachin' that Jesus is God's Son off of the Kabaa in Mecca. Like you said, if we fear losin' our lives, we've already lost; if we don't fear losin' our lives for the Gospel, we've already won."

Elijah was humored at the thought of David preaching on top of the Kabaa. He laughed and high-fived his friend.

David glanced at the SUV full of Minutemen driving down the dirt driveway, presumably to pick up Elijah. "I suspect your law enforcement experience might come in handy pretty soon in Seattle."

"We'll see." Elijah winced at the thought. "The Coalition's got a long way to go before we ever get to liberty and justice for all, and I'm not supporting any counterfeit criminal justice system. They're still putting murderers behind bars in the Coalition. I don't think we've fully realized that now that we're free of federal control, now we can do what the Bible says we should do to criminals."

"Patience, my friend. Let's restore one Christian ideal at a time."

"Justice is a package deal, David. It's Christ's way or the anti-christ's way."

"But the Promise Land was won by Israel one skirmish and one city at a time. Wait on the Lord. That battle belongs to Him."

Elijah meditated for a moment upon David's wise advice. They shook hands and Elijah headed for the vehicle. "I'm going to miss you, David."

David waved when Elijah shut the door. "Here, there, or in the air."

Seattle, Washington

Governor Boswell called for an internet meeting with the leaders of the CFC States. The legislatures of each state had voted to secede, but they needed to sign a document to unite the ten states and form an independent nation. Since the leaders had last spoken, the CFC States and their leadership had begun to suffer for their declaration of independence. The complaints were piling up.

"They've blockaded us." The nervous governor of the state of Nebraska was more worried than Boswell had ever seen him. "We're running out of fuel. Jobs are leaving. We can't export – our economy's going to go down the drain and quick."

"Montana's employment rates are improving drastically," Dreifuss, Montana's attorney general, rebutted. "We're getting businessmen from *your* state immigrating to *ours*. Why don't you lower your state tax rate and allow businesses to withhold federal deductions like we have. And if we go to a gold or silver standard like we're planning on doing, then when the rest of the country's economy crashes for all its debt, we'll have all the wealth."

The Nebraska governor sighed. "My point is that our move to secession has made things worse for us, not better."

"Hold on!" Boswell studied the governors' images on his computer screen over their encrypted internet connection. All of the whining was quite grievous to him. "Is that all the character we have? We get in a fix and we're ready to go back to Egypt? What about the freedom of religion we have, the means of self-defense we still possess, the elderly who are safe in the hospitals and nursing homes, the babies who are alive today because we've outlawed their slaughter?"

"Self-preservation is a consideration, Ben," the Nebraska governor asserted. "We have to be practical. We need to try to get other nations to recognize us *before* we become an independent nation."

"We're *already* independent! Nebraska voted to secede 60 to 40. This meeting is about uniting, not becoming more independent." Boswell was exasperated at the second-guessing of the Nebraska governor. "We can't be cowards when the liberals of this world throw temper tantrums in our streets and the president threatens to spank us. We aren't going to get recognition as our own nation if we back-peddle every time the president attacks one of our capitols or kidnaps and interrogates our families across the border. David Jamestown taught me a very important lesson. What good is recognition among the nations of the world if we don't have recognition from the God of nations, and if we have His recognition, then why do we need theirs?"

"If we're a beacon of liberty," the Idaho governor responded, "then shouldn't we be shining in the statehouses of potential allies in other countries and in sympathetic states?"

"Israel was judged by God for looking to Egypt for protection from the Babylonian invaders instead of looking to the Lord. Our victory does not depend in the slightest on whether we gain allies, but on whether we're allied to heaven."

"It's no lack of faith to distinguish friend from foe," Governor Wilson rebutted. "Our economy is severely wilting and the riots are growing in numbers. Without the federal government's safety nets, our social situation is tenuous."

"Oh please!" Boswell was growing frustrated. "Many of you are suffering because you still act like you owe submission to the feds. In essence, you're still in bondage. Be free! We'll have victory if we stand for the right, even if we stand alone."

The governor of Washington nodded, encouraged by Boswell's confidence. "I do apologize for my doubts," said Governor Littman humbly, leaning forward with his elbows on his desk as he peered into the camera affixed to his computer screen. "When I'm questioned in front of the leaders in our statehouse, well, I just don't have the confident responses that you do."

"You just keep your priorities straight and keep your head in the Word of God. Remember, the Bible says the righteous are as bold as the lion, but the wicked flee when no man pursues. Keeping your heart right with God is the hardest part of winning this battle." Littman pursed his lips and nodded soberly.

"Any activity around our nuclear arms?" asked the South Dakota governor. He raised the document that would formally begin their existence as a new nation. "If we sign this," he said, shaking it, "and the feds respond with invasion, then we must be prepared to respond to the president's predictable attempts to remove or destroy all nuclear armament within our borders."

"Our intel on the ground says there is no evidence of any attempt to move warheads within our borders. We have a cooperative team working on a plan to repossess nuclear warheads if open war commences, and we've a meeting scheduled with them tomorrow. Governor Littman, I've been informed that only one man in our Coalition – your whiz in Seattle – has the ability to break the codes at those nuclear facilities."

"Yes, that'd be our mathematics prodigy at Washington State University. He is presently training about 40 other geniuses to break the codes simultaneously at the nuclear silos in the Coalition."

"He's a target," someone opined.

Littman nodded. "And he's well-guarded. Well-concealed."

12

Seattle, Washington

"Hello ma'am." Arnie Oswald York greeted the receptionist behind the front desk at the Seattle Convention Center with a warm smile. "Here's my application." He handed her the typed application for employment.

"Uh, yes, Mr. York. Wow, you typed it." She thumbed the professional photograph that was paper-clipped to the front of the application. "Please have a seat over there and I'll call you when they're ready for your interview."

"Yes ma'am."

"It'll be just a few minutes." She reciprocated the young man's warm smile.

Arnie walked over to an area in the large foyer with couches and magazines. He sported a newly purchased blue pinstripe suit and a silk yellow tie. He had a crew cut with freshly dyed yellow hair. He bent down and picked up *Newsweek.* He read an article about several large corporations threatening to withdraw their business from the CFC States unless they submitted to federal authority. This worried him. It would ruin everything!

In two weeks, ACOG – the American College of Obstetricians and Gynecologists – was holding their annual convention at this facility. Twelve thousand obstetricians and gynecologists gathered to get their continuing medical education credits, which they would need to renew their medical licenses.

According to statistics Arnie had read, one-fourth of these physicians performed abortions. Almost all of the others, save a small remnant of pro-life physicians, sent their patients to other physicians to perform abortions on their patients. ACOG as an organization officially endorses abortion as a safe, legal alternative to childbearing, including late term abortion procedures when the baby is mature enough to survive outside the womb. Pro-life protesters have been rebuking abortionists at the annual ACOG convention for years. In vain has the American Association of Pro-Life Ob/Gyns borne witness to ACOG of the humanity of the preborn child. To ACOG, politics trumped truth and the love of money trumped healthcare. The babies continued to be slaughtered.

Thousands of baby-killers under one roof... How convenient.

It always bothered him that the death of one abortionist might possibly not save anybody, because the appointments that would be cancelled could be rescheduled with another abortionist. He had wasted months taking out one abortionist, one accomplice, one abortuary at a time. At that rate, it would take a whole lifetime to protect the babies! Or, a whole army of Arnie Oswald Yorks. But it was too risky to recruit others. There were Judas Iscariots everywhere. Even within the pro-life movement, he sensed no sympathy. The right-to-lifers hated him even more than the feds. They would rather see 30 babies die daily in an abortionist's five-decade career than see that abortionist snuffed out. Maybe the sincere pro-lifers did honor him in their hearts, but the fear of man had so paralyzed them that they offered stronger public condemnations of his actions than even the federal government. They even cooperated with the feds in compiling lists of activists and handing the lists over to the feds for their investigation of "the Chicago sniper." That is what they called him. They feared his actions were the corporate acts of the much-feared "Army of Yahweh." He chuckled as he mused, knowing that of all the so-called "Army of Yahweh" sympathizers, he was the only one who actually killed any baby-butchers. He enjoyed the idea that millions of dollars were being expended by the FBI to break up the ring of abortionist-snipers they feared were sweeping the country with waves of anti-choice violence, when, apart from the rare threat, the rare act of vandalism, or even more rare arson of an abortion clinic, it was only him doing the actual killing.

Arnie was getting too comfortable with the easy kills, so he knew it was time for him to get out of his comfort zone. It was time to slay the

Goliath of baby-killing in one historic act of vengeance. Babies were dying. Judgment neared for the mass murderers.

"Mr. York," the receptionist called out. "They're ready for your interview now."

Washington, D.C.

"We're being inundated with copperheads in the house," Congressman McGinnis informed the president and her cabinet. "Compromise for peace is popular."

The president glanced at McGinnis, the minority Speaker in the House, as if he had let her down.

"It's the footage of the failed FBI raid in Helena," he explained. "It has had a major impact. It's outraging our constituencies and winning the sympathy of too many congressmen and women. The FBI is seen as the aggressor. We are caught on video shooting our own men."

"The impact of the footage is over-shadowed by the arrest of James Knight, Madam President," Cameron added. "He had admirers on the right and the left. Taking him out expired a lot of your political capital."

"That's right," said Dena Halluci. "Josh Davis' booming online newsletter has become the most well-read in the nation in spite of our efforts to shut it down."

"Our attempts to shut it down have caused his popularity to grow," Cameron admitted.

"We still have no idea from where he's getting his leads in the White House," Erdman, the new director of the FBI, replied. "Our investigations are dead ends." Danny Connor's mouth went dry when Dena's gaze drifted briefly in his direction.

"Maybe it's the FBI investigators that need to be investigated," Danny proposed with a stiff lip. "Perhaps Todd Hamilton's incompetence trickled down."

Erdman took aught with the implication. "We have safeguards in place. Our investigators are clean."

The president looked up from her laptop and cleared her throat, informing the others with her body language that she would like them to be quiet so she could speak. "Remind me again, Mr. Erdman, why haven't we arrested Joshua Davis?"

"Hamilton couldn't find him, but I've got a whole arena full of our best cyber-prodigies looking for him. We'll catch him. We even have an army of the best hacks in the country working for us as free agents, searching full time for him in exchange for a hefty financial reward."

"Have you found anyone close to Ben Boswell who will help us?"

"As a matter of fact, we have," Erdman replied.

"Who?"

"I'll disclose this to you in private, Madam President." Erdman's shifting gaze informed her that he did not have full confidence in everybody in the room.

"Very well."

"Todd Hamilton's plan was pathetic. We'll succeed." Erdman waved the thin black bangs away from his brow, a fierce smirk of confidence upon his thin face.

"Washington State's a more promising venture than Montana, Madam President," said General Green. "Social outrage over Governor Littman joining the Coalition is growing and the situation on the ground is tenuous. It's the only state that hasn't criminalized abortion yet. Although the law is on the books, it passed with the slimmest of margins and enforcement of it is being held up until the state Senate finishes its impeachment debate."

"Which may not turn out as we had hoped," Cameron Weaver warned them. "With the release of this video footage of the raid to the public, the polls have turned and now" – he pursed his lips and shook his head back and forth – "I just don't know."

"The American College of Obstetricians and Gynecologists is having their annual convention there in a couple of weeks," Dena informed them, "and their leadership intends to take thousands of their doctors to meet with various influential members of the statehouse and to step up the pressure to get rid of Governor Littman."

"And they have begun a strong commercial campaign in tandem with Planned Parenthood, the ACLU, and NARAL to sway the public to urge their representatives to impeach the governor."

"Do you realize that if we eliminate the votes in the ten Coalition states," Cameron said, glancing at McGinnis, "then we'll gain a congressional majority by a landslide? I say we accept the secession until after the election."

"No, no, no," the president responded. "America needs leaders right now who govern on principle, not on what's going to get them re-elected. We have the most powerful, technologically advanced armed forces in the world. We need to stop the talk and draw some battle lines.

It's time to let America's big stick subjugate our enemies and unify our country."

Seattle, Washington

Arnie never thought it would be so easy. He walked the halls of the Seattle Convention Center in his pressed maroon employee outfit with his laminated nametag, studying the twelve thousand obstetricians and gynecologists as they scurried from one lecture to another, sipping their cappuccinos, chatting with one another about the stock market or their golf game. Anti-abortionists carrying posters of dead babies and preaching through megaphones on the sidewalks practically surrounded the facility. Arnie, like most of the employees and physicians, ignored them.

Arnie's duties were perfect for his mission. He had the responsibility of collecting the trash throughout the facility and disposing of it in the dumpster. He walked the length and breadth of the massive convention center and basked in his power. He held their security in the palm of his hand. He mentally frolicked in the terror that was soon to be unleashed upon them, and wondered how they and the government would react. In the next hour, horror would fill this place, the same kind of horror they inflicted on unborn children in their routine practice of medicine.

Having discovered the recipe for the scheduled luncheon, he shut himself into the kitchen the night before the conference. He took a tasteless, odorless white powder – a neurotoxin manufactured with a simple internet recipe – and mixed it well into the salt that would be used for the two dinner selections. He also mixed it into each of the three salad dressings to be placed on every table. Wearing rubber gloves and donning a surgical mask, he carefully sprinkled the poisonous neurotoxin in the powdered sugar for the topping of the three deserts. It was very tempting to mix it into the tea, but in his home testing, it made the tea less clear and he couldn't afford to arouse suspicion.

He tested the substance on stray cats and dogs, finding symptoms began within 30 minutes and death within an hour. The first three or four dozen victims would survive if intubated before the onset of respiratory symptoms, but the number of patients would soon overwhelm the hospitals. There would certainly be many deaths, possibly hundreds. The most difficult part of his plan was to make sure none of the staff consumed the substance and died before the luncheon, arousing suspicion.

He walked into the kitchen and gloated in what he saw. The cooks had beautified his recipe of death, and the waiters and waitresses were dutifully preparing it for delivery to the conference room. He began to bag up the trash in the trash receptacles. "S'up, Sandy?" He winked at a cook who looked his way.

"Hey Arnie."

"Say, Sandy." He moved closer to her and spoke softly. "Anyone got an upset stomach? I've been feeling kinda', you know, nauseated."

"Yeah." She nodded. "Marlo just went to the bathroom complaining of dizziness and nausea."

"Marlo?" Arnie's eyebrows furrowed.

"Yeah, the dishwasher. Why?"

Arnie looked at his watch. It was 11:30. The luncheon was scheduled to begin at noon. "Which bathroom? I think we've got the same symptoms."

"That one." She pointed down the hall.

Arnie dropped his replacement trash bag on the floor and headed quickly toward the restroom. He paused and turned back to Sandy. "If anybody else comes down with this bug," he said, holding his stomach, "let me know. I've got a remedy that helps."

Arnie walked into the employee's restroom. Two men were at the urinal and two men were in the stalls. "Marlo?"

He received no response.

"Hey, Marlo?" He walked toward the stalls. "Are you all right?"

Momentarily, he heard a groan. "Nah, man. I'm sick."

Arnie wiggled the door and found it locked. "Open the door and I can help you out, man."

"What? No, I'm not gonna," he paused, his words beginning to slur, "I'm not gonna open–"

Arnie grabbed the handle and wiggled the door again. "Come on, Marlo. Open the door. I've got something that'll help you feel better."

Marlo opened the door and Arnie was immediately shocked by how pale he looked. Arnie's face flushed with adrenaline and his heart skipped a beat. He was impressed with himself. His recipe was working well against his first human subject. He hoped that he could get Marlo to go home, but he knew if one person got a glimpse of this pale, Italian fellow, covered with sweat and weakly inhaling shallow breaths, they would immediately call the squad and his whole plan could be sabotaged.

Plan B. Arnie had prepared for several contingencies. He pulled out a four-foot strip of 100 pound fishing line, wrapped it twice around the neck of the sluggish dishwasher and pulled it tight. Marlo was too out of it to protest. “I’m sorry Marlo,” York whispered as Marlo began to choke and claw at the string constricting his throat. “You won’t feel any more pain. This is a better death.” He sat on Marlo’s legs until his jerking slowed. Only a small amount of blood dribbled down his neck from where the string cut into his flesh. “It’s for the babies, Marlo. It’s for the babies.”

Someone saw four legs under the stall, and tapped on the door. “Everything all right in there?”

“Uh, yeah. He’ll be okay.” Arnie put the line back into his pocket and propped Marlo’s limp body against the toilet.

Peaking through the narrow sliver between the door and the doorframe, the fellow worker didn’t appear convinced. “You sure? Want me to call 911?”

“He just needed some Tylenol.” Arnie exited the stall and shut the door behind him. He pointed to the stall with his right hand and reached into his pocket with his left to grasp the handle of a four-inch palm dagger. “I was just helping him with some drink to take it down.”

The fellow worker shrugged his shoulders and exited the bathroom just as two other employees entered. Arnie let go of the stall door and gravity swung it open and it hit Marlo’s leg.

Arnie cursed his luck and pulled the door shut. He couldn’t lock it from the outside. The two employees glanced at him strangely as he stood in front of an occupied stall with a half dozen unoccupied stalls all around him.

“I’ll wait here for you, Marlo,” Arnie said, holding the door shut.

He glanced at his watch. *11:45.*

One of the two employees had a similar pale appearance, and Arnie recognized him as one of the dishwashers.

“Whatcha’ been munchin’ on, buddy?”

“Huh?” He paused to study Arnie, his breathing labored.

“Looks like you and Marlo got sick on the same stolen deserts.”

“Huh?”

Arnie tapped on the door of the stall next to Marlo’s. “*Entre monsieur*,” he said in his nicest French accent, as he reached into his pocket for the four-foot strip of fishing string.

"I need to confess something to you, sir," Arnie told his manager, who sat patiently behind his office desk. "Marlo and some guys from the kitchen were smoking dope on the clock this afternoon…"

"What?!"

"A couple of the guys thought it would help Marlo's depression."

"You've got to be kidding me."

"No sir. Marlo was depressed. Suicidal, actually."

"Who?" The manager's countenance revealed concern and empathy.

"Marlo, uh, I don't remember his last name. He's a dishwasher in the kitchen. I didn't smoke with them," Arnie assured him. "One of the guys they invited to smoke with them was pretty sure they had some bad weed. Anyway, they all started getting sick about a half an hour ago. I thought you should know."

"Where are they now?"

"I don't know. I think they left. The kitchen's short right now. I can fill in washing dishes if you want."

Suddenly, the manager's phone rang. He glanced at the caller ID and picked up the phone. "Yeah?"

"Someone found four of the fellows from the kitchen puking in the bathroom. A dishwasher named Marlo Vasquez isn't breathing. Someone said it looks like he strangled himself."

"Strangled himself?" The manager squinted in disbelief. "You mean, he hung himself?"

"Yeah, it doesn't make sense. There was no rope, just a superficial cut all the way around his neck. The veins in his head were bulging like something out of a horror flick. The whites of his eyes were blood red. Another kitchen employee has the same cut around the neck, but's still breathing. Barely. An ambulance is on the way."

The manager covered his hand over the speaker and said to Arnie, "We found them. You go fill in for them in the kitchen."

"Yes sir." Arnie stood up and headed for the door.

The manager informed the lady on the phone, "They were sharing spiked marijuana this morning to try and help one of them with suicidal thoughts."

"What?"

"Yeah. I think we're looking at a volatile mixture of suicidal thoughts and bad marijuana. Don't call the squad to the front. We don't want to draw attention. Let's call EMT to the back of the building."

The topic of the noon lecture was "The Demise of Reproductive Healthcare in the Coalition States." The large banquet hall was filled with 200 round tables, each of them able to seat ten people. Halfway through the lecture, physicians started feeling ill. Many of them left for the bathroom. Others headed for their hotel room. Halfway through the lecture, only half of seats were filled. When the speaker started vomiting in the middle of his lecture, Arnie made a hasty exit.

The next day he learned the death toll: *1,393 physicians!* Five hundred more were still in critical condition.

He hoped the investigation sure to follow would not suspect him, but he was way too exposed on this mission. He could not go back to his home. It would just be a matter of time now. They'd figure out the physicians were poisoned from food in the kitchen. They'd figure out two of the dishwashers had been strangled. They'd figure out Arnie Oswald York had sent his manager on a wild goose chase with misinformation just to buy time. Everything would have to change.

Maybe the Coalition of Free Christian States would accept me.

Washington, D.C.

"I hope we all now agree that the time for diplomacy has come to an end," the president informed her cabinet as her gaze pierced her secretary of state, Beth Randolph, uninvitingly.

"Is there any evidence the CFC States were involved?" Danny Connor asked.

"Almost 1,400 reproductive health physicians have been murdered!" The president angrily thumped her fist on the table. "They've been killed in a state that has violated a constitutionally-protected right to abortion."

"They haven't arrested a single abortionist yet, Madam President." The president's chief of staff, Dena Halluci, thought it was hasty to blame the Coalition for this act of terror. She nervously combed her manicured fingers through her newly dyed black, shoulder-length hair, as if she intended to draw attention to her new style. "The implementation of their 'Life Bill' was postponed until their impeachment debate concludes."

"And coincidences are not proof, Madam President," said the wrinkled NSA director. "You're going to have to make your case to Congress and the public if you plan to use this to justify invading a state and causing the deaths of hundreds or thousands of American citizens."

"*All* of the Coalition states have abortion bans on the books. Whether they're enforcing them or not, they intend to. They've resisted the federal executive's anti-terrorism and gay rights measures. They've resisted the judiciary repeatedly, for goddess' sake!"

The secretary of state looked up from her laptop. "Please, Madam President, if the public hears you say that—"

"You're right." She nodded. "*Goodness'* sake." Her gaze fixed on General Green. "Isn't trying to secede an act of war? Cross-reference that with the murder of 1,400 abortionists in a Coalition state that's defied the judiciary to ban abortion and gay marriage, resisted our anti-terrorism statutes, protected hate criminals, and to top it off, *ticked me off*" – spit flew out of the corner of her mouth as she railed – "and you have the best excuse for an invasion ever!"

The secretary of state wagged her head and leaned on her elbows. "Make no mistake, Madam President, the Coalition states are not *trying* to secede. They *have* seceded."

"Well, I don't accept that!" She smacked both palms against the table. "They have not seceded until they've defeated our invasion force. End of debate." Beth Randolph bit her lip as the president's angry eyes shifted to the brass at the table. "General Green, brief us on our invasion scenario."

The general cleared his throat and motioned to a projected image on a large screen on the wall. "The united Guard forces in the ten insubordinate states are weak relative to their land mass they're defending. The major thing the Coalition has going for them is dozens of our nuclear silos," said General Green, "which we must take out with surprise precision strikes. The environmental damage will be minimal. If they get control of one of those warheads and relocate them, they will paralyze us militarily."

"And politically," Cameron Weaver added. "You want Congress's closet copperheads to come out and bite you in the rear, Madam President? Mention the nuclear threat we'd be under if the Coalition states had a nuke and we'll find ourselves in *bipartisan* impeachment crisis this time."

"We agree, Madam President," said Congressman McGinnis. "America doesn't want a vacation in Yellowstone bad enough to risk a nuclear attack for it."

The president's gaze shifted from the congressman to General Green. "Well, if that's the first battle line, then let's get to it."

"We agree" – General Green's gaze shifted to his Joint Chiefs – "we must first mobilize our Mobile Tactical High Energy Lasers around their border, so as to minimize their potential threat if they do acquire one or two nuclear weapons and equip them on ballistic missiles. The 'M-T-HELs' have an 84 percent success rate intercepting ballistic missiles."

"Reprogramming and mobilization will take a couple of weeks at least, maybe longer," the Air Force general responded pessimistically.

Danny swallowed hard and grew light-headed. His fingers went numb and his cheeks paled. He took several deep breaths to try to hold back the wave of nausea that threatened to expel his lunch. He couldn't hide anymore. The circumstances were demanding action from him if he was to make a difference at all.

"You were born for such a time as this," Josh Davis told him during their last conversation. That was a quote from the book of Esther, who risked her life to save her people. But what could Danny do that would make a difference?

Helena, Montana

Ben Boswell got up about 6 a.m. to get his coffee brewing. While waiting for his first cup, he checked his Email inbox and, lo and behold, he had an Email from a name he didn't recognize. "Beltway Help" was the author of the post. *Why didn't my spam filter catch it?* It suddenly occurred to him that this wasn't a name, but was help from inside the beltway.

His suspicions aroused. He quickly right-clicked the E-mail and screened it with his virus and worm eradication software. The E-mail was declared benign.

He clicked on it and a box opened up on the screen and informed him that the message was protected by ID handcuff software. A program in the E-mail began to hack into his computer, retrieving info about its owner.

Boswell sensed something was wrong and he hit delete, then control – alt – delete, but the hacking program was not deterred. The governor prepared to turn it off when it made a clicking sound and a video of Danny Connor began to show on his screen. The governor did not recognize the young handsome man who sat with his hands folded, back-dropped by a wall of books. Danny identified himself as a chief economics advisor in the president's cabinet and addressed Benjamin Boswell and the leaders of the Coalition of Free Christian States. He informed Boswell he had been secretly helping journalist Josh Davis expose the Administration's usurpations to the American public, and that he was supportive of the Coalition's principles and believed their resistance was justified.

Danny Connor's countenance then became very grave as he spilled his guts to the governor. "Prepare for an unexpected, massive, nocturnal air strike with stealth aircraft from California bases in six or seven days that will destroy all nuclear warhead locations within the Coalition territories. They will try to take out the Guard's jets and airfields and the fuel tanks with aircraft that will be visible to radar. They are also setting up devices around the border that have the capacity to intercept and destroy any ballistic missiles that the CFC States might employ to threaten the United States."

This can't be authentic, thought Boswell, astounded by the unlikely event that this could be real help from inside the beltway. *No, this can't be true. It's too good to be true.*

"I expect you are suspicious of the authenticity of this message. I'll confirm it by wearing my gray pin-stripe suit with a red and white striped tie, and a band-aid around my ring finger during a live C-span televised lecture on third world economics at George Washington University this morning at 11 a.m. eastern standard time. I'll also cough between the words 'third' and 'world' in the introduction of the lecture. In case you don't get this message until after the lecture, I'll see to it the video it gets uploaded to C-Span's accessible online archives immediately.

"But don't waste a moment," Danny warned him. "The president's preparing for the most massive invasion since the terrorists wars. I fear you will not be able to stop her unless you immediately begin to prepare for a defense of your coasts, cities, airfields, and most importantly, your nuclear arsenal. They may be monitoring me, or will be soon. Do not try to contact me. I will provide intel to you when I think it is necessary and safe. You will only be able to watch this video once more, and then it will self-delete. Press 'control-x' when you are ready to watch it again." Danny's countenance suddenly changed, and he appeared very fearful. "Pray for me," he concluded. The computer screen suddenly went black.

Ben Boswell's mind was buzzing and his body numb. He picked up the phone and dialed General Bob Bryan's cell number. His wife entered and set a cup of hot coffee on his desk.

She was concerned by the troubled appearance on his face, and his rigid posture. "Are you okay, dear?"

"We need to get on our knees and pray."

Within the hour, Ben Boswell had gathered as many staff members as he could to watch Connor's video once more from his home office. He set up a video camera in front of the computer screen, which broadcast the video to the other ten governors and their most trusted staff before it self-deleted. Then they watched Danny Connor's lecture live on C-Span and Danny confirmed his message with his dress, his band-aid, and his well-placed cough.

The threat was authentic.

13

Seattle, Washington

"In order for there to be such a thing as justice and human rights, there must be an objective standard of right and wrong." Elijah lectured from a podium in a packed auditorium of 3,500 at the Washington State University. "It can't just be a matter of personal opinion, else we would have no basis to condemn someone who assaulted another as long as he acted in accordance with his own opinion. Right and wrong can't be based upon a democratic consensus; else we would have no basis to condemn slavery where it was democratically popular. Americans have an infatuation with democracy, but its ethic is absolutely unsustainable. If ten white men and one black man were on a desert island outside of the boundaries of any nation's government and they were going to vote whether or not to legalize slavery, who here would justify their decision to enslave that black man if he lost the vote?" Not a hand rose. "We all know that the standard of morality and justice must transcend our opinions, as well the boundaries of nations and of time. There must be a Designer and Judge to impose this moral standard upon us."

Two of Mitch Paine's heroine-addicted college dropouts watched from the rear of the auditorium, wondering when and how they would be able to take out their target. Their movement could handle a brawl. They could be true through arrest and prosecution. They could survive the wrath of a theocratic state. But their movement may not be able to survive this man's series of lectures. This African American was too persuasive, and minds otherwise sympathetic with Mitch Paine's mission were being powerfully influenced.

"If there were no God, the atheist would have no basis from which to express his moral outrage at the execution of gays in Saudi Arabia," Elijah proposed. "If there were no God, the atheist would have no basis from which to express his moral outrage at the burning of witches at the Salem witch trials, or even the Coalition's prosecution of abortionists for that matter. Oh, the atheist is definitely morally indignant about the wrongs he finds around him, but he has no basis besides his own bias to be judgmental about anything. In arguing for relative morality and subjective truth, the atheist becomes his own worst enemy." Elijah paused to let the crowd meditate on the truth of his statement.

"The atheist says he will not believe what he cannot sense with his five senses; if he cannot see it, hear it, taste, touch, or smell it, then he says he doesn't believe it. First of all, which of his five senses told him that? Which of his senses told him only data that is sensed with his five senses is believable? Hmm? In just stating the proposition that only sensed data is believable, he contradicts it." As his congregation considered the apparent contradiction, it grew as quiet and still as if the room were empty.

"When the atheist – as we heard during Q & A last night – raises an objection about the evil influence of Christianity in colonial slavery or in the Crusades, how can he say for sure those things are evil? Can he sense evil with any of his five senses? Can he see, taste, touch or smell evil? See, the atheist contradicts himself when he tries to debate the problem of evil in the universe because in asserting that there is such a thing as evil he contradicts and therefore refutes himself. During Q & A last night the president of the Free Thought Club asserted that there was no such thing as absolute truth, but in just stating that assertion he contradicts it, for in the statement he shows that he believes at least one absolute truth, that there is no absolute truth. He has his feet planted firmly on thin air! He proves true the verse: 'The fool has said in his heart, there is no God.' Only a fool denies self-evident truths…"

The students were more receptive than Elijah predicted they would be. Many of them had never heard Christianity defended with such clarity. Even most Christians believed that the Christian religion was a matter of opinion and faith, not fact, and that trying to prove Christianity true was fruitless. The local church and campus ministry leaders would pat Elijah and his team on the back for their eloquence and their dedication to the kingdom of God, but the Minutemen knew that it was the churches full of prayer warriors all over Montana that brought the anointing upon them. Those saints were lifting their Seattle outreach up to God in fervent prayer at that very moment.

"Christianity is proven from the impossibility of the contrary." Elijah began to pace back and forth on the elevated platform. "If you reject Christianity, then you have no basis to call anything objectively good or evil. As Romans 1 in the New Testament says, we all know our Creator and His authority from creation and from our conscience. It is our rejection of these self-evident truths that brings God's condemnation. The United States of America has abandoned God's revelation of righteousness and justice as expressed in nature and in conscience and confirmed in more detail in His Word, the Bible," he said, hoisting his Bible into the air. "As a nation, we've turned from the true God to idols. The devil, since the Garden of Eden, has always offered mankind an alternative happiness and a counterfeit peace, but do not be deceived: it is a poisonous fruit that will destroy your soul and enslave your children. Until we have justice and righteousness in our land, we cannot have God's blessing and we cannot have lasting peace. Peace comes through knowing the Creator" – he pointed heavenward – "and His Son Jesus Christ…"

Mitch Paine's subordinates in the back of the packed auditorium grew troubled by the stilled silence among the students, many of them they knew to be Mitch Paine followers. "When are we going to stop this? We can't let this go on."

The college drop-out, wearing dark sunglasses and with an extinguished unlit cigarette butt hanging out of one side of his mouth, snickered at the anxiety of his peer. "He's got a weakness. We'll exploit it in due time." His eyes darted to his younger friend, the ambitious leader of the local chapter of Students for Social Action. "Tonight. Give everybody a call."

Helena, Montana

David sat on the edge of a platform of a high school auditorium as 1,000 aspiring Coalition Minutemen sat on the edge of their seats, hanging on his every word. His lecture on God's criminal justice system had concluded and it was time for Q & A.

"Yes." David pointed at a light-skinned African American young man on the second row.

He stood up and pushed the spectacles that were too large for his face up the bridge of his nose. "My name's Alex, from Salt Lake City.

One of my main concerns with this teaching is that if you accept the premise that God's Word has the answer for the crimes of abortion and physician-assisted suicide, then how can you reject the conclusion that God's Word also has the answer for other crimes like theft, adultery, homosexuality, and premarital sex? And if you accept that these are not just sins but crimes, upon what basis can we reject the penalty that God's law prescribes? I mean, the Apostle James said that if you keep the whole law and offend in one point, you're guilty of all. Why doesn't the Coalition defend those commandments and judgments of God's law?"

The young man sat down and David smiled broadly. "I love the questions I get from home-schoolers. They're just so far beyond where we public-schooled folks were at their age." The auditorium laughed and the young boy blushed as much as his dark skin would let him.

"Next question," he said, prompting more laughs throughout the auditorium. "Ah, I'm just kidding. The young man has a good question." David stood up for a moment and leaned against the platform. "If we reject the assertion that God's Word has the answer for crime, then aren't we rejecting our premise that God's Word has trustworthy answers? If we reject what God's Word says about any subject, then how can we trust it when it speaks of Jesus being the Son of God? Jesus said, 'Man shall not live by bread alone, but by…' – what?"

"Every word that proceeds out of the mouth of God," the congregation of Minutemen responded in unison.

"*Every* word," David reiterated. "If we reject God's Word, then by default we're left with some anti-Christ view that rejects the lordship of Christ. Jesus said, 'Why do you call me Lord, Lord, and do not the things which I say?' It's hypocritical to embrace what God's Word says about salvation and reject what God's Word says on criminal justice. Jesus said, 'If you love Me, keep My…' – what?"

"Commandments," the congregation responded.

"Correct. I certainly agree that God's Word is just when God declares penalties for certain crimes. Thieves should pay back to the victim four times the value of the object stolen – five times the value of the object stolen if it had sentimental value. Adultery, rape, and homosexual acts are capital crimes. The punishment for premarital sex is that the couple is forced to marry and the man can never divorce the woman for any reason. The man must also pay the father of the woman a fine for the shame he brought upon the family. Execution, restitution, flogging, and an eye for an eye are the only just penalties for crimes according to God's Word. And we would be healthiest and happiest if we obeyed God. God cried out in Deuteronomy, 'Oh that they had such a heart in them that they would fear Me and keep all My commandments always that it might be well with them and with their children forever.' God's Word is the path of life and peace, for individuals and nations. Why isn't the Coalition adopting and enforcing these other aspects of God's law?" David paused, adjusted his cordless mic tighter over his right ear, and sat back down on the edge of the platform. "There are only a few sins that God's Word specifically mentions that bring His judgment upon the whole nation. The shedding of innocent blood is one of them. Therefore, ending the shedding of innocent blood is the Coalition's first priority."

In the back of the room, a hand shot quickly up into the air.

David laughed at the man's enthusiasm. "Not so fast, sir. You're going to throw your shoulder out of joint." The crowd laughed as a middle-aged balding man stood up. "Are we obeying God's law when it comes to murder if we don't punish murderers like God says they are to be punished? We're still putting murderers in prison, aren't we? Two passages you cited in your lecture clearly teach murderers must be put to death in order to cleanse the land of the curse of innocent blood."

The man sat down and David grinned. "Good point. We are headed in the right direction in that we've stopped the killing of the innocents and incarcerated the guilty, but you are right. Justice is a holy appetite not yet satisfied in the Coalition states."

David did his best to keep his picture out of the newspapers and off of the television, but an undercover agent posing as a Minuteman finally identified him in spite of his shaved head and brown beard. Erdman and the NSA director urged the president to have him assassinated, but Dena and Cameron argued that the president should publicize the fact that a man wanted for the terrorist attack that slew President Fitzgerald was one of the lay leaders of the Coalition. "It's a blessing in disguise," said Cameron. "You couldn't pay for a better PR springboard than this."

It was General Green who proposed the answer that held the most appeal to Brighton, an answer she had always embraced. She needed to capture this David Jameson and convict him of the terrorist attack that killed President Fitzgerald and hundreds of pro-choice leaders. Nothing would appease the copperheads in Congress and bring the impeachment drive to a halt quicker than this.

In the rear of the auditorium where David lectured, a short, obese 45-year-old with dark, unkempt hair fondled a mini-DVD in his pocket. He had been personally instructed by Bill Erdman to get it into David Jameson's keeping. If possible, he was to remain anonymous. If he could only get to that open briefcase beside David's podium during the break.

"He's grown too powerful," Erdman had instructed him. "His influence is greatly increasing the resources of the Minutemen. These armed Talibanish fanatics could greatly prolong this conflict."

"Do you want me to kill him?" the undercover FBI agent had asked. "He's got bodyguards around him and it'll be difficult to capture him and make his death look like suicide, but I can poison him and frame a subordinate. If he murdered the president, we need to take him out." He hated to lose his cover for which he had worked so hard, but taking out the terrorist who killed President Fitzgerald would be an honor.

"No, no," Erdman responded, reminding himself that none of his undercover agents in the Bureau were aware that the death of President Fitzgerald was a convenient accident. Erdman's voice was gruff after a day of urgently directing subordinates all over the country. "That case has been made to the president, but she doesn't want to make a martyr out of him. She desperately needs the positive press of putting him on trial. She has made future Bureau budget increases contingent on good captures that result in positive PR for her. I'll tell you what we're going to do. You're going to be getting a DVD delivered to you. Don't watch it. You deliver it to Jameson anonymously. Don't be in the room when he watches it."

"What's on it?"

"I can't tell you that. If you're captured, you are going to want genuine ignorance. Just get it into his hands."

At the end of the lecture, as David was conversing with questioners at the front of the auditorium, the undercover agent made his way beside David and quietly dropped the DVD into the open briefcase. The DVD's cover read, "It's about Darlene." He glanced around to see if anyone saw him drop it, and then he looked down at the DVD, which teetered on a stack of loose notes. He watched the DVD as it slid down under the cover of David's black leather-bound Bible.

Missoula, Montana

"Oh, you cheer Governor Boswell now. You laud the bravery of Randy Woods. You praise the Coalition today, but how will you respond when you suffer for righteousness' sake?" Barry Friar preached his heart out, not only to the three thousand who packed the largest church in Missoula to hear him, but to millions who heard the broadcast all over the Coalition through radio, internet, and television. The applause and "amens" had become sparse as Friar reminded them of the cost they may have to pay for asserting their independence. The four dozen pastors shifted uncomfortably in the front five pews, much preferring the soft approach rather than the sledgehammer rebukes of the famed Minuteman leader. The television cameras zoomed in close during the conclusion of his sermon.

"'Beloved,' wrote the Apostle Peter in the fourth chapter of his first book, 'think it not strange concerning the fiery trial which is to try you, as though some strange thing happened to you.' Think it not strange, think it not odd, think it not unusual, saints, that you are going to suffer for Christ. All who live godly in Christ Jesus will suffer persecution. If they hate Me, said Jesus, they will hate you also. If they persecute Me, then they will persecute you as well. The servant is not above his master. If our Lord suffered for His opposition to sin, then we will as well. Daniel's righteousness was rewarded with a lion's den, and his three friends were cast into the fiery furnace because they wouldn't bow the knee to tyranny. We can never have the same spirit of glory upon us unless we are willing to drink the cup from which they drank.

"Peter goes on to tell us how we should respond to our suffering." Barry looked down to read from his well-worn Bible, which was open on the oak wood podium. "Does he say that we should whine, pout, murmur and complain, or quit?"

"No," his congregation answered his question in unison.

"Does he say that we should barter for a compromise, you know, make peace with the wicked so that they'll go easier on us?"

"No!"

"Peter says, 'Rejoice, inasmuch as ye are partakers of Christ's sufferings, that when His glory shall be revealed, ye may be glad also with exceeding joy. If ye be reproached for the name of Christ, happy are ye.'

"Oh, there will be grieving when our sons die in battle. There may be coffins filled with women and children. There will be prisons in far-away states filled with our fathers and husbands and sons, but through it all, we can rejoice. Why? Because we look forward to the day when the kingdoms of this world will become the kingdom of our Lord and Christ. Our hearts throb for it. Our heart is where our treasure is, and our treasure is stored in heaven, *not* in the Coalition of Free Christian States. The sufferings of this world don't compare to the riches of eternal wealth that await those who are faithful to the end. The Coalition's victory over tyranny is *not* the measure of our success, people of God." He shook his head: "If it were, defeat at the hands of the federal government would bring sadness. But we can be happy even in defeat and suffering. How?" He answered his question by singing the tune of a children's song. "This world is not my home, I'm just a-passin' through. My treasures are laid up somewhere beyond the blue.'"

As some youth finished singing the first verse of the song, he massaged his thick gray beard and smiled broadly, revealing a missing bottom tooth. "The measure of success is seeing God's smile and hearing 'Well done, my good and faithful servant.' That," – he pointed at the congregation with his right index finger as his eyes welled with tears – "that is what it's all about!" A rustle of applause spread across his audience.

He looked down again to read: "If any suffer as a Christian, let him not be ashamed; but let him glorify God on this behalf. For the time is come that judgment must begin at the house of God." Barry paused and looked up. He studied the faces of the stilled, large congregation, letting a moment pass as the truth of the passage sank into their hearts and minds.

"God will use persecution and suffering to clean His house. I heard a story of two Soviet soldiers who broke into a small underground church in Communist Russia, their machine guns cocked and loaded. Christians screamed and huddled against the walls in fear as one of the soldiers shouted: 'If any of you would rather live as a non-Christian than die as a Christian, then get out now!' Parents pulled their terrified children close as they wrestled with what to do. It was a moment of testing. One by one, families began to leave. Most of the congregation left. Those who had joined them week after week on their knees in prayer, hands raised in worship, so sincere and committed in days of ease, were now leaving when the call of the Gospel meant their lives. A minute later, the soldier shouted again, 'Last chance. Do you want to die for Jesus?' No one else left. Only a small remnant was prepared to die for their Lord and Savior. He that loves his life will lose it, but he that loses his life for Christ's sake and the Gospel's will find it. To everyone's surprise, the two soldiers put their guns down, took off their helmets, and began to embrace the saints nearest to them. Confusion was on everyone's face as the soldiers began to weep and bless those who cowered in fear from them only moments before."

"'What is all this about?' the pastor of the underground church inquired.

"'We are believers in Christ,' one of the soldiers responded. 'We just wanted to separate the sheep from the goats before we risked fellowship.'" Friar's listeners affirmed his story with strong "amens."

Barry stepped off the platform and stopped halfway down the steps. "Mark my words, people of God, our faith will be tried by fire. The church's suffering will separate the sheep from the goats and purify us. When you suffer, doubt not God's love for you, doubt not His goodness, doubt not the rightness of your cause, but rather, rejoice! 'Happy are ye!' When our hearts are heavy with mourning, trust Him. When the bombs are falling, trust Him. When our loved ones perish, trust Him. I don't know what the fate of the Coalition of Free Christian states will be, but I know that our faith in God will be tested. Before we conquer our Promised Land of 'liberty and justice for all' we must be faithful in the desert. In your day of testing, when all of heaven is sitting on the edge of their seats to see what you will do, rejoice that you are counted worthy to suffer for the cause of Christ. The Coalition need not win to glorify God, we must only fight." He lifted his Bible heavenward. "The lions are hungrier than ever and the fiery furnace is being stoked. Be faithful until death, and Jesus'll give you a crown of life. Lord willing, he'll even throw in freedom for our posterity to boot."

Berkeley, California

The annual convention of the National Council of Evangelical Churches rapidly deteriorated into a sideshow with national Christian leaders publicly venting their anger at the two Coalition Minutemen who had the courage to represent their cause in person.

"Can I at least finish?" Cal Manning sat beside Carson behind a table on a platform in front of a sea of frowns and snarls. He leaned into the mic that was propped on a stand in front of him. "You've asked three questions and won't let me answer the first one."

"To rebel against government is to rebel against God! You're persecuting gays and non-Christians in the name of Christ!" The denominational leader shouted into the microphone in the center aisle of the auditorium of 500 pastors and denominational leaders. "You're a shame and a disgrace to the cause of Christ!" The minister turned and stomped to his seat as those who filled the auditorium applauded.

"Your first question was–" Cal Manning spoke into the microphone but the moderator had turned it off. He glanced at the moderator, who was at a podium in the center of the platform. "Can I respond, sir?"

The moderator did not make eye contact when he replied, "We're running out of time, and his was more of a comment than a question. Let's go to the next question."

"Enough." Carson stood to his feet and turned to the moderator. "You are not being sincere. You let our critics spout their spite instead of encouraging edifying dialogue and understanding."

The moderator ignored him and read from the list of questioners. "Next question, Mr. Tom Duvall." A young man in a white suit and a rainbow-colored tie pranced his way from the rear toward the microphone at the front of the center aisle.

Carson took a deep breath and took his seat. "There are no Bible believers here," he mumbled.

Cal shot to his feet, fed up with their mistreatment. He projected his voice so as to be heard throughout the auditorium. "How many of you agree with the last reverend's comments? Can I have a show of hands?"

The moderator was about to protest when 99 percent of those in the room thrust their hands into the air. The moderator held his peace and let democracy have its say.

Cal shook his head as Carson commented, "We're wasting our time, Cal. They are not going to let us defend our cause."

Cal nodded and reached down to grab his briefcase. "Let's go."

"Your honorarium is contingent upon you staying the entire time you agreed to stay," the moderator announced as murmuring filled the auditorium.

Cal walked over and shook the moderator's hand with his right hand and grabbed the microphone off the stand with his left.

"I want to warn you all of divine judgment," he said boldly as the moderator clamored for his microphone. "Your salt has lost its savor. Your candlestick will soon be removed."

"Give me that!" The moderator snatched the microphone from Cal by the cord and the mic struck the podium with a loud bang and a whistle as Cal and Carson darted for a rear exit.

After their disappointing appearance at the religious conference, they were prepared to leave California immediately. However, a student leader from the Baptist Student Union met them in the parking lot and invited them to a Bible study. After a couple days of non-stop ministry to college students, Cal and Carson found the mission the Lord intended for them.

Deer Lodge, Montana

"Honey, check this out!" Dixie tossed a newspaper onto Jack's lap, covering the sandwich he clasped with both hands during their picnic on the lawn of their secluded log home.

Jack set aside his lunch, leaned back against the tree behind him, and read the title of the article out loud. "Civilian militias asked to defend border cites." He casually set the newspaper down beside him and picked up his sandwich. "Interesting."

Dixie's smile fit her perky curls. "Do you want to go?"

He dropped his sandwich onto his paper plate and gave her a confused look.

"Montana has the only strong civilian militia and if you read the article," she said as she thumped the paper, "you would see that Governor Boswell wants to strengthen civilian militias all over the Coalition. There's too much land to defend to trust the Guard to do it all. They made a specific call for previous military men, or men with experience – men like you." She intended for her child-like, wide-eyed gaze to awaken him to her implications. When he sat there quiet as if he couldn't read her mind, she went ahead and put her thoughts into words. "Maybe you and other Montana Militia leaders should go train civilian militias in other Coalition states."

A long silence followed as Jack tried to assimilate his wife's request. "I'm not a member of the militia anymore," he stated coolly.

"But you're so well-trained, Jack. You should do it."

Jack's eyes revealed his shock at his wife's suggestion. "I can't believe you're proposing this. You left me because of my over-indulgence in militia activities at the expense of my family. Do you remember? And now, you want me to go out for" – he threw up his hands – "only God knows how many months or years, to train civilian militias in other states?"

"I'll go with you, dear."

"You're pregnant, Dixie!" He crossed his legs Indian-style, leaned forward and put his elbows on his knees. "Do you know what it's like to live out of a tent for weeks or months at a time?"

Her cheery countenance transformed to gloomy and weepy with Jack's disappointing rant.

"I want my baby to live in a free country, Jack." Her eyes filled with tears as she reached for Jack's hand and clutched it with both of hers. He hated it when she cried. It was her trump card to victory in every disagreement, as rare as those disagreements were now-a-days. "You can help make it free, honey."

"Oh, please!" He felt like she was exaggerating his abilities.

"Just pray about it, hon. That's the very least we can do. All I am saying is that when I read that article a few minutes ago, I kept thinking, 'Jack should do this! Jack should do this!' I think it's your calling. My heart is warmed by the thought that we could help together."

"My calling is to be a husband and a father. It's a calling I abandoned for many years, and now that I've got things right with God, I've got my priorities straight."

"Fathers and husbands have to defend their families, too, not just single men. The Coalition almost died last week when the FBI raided Governor Boswell's office. There were dads and granddads who risked their lives for freedom. Some of them died, Jack. Died for freedom." She wiped her tears and forced a smile. "That's a good way to go."

Jack was silently contemplative, his eyes searching the leaves above as if looking for some answer written in the rays of sunlight that penetrated the branches. This woman had changed so much.

"Just pray about it." Her thoughts were along the same lines as her husband. Jack had changed so much.

"I'll tell you what I'm praying about." Jack raised the newspaper toward her and fixed his eyes on hers. When she took the paper from him he pointed to another article. "It looks like a group of Minutemen are headed to the University of Montana branch in Missoula tomorrow. Now, that's a military front to which I feel more called, defending freedom through winning souls. That's one type of war I'm not well-trained in, and I'd like to learn."

"Oh? I didn't see that. Let's go." She seemed more enthusiastic than he expected.

"You wanna go, too? We'll have to be incognito. There are probably feds infiltrated everywhere trying to find high-value targets."

"Ah, don't be paranoid. Didn't you know Montana seceded?"

Jack grinned. “Yeah.”

“Let’s go.” She squeezed his hands excitedly, like a child on the eve of summer break who’d just been told that she was heading to Disney World.

“Enough of this talk about taking up arms again, all right?” He kissed the back of her hand. “It just gives me a bad taste in my mouth.”

Dixie scooted up beside him and leaned against his shoulder with the oak tree to their back. “I so dearly love you.”

Part V

Wrath and Atonement

14

Helena, Montana

"You have got to be kidding me?!" Boswell spoke with General Bryan over his laptop computer from his car. He was in the backseat. One of his bodyguards drove and another one sat in the passenger seat in front of him. "They started this evening?"

"It looks like the feds started removing some of their warheads about ten minutes ago. Our men monitoring those facilities on the ground have noticed an increase in personnel and the presence of large semis designed for transporting heavy equipment."

"Does this affect our plan?"

"It actually helps our plan. We'll just stay away from those sites. Maybe they borrowed personnel from the other sites we'll be hitting. Plus, when we repossess a warhead and transport it by semi, it will be difficult for them to track us by any radiation emitted, because they'll have trucks on the road too."

"Well, General Bryan, with God's blessing you may commence."

"Yes sir. It will be done by sunrise. Lord willing."

The driver pulled into his driveway and the governor tapped him on the shoulder. "Turn around. We're headin' back to the office."

Boswell tapped a button on his phone and positioned his Bluetooth device over his ear. "Phone Dreifuss." His A.G. picked up momentarily. "Hello Chad. Call my cabinet and tell them that we've begun Project Fair Sunshine."

"Fair Sunshine?"

"Yes. Fair Sunshine."

Dreifuss grinned nervously. "Yes sir."

Missoula, Montana

"What's that?" One of the two federal employees at the underground nuclear silo north of Missoula was disturbed when the security system alarm sounded for two seconds, and then discontinued. "There's some disturbance in front of the motion detector on the south entrance." He turned his attention to the video surveillance, and didn't see anything.

"Those are birds." His partner briefly glanced up from his *USA Today* to one of the monitors spread out in front of him. " I've got some mild transmission disturbance on the sat dishes too. Probably turkeys. Man, I got a big one the other day hunting with Tom!"

"Ha! Turkey hunting with Tom. That's funny."

"Huh?"

"You sure that's just turkeys?" he asked, studying the radio waveform on the computer.

"It'll clear up. Just be patient."

Moments later, the elder guard became frantic. "Hey, hey! Humvees approaching!" On the security monitors, he saw several Humvees rushing up the gravel drive to the facility.

The second guard dropped the newspaper and picked up the phone. It was static. He tapped a receiver. "We're jammed! How did we miss that?!" He checked the satellite transmitter and heard only static on every channel. Cursing their luck, he thumped a button on the keyboard several times and then slammed both palms against it in frustration. "Computer's offline!"

"Let's see if my cell's functional." The agent searched the phone number in the address book in his cell. "Nope. Where's the sat phone?" He scurried about, opening several drawers in the wall. "Here it is!"

"I got the number here." The other agent placed his index finger on a number on the phone list tacked to the wall. "555-212–."

"Hold on, hold on." He turned on the special phone designed to be impervious to jamming technology. "What's the number?" He read the number and the agent with the sat phone typed it in and hit "Send." However, he heard only static on the line. "What? How are they blocking it? Check the computer again!"

"It's frozen! We've got to alert the Pentagon now!" On the monitors, he could see several men running from their Humvees toward the front entrance. He stood to his feet and headed for the stairwell toward the basement where critical communication equipment was locked in a lead vault that protected it from electromagnetic radiation.

The Coalition's munitions specialist affixed explosives in precise locations over the steel door of the nuclear facility. "Cover!" he shouted. Men ducked close to the wall out of the blast radius. A loud explosion fractured the bolts and the door swung open. Dozens of Guard personnel rushed into the facility.

"Hands up! Hands up!" the guardsmen shouted as they sprinted down a declining hallway to a platform where the federal agents worked. One stunned federal agent raised his hands in the air in surrender. The other one was captured halfway down the stairwell toward the basement.

"Get face down on the ground!"

"Save us some time." The mission commander towered over the two bound agents sprawled out face down on the floor. He pleaded with them, "Give us the codes to the warheads. We just want to relocate them for our protection."

"We have to get them from Defense Command Center in the Pentagon."

The mission commander turned to the code-breaker. "Your turn." The commander motioned toward the large computer terminal imbedded in the wall next to a thick glass door, behind which sat twelve warheads. "Do your thing."

The code-breaker was a professor of advanced mathematics at the Massachusetts Institute of Technology. He had been contracted by the federal government to beef up security at nuclear sites. He defected to the Coalition when the Coalition states outlawed abortion and euthanasia. A mathematics genius who mastered advanced calculus before the age of twelve, he had invented more mathematical theorems than most of his students could master in their lifetimes. At 30 years of age, he didn't look a day over 20. He wore silver, horn-rimmed glasses, and was so skinny, some of the men speculated that his briefcase was heavier than he was.

He opened his briefcase on the floor, connected a set of wires from his laptop into the appropriate outlets in the computer terminal embedded in the wall, and then sat cross-legged on the floor and began to type into his laptop.

"You're not going to get away with this." No one responded to the senior agent of the facility as he tried to get the guardsmen to relent.

"This is wrong. You are bringing destruction upon yourselves." There was no response from the guardsmen, who seemed more interested in the amazing speed at which the genius typed on his laptop. "Think of your kids."

"We are," the guardsman hovering over them responded.

"That code is impossible to break and the Department of Defense has a direct line to that computer. If the code is tampered with, they are immediately notified and before you'll have a chance to finish patting your computer hacker there on the back, a laser-guided Daisy bomb'll vaporize us."

"Just be quiet." The guardsman aimed his M-16 at them briefly.

"No, let him talk," the computer whiz said softly. "It's an interesting theory. Want to hear mine?" When they didn't respond, he said, "Math proves the existence of God. There." He hit "Enter" and the computer in the wall hummed, the lock in the wall clicked, and the thick glass door to the warheads popped open about an eighth of an inch. "Ta da," he announced in a dull tone.

"Very good," said the mission commander.

"The feds have not been alarmed. Not by the computer anyway." The code-breaker gathered his equipment back into his briefcase.

"You know what to do, boys," the commander ordered his men. They hung their guns over their shoulders and walked quickly into the room to prepare the warheads, which were packed in heavy lead insulation, for re-location on wheeled carts.

Two trucks carried live warheads. Twelve trucks carrying radiation waste in barrels headed out in different directions to try and confuse the satellite imaging the feds would surely employ to try and track them. The cabins of the trucks had also been painted with banned lead paint so as to minimize the radiation emissions.

"Good job." The mission commander patted the code-breaker on the back as he followed him out the door. "Larry," he said to the guardsman next to him, "take our genius here to the next site."

Washington, D.C.

"Madam President!"

The Secret Service guard who stood outside the president's room in the White House opened her bedroom door and tried to wake her.

"Excuse me, Madam President."

President Brighton had been unable to sleep, and was easily aroused from her superficial slumber. She reached for where her husband would have been if he were still alive. When she found herself alone in bed, she stared his unwrinkled pillow, blank-faced.

"Madam President?"

She sat up and stretched her arms over her head. "This better be important."

"Urgent call from the Department of Defense."

"Six hours ago, we started moving out our nuclear warheads as planned. Well, approximately one hour and 42 minutes ago, we began to lose contact with some nuclear silos in Montana," General Green told the president through an open laptop on his desk at the Pentagon. Beside him stood the NSA director, who had a worried look on his face. The president was in her bathrobe seated on the couch in the hallway outside her room, with her laptop rested comfortably in her lap. Two Secret Service personnel stood beside her, at her beck and call. "That's usually not a big deal," Green continued, "temporary transmission failures happen all the time due to weather changes and birds and the like, and the weather has been inclement–"

"Get to the point!" The president was growing irritated with the general's lengthy preface.

"Well, we have had six sites in the Coalition states lose their transmissions since that time and we cannot communicate with the agents at those facilities."

"Six?"

"…Much too high of a number to attribute to a chance event. There's a large low-pressure front over the area, but nothing to justify this. It appears the computer lines, the phone lines, and even their cell phone lines and our unjammable sat phones have been cut or transmissions jammed somehow. Don't ask me how." The general glanced at a text message on his cell phone. "Uh, oh no."

After a pause, the president blurted out, "What?"

The general hit a button on his cell, which sent an image up on his hardwired desktop computer screen. He and the NSA director were staring at it, disbelieving their eyes. "We just got an update here, Madam President, and it looks like 19 sites within the Coalition border are offline right now."

The president cursed angrily. Her eyes were wide and her lips were taut as she sat her laptop on the couch and stood to her feet.

"Those codes are an evolving 199 radioactive keys that makes it impossible to hack," General Green informed her, "even for our best supercomputers."

The elderly Warnell responded glumly. "No, it can't be done. Not impossible." The president sighed and the NSA director moved closer to the microphone. "Madam President, our protocol is kicking in and the system will instantly shift to an alternative lock via satellite that should deter any more breaks in our security. Our other facilities should be safe until we get our personnel to those sites. We'll send teams to those sites immediately, and our satellites will begin to try to track radiation emissions in vehicles large enough to carry warheads, just in case."

General Green took a step closer to the president. "How do you want to respond, Mrs. Pres–?"

"Attack!" she screeched, clenching her fists and startling her Secret Service agents with her tone. She sat back down on the couch and put her laptop on her lap so they could see her face through the webcam perched on top of it. "They're taking our nuclear warheads! Attack! Send up the bombers immediately! We have to destroy those warheads before they put them on missiles and point them at us!"

The NSA director and the general exchanged a surprised glance. "First of all, Madam President, we don't even know that we're being attacked at all."

"You've lost communications!"

"We just need to get our high res satellite eyes onto those locations and send a team to–"

"Attack, now! Are you blind? We can't let them take our nuclear warheads. Commence Operation Cat O'Nine Tails, immediately."

General Green bent over his laptop beside the NSA director. "We're not ready for that operation, Madam President. Half our tanks, artillery, and infantry are still being shipped to the bases in California, without fuel, without personnel to–"

"Send up what you can immediately, and we'll commence Operation Iscariot instead! Move to DEFCON 4."

General Green glanced at the NSA director, his lips tightening as his brow furrowed. "Yes, Madam President," the NSA director responded, "DEFCON 4." He opened his phone to begin to make the transition.

"Madam President," Green said solemnly, "if they have acquired nuclear weapons and fire them, we cannot stop it. Our Mobile Tactical High Energy Lasers are not in position to intercept a ballistic missile from the CFC States. That won't be ready for a couple of days at very least. And even if it was ready, they could fire a number of dummy ballistic missiles, and we could never get them all and would never know which of them was armed with the nuclear warhead until the missiles all reached their targets."

Margaret Brighton blinked hard as she considered the worst-case scenario. Her face went pale in disbelief that it had come this far.

Edwards Air Force Base, California

The screeching siren and flashing red light in the dormitory at Edwards Air Force Base awakened the pilots to the bitterest of realities. "Attention! Attention! All hands! Operation Iscariot underway! This is not a drill. Operation Iscariot is…"

"Operation Iscariot?" one senior pilot raised his head off his pillow and glanced at his watch: 0214 hours. He blinked hard, sat up, and reached for his flight suit with one hand and rubbed his crew cut with his other hand. He yawned loudly and tried to recollect the pleasurable dream he was having before he was awakened, but the urgency of the tone of the third-shift base radio operator drove away every memory of his dream.

"Correct me if I'm wrong." His defense systems engineer leaned over to quickly tie his shoes. "Isn't that the operation to commence if the Coalition acquires nuclear weapons and threatens to use them?"

"Yes sir, Captain." The senior pilot zipped up his flight suit. "Though I do find that hard to believe."

"Are we really going to bomb Americans?" the co-pilot mumbled. "I can't believe it!"

"Well, now, that's what this whole thing's about? Haven't you been readin' the papers?" the senior pilot responded mockingly. "We need to bomb 'em to keep 'em American."

"I've got two elderly grandparents in Flathead, Utah, who moved there from San Fran," the co-pilot responded. "Grandpa just got cancer and they just moved there because they don't want to be euthanized."

"Aw, come on! You're going to do your job and get your head out of the clouds!" The senior pilot grew irritated at the co-pilot's doubts on the eve of the mission. "We're going to keep this country one. My country, good or bad, right?"

The co-pilot swallowed hard and blinked away his doubts. "Good or bad."

An admiral charged into the room and started his characteristic shouting, interspersed with foul language. "Get your butts in those birds and do what you're trained to do! The Jesus-freaks have begun the DEFCON descent into nuclear civil war, and it's up to you to stop it!"

Camp Pendleton, California

Thousands of troops, artillery, and fighter jets were being shipped into the marine base in Southern California for a secret invasion the administration had been planning to execute in approximately two weeks. The transportation vehicles carrying Apache and Cobra attack helicopters were just pulling into Camp Pendleton when they were ordered to prepare for early deployment.

The crew hurriedly began to unload the munitions and equipment and started fueling, loading, and preparing their birds for take-off. After air superiority was secured and the Coalition's air force was completely destroyed, the Army Rangers were preparing to parachute in behind the enemy lines.

Northwest Montana

General MacIntosh huddled in a Coalition bunker over a large digital map of the Coalition, monitoring what could be monitored of the jets and bombers that sped toward critical targets and infrastructure within their borders. They could not identify the aircraft that were the greatest threat to them – the stealth bombers targeting their nuclear facilities. Coalition fighter jets appeared as bright green flickers of light on the screen. He occasionally discovered the whereabouts of stealth federal aircraft when one of the green blips disappeared on his digital map. Since the fighters and bombers charging them had the capacity to target radio signals, seldom did the Coalition aircraft risk communicating with him.

"Elder 452 reporting," came a rare report. "Two of ours down and two enemy jets destroyed." The Coalition fighter pilot's voice was more calm and subdued than MacIntosh expected it to be. "My co-pilot thinks he saw the Coalition pilots eject before a missile destroyed their F-22." Governor Boswell turned from the computer screen he was monitoring to more closely listen to the conversation. "I think it's a B-52 bomber. It is still on a coarse north last contact, sir. Its vector takes it over Helena…"

General MacIntosh leaned into the microphone on his desk. “What is your proximity to the bomber? Can you see him?”

“I got just a flicker on my radar before our boys were shot down. Those B-52s change frequencies fast with a very broad range. Radar lock was impossible.”

“Continue along the vector you believe that the bomber was in when you last saw him on your screen. Over.”

The look of despair on General MacIntosh’s face stole away Boswell’s peace. “We can’t stop ‘em if we can’t see ‘em, Governor.”

Isaiah Knabb, who sat beside the governor, felt like his stomach was turning. “I can’t believe it’s comin’ to this.”

Governor Boswell shook his head. “I always knew it would come to this.” His eyes fixed on his chief of security. “Liberty and tyranny have one thing in common, Isaiah. They cannot long be at peace with one another. One of them must be destroyed.”

Knabb took a deep breath. “Isn’t Governor Littman supposed to be getting us some satellite visuals to help us discover the location of their stealth bombers?”

Governor Boswell turned to a Guard communication officer across the room. “Get Governor Littman on the phone in Seattle. Tell him I need those satellite visuals, now.”

“I’ve got him here,” a subordinate responded, his hand cupped over a phone. “Their technicians are transmitting the images now.”

The Coalition leaders were speechless as they studied the projection that flashed up on the screen against the wall.

“They are trying to totally destroy us,” MacIntosh forewarned.

Their eyes were fixed upon the satellite images provided from Governor Littman’s former NASA engineer. The computer was programmed to detect all metallic flying objects in CFCS air space using powerful magnetism technology still in the experimental stage. The projected image showed stealth bombers flying over their border cities and heading directly toward their nuclear facilities, Guard command centers, and capitol buildings. The aircraft that were detectable with radar were white dots on the screen, and those aircraft that were stealth and not detectable with conventional radar were labeled in red. The stealth B-52 bombers were most worrisome to them. Unfortunately, a single federal bomber – without wingmen like the other bombers – was headed straight for the site where guardsmen and a team of nuclear scientists were frantically attempting to arm and insert a nuclear warhead into a ballistic missile for possible launch.

* * * * *

"Call off your bombers or we will fire on you!" Boswell warned the president over the phone as calmly as his adrenaline would let him.

"Excuse me?"

Governor George Pollock from Idaho was just entering the room with his staff and statehouse leaders when Boswell warned the president again in a stern tone: "Call off your invasion, or we will fire one nuclear-warhead-armed ballistic missile at Washington, D.C. and another at Edwards in California."

"You're crazy!" she screeched, the pitch of her voice rising with her rage. "Don't you think we will retaliate in kind?"

She cupped her hand over the phone and told General Green, "Get UN Security General Petri Urlich on the phone."

The general protested, "No, Madam President, please—"

"Now!"

"The playing field's level now," Boswell informed her. "The game board has changed. Leave us in peace. Call off your forces or we will defend ourselves."

"There's no need for this to escalate," she said, her tone more anxious than she wished it.

"That's all I have to say. You have been warned." He raised the phone and slammed it down into its cradle, startling the room full of CFCS political and military leaders.

Boswell took a deep, uneasy breath and leaned over the desk toward the satellite imaging that flashed up on a screen affixed to the wall. "God help us," he mumbled under his breath. "Dear God, help us." Moments passed, and much to his dismay, the images of the federal fighter jets and bombers continued their present vector against their targets.

When they saw the missiles entering Washington State's air space from the Pacific, Boswell saw a look of fright in the eyes of MacIntosh. He looked like a man who knew he was about to lose a fight but wanted to appear brave right to the end.

"MacIntosh!" Boswell called out as he pointed his finger at him. "No doubt! Trust God!"

MacIntosh nodded and licked his lips.

"You tell them to get that warhead ready now. We have a cause worth dying for, gentlemen. They" – Boswell pointed at the screen – "do not."

* * * * *

Millions of Coalition citizens were resting comfortably in their beds when, on direct order from Governor Boswell, the phones started ringing off the hook. The Minutemen immediately started igniting prayer chains in every church across the Coalition. In the middle of the night, the faithful began to gather.

"Oh God, hear our prayer!" David Jameson knelt, earnestly praying at the first stair of the altar of the largest church in Helena where they had been holding nightly meetings for Minutemen training. "Plead our cause with those who rise up against us. Defend us against those who seek to slay the innocent and take your people into captivity. Arise, oh God! Let your enemies be scattered. For the sake of our children and our children's children…" His mind involuntarily rushed to his wife and children and tears filled his eyes. "Oh God, keep Darlene safe. Bless my babies." He prayed with deep sincerity and passion, his fists clenched as sweat broke out over his body.

David reached down beside him to pick up his black Bible so he could pray the words of Psalm 91 when a mini-DVD fell out from between its pages. *What's this?* he wondered. The black words on the plastic yellow DVD jacket read, "It's about Darlene."

Behind him were 5,000 men, women, and children on their knees and on their faces in desperate prayer for their freedom and deliverance. The saints trickled in until there was no more room to kneel. They gathered in Sunday school rooms and hallways, nurseries and gymnasiums. Living rooms and churches all over the Coalition were soon filled with those who prayed as if their very lives depended on it.

* * * * *

MacIntosh began to study a message that had been sent to him on his cell phone. He halted conversation in the room as he read the update. "General Bryan and his men are in Nebraska and are putting up quite a fight with anti-aircraft artillery over southern Nebraska. They have some scores, but too many have died to justify their continued defense of Lincoln's remaining airfields. Federal bombs have killed hundreds of civilians." The room full of Montana and Idaho leaders and Guard generals gasped at the announcement. "The Nebraska Guard's viciously defended their territory, bringing down many enemy fighters." Governor Boswell nodded at the report, but never took his eyes off of the screen.

"Our nuclear bluff *has* to make them turn back," Governor Pollock said, motioning toward the screen. "They have no choice."

"If we get that nuclear warhead armed, then we won't be bluffing," Boswell responded. "If we lose tonight, then we lose *everything!* Our children and grandchildren will perish under an abortionist's instrument or be euthanized in death clinics. They've slaughtered more Americans every year in the Abortion Holocaust than our nuclear weapon will slay to stop their Holocaust. Tonight, our faith puts God on the spot, and He *will* show Himself strong on our behalf. If we're defeated in the end, at least D.C.'s destruction will give the next state who wants to secede a fightin' chance."

"Yes sir." MacIntosh nodded, encouraged by the Coalition chairman's confidence. "We're trying to wire these satellite images" – he pointed to the image projected on the wall – "to our fighters to help them locate the stealth attackers, but I am not confident it will be ready until most of the bombers have completed their missions." An aid handed General MacIntosh a satellite phone and he quickly put it up to his ear and hurried his team of scientists who were trying to arm the nuclear warhead and install it on a ballistic missile.

When General MacIntosh turned back to the governor he was taken aback at what he saw. Governor Boswell had dropped to his knees in the middle of the room, hands clasped, his face grimaced in intensive silent prayer. They all stood and watched him for an awkward moment, as his public prayer seemed so out of place in a war room bustling with anxious aids, intelligence gathering, and shouting orders. One at a time, they walked over to him, got on their knees around him, and joined him in prayer for a miracle.

Washington, D.C.

"They're bluffing," Brighton speculated.

"With all due respect, Madam President," said General Green, "it is possible that they have armed a nuclear warhead and placed it on a ballistic missile that is pointed toward us right now." His fingers hovered over a laptop as he spoke, as if preparing to give important orders any moment.

"They haven't had time to do it," another general argued. "No way!" His eyes were fastened upon a computer monitor as he perused his intel updates.

General Green's eyes darted to the general who dared to challenge him in front of the president. "That's unbelievably naïve, sir." The general did not respond, and Green turned to the president. "It's too risky, Madam President. Do you want to gamble millions of lives on it? We're dealing with a nuclear armed Coalition now and we have to play according to different rules."

The president's gaze fixed on the rather subdued Air Force General beside General Green. "How long until the bombers will have reached their targets?"

They both glanced at their laptops but it was General Green who answered the question. "The mission will be completed in 19 minutes, Madam President."

"Are the Guard's fighter jets posing a problem for us?"

The Air Force general glanced at his subordinate behind him who was on hold with mission commanders at Edwards Air Force Base for an update. "Well?" the general asked him.

"As of ten minutes ago," the aid responded, "fighter pilot casualties were even between us, but not a single one of our B-52s has been brought down."

"Those stealth bombers give us an edge, Madam President."

"When the bombing campaign is completed, send them to take out those semis that are emitting radiation. Some of them may be Coalition semis with stolen nuclear warheads." She pointed to the map of the Coalition on a screen against the wall, which was a satellite image of every point in the Coalition that emitted radiation compatible with the signature of a nuclear warhead. The lead paint that covered the eighteen-wheelers carrying the Coalition's warheads was insufficient to eliminate detection of all radiation.

"But *we* are removing warheads in trucks too, Madam President. It is difficult to distinguish between theirs and ours."

"Then take them all out. We can't take the chance of them having a warhead in the morning."

Northwestern Montana

"Do you see it?" one of the radio controllers for the Guard's Air Force asked two Guard pilots as they sped northeast in their F-22 fighter jet. "It should be on your accessory screens."

"Yes sir. It's coming through clear now." The rearward pilot, whose name was John, cleared his throat. "Dear God!" he exclaimed.

"Jesus, help us!" the short, lean pilot, Trevor, uttered from the front seat of the cockpit when he realized the extent of the massive air invasion.

"Coalition aircraft are green, sonar-detectable enemy aircraft is white, and stealth enemy aircraft is red. Those double red blips are the B-52 Halo Fortresses that have the primary payload. Those are our main concern. It's satellite based; the image may fade or go out completely, so burn those vectors into your mind. I'd save it on one of your hard-drives if I were you in case we lose it. Governor Boswell is warning the president that he will fire our armed nuclear weapon if they don't–"

"*Our* nuclear weapon?" Trevor thought he'd misheard the radio controller. "Excuse me?"

"You were left in the dark about it, but now you know. We're threatening to fire it on the invaders if they don't call off the invasion and leave the Coalition immediately. It's a bluff. Probably."

"Probably?"

"Probably. We've got to shoot those stealth bombers out of the sky before they reach their target in case they do not abandon their mission."

"Changing vector to intercept nearest B-52." The lead pilot Trevor banked and changed directions.

The co-pilot, John, had to swallow hard to compensate for his nausea with the swift turn.

"Where are we threatening to fire that nuclear weapon, sir?" Trevor asked the Coalition radio controller.

"You don't have clearance for that," he responded with a proud smile that you could almost hear through the radio. "You just do your job and get that Helena-bound bomber. He's solo – no wingmen. Keep radio silence."

"Yes sir."

"Godspeed."

Trevor accelerated the stealth F-22 as fast as possible. "We should be coming to within range soon. John, do you see anything on sonar?"

"No. Wait. Yes."

Trevor studied the image, his finger on his trigger. "Where?"

"He was there but he's gone again."

"If he's an occasional flicker on our screen, we're no less on his."

"Is that supposed to be comforting?"

Lieutenant Chad Calhoun, a scrawny engineer with a gnarled nose and over-sized spectacles, was responsible for the arming of the nuclear warhead and placing it on the ballistic missile in an underground Guard facility huddled in the mountains of northwestern Montana.

"That should do it." One of the scientists who hovered over two laptops and a manual nodded at Lieutenant Calhoun.

"It's armed?"

"Yes."

"Well, let's get it on the missile!" Lieutenant Calhoun's heart pounded with adrenaline as he told his aid to call Boswell. Before she could make the call, General MacIntosh was on the phone for him.

"General MacIntosh wants to speak to you." The aid stretched the phone toward him.

"Good." He grabbed the phone. "General MacIntosh?"

Without any introductory comments, he blurted out, "We've got satellite-imaging of the bombers and there's one almost within firing range of you!"

"Excuse me? What's in firing range?"

"We think you're a target for one of their stealth B-52s. We have an F-22 in pursuit, but you may not have much time."

"We've got the warhead armed and we're inserting it now."

MacIntosh paused to inform Boswell.

"Fire it!" Boswell said without shifting his gaze from the satellite imaging on the wall. Everyone in the room froze at hearing the order. It was completely silent besides the buzzing of the computers all around them.

MacIntosh returned to the phone. "All right, Lieutenant, we've been ordered to–" The general paused and glanced back at Boswell, as if wanting to confirm the order.

"Tell him to fire!" Boswell ordered, eyeballing MacIntosh. "Aim it at Washington, D.C. and fire it! Get those dummy missiles in the air as soon as possible as well."

MacIntosh simply froze. He never thought it would go this far, and now he was being forced to give an order than could result in the deaths of millions, not even counting the deaths that would result from the retaliation that the CFC States could face. He meditated for a moment on something Boswell had said: future generations of Americans all over the country would have their freedoms restored with the decentralization of power that would surely result from the destruction of the tyrannical federal government's hub of power. That hope put his mind at ease a little at the thought of firing a nuclear weapon on Washington D.C. He felt like he was a part of something so big that it could only succeed after his death. He was a small cog in a huge mission to establish justice and restore liberties lost in his country. He swallowed hard and repeated the order: "Get that missile in the air, now, sir. Fire!"

"We're trying…"

MacIntosh hurriedly updated Lieutenant Calhoun: "As far as we can tell, Lieutenant, none of the other teams have acquired their nukes besides you. The feds did something to lock up the codes, and many of those silos were bombed before the nukes could be removed. The semis that are transporting our nukes are also being targeted. You're the only ones that can retaliate."

"You tell Lieutenant Calhoun," Boswell shouted at MacIntosh as he pointed at him, "that he needs to fire now, while he still can!"

The lieutenant handed the sat phone back to the aid and shouted at the engineers, "Bombers overhead any minute! We'll be under fire soon! Lock and load and get this missile in the air!"

Up until this point, it had all seemed like an amusing drill to the scientists and engineers who had armed the weapon and were presently loading it into a ballistic missile. But now, they were being ordered to actually *fire* a nuclear-armed supersonic ballistic missile on the capital of the United States! As if that weren't enough pressure, they were about to be carpet-bombed by a B-52 bomber. They all stopped, stared at each other, and hesitated.

"Did you hear what I said? Get moving! We're about to be fired upon by a B-52 bomber and this missile is the last chance the Coalition's got!"

"We, uh, we still have to program the coordinates, sir, after the missile is installed," an engineer informed him as he hastily turned the pages of a bound manual.

"Well, get going!"

The chief pilot of the now solo B-52 Halo Fortress instructed his bombardier through his headset, "Closing on target, Tara. Prepare to fire."

"Aye, sir." She typed hurriedly into her computer to prepare the weapon for launch.

The co-pilot slowed the bomber for release of its bombs onto one of the critical targets.

An unexpected radio transmission came through suddenly from the admiral managing the invasion air force from Edwards Air Force Base: "Abandon mission, I say again, abandon mission! Abandon Operation Iscariot at once…"

The face of the co-pilot showed disbelief. "What did he say?"

The radio operator repeated, "Abandon Operation Iscariot and return to base. Confirm receipt."

The pilot grunted. "Ugh, I hate politics. Just let the warriors win, will ya?"

The co-pilot responded coolly, "I'll confirm."

"No." The chief pilot stretched his right arm toward his co-pilot and motioned for him to let go of the radio transmitter button. "I don't want to take a chance that enemy fighters will hone in on our radio signal." He tapped a button on the panel in front of him to communicate with the bombardier. "Fire, Tara."

"Preparing to fire," the bombardier responded. From her seat toward the rear of the bomber cabin, she had not heard the admiral's radio order to call off the mission.

The co-pilot and the engineer behind them were stunned. "You're disobeying a direct order!" the co-pilot blurted out. "Admiral Mince ordered us to stand down!"

"He's right," the engineer agreed with the co-pilot.

"This is where we suspected they were storing the nuclear warheads they stole last night," the chief pilot argued. "Now, we'll take it out, confirm receipt of the new order, and then we'll return to–"

"No!" the co-pilot raised his voice. He pressed a button to communicate with the bombardier and countermand the senior pilot's explicit instructions. "Hold fire, Tara!" he ordered her. He saw the scowl on the rigid face of the chief pilot and turned back to the engineer for some moral support.

"No, sir!" the pilot snarled. "I'm the commander on the field of battle – it's my decision. As the rural target nearest the capitol of Helena, this is the most important target in the Coalition territory. My order remains. Fire, Tara."

The bombardier shrugged. "Firing missile," she stated as she typed her last few keys and prepared to hit "Enter".

"Someone's locked on us!" the defense systems manager squealed suddenly. "Radar-lock! 2-1-3 – from the rear! Closing fast!"

Just as the bombardier was about to press the enter button to fire her satellite-guided missile at its intended ground target, the chief pilot dove and turned the bomber right. The bombardier swayed in her seat and removed her finger from the enter key to grab the arms of her chair to steady herself.

"You gotta be kiddin' me!" the chief pilot exclaimed as he tried to out-maneuver the missile. "How in the world did they sneak up on us? We're supposed to be the ones doin' the sneakin'."

"Another missile!" the defense systems manager announced.

"What are you waiting for, Miley?"

Miley, the defense systems manager, fired two Stinger intercept missiles at the oncoming heat-seekers and prepared to fire a rear air-to-air missile at the invisible target in the darkness behind them.

One of the Stingers made contact, but the second Coalition missile was too close…

The B-52 Halo Fortress made a spectacular explosion of fire and debris that earned shouts of ecstasy from the Guard pilots. "We got 'em!" the Coalition pilot of the F-22 congratulated himself. "I don't think that's ever been done before."

"Yeah!" The gunman celebrated with a clenched fist heavenward. "The other fighters and bombers look like they are turning back," he said, glancing at the screen. "They're retreating!"

"Whoa! What was that?!" Lieutenant Calhoun wondered when the ground shook as with a loud clap of thunder under their feet. The engineers were only briefly distracted from their mission of getting their nuclear-armed missile launched. They knew they could die any minute and their best chance of making their death worthwhile was to get that missile airborne.

"Call it off!" General MacIntosh ordered Calhoun over his headset. "I repeat, call it off! Do ***not*** fire the nuclear missile, Lieutenant!"

"Cease fire!" Calhoun ordered, pointing at the computer engineer.

The engineer, who had just finished typing in the coordinates for Washington, D.C. into the computer, had a confused grimace on his face. "Call it off? What?"

"Do ***not*** fire!"

The engineers and nuclear scientists who had been sprinting to launch the weapon now froze in their tracks. They had just crossed the finish line in the race of their life, and now they were being told they needed to run back the opposite direction.

MacIntosh explained to Lieutenant Calhoun, “The federal bombers and fighter jets are retreating, Lieutenant. One of our F-22s just blew the B-52 that was targeting you out of the sky just over your heads.”

“Yeah, I felt it.” He turned and shouted at the engineers, “Call it off! Abort launch!”

“Uh, you’re about five seconds too late, Lieutenant,” the chief computer engineer responded. “We can’t turn it off. We can’t stop it.”

“What?” Lieutenant Calhoun pushed his dark-rimmed glasses higher on the bridge of his long, pointed nose, dripping with beads of sweat.

“When we rigged the nuclear weapon to arm it, we disconnected the mechanism to de-activate it. We’d have to design a de-activation maneuver...” The computer experts and nuclear physicists around the table had a look of horror on their faces at just the thought of having to quickly engineer a method of de-activating the nuclear weapon.

“You’re kidding me!” The lieutenant frantically leapt to his feet and lifted his voice to be heard by every scientist and guardsman frittering about the facility: “Does anybody know how to disarm this thing? The feds are retreating and we have an order to call it off!” The dozen scientists and engineers immediately rushed to their manuals and laptops to try to discover an answer to the question that no one had bothered to investigate. “Get those captured feds up here and see if they know.”

“We can’t turn it off!” Lieutenant Calhoun informed General MacIntosh over the phone. “The federal employees on site have no knowledge of it either.”

MacIntosh turned to Boswell. “They can’t reverse it. It’s gonna launch.”

“Put it on speaker,” Boswell ordered as one of the technicians hurriedly complied. When the technician nodded at Boswell, he said, “What do you mean you can’t call it off? We’ve got to stop this missile from going off now! Pull the plug...”

“If we have to disarm this weapon before it launches, sir, it would not be a wise use of my time to explain why we can’t disarm it. We might be able to disable the ballistic missile, but this nuclear weapon is detonating here or in D.C. – one or the other. We just can’t disarm the warhead.”

“It’s got a power source, doesn’t it?”

“It’s a little more complicated than that.” Lieutenant Calhoun turned to a nuclear engineer beside him, a redheaded older woman. “How much time do we have?”

“Two minutes and 19 seconds,” she chirped anxiously.

MacIntosh overheard the engineer’s response over their phone connection. He immediately turned toward the Coalition computer engineer nearest him. “See that Coalition F-22 just north of Missoula?” He pointed at a green flicker on the screen with his laser pointer.

The computer engineer nodded.

“Get them on this phone right now.”

Trevor expected praise when General MacIntosh called him, not another urgent mission assignment. He was still on cloud nine from his successful engagements when the general popped his bubble.

“You only have two minutes to complete this mission, so both of you listen carefully. Millions of lives are at stake.” General MacIntosh’s voice was calm, but hurried. “Take your F-22 to the coordinates where you destroyed the B-52, and in 115 seconds a nuclear-armed ballistic missile is going to come flying out of the ground at the speed of sound, headed for D.C. You’ve got to intercept it and blow it out of the sky.”

“What? I thought the feds retreated!”

“When we rigged the warhead to arm it we disconnected the mechanism needed to de-activate it. Just head to those coordinates now and we’ll talk about it on the way.”

“Yes sir.” Trevor turned the jet around and picked up speed.

“What happened?” John, the co-pilot, asked from the backseat.

“I don’t have time to explain!” MacIntosh answered. “You have one opportunity to blow that missile up, because approximately six seconds after it launches, it’ll be going faster than you or your missiles can go. Got that? You have to blow it up.”

“I don’t have any more missiles.”

MacIntosh gasped. “Have you expended all of your air-to-air ordinance?”

“Yes sir.”

The general sighed audibly and John felt nauseous again.

“No one else is close enough. You know what you have to do.”

Without hesitating, Trevor nodded dutifully. “Yes sir.”

“You have 105 seconds. You come down on top of it because you will never hit it from the side or from underneath, and try not to hit it too close to the ground because the explosion will kill everybody in that facility.”

“Will the nuclear weapon detonate?”

"No. If you destroy it there will be an explosion but not a nuclear one."

"We will succeed, sir. Please, um, tell my wife and family that," he fingered the picture in front of them, "tell them I love them and I can't wait to see them again in heaven."

"I will. We're praying for you. The fate of the Coalition may rest with you. I'm signing off to let you concentrate. Godspeed you."

"Ah!" John cried out from the back seat once the general disconnected. "I don't want to die!"

Trevor took a deep breath from the front cockpit. "John, the Bible says, 'O death where is thy sting, oh grave where is thy victory! The sting of death is sin.' If the thought of death stings, it may be because of sin in your life."

"Ah, Trevor," he heaved, a sob rising in his throat. "I'm a sinner. I'm just a rotten sinner."

Trevor smiled, tears welling in his eyes as he sensed the conviction in his friend and the favor of his heavenly Father just as the sunrise revealed a pink glow on the eastern horizon. "Jesus!" Trevor passionately cried out with a broad smile on his face. "Say it after me, John."

"Jesus!" John repeated.

"I'm a sinner."

"I am such a sinner."

"I turn from all my sins."

"I turn from all my sins."

"Forgive me and accept me into your kingdom…"

The mission commander in the underground nuclear facility turned to the redheaded woman beside him. "How many seconds left?"

"Twenty-nine," she responded.

They watched the video projected on the large screen on the wall, which showed the missile in real time at the far end of the underground facility. Steam began to discharge from the rear of the 150-foot tall ballistic missile as it slowly rose through the hole that opened in the ground.

General MacIntosh paced the command center of the underground Guard bunker, surrounded by anxious Coalition leaders and senior Guard officials. "Can you redirect it, Lieutenant?" MacIntosh suggested. "Send it to the ocean, or to space?"

The engineers overheard the suggestion and it was as if a light bulb had gone off. "I think so," the senior engineer exclaimed. "Why didn't I think of that? Let's reprogram the coordinates!"

"Can we do it this close to–"

"We've got to try!" the lieutenant interrupted.

"What coordinates? I don't know any coordinates off the top of my head except my home."

Another engineer complained, "Twenty seconds doesn't give us much time to–"

"Those coordinates!" Lieutenant Calhoun pointed at the satellite images projected onto the large screen on the wall. "Those numbers at the bottom of that screen are the spatial coordinates of that satellite."

"We'll lose our satellite."

"Do it!"

"General MacIntosh," the lieutenant said as the chief engineer tried to insert new coordinates into the ballistic missile's computer. "We're trying to reprogram it for space."

"Are you sure? Is that safe?"

"I think so." Lieutenant Calhoun turned to one of his computer engineers, pushing his dark-rimmed glasses up his nose. "Can you lock in the new coordinates?" he asked nervously as the countdown neared zero.

"I may not know how to turn off a hijacked nuclear-armed ballistic missile," he responded with a nerdy grin, "but if there's one thing I do know how to do like the back of my hand, it's–"

"Please!" someone shouted at him. "Use shorter sentences!"

"It's done!" The engineer typing at the laptop removed his hands from the keyboard just as the ballistic missile began to eject brightly colored flames from its rear, rising eerily toward the dawn sky.

General MacIntosh shouted at the phone operator. "Get those F-22 pilots back on the line."

"Yes sir."

"Hurry!"

"I see it!" Trevor said as he turned the nose of the jet down and began to pick up speed in a vertical dive toward the ballistic missile as it rose from the ground toward them.

"Seven seconds to impact." John had a newfound confidence in his tone. "Don't miss it. See you in heaven, my friend."

In his mind's eye, Trevor tried to imagine what he would see when he crossed over.

"Trevor!" General MacIntosh called out to the pilot over the radio.

"Four seconds to impact..."

"Turn away! Abort!"

"Abort?"

"Abort!" MacIntosh shouted.

Trevor twitched his controls to the right and the F-22 twisted and barely missed the nuclear-armed ballistic missile, but the flames ejecting from the rear of the missile sent them into a spin toward the ground at the speed of sound.

"John! I can't control it! Eject!"

"Trevor!" MacIntosh shouted into his headset. "Trevor! John!" He glanced at the phone operator, who shrugged.

"Did they hit the missile?" Governor Boswell asked from one knee. "Has the missile changed course or is it still headed for D.C.?"

MacIntosh anxiously picked up the phone: "Lieutenant! What happened? What's the condition of the pilots?"

"Uh, the missile is still functional and–"

"Has it changed course?" MacIntosh shouted.

"It's too early to say."

The redheaded scientist beside Calhoun spoke up. "We'll know if the missile changes course in about 20 seconds when its trajectory would turn east if headed to D.C., but continue straight if it's headed to the satellite."

"Incoming!" another engineer across the room warned.

"What's incoming?" Lieutenant Calhoun barked.

"Collision in three seconds," the engineer said, reading a radar image on his computer.

Suddenly, the underground nuclear facility shook as if by a sudden earthquake. The lights blinked and sheetrock fell from the 20-foot ceilings.

Everyone braced themselves until the rumbling subsided. "What was that?" Calhoun wondered.

"That was the crashing of an F-22," the engineer in front of the radar screen said. He pointed at another screen that showed video surveillance of the west side of the facility. Huge balls of flames erupted along the fence line just 50 yards away from the front entrance.

"And there's our two pilots." Another engineer motioned to video surveillance screen that showed the north side of the facility. They saw two parachutes slowly drifting to the ground about a quarter of a mile away.

Washington, D.C.

"They launched it!" General Green exclaimed with alarm as he glanced at the satellite imaging of the retreating federal bombers and fighters.

The president exhaled a foul curse as she rose from her seat in the bowels of the Pentagon's underground bunker. She turned to face the chief of the Armed Forces. "They launched what?"

He took a laser pointer out of his pocket and pointed at the screen on the wall. "Right there! That's a ballistic missile."

"Retaliate!" the president shouted at General Green. "That's a nuclear armed missile aimed at us!"

The general wanted to cast doubt on the satellite imaging – he just couldn't believe that the Coalition would actually fire a nuclear missile at their own country. But he could see the Commander-in-Chief would not be prevailed upon. He made a call on his sat phone and began to hurriedly give orders to his chain of command to unleash their worst-case contingency response against the CFC States. They were turning the Coalition's capitals and large cities into wastelands.

"The missile has launched and has not changed course yet," Lieutenant Calhoun informed MacIntosh. "We will know in a moment."

"Madam President," a phone operator called out, "it's Governor Boswell."

She snatched the phone up from its cradle. "Have you launched a nuclear missile at us?" she squealed, her knuckles white around the black phone's handle. General Green waved to the phone operator and asked him to plug him in to the call so he could hear the conversation from a phone across the room. She nodded and he picked up the phone.

Governor Boswell responded calmly. "This one's going into space, and we will make a point with it. We are willing to defend ourselves."

"Are you telling me that this is *not* aimed at us?"

"The trajectory will continue into space, Madam President."

"It looks like he's telling the truth," General Green said, noting that the missile was not turning east as expected.

"Let this be a lesson to you, Mrs. Brighton," Boswell lectured her. "We will be free or you will perish trying to enslave us. Do you understand?"

She scratched her chin with a bright red fingernail, and did not respond.

"I'll call off the nuclear response." General Green tapped "flash" on the phone base and speed-dialed a number.

The president unexpectedly hung up on the Coalition chairman and waved her hand at the general. "No. Continue as planned." She stood over her desk with her palms on her desk and closed her eyes.

"What?" The general held the phone, which was ringing on the other end of the line, at arm's length. "You heard him. The missile is not heading toward us."

"The missile *is* going outside the atmosphere, Madam President," an admiral raised his voice. "It's *not* a threat to us now."

"It's an attack upon our satellites, and that's an act of war!" she barked.

"We don't know that! Please, call it off!" the Air Force general urged as he walked toward the president's desk. He became more emphatic when the president did not appear to be moved by his recommendation: "Call it off! Or millions of Americans will die needless deaths! Call it off!"

Someone picked up on the other end of the phone that General Green held in his hand. "Hold on!" General Green told them.

The president reluctantly realized that with so much protest among the high command of the armed forces, she could never get away with her nuclear response.

"All right," she mumbled at General Green. "Call it off."

Margaret Brighton plopped back into her chair as the staff in the room exchanged handshakes and sighs of relief.

"He's either insane or he's the bravest man alive," the president said softly with a blank stare on her face, speaking to no one in particular.

* * * * *

The headquarters where Governor Boswell and the Idaho governor huddled with their top aids and Guard generals erupted in clapping and shouting after they saw the bombers finally leave the borders of the CFC States. Shouts of praise and thanksgiving filled the room. Boswell's men gathered around and began to congratulate their governor with handshakes and hugs.

15

Helena, Montana

David entered the basement room of the church elder with whom he stayed, and it was as if his energy just drained out of him. He suddenly found his mind and body void of all the passion that had kept him encouraging and leading the saints in prayer for victory through the night. He felt like collapsing in a puddle on the floor and falling asleep right there.

On his heels was his bodyguard, Matt Wellington, the Austin sheriff.

"Praise God!" Matt exclaimed, inadvertently flexing his muscular arms as he clasped his hands in front of him. "God has given us the victory, David!" The sheriff-turned-bodyguard was as enthusiastic as a child on Christmas morning.

"Yeah." David's countenance was more forlorn than Matt expected. The last hour of victory shouts, handshakes, and hugs filled them all with euphoria, but David held a secret pain that his facial grimace only just now began to reveal. The mini-DVD he had found in the pages of his Bible during prayer was burning a hole in his back pocket.

"Are you gonna sleep or you gonna go ahead and stay awake?" Matt glanced at the clock on the desk that read 7:59 a.m.

"I don't know. We'll see how I feel." He retrieved the mini-DVD out of the back pocket of his jeans and kicked his flip-flops into the open closet.

Matt headed into the bathroom first and got the shower running and David breathed deeply as he flipped the DVD in his hand and studied the strange fluorescent pink hue underneath it. There were no marks on it.

He studied the message written in marker on the yellow DVD jacket, the words that had tormented him all night: "It's about Darlene."

He ejected the DVD player compartment of his computer, inserted the mini-DVD, and pushed the button and watched it retract into the computer. His heart throbbed rapidly. How did this DVD get in his Bible and who put it there? Who around him could know anything about his wife? And if someone knew something about his wife, why didn't they come to him instead of putting a message on a DVD?

"DAVID JAMESON, YOU MUST LEAVE THE CFC STATES IMMEDIATELY."

White words flashed up on the black screen and stayed on the screen for ten seconds. Then the screen went black. David's heart skipped a beat. He realized that this was definitely the handiwork of an enemy. Then the words appeared on the black screen: "IN ORDER TO STOP THIS…"

David's mouth went dry. He leaned into the computer for a long ten seconds until the next screen began to play.

The video showed a close up view of his nude wife with her arms and legs handcuffed to a metal chair. Electrodes were placed on her wrists and ankles as she shivered uncontrollably.

"Oh God! Darlene!" David wailed in horror, bursting into tears as he touched the screen with both of his hands, as if trying to conceal her nakedness from the faceless strangers that hovered over her.

"Please, please, please!" she squealed between rapid breaths as drool dripped down her chin.

David screamed in horror at the sight.

"We know your husband was behind the terrorist attack that killed the president," the unseen tormenter calmly stated in a thick French accent. "Where is he? Who were his accomplices?"

"My husband abandoned me!"

The interrogator pressed a button releasing voltage through the wires into her extremities and she convulsed uncontrollably, letting out a terrified gurgle.

"Oh God no!!!" David stood and grabbed the sides of the computer screen with both hands.

Matt heard David's frantic cry and rushed into the bedroom with a towel around his waste, his chest heaving with adrenaline. "What is it?! What's wrong?!"

Matt glanced at the computer screen that David grasped as if it were a life raft upon which his life depended. The screen was black with a message in bold white letters. “DON’T ABANDON HER DAVID JAMESON. TURN YOURSELF IN TO FEDERAL AUTHORITIES AND WE WILL SET HER FREE.”

Then the screen turned to static.

“It was there!” David exclaimed, his head in his hands, his sleepless, bloodshot eyes dry of tears. Jared sat beside him, his hand resting on his shoulder.

“I only saw the last message,” Matt Wellington said, staring at Governor Boswell who grasped a cup of coffee in his hands. Matt tossed the DVD in its clear case onto the governor’s breakfast table. “It had some kind of delete mechanism after one showing. It’s unretrievable.”

Governor Boswell sighed deeply, half dressed in an untucked T-shirt and brown dress pants, his fingers tapping against the red-and-white-checkered dining table cloth, casting shadows from the morning sun across the room and onto the wall. The governor leaned in to David, his elbows on the table. “David, why do they want you to turn yourself in so badly? Why are you so important to them? It doesn’t make sense.”

David sighed. He knew it was time to come clean with the Montana governor. “My name’s not David Jamestown.”

Jared took a deep breath and took a step back, observing the Montana governor’s reaction. Boswell didn’t appear upset. “It’s not?”

“No. It’s Jameson. David Jameson.”

Boswell turned his gaze upward and squinted, as if looking for answers in the contour of grain in the wood ceiling. “David Jameson,” he mumbled. “Where do I know that name?”

“I was accused of setting off the bomb in Ohio that killed President Fitzgerald.”

The governor stood to his feet and spilled his coffee, his body tense. “What?”

“He didn’t do it, of course,” Jared responded. “Josh Davis’ investigative reports have proven that.”

“But I put you in charge of the Minutemen, David! Didn’t you know what the accusation against you could mean to our cause, our Coalition?”

David sighed and turned away to face the window into the back yard, speechless.

The governor’s tension eased and he plopped back into his seat and laughed. “Oh God,” he mumbled as he rubbed the back of his neck with his right hand. “You truly work in mysterious ways, Lord.” His gaze turned to David. "You didn't volunteer for that position, David. I insisted. You tried to turn me down, remember?"

"Now you know why. You wouldn't take no for an answer."

"God wanted you in that position, David." Boswell took a sip of the last few drops of warm liquid that remained in his coffee cup. He took a napkin and sopped up the coffee puddle on the kitchen table.

Wellington nodded in agreement. "I think He still does."

David shook his head, his gaze fixed on an empty tire swing that swung in the Montana breeze in the Boswell's back yard.

"David," Jared ventured to say, "if you leave, you're giving them what they want."

"I agree," Wellington said, leaning back on the rear two legs of the kitchen chair in which he sat.

"It doesn't matter," David snapped. "My first obligation is to my wife and family."

"Don't you feel some responsibility to train the Minutemen?" Boswell asked. "You founded it. It was your idea, David."

David turned to Boswell. "You know that my first duty is to God and my second duty is to my family. Darlene is suffering. She–" ...*thinks I abandoned her* is how he would have concluded that sentence, but he forced himself to stop. Predicting that he would be unable to restrain an outburst of his incredible grief except by forced silence, he pressed his lips tightly together.

"Whoever gave you this DVD works for the federal government," said Matt Wellington, glancing back and forth from David to Governor Boswell. "You said that the interrogator in the video asked your wife where you were. They know where you are, David – that's how they snuck you the DVD! If they had evidence that you were guilty, they'd be broadcasting it in order to disparage the Coalition, but they can't prove anything and they know it."

"It doesn't make sense," Boswell added.

"The president claims that the evidence from the investigation of the Columbus explosion was lost in the Billings bombing," Wellington said. "They have no evidence to convict you besides circumstantial."

Boswell went to the coffee machine and poured himself a fresh cup. "They're wanting you to confess so that they can pin the attack on you without exposing their lack of evidence, David."

"I'll never confess," he assured them.

"Yes, you will," the governor replied.

"No, I–"

"Yes, you will!" The governor sat back down and grabbed the DVD on the kitchen table. "They showed you your wife's suffering and you are leaving the Coalition, something you otherwise wouldn't do."

"I was going to leave anyway to find my family, once things settled down in Texas."

"They'll make you do anything they want by flaunting your wife's suffering, David. You must see that. Can you bear to be in the same room and watch your children endure things like this?" He held the mini-DVD between his second and third fingers. "Do you think things'll go better for her if you turn yourself in, David?" He tossed the DVD back onto the kitchen table. "Your family is their upper hand on you. If you turn yourself in, you will have proven to them that they can use her to get you to do things that you would not otherwise do. If you leave, you will either be put to death or sentenced to solitary for the rest of your life. And your wife still won't be freed. Your kids will remain in foster care."

"They'll have no reason to keep her!"

"She'll be charged as your accomplice, David!"

David shook his head vigorously. "I've got to leave. I've got to! The Bible says that whatsoever is not of faith is sin. If turning myself in to the feds would even have a faint chance of alleviating Darlene's suffering, then I know it'd be wrong for me to stay. I, I, I couldn't live with myself," he stuttered.

"You're giving them what they want, Pastor," Jared said. "You've got to fight 'em. Don't bow to their will."

Jared leaned forward and placed his index finger on the DVD. "You said that your wife, in the video, told the interrogator that you abandoned her. Right?"

David sighed and said softly, "Yes."

"That's what you wanted her to tell them, right?" Jared exclaimed, his eyes lighting up. He nodded at David, who nodded back.

"That's good," said Boswell. He began to tap his finger rhythmically against his coffee mug.

"Yeah," said David, a glimmer of hope in his eyes.

"That tells me that she's holding up." Boswell stopped tapping his finger and took a sip of his coffee. "With what they can do with computer-generated animation now-a-days, making it look so realistic, the whole video could be a fake."

"When the enemy screams 'Stop!'" said Matt, "you double your efforts. You never, ever give up. You work harder training Minutemen and help lay a foundation for our new nation. Don't let the devil's will be done."

David kept his gaze fixed on the empty tire swing on the other side of the window. He tried to imagine his daughters playing in it some day, but he couldn't see it in his mind's eye. "I'm leaving. I'm sorry. You have men to continue the work. Lord willing, I'll be back with my family."

Matt glanced at the governor and shrugged, knowing that David had a made-up mind. "I'll go with him."

"I'll go, too," Jared proposed.

"No, Jared," said David. "You're a wanted man. You'll only make the journey more risky."

"Don't you know you're gonna get caught as soon as you're seen?" said Jared. "That shaved scalp and that stubble on your chin isn't much of a disguise." David was trying to let his beard grow out to better disguise his facial features, but it was a pathetic, scraggly beard.

The governor studied David for several seconds. "Well, how can I help you do what God wants you to do?"

David returned to the breakfast table and sat down. "It'd be nice if you could help me with some intel and give me a secure line to call some of our friends in Texas. Maybe they've heard something."

"What good's that going to do if you're just going to turn yourself in?" Jared wondered.

"Well, if there's a chance I can find her and break her out, then–"

"Break her out of a United-Nations-guarded facility in a martial-law-managed war zone?" Jared mocked the folly of the whole idea. "You and what army?"

"Me and the army of the Austin Sheriff," David responded. Matt Wellington laughed for a moment, and then stopped when he saw that David didn't mean that as a joke. "Didn't Jonathan and his armor-bearer defeat a squad of Philistine soldiers by themselves and lead the way into defeating an entire army?"

Matt set his coffee mug down as if he'd just lost his appetite for it. He crossed his thick, muscular arms over his bulging chest. "If you can have faith for a miracle, so can I." He looked at David and grinned. "Do all that's in your heart. I'm with you."

The governor gave David a strange smile. "I've got an idea of something we can do to increase the likelihood of them letting her go."

"What?"

Austin, Texas

"She's naïve. She trusts me. This plan will work." Janet, the undercover agent who befriended Darlene in the detention facility, sat around the room with five other UN and Army interrogators and officers. "Let me break out with her and she'll lead us to her husband."

Her superior, a British UN captain, shook his head as he sat, stiff-jawed, in front of a leather bound notebook on a wooden table in the windowless room. "You don't understand. There's…" He paused and sighed. "This won't be easy for you to hear."

"What?!" Agent Boltere's eyes darted from person to person.

"We already know where her husband is."

Janet Boltere sat still for a moment, expecting a punchline that would spark laughter throughout the room. Momentarily, she realized that the captain was serious.

"What?" Agent Boltere was furious. She stood up from her chair and smacked her palms on the table. "How long have you known this?" She paused to let the captain answer, but he remained silent, either unwilling or unable to give a satisfactory answer. "I have sacrificed a month of my life in miserable conditions to gain her trust. I even bore 20 lashes from Lieutenant Wenbrond's whip just to earn her trust!"

The UN captain looked down at his notes and thinned his lips. "Information is not being shared as freely as we would like," he said with a shake of the head, "but it's getting better."

"Has he been captured? Does he have accomplices? Can Darlene be interrogated for the answers to different questions?" she stammered out the questions quickly like a machine gun. "Does she–"

"No, no, no." The superior waved his hands out in front of him. "She's useless to us. We should re-educate her and then re-integrate her into society."

"She's as re-educated as she's going to get. She's harmless. But how can you say she's useless?" Agent Boltere asked with exasperation.

"Under interrogation, she's given us everything that's worth getting," another interrogator assured them.

"Don't we still want to capture this man? Even if you know where he is, you still may need my help in capturing him. He killed the former president and over a thousand abortionists and pro-choice leaders! He's a high value target." Even Agent Boltere's superiors were not high enough in command to know that he had been falsely accused of that.

"He's a leader in the CFC States," the UN captain stated. "We can't capture him because he's surrounded with armed guards. The president won't risk another catastrophe like the failed FBI raid in Helena. And the president needs David Jameson to be put on trial, not killed."

"Well, let me do it! Let us break free. I'll bribe the guard Ramone with stolen money. Darlene's already aware that he can be bribed and she already knows I've been hiding the means. When we're out, I know she'll lead me to her husband. She thinks I'm childless and my husband has a long federal prison term, and she has already invited me to be with her when we're released." Agent Boltere acted like this was the plan of the century, but her superior was not convinced.

"The Federal Bureau of Investigation already has personnel close to Mr. Jameson," the UN captain stated in his untempered British accent. "They're working on a plan to take the Coalition leadership down in one fell swoop. It's just a matter of time."

"Well, what am I good for?" Agent Boltere complained as she plopped back into her chair and crossed her arms over her chest.

"This isn't about you," the UN captain reminded her.

A senior interrogator glanced at the captain with raised eyebrows. "Why not let them break out?" Agent Boltere measured the senior interrogator's every word and the captain's facial cues as they carefully weighed their options. "What do we have to lose? We were going to let her go anyway. Maybe she will get some unique intel as Darlene's friend and she'll be able to help out the Bureau."

The UN captain twitched his nose and looked down at his pad. He scribbled himself a note and then put his pen back in his top pocket. "I'll speak to the FBI director and see if he can use you."

Helena, Montana

"All right." Matt started the ignition in the loaned Coalition van, and then turned to look at David in the passenger seat. "Are we ready to do this?"

David tightened his seat belt and nodded confidently.

"Let's go get her."

On the outskirts of Helena, they turned off the interstate and headed south on a back road. David's thoughts were on Darlene. How David missed his wife! The thought of seeing her again brought tears to his eyes. He could only imagine where his children were. He began to pray silently for them, his eyes fixed on the mountains on the western horizon.

"Hang in there, David. It won't be long now."

"You think so?" David turned to glance at Wellington briefly, then turned his gaze back out the open window as the breeze teased the dirty blond hairs on his chin.

"Sooner, rather than later."

Without warning, Matt pulled the van's steering wheel to the right and drove the van into a ditch. The front bumper stuck into the mud and the vehicle began to flip end over end, sending glass and scraps of the van's frame all over the road.

An oncoming vehicle skidded to a stop and the driver rushed to offer aid. He discovered the van's driver and passenger unconscious in the upside down van on the far side of the irrigation ditch on the edge of a cornfield. David was breathing rapidly and bleeding profusely from a scalp wound.

He cut David's seatbelt with a pocketknife and David fell to the glass-shard-covered crumpled van ceiling.

Austin, Texas

From his office at the detention facility, the UN captain watched the news report in astonishment.

"David Jameson, wanted for the bombing of the Reproductive Rights Convention in Ohio that killed President Fitzgerald, died this morning in a tragic auto accident," the newscaster announced. "He was an influence on Texas Governor Henry Adams before he rebelled against the government. Some say he had become a renown religious leader hailed by some as the prophet of the Coalition of Free Christian States, who went by the alias David Jamestown…"

The television showed footage of him covered with blood and being rushed from an ambulance through an Emergency Department's double doors.

"A group of anti-government religious extremists who call themselves the Minutemen is honoring David Jameson with a special funeral on Friday…"

The UN captain picked up the sat phone and got the Bureau on the phone. This changed everything.

Uninformed of the publicized death of David Jameson, the undercover personality of Agent Boltere was preparing to break out of the FEMA camp with Darlene. "Shhh!" Janet quieted the dreamful stirring of Darlene Jameson at 3 a.m. Darlene roused from her bunk and sat up. “Quiet!” Janet whispered. “Ramone agrees and–”

“Really?” Darlene exclaimed in a hushed whisper.

“He took a little convincing, but we have a doorway of opportunity through the south exit. Here.” She pushed a pair of sweat pants at her. “He gave us these. There’s no guard at that tower right now and there’s a hole dug under the barbwire that hasn’t been re-filled yet. Apparently someone else tried to escape two nights ago. They’ve got a board over it with some bricks.”

This sounded too good to be true to Darlene. How could they not have a guard at the same place where there was a hole dug under the barbed wire? “I think, on second thought, I’m not going to go. You go.” Darlene nudged her friend Janet to the door. “I’ll be getting out of here soon and I don’t want to blow it.”

This stunned Janet. “What are you talking about? I’m doing this for you.”

“Shhh!” someone urged from a neighboring bunk.

Janet spoke more softly, “Ramone told me that they are moving you up to Ivan in the morning.”

“What?!” Darlene had a look of horror on her face. Ivan was the most severe and sadistic of the male camp interrogators, who tortured, mutilated, and sexually abused men at the men’s camp two miles away. They called him Bluebeard, after the pirate who was renown for raping and murdering over 800 little boys. Ivan only occasionally came to the female camp. Of the three women Ivan had interrogated, one was dead, one went insane, and the third had disappeared, presumably because she shared information that secured her release. “Why?” Darlene asked the question that she knew Janet couldn’t answer. “What did I do?”

“Darlene, if you stay, you’ll die. Or worse – there are some things worse than death, you know. I can’t stand the thought of you in Bluebeard’s grip. He’s a sadist. He enjoys causing extreme physical and emotional suffering. Please, this is our chance. God’s making a way for us.”

Darlene appeared deep in thought. Janet patted her on the shoulder. “There’s something else Ramone told me that you should know. Your husband is working with the Montana government.”

“What?”

Janet nodded, measuring her facial cues to try to discern whether this was something Darlene already knew and had concealed from them.

"He heard it on the news, Darlene. You're husband's like a famous spiritual leader."

Without warning, Darlene grabbed both of Janet's hands and began to pray, "Dear Father, keep us safe. We need your help to protect us from those who would do us harm…" Janet was taken aback at the sudden, sincere prayer of Darlene. She judged her to be a sweet, homely woman with a pretty face who had the unfortunate curse of being married to a maniacal terrorist. But we all are the property of the state, Agent Boltere reasoned, and property must be managed for the good of all. Personal comforts and natural rights take a back seat to social order. Agent Boltere's face flushed as Darlene concluded her passionate prayer: "Our lives are in your hands now. Unite me with my husband and all my children, dear Lord. In Jesus' precious name, Amen."

"So we're going?" Janet asked, bright-eyed.

"God will keep us safe." Darlene declared her faith with a tearful nod.

After they made their way past the unmanned tower and the barbed wire fence, they jogged through the desert, evading cactuses and jagged rocks in the light of the full moon directly over their heads. They found an abandoned car on a narrow dirt road about a mile away. "Come on! Maybe the keys are in it," Janet said, jogging ahead.

Darlene was exhausted from the jog through the desert sands, but she still had her wits about her. "You're foolin' yourself. What are the chances?"

"It's open!" Janet said, opening the door to the two door royal blue Sedan. "And the battery's still good," she said when the light came on in the car. "Maybe they arrested someone here and haven't gotten the opportunity to tow the car yet?"

Darlene's jog slowed to a walk as she came upon the vehicle. She fell to her knees beside the passenger door and grunted.

"You okay?" Janet asked, coming around the car to check on her.

Without a word, Darlene leaned forward and vomited on the dirt road. Janet knelt beside her. "What happened? Are you comin' down with something?"

Darlene sat up and wiped her mouth. "Just a nervous stomach, I guess."

Janet helped her to her feet and into the passenger seat. Janet sprinted around to the driver's side and plopped into the seat. Suddenly, she squealed gleefully.

"Shhh," Darlene reproved her. "Keep it down."

Janet pointed underneath the steering wheel, informing Darlene why she was so elated. "Keys! There are keys in it!" She cranked the car as Darlene opened the door and stepped out with a troubled grunt. Janet got out and spoke to her over the roof of the car. "Come on! What are you doing?"

"It's not our car."

"We're going to die or get re-captured in this desert if you don't get in. They must have arrested the owner. The owner would want us to use it to get free. We'll get it back to them…"

Darlene planted her hands on her hips. "This is not our car, Janet. Someone could be walking around here somewhere. We're not taking off in their car."

Janet lifted up her voice and yelled at the top of her lungs. "Hello? Anybody there?" After a moment, she turned to Darlene. "People don't go for walks around here, Darlene. This is no man's land. God's given us manna in the desert and you'd rather starve. I don't understand you sometimes."

Darlene pointed at Janet over the roof of the car. "We *will* find out who owns this car and get this back to them."

"Of course." When they sat in the car, Janet looked at Darlene and could immediately discern that Darlene was suspicious of all of the extremely convenient circumstances.

"Darlene, you prayed for God to help us, why should we be surprised when he does?"

Darlene did not say a word, but buckled up as Janet started the car and shifted into drive. "Let's just get as far away from here as possible."

Looking in the storage area between the two front seats, Darlene found a dead cell phone. She found a power cord in the glove compartment.

Janet looked at her and laughed. "I'm half expecting to find some warm biscuits in the glove compartment."

Darlene gave Janet half a grin and plugged the cell phone into the dash power outlet.

After breakfast at a fast food drive-thru an hour away, Janet urged Darlene to call her husband. "The governor's office should be open now. You should call and find out where he is."

"Don't you think that the feds are monitoring any calls to the Montana governor's office?"

"You have to at least try it." Janet was growing impatient with Darlene's skepticism.

Darlene dialed 411 and asked for the phone number for the governor's office in Helena, and the operator put her through.

"Governor Benjamin Boswell's office, may I help you?"

"Yes ma'am," Darlene spoke with a slight tremor in her voice. "I'm looking for information about somebody who I think is probably close to the leadership. I need to see him."

"What's his name, ma'am?"

"David Jameson."

"Of course. The funeral will be Friday at noon at the Helena Christian Church."

The color drained from Darlene's thin face. "Funeral? What? David's dead?"

The secretary paused. "He died in a tragic car accident yesterday." When there was silence at the end of the phone, she asked, "Are you all right ma'am? May I ask who's calling?"

When Darlene did not answer, the secretary asked again. "Who is this?"

"Darlene," she mumbled, still in a state of shock.

"Darlene who?"

"I'm, I'm, I'm sorry to bother you." Darlene's tears began to flow freely, and a deep sob erupted from within her. She dropped the cell phone on the floor and began to sob with her head between her knees.

"Darlene! What is it?" Janet placed her palm on the back of her head.

"He's dead!" she wailed pitifully. "David's dead!"

"Darlene? Hello?" The secretary called out to the mourning woman just as Governor Boswell was walking past her into his office. "Governor, isn't David's wife named Darlene?"

"Yes." His eyebrows raised in anticipation. "Is that her on the phone?"

"She asked for David's whereabouts, and when I told her about the funeral, she started weeping, just bitterly weeping." The secretary raised the phone. "She called him David Jameson, but I think she was referring to David Jamestown. She could be asking about someone else, I don't know. I can still hear her weeping on the other end of the line, but she won't respond to me."

Ben Boswell took the phone and put it to his ear. "Is this Darlene Jameson? Darlene?" He raised his voice to be heard over her weeping. "Darlene! Can you hear me?"

They could not hear the governor's voice on the cell phone because Darlene had dropped it on the floor. She alternated between loud sobbing and fervent prayer. She pounded her chest with her fists, overwhelmed by grief. Over and over she implored for God to help her and to be her comfort.

Boswell turned to the secretary. "Do you have a caller ID?"

She nodded and grabbed a pen. "I'll write down the number."

"You!" He pointed to an aid who sat at another desk beside the secretary, opening mail. "Listen to that line and shout into the receiver intermittently, trying to get her attention. Let me know if they start talking into the phone again."

Darlene felt her heart would break. She opened the door to the car and began to run into a field of tall grass beside the fast food restaurant. Janet called out to her, but Darlene's pace did not slow. About 50 yards into the field, she collapsed. Janet caught up to her, her eyes moist at the sight of such pitiful grief.

"He's dead!" She wept on her knees, her forehead against the ground still wet with dew. "Oh, my God! He's dead!"

After an hour of praying and weeping in the middle of the grassy field, Janet was growing impatient. "Oh, Darlene." Janet fell to her knees beside her, her hand gently caressing her back. "I'm sorry, but a police officer could see our car and call in the license plate. We really need to head back to the car."

Darlene had wept all her tears out. She raised her head and turned her eyes to Janet. "Why didn't I pray for my husband more? I was so caught up in my own suffering, that I neglected to pray for my husband." Her eyes were red and eyelids swollen. Her mouth and lips were cracked and dry. Janet pitied her. "Janet, what am I going to do now?"

"I'll tell you what you're going to do," she said confidently, putting an arm around both shoulders and squeezing her tight. "We're going to visit every elementary school within 30 miles of where you were captured and we're going to find your oldest daughter. Once we find her, we're going to follow her bus to the home of her foster parents and, hopefully, to your other daughters. Then we're going to get your kids back with their mother who loves them." To this point, it was all about capturing David Jameson. But now she sincerely wanted to help the poor woman find her kids.

Darlene didn't even bother to look at the phone when it rang. As Janet found a parking spot on the far edge of a Walmart parking lot, Darlene was pre-occupied studying the phone book in the back seat, putting the location of the elementary schools in Austin on a map with a dot of red marker and designating them with a number in pencil.

"Who could that be?" Janet mumbled.

"It could be the government trying to track us. Don't answer it."

Janet picked up the phone to examine the caller ID, and then she turned the ringing phone toward Darlene. "It's the same area code as the office of the Montana governor."

Just the thought of Montana renewed the grief in Darlene's bosom. She winced, and looked back down at her map.

Janet answered the phone. "Hello?" she said softly. After a moment, Janet's brow furrowed. "Who's this?" Her eyes suddenly brightened and a thin smile shone up her face. "It's for you." Janet extended the cell phone to Darlene.

Darlene had an inquisitive look on her tired face. She put it to her ear. "Hello?"

"Darlene, is that you?"

Darlene couldn't believe her ears. "David?"

"Yes, it's me!" Tears gently flowed down David Jameson's unshaven cheeks. "I'm so sorry for how you have suffered. How were you freed? What happened?"

"David? You're alive?" Was she dreaming? Was her husband really alive?

"Yes, of course," he faked a laugh, trading broad smiles with Matt Wellington. "Faking my death was Governor Boswell's plan to convince your captors that there was nothing to gain from keeping you anymore. I never thought it would work so quickly..."

"David, you're alive?" she repeated. It had not yet begun to sink in. She had grieved so deeply over her husband's death that the whole conversation seemed like a hallucination she found difficult to believe. "David, is it really you?" She clutched the phone to her ear with both hands as if she had a direct line to heaven.

"Yes, it's me! And I love you with all my heart, my dear."

At hearing these comforting words, Darlene finally began to cry tears of joy. "Oh, thank you Jesus!" She raised her right hand toward heaven as the tears flowed down her cheeks in rivers. “You’re alive! And you love me.” Janet watched Darlene rejoice in the rear view mirror, and her ambition was stirred at the thought that this poor, naïve woman was going to lead her right to the nation’s most dangerous enemy combatant.

“Do you *really* love me?”

At hearing Darlene’s words, David began to cry more freely, trying to hold back the sob in his throat so he could be understood over the phone. “Of course I love you! You are the love of my life. Soon we will be together again, and I will hold you in my arms and whisper it in your ear.”

“Oh David!”

“Where are you?”

“We are in Austin. Um, Janet?” Darlene wiped her tears and glanced at her ecstatic friend in the driver’s seat in front of her. “Where are we in Austin?”

“He can’t come to us.” Janet shook her head sternly. “Not now. Here,” she said, extending her hand, “hand me the phone.”

“David? Hello. I’m Janet and I escaped with Darlene. I am so glad you’re alive. You have no idea how terribly your wife grieved when she learned that you had been killed.”

“Well, thank you for being there to comfort her, Janet. Where can we meet? Going by back roads, I’m at least a two day’s journey away from you right now, if I don’t stop for anything but gas.”

“We’ll try to talk to some locals and we’ll find a meeting place away from the troops. There are UN and Army troop movements all over northern Texas. Don’t try to come in until we find a safe route for you…”

16

Missoula, Montana

Jack and Dixie were joining Barry at one of his scheduled lectures on the campus of the University of Montana. Their hearts were heavy with the thought of how the recent conflict came so close to destroying the Coalition. The world seemed to move in slow motion as Jack and Dixie drove the interstate to the Missoula campus. No one smiled, as Montanans normally did, when he nodded kindly to them as he pumped his gas. Everyone was sober and quiet when he stood in line at the counter to get coffee and a newspaper. All seemed to realize how grave the consequences could be for seceding.

As they walked on campus toward the auditorium where Barry Friar was speaking, Jack gazed up into the crystal blue sky and tried to imagine Coalition jets chasing federal bombers, with the ensuing explosions and dogfights. He shook his head incredulously. It was all so surreal.

Colleges and universities all over the Coalition sponsored lectures in their large auditoriums wherein Minutemen defended the Coalition's cause. Campus ministries frequently co-sponsored the lecture series. At the end of the long day of lectures, and even some formal debates with political opponents, the Minutemen would have a long Q & A time, conversing with students late into the night.

There had been so much unrest on campus among the leftists that Barry decided to focus on the basics during the day's lectures. Is there a God? Has He revealed His will to us? Is it wise to disregard God's Word for the opinions of men? Barry intended to draw the battle line between a loving God and sinful man, and make it plain to all that dissension from His Word is rebellion to His will and harmful to man's well-being.

After the first lecture of the morning, the students mingled in small groups in the front, discussing and debating the day's topics with several Minutemen. Dixie engaged a young freshman brunette in the aisle, who informed her of riots on campus the night before. "You haven't heard about it?"

"No." Dixie glanced fearfully at her husband, who stood about ten feet away, listening to a different conversation. "We have not."

She looked over both shoulders, then said softly, "I live off campus, so I didn't even know about it until I got to class, but let me give you fair warning, some of the progressives were pretty stirred, and," she paused as she looked to the left and right again to make sure nobody was listening, "and I was told that they're going to start some trouble here today. A building full of classrooms was set on fire last night, gutting part of the building. Two students have been taken into custody for questioning."

Jack saw the trepidation in Dixie's countenance and stepped in closer to give his full attention to her conversation. Dixie asked the student, "Who were they?"

"Some guys that are a part of Students for Social Action – they're completely against the Coalition and they can get pretty violent making their point."

As the young woman spoke, the next group of classes began to file into the auditorium. Jack noticed that interspersed among them were several students carrying small signs with liberal slogans.

"Get your religion out of my crotch!"

"Keep your laws off my body!"

"Free Montana from fascism!"

"Eat the rich!"

One large banner was unfurled in the back, held by two young women. The banner read "Equal Rights NOW" and had a large equal sign underneath a rainbow.

Barry, who was engrossed with students' questions in the front of the auditorium, saw the signs and was immediately taken aback at the number of leftist protesters sprinkled throughout the 2,000 who filled the lower floor and balcony.

He motioned to Jack, who climbed the stairs onto the stage and walked up to him. "Jack, I'm afraid we're gonna have trouble with this class."

Some other Minutemen gathered around, and Barry proposed that they call it a day and head back. But the others were too encouraged by the promising dialogue after lectures.

One of the Minutemen opened his cell phone. "I'll call school security."

Barry took a deep breath as a campus minister headed to the podium to introduce him. Ten minutes into his lecture, as if on cue, Barry's crowd at the University of Montana's auditorium grew rowdy. The university security, however, would not intervene. The heathen poster-wavers gradually moved toward the front of the lower seating level right in front of the stage, and began to chant "Stop the hate!" They tried to raise their posters so that Barry could not be seen. He spoke more directly into the cordless microphone to try and be heard over the shouting protesters, but their distractions were difficult to overcome. Barry abandoned his lecture notes in an attempt to engage the protesters in the front, but they were stubborn and unreasonable.

"Raise your hand if you're an atheist!" Dozens in the front stopped their chanting and began to wave their hands enthusiastically.

"No, you're not an atheist." Barry made eye contact with one of the better-dressed protesters in the front. "You're kidding me."

"Yes I am!" he howled as his friends egged him on. "God is a fairy tale."

"Speaking of fairy tales, are there any homosexuals in the room?"

The well-dressed student in the front raised his hand and squealed with glee as the audience howled.

"So you're an atheist and a homosexual, too?"

The students cheered their local SSA leader, whom Barry Friar had singled out.

"Gloriously so!"

Barry waved him up beside him on stage, but the young man was reluctant. "I want to know why you're an atheist. Come on, tell us."

The student grinned sheepishly and wouldn't respond.

"Come on! My mind's a true open door," he said, employing a reference to the gay club "Open Doors" that was active on campus. "Tell us why you're an atheist." The crowd began to quiet down to hear their student leader's response.

The young man stood on a chair in the auditorium and turned to face the two thousand students. "Because Christianity is trash!" He thrust his right hand into the air as his admirers cheered and clapped.

"Okay, all right." Barry massaged his gray beard and grinned at the young man's overblown enthusiasm. "Tell us, why do you think the religion Jesus founded is trash?"

The crowd grew quiet again to try to hear the man's answer. "Christianity is intolerant of gays!" he snarled.

"Wait," said Barry into the microphone as he waved the crowd quiet. "I thought you were an atheist. I'm confused. I thought atheists didn't believe in absolute truth. I thought they didn't believe in right and wrong."

"We don't!" he responded. "Religion is a crutch for the weak-minded. Right is wrong is whatever you want it to be."

Barry turned to the crowd. "Do you all agree?" He extended his microphone at the crowd as if asking them to respond. Half of the students cheered their answer. Barry pointed at the SSA leader. "Let's talk about it. Come on up here, man!" He motioned for him to come up beside him on stage and he finally agreed. He loosened his silk black tie as he proudly ascended the stage.

"If morality is whatever you believe it to be, how can you condemn someone who condemns gays to hell? Aren't the Christians just following their personal beliefs?"

"It's my opinion," the student said proudly, puffing out his chest as he spoke into the microphone that Barry Friar extended toward him, "being intolerant is wrong. Intolerance provokes gays to commit suicide! It's why reproductive healthcare providers have to do abortions in back alley clinics in the Coalition states. Intolerance is, is evil!"

"Intolerance is evil?"

"Absolutely!"

Barry scratched his head. "Interesting. Remind us all again," he said as he waved across the auditorium, "we *all* would like to know *why* you think your opinion is absolutely right and alternative opinions are wrong? We're hanging on your every word now."

When the young man did not immediately respond, a student beside him screamed, "It's his opinion, dude!"

"No duh!" Barry shouted back. "But if the basis for his opinion is his opinion, then he's engaged in circular reasoning, and being illogical. None of us want to entertain the notion that a progressive opponent of the Coalition would be illogical in any way." Barry had discerned that the well-dressed student in the front was the chief instigator of this protest of their lecture. The crowd grew still as they sensed the uneasiness building in the SSA leader, and they were anxious to hear his response.

"Christianity has a basis for its opinion that homosexuality is unhealthy and unnatural," Barry continued. "The word of our loving Creator forbids it because adultery and homosexuality are both violations of our design to enjoy sex in a lifelong physiological natural commitment."

"I was born gay," the well-dressed student insisted. "It's scientifically proven!"

"Did you know," Barry asked him, "that every homosexual has a *heterosexual* design, physiologically? Did you know that the bodies of homosexuals are designed for heterosexual sex? Our holy God didn't give us rules to hinder our pleasure, but to maximize it – because He loves us! He loves us so much that when our sinful choices separate us from Him, he doesn't leave us in our sin and misery. No – our loving Father sent His Son to die on the cross for us so that–"

"Stop the hate!" The student leader started chanting the slogan again, and in five seconds, half of the students in the auditorium had shut their ears to the Gospel and were screaming the slogan. "Stop the hate! Stop the hate! Stop the hate!" Some of the students began to climb onto the stage beside Barry and surround him with their signs. Some Minutemen tried to stand between Barry and the protesters, but in just a few seconds, they were surrounded on all sides.

"You have got to stop this!" Jack insisted to the chief of security on the side of the stage. "At least put these protesters off the stage."

"If we start arresting people," the chief of security responded, "the situation will just escalate and get violent. They're harmless."

"We have permission to be here. Governor Benjamin Boswell has predicated your school's state funding on these lectures. The university president personally invited us and several campus ministries are sponsoring us. If you let this lawlessness continue," he said, pointing to some students who began to throw food, "it's going to get violent anyway." The two security guards on each side of the chief of security had a look of wonder on their faces as they watched the unruliness of the crowd grow with every passing minute.

Another Minuteman standing beside Jack put his index finger to within six inches of the chest of the chief of security. "We will tell the university president that this riot's your fault because you would not intervene to protect us when the situation was more manageable!"

When Jack saw that Barry had been completely surrounded by poster-wielding students, Jack left the conversation and came to stand beside Barry.

"No, no, you don't," said Jack, as he tried to wedge himself between the heathen protesters and Barry. He could smell the pungent stench of alcohol and marijuana on the breath of the intoxicated students nearest him. "Barry!" He looked over his shoulder at him. "This isn't profitable. We're casting our pearls before swine. We need to leave while we can."

Barry nodded, but then continued engaging in the conversation with the SSA leader and two students beside him. He tried to pick pieces of chewed gum out of his beard that students nearby threw at him as he spoke. In spite of the melee that was growing all around him, Barry kept his composure and tried to reason with those who would be reasonable.

"Hey, back off!" Jack ordered, stiff-arming an enthusiastic transvestite who pressed a little too close for comfort. His heart thumped with adrenaline, and he became concerned for their safety. The sodomite acted as if he were going to punch Jack, but backed off when Jack did not appear intimidated. Barry stayed calm, however, as he continued to try to engage the crowd on an intellectual level.

"Hey! Dixie!" Jack tried to get his wife's attention. She stood on the outskirts of the crowd that had gathered around them on the stage. "The security's not going to do anything." He motioned to the chief of police on the side of the stage. "Call the police!" Dixie made her way through some ruffians toward the chief of security, who was leaving the stage through the side door.

One of the security officers began to flash the lights in the building off and on, trying to urge the crowd to leave, but no one moved.

Suddenly, one of the students who held a poster in Jack's face sent a head-spinning blow through the poster to Jack's jaw. Being unable to see the oncoming fist, he was not able to brace for it. His head snapped back and he crumpled to the hard wooden floor. He hit the back of his head on the corner of the podium.

"Hey! Hey!" Barry shouted as he witnessed the assault. "Get away from him!"

This was turning into a riot, and Barry felt seriously threatened as he stooped over to check on Jack. He tried to keep the throng from trampling his semi-conscious friend as a pool of blood grew under his head. Fists began to fly all around them as the verbal conflict between protesters and Minutemen suddenly turned violent.

The mass of chanting students were thrilled that they had effectively silenced the Minutemen's leader. The SSA leader shouted, "To the administration building!"

The growing throng of angry students marched to the administration building on campus, leaving a path of vandalism and carnage in its wake. Another riot at the University of Montana had begun and the police force would not be able to quench it for several hours.

"Jack, Jack." Dixie's voice sounded distant and hollow. Her face was a blur in front of him. "Everything's going to be all right, Jack." She touched his cheeks with her hands. "Your wife and your baby are fine..."

Jack startled to consciousness as if from a troubling dream. A physician was gently swabbing streaks of dried blood off his scalp with a hydrogen-peroxide-soaked gauze. Bright rectangular-shaped lights blinded him. For a moment, he wondered where he was. The throbbing pain in the back of his head reminded him of what had happened to him.

"Dixie? Where's Dixie?"

"Down boy, down." The physician pressed Jack's chest back against the cot in the Emergency Department of Helena General Hospital. The physician hovered over Jack's head as he cleansed his scalp laceration.

Calling out for his wife caused excruciating pain in his right jaw. He reached up to hold his jaw and the physician replied, "It's not broken, but you're probably going to want to eat through a straw for a couple of weeks. You've got a pretty nasty gash on top of your head."

"It hurts in the back of my head."

"Apparently," the physician responded, "the back of your head hit the ground. No laceration there, just a bruise. CT scan was negative for a subdural hematoma..."

"A what?"

"It was negative for a bleed on your brain. I'll have to put at least a dozen stitches in this laceration though." He draped his head with a sterile towel as he spoke. "You won't be able to see while I'm doing this, because I need to keep a sterile field here. Don't touch the towel, all right?" He began to inject anesthetic into the tissue around the wound on top of Jack's head: "Little sting here..."

"He got a brain in there, doc?" Barry asked light-heartedly as he stepped into the exam room.

"Barry!" Jack recognized Barry's voice and put up his right hand. Barry walked over and grabbed it.

"Did anyone ever tell you that when someone swings a right fist, you shouldn't move your jaw in the way?"

"How's Dixie?" Jack asked. When no one answered, he grew nervous. "Where's Dixie?"

"Calm down, Mr. Handel," the physician responded. "We'll talk to you about your wife after I finish sewing this up, okay?"

Jack would not be consoled. "Barry! Tell me what happened to my Dixie! She's pregnant, you know."

"I told them, Jack."

"Where is she?" When they would not answer, Jack let go of Barry's hand and tried to pull away the sterile drape that covered his vision.

"Keep still, sir," the physician responded. "You'll be able to see your wife in a few minutes."

"She got hurt, Jack," Barry informed him, grasping his trembling hand with both of his. "She was outside the office of campus security when a mob of students flooded into the building…"

"What happened? Is she all right?" Jack asked in a frantic tone. "Tell me!"

"She got trampled, Jack," Barry softly responded. "She's in the Intensive Care Unit right now. Seven people have already died in that riot, and there are many severe injuries…"

"Oh no, please no." Jack began to cry uncontrollably and squeeze Barry's hand more tightly.

"Dixie's got internal bleeding, and she's about to go into surgery, Jack."

"Is the baby okay?"

"I don't know." Barry wept with his friend. "It's all right, Jack," he said, unashamed of his tears. "Give it to God. Give it to God."

"We prayed for her healing before we sent her into surgery," the physician added, being moved to grief at the sight of these two men weeping. "It's in the Lord's hands now."

Jack waited three hours in the surgical waiting room with his faithful friend at his side. Barry and Jack took turns pacing and praying and Barry tried futilely to comfort the nerves of his stoic friend who seemed impervious to encouragement. Every time the mechanized doors that led to the surgery suites opened with their characteristic click and hum, Jack's heart stopped. Then the physician would call on someone else's family, and Jack would begin pacing again.

"How long can they be in there?"

Barry patted the seat beside him, motioning for Jack to take a seat. "Calm down, Jack. Hey, why don't you let me get you something to eat?"

"No," he mumbled. "I'm not hungry." He plopped down into a vacant seat beside his friend.

"Y'all really loved each other again, huh?"

Jack turned to look Barry in the eye. "Yeah. We really did." In spite of the faint smile that shone on Jack's face, his eyes welled up with tears. He took a deep breath, trying to suppress the wave of emotions that threatened to undo his composure. "It was just like you said on your farm the day the siege began…"

"Oh, I remember. And what a day it was."

Jack winced with the recollection. "Yeah. I had to make the choice to love her, Barry. When she rejected my advances, I had to persist. I had to pursue her, just like Jesus pursued me. And you were right. The flame rekindled, and she fell in love with me all over again."

"I thank the Lord, Jack."

Jack placed his head in his hands and let out a long, hard sob. Barry sniffed and placed his right hand on the back of Jack's neck.

"If she were to die, I, I don't know." Jack shook his head and mumbled inaudibly.

"Just trust the Lord, Jack, just like you've been doing. We've committed this thing to God. We just have to trust Him now and receive the peace that He promises."

The large surgery doors clicked and hummed as they opened. A face-mask-wearing surgeon stepped through them, accompanied by a nurse in surgery scrubs. The surgeon read from the clipboard in his hands. "Jack Handel?"

"That's me." Jack stood up and walked over to the surgeon. "Tell me the good news."

The surgeon pulled his surgical mask down around his neck. "Come with me," he said without emotion. Barry and Jack glanced uneasily at each other and then followed him and the nurse into a small room with four leather seats and a phone.

"I don't have good news for you, Mr. Handel." The surgeon ripped off his mask from his face and threw it into a trashcan in the corner of the small room. He took a deep breath. "Your wife didn't make it."

Jack felt his arms and legs go numb and tunnel vision set in.

"We did all we could, but the bleeding from her trauma was too severe. Her spleen ruptured from the trampling. We transfused her constantly, but the large hematoma in her abdomen had used up all her platelets and she wouldn't clot. She bled out as fast as we could put it in. I'm sorry. We did the best we could."

The numbness evolved to a faint tingling in Jack's fingers and toes, and he felt dizzy as if his heart had suddenly stopped. Barry reached to put his arm over Jack's shoulder. Tears welled up in Jack's eyes and his chest heaved in pain. He felt like his heart had broken like a dam and the floodwaters rushed down his cheeks. When the physician moved toward the door, Jack's gaze remained fixed upon the same location where the doctor gave the grave announcement. His gaze wandered lazily to an oil painting of a leafless tree in front of a snowy winter prospect.

Jack knelt beside the surgical bed and held Dixie's pale white hand. He caressed it, squeezed it, kissed it, and fondled the wedding ring with affection. He prayed and wept, and begged God to relieve his heart-wrenching grief. She was the love of his life, and now she was gone.

"Hey, bud." Barry whispered through the cracked door. He walked in and stood beside Jack, who was still on his knees holding his wife's hand, the same position that Barry had left him in an hour earlier. Barry spoke softly, "The nurse says that we need to leave. They need this room for a patient."

Jack heaved a painful sigh. "What am I going to do now, Barry? What am I going to do? She's gone."

"She's gone to heaven, Jack. She's with your baby. You'll be with them soon enough. Life is so short, Jack, compared to the endless years you'll be with her; being without her will be like a nap. You'll miss her, but in just the first few moments of heaven this hardship and grief you're going through will seem so small to you."

Jack took a deep, painful breath and exhaled it with a sob. He kissed her hand again. "What am I going to do now, Barry? My life has revolved around her." Barry handed him a tissue and he wiped his nose.

"Your life's going to revolve around your Savior. He promised that He is the living Water of which we can drink and never thirst again. He's our Comforter. He's going to take care of you, Jack." After another moment of silence, Barry repeated: "We need to go, bud."

Jack couldn't stop thinking about their last conversation. She wanted him to train the civilian militia in other states. She wanted him to teach others how to defend themselves. She, of all people, wanted her husband, whose militia activities she had despised for so many years, to go back into the militia.

Jack stood to his feet, eyes dry and burning from the many tears he had shed. His knees were sore and both feet were numb from being in that position beside her bed for so long. He reached for Barry.

"Lord, help me." They hugged each other tightly until they wept out the rest of their tears.

Washington, D.C.

"Danny Connor, that's who!" President Brighton was heaving self-criticism upon the listening ears of Dena Halluci in the privacy of her office. "How could I have never seen it?"

"Danny Connor?" She shook her head more vigorously than normal, sporting her most recent style. She sighed wearily when the president didn't even notice. "Are you sure it was Danny?" She found it hard to believe that Danny Connor would resort to treason.

"Oh, we all should have known it," she said with a wave of the hand. "He was playing us. I can't believe we were so naïve to let it go on so long." Her face was red and her extremities fidgety as she braved the waters of regret; so much so that Dena wondered if she had consumed one too many cappuccinos that morning. "He told the Coalition that we were taking out the nuclear weapons within their borders and Ben Boswell got a head start on us. He's been the one feeding Josh Davis's conspiracy theories all along." She looked away from Dena and began to type on her laptop. "Stupid! We were so stupid not to see it! Now we've lost the initiative."

"What are you going to do about him?"

"Let me put it this way. You won't see Danny Connor at any more cabinet meetings."

"Of course."

"As for the media, you tell them that we're pursuing a blockade and a diplomatic solution with the Coalition."

Dena took a deep breath. She hated to be the one who had to tell Margaret Brighton what she needed to hear, though she might not want to hear it. "Madam President, the American people want to know who was bombed and why. They want the number of casualties. They're asking for confirmation of the rumors that the Coalition has obtained nuclear weapons. They're asking about the massive military build-up in California. They're asking about the influx of UN troops from Texas into Oklahoma. Obfuscation is an inadequate response, Madam President. Arresting Texas' leadership was acceptable, but—"

“It better be,” the president mumbled.

“*Barely* acceptable,” the president’s chief of staff added, “but sending UN troops into Oklahoma and other border states, is not.”

“Just do what I said, Dena!” the president blurted out with a tone of frustration in her raspy voice. “Read the statement I put out. We’ll talk about it at the cabinet meeting in the morning.” Dena appeared jolted by the president’s abrupt shouting, and stood up to leave. “Wait.” The president stopped her. She sighed and put her elbows on the table and her head in her hands. “I’m sorry, Dena. I’m just pretty stressed out right now.”

Dena stared at Brighton for a moment, trying to discern the sincerity of her apology. “You need to appear strong and confident right now, even if you don’t feel like it.” She waxed bold and said, “If you give the media any more Xanax moments like that, your presidency won’t survive till November.”

“I really,” she paused, and Dena noted light red splotches arose on the president’s face and neck. “ I really, I really miss Raymond.” The president stunned her chief of staff with her unexpected tears.

Dena sighed deeply for an uneasy moment and was at a loss of what to do. She was tempted to exploit the president’s lapse of tenacity to be more insistent with her suggestions; however, her empathetic inclinations won over. She stood stiff and silent in front of the president’s desk as the president wept quietly with her head in her hands. Finally, Dena walked around the desk and put an arm around her.

The president did not reciprocate the half-hearted hug but rather grabbed a tissue off her desk to wipe herself and keep her mascara from running. “I’ll be all right, I’ll be, I’ll be okay.”

Dena Halluci glimpsed at the president’s private E-mail, which utilized an encryption program with which the chief of staff was unfamiliar. The letter was addressed to “Nightfall” whose E-mail address had a CIA suffix. “1. UN engaging. 2. D. Connor can go now.” It was signed “1womyn”.

“Where is he?” Josh Davis reluctantly picked up another cold french fry from the front seat of his RV in the Wendy’s parking lot. He lost his enthusiasm for the fries when Danny failed to arrive on time. That was unlike Danny Connor, especially without a phone call.

He considered dialing his cell phone, but it was too risky, and he talked himself out of it. An hour later, he drove by his home and saw a police car in the driveway behind Danny’s car. He caught a glimpse of

Danny's wife standing in the doorway, distraught, speaking with the officer.

Josh learned the next day that when Danny's wife came home from work, she found his unlocked car in the driveway with the keys still in the ignition. But there was no sign of her husband.

Danny Connor was never seen again, an extensive FBI investigation notwithstanding. The investigation would conclude that Danny Connor's mental instability had been increasing for months before his disappearance. Furthermore, it was proven that he had been living a double life with his online gambling and pornography addictions, stealing tens of thousands of dollars from his bureaucracy's budget over the years to fund his habits. It was speculated in the media that Danny had fled to Bangkok to lavish his appetites in that region's thriving child sex prostitution rings. When *60 Minutes* received a tourist's grainy video showing someone who looked like Danny Connor in a Bangkok bar with a young girl under each arm, they ran a segment on it.

The president ordered a nationwide mental health awareness campaign in honor of her missing cabinet member. A monetary award of $100,000 was offered for information leading to the discovery of his whereabouts. His disappearance, however, would remain a mystery, and his friend Josh Davis was suddenly blind.

17

Boise, Idaho

Chairman Boswell called an emergency meeting in Boise with all ten Coalition governors and their cabinets. Half of the leaders were present via the internet, and their images showed on flat-screens all around the walls.

Ben Boswell opened up in a word of prayer. When he concluded and looked up, he saw that General Bryan's image was present on his computer screen. "General Bryan, I want you to know that we are so proud of you and our Guard forces for the defense you put up two nights ago. Why don't we give him a hand?" He began to applaud and the other Coalition leaders joined in.

"Thank you." When the applause subsided, Bryan said, "All the glory goes to God."

"Do you have an update for us?"

"We lost about a fifth our fighter jets. We were only able to capture the nuclear weapons at nine sites before the federal attack vaporized the other nuclear silos, but then they targeted our transports that were re-locating the warheads, probably through incidentally-emitted radiation tracked through satellite imagery."

"Any detectable radiation at those destroyed sites?" someone asked.

"Yes, but minimal. We have seven nuclear weapons left, hidden at various places at underground facilities. We have plenty more firepower and pilots, but we're short on fuel. That's our weak link. If we have many more massive air battles like we did this week, we'll bankrupt our entire jet fuel supply or be forced to confiscate private supplies so drastically that we will risk insubordination."

"We're not going to confiscate private supplies," Governor Boswell responded.

"Their blockade has crippled us," the Nebraska governor regretted.

"We're working on meeting your needs," Chad Dreifuss commented. "We have delegations in Canada, Mexico, and even overseas working on resolving our fuel shortage right now."

Bryan nodded. "I've faxed our casualty report from the air conflict to each of your offices." Countenances were downcast as he read the number of deaths and injuries from the slip of paper. "I estimate civilian casualties to be half that."

"We had 25 perish when our capitol and state office buildings were bombed," Governor Pollock of Idaho said solemnly.

"We lost 14," Governor Sam Reynolds of Utah added.

Governor Littman placed his hand on the shoulder of Reynolds, who sat beside him. Governor Reynolds appeared slightly choked up about the destruction of his state's capitol building. "We are calling for a day of prayer and fasting tomorrow," Littman said, "for the families of the victims and the future of the Coalition. We need God now more than ever."

Boswell grinned, excited to hear the leader of the least spiritual of the Coalition states speak so freely of his reliance on God. "I think we all should do that, Governor Littman."

Governor Boswell turned his attention to General Bryan. "Well, we have a huge slab of desert, mountain, and prairie under us. How do you propose we defend it, General?"

"If we had unlimited fuel, then it wouldn't be a problem for our air force. Thank God we have not lost the satellite imaging Governor Littman's team provided for us. The nuclear engineers were able to direct the missile off course and save the satellite. The feds still don't know we're hijacking those images."

Governor Littman smiled and those adjacent to him patted him on the back and shook his hand.

"Our nuclear arsenal," Bryan continued, "is limited, but the feds don't know that. Warheads are being placed on conventional ballistic missiles and aimed for strategic sights at the nearest military facilities over the border." With the touch of a button, the screen changed to a computer chart of the United States and Bryan pointed out targets on the computer, which lit up on the screen in the meeting room. "We can destroy the United States of America as we know it. That'll keep them awake at night." He paused. "Unless…" He paused again, deep in thought.

"Unless what?"

"General Knox with the Colorado Guard has worked for years at the nuclear defense facilities in their state, and he thinks the feds can mobilize their Mobile Tactical High Energy Lasers within two weeks. They'll be able to intercept and destroy our ballistic missiles before they can reach their targets. Those will tremendously weaken our ability to propel an invasion."

"We just have to fire a lot of ballistics all at once. They can't get 'em all."

"Yes, but they can have multiple defense systems between us and potential targets, such as D.C., and that will protect their military infrastructure and their leaders, and decrease their risks greatly."

"Well, General Bryan, what do you propose?"

The General touched a button on his laptop and a map of the Coalition shone up on their screens. "First, ignore the map. We won't be defending borders as much as we will be defending cities. The stretches of land are just too vast to protect it all, and our fuel is inadequate." He tapped on his computer with a magnetic pen and highlighted large tracts of mostly vacant land along the border of the Coalition States and the United States. "The consensus among the Coalition generals is that we re-locate our forces along the borders where we would most likely see a ground invasion."

Governor Mackenzie of Nebraska harrumphed with a puff of his pendulous cheeks, realizing that his state was one of the states most likely to see a ground invasion.

"The feds are unlikely to risk any more massive air strikes," Bryan speculated. "It's too risky for them. We suspect they may try and inch their way toward us one town at a time and try to choke us into surrender." He tapped on cities around the Coalition border, which highlighted them. "They'll squeeze us on the ground, crack the whip mile by mile, state by state, trying to make deals with the mayors and leaders of each state. They'll try to force local leaders to choose between two options: execution for treason or a hefty federal handout to make their military occupation more palatable…"

"It's a false dichotomy," Boswell interjected with a raised index finger. "Obedience to God and the blessing of God may give us victory."

Some of the other governors nodded, but his sentiment was far from unanimous.

"They'll exploit our weaknesses," Bryan continued, "which is our size and our independence, until Montana is all that's left. Then they'll be able to move their MT-HEL's around the border of Montana, which will have a greater effectiveness at neutralizing our nuclear threat."

"We aren't going anywhere," the Wyoming governor stated. "We're committed. Our unity is strong. We're unbribable."

The Nebraska governor grunted uneasily, and the doubtful grimaces of the other Coalition leaders revealed their lack of confidence in the Wyoming governor's prediction.

"How hard will it be to take Walla Walla?" General Bryan pointed at a city on Washington's southern border. "Or Chinook, or St. George, or New Plymouth, or Fairbury, or Sioux City." He tapped small towns on the map along the CFCS border. "Your commitment to the Coalition may be measured in the blood of the citizens of your own states."

Boswell sighed heavily. "You sound like it's a pretty sure thing."

"Governor, I think the Joint Chiefs are sitting around their maps at the Pentagon, congratulating themselves for already check-mating us. To them, it's just a matter of time. They will try to amputate us into submission one town and one state at a time."

"Submission to tyranny will *never* become a reasonable alternative for any of us." Boswell's comment was more of a statement of faith than fact, he knew.

"Of course," Bryan nodded. "For the Coalition. But I suspect Walla Walla may surrender if invaded, and I suspect Walla Walla's capture won't motivate the kind of nuclear threats as when the feds were bombing our airfields and capitol buildings, especially if they have activated their MT-HELs." The computer screen returned to the images of the Coalition leaders. "The state of Washington is particularly vulnerable given the proximity to the large California bases and the ocean. Our ability to defend against a naval attack is dismal indeed."

General Bryan glanced at Governor Littman of Washington. "Keep your eyes on the Pacific, Governor."

Littman took a deep breath, and spread his palms out on the table, as if to steady his dizzy head. "There are rumors that Mitch Paine is back in Seattle stirring up trouble and that a major riot is in the works." Littman clenched his teeth, frustrated. "I can't believe we had him and he got loose."

"What about your civilian militias?" Boswell surmised. "Have you thought about giving them the firepower and artillery to defend their own cities? We have no shortage of weapons and artillery…"

Wilson and Littman laughed, and many of the other leaders found their laughing contagious; they all laughed heartily for a long moment.

"Did you say, *our* civilian militias?" Littman responded. "We aren't Montana, Ben. We do not have civilian militias because we're, well, we're…"

"Civilized!" Governor Wilson added, sparking more laughter.

Boswell maintained his sober countenance. "If you don't have civilian militias, then arm your men. Get your veterans involved in training your civilians how to defend their own towns. The second amendment, after all, requires a well-armed civilian militia. Montana has a very strong civilian militia, and we can send some of our best out to your major cities to teach your men how to fight."

"I gotta better idea," Pollock bravely proposed. "Why don't we give the feds a taste of their own medicine? They'd never suspect it. Let's bomb the major cities in each of the surrounding states with a few of our stealth fighters."

"No, no, no." Boswell stretched a heavy hand toward the Idaho governor. "That Gettysburg spirit didn't fare well for the Confederates, and it won't fare well for us. It's not the kind of spirit we want to have."

"Gettysburg spirit?" Littman had a confused look on his face.

"When the Confederates fought defensive battles, they won. When they crossed north of the Mason-Dixon to fight offensive battles, their defeats were devastating."

"We are at war, Ben," Pollock asserted with a vigorous wag of hid index finger. "We need to treat them like enemies. What did we do to neighborhoods in Dresden, Germany, during the Second World War? We bombed them to rubble! What did we do to Nagasaki and Hiroshima?"

"That our forefathers slaughtered tens of thousands of women and children because they couldn't catch their enlisted fathers and husbands in no way justifies us behaving in the same way."

"But, but…"

"We won't have God's blessing if we intentionally maximize collateral damage," Boswell insisted. "The immoral tactics of D.C.'s tyrants do not justify immoral warfare on our part. War does not exempt us from our obligation to obey the golden rule. We will take careful aim and we will be defensive and precise with our weapons. Violence is a last resort to be employed in self-defense, and we will employ no more violence than is necessary to win our freedom."

"Why don't we send our stealth bombers over the major cities of nearby states, cities that don't have fighters patrolling overhead," Governor Wilson proposed, briefly removing his cigar to grin. "Let them drop millions of leaflets that say, 'The Coalition could have bombed you.'" He laughed with the other governors at his own humor, but Boswell was surprisingly somber.

"I think it's a good idea," Boswell said with eyebrows raised. "We could even add a Bible verse or two."

"What?"

"The Bible says when your enemy hungers, feed him, when he thirsts, give him drink. Don't be overcome with evil, but overcome evil with good."

"You've got to be kidding me! You want to drop Bible verses on cities across the border?"

"Yeah, let's attach a Cabella's gift card to it," someone added jokingly.

"Hold up!" Dreifuss, Montana's attorney general, raised his voice and lifted the Guard casualty report in his right hand. "Do any of you find anything strangely telling about these casualty statements?" The governors glanced at their notes and their copy of the lists of casualties.

Boswell shook his head, curious as to what prompted the normally reserved and respectful Chad Dreifuss to interrupt. "What do you see, Chad?"

"Every state that has actually shut down abortion clinics and arrested abortionists did not suffer any casualties at all, whereas every state that hasn't done so suffered deaths."

Their eyes raised and they all nodded as they noted the interesting finding. Boswell's head hung low, and he closed his eyes for a moment. The silence in the room was telling. They all were introspective, wondering if this were a magnificent coincidence or if God had divinely protected the states that actually banned abortion with action instead of just rhetoric.

Governor Boswell reached into his briefcase and pulled out a hardback book. He opened it to a marked page and read from it solemnly: "Virtue, morality, and religion: this is the armor, my friend, and this alone renders us invincible. These are the tactics we should study. If we lose these, we are conquered, fallen indeed… So long as our manners and principles remain sound, there is no danger." He closed the book and read the name of its author, "Patrick Henry."

"Amen."

"Let this be a stern reminder to us that our victory rests upon obeying God and doing justice. There will be no mercy for us until there is justice for the preborn." His eyes roamed from governor to governor, whose sober countenances revealed that they grasped the extraordinary implications of these findings. "End the child-killing, or we will suffer defeat. Thus saith the Lord."

Washington, D.C.

Unbeknownst to most Americans, the president hastened the order for UN troops to amass at Camp Pendleton and Vandenburg Air Force Base in California. Operation Cat O'Nine Tails was the title given to the anticipated major ground assault. American forces gathered at Edwards and Nellis Air Force Bases, Fort Irwin, and China Lake Naval Weapons Center.

At the president's cabinet meeting, the Joint Chiefs began to turn up the pressure on President Brighton to get as much done as possible militarily before the UN was prepared to steal the glory.

"We're convinced that right now, Madam President, not next week, but right now," General Green exclaimed as he stood up and tapped his index finger at the mahogany table, "we can exploit a critical weakness and end this military conflict quickly!"

She sighed at the General's predictable enthusiasm. "Okay, General Green, okay. What do you propose?"

He flicked on his laser pointer and prepared to make his case. "It'll be a two-pronged attack. We'll be ready for the *coup d'etat* on Tuesday. The UN forces will be helpful in a policing role, but this mission will conclude before General Petri Urlich gets over his jet lag."

"You're that confident?"

The general grinned mischievously. "Madam President, our boys can do this drunk."

Helena, Montana

Governor Boswell got a call at 5:10 a.m. He painfully roused from his deep slumber and picked up the phone. "Governor Boswell! This is

Trey Storms with the Washington State Guard. Federal forces are moving north on I-5 and east of Olympia on the coast–"

"Hold on, hold on." Ben Boswell mumbled as he sat up in bed.

"What is it?" Mrs. Boswell rolled over to face him.

"Slow down, General Storms," Boswell urged. "I can't understand you."

"There's a ground assault into Washington State right now. It looks like an attack toward our capitol in Olympia, with two forces converging onto her from the south and the west. Governor Littman told me to call you."

Boswell put the phone on speaker and began to dress as he spoke, "Have the Coalition Guard forces been mobilized?"

"Too little, too late, from too far away, I'm afraid, to do much good. The Washington Guard's stationed around the capital city, but we're pretty much surrounded…" Boswell heard a mortar round blast in the background as the general spoke.

"Oh! That was close!"

"Are you all right, General?"

"Barely. A large combined force of guardsmen were on the way here to help with the threat of rioting, but they're 300 miles out. It's a real mean artillery battle right now. We have a few jets in the air, but their jets are keeping out of range and not engaging our air force or our ground forces, and so the air forces are just staring each other down right now. It's a bloody ground battle, and it's spilling into the streets in a thrust to the capitol building."

Seattle, Washington

Elijah was snoozing in a cozy hotel room across the street from Washington State University when there was a sharp bang on the door at the crack of dawn. He roused and heard the thick Indian accent of the hotel's owner, whom he had befriended.

"Mr. Slate! Mr. Slate!"

Elijah rose from his slumber and opened the door. The middle-aged Indian with a thick black mustache stood there with a suitcase in each hand. His wife was sitting in an idling car behind him in the parking lot.

"Pallay, what's the matter?"

"The Army is attacking. I've heard that the roads westward are open, so I'm leaving with my family. You can stay in the hotel if you like, but would you please keep an eye on everything for me if you decide to stay? I won't charge–"

"What?" Elijah stepped through the doorway, rubbing his eyes.

Suddenly, a faint rumble like distant thunder and a flash of light on the horizon stole their attention.

"See?" said Pallay, pointing. "We are leaving!"

"What was that?" Elijah's evangelist friend, who slept on the bed behind him, awoke and came to the door.

Another artillery shell struck along the southern horizon, bellowing like an angry thunderstorm.

Elijah then heard the faint sound of someone screaming on a megaphone on campus nearby.

"Goodbye, my friend, and good luck." Pallay rushed to the car and skidded into the congested road. Drivers were filling both lanes heading west, as there were no drivers going eastward.

Elijah shut the door. "Get dressed, Andy. Grab your Bible and your sidearm."

Elijah called the other rooms to wake up the other 150 Minutemen, comprised of patriots and evangelists from all over the Coalition. Most of them had already been awakened from the distant explosions. He assigned them to a dozen potential hot spots all over the city.

"Where are we going?" Andy asked.

"Campus. We've got to put a stop to the squall before it becomes a hurricane."

Olympia, Washington

Trey Storms, the Adjutant General of Washington, had a difficult time discerning what his men were doing on the ground as the feds pressed toward the city.

"They're on Fifth, between Hutchins and Main!" Captain Kammler's voice was back-dropped with the chatter of automatic gunfire and the explosions of mortar rounds.

"Put Grayman's company south in the bank and the shopping center," Storms ordered.

"Artillery has shattered Grayman's company, sir."

"Where's Kory's artillery company?"

"They're on... Hey! Hey!! There!" The sergeant shouted and pointed to a subordinate. "I want your men on that corner! Put that M-

198 into action, now!" He returned to the phone. "Kory's on the north side of the statehouse."

"On the north side? Why?"

"Marines are coming in on the bay."

"What?"

"Kory's shelling them before they get to shore. But things aren't holding up as well to the west and south, sir. Lots of casualties…"

"Fire!" shouted Kory Campbell from behind a four-foot brick wall that served as a fence to a city park in downtown Olympia. The blast of artillery shook the ground beneath their feet as they picked off the flatboats of Marine invaders 100 yards off shore. The last of the Marine flatboats shattered to pieces as the Marines abandoned it at the last moment and began to swim to the western shore of the bay, away from the Guard's forces.

"Sergeant Kory!" his radio operator shouted, tugging on his arm.

Kory ignored his radio man and ordered his 60 men to the northwestern shore: "I want you to scour that shoreline and pick up survivors..."

The man beside Campbell suddenly cried out in pain. "Ow!"

Campbell looked and saw blood pooling in the dirt from a shrapnel injury to the calf of his right-hand man. "You okay?"

"No, I'm not okay," the soldier grimaced with pain.

Campbell looked around for a medic, and not finding one nearby, he tapped another soldier beside him. "Get a medic for this fellow."

"Sergeant! General Storms wants to talk to you." The radio operator yelled at him, as he nursed his wound.

"What?" Kory turned his attention to the injured radio operator.

"The general wants to talk to you."

Campbell took the phone and put it to his ear. "Kory Campbell here."

"I want you to take your men at full pace to the southwest and stop those troops comin' up I-5…"

"I've got dozens of casualties and injured, sir…"

"Leave some babysitters and get over there. In 15 minutes, Olympia'll be occupied if we don't repel those Marines coming up the interstate!"

"Where's Kammler's company?"

"They're getting torn to shreds southeast of you. You get to that southwestern flank now!"

Washington, D.C.

The president was entertained as she watched the generals at work in the Pentagon war room.

"This phase will conclude soon, Madam President." Everyone's eyes were fixed on the satellite images projected on the wall.

Brighton called out to an aid as she sat with her wiry arms across her chest. "Someone get Governor Littman on the phone. Maybe he will be reasonable now."

"Yes, Madam President."

Olympia, Washington

"Governor Boswell!" Governor Littman spoke to Boswell over his cell. "We're under heavy attack! We've got heavy casualties! Downtown's a war zone…" He was hyperventilating between sentences and spouting his complaints in a staccato-like fashion.

"Calm down, calm down." Boswell was in the back seat of a bulletproof Lexus as his security team escorted him to the Guard headquarters just north of Helena.

"I need the entire Coalition Guard here now – right now! – or I won't have anything left to defend."

"They're on their way…"

"I don't know how much longer we can hang on. Olympia and Seattle's going up like a bucket of gunpowder in a bonfire – there's rioting and vandalism everywhere. Every fourth building's on fire, they're being set faster than the fire engines can put them out. Fire trucks are being vandalized and firemen and police officers are being assaulted. I don't think we can take much more than this…"

"Listen to me, Frank! Don't waver on our mission. We knew our faith was going to be tested. Stand firm!"

"Waver!? I don't think we're going to survive this night if our entire Coalition Guard force doesn't engage soon!"

"You won't survive if you shake the devil's hand for peace. Do you understand me? Don't put your faith in the strength of men and guns, sir, or defeat is *certain*, Frank, with or without the Guard there to defend you. You commit this thing to the hands of God right now, and the peace of God that passes understanding will keep your heart and mind through Christ Jesus…"

Somebody opened the door to Littman's office and shouted, "The president's on the phone for you…"

"I gotta' go…"

Boswell overheard those words and grew concerned. "Wait! Frank!"

Click.

Boswell was stumped at what to do next. His driver drove to the front entrance of the facility and opened the door for him. He put his cell back into its holster and rushed through the open door. As he jogged down the hallway, it occurred to him he would be unable now to bluff the president into withdrawing her forces. Their Mobile Tactical High Energy Lasers must be in defensive positions to intercept any ballistic threat; otherwise they wouldn't be attacking like this. Ballistic missiles, whether armed with conventional munitions or nuclear warheads, had to remain a last resort. Bluffing is inflationary; the more you do it, the less valuable it becomes. The president was keeping her fighter jets at a distance, which told him they weren't completely disregarding the ballistic threat of the CFC States. They clearly thought very little of the ability of the Washington Guard to put up an effective ground defense.

Ben Boswell began to realize that the feds were executing a "divide and conquer" strategy, just as General Bryan predicted. The feds wanted to subjugate them piece-by-piece. "If there was no God, they'd win," he reminded himself out loud. "But the Lord God Almighty is our defender." He burst into a room and into the presence of several Guard officials.

The grayest and thinnest Guard general in the room had just picked up the phone and was preparing to call Governor Boswell when an inferior said, "There he is now."

The general rushed up to him to hand him a fax. "This came just now."

The fax was entitled, "Critical intelligence information" and was from a state trooper in Oklahoma.

It read, *I saw miles and miles of armored personnel carriers, tanks on semi-trucks, and buses carrying infantry, heading north on I-35 just south of Oklahoma City about 3 a.m. I suspect these are coming from Camp Bullis Military Reservation in San Antonio. I didn't think much of it until the conflict broke out in Washington State.* The letterhead on the fax read Oklahoma Highway Patrol. *P.S. Thank you for not bombing us,* he concluded. *My family is appreciative. (We got your leaflets.)*

His first impression was to be glad that he had his stealth bombers drop those leaflets instead of bombs in major cities just outside the

Coalition border, but upon further thought, he began to suspect this was counter-intelligence to affect their ability to defend themselves on the western front.

Governor Boswell set down the fax and walked over to the map on the wall. “If I were Margaret Brighton with almost all of the Coalition’s Guard 1400 miles away,” the governor said, while rubbing his chin, “I’d attack now from the east. I’d attack Denver, or Lincoln.”

“That’s right.” The elderly Guard general nodded. “General Bryan’s right. They’re going to inch their way toward us one town at a time. They’re going to tighten their grip around us like a noose.”

“Get General Bryan on a secure line for me.”

Olympia, Washington

As he sped in his Bradley westward with 5,000 soldiers in his wake, Rod Sanders could see the fighting from a half a mile away. The federal infantry was shelling Guard armored personnel carriers and Bradleys on the street and on the lawn in front of the statehouse. The Washington Guard was putting up a stiff fight with rifles and mobile artillery, but the Guard positions were being crippled with tremendous efficiency. The guardsmen frequently abandoned their haphazardly erected artillery fortresses and spread out to take cover under vehicles and behind bushes. It soon evolved to a rifle-shooting battle – shoot or be shot. Some brave citizens unexpectedly began to shoot semi-automatic handguns and rifles down on the federal infantry from second and third stories of buildings and apartment complexes, provoking some cheers from the guardsmen who ducked for cover. A Molotov cocktail was thrown down on a federal personnel carrier, impeding it only temporarily, but long enough to make it a good target for an anti-armor missile from one of the Guard’s Bradleys on the western edge of the statehouse.

The federal Bradley vehicle exploded and sent flames past them into the sky, and the brave young civilians cheered with their fists sticking out of the second story windows of the apartment building.

“Fan out!” Sanders ordered to his sergeants and captains over the radio as he studied the digital map of downtown Olympia on the big screen GPS affixed to the dashboard. “Dana, take 12th, Masters, 11th, Whitlow, 10th Avenue. Paltrow and Westling, get to the statehouse and set up a perimeter! Nader, to the western flank immediately and set up a defense against the oncoming Marines on those streets…”

Sanders ordered his troops hurriedly into position as they pulled in close to the action with .50-caliber machine guns on top of their Bradleys spitting out bullets as fast as they could. Their TOW long-range anti-armor missiles and Bushmaster 25 mm electric cannons engaged every federal armored personnel carrier, tank, and Hummer in sight.

A 55-year-old lieutenant shouted over the radio to Colonel Sanders from the inside of a culvert ditch: “We’re getting killed over here! We had to abandon our Bradley, three of my men are hurt pretty badly. My squad is out of artillery and almost out of bullets…” Sanders could barely hear over the non-stop automatic machine gun fire in the background. “We need support, and we need it now. Can we get air support?”

“Lieutenant, I’m sending ground support over now…”

The lieutenant dropped the phone and began to fire his machine gun in three round bursts toward a row of Marines hugging a wall as they made their way eastward, their path protected by artillery fire behind them. The top of Nader’s helmet and the flash of gunfire made a target for an M-198 cannon shell that disintegrated him and three of his subordinates as they hugged the ground inside a culvert. A cloud of smoke and blood vapor over a crater four feet in diameter was all that was left of them.

The federal infantry clearly were not prepared for Sanders’ sudden assault from their eastern flank, and those who were targeting the Washington Guard positions and guardsmen were now being shot at from both the north and the east at every intersection. Sanders’ artillery and .50-caliber machine gun fire soon cut the feds to pieces and forced them to retreat several blocks.

If the federal infantry slowed at the intersections to avoid the vicious cross-fire in the streets, they felt the wrath of civilians upon them from above. The federal advance was on its heels and they were forced to set up a defense within some brick buildings five city blocks away from the statehouse. They called for reinforcements to make their retreat more palatable.

Washington, D.C.

When the president concluded her conversation with Governor Littman of Washington State, Halluci could see from her grimace that the conversation was a disappointment. “Littman wasn’t ready to bargain?”

The president answered the question by tossing her cell phone carelessly on her desk in the heart of the Pentagon’s war room. “He tried to sound brave but he was scared out of his wits.” She turned away from her chief of staff and walked over to General Green.

General Green turned around from where he sat in his swivel chair in front of a number of phones and laptop computers, through which he communicated with his men on the field. “The rest of the Coalition forces have arrived from the east, just as we expected. They stopped our advance before we could take the statehouse.”

“Pull ‘em back and tell them to take a breather, General. We don’t want any unnecessary loss of life.”

“Commence Phase Two?”

She nodded. “Yes, commence Phase Two.”

Helena, Montana

While Boswell was on the phone with Bob Bryan discussing the trustworthiness of the new intelligence from the highway patrolman in Oklahoma, another call came through on a special private line. It was the technician in Seattle who managed their satellite imaging. “Hold on, Bob. I’ve got to get another call.” He tapped the flash button on his phone. “Hello?”

“Yes sir. This is Don Barker. We’ve got some infantry movement, it appears on the…”

“Denver or Lincoln?” Boswell interrupted him.

“Uh, you know already?”

“Denver or Lincoln?”

“Lincoln.”

Boswell sighed heavily. “How far off?”

“Um, give me just a sec.”

“Let me take this other call and I’ll be right back.”

“I’ll have more details for you in just a couple of minutes.”

Boswell tapped the button on the phone again to return to his conversation with General Bryan: “It’s confirmed Bob, Lincoln is going to be under attack soon. We need air support to defend those cities or they’re already gone. The Guard is pre-occupied in Olympia and Seattle...”

"If we bring in the air force, this may be the last time we'll be able to do it. Their blockade has choked us dry. In addition, enemy jets outnumber our jets…"

"We won't be able to do it at all if we lose Nebraska and Colorado, understand?"

"That's not necessarily true sir. The Coalition *can* survive without two border states. You must understand that our strategy today must take tomorrow's defense into consideration. Engaging in the air would be suicidal right now."

"Well, let's at least get some guard forces shipped down there in an air transport vehicle. It's all or nothing now, Bob. It's all on the line in this battle."

"I'll do it. They'll be there in about four hours…"

Boswell notified Governor Mackenzie of Nebraska and Governor Wilson of Colorado, who were both still on their way back to their underground bunkers. *What are they going to do?* Boswell thought as the phone rang. *They'll be under attack without even their own Guard to defend them. They need to hold on for at least four hours until Guard reinforcements arrive...*

"Ben Boswell! Just the man I wanted to speak to," said the gray-headed governor of Nebraska from the back seat of his SUV. "How's the fight in Washington State?"

"They've stopped the federal advancement on Olympia, but you'll get a taste of the battle soon enough, friend. I have just received intelligence that the feds are heading toward your position from the east right now."

"What?" the exasperated Nebraska governor exclaimed.

"I'll have more details for you in a few minutes from the man with the eyes in the sky…"

Olympia, Washington

After Rod Sanders halted the federal military assault on the statehouse and capitol buildings, courageous armed citizens began to harass the federal troops on their flanks and from the rear. Fuel tankers that had been strategically placed along the interstate during the feds' trek north were being systematically destroyed, thanks to bands of enthusiastic, tyranny-hating locals. Others captured and drove the fuel tankers to the rear lines of the Guard's forces, where fuel was transferred to the Guard's armored fighting vehicles.

Dozens of civilian snipers sacrificed their lives for an opportunity to take out just one of their invaders. This was their home. They defended their families and liberties with their blood, impressing even the federal generals with their fearless tenacity.

Seattle, Washington

With the relief at the front lines on the outskirts of Olympia, many of the guardsmen were ordered into downtown Seattle. The situation there was becoming critical. Police forces were engaged in gun battles in the streets with roving bands of angry anarchists and looting students. Intoxicated rioters were burning down buildings and assaulting citizens who dared to challenge them. Firemen and policemen were harassed, pelted with beer bottles and bricks, and beaten without mercy. The guardsmen carried wooden clubs, tear gas, and automatic weapons with mags carrying rubber bullets and other mags carrying live ammo.

Hundreds of well-armed civilians and Minutemen enthusiastically volunteered to assist the Guard and the police force in restoring peace to their city. They scoured the streets for rioters and vandals, helping with arrests, and documenting testimonies of eyewitnesses as well as video and photographic evidence that revealed the identity of the perpetrators. They also aided in putting out the raging fires.

When the police force reached Washington State University, they found a crowd of 1,000 students shoulder-to-shoulder, 75 yards thick in every direction, surrounding an African American man standing atop an overturned trash receptacle, megaphone in hand, preaching his heart out with a painfully hoarse voice.

The crowd of Minutemen, who had endured the spit and the curses of the throng of heathen for several hours, began to cheer as the police force made their way across the campus green toward them. The students grew fearful of getting blamed for the vandalism all around campus, and so fled before them. Elijah hopped off the trashcan and took a deep breath. He extended a hand to the overweight sheriff with the thick, black mustache and goatee.

"How's it going, uh," – he hesitated as he read his nametag – "Sheriff Miller?" Elijah's voice was all but gone.

"You know, I'm gonna have to give you a ticket for turning that trash can upside down," he said as several officers around him chuckled. "Just kidding. How in the world did you do that?" The sheriff of Seattle grinned widely. "This is the only part of campus that isn't on fire."

As the sheriff inquired further, he discovered that it started when Elijah began to preach to a group of about 100 students who were conspiring destruction on nearby dormitories. The crowd of lawless students grew and the Minutemen were soon surrounded. Elijah's defense of Christianity and the Coalition had them all in an erratic frenzy, but aptly placed humor and Elijah's occasional soft answers kept their tempers to a minimum. Even those among them that were most immune to conviction of sin simply set down their Molotov cocktails and their baseball bats to be entertained by the lively dialogue between the boldest leftists among them and the African American evangelist who had become known as "the preacher."

In other parts of the campus and in sections of the city where no Minutemen were stationed, the rage was unhindered and much of the campus and many buildings and restaurants were destroyed. The rioters spread their violence and mayhem throughout the city. Anyone who did not join in the reckless destruction of private property was a candidate for destruction themselves from the merciless mob of drunken college students, drug-crazed hippies, gothic head-bangers, illegal immigrants, welfare recipients and unemployed citizens whose government checks were late, and frothing-at-the-mouth communists and anarchists.

18

Lincoln, Nebraska

As an overwhelming federal force invades his state with 80% of his guard forces several states away, Nebraska's Governor Mackenzie was growing desperate. Every spare employee in the capitol building was ordered to begin calling up State Guard reservists and military veterans to active duty – particularly those who might have the ability to man artillery weapons. Several staff members were assigned the duty of contacting the members of gun clubs and hunting clubs to request that they come to Nebraska's defense. Through radio and television, Governor Mackenzie requested every able man who had a gun to come out and defend his state from the federal troops that sped toward Lincoln by two routes: State Road 2 and Interstate 80.

A pawnshop owner informed one of the governor's callers, "A guy was here several of days ago, uh, what was his name? He was recruiting guys to train in a local militia he was starting up…"

"What was his name?" the governor's aid asked.

"I, I don't remember. Had about 500 volunteers last time I spoke to him. He was going to train them in a ten day boot camp, and then a second-string group in the evenings three nights a week…"

"Do you know how we can get in touch with him?"

Dillon State Park, Nebraska

Jack Handel had wasted no time. Even before his wife's funeral, he was on the phone with the leaders of the Montana militia and gun and hunting clubs, planning a massive campaign to raise up independent state militias in the other Coalition states. The morning of Dixie's burial, he met with 75 interested men and planned a trip to the border states to train civilian militia.

Jack was in the middle of his ten-day boot camp about 30 miles north of Lincoln at a large state park. He had to limit attendance at this training camp to those who intended to lead and train militias in their neighborhoods or churches, and even then he had to turn people away when their number reached 1,000. This was a leaders-only camp for men who were already skilled shooters. He taught basic lethal martial combat, warfare strategies, sniping, survival techniques, and he trained them in the use of artillery with weapons donated by the state's Guard unit. They were a rag-tag bunch of attorneys and mechanics, hunters and Sunday school teachers, business shop owners and farmers, mayors and janitors, young and old.

Jack sat at a picnic table at the end of the line of about 100 of his best shooters who lay prone on the ground as they shot at targets 300 yards away. He had assigned several other skilled militia members to set up spotting scopes along the line of shooters, offering advice and correcting bad habits. Jack was looking through his sighting scope when he received a tap on the shoulder.

"Mr. Handel?"

"What do you want?" Jack snapped, undistracted from his scope.

"Terry said I could join."

"Which Terry? That Terry?" Jack pointed to the third man down the row who aimed his .308 at a distant target.

"Yeah, Terry Rowles."

"Well, Terry's wrong. We've got too many. Sign up with Sara at the office, and we'll call you." Jack pointed in the direction of the state park office.

The young man extended a target in a plastic ziplock bag with a tight group of bullets around the bull's-eye of the target. "But sir, this is my grouping at 500–"

Jack interrupted him without even looking at him. "Do you live near Terry?"

"Yes sir."

"Terry's starting a training camp in his church next week, so you can sign up with his church, or you can sign up with Sara. In the meantime," – Jack pulled away from his scope and turned to look at him for the first time – "you can do some good for the cause if you'll get on the phone with other churches in your area and see if you can get the pastors to urge their men to sign up with Terry's militia training classes."

The young man shoved his paper target into his pocket, hung his head in disappointment, and walked away.

"Heads up, boy," Jack encouraged the young man as he shuffled away from him. "It may be a long war and there'll be plenty of blood-spillin' to go around."

"Yes sir."

"Slowly! Slowly, Travis! This ain't no track meet. One bullet, one kill. If you miss him by an inch at this distance, you'll miss him by twelve inches at twice the distance. And if you miss, you'd have done better by not pulling the trigger, because their snipers might locate you from the blast of your gun."

"Mr. Jack Handel." A camouflaged guardsman tapped him on the shoulder.

"Come on, Ricky!" Handel shouted, ignoring the tap on the shoulder and gazing at distant targets through his spotting scope. "You're low and left. You're anticipating a little. Slowly, Ricky, slowly squeeze the trigger until the blast surprises both you and the gun."

"I hit the circle!" the scrawny African American lad complained.

"The most consistent shots in your group are all scraping the outer rim," Jack rebutted with his spotting scope fixed on Ricky's target. "That rifle and those bullets are better than that. With that aim you'll injure a UN private at 300 yards, but miss his general at 600. And the injured soldier will still shoot his grenade launcher at you. Quit anticipating." He pulled his eye away from the scope to make eye contact with his student. "Do you want to injure new recruits at 300 and run? Or do you want to kill a general from 1,000 and win the battle?"

Ricky smiled. "Win the battle."

"Then put 'em in the center! Let's go."

"Mr. Jack Handel!" The man who tapped on Jack's shoulder shouted so as to be heard over the gun blasts.

"Come on, Will!" Jack turned to a fellow Militia of Montana member to his left who was acting as his assistant. "Stop letting people interrupt me while I'm working."

Will had his back to Jack, chatting with a highway patrolman, when Jack reproved him. He turned to face Jack. "Sorry, sir."

Jack turned and saw the man dressed in camos who had tapped him on the shoulder. He held out an open cell phone. "The governor's office wants to speak to you." He extended the phone to Jack.

Jack didn't accept it, but lowered his eye back to the scope. "Give it to Will. I'm busy."

"It's the governor, sir."

Jack looked back at the camouflaged fellow, and saw the patch for the Nebraska Guard on his right shoulder. "Of Montana?"

"No, Nebraska."

Jack took the phone. "This is Jack Handel."

Austin, Texas

Darlene and Janet busied themselves scoping out a large elementary school in downtown Austin, looking for Darlene's kindergartener, Charlotte. They found a stray dog, crafted a leash, and feigned that they were women going out for some exercise. They walked along a sidewalk near where yellow school buses released children in front of the school. During the mid-morning hours, they scouted playgrounds at other elementary schools. Then they went to a third school in the afternoon and watched children board the buses and cars. Darlene was shocked at how normal everything appeared in the streets of Austin. Though they were under martial law, though there were armed civilians holed up in their homes against federal forces just 12 miles away, and though Christians were tortured for their faith in detention facilities 20 miles north, everybody just went about their business without bother.

"Where could she be?" Darlene said, as she took another lap with Janet past the elementary school.

"Ugh! I'm not in very good shape, Darlene. We should have found a dog that walked just a little bit slower."

"Beggars can't be choosers." Darlene's gaze was fixed on the playground on the other side of the fence. She was desperate to find her babies.

"Don't stare so long, or you're going to arouse suspicion."

Darlene sighed a weary sigh, and with a soft voice tenderized through a thousand tearful prayers, she prayed, "Dear God, let us find my girls before David gets here."

North Omaha, Nebraska

David and his bodyguard, Matt Wellington, were heading south when they learned on the radio that the feds had invaded the state of Washington and threatened to take over the capital city of Olympia.

They decided to change their route to Texas by going though South Dakota, and then southward through Nebraska, Kansas, and Oklahoma. He had also learned through intelligence obtained from Governor Boswell's office that the federal roadblocks were thinner along the Oklahoma-Nebraska border than elsewhere, in part because of Oklahoma's sympathy with the Coalition. Although Oklahoma was reluctant to join the Coalition, their governor refused to call the Guard up to monitor their northern border with the most eastward state in the Coalition, Nebraska. Moreover, most Oklahomans were furious about the UN troops who ventured into southern Oklahoma to set up camp.

David and Matt followed State Route 75 on the west side of the Missouri River and were ten minutes from Omaha when they learned through the radio about the federal advancement into Nebraska.

...The federal ground forces are pressing into Omaha from the south and the east. They have completely destroyed Offutt Air Force Base in southern Omaha with mortars launched from a long train of Army vehicles. Federal forces are moving quickly toward Omaha westward along Interstate 80 over the river and northward along State Route 75 just south of Omaha...

Matt shook his head, disturbed by the news. "This changes everything, David. They're on the same road we're on."

"They're south of Omaha," David said, studying a map and running his fingers through his light brown beard. "We're north."

"We gotta turn around, David." He slowed their red Jeep Cherokee and pulled over to the side of the road. "We need an alternative route south. We're driving into a war zone."

"Shhh." David turned up the volume on the radio and spread the map out on his lap.

...We just got this in from Governor Mackenzie's office, the radio station disc jockey announced. After a moment of silence, he paraphrased the fax. *Governor Mackenzie is calling every freedom-lovin' Nebraskan to arm themselves and resist the federal advancement. The federal troops aim to conquer Nebraska but we must resist, he says. With God's help, we will turn them back and maintain our sovereignty...*

Upon hearing this, Matt grinned and put a palm up in the air toward David, who reluctantly slapped him a high five. "Rally the lesser magistrates!" Matt exclaimed. David was more preoccupied with finding a way around the conflict to his wife in Texas than he was about cheering on any resistance to the federal invasion.

"Look at all the traffic heading north." The traffic moving quickly the opposite direction on the two-lane road was bumper-to-bumper and getting thicker by the moment. "Everybody's fleeing Omaha."

David didn't look up from his map. "We gotta go west to Fremont and south to Lincoln."

"That's not gonna work." Matt pointed at the map with his muscular arm. "The feds will probably be in Lincoln before we get there. It's Nebraska's capital. I'm sure they mean to occupy it."

"There's no quick route around Omaha or Lincoln."

"We could wait until they leave Omaha and then–"

"No. I'm sure they'll leave forces in Omaha."

"Well, we could go east on State Route 30 into Iowa and then south toward Texas. The feds may have roadblocks at the border, but it's a chance we need to take. We passed that exit a couple of miles back." Matt pointed northward behind him with his thumb.

When David looked up from the map, he exclaimed, "Whoa! Matt, what now?"

A long caravan of camouflaged Army vehicles sped north on the opposite side of the two-lane highway, right toward them. Cars that were in their way were waved to the side of the road at gunpoint.

David threw the map in the back seat. "Turn around. Go north!"

Matt skid the tires in a quick U-turn and headed north.

"Hurry!" David urged him.

Matt began to weave in and out of traffic, prompting other cars to beep their horn at him. Soon, the approaching military vehicles could no longer be seen in the rearview mirror, but within view of the city limits there were bright red brake lights as far as they could see ahead of them. Matt speculated that a traffic accident had slowed down the northbound traffic.

"This is the town of Blair." David pointed at a green street sign on the side of the road. "That's where we get onto State Route 30 to cross the river into Iowa." Both sides of the two-lane highway were filled with cars driving north. "Drive along the grass. We've got to get around this accident and get to that exit."

Matt followed David's suggestion and drove north along the soft shoulder of the road. They made it to the small town of Blair to the intersection of S.R. 30 where they came upon what they thought was a motor vehicle accident. They were shocked to discover that there was no motor vehicle accident, but the feds had blockaded the road just inside Blair's city limits. The federal forces must have anticipated the flight north from Omaha and were stopping and searching vehicles. When they saw Matt and David driving the shoulder, two camouflage-clad soldiers approached their vehicle with their weapons aimed at them, ordering them out of the car.

"What do we do?" Matt asked.

David did not respond, but opened the door and stepped out of the vehicle. The soldier approached David, grabbed his shoulder, turned him toward the car, and ordered him to put his hands on top of the vehicle and spread his legs.

"I'm sorry. We thought there was an accident and we–"

"You were trying to evade a federal roadblock." The soldier flung his rifle over his shoulder by the sling and began to frisk David. "That's a federal crime."

"We thought it was a motor vehicle accident."

"Do you have any weapons, ammo, or food in the car?" The cell phone between the driver and the front passenger seat of their red Jeep Cherokee began to ring. David ducked his head to glance at the LCD display and saw it was Darlene calling. "Sir, can I get that phone call?" He turned to face the soldier. "That's very important. It's–"

"Shut up!" The soldier screamed at him with a voice hoarse from shouting orders, and smacked him against the face with the back of his hand. "When I tell you to put your hands on the car you keep them there! Do you have any guns in the car?"

"Of course they do," a soldier behind him answered. "All these cars do…"

David licked the blood off of his lip and did not immediately answer. He had to find a way to answer that phone. The soldier thrust David's chest against the hood of the car. "Answer me!"

"That call is my wife, sir. It's a matter of life and–"

The soldier was irritated with David wasting his time, so he reached into the car through the open window, grabbed the cell phone, and threw it into the ditch on the side of the road. David hollered in shock at losing his only connection to his wife, "No!"

David turned toward the ditch to try to discover exactly where the cell phone would land when the soldier smacked him hard with an open palm, snapping his neck to the side and flinging him against the car and to the ground.

Matt had gotten out of the car and was exchanging feisty words with the soldier who wanted to frisk him. The soldier called for assistance and two other soldiers flung Matt against the ground and removed a .45-caliber semi-automatic from a holster in the small of his back. Under the space between the Cherokee and the asphalt, David watched Matt vainly try to reason with the two soldiers.

"Dear God, help us," David moaned, tears coming to his eyes as he realized he would not be able to see his wife anytime soon – if ever. If they discovered who he was, he may never again see the outside of a cell. Matt was at risk of doing hard time, with his handgun and a loaded semi-automatic assault rifle and several loaded mags under the tarp in the back seat of the car.

"I have rights," David insisted. "This is America. We're brothers."

"I thought this was the Coalition. That makes you my enemy." The soldier raised his rifle and thumped David on the head with the butt of it, knocking him unconscious.

Austin, Texas

"David! You won't believe it!" Darlene's voice was full of excitement as she left the message on his answering machine. "We found Charlotte! Can you believe it! We found her! We just watched her get onto a bus in downtown Austin." Darlene glowed as she glanced over at Janet, who had a broad smile on her face as she pulled in behind the yellow school bus into traffic. "We're following the bus to discover where she lives," she said through tears of joy. "Pray that they're all staying at the same foster home. Pray that we can get them without getting caught. You're right, honey. God won't give us more than we can handle. He's lookin' out for us. Call me back as soon as you can."

Darlene and Janet followed the yellow school bus to a small farm house outside of the city limits. The house appeared old but clean. There were farm fields on each side.

When Charlotte got off the bus, she glanced back a moment at the car behind the bus, and Darlene's heart felt as if it would just burst. She gazed into her eldest daughters' eyes, and her heart throbbed with anticipation. Soon, she would hold both of them again.

"That's her, huh?" Janet asked.

"Yes it is." Tears flowed down Darlene's pale cheeks. "That's my Charlotte."

"Do you see any of the other girls through the window?"

Darlene squinted to try to look for any signs of life through the windows, but it appeared as if no one was even home. Charlotte knocked at the front door and twisted the doorknob, but it appeared to be locked.

The bus began to drive ahead and Janet picked up speed to follow it closely.

"Where are you going?"

"We gotta keep driving. We can't arouse suspicion."

"Don't leave!"

"We'll scope it out, and pick just the right moment to–"

"There they are!" Darlene squealed with joy and grabbed Janet's right arm. "There's my girls!"

Janet looked back to see the two younger Jameson girls open the door and rush to hug their big sister on the front porch of the old farmhouse.

"There's my girls!" The tears flowed like a river down her cheeks and onto her blouse. Janet stopped the car just past the edge of the property as Darlene kept her eyes fixed on her three children, her heart bursting with ecstasy. "Oh, Charlotte! Mary! Johanna! Johanna's walking now! Oh my!" Without warning, Darlene opened the door and jumped out of the car.

"Darlene!"

Darlene left the door open and began to sprint as fast as her little legs would take her toward her children. She jumped the ditch and almost fell down. "Charlotte! Mary! Johanna! It's Momma!" She regained her footing and ran toward them with her arms out-stretched.

"No! Darlene!!" Janet exclaimed, thrusting the transmission into reverse and backing up the car until it was directly in front of the home. Fortunately, there wasn't much traffic on the road and there were no cars in the driveway.

"It's me!" Darlene cried. "It's Mommy!"

"Mommy? Mommy!" They began to cry and run toward their mother.

"I'm here, babies!" Darlene fell to her knees and embraced her two oldest daughters, who reached her first.

"You're not a bad person, are you Mommy?" Charlotte's eyes were full of painful tears, and Darlene thought she looked way too grown up.

"No, baby. Mommy loves Jesus." She pulled little Johanna, the toddler who lagged behind, close in a tight embrace. "Oh, Johanna! I have prayed for you all every day."

"Because Mrs. Jones said you were bad." Charlotte motioned to the house.

Darlene froze, realizing that an adult may be in the house. "Is she there?"

She shook her head. "Not yet."

"Get them in the car!" Janet shouted as she opened the rear passenger door and turned her face away from a driver who passed them on the two lane road. "Come on!"

Lincoln, Nebraska

In response to the governor's call for men to aid in the defense of their city, 5,000 men and 1,000 women gathered with weapons and ammunition outside the capitol building in downtown Lincoln. Those who did not have a gun were given one by Guard reservists commissioned to distribute them to civilians. Some of the men with experience in the armed forces were given automatic weapons and smaller artillery such as RPGs and grenade launchers. More experienced vets were given charge of larger mortar equipment.

The men were somber and still as a Marine brigadier general who had defected from the federal government informed them over a megaphone of the details of the federal advancement and the plan to defend their city. "Our fathers, sons, and brothers in the Guard are laying down their lives in the state of Washington trying to resist the federal advancement there. Now it's up to us to protect Nebraska. We have to be the ones willing to lay down our lives for liberty. If anyone rats these plans to the feds," the Marine warned them, "we have permission to shoot them on site. We are at war and traitors will be executed."

He then described their defense strategy to them. Defected military and vets made their way to the front of the growing crowd and stood at attention in front of the aging brigadier general. "We must work as a team," their commander instructed them. "Every one of you must obey your leader, and every leader must obey the orders given to them from above."

Gun shop owners distributed ammunition to all who lacked. Men with walkie-talkies roamed to and fro among the crowd and divided the men into companies, writing down the names of their impromptu leaders. Pastors led their churches, professors from the local Christian university led their students, employers led their workers, physicians led their patients, high school football coaches led their players, and fathers and grandfathers led their children.

The Marine promised the men that many of them would die. "Be brave. Be true to your God today. Fear nothing but God's displeasure," he shouted, to the cheers of all of Lincoln. "Better to perish fighting for liberty than die a slave. Let the victors when they come, when the forts of evil fall, find my body near the wall!"

These civilians had counted the cost and were preparing to pay it. They were no longer simply defending the Coalition, their governor, or their state – now they were defending their families and their religion. The Marine led them all in a passionate prayer for God's help, and then ordered the laymen to their respective positions on the battle line.

Men rushed to the front line outside the city limits in pick-up trucks, vans, and SUVs. Semi-trucks blocked interstate overpasses at the necks of bridges. Pick-up trucks, with artillery bolted to their truck beds, fanned out to strategic locations in the trees along the roadside, so as to conceal their location.

Jack Handel, still trembling with adrenaline over the mandate the Nebraska governor had just given him, was ordered to immediately lead the 1,000 men at his training camp to the front line. They raced to the eastern city limits of Lincoln in 200 vehicles.

When Handel, the roadblocks of semi-trucks across the necks of bridges around the city was almost complete. Jack walked up to a short, white-haired Guard reservist and identified himself. "Been waitin' for ya. Thanks for coming. Call me Wickard," the stubby Guard reservist told him. The reservist handed him a walkie-talkie and they discussed the most strategic place to position his men.

"This is the primary attack route according to our satellite intel." The reservist motioned eastward along the four lane highway that led to the bridge upon which they were standing. "Omaha's 30 miles that way. I was told 30 minutes ago that they'd already be here," he said, studying the sky, looking for the drones that he knew must be flying overhead, relaying their positions to federal officers.

Jack Handel gave his men orders and situated 200 of them directly behind the semi-trucks. He barely had time to catch his breath when someone yelled, "Artillery! Hear that?"

Wickard studied the horizon with his binoculars, and saw a flash of light along the horizon, like the flash of lightening on the edge of an approaching thunderstorm, followed by a bellowing rumble.

Wickard looked to his left and saw two large pick-up trucks driving just behind the tree line with M-198 artillery canons freshly bolted to the floor of the truck beds. “I want them out of sight!” Wickard ordered a fellow reservist. “They have a five mile range, they need to back up and try to camouflage themselves with branches and stuff.”

“They know, sir.”

“How many of those do you have?” Jack pointed to the trucks with the M-198s.

“Twenty-five were in storage in Lincoln. A few Bradleys were being repaired, and we got them up and running. They have TOW long range anti-armor missile launching systems.”

“That’ll level the playing field a little bit.”

“I don’t know,” Wickard responded wistfully. “If they can shoot tanks, they can be shot by tanks. The feds have superior firepower, numbers, experience.” Wickard sighed and looked down. “Oh man,” he mumbled, the sound of fear in his voice. “I can’t believe this is happening. This may be the bravest few minutes in Nebraska’s history, but it still may only be a few minutes.”

Once Jack discovered where Wickard had stationed his fellow reservists and retired vets, he got on his walkie-talkie and started ordering his men into buildings beside the road back further toward the city. He ordered his snipers on the top of the hills to the south.

“Hey, Mr. Wickard!” Somebody called out to the reservists from behind them.

Wickard turned to see a businessman with well-ironed slacks and a starched white shirt lift his cell phone into the air. “It’s my parents in Omaha. Omaha’s putting up a fight! They’re putting up a *good* fight!”

Those who were within earshot of the bank executive cheered wildly. “You!” Wickard said as he pointed to the businessman. “You’re my radio operator! I need your cell – the batteries are getting weak on my radio and the guy I sent out to get new batteries has been gone 15 minutes. Get Governor Mackenzie on the line for me if you can.”

“When they break through,” Governor Mackenzie told three veterans from the Terrorist Wars on the telephone, “why not have the ladies on the sidewalk cheer the feds on? Have them hold flags and cheer, clap and wave at them. They’ll probably come right down 77 and then exit off the interstate at the statehouse exit. Have the ladies on both sides of the road clap and cheer like it was a ticker-tape parade. The feds expect it to be a cakewalk, so we’ll make them think they’re going to get one. Then we'll have the men stationed in the upper floor of those buildings" – he pointed at the buildings on the east and west sides of the street. "When the feds are well into the city, have the ladies flee down the alleys on cue and have the men rain hell down on the invaders with the Guard's .50-caliber machine guns and artillery…"

The vets chuckled giddily. "I like it."

"Uh, governor? You said, *when* they break through. Do you think we stand any chance at all of stopping them outside the city limits?" This Army veteran was responsible for setting up an inner perimeter of defense with the 250 civilians who were placed under his command, and he didn't like the notion that most of their forces were already given up for dead.

"Well, Omaha has put up a good fight and slowed them down, but we're not going to be any more of a match for their professional fighters and their firepower than those laymen were in Omaha. Even if they don't engage from the air, they're still coming in here with some major firepower."

"But I've seen the numbers. It seems to me that we'll greatly outnumber them."

"It ain't going to make a difference, gentlemen, unless we're aimin' to drown them in our blood. Short of a miracle, the feds *will* make it into Lincoln. Unless the Coalition air force engages their vehicles on the ground."

"But if our jets and Apaches engage, then theirs will too, and this is just going to escalate all over again, except this time, they're probably prepared to defend against a ballistic threat."

"Don't you think I know that?"

The veteran shook his head in disbelief. He sure hoped that Governor Boswell and the Coalition generals knew what they were doing. "Well, Governor, if we're going to be ready for them, we have to get busy."

"Godspeed ya'. Call me on this line in 15 minutes to let me know how you're doing and I'll brief you on any intelligence I get."

A civilian's pick-up truck sped from Omaha toward their blockade. The driver, a scruffy-faced farmer in blue overalls, found himself unable to pass through the roadblock, so he parked his pick-up truck in front of it, and scrambled between the trucks and cars with his three teenage boys right behind him, rifles slung over their shoulders.

The farmer shouted out to Hammel and Wickard, “Get ready, fellas! They’re coming!” About 250 men squatted in rows on the side of the road, clutching their rifles.

A satellite-guided, roving eco-car about the size of a go-cart was 100 yards behind the truck. It careened toward the roadblock, oblivious to the thousands of crosshairs that were fixed upon it. It was one of the Army’s unmanned scout vehicles.

Jack Handel ordered one of his artillery gunners to take out the eco-car just for an opportunity to get their feet wet, which they did. “Good shot! Move your vehicles 30 yards to the north and prepare to fire again. Remember, you gotta keep moving, because they’ll aim their weapons at the location from which you just fired…”

“Come on, come on!” Wickard reached for the walkie-talkie as one of his men installed fresh batteries.

“There you are, sir.” He turned the radio on and handed it to Wickard.

Wickard hit a button on the radio. “Get ready. Prepare to fire!”

“I got the governor,” the businessman with the cell phone told Wickard. “Here’s Governor Mackenzie.”

The reservist snatched the phone from his newly commissioned radio operator. “Any new intelligence, Governor?” After a pause, he concluded the phone call. “Thank you sir. I’ll keep you informed. Pray for us.” He handed the cell phone back to the businessman and told the artillery gunner over his walkie-talkie: “You fire on them as soon as they get within range.”

“Uh, yes sir… Um…” Wickard heard pages flipping in the background.

“Why that hesitancy in your voice?”

“Uh, remind me, what’s the range of this thing again?”

“I thought you knew how to operate that thing?”

“I’m a reservist, sir, and a full-time 18-wheeler driver. I’ve loaded these onto Bradleys but never fired one before.”

“Oh brother. You just shoot ‘em when you can see ‘em on the horizon. Do you know how to operate the rangefinder?”

“Yes sir. I think so.”

“They’re coming up within range. Fire on them once they do. If you hesitate, they will kill you before you have an opportunity to fire one single round at them! Got that? It’s kill or be killed, understand?”

The Guard reservist Wickard motioned for Jack, who ducked behind their semi-truck roadblock. “Hey. What’s your name again?”

"Jack Handel with the Militia of Montana. You know, we're sitting ducks behind this semi, because this is the first thing they're going to blow up once they get within range."

"Good point," Wickard mumbled. "Perhaps we should move down into that culvert over there."

"I've already got some men down there. I've got a plan."

"Maybe you should stick with the plan that's been given us."

"You stick with the plan that you've been given, but I've got free reign over my own men."

"You think you can stop the feds' advancement?"

"Oh, we won't stop them. But we'll slow them down. Just face it." Jack kept his gaze fixed on the horizon that was visible between the two semis in front of him. "We're going to see Jesus today. Our job's to take out as many of them as we can so they'll have time to prepare a better defense back there," he said, pointing his thumb west toward the other roadblocks that were being set up miles behind them.

"Waverly's putting up a fight!" Wickard's makeshift radio operator informed him. There was armed resistance in the small town just seven miles east of them. A few of the men around them who were able to overhear the comment cheered.

"All right! Come on, boys, hold on." Wickard studied the horizon with his binoculars.

"See ya' soon, Dixie," Jack whispered to himself.

Wickard lowered his binoculars. "So, tell me about this phenomenal plan of yours."

19

Olympia, Washington

"Colonel! Colonel!" A Guard captain addressed Rod Sanders over the radio in downtown Olympia with the chatter of machine gun fire and the screams of a wounded man in the background. "The feds are moving into the mall on 14th and Main. They're taking artillery and RPG's into…"

"Get Masters into that building! The feds have been firing down on us from those top floors and they're crippling us on those streets. I told him to occupy that building 20 minutes ago!"'

"They're held up on 11th and Main, sir, with a heavy gun battle that's spreading room to room in the office building. They have someone shooting from the buildings over there, too. Feds or friendly citizens – not sure."

"Tell him that he… never mind. I'll tell him myself. You get to his position as soon as possible and provide support."

Guard Lieutenant Masters, the fuel station owner from Lasseter, Montana, was point man in a room-to-room search through an office building, trying to catch snipers who fired on them from above, severely crippling their ability to move on the streets. He stood with his back to the door and motioned to his men, who assumed their foreordained positions along each side of him. A large man next to him kicked the door with a grunt and then two on each side of him burst into the room shouting.

A woman in a pants suit screamed and ducked behind her desk. “It’s all right, ma’am,” the aged Lieutenant Masters told her as he walked carefully toward her desk. “Where are they?”

Through a torrent of tears that flowed over hives that had broken out on her face, she pointed to a door on the other side of the room. “Ten minutes ago, some men ran down that hall that way, talking about shooting down on the Guard.”

Masters opened the door on the other side of the room, and peaked out to look down the hall. There were four closed doors on each side of the hallway that led to a stairwell. He pointed down the hall. “That way?”

“Yes.”

“Get outta here,” he told her as he pointed back the way he came. He quickly took off down the hall, trying to move as quietly as possible.

“Lieutenant Masters!” came the call over his radio.

He tapped his receiver and spoke into his shoulder mic as his men began to clear the rooms down the hall. “What?”

“You’ve got armed civilians in the building as well. I just saw about four or five young men run up a stairway with guns. I think they’re on our side.”

“Oh, great,” he mumbled sarcastically.

Muffled gunfire resounded down the hall. Masters suddenly understood that they had stumbled upon the snipers who were shooting down at them. The guardsmen kicked down the last door on the left and bursts of machine gun fire echoed throughout the building. Masters started running down the hall. He saw one of his men take a flurry of bullets in the chest and abdomen, falling to the ground with a scream. He witnessed one of his men fall through the open doorway on the right, clutching his weapon with one hand and clawing the ground in pain with the other. Another round from a weapon in the room made him go limp.

Masters and the stunned soldier next to him quietly rushed toward the conflict, and ran headlong into two federal soldiers coming out of the room on the left. Before he even realized he had just collided with the enemy, Masters found himself face down on top of a soldier half his age and twice his strength.

The Coalition guardsman besides Masters got off a shot at one of the federal troopers, but the soldier pulled him close and wrestled the gun out of his grasp. The Coalition soldier traded punches and knees with the federal trooper and was flung against the wall.

Lieutenant Masters let out a yelp and reached for a twelve-inch dagger on his calf. As the federal soldier reached for his own knife, Masters grabbed the soldier's right arm to prevent him. Masters pulled his legs around his opponent's hips until he was sitting on his abdomen in the full mount position. He tucked his feet under the soldier's hips to keep from being bucked off. He raised his dagger his right hand, but not before the fed had grabbed his fallen rifle. The fed raised the black M-16 and pointed it at Masters' face. Masters let go of the knife to grab the barrel of the rifle and direct it away from his face. The fed pulled the trigger and the heat of the machine gun barrel singed Masters' hand.

"Ow!" Masters screamed. He let go and with his left forearm pushed the barrel against the fed's face. He pulled the trigger of the federal soldiers gun, burning the federal soldier's face and shooting the leg of the soldier that was wrestling with his partner. As the federal trooper cursed in pain, Masters snatched his knife and swung it toward the chest of the soldier beneath him, but the soldier caught his swinging arm and used Master's momentum to flip him over.

"Ah!" Masters yelled again, more from the arthritis in his back than from any pain the trooper inflicted on him. With Masters underneath him, the federal soldier, bigger and stronger than the aging Coalition lieutenant, was thrusting Masters' own knife toward his throat. Masters thought that his life was about to end.

Just as the knife was one inch from the pit in Masters' throat, a bullet blasted through the federal soldier's head causing him to fall limp onto Master's chest.

Masters thought for a moment that the blood was his own. He rolled the soldier off of him and gasped as he watched his partner, still breathing heavily from his own bout of hand-to-hand combat, eject an empty magazine from his M-16 and insert a fully loaded magazine in its place.

"Thanks," said Masters, breathing heavily, his face and neck covered in the warm blood of his enemy. He sat up and put his right hand on his left shoulder and moved it around, grunting in pain. As this aging vet of the first Gulf War massaged his aching shoulder, he felt the squishing of blood between his shirt and his chest and he winced in disgust. "You could have shot him from the side and spared me the bloodbath of some dope-smokin', HIV-infected–"

"Hey," the guardsman responded jokingly. "Ain't that hate-speech? Don't ask, don't tell, remember?"

Masters didn't find that humorous. He struggled to his feet with a grunt. "Ugh, I think I—"

The sudden footsteps of several men down the darkened hall got their attention, hushing the complaint on Masters' tongue. Masters' eyes tried to make out the images rushing toward them, but it was too dark. His mind buzzed with troubling thoughts. *Were these good guys or bad guys running toward them?* They quickly darted into an empty room beside them and tried to shut the door quietly, but the doorknob was broken and it swung back open of its own accord. Masters hugged the wall and held the door shut with his right hand, panting heavily from his adrenaline.

Master's subordinate had the look of fear on his sweaty face. He motioned to a door that led to another room and Masters silenced him with a twitch of his head back and forth.

Masters kept his ear to the door. He listened carefully to the voices in the hallway, trying to discern whether they were civilians, guardsmen, or federal infantry. When he heard the whispered phrase, "That's Donny, stationed out of Ft. Bliss. Oh man," he let go of the door and fired a three-round burst through the sheetrock.

At least one body collapsed outside and blood pooled under the door. Another wounded federal trooper had a grenade in his fist. He pulled the pin and threw it into the room through the open door. Masters didn't see the grenade but heard the metallic thumps of it bouncing against the floor into the corner of the room. The guardsman with him instinctively kicked in the door of a closet, grabbed Masters by the shirt, and they jumped into the unlit room together. The grenade detonated a second later, sending shrapnel through the walls and casting eerie streaks of light and smoke into the closet in which they found themselves.

Masters had never had a grenade blow up so close to him, and the blast was louder than he ever thought it could be in such closed confinements. He was knocked senseless for a moment, but soon regained his composure and rushed out of the closet, taking advantage of the cover of the smoke. He peaked through the splinters of the door and saw the hallway empty except for the carcasses of dead or dying soldiers. Apparently, a water pipe in the ceiling above them was punctured from the shrapnel and hot water sprayed through the fractured ceiling onto the floor.

He turned to tell the guardsman still in the closet, urging him to update Guard command when he noticed that the man did not move from his crouched position. He bent down to check on him and saw blood coming out of his mouth. Masters searched for a carotid pulse with his index finger and felt the last heartbeat. A jagged piece of shrapnel had entered just under the guardsman's helmet where it severed his spinal cord and pierced his brain.

Suddenly, Masters heard footsteps down the hall, young voices shouting, and gunshots from at least three guns. The door hung erratically on its hinges. He pushed gently it on its hinges so he could see through the cracks in the wood to get a look down the hall at the soldiers to discover if they were friends or enemies. Unexpectedly, half the door fell onto the ground with a loud crash. "Shoot," he mumbled.

"Who's there?" he heard a young voice call out down the dark hall.

"Guard," he responded, finger firm against his trigger just inside the doorway.

"We're on your side."

Masters stepped into the hall cautiously and saw three young teenagers carrying three Chinese-made SKSs and a fourth youth carrying a military-crafted automatic assault weapon. He sighed heavily at the realization that all six men previously with him were now dead.

"We got four of 'em upstairs," said the young man who appeared to be a leader of the clan and who held the military weapon.

Masters picked up his radio and informed Guard command, "Sanders, this is Masters. We got the snipers. I'm the only survivor."

The leader of the clan of young civilian militia moved in closer and recognized the lieutenant. "Is that you, Mr. Masters?"

"Charlie? I thought I recognized one of those young voices from down the hall."

Charlie reached forward to shake the hand of his former employer at the only gas station in Lasseter, Montana.

"What are you doing here? Last time I checked you were still managing that two pump gas station and muffler shop?"

"Last time I checked, *you* were late for work, and you sure didn't own any military-spec machine guns." Masters gently thumped the stock of Charlie's military-issued weapon.

"Boys," Charlie said, looking at the young men under his command, "gather ammo from the dead. I'm runnin' low on .223."

"I've got to get back in the street, Charlie. You guys could be of help. Come with me."

Masters overheard a call come over the radio of one of the dead feds. "If you're alive, Sergeant Major, get out of that building. We're shelling it flat in ten seconds."

"Ten seconds?" one of the young men blurted out. "What did he say?"

"They're leveling this place," Masters responded, his gaze darting back and forth down both directions of the hall to try to decide the best route out of the building.

"We gotta get out of here," one of Charlie's partners yelled as he rushed for the door.

"Don't have time!" Masters responded, darting into the room to the broken window to see a tank in the street raising its huge barrel toward them. "There are civilians holed up in rooms all over this building…"

"They can't level the whole building…" Charlie objected.

"Take 'em out," Masters ordered as he and Charlie instantly lifted their weapons to their shoulders and pointed it at the tanks. Charlie began to fire indiscriminately at the tank when Masters stopped him: "No! Aim down the tube!" He reached for a .50-caliber bolt-action rifle that one of the dead federals still held in his clutches. He raised it, assured that a bullet was in the chamber, and aimed it at the tank. **Blam!**

"Come on!" Masters reproved himself for his bad shooting. He ejected the smoking shell and flipped the bulky bolt-action to insert another round into the bull barrel.

Charlie's friends joined him at the window trying to shoot down the tube but returning fire from the feds in the street hindered them. Charlie screamed and ducked below the window. For a moment Masters thought that he was shot.

"I'm all right." Charlie dabbed his head with his hand and saw blood. "Just grazed. Whoa." He sat on the ground, feeling dizzy for a moment. He returned to the window quite tipsy, and tried to aim his heavy caliber rifle down the tank's mortar tube.

"Shoot accurately, fellas!" Charlie yelled at his friends who intermittently fired a round or two then ducked below the window.

One of his friends held his gun up and fired indiscriminately across the street. "They're shooting on us, Charlie! We can't!"

"Take out these tanks now!" Masters shouted at them as the tank barrel slowly rose to aim at their position.

"I'm outta here." The fellows with Charlie decided to take their chances with the soldiers in the streets. They fled from the room in a panic.

"Mick! Jerry! We need covering fire!" Charlie screamed as he took careful aim down the mortar tube, bullets whizzing around his head. He glanced behind him and saw that his men had abandoned him.

Lieutenant Masters braved the hail of bullets speeding around his head, took his time, and fired one shot of his .50 cal down the mortar tube. His bullet collided with the mortar round just as it was inserted into the tube, readied for firing. This caused the shell to explode inside the tank and turned the vehicle full of mortar shells and ammunition into a massive bomb. Twisted masses of steel and burning debris spewed into the street and nearby buildings, crumbling brick walls and mutilating corpses with speeding shrapnel. Eardrums ruptured and windows shattered a block away from the magnificent concussion.

"Yeah!" Charlie cheered.

Masters ducked and spun down the volume on his hearing aid, finding his ears ringing painfully from the loud explosion. "We've still got enemies out there, Charlie. Let's get out of here."

Lincoln, Nebraska

The Guard reservist Wickard again reiterated the order to his artillery operators to fire when the enemy was within range. He could just barely see the haze of dust kicked up from the line of green vehicles creeping toward them in the distance. Behind the advancing troops, along the horizon, he could see the glitter of an Air Force fighter jet patrolling the sky.

He braced for the hellish rain of mortars.

A loud blast sounded to the south along the tree line in the hills and a huge explosion destroyed the Bradley in the front of the approaching line of federal vehicles.

"Yeah!" Wickard and his men shouted as they began to fire a few volleys at the oncoming forces.

"Hold your fire!" Jack shouted. "Save it!"

The second blast came from the approaching feds in the east. What started as a faint, high-pitched squeal, grew louder and louder as it approached. The feds quickly fired a second and third mortar before the first one struck. Jack hugged the gravel on the side of the road behind a small stack of old railroad posts. He cupped his hands over his ears and prepared for the torrent.

After two minutes of constant bombardment, the roadblock of cars and trucks were in flames. Several of the Coalition's Bradleys and automobiles that were in plain view were destroyed, as were half of the M-198 cannons along the tree line. The federals were closing in fast, undeterred at the occasional explosion of one of their armored personnel carriers resulting from Coalition mortars. The federal Bradleys were close enough that they began to fire heavy machine guns at the Coalition forces huddling the ground around the roadblock. Coalition casualties near the roadblock mounted. The Nebraska militia fired artillery back as quickly and as purposefully as possible and made many hits that slowed the federal advancement, but they were no match for their firepower and accurate aim under fire.

Moments later, Jack saw the federal infantry make the move off the road, a transition for which he had been awaiting. Soldiers rushed from the armored vehicles and some of the damaged Bradleys and sprinted toward the town in an attempt to flank the Guard's forces.

"Here they come!" Jack told his men on the radio. "They're trying to flank what's left of our forces at the roadblock. They're heading right for you, get ready."

He sprinted down the grass between the highway and the Interstate entrance ramp in the direction of where his men were stationed toward the town. "They've got a lot of troops there," he said into his radio. "At least 500 north and 500 south of the interstate." The federal troops rushed onto the field between the hills to try and get around the Coalition's defensive line on the bridge. "Do not fire until I give them the signal," Jack ordered, breathing rapidly as he ran.

Jack changed his walkie-talkie to a different channel: "Nebraska militia's mortar company: commence firing your mortar cannons now!"

The federal troops attempting to flank the roadblock were halted dead in their tracks with the sudden engagement of dozens of heretofore unengaged Coalition artillery munitions concealed in the buildings and in the hills. The barrels of the cannons were situated so that their flashes were concealed to the eyes of the federal artillery on the road. The federal infantrymen were forced to hug the ground in the open.

"Down! Down! Everybody down!" An Army captain's order went mostly unheeded as the deafening explosions sent clouds of smoke, dirt, and body parts high into the air. "Stay down!" he screamed. "Devon! Where's our artillery?"

"I'm calling for it!" The radio operator held the phone close to his ear before an artillery shell landed directly on top of him, disintegrating him and slicing the bodies of three soldiers around him with hot, bloody shrapnel.

"We can't stay here!" a trooper next to the captain complained at the top of his lungs to be heard over the continuous barrage of artillery. "We're getting torn to pieces!" The Coalition artillery decimated their ranks, leaving the wounded clawing the sand for cover.

The captain lifted his head, looking around for better cover. Fifty yards west was a string of buildings along a narrow road. A sniper's bullet grazed off of the top of his helmet, thrusting him on his back against the dirt. "Let's get out of here! Everybody, get to those buildings due west! Now!"

The captain stood and made it two steps before a spinning lead projectile collided with his right shoulder at 1,800 feet per second and mushroomed into his chest. He fell on his back, hemorrhaging. "Go! Go!" he gurgled as he waved his men westward.

Jack spoke clearly into his walkie-talkie as he saw the federal troops in the distance continue their lethal race westward: "Wallace sniper company! Commence firing! Make the hills come alive…"

The federal troops were quickly cut down from his snipers in the trees and the hills. Jack heard several tanks and Bradleys fire mortars in response to the Coalition's effectiveness against the enemy infantry, and he warned his men in the hills: "Sniper company! Prepare for federal mortar fire any moment, but you must not let up! You *must* make them flee for the cover of that building."

He switched channels as he continued his sprint down the road toward the town. "Mortar company! Prepare for incoming mortar fire!" The federal artillery was effective at annihilating some of the sniper's positions, but the Coalition snipers were spread far enough apart and concealed well enough to prevent any considerable damage to their ability to fire down on the fleeing troopers.

He switched channels again: "I'm almost at your position! Hold your fire!" Jack broke through the high grass at the edge of a field and into the parking lot in front of several office buildings where some of his men were hiding.

He leapt through an open window. "Get ready, boys!" Jack Handel told the 50 men hiding in the shadows, under tarps, behind desks, and in the back rooms on the eastern side of the office building toward which the federal troops were sprinting. "They're 200 yards off, closing fast!"

Handel changed channels again, his chest heaving from his sprint. "Wickard! Make sure Coalition artillery knows we're in that building to which the federal infantry is sprinting!"

"They know, they know. More troops are coming your way!"

Handel opened the channel to speak to the man he had put in charge of the artillery gunners and snipers in the hills to the south. "Wallace! Take 'em out!"

"About 500 more troopers are on your tail heading west…"

"I know, I know! Take 'em out!"

"We're gettin' hammered! But the half of us that are still alive are still firing…"

"Do not let up, or they'll overwhelm us!"

Jack re-positioned the few straggling militia in the front room to hide in back rooms. He went to the soldier who manned a .50-caliber machine gun in the shadows of the hallway facing the entrance, and draped over him a loose black tarp abandoned by a painting contractor. "Let them get well inside before you open fire."

"Yes sir."

"If they stay outside the buildings and hug the walls southward," Handel said, pointing to his right, "then we'll let the guys in the south side buildings and on the roof take them out. You hold your fire until at least half the men have passed your position."

"Yes sir."

He handed a fellow beside him two grenades. The young man, who didn't look a day over sixteen, grasped them tightly, wide-eyed with wonder like they were million-dollar diamonds. "Do you know how to use them?"

"I tossed one in training. This is the pin, right?"

Jack rolled his eyes and turned to the machine gunner. "Make sure he throws them high on the far side of the room before you start to fire. And keep your head down. Got it?" The Guard reservists nodded, and Jack pulled the tarp the rest of the way over his head.

Jack rushed down the hallway, shouting to the men in the adjacent rooms, "Ya'll just shoot through the sheetrock at thigh level once you hear the grenades go off. Got it? Don't fire toward the hallway! There's friendlies over there..."

Jack rushed to the men stationed to the south of the building to inform them of the oncoming hordes of troops. He led some of them onto the roof, where he saw the secondary wave of forces heading across the field toward them.

When the feds reached the building, half of them rushed into it. Half headed toward the southern flank of the building, breathing heavily from their sprint across the open field under heavy mortar attack and sniper fire. The long field was littered with the dead and injured.

The federal troops finally found a place of shelter from the bullets and shrapnel that had shattered them to half their strength. As they took deep breaths in the refuge of the first floor of the building, they felt lucky to be alive. Many collapsed exhausted in the cover of some bushes outside of the building and in a culvert at the edge of the parking lot, thinking that it was a finish line after their race through the gauntlet of Coalition snipers and artillery.

When the Guard finally started firing from inside the building and from the roofs, the feds were slaughtered in a thick hail of grenade shrapnel and automatic gunfire in 20 terrifying seconds.

"All right!" Jack cheered with the Coalition militiamen, who were grateful they had only suffered minor casualties. "Quiet down while I call Wickard!" He tapped his radio: "Wickard? Are any more infantry advancing? Has the federal advancement to your position stopped?"

"Federal artillery's holding their position at a distance. How'd you fare?"

"We killed 'em."

"All of them?"

"All of them that tried to flank you southward. My men did well on the north side of the interstate as well." The few soldiers within earshot of Wickard's radio heard the news and began to cheer.

"You didn't take any prisoners?"

Jack laughed. "Ha ha. Very funny. We're civilian militia defending our families. Of course we didn't take prisoners."

"The feds are retreating," Wickard informed him, "both south along the interstate and east on some smaller roads. You stopped their flanking maneuver cold."

"All right!" He set the walkie-talkie back on his hip. "Good job, boys! But we are not done. Hold on!" He raised his hands to calm the cheers. "Gather what extra ammunition you need from the dead and injured." Jack stood erect, clenched his fists, and raised his voice. Spit flew out of the corner of his mouth as he preached, "Those butchers came here to murder your babies and enslave your wives! That's what they're fightin' for, and we're not going to let them live to try it another day!"

"What? We're charging?"

Jack checked the ammunition in his rifle. “Prepare to attack! If we give the feds a breather, they’ll regroup and attack by a different route.”

“What about the injured federal soldiers?” a guardsman said as he eyed through his scope an Army infantryman grasping his handless arm and crying in pain in the parking lot.

“God willing,” said Handel, “they’ll survive till their execution.”

A nearby history teacher smiled as he patted his weapon. He quoted the famed Confederate General Stonewall Jackson: “No quarter to the violators of our homes and firesides.”

Jack recognized the quote and affirmed it. “That’s right, no quarter.”

“Doesn’t that violate the Geneva convention?” someone rebutted.

Jack snapped, “That only applies to lawful war. Congress doesn’t have the authority to make war on us, much less declare it in a constitutional fashion. They’re terrorists, that’s it. Get our boys off the hills and out of the buildings and onto whatever vehicle they can find and tell them to prepare to sprint east on my order. The feds gotta be low on munitions. Haden!” He called out to another man across the room. “Get your squad out there in the streets and see if some civilians will loan us their cars so we can pursue these invaders east.”

He unlatched his radio and handed it to a subordinate: “Update Wickard. Tell him that we’re attacking. Tell Wickard that artillery support would be appreciated.”

20

Blair, Nebraska

David and Matt's hands were cuffed behind their backs and their feet were shackled to a stainless steel chain clamp that was fastened to the floor beneath their feet in the long black FBI van. They sat on shallow metal seats bolted to the floor along the walls. David and Matt were the last prisoners to be loaded before the doors were shut.

When it grew silent outside, the chained Nebraskans began to complain and vent their frustrations. They soon discovered that all of them either resisted having their vehicle searched or had illegal guns on their person.

"Are you all right, David?" Matt asked.

The right side of David's eye had almost completely swollen shut and the right side of his nose looked swollen. David's eyes appeared to be dimming. It had been a frustrating day for the trooper who frisked David, and David suffered for it.

"David?"

"I'm all right." David tried to force his bad eye to open to look at his friend. "I just have a headache, and I can't breathe through my nose."

The back door opened and a short, muscular federal Army captain pointed at David through the open door. "You! What's your name?"

When David did not answer, the captain repeated the question, extending his thick arm toward David, pointing at him. "You don't have ID on you and I need to know your name! Now!"

Again, David did not answer.

The captain was furious. “All right, who was with him?” He looked behind him at a subordinate, who handed him a clipboard.

“It’s the third name from the top, Captain Wyndham.” The subordinate pointed at the clipboard.

“Matt Wellington! You!” He pointed at the lean, tall, muscular fellow across from David. “You said you were his friend, huh?” Matt nodded. “What’s his name?” Matt was silent. “You don’t want to get on my bad side today. Tell me his name.”

“I don’t know. I picked him up on the side of the road, and it turns out he’s got amnesia. He don’t even know his own name…”

“Oh really!” The captain knew he was the subject of a joke, and he didn’t like it.

“I’ve been calling him ‘dude.’”

“So that’s his name? Dude?”

David turned his head toward Matt, and Matt saw it and told the Army captain, “See?”

The dialogue provoked poorly concealed chuckles throughout the van. The soldier climbed into the van and walked toward Matt. He stood in front of him and just stared at him for a moment. The captain’s jaw muscles alternatively contracted and relaxed, making Matt wonder if he had a tic or was chewing something. Without warning, the captain slapped Matt on the face as hard as he could with his right hand. Matt braced for the first blow, but he could not have prepared for the slap from the left hand that followed up. He cringed at the stinging pain and his lip began to bleed.

The soldier grinned at Matt’s fear and turned back to David, wincing when he caught a glimpse of David’s purple, swollen eye. Captain Wyndham glanced back at the subordinate by the back door of the FBI van. “Man! Jarvis did a job on this fellow.” He slapped David gently on the cheek to arouse him. “Hey! You conscious?” David moaned in response to the physical stimulation. Captain Wyndham looked back at the subordinate. “Hand me the scanner.”

The private reached in a satchel, retrieved a black plastic laptop, and handed it to Captain Wyndham. Wyndham opened it, turned it toward David, and said, “Open your eyes and look at me!” When David opened his good eye, the flash of the digital camera embedded into the narrow laptop computer temporarily blinded him, and he squinted hard and turned away. Captain Wyndham then took David’s right hand and pressed it against the inside plate of the computer. Then he did the same with David’s left.

"I'd love to have some fun with you to make you talk," the hardened Army captain told David, "but frankly, I'm plum tuckered out from smackin' you Jesus freaks around." The privates watching through the open rear doors of the van laughed as their captain showed him his raw and scraped knuckles. "Look at that! Now I'm going to have to take an antibiotic to kill the germs from all the slobber from all the religious nuts I've been knockin' around."

It wasn't long before the phone inside Captain Wyndham's tent rang. He picked it up on the first ring. "Captain Wyndham."

"Got an answer for you, Captain," the Army intelligence agent responded spryly.

"Who is he?"

"David Jameson's his name," the corporal said through his Bluetooth as he perused the computer file of the man on the FBI's Ten Most Wanted List. "You know, the guy who blew up the National Reproductive Rights Convention that killed President Fitzgerald? He's one of the most wanted men in the–"

The captain's eyes grew wide. "Oh yeah!" He set his sandwich on the table beside him, stood and began to pace excitedly. "What a catch!" He walked outside of his tent on the bank of the river that separated Iowa from Nebraska. He heard the faint, unmistakable sound of a whistle growing louder with every second.

Suddenly, a mortar struck the center of the outdoor tent nearby, where officers chatted, rested, and ate lunch together. The collision filled the air with bloody dust.

The captain was knocked onto his side with the force of the blast. A siren sounded and officers began to rush to and fro in a panic.

Captain Wyndham sat up and looked around, unsure of his bearings for a brief moment. "Where'd that come from? What happened?" He grabbed a Hispanic soldier by the arm. "Where'd that come from?"

The terrified private pointed east. "That way, from across the river."

"What? Who's doing the shooting?" Captain Wyndham stood and studied the eastern horizon through the trees on the riverbank. He heard the faint whistle of another mortar gradually getting louder. "Incoming!" The mortar round struck a nearby Bradley, sending flames and debris into the air.

The force of the blast knocked the captain onto his stomach this time, and temporarily knocked the breath out of him. He lifted his head out of the sand, and blew the dirt out his nose. To his right was the headless corpse of the soldier with whom he was speaking. Suddenly, dozens of mortar rockets began to whistle toward them. When he came to his senses, there was only one thought on his mind.

Get David Jameson and get outta here!

Washington, D.C.

Unbeknownst to the Coalition militia, unmanned stealth predator drones flew silently overhead, their 80 horsepower engines carrying them in broad circles over the battle lines. They carried heat-sinking stinger aircraft missiles to defend from air targets and hellfire missiles to engage ground targets. They had been patrolling for almost two days without stopping and transmitting images to the Pentagon in Washington, D.C.

"We're retreating." The Army tech expert beside General Green read what they all saw.

No duh! is how General Green was inclined to respond, but instead he mumbled, "I can see that." The generals in the Pentagon war room were stunned as they observed the action on the drone images.

A soldier with a sat phone called out to General Green. "General, the Coalition rebels are in vigorous pursuit. We're suffering heavy casualties. General Willis is requesting permission to engage ground targets from the air."

General Green glanced wearily at the CIA director who presided over the mission of finding and destroying the Coalition nukes. The CIA director looked up from his computer screen, and trading a troubled grimace with General Green, responded, "No. Not with the threat of nuclear engagement."

"And, hold on!" the phone operator cupped his hand over the earpiece. The generals sat silently, awaiting the report from the field of battle. "They're being attacked from the east now."

General Green stood to his feet. "From the east?"

"Mortars, military, armored vehicles…"

"What?"

The phone operator stood to his feet. "It's the Iowa Guard!"

"We've got to inform the president," a general at the table recommended.

General Green leaned against the table in front of him with his palms down. He mumbled with his eyes closed, "I'm not looking forward to this. Call the president back."

* * * * *

"I'll get to first, honey, and you bring me home with a grand slam." The president winked and smiled at her chief spin master.

Cameron Weaver winked back without as much enthusiasm as usual. He knew what the president meant was that he would have to respond to the difficult questions the president's statement would raise among the press corps. He knew that his answers would not satisfy them, and he hated that. *Obfuscate*, he reminded himself. *Smoke and mirrors. Don't be deterred by the facts. The men and women behind the pens and cameras are your allies...*

Cameron stepped onto the stage and introduced the president. As the president and Dena climbed the stairs to the lighted platform, one of Dena's staff members walked up to her and whispered into her ear. Dena reached over and grabbed the president's forearm as she ascended the stairs. "Madam President. General Green needs to speak with you."

"Can it wait?" She plucked her forearm out of her grasp.

Dena glanced at the staff member, who whispered, "I don't know."

"Dena, let's get this over with first. This won't take long."

"Citizens of the world," Margaret Brighton said in her prepared speech, "your government has taken measures to put an end to this bloody rebellion within our country. Exploiting a critical weakness, we have attacked, and we have high hopes that the conflict will end and our differences resolved very soon. This conflict has placed a great stress upon your armed forces. With an escalating threat in the Middle East, our armed forces are dangerously over-extended. Upon the urging of the Joint Chiefs, the United Nations has been called upon to lend their peace-keeping forces to help us to restore peace and justice in the troubled areas of our country..."

Two minutes after she concluded her speech, the president wished she had taken General Green's phone call first. The diversion on the western edge of the Coalition of Free Christian States was successful, drawing the Guard forces away from the eastern border. But the eastern invasion was a catastrophic failure. The overwhelming force of civilian militia sent them fleeing back the way they had come. They just didn't expect citizens inexperienced in warfare to be willing to kill and die for their cause. Nor did they expect to face so much automatic weaponry and mortars. Nebraskans suffered five times more casualties than the federal forces, yet still beat all odds and repelled the invasion.

The president cursed out General Green and slammed the phone down so hard it cracked in the middle and pinched her palm.

"Madam President, please calm down!" Dena said, attempting to soothe her irritation. "Please!"

The president cradled her bleeding hand and rushed from the room without so much as looking at her chief of staff. She locked herself in the bathroom, took two Xanax, and dialed a number on her cell phone to consult her medium.

Des Moines, Iowa

"What in the world are you doing?" The Speaker of the Iowa Assembly raised his voice in frustration as he hovered over the desk of the Iowa governor. "Are you crazy!?" The Speaker couldn't believe that the governor seemed more intent on reading his E-mails on his laptop than paying attention to the Speaker's heartfelt reproofs. "You can't send the Iowa Guard to... Are you listening to me?"

"I already have."

"What? I thought the resolution said that force *may* be a consideration."

The governor sat back in his chair and took a deep breath. "That was a compromise that we didn't have to make after all. The executive branch of the state of Iowa is not going to sit idly by anymore," he calmly stated, "while the federal government tramples over our brothers and sisters next door."

"But–"

The prematurely balding Governor Beverly raised his palms toward the Speaker, halting the hasty objection. "Hold up. I might not ban abortion in all cases as they have, but I know the color of tyranny. I will not tolerate this invasion force in Iowa one more day! I'm sending my Guard and my highway patrol to help evict the federal troops out of Nebraska and out of Iowa."

"You're insane! You know what's going to happen?" The Speaker stepped in closer to the governor and leaned on the desk. "The federal government is going to take our funding and your people will turn on you! You'll go to prison and be impeached in absentee!"

Governor Beverly did not make eye contact, but tapped on something on his laptop with his mouse. Whatever he saw made him grin broadly.

"What?" The Speaker was curious as to what could make him smile at a time like this.

"Well, I'll be in good company then," Governor Beverly said, not taking his eyes off the computer screen.

"What do you mean?"

"Iowa's joining Kansas and Oklahoma in the Coalition of Free Christian States."

"You've got to be kidding me! You can't do that without the consent of the statehouse. I'm the Speaker…"

"Ex-Speaker. We didn't need you after all."

Blair, Nebraska

"Where's the van that was just here?" Captain Wyndham inquired of a private who was ducking down in a ditch. "Which way did it go? Who was driving it?"

Captain Wyndham lost his personal radio and his M-16 when the mortar round hit his tent and he was having a difficult time locating his trophy prisoner.

"What?!"

"The black FBI van that was parked right there." He pointed at the parking lot in front of the small grocery store at the main intersection in downtown Blair. "It was full of prisoners. Where did it go?"

The private screamed to be heard over the gunfire and mortar rounds. "The prisoners were moved south towards Omaha! Netter and Trapper's companies are retreating from Lincoln and they wanted to pull the prisoners back and join with–"

"What?" Captain Wyndham misunderstood the private because of the explosions and gunfire all around him. Before the private could repeat his answer, a .308 round grazed the private's helmet.

He squatted lower in the ditch and pulled his Kevlar helmet lower over his brow.

Captain Wyndham turned and screamed at the two dozen soldiers who huddled down in the ditch for cover. "Come on! Return fire!" When the private with whom he was speaking began to return fire, he slapped him in the back of the head. "Not you! Tell me where the van went!"

"South. We need air support!"

"That ain't gonna happen," Captain Wyndham mumbled as he peaked over the edge of the ditch to witness the Iowa Guard crossing the bridge over the Missouri River into Nebraska, followed by Highway Patrolmen in SWAT vehicles. The mortar rounds were coming from the Iowa Guard's Bradley Fighting Vehicles.

Captain Wyndham reached into a satchel that hung over his shoulder, pulled out an M-16 magazine, and snatched the private's weapon. He ignored the protests of the private and peaked above the ditch again, flinching with every round that whizzed by his head. The soldiers stationed at the roadblock quickly abandoned their mission of searching passengers in the vehicles that were as far south on State Route 75 as the eye could see, and became occupied with finding cover and defending themselves. Most of the civilian passengers in the traffic jam had gotten out of their cars and were ducking in a ditch on the west side of 75, or were fleeing west across a corn field to get as far away from the firefight as possible. A few of the Nebraska civilians were encouraged at the charging of the Iowa Guard, and so the ones who had small arms began to fire them at the federal troopers from behind their cars.

Captain Wyndham was at a loss for what to do. Mortars and machine gun fire from the east and small arms fire from angry civilians to the south and north were a volatile threat to the 150 Army infantry that occupied Blair. Without guidance and without the ability to accomplish their mission, soldiers fled in different directions and holed up wherever they could. Captain Wyndham had to get south toward Omaha as quickly as he could to try and catch up to the van that held David Jameson.

He saw a motorcyclist whizzing past the traffic jam northward on the west shoulder of State Route 75, trying to bypass the federal soldiers at the roadblock on his 350 Honda dirt bike. Captain Wyndham saw this as his only opportunity. He loaded the magazine into the M-16, chambered a round, and put the sling over his shoulder. Then he jumped out of the ditch and took off in a sprint toward the road to try and intercept the motorcyclist. Bullets whizzed around his head but he did not detour. He crossed the road and, just as the motorcyclist was slowing to turn west on 30, he pushed the motorcyclist off his bike. The motorcyclist fell onto his back and spun into the center of the intersection. The motorcycle slid and came to a stop under a burning Hummer. Captain Wyndham pulled on the back tire of the motorbike, set it upright, mounted it, and spun out heading south in the middle of the two lane highway. He picked up speed quickly to make a difficult target for the civilians who were firing on him from ditches on the west side of the road. Two miles down the road, right where the traffic jam began to thin, he saw the vans full of prisoners pull off the shoulder of the road onto the now clear two-lane highway.

He picked up speed and tried to wave down the vans. The six vans in the caravan came to a halt in the middle of the road. He jumped off the bike and then caught site of what made the vehicles stop. Five hundred yards ahead, across the treeless horizon, he could see federal soldiers on foot and in vehicles heading over an overpass back into Omaha, attempting to flee heavy fire from the west. When those troops crossed the overpass, they came headlong into oncoming fire from Omaha civilians who shot at them from every window and alley. Jack Handel was leading the Nebraska civilian militia in an all out sprint toward the fleeing troops to push them out of Nebraska, but the Omaha civilians preferred them dead. Handel's men rode in their pick-up trucks with M-198 cannons mounted in the truck beds, in their patched up Bradley fighting vehicles, in Jeeps, convertibles, dune buggies, four wheelers, and every other kind of civilian vehicle from which Nebraskans could fire weapons at their invaders.

Captain Wyndham would not be dissuaded from his task. He ran up to the passenger door of the first van he came to. "Is David Jameson in here?"

The soldier in the passenger seat of the car rolled down his window: "Captain! We have a situation. Do you want us to offer our assistance and–?"

"Open the back door!"

"Shouldn't we–?"

"Now!"

The soldier in the driver's seat typed in a six-digit code on the security panel on the dash, and the rear door clicked open. Captain Wyndham ran to the back of the van, opened the door, and poked his head inside. No David Jameson.

He slammed the door shut and ran to the next van. "Open the back door," he shouted at the driver.

"Captain Wyndham? Netter's company is getting torn apart up there–"

"Just open the door!"

"We can't go north or south, and there's a river to the east and nothing but farm field—"

"Shut up and open the door!"

The rear door clicked open and he ran around to the back and poked his head inside and caught of glimpse of his prize prisoner on the end of the aisle. "There you are."

"Sir!" the anxious driver turned his head and called out to Captain Wyndham. "The civilian fighters are coming right at us! They're not firing at us yet. Do we fire, sir?"

Captain Wyndham jumped into the vehicle and looked at the number under David's seat. "Unlock 14!"

Matt, who sat across from David, objected, "Where are you taking him?"

"Do we fire?" the driver asked Captain Wyndham as he hit a button on the dash. The thick steel clamp that held David Jameson's ankle shackles to the floor opened and descended into the floor of the van.

"You're a soldier!" Wyndham glanced at the driver through the grate that separated the two soldiers in the front from the civilian prisoners. The passenger in the front grabbed his M-16 that he had on the floor between the two front seats, and he switched it off safety and chambered a round. "When I get out of this van with this prisoner," Captain Wyndham ordered, "you will discharge your weapons!"

Captain Wyndham grabbed the injured David Jameson by the scruff of his shirt and dragged him out of the back of the van.

"He needs medical care!" Matt shouted. "Where are you taking him?"

Captain Wyndham ignored the question and pushed David into the road and into the cornfield to the west.

"David!" Matt screamed as the door was shutting. "I'm praying for you David!"

"Pray for my family," David shouted back. David was at peace with his crucifixion. He just prayed that it would be sufficient to win his family's freedom. The blood of the righteous is the price of liberty. Jesus demonstrated that for us when He gave up His life on the cross. David was willing to walk in Jesus' footsteps and make the sacrifice.

As David was pulled by the scruff of his T-shirt through a shallow ditch and into a field of standing corn, his thoughts went to the high priest Aaron, who grabbed a censer full of incense and ran through the Israelites who were perishing from a plague that God's wrath had sent upon them. Aaron, the Bible says, walked between the dead and the living. The Bible says that Aaron atoned for Israel with his sweet-smelling incense in that field of suffering and death.

The Apostle Paul said through his sufferings he filled up that which lacked of the sufferings of Christ. What lacked of Christ's sufferings? Did Jesus not taste death for every man and suffer for the sins of the world? Absolutely. What lacked was its impact upon the world. For that, Jesus would need disciples who would take up their cross and follow Him into the world to spread the message. He would need people to demonstrate His love to the sinful world He died to save. Peter said that we should arm ourselves with a mind to suffer in the footsteps of Jesus Christ, and in so doing we would cease from sin.

David prayed that the incense of his ceaseless praise in the fields of suffering through which he was dragged would save lives, change hearts, and win liberty. David prayed that his crucifixion would enlighten more Americans to the life-changing reality of Jesus' death and resurrection. For the joy that was set before Him, David embraced his cross and kept his eyes on the prize.

* * * * *

"There you go." An overall-wearing corn farmer-turned-militia-fighter unlocked the shackles binding Matt Wellington's feet. Jack Handel and the Nebraska militia had killed or captured almost every single one of the ten thousand American soldiers who invaded their state, and this beer-bellied farmer was given the responsibility of guarding about 100 prisoners and setting free all of the civilians who had been incarcerated in the black vans on State Route 75. The six digit codes needed to unlock the vans' shackles were not too hard to come by. With his father's hand-me-down Buck knife and a lighter, the corn farmer turned out to be quite persuasive.

"Where's the driver of the van behind me?" Matt asked him.

"Why?"

"Where is he?"

"That's the stubborn one. Over there." The farmer pointed to a line of bound federal soldiers on the west side of the road. "It's the guy with the black goatee, I think."

Matt walked over to the soldier with the scraggly black goatee, dripping with coagulated blood. He aimed his M-16 at his forehead.

"Whoa!" The soldier protested when he saw the weapon aimed at his face. "Whassup?" He raised his tightly bound hands in protest. His hands, Matt saw, had been tied together with 30-pound fishing string. The farmer apparently had run out of rope and was improvising. A couple of his fingers were bleeding from being ground between the hot asphalt and the heel of the corn-farmer's boot. That and a few lacerations from the lighter-heated Buck knife scraped under his eye was apparently how the farmer pulled the codes out of him.

"One of your superiors took a prisoner out of the van in front of you and fled – that van there," he said, pointing. "Where'd he go?"

The corn-farmer had already driven away any resistance this army private had. "He went west. Who was he anyway?" Matt glanced over his shoulder at the endless cornfield behind him.

Matt was about to answer when the young 17-year-old son of the corn farmer came running toward him, screaming, "I found it! I found it!" The boy had become mesmerized with the former Austin sheriff's story about Jameson. He had ridden to Blair on an abandoned motorcycle and found David's cell phone right where Matt told him it would be, on the banks of a grimy ditch.

He handed it to Matt, who grinned ear-to-ear and high-fived the young man. "Thanks, man."

"You're welcome. I hope you find him."

"Hey!" Matt Wellington called out to the beer-bellied farmer, who had his back to him on the side of the road. The farmer did not hear Matt, but surprised everybody when he raised an M-16 he had taken from one of the feds and aimed it at one of the black FBI vans. He pulled the trigger and ten bullets sped from the gun with just three seconds of holding the trigger. The farmer not only blasted the tire but struck the engine as well, sending smoke spiraling into the air. The prisoners closest to the van on the side of the road shrinked away from it, fearing that it would blow.

"Whoa!" The farmer shouted with glee. "Cool gun! I think I'll keep this…"

"Hey!" Matt called out again. The farmer turned to him. "Is this really a good time to practice shootin'? Would you set that thing down and get these guys some water?" Matt motioned to the bound federal soldiers on the side of the road.

"We don't have enough water," the farmer complained. "My main man said they'll be heading back this way 'fore long."

"Your main man?"

"Yeah. If Jack Handel's with 'em, he'll probably just shoot 'em dead. Why waste water on them?"

"He'll shoot 'em?"

The farmer nodded. "He's very Stonewall-Jacksonish, you know, no quarter to the violators of our hearth and home." His furry eyebrows lifted. "Maybe we should call him Stonewall Jack!"

Matt sighed and turned to the young man who had fetched the cell phone. "Will you get those prisoners some water from the ditch, or something?"

"Sure, man."

Matt slung an M-16 over his shoulder and headed across the road toward the cornfield. At the edge of the field he turned and yelled at the farmer, "Don't shoot this way! All right?" The farmer nodded and then Matt took off into the cornfield, briefly pausing when the farmer raised a confiscated .50-caliber sniper rifle and took a pot shot at a van further south, causing it to explode in a ball of flames.

"Hey!" a soldier on the side of the road called out, surprised by the blast.

"Cut it out!" another shouted. The farmer was too busy shouting with excitement to hear their criticism.

"Can I take a shot at one, Pa?"

Matt laughed at the thought of it all as he began to run through the corn.

He opened David's cell phone as he ran westward. He wanted to call Ben Boswell with an update.

Captain Wyndham heard the van explode and he stopped his running through the rows of corn. He had his hand clenched around a fistful of David's T-shirt.

"Where are... you taking me?" David inquired between heavy breaths, his hands still cuffed behind his back.

"Shut up!" the Army captain ordered. He tugged David's shirt, practically dragging him through the standing corn toward the tree line in the distance.

David's head was aching severely now, and his mouth was dry from thirst.

They stopped at the crossing of what appeared to be a four-wheeler trail across the rows of corn, and Captain Wyndham paused to look left and right.

"I was headin' to see my wife in Texas," said David as he tried to catch his breath.

"Your wife, huh? She in on your terrorist activities?"

"I'm not a terrorist. I'm a Christian."

"Aren't you all." Captain Wyndham turned left onto the four-wheeler trail.

Matt finally found their trail when he stumbled upon the footprints of two men in a shallow, muddy area of the field. He ran through the tall rows of corn as quietly as he could, stopping every minute or so to catch his breath and listen for voices.

Omaha, Nebraska

"Jack! It's the governor's office." The businessman with the functioning cell phone leaned out of the driver's seat of the SUV.

"Of Nebraska?" Jack Handel was pumping fuel, donated by the fuel station owner.

"No." He extended the phone toward him. "Montana."

Jack reached for the phone. "I get to chat with two governors and destroy two federal Army companies in one single day. What a day!" He put the phone to his ear. "This is Jack Handel."

"I heard all about your exploits, Jack. We share a common friend – Barry Friar."

"Oh yes, how's he doing?"

"As tenacious as ever."

"You've got a good warrior there, Gov." Jack hung up the gasoline dispenser and walked back around to the passenger seat of the SUV. "We sure are thankful that the Iowa Guard and Highway Patrol stepped in to help like they did. We whooped 'em today! A lot of good folks died, but we birthed a strong militia in Nebraska."

"The reason I called is that I need someone for an important mission." Boswell held a post-it note with a message scribbled upon it. "I want you to help me on something personal."

Blair, Nebraska

The Army captain fled with David past the farm fields and deep into the sparsely populated woods of eastern Nebraska. He felt inclined to avoid roads, as an enemy soldier or a traitorous civilian would be more likely behind enemy territory than a friend. If he could sneak up on a home, he planned to break in and use the phone as he held the homeowners at gunpoint. He had in his grasp one of the most wanted men in America, and he wasn't going to surrender him to the rebels without a fight. If he could only find a phone, he could call in an Apache to pick them up. He walked the fields by the light of the moon with his trophy prisoner in tow for most of the night. When the moon set, he found a dry place for them to sleep.

As the morning sun rose in the east, the reddish glow on the horizon reminded Captain Wyndham that his life would get so much easier if he could just get this prisoner out of the Coalition and back into the United States.

"Wake up!" Captain Wyndham kicked David in the side. To keep David from escaping in the night, he had tied his handcuffed hands to one small tree and his ankles to another. Wyndham reached down with his pocketknife and cut the ropes off of David's ankles and wrists. "This ain't Holiday Inn Express. Get up."

David grunted as he lifted his head off of the dirt, and Wyndham seemed impressed by the amount of swelling above David's left eye.

"Man, Jarvis must have one heck of a backhand, or your platelets don't work right."

David sat up and tried to open his eyes, but his left eye was completely swollen shut. "My busted lip was from his backhand," he mumbled. "The eye was from the butt of his gun."

"Yeah," said Wyndham with a chuckle. "Treason hurts, don't it?" David forced a smile at him. For some strange reason, David had an unusual affection for this man. He felt that he was to be God's grace to this soldier, regardless of how he mistreated him. Through him, God would grant this unworthy prodigal one more chance to come home to the golden ring and the fatted calf.

"Thank you for untying me." David spoke more kindly than the captain expected. "How about these cuffs?" He extended his wrists toward him.

The captain laughed at the question as he relieved himself behind a tree.

"Can you at least cuff me in the front, so I can run with you better?"

"I think I'll leave them just like they are."

Rather than stand up, David fell to his knees and began to pray. The captain felt uneasy when he witnessed the passion of David Jameson's prayer. David cried out to God for his wife and family, and then for the soul of the one who had kidnapped him, provoking Wyndham to curse under his breath. When David concluded his prayer, he stood painfully to his feet.

“Today’s the day of our salvation,” Captain Wyndham said mockingly. David held his peace. Wyndham tossed his assault weapon over his shoulder and prodded David down a deer trail. “We can’t be far from a town. Giddy-up.”

After 45 minutes of a slow jog through the woods and through a large meadow, Captain Wyndham was fed up with Nebraska’s houseless expanse. They had been walking parallel to a road westward, and every few minutes or so, he could faintly hear a car coming.

Wyndham stopped, sighed, and then let out a string of curses.

“Thou shalt not,” David paused, breathing heavily, his eyes dim with fatigue. “Thou shalt not take the name of the Lord thy God in–”

“Shut up!” Wyndham screamed. “Enough of this nonsense, I’m hijacking a car.” He jerked David by his collar a little harder and picked up the pace toward the road in the distance.

He walked into a clearing beside the two-lane road and pushed David flat on the ground. “Stay!” Without warning, he kicked his prisoner in the stomach, knocking the breath out of him.

Traffic in the road was sparse, so Captain Wyndham had time to choose his vehicle carefully. He walked in the middle of the road to obstruct the silver Mustang that drove toward him. He aimed his M-16 at the driver. “Stop the car!” The driver slammed on the breaks and skidded the car partially sideways, finally coming to a stop just ten yards in front of Wyndham.

Wyndham ran up to the car window and pointed his rifle at the young male driver. “Get out!”

The driver put up his hands. “What do you want?”

“Unlock the car and get out! Now!”

The driver unlocked the door, and when Wyndham reached to open the door, the driver surprised him by slamming his foot on the gas pedal. The tires began to spin.

“No! Open the…!” Wyndham had only a moment to respond. If the citizen fled, he could notify the state authorities of their location and a thousand Coalition guardsmen could be hunting them within minutes. They were at war, and difficult decisions had to be made.

A single pull of the trigger delivered a three round burst through side windows and into the head and chest of the driver.

David shouted in protest, “No!” He rolled out of the way of the coasting Mustang and it slowed to a stop on the side of the road next to him.

“You didn’t have to kill him!”

“Shut up and get in the car!” Wyndham ran up to the car and flung the door open. He grabbed the driver by the hair to keep from getting his blood on him, and he dragged the dying man into the road.

“No!” David shouted, slowly rising to his feet on the side of the road.

Captain Wyndham turned and shouted at David, “Get in the car! Now!”

When David again refused, Captain Wyndham stomped over to him and grabbed him by the scruff of his shirt. David hoped he could put up a resistance long enough for another car to drive by and spot them.

He struggled and freed himself from Wyndham’s grasp and began to run eastward down the side of the road, away from the Mustang and the enraged Army captain.

David’s hands were tied behind his back, so it was only seconds before Captain Wyndham caught up with him. Wyndham swung his M-16 by the barrel and connected with David’s right temple. David fell hard to the gravel on the side of the road. Wyndham grabbed David by his collar and tried to pull him up to a standing position. “Get up!” David feigned as if he were teetering on the edge of consciousness. If Wyndham was going to get him into that car, he would have to drag him. Wyndham caught on to David’s subterfuge and was determined to make him pay for it. He threw David on the ground and thrust the butt of his rifle against the side of David’s head, knocking him unconscious. “There,” said Wyndham, slinging his rifle over his shoulder. “That’s better.”

Wyndham reached down and hoisted David over his shoulder with a grunt. But when he turned toward the Mustang, a tall muscular man with a crew cut stood at the rear of the silver Mustang, aiming an M-16 at him.

Matt Wellington activated the laser pointer on the weapon and pointed it right at the mid-section of the Army captain. “Put him down!”

The captain instinctively dropped David’s body in front of his, and then held him in front of him as a shield. He swung his rifle around his shoulder until it was aimed at Matt.

“No!” Matt responded, frustrated at his own hesitancy in firing at the captain when he had an open shot. He fired at the federal soldier’s legs just as the first rounds of the captain’s .223 bullets whizzed all around him. He tried to rush around the Mustang for cover, but one of them connected with his right leg before he could make it. Though it was only a graze, he screamed in pain and fell to the ground behind the car. His gun dropped a few feet away from him.

One of Wyndham's bullets ricocheted off the ground and struck the fuel tank of the car, causing an explosion that knocked him even further away from his weapon. Wyndham winced from the billowing heat that singed his forehead and the hairs on his forearms.

Matt shook his head and tried to get his bearings. The heat from the raging fire in the Mustang provoked him to turn and move away, but his weapon was between him and the flaming engine. It beckoned him to brave the heat and get that gun at all cost. He growled in pain as he pondered his dilemma. The wound that pierced his left thigh muscle felt worse than it looked. His lower leg seemed paralyzed, and it wouldn't move when he ordered it to move.

"Where ya' going?" Captain Wyndham asked mockingly as he stepped around the flaming Mustang.

Matt looked up at the soldier, the evening sun to the captain's back. David was still unconscious, drooped over Captain Wyndham's shoulder. Windham carefully aimed his gun at Matt's chest with one hand. Matt caught sight of the rapid dripping of blood from David's scalp splattering on the hot cement at the captain's feet.

"To heaven, I suppose," Matt mumbled.

Captain Wyndham's finger had half-pulled the trigger when, unexpectedly, a bullet whizzed right past Matt's head. Matt's jaw gaped open, stunned as he watched the Army captain drop to his knees.

Three hundred yards behind the captain, Jack Handel was leaning out of the side door of an Apache helicopter with his sniper rifle. They had scoured the area for hours, looking for signs of Matt and David. Then the pilot caught sight of the explosion, and they arrived just in time.

Matt was horrified as he watched the last moments of the Army captain's life. Wyndham's stare was blank, his jaw was loose, and his face white as his life's blood spilled out of his aorta onto the ground. His weapon tumbled out of his hand onto a pool of his splattered blood and tissue. Matt wished that there was something he could say that would impact this soldier for Christ, but he knew it was too late for him. Death snatched his soul from his body, ushering him into an eternity of regret and pain. Wyndham fell down on his face with a thud, and David crumpled to the ground, his fall partially cushioned by the corpse of his captor.

"David!" Matt exclaimed as he crawled toward him. "David!"

David's collision with the ground restored his consciousness. He moaned and shook his head. "What's that noise?"

Matt laughed as he pulled David away from the steaming pool of blood that was spreading under the federal captain's carcass on the hot black asphalt. "It's one of our copters, David." He waved at the copter with one hand and tried to help David to a sitting position with his other. "You're going to be all right, brother."

"Oh, God help me." David would have grabbed his aching head, but his hands were still tied behind his back, so he just shut his eyes and let his head bob toward the ground.

Matt retrieved the handcuff keys from the dead captain's pocket and unlocked David's cuffs. The Apache landed about 20 yards away in the median of the four-lane highway. David stretched his arms around Matt in a hug, thanking God that he had survived. "Oh God," David prayed, "help us get to my family."

The cell phone vibrated on Matt's hip and he unlatched it, opened it, and put it up to David's ear.

Darlene's sweet voice was crystal clear over the phone. "You gonna sightsee forever, or you gonna come to the border of Texas to pick up your wife and daughters?"

David's eyes widened and for a moment he thought he was daydreaming. He looked at Matt and saw the phone.

"Ain't God good?" Matt's eyes began to brim with tears of joy.

David grabbed the phone with both hands as if it were a fragile, long lost family heirloom finally rediscovered. A sob of gratitude swelled in his throat. He felt like he was standing beneath a waterfall of love, peace, and joy, flowing straight from the throne of His heavenly Father. He found himself unable to speak, and just held the phone to his cheek, feeling completely overwhelmed by God's grace. He was ushered from the brink of the grave to the gates of heaven in a single moment.

"Oh, Darlene," he exclaimed through his tears, "my cup runneth over."

Part VI

"Zion will be redeemed with judgment" (Isaiah 1)

21

Olympia, Washington

"Elijah Slate! I can't tell you how good it is to finally meet you." Governor Littman strutted to Elijah and shook his hand vigorously. "Hold on for a sec."

Littman returned to his desk phone and told the attorney general and the chief of police to wait a moment. He then put the director of the Highway Patrol and the adjutant general of the State Guard, who were present online, on hold. He waved Elijah to the seat in front of the desk. "Have a seat."

Elijah's bands of armed Minutemen not only kept a large part of Seattle's college campuses safe from vandals, but they also were of great assistance in apprehending criminals and gathering video evidence and eyewitness testimony. His exploits had impressed Governor Littman so much that he personally invited Elijah to be present at his next staff meeting.

"Sorry I'm late."

"You're not late," the governor assured him with a smile. "You're right on time."

The sheriff of Seattle called out to Elijah from a seat against the wall. "How are you handling things, brother?"

"Things are calming down on the street," Elijah responded as he took a seat, "thanks to a practical martial law that we've enacted. I suppose you know that."

The sheriff discerned some disapproval in Elijah's comment, but maintained his warm smile nonetheless.

"I wasn't sure if we would survive the evening," Governor Littman commented with a heavy sigh. "Sheriff Miller here" – he motioned to the overweight law enforcement officer with the thick black mustache and goatee – "says you and your Minutemen were of indispensible assistance."

The sheriff nodded as he walked over to shake Elijah's hand. "I don't even want to think about the extent of the catastrophe if you and your men had not been there to help."

Elijah kept a straight face as he shook the sheriff's hand vigorously. "Thank you."

"I'd like to keep most if not all of your men," Sheriff Miller said, "under my command for a few weeks, at least until things settle down."

Elijah grimaced, and both Sheriff Miller and Governor Littman sensed his discontent.

"We are terribly understaffed and could really use your help," Sheriff Miller said as his smile faded to a frown. "We have had riots in every single prison in the state, several of which are not yet under control. We have a lot of work ahead of us the next couple of days. We couldn't pay anything now, but we'll hit up City Council for stipends for you, and I think we'll get it."

"We'll find some state funds to defray your expenses," said Governor Littman with a wink, "if you think that–"

"Money's not important," Elijah interrupted. An uneasy silence followed.

"Well, can we expect your help in restoring peace and order?" the sheriff asked again.

Elijah suddenly felt like the Minutemen had become cheap labor to an overwhelmed police force, and he reluctantly nodded.

Sheriff Miller had a puzzled look on his face as he gazed at Elijah. "Why do I feel like you're not a big fan of what we're trying to do here?"

Elijah wagged his head and sighed. "I'm sorry, gentlemen, but I do have some concerns."

"Hold on." Governor Littman was clearly perturbed by the change in Elijah Slate's countenance. The governor tapped a button on his phone: "Veronica, tell the men I have on hold that I'll have to get back with them within the hour."

"Yes sir."

Governor Littman studied Elijah for a moment. He had the feeling that this lean African American man sitting in front of him was not an underling, but more of an equal. This wasn't a man who cowered before men of esteem and authority, but rather who mentored men of esteem and authority. "We're in debt to you, Elijah, for your heroic efforts. You and your Minutemen salvaged probably hundreds of millions of dollars of infrastructure..."

"And saved lives," Sheriff Miller added.

"Yeah, you said that." Elijah wasn't comfortable with the level of flattery they were heaping on him.

"So the least we can do is talk through our differences." Governor Littman leaned back in his chair and clasped his hands together in his lap. "Speak freely."

Elijah took a deep breath. "When we founded the Coalition of Free Christian States, we really only departed from the United States in a few major areas. Abortion, physician-assisted suicide, free speech, and the second amendment."

"Those are some pretty major areas." Governor Littman chuckled and rocked in his chair for a moment. The sheriff crossed his arms over his barrel chest.

"There are many, many other areas in which we did *not* depart from the status quo, areas which are just as far removed from God's prescription for governing as the killing of children in the womb."

The governor had a puzzled look on his face. "Like what?"

"Our pathetic criminal justice system, for one. Those rioters laugh at our prosecution. We punish crime by forcing the innocent and the law-abiding, upon pain of fine or property confiscation, to pay for the grocery bills and rent of those who terrorized them. The taxpayer'll be paying for their air-conditioning in summer, their heat in winter, their defense attorneys, their groceries, their medical care, their education, their entertainment…"

"Well, that's how the system works!" Sheriff Miller raised his voice, apparently disturbed that Elijah would question that which appeared impossible to change.

"That's not how it *should* work. Law-abiding citizens should not be forced to pay 50 thousand bucks annually for the upkeep of each rapist, vandal, and assailant – that's fundamentally unjust. And the penalty for lawlessness should be severe enough to provide an adequate disincentive. This state has arrested two physicians for murdering preborn babies, but what are we doing to them? We're feeding them, letting them play basketball, lift weights, watch television, and we're letting them give telephone interviews to encourage our enemies." Elijah shook his head. "I'm sorry, gentlemen, but delayed justice is injustice. Our system of criminal justice is an abomination to God," he dared to say.

Governor Littman raised his eyebrows and licked his lips, stunned at this unexpected turn of events. He glanced at the sheriff, who shrugged. The governor leaned forward with his elbows on his desk. "I suppose we have just all taken the present system for granted that it couldn't be improved. What do you propose we do about it?"

Elijah walked over to the governor's bookshelf and pulled out a blue Gideon Bible. "I propose that we adopt the Bible as our criminal justice system."

Sheriff Miller briefly laughed, but regained his composure when he witnessed the somber grimace on Governor Littman's face. "The Bible?" Littman wondered aloud. "How's that help us fight rioting? It'll get you to heaven, but how does it help us protect the people from crime?"

"The good book gives principles to live by, yes," Sheriff Miller added, "but principles to govern by, in a democratic society?" He shook his head, disturbed by the very idea.

Now it was Elijah who briefly laughed as he took his seat. "All right, Sheriff. You've got man over here" – Elijah set the Bible in his lap and raised his left fist – "and God over here." He raised his right fist. "When God and man conflict" – he clashed his fists together – "who's right? Who trumps who?" Elijah let that question hang out there for a moment as the governor and the sheriff of Seattle considered it.

"I suppose God is right," the sheriff responded. "God trumps man."

"You suppose?"

"No, I mean, God's always right."

The governor nodded. "Of course. Judgment Day will prove that."

Sheriff Miller grunted. "And He always wins. Every knee shall bow."

"Then why should we act like a democratic majority or a godless judge can overrule God?" Elijah lifted the Bible in the air. "God's Word speaks to all matters of life, and when He speaks, we are fools if we side against Him in favor of the devil's alternatives. I promise you, Governor Littman, if you will give me the liberty to enforce God's criminal justice system, that crime will come to an end almost immediately and our citizens can save their money rather than spend it on the upkeep of society's lowlifes. It'll be very good for the economy, because the prison systems will basically be privatized…"

"Privatized?" Sheriff Miller exclaimed.

"If we followed the Bible's remedy for crime, what we now know as prison would simply be converted into privatized labor camps and the number of prisoners will drop 90%." The governor and the sheriff traded a puzzled glance. "God's criminal justice system," Elijah said as he smacked the Bible against his palm, "would punish criminals severely, quickly, efficiently, with a disincentive significant enough to bring crime to an end almost overnight. Then our military occupation of this state, which is presently about as oppressive to our law-abiding population as anything Margaret Brighton could conjure up, could end."

"My powers are limited by my oath and by law, Elijah," Governor Littman said.

"Your powers are limited by God, Governor," Elijah insisted. "You are not presently fulfilling your God-ordained role. Not yet anyway. You are the head of the executive branch. You have the duty and the authority, from God Almighty and the state Constitution, to enforce the law in a manner consistent with your Christian faith. You have the power of your executive orders in times of emergency. There are many old laws on the books that have been ignored for close to 100 years, laws against adultery, against sodomy, more strict laws against theft and assault, laws in favor of capital punishment—"

"Those old laws have been overruled by the…" The governor paused, realizing how Elijah would respond since they had seceded from the United States.

"Welcome to the Coalition, Governor," Elijah said with a contagious grin. "We don't respect the Supreme Court's tyranny anymore when it comes to physician-assisted suicide and abortion, now do we? Well, we should also disregard the Supreme Court's decisions when it comes to criminal justice. When God and man contradict," he said, holding his Bible aloft, "who trumps who?"

The sheriff and Governor Littman nodded. "God trumps man," they admitted simultaneously.

"And He," Elijah said, pointing heavenward, "cannot be overruled. We can rebel, and believe you me, this state has rebelled to what God's Word says about criminal justice."

"Give us some examples," said Governor Littman, his countenance softening toward Elijah. "How would you punish crime if you took the Bible as your instruction book? Be specific."

Elijah smiled. "Gladly," he said as he cracked open the Bible.

The governor put up a palm. "Wait." He tapped a button on his desk phone. "Veronica, get the entire cabinet back online now."

"Yes sir."

* * * * *

"The armed and courageous citizens of Nebraska have stopped the unlawful federal invasion in its tracks," Governor Littman happily informed an elated crowd of thousands of Coalition patriots who gathered on the pocked and blood-stained capitol steps in downtown Olympia. The sheriffs of Seattle and Olympia stood to his left, backed by several state reps and state senators. On the other side stood Elijah Slate, still grasping the blue Gideon Bible he'd picked up off of the Washington governor's bookshelf. "The valiant defense of the Coalition Guard," Littman announced in a celebratory tone, "forced the federal troops to retreat south back into Oregon under constant fire from armed civilians. We suffered many casualties today, but our men and women, professional and lay warriors, fought with valor. You are all to be commended for your bravery and your willingness to lay down your lives for liberty and for Christianity. The rioting would have been much, much worse, if it weren't for the civilian leaders who kept the rioters at bay and apprehended many of the suspects. One such civilian leader is Elijah Slate, one of the leaders of the Coalition Minutemen who has been ministering at the University of Washington. Sheriff Miller of Seattle," he said through a rustle of applause, "has commended Elijah and the Coalition Minutemen for keeping the University of Washington from being burned to the ground. He and his men single-handedly brought hundreds of perpetrators to justice." He paused and corrected himself, "Well, we captured them but haven't brought them to justice yet. Elijah Slate, a police officer from the sovereign state of Texas," he turned and placed his right palm on Elijah's shoulder, "is going to help us with that." At the mention that Elijah was from Texas, the crowd of thousands erupted in a thunderous applause that lasted for a full minute. Littman turned to Elijah and winked. "Elijah?"

The governor stepped aside as Elijah Slate stepped up to the podium. The television cameras zoomed into the face of Elijah Slate, the mysterious African American evangelist who suddenly became important enough to be singled out and given the microphone with a statewide audience on the heels of the greatest catastrophe their state had ever endured.

The cheering and clapping had barely settled to a soft rumble when Elijah coolly informed the attentive citizens of Washington State that

Governor Littman had just appointed him to preside over a drastic change in the state's criminal justice system that would be effective immediately. "Our present system of criminal justice is a complete failure because we have replaced God's Word with man's. As a result, we have the highest crime rate in the world and the highest percentage of citizens incarcerated in prisons in the world. One-quarter of all the prisoners in the entire world live in the U.S. With all of those correctional institutions, you'd think we'd be, well, corrected. Not at all. We have the highest rate of repeat offenders in the world. And all this is in spite of having the most expensive criminal justice system in the world. It doesn't serve the public who pays for it; it primarily serves the billion dollar prison bureaucracy and the hordes of wealthy attorneys and prosecutors who profit off of the crime and injustice. How have we gone from the land of the free to a police state? We have abandoned God's Word for the words of man." His listeners couldn't deny his premises, but they didn't know quite where he was going. So they just stood there attentively, hanging on every word, as they were in living rooms all over the state. Sheriff Miller stayed on the stage during Elijah's speech, while the governor and the statesmen slipped out the back under careful guard.

"From now on, this state will adopt God's Word as the standard for justice," Elijah stated emphatically. "The Bible will be our rule book." He smacked the blue hardback Gideon Bible in his hand.

"Why is murder wrong?" He paused to let his audience think on the question for a moment. "Is murder wrong just because we vote it to be wrong? If so, we could vote it to be legal and then murder would be okay." He shook his head back and forth. "That cannot be. Is murder wrong just because our leaders say it's wrong? If that were the case, when our leaders committed genocide and said it was right and legal, then it would be right. But might does not make right. Murder is wrong because it violates the law of God. In Exodus 20, God's Word says 'Thou shalt not murder.' But what should be done to those who violate this commandment? It's not just a sin, but a crime. In the very next chapter, Exodus 21, the same Lawgiver who insists that murder is wrong commands civil authorities to enforce penalties against those who commit this and other crimes. The penalty He prescribes for murder, kidnapping, and rape is death, effective immediately…"

At hearing those words, an eerie restlessness swept over the crowd. Some were giddy with excitement, whereas others grew skeptical and anxious. Most, however, were simply stunned. Elijah continued, "On the testimonies of two or three incontrovertible pieces of evidence, like eyewitnesses, video evidence, DNA evidence, and uncoerced voluntary confessions, capital criminals will be put to death immediately. No more coddling of capital criminals at taxpayer expense. These executions will take place publicly every evening immediately after the conviction." A rumble of scattered applause resounded throughout downtown Olympia. Several people in the crowd could be heard briefly shouting a word of protest. Elijah appeared unmoved at the praise and undeterred by the occasional outburst of disagreement.

When it quieted down, he continued: "God told the nation of Israel that the nations around them would recognize the wisdom of their commandments and would know that God was in them, *because* of their law and their judgments. Think about that! Gentile nations would see the wisdom in Israel's law. Why? Because it's self-evidently wise. Oh, the folly of those who think they're smarter than God! God's criminal justice system provides the *best* protection of our God-given rights. Perjury in a capital case is a capital crime because it secures against perjury and makes testimony more trustworthy. God promises us in His Word – in Deuteronomy 13:11 to be exact – that crime will stop when we follow His instructions in punishing crimes. God's laws against murder protect our lives, God's laws against theft protect our property, and God's laws against sexual predators and perverts protect our children's innocence. Humanism will no longer be the standard for justice. God's Word," he said, extending his Bible toward the television camera broadcasting his speech all over the Coalition, "has the right remedy for crime. Under God's leadership, we will begin to follow His plan for restoring peace to our troubled land. First justice, then peace. That's God's way. He's a good God, and in accordance with His love and wisdom, justice will commence this evening, beginning with child-killers and those who have been witnessed committing capital offenses in the riots." This comment prompted some vigorous clapping through the large and growing audience. The common people were absolutely furious about the devastation of downtown Olympia and Seattle, and they were in the mood to get severe with those responsible.

"All rioters should take heed." Elijah looked directly into the camera. "Restitution will replace imprisonment for theft or vandalism. A vandal or a thief who has destroyed or sold that which he stole will pay back to the victim four times the value of the object stolen. Four times! Five times the value if the object had sentimental value. If the thief is caught with undamaged stolen goods, he must repay double. If the thief returns the stolen goods of his own free will, God's law prescribes that

He will only have to repay one-fifth of the value of the object stolen. See the wisdom of God's law?" Heads nodded throughout the square. "God's criminal justice system encourages thieves to turn themselves in.

"All you rioters who broke the law yesterday and today, listen to me." He pointed into the camera. "We have video footage and many eyewitnesses. If we catch you, you will pay as the law demands. Make amends by returning the stolen object plus one-fifth of the value of the object you stole. Make restitution on their own, because if we catch you, you are going to owe a lot more. If you cannot pay for your crimes, and the one you victimized isn't willing to work out a payment plan for you, then you will be placed in privatized labor camps, where you will work to pay off that which you owe. We have a number of companies on the verge of bankruptcy who will start lining up to take advantage of the free labor force. Forced laborers will be kept for six years max, then on the seventh year, they will go free, but your tour of duty will be punishment with a capital 'P'. Turn yourself in, rioters and thieves, and save yourselves!" A surprising applause rippled through the crowd.

Governor Littman, who watched the speech on television from a private room in the statehouse, raised his eyebrows and commented, "They're clapping! I can't believe it."

"I certainly didn't expect that," the director of the Highway Patrol added in disbelief.

The attorney general wasn't as surprised. "So many homes and businesses were destroyed by the riots, I think they're fed up with coddling criminals and they're ready for some hard-hitting justice."

"Assault will be punished as God's law instructs as well. If the victim recovers, the assailant will pay for the medical expenses and for the lost wages of the victim until recovery is complete. If permanent damage results from the assault, an eye for an eye, a tooth for a tooth, hand for hand, foot for foot.

"Justice will be blind to money. Wealthy CEOs and homeless beggars will receive the same number of stripes across their bare back for the same liability. Nations that resort to flogging for crime do not have to do it that frequently. It works! There'll be no getting people off on technicalities, and there'll be no plea-bargaining. All those who have shed innocent blood in our state will face the justice that God's Word demands. Genesis 9:6 and Numbers 35 make it clear that only justice can cleanse the land of the curse of bloodguilt.

"All mature Christians who are interested in becoming a judge under this new standard of justice are welcome to go to the Reformation Civic Center over there," he said, pointing at a large building about a quarter mile away, "every night for the next ten days from seven to nine p.m., beginning in about two hours.

"I'll conclude with this passage from the New Testament. It is found in Romans, chapter 13." Elijah opened to the passage in his blue Gideon Bible. "Let every soul be subject unto the higher powers. For there is no power but of God: the powers that be are ordained of God. Whosoever therefore resisteth the power, resisteth the ordinance of God: and they that resist shall receive to themselves damnation. For rulers are not a terror to good works, but to the evil. Wilt thou then not be afraid of the power? do that which is good, and thou shalt have praise of the same: For he is the minister of God to thee for good. But if thou do that which is evil, be afraid; for he beareth not the sword in vain: for he is a minister of God, a revenger to execute wrath upon him that doeth evil. Wherefore ye must needs be subject, not only for wrath, but also for conscience sake."

Elijah shut the Bible and took a hard look across the width of the silenced crowd. "Justice begins right here, at nine o'clock tonight. May our land be cleansed of the guilt of innocent blood, and may God's wrath be quenched. May God's law be a schoolmaster to lead us to Christ. Amen."

Seattle, Washington

Mitch Paine clapped mockingly in an apartment full of campus radicals in downtown Seattle. "That a' way, bloodthirsty fanatic! Way to go!"

Shouts and curses at the screen filled the room.

"Fascist!"

"Bigot!"

"Neanderthal!"

"Misogynist!"

"What a homophobic fanatic!"

"Racist!"

"Capitalist pig!"

"The crazies are runnin' the asylum now," Damon commented, still favoring his ribs that were sorely bruised by a guardsman's rubber bullets. "It's just like you've been saying all along, Prof." Damon had become Paine's right hand man since Nick was killed when they captured the professor in Montana.

Mitch Paine nodded. "Oh, he's done it now. The people aren't going to take any of this load of–"

"We're going to crucify him!" someone exclaimed.

"How in the world did this fruitcake get the reins of the criminal justice system?" someone asked. "How?"

"This is where God-led government leads," Paine lectured with an I-told-you-so nod. "If you start with the premise that your God is the true God and the Bible is His Word, then there's just a small step to take before you start killing gays."

"He didn't say anything about gays, did he?" someone asked worriedly.

"Give it time, he will," someone responded.

"The Christian reconstructionists control Governor Littman now," Paine speculated. "He's scared of them because his soul's at stake. The Jesus freaks are pulling his strings. That's the risk of democracy, you know. Popular religion will destroy freedom in a democracy. Karl Marx had it right."

"The people will rise up and say enough is enough once he starts killing people on live TV. Let's take him out and start an uprising!"

"But they're looking for us," a fellow lying on one of the two twin beds in the room protested with a large bottle of beer in his hand. "We don't want to take a chance getting caught, do we? Especially now that they're going to start killing people and flogging them and stuff. Man!" He took another swig of his domestic ale. "I'm moving to California first chance I get!"

Someone else thought out loud: "Wonder what they're going to do to Tommy?"

"Or Callie and Ben," someone else added, worried about their friends who had been caught rioting.

"The freaks are going to whack those two abortionists tonight."

"Yeah, they're going to kill them for sure."

"I don't know about you guys," said a fellow with long brown hair who sat in a chair with one hand in a bag of Doritos and another on the mouse of his laptop. "I'm going to that guy whose store I trashed and robbed, and I'm going to try to make a deal with him to pay him back. I know they had a video camera in that store, and I'm not just going to sit around until someone recognizes me. The jail's already got my mug shot for a DUI – it's just a matter of time. I cannot afford to pay quadruple, and I sure ain't going to take a chance of going to some slave labor camp. It says here," he said, reading from an online Bible, "that slave-owners can beat the criminals in their possession. Even if they die from the beating, the slave-owner's innocent, so long as the criminal lived for a couple of days before dying. If the slave dies right away, then that supposedly shows the slave-owners intent to kill, and that's a capital crime. If they cause permanent injury in the beating, then the slave goes free."

"At least nobody gets a prison term longer than seven years!" a tattooed woman in a tank top commented. "I've been to prison. Prisoners get beaten anyway already."

"Yeah, but, man," the fellow with long brown hair retorted, "the slave-owner can make us work as much as he wants to. I'm paying back whatever I have to and coming clean. I'm not taking any chances."

"I think I'm comin' clean, too," a woman with a butch haircut and a halter-top commented. "If I return these CD's I stole" – her gaze darted to a plastic bag full of CDs at her feet – "I just have to pay one-fifth of the value back to the owner – that's 250 bucks. But if they catch me, I'll have to pay two-fold. That's $2,000 bucks! If I sell them on Ebay like I was plannin' to do, and they catch me then I have to pay $4,000 bucks! I don't have that kind of money and I'm not taking a chance of being locked away in an industrial prison for seven years."

"This place has gone crazy, man. I'm getting outta' here," the fellow with the bottle of beer repeated.

"You cowards are proving his point!" Mitch Paine scolded them as he thumbed the TV to mute with the remote. He stood to his feet and pointed to the television. "This fanatic just got done saying these laws would make criminals turn themselves in. You're thinking exactly what he wants you to think! Don't let him intimidate you."

"Everything's changed, man," the fellow long brown hair rebutted. "They're going to start killing and whipping people publicly. Jail ain't bad, man – three square meals, television, workin' out, getting credits toward your degree – but who wants to risk getting flogged on nationwide TV? Or getting shipped off to a labor camp where they can beat you?"

"None of us are going anywhere." Mitch Paine leaned against the table upon which the television rested. He bit his lip, frustrated. "Damon's right. It's time to make our move. There's no way the people will tolerate this. I don't care about what kind of Jesus-revival they've had. It's time to lead. We need to show the people they have nothing to fear from Elijah Slate. Damon?" he said, looking over at him.

"Yeah?"

"Why don't you get about 30 guys together to bust 'em out tonight?"

"You mean, bust the abortionists out of custody?"

Paine nodded. "We need about 30 clean-cut lookin' guys and girls."

"We don't have any clean-cut guys and girls," he said to laughter.

"Well, cut some hair then! I've got a contact that'll get us some guns."

"Guns?" someone protested. "That'll get us hard time."

"All time is hard time now," someone mumbled.

Paine ignored the interruptions and continued to instruct Damon. "We need some committed people for this mission."

"What do you want us to do?"

"You're to downtown Olympia. You just get on the ringer and get the group together and I'll come up with a plan. We need at least 30 to 50 volunteers, people who aren't afraid to bust up some fanatics like Elijah Slate and his henchmen to rescue those doctors and our captured friends."

Berkeley, California

It was 9 p.m. and Cal Manning had just concluded a lengthy Bible study and prayer meeting in the basement of a Berkeley dormitory. A student was plucking his guitar melodically as Cal Manning concluded with prayer. A hundred students mingled, shook hands, and hugged as they prepared to leave. Cal had a grin from ear to ear. He plopped down on a leather couch beside Carson. Carson raised a hand for a high-five, and Cal gave him one.

"You look exhausted," a campus minister who sat in a chair across from him commented.

"In my weakness" – Cal pointed heavenward – "He is made strong."

Several campus ministry leaders, two church college group leaders, and several students sat around them on the ground and on chairs, reluctant to leave.

"Hey, Cal." A college ministry leader got Cal Manning's attention.

"Yeah?"

"I've been thinking. With what Elijah Slate's doing in the state of Washington and with the armed conflict and all, I'm concerned about your safety."

Cal grinned, confident and fearless. "No suffering will come to us unless God finds us worthy of it."

The campus minister took a deep breath and glanced at Carson.

Carson kept his eyes fixed on the dirty gray carpet. "We've kindled a fire here, and it will continue to burn when we go home." Cal glanced at Carson as if he had just insulted him.

"We don't want to see you two arrested," a college ministry leader added.

"If you feel your time here's done Carson, you can go home." Cal snapped. "We're in a revival. I can't leave."

Sensing the contention, a church college group leader said, "Y'all don't get all Paul-and-Barnabish on us. The Lord'll give you peace about what to do."

Carson looked at Cal. "I can't leave you here by yourself."

Cal leaned back in his leather chair and turned his eyes to the ceiling, as if studying the design of the water stains above him. "Carson, if I leave now, it'll be like leaving the battlefield on the eve of a great victory. It would be unbelief, because if you knew God was about to answer our prayers and we were on the eve of a great city-wide revival, you'd stay, wouldn't you?"

"Cal, the Coalition was just invaded." Carson opened a folded piece of notebook paper out of his pocket and handed it to Cal. "We launched a nuclear missile into space to prove a point, and these kinds of death threats are not to be lightly discarded."

Cal had one look at the marker-scribbled note, and stretched out his hands, frustrated. "I told you, Carson, I don't care about these! This is the devil." He shook the note in front of him. "Satan doesn't give us commands! We shouldn't be motivated by the fear of man but the fear and love of God." He wadded the paper into a ball and threw it on the floor.

"But you need to use wisdom," the campus minister urged as he picked up the crumpled note. "That death threat was *before* Elijah's televised speech. You just can't keep ignoring these…"

A campus minister beside him reached for the note and asked, "Let me see that," and he handed it to him.

"Well," said Cal, "we can't rightly complain to the godless secular authorities about death threats, can we?"

Carson shook his head back and forth. “Not without risking arrest.”

Cal rolled his eyes. “I don’t mean any disrespect, brothers, but the fear of man and carnal wisdom has been an excuse for cowardice since the dawn of time. Would the prophet Elijah have ever taken on the prophets of Baal on Mt. Carmel if his faith had taken a back seat to the fear of man? Would David have ever charged Goliath? Would Jonathan and his armorbearer have ever taken on a garrison of Philistines all by their lonesome? The foolishness of God is greater than man’s wisdom, and God’s strength is exalted in our weakness.”

Carson nodded at the truths in Cal’s sermonette, and felt cowardly for thinking they should leave. Cal saw his struggle, reached forward and placed a hand on his friend’s shoulder. “We’ve been invited to speak in three classes tomorrow. Three classes! That’s hundreds of students! We’ve got about 20 converts so far and, you know, about twice that many convicted people coming to these dorm meetings. We’ve got invitations to speak at Intervarsity and Campus Crusade this week.” Two of the campus ministers around them nodded. “We’re on the verge of a big breakthrough with Pastors John and Mike – they’re getting on board with the open-air campus preaching. They’re planning on joining us at the SSA rally in a couple of days.” Cal could tell by the grimace on Carson’s face that he was way out of his comfort zone. “Listen, Carson, God has not given us the spirit of fear, but of love, power, and a sound mind. Any suffering we endure will be a megaphone through which we can promote God’s kingdom. Trust in Him.”

Cal could see that the leaders who surrounded them held Carson’s opinion. They thought they should leave to avoid capture. “Do you remember what we read tonight in Acts?” Cal asked. “The prophet informed Paul that he would be captured if he went to Jerusalem. All of his friends urged Paul to stay away. But do you remember Paul’s response?”

They nodded, and Carson whispered, “He said he was ready to die for the Gospel.”

“That’s how you overcome the principalities, powers, and wickedness in high places: your testimony, the blood of Jesus, and loving not your life unto death. I wouldn’t miss that SSA rally on campus even if I knew it would mean my death.”

After a moment of reverential silence, Carson responded, “You’re one brave dude, Cal. I wouldn’t miss your preaching outside that SSA rally for anything.”

“Outside? I want the microphone, Carson.”

Carson laughed, and Cal said, “And when I get ‘em all riled up, I’m going to hand the mic to you, so be ready!” The leaders around them burst into laughter.

A student rushed into the room. “Hey! It’s about to come on.”

Cal and Carson exchanged grins, and a campus minister said, “Let the executions begin.” They went into the next room where a large screen television was about to play the most-watched television program of all time.

Olympia, Washington

Mitch Paine’s motley crew of 40 volunteers arrived at the courthouse steps of Olympia a little early, but downtown was already thick with people. They roamed around until one of them recognized two camo-clad men the courthouse with exposed sidearms.

“Hey, hey!” An SSA student from the University of Texas tapped Damon on the arm. “There they are. Those guardsmen are the ones that busted Todd and Wes.”

Damon recognized them. “They aren’t guardsman. They’re Minutemen.”

“Oh no,” he whispered as he jerked his head away. “They saw me. Are they walking this way?”

“Let’s go.” Damon started walking away from the gathering crowd of citizens. “Try to look inconspicuous.”

A sudden scream came from the area near the two Minutemen. “No! No! I didn’t do anything!” Two civilians were wrenching the wrists of a male student who had joined Mitch Paine’s group in California.

“That’s Gary!” Damon said. “One of them must have recognized him.”

They watched as the two civilians tied the college student’s hands behind his back. “I’m just here to watch!”

“Oh no,” one of the civilians said. “I saw you hit my sister in the face with a brick! I’ll *never* forget your face! You laughed!”

“I don’t know what you’re talking about.” The crowd was gathering around to observe the citizen’s arrest.

“If she recognizes you as clearly as I do, that’s two witnesses. Then you’re going to face justice, pal! Too bad she can only see out of one eye, thanks to you!”

“I’m sorry, it was an accident,” the student insisted just as a police officer arrived.

“A confession and a lie,” the policeman judged, patting the arresting civilian on the back.

“At least we got a confession,” the irate civilian responded. “This guy totally smashed my sister’s face!”

“I haven’t been read my rights! My confession won’t stand up in court.”

“We’ve got new law, pal,” one of the observers responded.

“Not laughing now, huh? Eye for an eye has a way of sobering you up, doesn’t it?” The arresting civilian tugged the rioter away from the crowd in the direction of the jail one block away. Two other armed civilians accompanied them toward the jail.

“Oh man,” one of the students beside Damon whined. “This ain’t good.”

The headlights of five large trucks came rumbling down the road toward the capitol steps. “Who are they?” one of the students wondered.

“That’s the Guard.”

“Man, this ain’t good.”

“Would you shut up?!” Damon turned to the young student and rebuked him in a harsh whisper. “Why don’t you go back to your parent’s house, you sissy!” The student’s eyes were filled with regret for his display of fear. He looked down in shame and Damon leaned forward and whispered in his ear. “Don’t wimp out on me. Have some courage, dude.” Guardsmen filed out of the trucks and positioned themselves at pre-assigned points around the block. “There’s 40 of us here, armed with weapons this time, and we’re just the fuse in a bomb of the people’s power.” The young man made eye contact with Damon and forced a smile.

“For the little guy?” Damon extended a fist and the student smacked Damon’s fist with his own, a sign of camaraderie.

“Yeah, the little guy.”

Thousands of people flooded into the downtown area to witness the first executions of Washington state’s new justice system. Clusters of Christians and patriots gathered tightly together at the front of the stairs. Damon and his entourage stayed on the outskirts of the crowd, but their low hats, baggy clothes, and multiple piercings, coupled with their reluctance to gather with the gathering throng made them stand out, and many passers-by stared at them suspiciously.

“This has all the makings of a funeral,” Damon commented. “Oh man!”

"What?" the fellow next to him was startled by Damon's exclamation.

Damon's eyes were focused on the stairs that led to the platform where the executions were due to take place within an hour. "What in the world is Don doing up there?"

"What are you talking about?"

"Don's up there talking to those two officers in cams, there," – he pointed at the foot of the stairs. "Go see whassup."

"You mean, go up there?"

"Yeah."

The student pressed through the crowd and listened for a few minutes as a fellow leftist, arms flailing, dialogued with the two guardsmen.

One of the two guardsmen took out a cell phone, dialed a number, and handed the phone to the young man.

After a minute of listening to the conversation, the student had heard enough. He casually returned to Damon's side.

"What's Don doing?"

"He wanted to turn himself in. He was scared crazy."

"Turn himself in?"

"He was worried someone would recognize him, and he'd rather pay a fifth for what he stole and can return, and double for what he broke, than quadruple."

"What did they tell him?"

"They got the store owner on the phone, and Don and he worked something out."

"Oh, they did, huh?" a disbelieving Damon mumbled.

"Yeah. The store owner's only going to make him pay back what it costs to fix it up, as long as Don helps him out until things get up and running again."

"That's cool."

"Yeah. Don was tripping. Oh, another thing."

"What?"

"There are buckets of large stones on the sidewalk in front of the stairs."

"Large stones?" Damon wondered aloud. "You gotta be kidding me," he mumbled under his breath. "Barbarians."

"There he is!" The student motioned to the platform as Elijah walked up the stairs onto the stage with four armed citizens, one in cams and three wearing T-shirts with Christian messages on them. Elijah grabbed the sides of the podium with both hands, and looked into the video camera that was stationed on a tall tripod about 20 yards away.

* * * * *

"I'm not abandoning you." Mitch Paine held the dorm exit door open with one hand. "I'm going to California to get some more people and to try to get some media cameras to follow us back. You think you can go down there and get hundreds more followers as well as I can?"

"No, no." A leader of Earth First, with 200 activists under his command, certainly didn't mean to imply that Paine was abandoning them.

"You just do what you're supposed to do, got that? Watch it on television and when Damon and the others get their wrecking machine up and running, make your way to the courthouse, busting every window and burning every car and store on the way. Got that?"

"Okay."

"We need big-time havoc, you understand?"

"Yeah."

"Remember. Chaos is how we build. Our new society will be erected on the ashes of the old one."

"How are you going to get back across the border? They're probably stopping people on the way in."

"You let me worry about that." Sensing fear in the eco-terrorist, Paine placed his right hand on his shoulder and winked at him. "We're going to win this thing." Paine then walked through the door, covered his face with the hood of his jacket, and jogged to his car.

The environmentalist turned to another activist beside him. "He's abandoning us."

22

Olympia, Washington

"Good evening, saints," Elijah spoke into the microphone to the crowd that had grown to at least ten thousand, with many more continuing to flock in. The courthouse had an eerie backdrop of the colorful orange and red glow from a sluggish sunset, made more spectacular from the pillars of smoke that still crept heavenward from the riot's fires.

"I hope all of you were able to be a part of the meeting in the Reformation Civic Center, or at least, were able to watch it on television. We are not here tonight to revel in blood, or to glory in the fall of those who have committed these crimes. We are here for a holy purpose," Elijah solemnly stated. "Like marriage, like a baptism, like the birth of a child into the world, executing civil justice is a holy duty which should instill fear and awe into every one of us. Let the events tonight remind us that God is just and that his wrath is severe. Let's look, learn, and let the wickedness these criminals represent be purged from among us."

The few 'Amens' were confident and bold and cut the windless silence like a knife.

A group of teenagers near the front began to grow rowdy, and chant, "Eli – jah! Eli – jah! Eli – jah!…" The cheer caught on and many joined. Elijah surprised them all when he suddenly reproved them for it.

"Enough of that!" He pointed a critical finger at the cheering youth. "You think this is some kind of football game? This is serious business! Human beings made in God's image are going to die tonight." The cheering immediately died down, and a quiet fear and respect stilled the crowd.

Elijah took a deep breath and lifted his Gideon Bible. “The Bible says that if man sheds innocent blood, then he should be put to death, quickly and publicly. The Bible says that if we do not execute the shedders of innocent blood, then God will curse us and our land. Exodus 21 plainly teaches that if someone kills an unborn child, even through carelessness, the state should take ‘life for life.’ Jesus supported the death penalty during his ministry. The apostles supported the death penalty in the book of Acts and in their Epistles. The Bible says that if we delay the punishment for a crime, criminals will be emboldened and crime will be more prevalent. So in obedience to God’s Word, we are going to begin with executing two abortionists.”

Elijah turned as three policemen escorted a balding gentleman with pepper brown hair in his late 40’s. His hands were tied behind his back and his feet were shackled. His teeth were clenched in anger. When he saw Elijah, he began to heave the foulest curses on him, the Minutemen, and the Coalition. Elijah just stared at him blankly as the tirade of abusive language continued for about 20 seconds. So foul was his tongue that the crowd tried to drown out his cursing with loud boos and shouts. Dozens in the crowd walked to the buckets of large stones and began to pick out the larger ones for the coming execution.

When the abortionist slowed his tirade to take a breath, Elijah spoke into the microphone: “Mr. Daniel Wallace. In the past 15 years, you have killed thousands upon thousands of innocent children…” The abortionist continued to threaten and verbally abuse Elijah and the Coalition, so Elijah spoke directly into the microphone to be heard over his screaming. “We have dozens of witnesses to your cruelty. We will mention two; that is all that God’s law requires. The names and testimonies of other witnesses can be found on my website, RightRemedy-dot-org. Actually, Mr. Wallace’s confession amounts to a third witness of his guilt. Okay, Tanya Paris, are you there?” Elijah glanced to his left, and then his right.

When Elijah spoke her name, the crowd stilled. Tanya Paris was a world-famous actress who had graced the cover of every glamour magazine from Hollywood to New York City.

A young blond woman in her twenties raised her hand on the left side of the stage, and everyone stood on their tip-toes to try to get a glimpse of her. The doctor looked over and recognized his former patient, and his cursing stopped immediately. For a brief moment, Damon thought he saw fear in the physician’s eyes.

"Come on up here and tell us what happened to you."

Tanya walked to the podium, exercising caution to not come near her former gynecologist, Dr. Wallace. She walked up the podium, and Elijah stood beside her with a hand on her shoulder as she testified. "Five years ago, I was raped by a boy at school and got pregnant. My parents were displeased, of course, as my career was already up and running and a pregnancy could end it. Mom and Dad told me that if I was going to stay in their house, I had to get an abortion." She vigorously shook her head side to side as tears welled in her eyes. "I did not want to, but they insisted that I at least meet to talk about it with Dr. Wallace. We did, and Dr. Wallace promised me that—" Her voice cracked, and she paused when her emotions started to show. She held a tissue up to her face, and tried not to cry.

"It's all right," Elijah whispered to her. "It'll be over soon."

"He told me that my baby was just a blob of tissue. That it wasn't alive. Then he killed it." She sobbed for a few seconds, and then quickly gained control of herself.

"My parents – they forced me! – and once Dr. Wallace started giving me the medicine, I don't even remember anything after that. Honestly! I would never have killed my baby. Never…" She started weeping bitterly now, and Elijah called a modestly dressed woman in the front of the crowd to come and comfort her. She placed an arm around her shoulders and whispered something into her ear.

Momentarily, Elijah asked her, "Where are your parents?" She stopped crying and looked up into his eyes once she realized why he asked.

"I, I can't turn them in."

* * * * *

"We gotta leave! We gotta leave!" The 50-year-old millionaire stood up from his Lazyboy and plucked the keys of his Lexus from his pocket. Their daughter had told their secret to the world. Their sin had found them out.

The woman beside him wept in the couch of their Beverly Hills mansion directly in front of their big screen television. "We deserve what we've got coming to us. We are accomplices in the death of our grandbaby."

* * * * *

A 50-year-old engineer sitting on the edge of his couch under the glow of his flat-screen looked over at his 33-year-old mistress, who sat beside him. Her eyes were filled with trepidation over what she was witnessing on the screen.

She looked over at him, and he said, “We can’t do it, hon.”

The woman burst into tears. She pawed her tears with her well-manicured hands. “I can’t have this baby! What will it do to my career?”

“I’m sorry, but we can’t.” He shook his head back and forth, keeping his eyes fixed on the screen.

“But I’m married to another man. He’ll kill me!”

“We’re not gonna punish the baby for our affair, and they” – he pointed at the television screen – “aren’t gonna let us.”

* * * * *

Elijah leaned down to whisper in Tanya’s ear. “Who was the boy?”

“The boy?”

“Who raped you?”

Tanya’s mouth went dry, and Elijah saw the color drain from her face. “If you want to pursue justice for your baby, and cleanse this land and your conscience of bloodguilt, you’ve got to come clean, Tanya.”

She turned toward the crowd, the bright flashes of the media’s cameras distracting her from the tug of her conscience. “We’ll talk about this later, Tanya.” A guardsman escorted her down the stairs beside a bucket of stones.

“Jerry Chavez! Where are you, Jerry?”

A jubilant Hispanic fellow in his twenties with a bounce in his step and a sheathed sword hooked to his belt came up with a bellowing shout of “Praise the Lord, Washington State!”

The abortionist recognized the man who was a faithful witness for years on the sidewalk in front of his office, counseling his patients to keep their babies.

“You’ve given our AV guy the pictures?”

Jerry nodded, and spoke into the microphone. “These are the victims of children Dr. Wallace killed…”

Two young men from the balcony of the capitol building dropped white sheets that had been sewn together, which served as a screen for the elevated projector. “I saw these carcasses in the dumpster behind Dr. Wallace’s abortuary. He was the only abortionist employed there.” Jerry pointed at the photographs of contorted aborted human fetuses that were flashed up on the screen, and the crowd gasped in horror with each photograph of the dismembered, bloody children.

Wallace, for a moment, was speechless as his face reddened with rage. Damon thought that he had never seen a man more angry in all of his life.

"All right. That's enough." Elijah patted Jerry on the shoulder. "It's time."

Jerry descended the stairs and lifted a large stone from a white bucket.

"Come on, Damon. Do it!" Damon's partner whispered. "Now or never."

"Shhh!" Damon ordered. "There are too many people around here. Let's go over there next to that flowerbed."

They were in the middle of a throng of people, and Damon was concerned that those around them could overhear what they were saying.

"Just follow me," Damon whispered before turning and walking briskly away.

The execution was a horrifying thing to watch, but difficult to pull your eyes away from nonetheless. It was cold, swift, and bloody. It was justice, a rare thing to the eyes of most Americans. And it was effective; every single scheduled abortion in the state was now cancelled.

The crowd of ten thousand was aghast. They stood there as silent as death, horrified at what they had just witnessed.

Elijah walked to the microphone and spoke to the stilled crowd as two police officers wearing rubber gloves began to remove the stones off of the abortionist's body. "Let this be a reminder to us that we will not require often: God does not tolerate the killing of innocent people."

The officers began to drag the body to the side of the stairs and Elijah stopped them: "No! Wait! Take him through the crowd." He pointed straight into the middle of the throng. "They'll make a path." As they dragged his corpse through the crowd, it left a trail of blood behind.

"Washington State, you have shed innocent blood, and now look at the wages of sin. I hope all child-killers realize they will not get away with it." He looked into the camera lens. "You will not commit any more abortions or physician-assisted suicides in Washington State. And unless you repent, you won't get away from it on Judgment Day either."

"Amen!" shouted many in the crowd of ten thousand.

"Bring out the next abortionist."

Every single abortionist, abortion advocate, and murderer that remained in the state of Washington immediately began to pack up and head south.

"Come on, Damon!" The student beside him was beginning to tremble.

Damon still held the gun hidden under his jacket. He looked back and forth, fearful of those nearby who glanced suspiciously at him. With his back to an elevated flowerbed and with his partner standing in front of him, he pulled the stainless steel .22 magnum pistol with a long barrel and scope affixed to the top. He stabilized it on the shoulder of his friend.

"Hey!" Someone a few feet to his right shouted at him. "Hey! He's aiming a gun at the stage!"

Damon cringed in fear as those around him began to scream about the threat. Damon was tempted to make for the comfort of the nearest dark alley, but the fear of Professor Paine's disapproval prodded him toward courageous defiance of Washington State's religious totalitarianism. He jumped on top of a cement barricade, turned with his gun, steadied it on a light pole, and took careful aim.

Blam!

Elijah heard the blast of the gun in the back of the square. The bullet struck the top stair that led to the platform, sending up a flash of gray dust. Those nearest the platform instinctively ducked. Four guardsmen and the Seattle sheriff unholstered their weapons and moved in front of Elijah, guarding him with their own bodies.

Damon concentrated more carefully for his second shot, steadying the pistol-scope's crosshairs over the back of Elijah Slate's head, when a bystander nearby grabbed him by the shirt. "Stop!" he screamed as he flung Damon onto his back against the ground.

That would be the man's last word. Damon instinctively raised his gun and put a bullet through the man's forehead. He fell limp to the ground beside Damon, and then began to seize. The entire crowd pounced on the murderer at once. They pressed him to the ground and wrestled the gun from his sweaty grasp. You could hear Damon's scream at the bottom of the pile: "No! Let go! No! Get off me!"

"They got the shooter," an officer said to Elijah. They watched as Damon was dragged, kicking and screaming to the front of the crowd, his hands cuffed behind his back.

"No!" Damon screamed. "It was Mitch Paine! He put us up to it!"

A Minuteman who gripped Damon's bicep informed Elijah, "This young man shot a man in the head back there."

"With this gun." An officer handed Elijah the stainless steel pistol in one hand and the bullets they removed from the gun in the other. "It was a fatal wound."

"Mitch Paine wanted you to kill me, huh?"

"And President Brighton put *him* up to it!" Damon added as the television cameras zoomed close. "There are about 40 of us here." Damon appeared happy to try to accommodate Elijah Slate in hopes of winning his favor. "Thousands of us are staying in hotels and college dorm rooms…"

"Us? Who's us?"

"Rioters, Marxists, environmental activists, gay activists…"

Elijah motioned for some guardsmen to begin scouring the area. "Their names?"

Damon gave him about 15 names that he could remember off the top of his head, including the leaders of many of the liberal groups who met with the president. "President Brighton told them they could get their criminal records cleared if they helped bring down the Coalition from the inside with rioting…"

After watching this exchange on television, it took two minutes for every single one of the thousands of hippies and students who worked for Mitch Paine in Washington State to be on their way toward the nearest Coalition border, following the speed limit very carefully, of course.

Washington, D.C.

"Noooo!" Margaret Brighton screamed from her living room as she watched the live broadcast. She stood to her feet and stomped. "No! No! No!" She grabbed her dinner plate that sat on the coffee table next to her and threw it at the television set. The plate missed the TV and hit one of her stereo speakers. So she picked up the lamp, and threw it at the television, and the LCD screen exploded with a zap.

"Madam President!" Two secret servicemen came running into the room, startled by her outburst. "Is everything all right, Madam President?"

She ordered them to leave the room, picked up her cell phone, and speed-dialed her press secretary. "Cameron! Get that off the air, now!"

"We can't…"

"I want it off the air!"

"Madam President, is what that student said true? Did you meet with those—"

She hung up on Cameron and speed dialed another number.

General Green was at the Pentagon when he heard the characteristic ring informing him that the call was coming from the White House. He tapped the Bluetooth device over his left ear. Having just been informed of what had transpired in Olympia, he wasn't surprised by the hasty phone call, nor by the caustic tone of voice at the other end of the line: "Good evening, Madam—"

"Tell the UN to get in there and destroy that Coalition, **now!**"

"They're not in position yet."

"I don't care! Do it now!" she squealed her orders. "Take him out now!" She stood to her feet so she could stomp for emphasis.

"Madam President, we can't fight wars like that. Calm d—"

"Don't you tell me to calm down!"

Margaret Brighton threw the phone at the wall and stomped up to her bedroom for an extra dose of Xanax.

The general shook his head and slowly lowered the phone back down to the receiver. The thoroughly suppressed chauvanist in him, buried deeply in the course of a dozen sensitivity seminars, bubbled to the surface. *A menopausal commander-in-chief! Whew! Who ever came up with that idea ought to be shot!*

It was the end of violent crime in Washington State. The thousands of bureaucrats, attorneys, and state employees who profited off of the disastrous criminal justice system of Washington State began to look for jobs in the private sector. With the low tax rate and the influx of cheap slave labor available in the new justice system, many citizens ventured into entrepreneurial opportunities. The jobless rate dropped to zero, even as the state began to wean its citizens off of welfare and unemployment benefits.

Washington, D.C.

Josh Davis, the Coalition's only journalist inside the beltway, watched the executions in awe. With the disappearance of his friend and co-conspirator, Danny Connor, he had given up hope and descended into a deep pit of loneliness and isolation. However, seeing Washington State's initiative to resist the federal government had given him hope. He didn't necessarily agree with the swift public executions, but he appreciated the fact that local authorities were boldly and publicly operating within their lawful rights to manage their own criminal justice system in defiance of federal usurpation.

When he heard Damon's testimony about Brighton's involvement with Mitch Paine's activities, his mind began to buzz like a hive of angry bees. He began research on another article that would rock the nation. He confirmed the personal connections between Margaret Brighton and many of the liberal clubs and left-wing organizations that were involved in the rioting across the border. Many of their benefactors were also major contributors to Brighton's election campaign. Under a pseudonym, he conducted phone interviews with dozens of incarcerated rioters who confessed to operating under Mitch Paine's authority. The list of their leaders read like a "Who's who" of the liberal left.

The connections between Brighton and these Marxist groups were irrefutable. Damon's testimony was firmly established. Josh Davis finished the article in a couple of days and blitzed the internet with it. He distributed it to thousands of religious conservatives all over the nation who expressed a willingness to help him. Hundreds of thousands of copies had flooded the nation by the end of the week. Congress responded by issuing a subpoena for Mitch Paine and fiercely debated another investigation of the president and the FBI. The Republican congressmen and women who were most vehemently opposed to James Knight's obsession with impeaching President Brighton were now publicly sympathetic.

23

Berkeley, California

During Cal Manning's lectures in classes at the University of California in Berkeley, questions on the new, radical criminal justice system of Washington State filled the air.

"Not only does God's law forbid murder with the sixth commandment in Exodus 20," Cal raised his voice to be heard over the whisper of his dissenters, "but it also forbids letting murderers live according to Exodus 21. It's a question of who is Lord. If the God of the Bible is the true God, then we all should obey Him. Being a politician doesn't exempt you of your duty to obey God's Word. It's that simple."

A freshman in the front of the criminal justice class raised her hand and he called on her. "Go ahead, ma'am."

"God's a God of love. I can't imagine him killing someone. Look how Jesus treated people."

"You might not be able to imagine Jesus doing a lot of things that even you would justify, like spanking kids, like putting rapists and murderers in prison. Could you imagine Jesus doing that?"

The woman shrugged.

"Read the book of Revelation, ma'am. Jesus is going to judge the world for sin, and His punishment will be fierce. Just because He came the first time as a Lamb doesn't mean that there's something wrong with being a lion – the Bible actually calls Jesus the Lion of the Tribe of Judah."

"What about the woman caught in the act of adultery?"

Cal repeated the question: "You mean, the prostitute in John chapter 8 whom Jesus did not execute?"

"Yeah."

"That's a very good question, young lady, and I'm glad you asked it. The Pharisees testified that they caught this woman in the act of adultery. They brought her to Jesus with stones in their hands. The Bible says that they were trying to tempt Jesus, probably trying to get him to contradict the law of Moses. They said to him, 'Moses said that this adulteress should be put to death, but what do you say?'

"At first, Jesus just ignored them and wrote on the dirt. When they asked again, Jesus responded, 'Let him that is without sin cast the first stone.' They became convicted of their own sin, dropped their stones, and walked away. When Jesus was alone with the woman, He asked her, 'Woman, who's here to accuse you?' She responded, 'No one, Lord.' Then Jesus said, 'Neither do I condemn you, go and sin no more.'"

"There! You see, he didn't stone her for her adultery. Elijah Slate would have."

"No, no," Cal shook his head. "Elijah would *not* have executed her for the same reasons Jesus didn't. It was *unlawful* to execute her in those circumstances."

"Really?"

"God's law demands that both the woman *and the man* in the adulterous relationship be executed. Where was the man? I mean, they said that they caught her in the act, so where was the man? Maybe Jesus wrote 'Leviticus 20:10' on the ground, implying that they were guilty of *not* charging the man. You know, in a capital case, false witnesses were to be put to death. They may have thrown down their stones to keep them from being thrown *at* them. Maybe Jesus wrote on the ground the names of the women that these religious hypocrites had committed adultery with. Maybe that's why they got so sensitive to conviction all of a sudden and scuttled away. They were hypocrites. They were not without sin and therefore not qualified to judge. Matthew 7 verses 1 through 5 says that only those free from sin are qualified to judge their neighbor.

"The Bible also says witnesses are to be the first to put capital criminals to death, but the witnesses had all dropped their stones and walked away. The Bible also says that they should be executed publicly. Jesus wasn't an eyewitness and he was left alone with the woman, so it would have been unlawful for Jesus to stone her. When I look at the passage, I see just more evidence that Jesus promotes the death penalty for crimes worthy of it. After all, he told them to execute her."

"But Jesus forgave her of what she did."

Cal nodded. "That's not unique to the New Testament. Remember, God forgave King David in the Old Testament for adultery with Bathsheba and for killing her husband to cover it up, so there's no new standard set in John 8. God forbids our leaders and judges to extend leniency to convicted criminals. If the state started forgiving all the rapists and murderers, our streets would be filled with rape and murder. God ordained the state to be the agent of justice to protect the innocent. Elijah was appointed by the executive branch of Washington State to execute those murderers."

"But what about eating shrimp and catfish?" another student asked.

Elijah grinned. "$12.99, all you can eat at Billy's Crab Shack across the street."

The crowd laughed at his humor.

"Seriously, that is a good question," Elijah responded. "The New Testament renders dietary commandments, feast day commandments, and circumcision optional for the Jews in the New Testament. You can read about it in Romans 14, in Galatians and Colossians. So those commandments that were unique to the Old Covenant are not obligatory for Jews or Gentiles today. We enter into the New Covenant with God through faith in Jesus' blood, not in circumcision rituals, animal sacrifices, and feast days."

Cal was ecstatic about the many lectures they were invited to give in various classes on campus. The events in Washington State were a topic that fascinated everybody, and his friendship with Elijah, the new chief law enforcement officer in the state of Washington, made Cal's lectures all the more captivating.

When lectures for the day ended, Cal and Carson were drawn as if by a magnet to the free speech area of U.C. Berkeley's campus, where SSA was setting up for the much-anticipated rally.

Cal planned to go back to their hotel across from campus to retrieve a box of "Chick tracts", whereas Carson wanted to mingle with the students on the green to discover what he could about SSA's plans for the day. Cal and Carson planned to meet up on the sidewalk beside the free speech area in an hour.

Cal retrieved his box of tracts and followed the sidewalk through a tunnel under a four-lane road that bordered the campus. Two large athletic students stepped out in front of him about ten yards ahead. The light was dim in the tunnel, but the way those two large men just stood there staring at him concerned him. He stopped, turned around, and acted like he forgot something at his hotel. A quick look back revealed that the jocks were closing on him at a rapid pace from 20 yards back. He turned around and saw two more young men step out from behind a tree and stand in the middle of the sidewalk. They just stood there, with their hands on their hips, staring him down. To his left was a canal and to his right was the side of a student dormitory. He didn't have a lot of options.

Cal banked right up the grassy hill on a foot trail toward a side door to the dormitory with the four students in chase.

Lord, keep me safe. Let that door be open.

Cal made it to a side door of the dormitory just as two female students exited. He entered the stairwell and pulled the door shut behind him. The student who was closest tried to open the door, but it was locked. The second student to reach the door was removing a plastic card key from his wallet to unlock the door. The two jocks made it to the door and began to breathe out threats to him. One of the students began to talk on his cell phone.

Cal bolted up the stairwell just as the students unlocked the door. Up two flights of stairs he found two more beefy students waiting for him. He was trapped.

"Where ya' goin', Mr. Minuteman?" one of the men behind him said in a mocking tone.

Cal grabbed the metal handrail just in case one of the men on the stairwell above him tried to push him down.

"We were just wonderin' if you'd like to make a deal. Get your pathetic self off our campus in exchange for living another day."

Cal turned to glance at the two students above him at the top of the stairwell and was about to order them to move when he heard a gun cock below him. He looked down to find the largest of the four men pointing a .38-caliber revolver at his head. Cal fearlessly swatted the gun away from him and pushed the gun-holder away from him two or three steps down, surprising the men with his fearlessness.

"Do you want to die!" the fellow with the gun said, raising it again and leveling it at Cal's chest. Cal kept his peace, praying silently.

"Let's give him a boot party!" another one of them said, laughing.

Without flinching, Cal responded, "What makes you think I'm going to let you do that?"

"I thought Christians turn the other cheek."

"Don't pretend like you're going to shoot me with a gun in the dormitory stairwell. Let's be realistic," Cal said calmly. "Everybody within two floors will hear that blast and there'll be too many witnesses to kill. So here's how we're going to do this, boys. I'm going to fight the six of you right here, and probably get ten or twelve good blows on a few of 'ya before I lose, but *you*" – Cal pointed at the short blond fellow below him, who was clearly the most nervous-looking of the six college students that surrounded him – "are going to get severely injured during the exchange. Maybe even killed. The choice is yours. Shoot me, and I go to heaven and you to jail. Fight me, and you" – he pointed at the young blond student below him – "may not survive."

"Get a load of this guy!" said the gun-holding jock.

"If you think that you're going to intimidate somebody who has no fear of dying, better think again, boys."

The pale-faced blond student responded, "Ah, we scared him. Let's get outta' here. No more preaching on campus, got that?"

"We just want your wallet," the brave fellow with the gun insisted.

"Well, you'll have to fight me for it." Cal put his back up to the wall and spread his legs slightly to lower his center of gravity on the stairwell. He raised his arms and clenched his fists, prepared to fight.

"Let's get outta' here," the nervous-appearing blond student responded.

"No, let's take him out," one of the students on the stairwell above him responded.

"Better kill me, or he is crippled or killed," Cal repeated, pointing briefly at the blond student below him again. He was their weak link, and Cal was exploiting it.

"Shoot him, Pat! Shoot him!"

The fellow with the gun stretched his gun toward Cal again. "Your wallet!"

Cal saw that the hammer was not pulled back on the pistol, so he knew that the trigger pull would be long. So he quickly slapped the handgun away as he stared in the direction that split the difference between his attackers, so as to see them all out of his peripheral vision.

"What are you, crazy?" the fellow with the gun shouted.

"Let's get outta' here, man. He's insane!" the blond student responded, pulling at the forearm of the student with the gun. "Let's go."

"What are you talking about, man?" the fellow with the gun scolded the blond fellow.

"He's talking about saving his own life," Cal responded, "or at least staying out of a wheelchair."

The door above the two students suddenly opened up, and a group of girls started heading down the stairwell. The students on the stairs above Cal looked up and appeared nervous. The fellow with the gun placed the weapon behind his back so as to hide it. "Just let 'em pass."

When Cal noticed the gun was no longer pointed at him, he wasted no time. He swung his left foot and caught the fellow with the gun under the chin, sending him hurling down the remaining five stairs, knocking down one of the three jocks who stood directly behind him. Cal punched one of the students above him in the groin, and then grabbed the shirt of the other student above him and flung him over his shoulder and down the stairs, knocking down the other students below him. Cal could hear one of their heads smack the cement at the bottom of the stairwell with a nauseating thud.

They were bleeding and breathless in a state of shock on the landing. One of the uninjured students at the bottom of the flight of stairs reached over to grab the gun that landed on the ground next to him. Cal pounced on him and delivered a right fist that snapped the student's head back.

One of the students reached for Cal's arm that held the gun, and Cal instinctively backhanded him across the face. They were a bloody, pathetic mess. He pointed the gun directly at the short, blond student, who put his arms up and cowered in fear. "No, please don't!"

"You could have died today, son." Cal spoke with a calmness that surprised even him. "Evil company corrupts good morals. Get right with God, son. Do you hear me?"

The young man nodded, "Yes sir."

"I'll be speaking at the Baptist Student Union tomorrow at 7 p.m. I'll meet you right at the bottom of this stairwell at 6 p.m. for dinner, then church at the B.S.U. My treat." He gave the young man a genuine smile and lowered the pistol. "Got it?"

"Yes sir."

Cal pointed the pistol at the fellow he kicked, who was just now coming back to consciousness. Blood was pouring from his mouth, and when the student opened his mouth, Cal saw that his tongue was almost completely severed. "Go on, get outta' here. Get to an ER for stitches." The students struggled to their feet and began to make their way down the stairs. He gently kicked the rear end of the student who was the slowest of them. "Y'all come to the B.S.U. tomorrow at seven and I won't turn you into the police."

"B.S.U.?" one of them wondered aloud.

"Yeah, the Baptist Student Union. You better be there."

Cal sighed, whispered a prayer of thanks to God, and thought, *What did I do with that box of tracts?*

When Cal approached the free speech area, his adrenaline from his confrontation in the stairwell had begun to subside, and he felt a new kind of anxiety. Thousands of students had begun to gather at the foot of the stage in the middle of the Berkeley green. A large banner that read "Students for Social Action" was being draped as a backdrop behind the stage.

Cal walked up to Carson and patted him on the shoulder. "Learn anything interesting?"

"Yeah. Mitch Paine's speaking."

"*The* Mitch Paine?" Cal's eyes widened, and Carson nodded.

Cal approached two university policemen who were standing nearby. "Excuse me, sirs."

"*The* Cal Buckner!" The younger officer recognized him, knowing him by the pseudonym he had been given before he left Montana. "Well, it looks like I lost," he said as the other officer snickered. "We had a bet on whether you'd even show up today. After what's been going on in Washington State, we figured you fellows would stick to formal debates, Sunday schools, and lecturing in classes and give up the more controversial open air preachin', especially with this crowd." He motioned to the growing mass of leftists on the green.

"I want to thank you for being here," Cal said with a smile and a handshake. He knew that the presence of the officers might soothe fragile tempers.

A punk rock band ascended the stage and began to play a song with the sound cranked up as loud as the school administration would let them. Over the course of ten minutes of rock music, the crowd grew to at least 5,000 students and Berkeley hang-outs, those drop-outs and hippies from previous generations who never managed to leave the college scene.

To Cal's delight, he saw Mitch Paine step out of a limo next to them on the sidewalk. As the renown professor walked past them, Cal called out to him, trying to shake his hand. "Mr. Paine! Professor Paine?" The professor, flanked with several other student leaders, ignored the dense crowd of students who called out to him and ascended the stage to the microphone. He thrust his fist in the air and shouted into the microphone,

"How many of you'll are ready to fight the religious totalitarians!?" The crowd erupted with loud cheers.

"Well, do I have a community service project for you!"

Cal stood up on his folding metal chair on the sidewalk and prepared to rebuke the notorious communist professor. He leaned forward, raised a rigid index finger at Paine, and shouted, "The Bible says God *hates* the violent man! Get right with God or you're gonna burn in hell, Mitch Paine!"

Cal could tell Paine heard him well by the stunned look on his face. Paine cocked his head and raised his voice into his mic, "We are going to take back the country and drive the religious fanatics out of our statehouses and courtrooms – and off our sidewalks!" He cast an irritated glance at the preacher on the folding chair. His crowd erupted with laughs and cheers.

Paine turned to address the security officer in the rear of the stage. "Are you just going to stand there and let him interrupt me like this?"

"The sidewalk's a free speech zone," the officer responded, reluctant to arrest the Coalition Minuteman he had grown to respect the past two weeks.

"Why aren't you enforcing the hate crime statutes then?"

"We're university security, not city cops. U.C. Berkeley is the free speech capital of the world, and the campus president has extended leniency."

Although Cal could not hear the conversation between Paine and the officer, he saw the officer's uneasiness and intervened. "Officer Merrill? Will you please arrest this man, Mitchell Paine? He has orchestrated riots that are responsible for the deaths of hundreds of Americans and billions of dollars of property damage!"

Paine pulled in close to the microphone to try and drown out the Minuteman's accusations. "How many of you are fed up with the religious fanatics in this country robbing us of our freedoms?" Paine's shouting turned the crowd's attention away from the preacher standing on a chair on the sidewalk. "The freedom to be gay!" The crowd cheered him on. "The freedom to have sex! The freedom to get drunk! The freedom to get an abortion!" Again, the crowd cheered loudly and Paine paused to bask in the glory.

When the applause began to subside, Cal shouted, "The freedom to execute abortionists!"

"Whoa!" some students nearest to Cal jolted at the Minuteman's quick wit. Most students appeared to enjoy the interchange. Cal noticed

Paine speaking to Officer Merrill on the stage again and he discerned that he was trying to have him arrested. He took a pro-active stance against Paine's conspiracy against him. "Since your hero, Mitch Paine, can't beat the 'know-nothin' Christian in public debate, watch him act like a fascist and censor dissent by pestering an officer into arresting the dissenter!"

Paine paused and turned away from the officer as the crowd responded with a booming, "Ooooh!" Everybody loves a fight, and Mitch Paine and the Coalition Minuteman were putting on a show. Someone called the news station and they showed up to get some live footage.

"Go ahead and try to violate my free speech rights by getting me arrested, Mr. Paine! That'll just give me ample opportunity to talk to investigators about your mayhem and violence that resulted in the deaths of so many Americans, including women and children! Some warrior you are! Pathetic communist weasel throws bricks at children and calls it a revolution. Tell us about all of the old ladies your students robbed and raped, and about all of the firemen you assaulted. See, students. Your hero's a farce. He's as bankrupt as sodomite's innocence."

Frustrated, Paine started a chant to drown out the zealous sidewalk protester. "Fascist, go home! Fascist, go home!"

Cal and Carson joined in the chanting, pointing at Paine as they shouted, "Fascist, go home!"

Paine clenched his teeth, furious that these two Jesus freaks were crashing his party.

Vandenburg Air Force Base, California

"Hello, Madam President." General Green spoke to the president over the encrypted internet connection. "I have Petri Urlich, UN Security General, here to speak with you."

The president leaned forward in her chair behind her desk in the Oval Office. She stared into the screen as a dark-haired, thick-skinned fellow with a burley brown mustache and a baby blue UN beret on his head stepped up next to General Green. "Update me on your progress, General Urlich."

"Yes ma'am." He spoke in his thick-tongued Bulgarian accent, his upper lip veiled by his thick mustache. "We will be prepared for our massive attack with our combined armed forces at the beginning of next week."

She nodded. “I was hoping that we could have done most of the work for you before this point, but we have been quite impotent to deal with their armed civilian population and their nuclear threat. I have read the updated invasion strategy, and I am so much more impressed with your additions…”

General Green blushed when the president dishonored him in front of the UN Security General. He was growing to hate this woman.

* * * * *

At a meeting of the Joint Chiefs and the UN generals, the Bulgarian commander adopted the president’s demeaning condescension of General Green.

“General Green, please!” General Petri Urlich shouted at the chief of the armed forces of the United States. “I would expect this from a member of Greenpeace, but not a famed general of the most powerful nation on the planet!”

General Green just shook his head at the reproof and searched for the right words with which to rebut the UN general’s argument. “We know where they are,” Urlich argued, “they’re easily accessible, and we know that they are active members of the government with whom you are at war! Now, for the sake of your men—”

“No torture of American civilians! No!” General Green snapped. The others at the table stayed out of the conversation, knowing the implications of the conflict. There was a major divergence of opinion regarding the torture of peaceful American civilians to extract information. Many of the American generals had received security training from the Israelis during the Terrorist Wars – the Israelis were not ashamed of their torture of civilians, even juvenile civilians, in attempts to extract intelligence that would aid them in their conflict with the Palestinians. But General Green was “old school.” Ingrained within his character was the distinct impression that peaceful civilians were not to be treated with the same cold cruelty with which captured enemy combatants could be treated. Even the torture of captured soldiers in battle had to be kept quiet, lest politicians face civilian pressure to enforce the laws against it.

“You need to stop thinking of the lay leaders of the Coalition of Free Christian States as United States civilians, sir. They are the enemy. They have seceded from your country. They are traitors. Their Guard and even their civilian militias have spilled the blood of your men.”

"These are civilians on a peaceful mission. They received a personal invitation from religious leaders and even a university president to—"

"They could be spies!" the UN general interrupted.

"I have personally investigated their mission already. They are Christian proselytizers, sir. Their weapon is rhetoric. They are harmless."

"They are propagating a religion that could undermine your nation's unity and turn others against your government! Don't you know that propaganda is the fuel of revolutions? They are probably violating your president's hate-speech laws!"

"I'm a military officer, not a police officer or an FBI agent." Green stood up at the table and leaned into the UN general. "Even non-Americans, even illegal aliens have freedom to speak their mind in our country."

"You Americans are so arrogant and sentimental," General Urlich mocked, pushing his notes to the side and waving his hands erratically. "You think you are so superior in your morals and ideals." He grunted in disgust. "Do you think you are special?"

"I am an American, sir."

"You are a **soldier!**" General Urlich stood up until they were nose to nose, and thrust both of his fists against the table between them. He stared into General Green's beady eyes. "A soldier!" General Green turned his gaze away from the UN general's cold blue eyes and sat back in his chair. For a moment, others at the table fully expected that he would stand up and leave the room in protest to the UN Security General's public disrespect of his moral authority and his leadership. However, General Green knew that this would result in his dismissal from the president's cabinet, as the president had expressly ordered General Urlich to have authority in this mission.

"The UN charter protects the right to free speech," Urlich lectured him, "the right to follow conscience, the right to religion, the right to life, liberty, and the pursuit of happiness, just like your Bill of Rights, General. But we are not naïve to the unique circumstances of war."

"Your Charter states that those rights come from the UN and may be limited by the UN. Our rights don't come from the state, nor are they subject to the state's whims. Our rights come from—" He was going to say that they came from God, but all that had changed with this administration, hadn't it? General Green wasn't sure what he believed anymore.

General Urlich cursed General Green with a loud voice. General Green leapt to his feet in protest, his back straight and chest thick with medals. “I will have respect, General Urlich!”

General Urlich glanced over at a UN admiral who sat next to him and said, “Get President Margaret Brighton on the line, now! We will see what she thinks of your sentimental incompetence!” The admiral began typing on the laptop as the UN Security General shouted at Green, “I will apprehend these spies and traitors and utilize the information within their minds to fight and win this war against our enemies! And I will do it with or without your tacit approval. These Christian advocates are just dust and water stuck together by ideas. We are at war, and we need to use all the resources at our disposal to win this war and win it quickly. If we can wrench this traitorous matter and obtain information about our enemy’s offensive capabilities and defensive positions and strategies, it may help us win the war. Matter is a means to an end – *our* end! Karma has delivered these traitors into our hands right when we need their intel the most. The Mobile Tactical High Energy Lasers are in position and our soldiers are ready for the invasion. I can send my intelligence officers to apprehend them and you can have nothing to do with it, if you so wish. But we must do it quickly, before they leave and the opportunity is gone. If it can save just one of your men, General, just one of your men, would it be worth it?”

General Green gritted his teeth and looked away as he tapped his ink pen against the table. The UN general was circumventing him to go directly to the president. “You are helping in this conflict at the request of the president,” he reminded him, “and you command our invasion forces, but U.C. Berkeley is outside your jurisdiction. You are not the supreme Commander of the Armed Forces of the United States.”

“I’m sorry, General Green, but I soon will be.”

The UN admiral with the laptop turned the screen toward the UN Security General and the president’s face showed up on the screen. “Good morning, Madam President…”

24

Berkeley, California

"Mitch Paine is a terrorist!" shouted Cal at the top of his lungs. Cal cupped his hands around his mouth to amplify the sound in the direction of the SSA platform. He had managed to attract most of the idle students on the green.

Mitch Paine continued delivering his speech from the podium, but the uptight religious fanatic on the chair near the sidewalk was stoking his temper to an inferno, distracting him from his prepared speech.

"Your hero cannot save you," Cal shouted. "He's no better than the radical Muslims who hijacked airplanes and flew them into malls! He has the blood of innocent Americans on his hands."

A dark-skinned Arabic student on the outskirts of the crowd took offense. "Have you ever read the Koran?" he shouted in a heavy accent as he pressed his way to the front of the crowd of hundreds.

"Yes," said Cal from on his folding metal chair, carefully projecting his voice to be heard at the back of the crowd, "I have. When people wouldn't convert to his religion voluntarily, Mohammed tortured them to force them to convert. He fought 81 war campaigns against non-Muslims, whom they murdered, raped, and burglarized. When the treasurer of a conquered city wouldn't tell Mohammed where the treasure was hidden, Mohammed kindled a fire on his chest. He violated women in the presence of their weeping husbands, and ordered his followers to do the same. If you think that's a holy man, you're sadly mistaken…"

"Mohammed was the prophet of Allah!" the Arab shouted. He stepped closer to Cal, his eyes blazing with rage. "Are you saying Mohammed was not a holy man?"

"Mohammed was a false prophet and a sex pervert. He married Aesha when she was six. The only reason he was hailed as a prophet in his day is because he murdered everyone who objected, and his followers got to loot and rape for reward."

The climax of Mitch Paine's speech was more of a drizzle than the tornado Paine anticipated. The preacher had stolen his thunder. Paine handed the microphone to the SSA student leader and walked off the stage. Hundreds of students in front of the SSA stage gravitated to a confrontation on the sidewalk between the angry Muslim student and the Minuteman with the booming voice.

A black sedan with an international license plate pulled up beside the curb, and two tall gentlemen in trench coats stepped out onto the sidewalk, just 20 yards behind the preacher on the folding metal chair. "Drive around the block," the senior UN intelligence officer told the driver.

* * * * *

"This is the place!" The Arab student was trembling with rage as he walked to his car in the parking garage. He pressed his cell phone tight against his cheek, careful to keep his voice down. "There's a Christian here on campus publicly blaspheming Mohammed and mocking our holy jihad. There are very large crowds." He paused. "Yes Radja! This is the sign we've been waiting for."

The student jumped into his silver Saab and shifted his car into "drive". He flipped on his laser-finder, got on the highway, and sped east as fast as possible.

Carson stood directly behind Cal, witnessing and distributing tracts, when he got a tap on the shoulder.

He turned. "Yes?"

A tall man in a trench coat leaned forward and whispered to him. "I think my friend over there is prepared to get saved."

Carson stared into the aftershave-scented, muscular face of the tall fellow in the long trench coat, and sensed insincerity immediately.

"Good," Carson responded. "Tell him that we have a prayer meeting tonight in the basement of Smith Hall."

"You don't understand. He wants to get saved right now, and I don't think he will make it another minute unless you go and talk to him."

Carson glanced in the direction of the man's pointing and saw a similarly attired bald man, his head drooping as he leaned against a brick ledge that separated the sidewalk from the lawn.

Carson walked toward the quiet gentleman, praying softly for his conversion.

* * * * *

"Where is the nuclear armament?" the senior United Nations intelligence officer inquired.

Dressed in only his underwear, Carson's hands were tied with cuffs to a pole over his head in an abandoned warehouse next to Berkeley's campus. Each foot was bound with rope and tied to opposite walls so as to keep his feet one meter apart. He kept the weight off of his cuff-lacerated wrists by standing on his tiptoes with his legs spread. His whole body was criss-crossed with stripes from a beating with thick rubber rods. His cries were muffled by duct tape over his mouth.

"You represent the traitorous Coalition of Free Christian States. You are a leader. Tell us!" The senior officer nodded at the junior officer, who walked over and ripped the duct tape off Carson's face.

Carson's eyes dimmed. "Tell us!" the officer ordered again, "or we will do much worse."

Carson began to drift gently out of consciousness. "Wake him up," the senior officer insisted. The junior officer reached down, picked up a small bucket, dipped it in a cooler full of icy-water, and threw it into Carson's face.

Carson startled awake. He began to groan pitifully. With a voice hoarse from screaming, he tried to speak: "I, I, I'm not even a leader. I'm—"

"Speak up!"

"I know nothing of the Coalition's military." Carson was beginning to realize that if he convinced them he was totally ignorant of the Coalition's defenses, they would just capture his friend and mentor Cal Manning and extend to him the same treatment. He hoped that his patient suffering would give Cal more time to get away. "But even if I did," Carson bravely added, "I wouldn't tell you a thing."

The junior agent reapplied the duct tape as Carson began to writhe futilely.

"His fingernails." The senior agent nodded at the junior agent, who grabbed a pair of needle-nose pliers off the table.

"We *will* discover what's inside that brain of yours. How much you must endure before we succeed is up to you!"

* * * * *

"There they are." Radja pulled the wheeled suitcase toward Cal's crowd.

"Let us see if he will blaspheme now." Mohammed's thick accent grew more coarse and his snarl more fierce as he gripped the radio-operated detonator in his pocket. They made their way toward the preacher on the folding chair, pulling the heavy wheeled suitcase behind them.

* * * * *

Cal began to sense soberness in the crowd of students that he had not experienced before. He discerned true conviction settling into the hearts of many. Their defense of Mitch Paine and their justification of their sins had ceased and humility filled their eyes as they contemplated eternity. He looked beside him and saw many campus ministry leaders praying silently.

A sympathetic Christian student who had been attending his nightly prayer meetings tapped him on the back from behind. Cal turned and the student pointed down the sidewalk. "What do you think of that?" Two Muslim men in white gowns and white skull caps headed toward them, one of them pulling a large suitcase that was apparently quite heavy judging from the effort it took to pull it.

* * * * *

Carson prayed as he suffered. He stopped fighting the pain and embraced his cross. As they wrenched each fingernail from his hands, one at a time, he offered each fingernail to God as a sacrifice of praise. He could sense the smile of God upon him as he wept to the Lord. After a fingernail was removed, they would rip the duct tape from off his raw, bleeding lips and grant him an opportunity to give them some valuable intelligence. Yet he continued to insist through hurried breaths, as the blood flowed freely down his arms in rivers: "I don't know anything!"

"It says here," the senior officer said as he referred to a handheld mini-computer he held in his hands, "that Montana Governor Benjamin Boswell says the Minutemen are the heart and soul of the resistance. He said that the Coalition could not have seceded without you."

Carson hung his head and wept bitterly. His calves began to ache and his legs spasmed. He let his body hang and supported his weight by the cuffs around his wrists. He felt the sharp-edged cold steel cut through his skin. "All I know, all I know," moaned Carson, as the pain and exhaustion pushed him to the edge of consciousness, "is that I'm going to heaven when I die."

"Heaven?" The intelligence agents laughed at each other. "We won't be so gentle as to send you there," the senior agent replied, hands in the pockets of his trench coat.

The senior agent nodded to the younger agent, who reapplied the duct tape to Carson's face. "Right side of face only. We might need pictures of him, so keep the left side of his face clean."

* * * * *

Cal stared at the two middle-eastern Muslims for a moment, and then took the opportunity to call everyone's attention to them. "Students of U.C. Berkeley! See those two Muslims over there?" He pointed. "See the one in the front pulling that heavy briefcase?"

"Is he pointing at us?" Mohammed's laser-like gaze pierced the preacher who stood on the folding metal chair.

"I think he is." Radja stopped tugging the suitcase and carefully studied his surroundings, paying special attention to the two officers who stood behind the preacher.

"Let's get closer, and listen to what he has to say."

"What if there was a bomb in that suitcase right there?" Cal pointed at the two Arabs. The fear of terrorism was fresh in everybody's mind after the terrorist attacks that killed and crippled so many. "What if those men are terrorists, and have planned to detonate a bomb on your campus today?" He looked at the crowd and noticed the fear that filled their countenances. "That's just the kind of devastating national judgment we deserve. You're not promised another day, students. You're living on borrowed time, and the God who created you is offended at your sins. We all could be dead in the next 20 seconds. Where will you spend eternity? You're each going to stand before God and give an account for the sins of your life. Good works won't get you to heaven. Mitch Paine ain't going to get you to heaven. But Jesus died on the cross for your sins and rose from the grave, and only he has made a way that sinners can be forgiven. Turn from your sins and trust in Him. Do it now!"

Olympia, Washington

"Yeah! Preach, Cal!" Elijah cheered on Cal Manning with a room full of Minutemen. They halted their Bible study when they learned of the exchange being played live on television.

Lovington, New Mexico

The exchange was being played live on the radio stations of the Coalition, and Matt Wellington was ecstatic. "Slay that evil spirit of Islam in Jesus' name! God bless Him!"

David was distracted and not paying attention to the radio. He was only a few minutes from meeting up with his wife and daughters, and his heart pounded with enthusiasm like a little boy's on Christmas Eve. He could not wait to see them again. The past six months of being apart seemed like an eternity.

They discovered through Janet, the woman who broke out of the UN detention facility with Darlene, that north Texas was swarming with federal troops. Every road in and out was blockaded and every vehicle was searched. The safest route for Darlene to take out of Texas was west toward New Mexico. They planned to meet in the parking lot of a restaurant in Hobbs, New Mexico.

"Just step on it, Matt." David reached for two more ibuprofen from the glove compartment to remedy his sore facial wounds and his aching head. "She should be there by now."

David reached into his under-the-belt pants holster and pulled out the .45 caliber handgun that Jack Handel had given him. "Jack didn't tell me how uncomfortable this thing would be."

Matt laughed. "They're designed to keep you alive, not comfortable. You know how to handle that thing, right?"

David nodded, putting the gun back inside the holster.

Berkeley, California

Radja and Mohammed moved closer toward the preacher on the folding metal chair. The crowd moved aside for them. Mohammed placed a death grip on the detonator in his pocket, his thumb firm against the red button on one end. When the two officers behind the preacher began to make their way toward them, Mohammed pulled out the detonator. He held it up, pushed the button, and held it in a pressed position.

"I have just detonated a nuclear weapon!" Mohammed shouted, his black eyes blazing with hate. "When I release this button, we shall all die, then *you shall be damned!* Allah be praised!"

Cal's eyes met his, and he had the strange sensation this was not just a threat.

He turned to the crowd. "Students, if this Muslim terrorist is right and he is about to detonate a nuclear bomb, then very soon you're going to stand before God and be judged. Turn from your sins and call out on the name of Jesus!"

At hearing these words, many of the students in the rear thought the threat to be real, and they began to flee from the vicinity. "There's no use in running," Cal called out to them. "You can only escape judgment through Jesus Christ!"

Then a remarkable thing happened that even calmed the temper of Mohammed, who stood holding the detonator aloft. Some students in the front of Cal's crowd began to bow their heads and tremble. Some of them expressed contrition and humility, crying aloud for Jesus to save them. The conviction spread like wildfire across the crowd, with student after student expressing contrition for their sins.

"Whosoever shall call upon the name of the Lord shall be saved. Do it!" Cal paused as most of 1,000 students, lead by the faithful Christian students who had been laboring with Cal for souls, broke out in a spontaneous prayer on the Berkeley green. Tens of thousands did the same in their living rooms all over the country. He placed his hand on the head of a dark-skinned Arabic girl with a drape over her bowed head at the front of his crowd, her hands clasped tightly in front of her. "Trust in Jesus," he whispered to the Muslim woman.

"They will kill us," she whispered back. She lifted her tearful eyes to look into the preacher's face. Cal could see the fear in her eyes. It was as if she knew something he didn't. She recognized the two Muslim men, and she knew this was their end.

"Fear not, my sister. Jesus died on the cross and rose again for your forgiveness. Peace, in Jesus' name."

Mohammed was in a state of disbelief. He lowered the detonator he held aloft, still holding the red button down. He had never witnessed such humility and piety in this pagan nation. Here were 1,000 students at one of the most liberal universities in the nation publicly praying a prayer of repentance and faith.

The officers approached Radja, but Mitch Paine came pushing through the crowd, flanked by a dozen leftist leaders. Paine wedged himself between the officers and the Muslim with the suitcase on wheels.

"Stop persecuting these Arabs, you xenophobes!" Paine reproved the police officers. "Islam is a religion of peace. There's the man that should be arrested!" He pointed to the preacher on the folding chair.

The officers appeared unsure of what to do until Mohammed screamed, "I shall release this detonator and we all shall die!" That comment confused the professor. He turned to the students who knelt at the front of Cal's crowd, and reproved them. "Suckers! Have you no respect for yourselves? Get up! You don't need Jesus! You need each other! *You need me!* You need to join the revolution of the people's power!" His eyes were ablaze with vision and ambition.

"They're joining God's revolution, Mr. Paine," Cal spoke calmly. "Your time is short. Get right with God…"

With the Mohammedian distracted, one of the Christian students who stood beside Cal lunged for the detonator and Mohammed pulled it away from him and removed his finger from the red button. "Allahu Akbar!" He raised the detonator into the air. "Allah is most wise and compassiona…"

25

Berkeley, California

After about a dozen strategically placed punches, the left side of Carson's neck jolted with electrical pain that shot up his left arm. His screams became more desperate and extreme, and the senior agent responded to the younger, "Good Romano, good!" The punches continued, all on the left side of his face, and with each blow, excruciating waves of electrical pain shot down into his arm until his arm was on fire, from his shoulder to his mutilated fingers. A cervical disc had ruptured and was bulging into a nerve that innervated his left arm. He longed for unconsciousness, but the punches were well placed and the strength behind them well calculated.

Carson could stand it no more. In the seconds between punches, he glanced at the senior agent, and blinked repeatedly, as if to let him know he was giving up. Another punch fractured his nose. He looked quickly at the agent again, then blinked again, vigorously. Another punch underneath the eye. His eye had begun to swell so much that he could barely see from where the erratically-timed punches were coming. He looked at the senior agent and blinked again.

One more softer punch to the jaw and then the senior agent put out his hand to stop his subordinate. "I think he wants to tell us something, Romano." Both agents smiled broadly. They won. They always won. The traitor's resistance had finally melted. Self-preservation is the most basic of all desires. The senior agent pulled his mini-computer out of his trench coat pocket and prepared an Email that he would send to his superiors with any intelligence gained.

The junior agent rubbed his gloved knuckles, and then ripped the duct tape off of Carson's mouth. Blood and chipped teeth drooled down his chin and dripped to the ground as Carson breathed heavily and groaned sorely. The entire left side of his face was swollen purple, bleeding, and aching from the top of his head to his chin, but the pain in his neck was the most extreme he had ever felt. "I, I, have something…" he said through raspy, hurried breaths, "to tell you…"

"It's good to see that you've come to your senses. It was foolish of you to resist and bring such pain upon yourself. Tell us everything you know, and we'll let you live."

"A second, give, me, a second." Carson groaned as he tried to catch his breath.

"We'll give you ten," the senior agent said as he glanced at his watch. He then began to count.

"10, 9, 8, 7…" The UN interrogator counted off the numbers coolly, even pausing to yawn and wipe the sweat off his brow with a white handkerchief.

Be strong, Carson. God will help you endure. Don't tell them anything, Carson's conscience prodded him. *If you do, they'll apprehend Cal Manning and do this to him. Don't give them anything!*

"…6, 5, 4, 3…"

Tell them, Carson, another part of his being argued. *Tell them everything you know about the Coalition – make stuff up to satisfy them if you must. Do it, or you'll never see your family again. Stop this torture! You did the best you could. No one would fault you…*

"…2, 1." The senior agent lowered his wrist watch and stared into Carson's eyes. "Time's up. What do you have to tell us?" After a few seconds without an answer, the senior agent nodded at the junior agent, who reached for the pliers on the stool. "Toenails?"

"You," Carson suddenly spoke with a bloody gurgle as he looked up into the eyes of the senior agent, and then the junior UN intelligence agent, "you punch like, like a kitten. A sissy," he said with a barely distinguishable grin.

The senior agent pulled out his gun and removed a silencer from his pocket.

"You're going to face Jesus and be judged, you know that?" At Carson's reproof, the UN agent began to screw the silencer to the end of his handgun more quickly. "You're going to fall into the pit you've dug for me."

With these words, the junior agent flew into a rage. He cursed in his foreign tongue as he picked up a long fiberglass rod on the bloody counter covered with the tools of their grisly trade. "Don't kill him quickly, sir! Let me have a turn at him again."

"God, help me," Carson mumbled, his eyes drooping. "Jesus, defend me."

The senior UN agent clenched his teeth as he pointed his handgun between Carson's eyes. He was torn. They needed the intel and any amount of suffering was necessary to discover it. However, he was growing to admire this man more than any he had ever worked on. The Minuteman's words were painfully penetrating. At Carson's mention of Jesus, memories from his youth flooded back into his mind. He couldn't quite pin-point the source of the discomfort in the pit of his stomach. He couldn't shake the feeling that the young man held the key to what he had searched for his whole life, a need he couldn't quite put into words. He stuck his weapon under his belt, and crossed his arms over his chest, contemplating his options. Carson raised his eyes to meet his.

"Can I go at him?" the younger agent asked, the rod grasped tightly in his trembling hands. The senior agent looked at him, blank-faced.

"Well?"

The senior agent reluctantly nodded.

The junior agent wound up his swing and aimed for Carson's stomach.

Carson braced himself. "My Jesus!"

The rod never reached its destination.

A loud roar and white-hot blast incinerated the vacated building across the street from U.C. Berkeley in a single second.

Oakland, California

The 33-year-old CEO cruised the streets of Oakland in his convertible Mustang, driving slowly to study the scantily clad professional seductresses strutting the cluttered sidewalk. His wife suspected that he was cheating on her, and she walked on eggshells at home because their fights and arguments seemed to exacerbate his manic tendencies. She wouldn't leave him, however, because she knew she'd have to part with so many luxuries to which she had become accustomed.

One brunette in a black leather miniskirt caught the playboy's attention. Though the light was green, he stopped, and she slithered up to his car with an intoxicating swagger.

"Hey, baby." He raised an eyebrow and revved his engine in neutral.

"Hey, handsome." She leaned into his convertible.

His mind was on her body. Hers was on crack cocaine. They both had three children at home.

For a brief moment, his heart spasmed with guilt, but the woman's flirtatious smile distracted him. He smiled back at her – until he heard the sky roar. The sunny sky brightened with rushing white flame and the windows in the skyscrapers on each side of the road shattered, showering glass down toward them. The glass melted before it reached them. The bright sky suddenly darkened as chunks of building disintegrated into ash. A mighty rushing wind threw the debris down to the streets, followed by a wave of white heat that would turn six inches of concrete into black dust. He breathed his last with a scream of horror he never heard.

San Francisco, California

Reverend Mel Whitlow concluded his sermonette as the 200 who filled his congregation nodded in approval. He looked down at the pair of couples in front of him. On his right were two men, lovers for five years. They gazed into each other's eyes with a steadfast passion that stirred his emotions. The shorter of them wore a tuxedo with a top hat and a fluffy gray tie, his well-manicured five-o'clock shadow highlighting his wide set jaw and deep blue eyes. Mel recognized him. He modeled in a gay magazine for which Mel had a subscription. The more effeminate of the pair wore a short red dress to show off his tan and rainbow tattoo.

To the reverend's left were two women, enraptured in the other's embrace. One looked nearly male in a black and white tuxedo, while the other was decked with make-up and jewelry.

They were brave souls, defying the hatred and bigotry of their culture. He was proud of them. They were in love and love was of God.

"I now pronounce you," he said, smiling at each couple in turn, "husband and—." He paused, forgetting if he had planned to say "husband and husband" or "lover and lover" or some other afore agreed upon invention. The confusion awakened some part of his nature deep within him, startling him as if a long forgotten memory had awakened a long denied reality. He winced with a fresh stab of conscience and, at that moment, longed for a sip of Jack Daniels. He licked his lips and tried to regain control of himself.

"Are you okay, Reverend?" the gay model whispered to him.

Mel nodded. "I now pronounce you…"

He said the word "lover", but no one could hear it, because of the sudden thrashing of the church building. The walls rocked to the left and then the right, and then the beautiful stained-glass windows shattered. A speeding wave of heat instantly ignited every one who sat near a window. Less than a second later, the 200-year-old church building in downtown San Francisco disintegrated with unfathomable force, leaving no trace of its previous location beside a foundation burned as black as the hearts of its inhabitants.

Hollywood, California

A Supreme Court justice, the secretary of state, and Richard Faulkner, the liberal Republican who had the privilege of being the Speaker of the House, were special guests at a night of fundraising for the UN Population Fund at a Hollywood gala. As a former Marine, a fiscal conservative, and a pro-life-with-exceptions Republican, the Speaker was the recipient of many cold shoulders and colder stares from the Hollywood elites. But Faulkner was on his way to the top in D.C., and in order to get there, he had to reach toward the middle.

The UN Population Fund financed abortions in poor countries, administering contraceptive injections to women in exchange for clean water or admission to refugee camps in war-torn countries. They officially endorsed forced abortion of all unlicensed children. A burgeoning population, they believed, was the greatest threat to the future of the human race. With China abandoning their one-child-per-couple policy, the U.N.P.F.'s good name and their bank account had taken quite a hit. They needed money – a lot of it! – in order to stop the exponential growth of the population of 100 poor nations all over Africa and the Middle East.

Society's elites mingled, drank wine, laughed, and rubbed shoulders with the wealthiest movie-producers, the most beautiful actors and models, and the most powerful judges and politicians in California. Life was never better for Rich Faulkner. This was where he always wanted to be.

Someone tapped him on his shoulder. He turned to see an outstretched hand framed with several layers of a diamond bracelet. He suspected they were fake until he saw her face. She was a well-known actress, though he couldn't place her name. She wore a candy-apple-red mini-skirt with six-inch-long high heels.

"Congressman Faulkner?"

"Yes ma'am," he said, gently shaking her outstretched hand. "Good to meet you."

She jumped straight to her point. "I have a question about your position on something."'

"Go ahead." He smiled broadly with his hands on his hips.

"If the fetus is a person, then why would you justify killing the person in cases of rape or incest? If it's not a person, then why would you infringe on a woman's right to do whatever she wants with her pregnancy?"

Faulkner was stumped. He turned his eyes to the chandelier overhead, trying to recall the talking points he was coached to share when asked such a question. "Well, it's not really, uh, it's not really a, um…"

The actress leaned in closer. "A person? They why won't you defend a woman's right to choose?"

Faulkner crossed his arms and tapped two fingers on his chin, trying to figure out a way to get out of this conversation. Several around them paused in their own conversation to listen to the popular actress engage Richard Faulkner, the Speaker of the House, on his most unpopular position among such social elites.

Her condescending attitude toward him provoked him to lash back at her. "Well, if it's not a human being," he snapped, "what is it? It's growing, it's human…"

The woman raised her voice. "If you believe it's a person, then why do you justify killing some people? You can't have it both ways…"

I don't really care about abortion, but I've got to take at least a weak pro-life position to get pro-life leaders to endorse me and get elected in my district, is what he wanted to say, but just the thought of the truth made him feel like such a liar, a cheap prostitute, a two-faced hypocrite.

As she rambled on, he turned his mind to the waitress with the platter full of glasses of Chardonnay. As the scantily dressed waitress pranced by, he raised his eyebrows at the beautiful actress and reached for two glasses. "The inconsistencies of partisan politics are so easily remedied with a couple of glasses of liquid pleasure." He extended a glass toward her. At first she didn't take it, but he persisted. "Please, entertain me."

She smirked and took it from him, thinking that if the hypocrite could be bought, maybe she'd buy him. He read her thoughts, winked at her, and took a sip he never tasted.

The walls suddenly caved in on them in a brief, intense spasm of flame and fury.

Los Angeles, California

Dr. Wagner's mind was on the golf course as he concluded the procedure.

"Pulse is low, 48," the nurse told him, "respirations are low, less than ten."

"Whoops." The gynecologist raised his eyebrows and turned to his nurse. "A little too much Dilaudid. One milligram of Narcan, please." With women in the state of Washington testifying against their former physicians, he wanted to maximize the patient's comfort and be assured that she would have absolutely no memory of the procedure. He stood and walked over to the suction machine while the nurse dumped the "products of conception" out of a pan into a strainer. The physician stuck his gloved hand into the mound of tissue and began to separate body parts from placental tissue. He hated this part of the procedure, but he had to make sure he got all of it.

"What if the Coalition tries to take California?" the nurse nervously inquired. "What if they try to conquer the coast country?"

"They don't want to conquer California," the physician said, irritated at the suggestion. "They want to be left alone. The only people moving south will be women with unwanted pregnancies. Where is the head?" He angrily tossed tiny extremities and chunks of flesh around the stainless steel strainer. "Man! I'm behind schedule and I need to go back in." He resumed his perched position on his stool between the Hispanic patient's nude legs.

"She's waking up, Dr. Wagner." The nurse saw the patient lick her dry lips and flicker her eyelids. The patient moaned and briefly opened her eyes. "Narcan's kicking in, Doctor."

Dr. Wagner cursed the patient in a loud voice, making the nurse flinch. He caught the nurse's critical gaze, and became overwhelmed with so much hatred right at that moment. Violent imaginations and lust-filled images were tossed to and fro in his sin-soaked soul, as a tsunami would toss long forgotten skeletons and putrid sewage onto the bare, sun-lit shore. The wave of fury flooded over his body and reddened his cheeks. A thoroughly suppressed conscience punished him for the animosity he felt, stabbing him with a pinprick of guilt and regret deep in his gut. *You're not in this to help women,* a voice deep inside him uttered, ripping his cloak away and exposing his nakedness. *You're in this for money and lust.*

Another foul word walked the plank of Dr. Wagner's tongue, but was never uttered.

The sky seemed to explode outside. The roof was sucked off the building and they all got a brief glimpse of a red sky full of flames and debris. Then the walls collapsed, crushing them to death in an instant hurricane of roaring flames and radioactive wind.

Vandenburg Air Force Base, California

After three hours of planning and discussing contingencies at the largest Air Force base on the coast of California, the generals were ready to break for the day.

"How long do you think it will take?" an admiral asked UN General Urlich. The general, bristling with pride over his newly established superiority over the Joint Chiefs, paused from gathering the reports. He pulled his baby blue beret lower on his brow.

General Green answered the question that was not intended for him. "One day." His mind recalled the high level of collateral damage predicted for the bombing campaign, and he thought for a moment on his reasons for initially joining the military as a high school senior. He wanted to protect Americans from terrorism. He loved his country. He wanted to be a patriot. Now, he would be the one dropping bombs on crowded city streets and homes. A flash of guilt darkened his eyes, and he squinted hard. "It'll take one day." He opened his eyes to see the UN general snarl at him, as if to object to the demoted U.S. general's opinion. *How did it come to this?*

General Green thought he saw a grin underneath the UN general's bushy brown mustache. General Urlich glanced at his watch, and wondered, *What's taking my intelligence agents so long with that Minuteman? I expected notification an hour ago…*

Suddenly, the lights went off. Then the emergency lights came on and sirens could be heard in the distance. "What is that?" General Green stood up suddenly. "Did you feel that? Did you feel that, that tremble?"

One of General Green's personal assistants rushed into the room with a pale look of fright on his face, a cell phone in his right palm. "General Green!"

"What?"

"There's been, nuclear, some sort of nuclear–"

"Slow down, slow down…"

Before the men could even comprehend what he was saying, an escalating indescribable roar as of 1,000 distant, oncoming trains, could be heard from the north.

The assistant ducked under the table, re-reading the cell phone message that informed him of the oncoming disaster. "Nuclear bomb, General!"

First, the hot wind that blew through the open door into the windowless room made them all gasp in terror. The radioactive wave of flaming debris rushed through the windows and through holes torn from the outer rooms of the building. The blistering heat melted steel like butter, vaporizing the shattered glass before it hit the ground. The wave of radioactive heat raced its way through every room as if looking for every ounce of combustible material in every nook and cranny in the entire four story headquarters of Vandenburg Air Force Base. The wave from the bomb instantly scalded every piece of exposed flesh – their faces, their hands, their mouths, and even their ankles under the table. As they sucked the noxious flaming fumes into their lungs with gasps of horror, their throats, their air passages, and their lungs received severe burns. They fell to the ground frantically trying to put out the flames that tormented them. Not one of them was able to escape the room, which was actually one of the most comfortable places in the entire building. As their flesh boiled and lungs burned, they all slipped into unconsciousness within 20 seconds, the most painful and horrible 20 seconds in each of their lives.

These were the lucky ones. The few survivors fortunate enough to be in one of the basements of the many structures at Vandenburg faced a misery more prolonged than the others.

Pacific Ocean, off the coast of California

The state-of-the-art nuclear-powered aircraft carrier, the U.S.S. Bush, was 160 miles off the coast of San Francisco, heading toward the U.S. Naval Air Station in San Diego. Four men were tossing quarters against the deck wall in a popular gambling game.

"That's mine!" the African American said as he slapped his palm against his thigh excitedly.

"No it's not!" the tallest of the four responded. "My quarter's closer."

"What are you, blind?"

"It's Midge's," another sailor responded.

The fourth affirmed, "Midge has it!"

"Awwww," the tall fellow responded.

The black sailor, the shortest of the entire crew, smiled in spite of the fact that the men were still calling him "Midge," short for "midget." He picked up the four quarters, and shoved three of them in his pocket.

Suddenly, and without warning, a distant boom in the east made them each flinch and turn their heads.

"What in the world?" Midge had a look of awe on his face as he studied the horizon.

They walked to the edge of the deck, stunned as they watched a sight that chilled them to the bone. A huge billow of smoke began to spiral heavenward – something they had only ever seen in pictures.

The ship's siren began to scream and the men raced toward their respective stations.

Midge was the first one to make it into the cockpit of a jet. Men hurried to prepare his F-18 for emergency launch. He couldn't help but look to his left where it appeared a mountain of water was swelling right up out of the ocean between the shore and their ship.

"What in the world!"

The massive hill of water began to spread outward and speed toward them. Soon the rising ocean totally obscured the nuclear billow on the horizon.

The lineman was waving him for launch as the ocean began to push them rapidly toward the sky, like an elevator going too fast up a skyscraper. He felt pressed against his seat. He saw the lineman with his glowing sticks get knocked off balance by the sudden upward surge. The ship began to rock precariously, and the men on the platform threw themselves prostrate on the deck to keep from rolling off the precipice like marbles off a crooked table.

"Go! Go! Go!" the general shouted to Midge through his helmet headset. His engine was burning and he was finally hooked up to the launcher and ready to go. With the push of a red button, the launcher accelerated him and, in a second, he was off the ship. As he sped off the edge of the aircraft carrier, he noticed the sea rushing to meet him.

"Come on!" He thrust the jet engines and pulled up the controls. The landing gear scraped the angry seas before heading above the waves into the uneasy sky. He banked and came back toward the aircraft, and was shocked to realize he had to continue his climb in order to stay level with the horizon. The huge aircraft carrier flipped onto its side and sailors threw themselves into the ocean to avoid getting sucked into the depths of the ocean by the sinking ship. Hundred-million dollar fighter jets slid across the deck, crashing into each other, crushing the men who rushed about, and falling into the ocean like toys into a bathtub. One of the huge rotors on the aircraft carrier was lifted out of the sea, spinning wildly. Smoke began to bellow from the engine vents.

Midge now realized he was the only jet in the sky.

He continued to climb as the aircraft carrier slowly turned completely upside down. He looked to the east, and realized that he was on the top of a wave that must have been 250 feet high! The ocean looked like a deep bowl. He thrust his engines into overdrive to try and get above the draft that he knew could easily cause him to lose control of his fighter jet.

Midge always thought that tsunamis were shallow in deep water and increased in height as they grew closer to shore, but this tsunami was already hundreds of feet high. The massive wave continued to grow and began its trek eastward toward the shore. It was 100 miles wide, and 250 feet high at its center, over which Midge flew eastward, trying to beat it to shore. He frantically called out on his radio on various frequencies. "U.S.S. Bush is down! U.S.S. Bush is down! This is Captain Andrew Neville. The U.S.S. Bush has been toppled by a huge tsunami that's heading eastward about 55 miles per hour and gaining fast… 85 miles per hour now! Anybody there?" There was no response.

He continued to study his sonograph images as he broke Mach 1. The tsunami approached 125 miles per hour and continued to climb. It didn't make any sense. The ocean was hundreds of feet deep here. There must have been a massive shift in the plates of the ocean floor to cause a tsunami to rise up out of the water this far away from shore.

"Is anybody there!?" He maximized the speed of his F-18 toward the cloud that mushroomed miles into the air. The thought occurred to him that that was probably not a good idea, so he turned southward toward the base in San Diego.

He tuned into the frequency of the U.S. Naval Air Station in San Diego Bay, which was at the southwestern corner of California, and began to sound an emergency mayday signal.

He heard a man's voice over some static on an emergency channel: "…we … station… landing…"

Midge boosted the power to the radio. "I can barely hear you. Do you copy?"

The signal cleared: "This is Naval Air in San Diego, can you hear me now?"

"Yes sir."

"We've heard your signal but we're knocked off-line because of the nuclear blast and couldn't respond."

"What happened? Were we attacked?"

"Unknown. You can land at runway—"

"There's a tsunami headed eastward of catastrophic potential!" Midge shouted. "I'm right in front of it. It's about 120 miles wide and 280 feet higher than sea level, and picking up speed." He glanced back down at his sonar. "Make that 140 miles wide."

"What? Oh. I, I think I see it. Hold on," he said as he studied the doppler. "Oh no! Admiral!" he shouted. "Admiral! Look at this!" The radio operator projected the magnified sonar image on the large screen of the intelligence headquarters and the face of the highest-ranking naval officer in the room turned as white as a ghost.

"Please tell me that something's wrong with that reading," the naval officer said, pointing at the screen.

"It's on multiple screens. It's accurate," the radio operator replied, moving his chair away from the panel as if planning to get up at any moment and run.

"I'm trying to get the satellite image," a nearby operator said, "but I can't get anything. Oh, wait!" He tapped his keyboard. "There it is."

"No matter, son. It's a tsunami," the admiral said matter-of-factly as he studied the sonar screen. He looked like a man with a fatal illness who was studying the etching in his own tombstone for the first time, horrified, yet trying to appear brave for the onlookers. "Captain Terrence, give the order to get everybody in the emergency bunker, now."

"The emergency bunker?"

"Hurry! Get everybody in the airtight emergency bunker now!" He headed toward the door. "Those doors are shutting in 15 minutes, and if they're not in it by then, they're going to get shut out."

Captain Terrence gave the order over the intercom as the radio operator protested, "But Admiral! That tsunami is 400 miles northwest, heading due eastward. Is that going to affect us?"

"And it's gone from 200 miles per hour to about 250 miles per hour in the past 55 seconds! And it's still in deep water! If it's growing sideways as fast as it's growing in height and speed, it'll kill us all. You do the math if you like, son, but we're going underground. The nuclear bomb must have caused an oceanic quake. That's the largest tsunami in recorded history. About twice as large! That has Armageddon potential. That monster's going to suck California into the Pacific!" He held the door open, "Everybody out!"

The radio operator protested: "But the pilot—"

"You tell him to land at a base in Arizona," he said as the personnel began to rush past him down the stairs. "Landing at a base in California would be a death sentence for him."

"Yes sir!"

"Get our pilots in the air, ASAP! Then get the president on the mobile line for me on the way to the bunker."

The ground beneath their feet began to tremble.

"You have got to be kidding me!?" the admiral shouted as the earth tremors began to escalate.

"That can't be the same quake. Call Vandenburg!" the admiral bellowed.

An engineer picked up the phone and punched a button.

"Can the bunkers hold?" someone asked as the tremors continued to escalate.

"We don't have a choice." The admiral turned to look at a video image of the runway, and saw cracks forming across the asphalt. *Oh no! Those jets won't be able to take off...* "Change of plans. Get the pilots up in our copters, now! Fill those copters with all the personnel they can hold."

"If that tsunami covers us, one crack in the bunker's seals and we'll all drown," one of the radio operators said as he passed the admiral.

"The phone at Vandenburg isn't even ringing, sir. I'm getting a disconnect beep."

"To the bunker!" the admiral shouted.

"But–"

"You don't understand, son!" The admiral pointed to the stairs. "Everybody outside the bunker's gonna die. Now go!"

* * * * *

President Margaret Brighton was receiving intelligence reports from CIA, FBI, and armed forces intelligence personnel about conflicts not only in the Coalition, but around the globe. The room was filled with her most trusted sycophants and bureaucrats.

"We think that China's Prime Minister Ching tse Tong begrudges the United States," the CIA agent informed the president.

No duh! the president wanted to say, but didn't.

"Our ambassadors have been disallowed audience with the Prime Minister, and their ambassador to the United States, Zao Zisheng, simply reiterates the same rhetoric, that they are displeased with our Tiennamen Square-like violations of God-given rights of *fetuses* and *fetus*-defenders, and that they support the Coalition's right to exist independent of tyrannical rule."

"Oh please," the president waved off the bad news as if she didn't care. "Give me something positive." Flustered, the CIA administrator dropped his notes haphazardly onto the table and sighed noisily. The president's suspicious glare measured his displeasure.

"Tell me what's going on with Iowa, Nebraska, and Oklahoma," she asked. "Has Iowa's legislature begun its impeachment proceedings yet?"

Bill Erdman waved his thin, black bangs to the side and opened his mouth to answer when the door swung open and in stepped four Secret Service agents. "Madam President, come with me!" one of them ordered as they took her by the arm and practically dragged her out a side door toward the stairwell.

"What?"

"We'll inform you of the crisis *en route*."

One of the S.S. agents informed the intelligence agents in the room that they were welcome to accompany them.

"I can walk!" She tried to jerk away from their grasp, but they held their grip and kept up their pace.

"Quickly ma'am! There's been an explosion in the San Francisco area."

"And that justifies this!?" she snapped as they turned to head down a stairwell.

"A *nuclear* explosion."

The president delivered a stunned glare at the S.S. agent on her left. "Nuclear? Was it the Coalition?"

"Unknown. You'll be given a full update once we reach the bunker…"

Hobbs, New Mexico

David's whole body tingled and his hands trembled as they pulled into the McDonalds parking lot. He felt like his speeding heart dropped into his abdomen when he saw the blue Sedan Darlene and Janet were driving. His eyes welled with tears as Matt looked for a parking spot near the Sedan. This was a dream that he had replayed over and over in his mind for half a year, and it was finally coming to pass. His anxiety was all the more intense because this was the first time he had seen her since he confessed his sin of adultery to her. That seemed like a lifetime ago. He searched through the windows of the Sedan, looking for those familiar eyes, but the windows were reflective.

Just as his faithful bodyguard pulled the Navigator into the parking space next to the Sedan, its back door opened and Darlene stepped out of the back seat with a wide smile on her thin face. *Is that her?* David hardly recognized her. Her hair was only one inch long and her face was thin and pale. He knew by the wounds on his face that Darlene would have a difficult time recognizing him as well. He had told her about his injuries on the phone, so she would not be too distraught. When he ran to her, wrapped his arms tightly around her, and pressed his lips against hers, he knew he was in the embrace of the love of his life. His heart melted in her arms. His kiss was an act of worship to his Maker, accompanied with rivers of tears. He prayed so hard to see this day, and here he was, in Darlene's arms once again. He tightened his grasp around her thin waist and moved his lips to her ear as she began to sob.

"I always loved you, Darlene," he whispered into her ear. "I had to leave because it was the only way we could ever be together again. I'm so sorry you suffered…"

"It's okay," she said, trying to settle her trembling voice. "Jesus gave me such strength. Everything's all right now…"

"I'm so sorry I sinned against you."

"It's under the blood of Jesus. It's all forgiven…"

"Daddy! Daddy!"

Three little girls climbed out of the back seat of the car and grabbed onto his legs. He bent to hug and kiss each of them as Darlene wiped her tears.

"What a sight!" Matt exclaimed to the thin, tan, dark-haired lady who stepped out of the driver's seat and came around the car to watch the reunion.

"Yes it is," Janet said, her hands on her hips and a smile on her face. "A beautiful sight."

"Matt." He extended a hand toward Darlene's driver and introduced himself. "Matt Wellington."

"Janet," she said, shaking his hand. "Excuse me, but I need to run to the restroom." She turned to head inside the McDonalds. "I'll be right back."

"You're supposed to be here by now!" Agent Boltere barked on the cell phone at the South African UN commander. "You told me yesterday that you would have an undercover team here."

"We're just now evaluating an emergency on the west coast," he responded, "and we had to reassess our priorities with our limited resources."

Agent Boltere could hear the tension in his voice. "What kind of emergency?"

"Later. The team'll be there in five minutes. Just keep an eye on them."

When Janet stepped out of the restaurant into the sunny blue sky, she became startled when she did not see David, Darlene, or the girls. The silver Navigator that David arrived in was gone!

She rushed toward the car and let out a curse as she opened the door. She halted when she saw David's bodyguard sitting in the passenger seat, eating a hot fudge sunday. Matt seemed disappointed with her use of foul language and didn't understand why she appeared so disturbed and angry. "Everything all right?"

Janet put her hand in her sweat pants pocket and wrapped her palm around the .380 she had purchased from a drug dealer off the street. "Where'd they go?" she asked nervously.

He swallowed his mouthful of ice cream. "Ah! Brain freeze!" He feigned a grin and fastened his eyes on her right hand, concealed under her untucked shirt.

"Where are they?" she barked, a little louder this time.

Matt intentionally tried to keep his facial features from revealing his growing concern. "There's a playground at the BK across the street. They need a few moments of alone time."

Janet looked across the street and saw David and Darlene holding hands as their three children played on Burger King's outdoor playground. Janet tried to suppress her adrenaline and relax her tense facial features. Armed UN agents would arrive any minute to arrest David and Darlene Jameson, and they weren't here!

"Well, let's go over there." Darlene sat in the driver's seat and cranked the car.

"No, let's not." Matt reached over and turned off the ignition.

Janet looked over at him, perturbed.

"They want some alone time, Janet, and we're going to give it to them."

Now what? she wondered.

"I still can't get over it," Darlene said with a toothy smile. "We're together again."

David smiled as broadly as his scraped and lacerated face would let him. "I'm so thankful."

"Watch, Daddy, watch!" Charlotte cried out from the top of the slide. Those words warmed David's heart anew. His little girls seemed to have grown up so much since that day he left them at a hotel so he could participate in the sit-in around the last abortion clinic in Austin, Texas. He had struggled so long with fear of what the enemy would do to his children that he was continuously overwhelmed with gratitude that they were finally safe. Those girls were so resilient. God truly answered his prayers.

David and Darlene turned and watched as little Charlotte slid down the slide, and then they both cheered. David turned to see Darlene holding her stomach, her face pale. He reached for her hands. "Are you okay?"

Immediately, Darlene burst into tears as she rubbed her stomach with both hands. He went around the table to sit beside her. "What's the matter?"

"David?" She wiped her tears and turned to face him, careful to conceal her emotion from the children. A strange pause followed that made David's heart sink. She had bad news.

"What is it, my love?" He wrapped an arm around her shoulders.

When she was reluctant to forthrightly answer, David feared the worst. She must have a painful confession to make. He hugged her tightly. "Darlene, you have forgiven me for such grievous sins, for adultery, for the sin of murder, for living a lie for so many years. Whatever you have done, whatever it is, I will forgive you and love you just the same."

Her mouth went dry. Instead of speaking, she reached into her back pocket and plopped a pregnancy test down on the table. David stared at it, confused. The reading was positive. He quickly did the math in his mind. He glanced at her thin abdomen, then turned back to study the pregnancy test, taking it in both hands. She was pregnant all right, but it wasn't his child – they had been apart for too long. Tears poured down out of Darlene's sunken eyes and into the palms that she pressed against her face. "The U.N. guards were so, so cruel," she said without looking at him. "They told me they'd let me be if I would give you up, but I couldn't!"

He studied her for a moment, coming to grips with how much she must have suffered for him.

When the three children heard her grief, they came running to their mother, surrounding her. "What's the matter, Mommy?"

David realized that God was trying to prove him, test him. How many times had he vowed to love the baby that was conceived through rape, but to this point it was always hypothetical. Now, the horror was his own – intrusive, vile, disgusting.

"That's just like you, God," David whispered under his breath. *You know how to bring love out of hate, flowers out of deserts, blessings out of dungeons, and life out of a graveyard.*

Char overheard her father's mumblings. "What, Daddy?"

"Everybody, look at me!" David beckoned his daughters to look at him. He wrapped two arms around their mother. "We're going to take a minute and give thanks to God for one of the greatest blessings God could ever give us. Can you guess what that would be?"

"Being together again?" Char responded.

"No, better than that!" David's lips trembled as the tears flooded down his face. Darlene heard the emotion in his voice and turned her eyes up to meet his. With their eyes glued to each other, he smiled. "Let's thank God for the baby in Mommy's tummy."

All the children squealed with joy, David and Darlene kissed tenderly. Then he whispered into her ear. "I admire you more than anything, my dear sister, my best friend, my lover."

His words provoked within Darlene an eruption of spontaneous prayer of thanksgiving to God. They hugged, prayed, and wept together, oblivious to the gazes of those around her.

"I'm not very comfortable with just waiting here," Janet said, eyeing the thick biceps of David Jameson's bodyguard. "I mean, we've been like this," she said, crossing her fingers, "through the valley of the shadow of death in a UN detention facility in Austin. You know she's pregnant, right?"

"Really?"

"Yep. Raped. We all were."

Matt grew nauseous at the thought. "Let's just give them a few more minutes, all right."

"Can we at least drive into their parking lot?"

"So what did you do to get incarcerated, Janet?" Matt stretched his arm out of his rolled down window and gripped the top of the door with his hand. As he asked the question, his gaze searched Burger King's outdoor playground across the street. Matt didn't trust this woman who went by the name of Janet. At best, she had developed a co-dependency problem with Darlene. Not to mention her use of foul language when she saw that the Jamesons had left. Anyone who'd curse like that under stress was unlikely to have remained faithful under UN interrogation, but would have done whatever they needed to do to be set free. Janet was obsessed with re-uniting with Darlene, and Matt wanted to hold her back as long as possible. His eyes darted back and forth from the BK playground to Janet's right hand. "How did you become a believer, Janet?"

As he asked that question, Janet suddenly started the car back up and thrust it in reverse before Matt had the chance to protest.

He reached over and grabbed her right arm with his left hand, keeping her from switching the gear from reverse to drive. He whipped out a 357 magnum revolver from its resting place in the small of his back, a handgun that Jack Handel had kindly given him. He pointed it in her face and calmly said, "Not so fast there, Miss Undercover Agent."

Janet's face turned red as she pressed on the brake with the gear in reverse. "What are you talking about? I just want to go be with Darlene. I don't know you, and I'm uncomfortable being alone with a man I don't even know. Now, why are you pullin' a gun on me?"

"Because of the way you keep reaching under your T-shirt." He reached down with his left hand and felt her small handgun in her pocket holster. "Where'd you get that?" he said to her as if he had just caught a little child with her hand in the cookie jar. "A UN detention facility?"

"I stole it from a street thug who tried to rob us with it!" she piped up. "Just who do you think you are? You have no idea what Darlene and I have been through together!"

"You're right, I have no idea," he said mockingly. He tried to retrieve the gun with his left hand, but her pants were too tight. A couple came out of the restaurant and he lowered the gun.

Suddenly, he heard the cocking of a gun by his right ear. "That's not David Jameson, Agent Boltere," the UN officer stated with a thick Russian accent.

When Matt looked over his shoulder at the stainless steel .44-caliber Desert Eagle pointed at his head, he realized this was not a U.S.-government-issued weapon and these were no ordinary government agents. Janet reached over and took the handgun out of Matt's right hand. In the mirror on the right side of the car, Matt could see a white van right behind his vehicle with two large men sitting in the front. The passenger slowly stepped out of the van and came around it until he stood between the van and the back of the blue Sedan.

"They're across the street at the Burger King playground," Janet Boltere coldly responded to the agent in her Romanian accent.

Suddenly, with his right hand, Matt grabbed the Desert Eagle handgun and pulled it hard over his right shoulder, slamming the chin of the UN agent into the top of the door. He pressed the Desert Eagle against the dashboard with his right hand and, with his left hand, he pressed Janet's right hand that held his pistol against her right thigh.

Blam!

"Ahhh!" Janet screamed after shooting her left knee with Matt's .357-caliber pistol.

"What was that?" David and Darlene lifted their eyes toward the McDonald's parking lot across the street. David stood and went to the edge of the playground, trying to discover the source of the gunshot when he saw the struggle inside the blue Sedan.

"Matt!"

"Run! David! Run!" Matt screamed at the top of his lungs. "Run!" The UN agent reached in and tried to jerk his handgun out of Matt's grasp, cursing as he strained to gain possession of his weapon. With both hands on his gun, he began to gain in the tug-of-war with Matt.

Matt violently raised his left elbow and struck Janet's jaw, and she went limp. Grabbing the Desert Eagle tightly with both hands, he pressed his right elbow on the button on the door to raise the window. The UN agent cursed as the window rose against his arms. He screamed at the other agents in the van to come to his aid.

As the window squeezed the agent's arms against the top of the door, blood began to trickle down the window from the gash in the agent's chin. Just as Janet stirred from her brief lapse of consciousness, the UN agent wrestling for control of the .44 magnum managed to squeeze the trigger of his weapon.

Blam! Blam!

Janet received two 44 magnum bullets to her right thigh, nearly severing her thigh in a puff of blood and flesh. Matt screamed from the pain of having such a large caliber handgun go off so close to his head in a closed space. Blood spurted from Janet's leg arteries onto him as he held the Desert Eagle aloft with his right hand. He ducked just as a UN agent behind the car fired, piercing both windshields. Matt pressed all the way down on the gas with his left foot just as Janet's left foot involuntarily released from the brake. The UN agent directly behind the car was not prepared for the sudden rearward direction of the vehicle, and was struck by the car and run over by a rear tire.

The agent with his arms trapped in the door continued to scream the vilest curses as the car lunged rearward with both of his arms still stuck in the door. Matt thought he heard a crack. He smashed against the van as he continued to press against the gas pedal, lurching the parked white van backwards just as two more UN agents were trying to get out of it.

Janet aroused from her unconsciousness and reached for the .380 in her blood-soaked right pants pocket. Matt delivered another vicious left elbow to her chin, fracturing her jaw. She clawed at his left arm, screaming inaudibly in a high-pitched voice like a cat half run over.

Matt was surprised by her tenacity, having lost as much blood as she had through her leg wounds. "Die already!" he blurted out.

He then grabbed the agent's arm that was trapped in the door, and began to twist it. "Let go of the gun!" he shouted at the agent, who cursed loudly in Russian.

When David heard the gunshots and saw the blue Sedan run over a man in the parking lot and collide with the front of the white van behind it, he knew their moment of bliss was coming to an end. He saw two agents get out of the white van and take off in a sprint in their direction.

"Let's go!" David hollered, turning to Darlene. "They're onto us." Other families around them began to flee to their cars at the sound of the gunfire.

"What? Who?" Darlene said, pulling her children near. "What about Janet?"

"I don't know," he said, picking up their three-year-old with his right arm and reaching down to get his one-year-old with his left. "But we've got to go!" They rushed to their SUV and David opened the rear door and set the two children into the back seat of the car. "Mary! Hold Johanna," he said before shutting the door.

Darlene stopped in front of the Navigator, her eyes focused on the melee across the street. "But Janet—"

"She and Matt are on their own. We've got to get you and the kids to safety. Get in!"

Darlene got in the right rear passenger seat, helped Mary buckle up, and held Johanna and Charlotte on her lap as David started the car and thrust it in reverse. He saw the agents beginning to cross the street, and he searched frantically for a rear exit that avoided the road. "Oh no," he mumbled.

"What?" Darlene inquired.

"We can't escape." The only exit took them past the agents who were rushing toward them with their weapons drawn.

"Oh, God help us!" Darlene prayed.

Suddenly, the ground beneath the car began to tremble.

"Dear God!" David exclaimed. "What in the world is that?" He let go of the steering wheel, concerned that something was wrong with the car. That's when he saw the windows of the McDonald's restaurant shatter, scattering glass inside and outside the store.

Four-year-old Charlotte cried from the back seat, "What's happening?"

The rear wheels of the large SUV suddenly dropped into a crack that opened in the ground beneath them. A minivan behind them was pulling out of the parking lot and drove right into the four-foot wide crack in the ground that descended down into a pit of darkness.

"David!" Darlene squealed, holding her children tight. She looked out the window. The gaping pit in the asphalt behind them seemed to widen by the second. She looked over at three-year-old Mary in the seat beside her, who screamed in horror. "Oh Jesus," Darlene squealed, "help us!"

David tried to accelerate the SUV out of the crack into which the rear wheels had fallen, but the tires began to spin, sending smoke into the air. He flipped the switch on the dash to put the car into "4 low," but the crack in the parking lot was too deep. The front tires could not pull the heavy SUV out of the crevice.

"We've got to get out!" David hollered. He pressed down the emergency brake as the rear of the SUV continued to drop into the deepening crack. It felt like the car was being sucked into the ground. He tried to open the door, but gravity pulled it back shut. He quickly pushed the buttons on the door to roll down all the windows. "Out of the windows!" he urged his wife and children. He climbed out of the window and stood on the footstep of the side of the SUV. He reached into the driver's side window and hollered, "Come on, Mary! Come to me!"

Little Mary screamed hysterically and he ordered her again, "Mary! Obey me! Come to me now!"

Three-year-old Mary stopped her crying, took a deep breath, and began to unbuckle her seatbelt. "I'm coming, Daddy."

"Quickly! Be brave!" At that moment, he was so thankful that they had always trained their girls to instantly obey. He had always worried that he would urgently order a child to "Stop!" or "Duck!" and their reluctance to instantly obey would cost them their lives. Mary reached for her father and he carefully pulled her out of the window.

The bumper of the SUV gave way on the edge of the crack and the vehicle suddenly dropped two more feet into the ravine in the parking lot. David's foot slipped and he hung onto the window frame with one hand, holding Mary tightly with his other. Their feet dangled over the five-feet wide bottomless darkness in the bowels of the cracked earth and shaking earth. Chunks of asphalt and dirt under their car's rear crumbled into the crack and a foul sulfur-smell belched out of it and into the sky. "Darlene!" David shouted. "Help!" His fingers began to slip.

"Hold on!" Darlene screamed. "Don't let go!" Darlene lifted Charlotte and Johanna up into the front seat and then climbed out of the rear passenger window where she stood on the footstep outside of the car. The earth's trembling grew more violent. The car was now at a 45-degree angle as the crack in the ground. "Give me Johanna!" she ordered Charlotte, who complied as quickly as she could.

A huge crash in front of the car got Darlene's attention. Burger King had just crumbled to the ground. "Don't let go! David!"

"Come get Mary!" he shouted back. "I'm slipping!" The shaking threatened to undo his grip on the driver's side window frame.

"Don't you let go!" The SUV dropped another two feet into the ground and the front tires came to the edge of the crack.

Darlene put Johanna on the hood and David cried out, "Come get Mary!" David attempted to pull his right leg into the open window of the car, but his body ached from the beating he had received in Nebraska. "Come on!" he reproved his sluggish joints.

The progress of the two UN agents was slowed by long, wide cracks in the ground from the earthquake.

David's fingers slipped and Darlene screamed, but he managed to grab the posterior part of the open rear window, defying the black abyss that hungered for him like an angry monster beneath his feet. He gained a better grasp on the car as he used the rear tire as a foothold, and he pushed himself toward the driver's window, still grasping onto his terrified three-year-old with his right hand. "Mary! Climb onto my back!" he ordered her.

"Daddy!" she wailed as she clawed his arm for dear life.

"Now! Or we're both going to die!" That was all the encouragement Mary required. She courageously did as she was told.

Darlene retrieved Charlotte through the front passenger window, and put her on the hood beside the baby. "Jump down to the ground, Char, and back away!"

Darlene climbed onto the hood herself, grabbed Johanna, and then scooted off the hood of the car onto solid ground.

Mary was choking David with her tight grasp on his neck, but he could live with that. At least now he had two hands to climb up the side of the SUV and out of this foul-smelling ravine into which their car was slowly descending. The rear bumper, which was hung up on the far edge of the widening crack, began to creak and groan, and David knew it would be giving way any second.

"Toss me Mary!" Darlene insisted, her hands outstretched to them from the edge of the crumbling black asphalt. He was about three feet away from her now, holding onto the driver's side rear-facing mirror. It began to give way, and he grabbed for the hood, his hand sliding on the windshield until it came to the base of the windshield wiper. He grasped it hard at its joint, and tried to pull himself up just as a bullet shattered the windshield of the SUV, barely missing Johanna.

"David! They're shootin' at us!"

"Mommy! Mommy!" Charlotte cried as she hugged Darlene's legs, her eyes fixed on the two agents who were now rushing into the parking lot.

David put his right leg half way into the driver's window so he could hold onto the door and toss Mary toward Darlene with both hands. He reached over his left shoulder, pulled Mary over his head and with both hands, he tossed her up to Darlene with a grunt.

"I gotcha! I gotcha!" Darlene caught Mary by the arms over the edge of the ravine and pulled her close and away from the edge.

The UN agents were now shouting orders at Darlene: "Put down the girl and get on the ground!" Darlene was reluctant to obey, and one of them shot at her feet.

David unholstered the handgun Jack Handel had provided him, put his right foot up on the bottom edge of the open window, and jumped toward the lip of the cracked asphalt. His chest slammed against the precipice and his feet dangled into the dark hole below him. The collision knocked the breath out of him, but he kept his grip on his handgun. He kicked against the cliff of soft dirt, but it crumbled underneath his feet and failed to provide any traction to push himself out of the crack. He aimed the handgun at the nearest UN agent just as the agent noticed him.

David pulled the trigger with the nearest agent in his sights, but nothing happened. The gun was still on safety.

"There he is!" the agent shouted, turning and fixing his sites onto David's head. David quickly flicked off the safety mechanism and aimed at the agent, but the agent pulled his trigger first and sent shards of asphalt flying into David's forehead. David kept his composure and pulled his trigger, but, unfortunately, the gun failed to fire once again.

"Come on!" David screamed in anger at himself. He had not chambered a bullet into the barrel.

The second agent, who was further away, screamed, "Don't shoot!" he ordered his subordinate. "Put down the gun now, Mr. Jameson, before you fall!" They had explicit orders to take David Jameson alive. They kept their sites aimed at him as they continued to walk toward him, their feet spread wide apart to help keep their balance in spite of the erratic shifting of the ground beneath them.

David ignored the command, chambered a round, and climbed up until his elbows held his weight on the edge of the crack. He aimed the gun again just as another bullet whizzed past his right eye piercing his right ear lobe. The whistle of the speeding bullet caused him more pain than the bullet. However, he managed to aim his gun again at the nearest agent and pull the trigger. The bullet struck the senior agent in the lower abdomen under his bulletproof vest, and he fell onto his back, groaning. Another bullet whizzed past David's head. He turned his gun on the second agent, pulling the trigger and missing twice. His wife and children screamed for fear as the agent fired at him striking his right hand, sending his handgun flying past his head and into the widening crack in the ground. He had been holding himself out of the crack with his elbows, but with the force of the bullet that penetrated his hand, he slipped and was dangling by the precipice by his one good hand.

"David!" Darlene screamed, as she rushed to try to help him up. A gunshot blast struck the asphalt at her feet and she and her children screamed.

"Stay where you are!" the agent ordered.

The frame of the SUV crackled and groaned until, finally, the rear bumper gave way and fell into the earth, getting stuck in the crack 50 feet below David's dangling legs.

"Don't shoot!" Darlene shouted. "Please! We'll do what you want!" She pulled her three children close to her as the agent's handgun shifted from David, back to Darlene, back to David. He only saw four fingers of one hand clinging to a cracked chunk of asphalt that wobbled on the precipice.

"Help," David mumbled. His strength waned and he thought he might fall. He reached up with his bad hand to try and pull himself up, but his hand was as useless as it was numb.

"Let me help him," Darlene begged as the children clung to her, horrified.

"Daddy!" they screamed. "Please help Daddy!"

"Please, he'll fall," Darlene pleaded.

"No!" the agent coldly responded, an evil grin creeping onto his sweaty face. He was angry that this traitor had the audacity to shoot at him and injure his partner, yet he had orders to capture him alive. He unlatched the radio on his hip and put it to his mouth. "We made contact with David Jameson, but he was armed and resisted. He severely wounded Agent Wilkowitz. I don't think Jameson survived." He tarried for a response, as his decision to kill the traitor or save him would depend upon his superior's response.

"Nooo!" Darlene screamed as the agent stepped closer to David and steadied his handgun with two hands.

The ground tremor began to slow as the agent placed his toes on the very edge of the precipice, setting his sites on David's forehead. David looked up at the agent and thought to beg for help, but behind that gun he saw only cruelty. There was no mercy in those cold brown eyes.

The agent's radio sounded, "Bring Jameson's body if possible…"

"God, help us," David whimpered.

The agent heard David's prayer and mumbled, "Even God can't help—"

Blam!

Darlene screamed the longest and loudest she had ever screamed in her entire life! The UN agent lowered his gun and fell to his knees. Matt Wellington had taken careful aim from 50 yards away at the edge of the large crack that went parallel along the road. The agent fell forward head first into the crack and brushed against David's back, causing David to loosen his grip on the edge of the crack. Darlene thrust the children away from her and lunged for him. She managed to grasp his good hand with both of hers just as the chunk of asphalt that he grasped broke loose.

"Mommy!" the children screamed. She looked as if she would fall in herself, as her upper torso was pulled over the edge by the weight of her husband. The three girls grabbed their mother's legs with all their might, holding their parents above the black abyss.

"Don't let go!" Darlene screamed. "David! Hang on!" She felt herself being pulled over the edge. "Charlotte! Hold onto my legs! All of you! Hold on!"

"Let go of me, honey," he pleaded with her, fearful of both of them losing their lives.

Matt sprinted up the road toward a place where the crack was narrow enough for him to jump the distance. Momentarily, he came running into the parking lot.

He had been shot twice in the exchange with the UN agents, once in the right shoulder and once through his left forearm. His shirt was covered with blood.

He grabbed Darlene's waist and started trying to pull her out of the crack. "Don't let go of him, Darlene!"

"Help!" she screamed. "He's too heavy!"

David was too far down into the ravine for Matt to reach. David tried to push himself up with his feet, but every protrusion of the brittle chunks of dirt gave way when he kicked against it. The pit below him went as far as they could see into blackness.

"Help Daddy!" the Jameson girls pleaded.

"Hold onto your Mommy's legs!" Matt ordered the children.

"Where are you going?" Darlene screamed as Matt ran off.

David begged her. "It's all right. Just let go, Darlene, please."

"No, David! I'm not letting go of you again!"

Matt rushed to the fallen UN agent and took off his belt. He connected his leather belt to his own, and let it down into the crevice toward David just as another tremor began to grow in intensity and cause the crack to separate even more.

"Grab it! David! Grab the belt with your bad hand and don't let go!"

"I can't…"

"Do it! Grab it with your teeth if you have to!"

Sensation had begun to return to David's injured hand as his numbness evolved to pain. He grasped onto the belt with his bad hand and brought it to his mouth. He clenched onto it with his teeth. They pulled his upper body out of the ravine the very moment that the SUV, which was hung up in the crack below them, came loose and dropped deeper into the earth. It fell for several seconds and crashed against an unseen obstruction in the blackness, causing it to explode. This ignited flammable methane that had leaked from a broken underground pipe. Flames shot 20-feet into the air just as David's upper torso was pulled out of the crack. The flames caught the bottom of David's pants on fire, but Matt and Darlene patted them out with only minor burns.

Darlene and Matt pulled David out of the crack and the crying children rushed to their father's side. Darlene knelt beside him, exhausted. She rested her hands on his chest, grateful. She held David's face with both of her hands and told him, "Don't you go to heaven before me, do you hear?" The blood from his bullet-pierced right earlobe congealed disgustingly on the side of his face. His bandages had loosened with his sweat, and his wounds were all exposed.

Breathing heavily, he opened his eyes and looked at her lovingly. "Yes ma'am," he said with a faint smile.

Darlene reached over and grabbed the handgun of the dead UN agent. She put the safety back on and set it on his chest. "If we survive this day, you're going to practice your shooting some more."

They looked into each other's eyes and laughed. Matt was reluctant to find humor in the comment, finding the timing premature. His adrenaline was keeping him conscious, but he'd lost a lot of blood.

David sat up and saw Matt's blood-soaked shirt. "Are you all right?"

"Shhh!" Matt responded. "Quiet. Do you hear that?"

"What?" Darlene asked.

David slowly stood to his feet, placing the handgun under his belt. He cradled his wounded hand to his chest and studied the eastern sky. "Is that a helicopter?"

Matt looked through the billows of smoke rising from the burning ruins of the restaurant beside them and saw three black helicopters speeding low to the ground straight toward them. "Those don't belong to the Coalition." He glanced at David, his face pale from his blood loss. His eyes showed fear.

"Run!" David picked up Mary, Matt picked up Charlotte, and Darlene picked up the one-year-old Johanna. David took off toward a three-story bank beside the collapsed Burger King restaurant. The bank appeared undamaged from the quake except for shattered windows.

"Go!" Matt shouted, handing the child he carried to Darlene. "I'll hold them off!" Matt ducked behind the restaurant's dumpster. When the helicopters drew near, he began firing on them with his handgun.

David sprinted as fast as he could around the large crack in the ground, and then toward the bank, with a child over his shoulder. As they neared the bank, they were astounded at the piercing shrill scream of a siren coming from inside. Their girls clasped their hands over their ears. The door to the bank was locked and there did not appear to be anybody inside. Stepping through a broken window beside the front door, they entered just as the Cobra helicopters spotted Matt and began to return fire.

David helped his wife and children enter first, and stepped into the lobby of the bank just as the nearest helicopter began to spew .50-caliber bullets in their direction. Bullets whizzed all around them as they rushed in and ducked behind a counter.

The helicopter hovered two feet above the ground as it fired into the first floor of the bank. Darlene screamed as she and David knelt over their daughters to protect them from the bullets, the flying debris, the shattering lights overhead, and the splintered pieces of wood and drywall dust that filled the air.

The firing stopped and David and Darlene looked at each other, wondering what was going to happen next.

"How many bullets do you have?" She had to scream to be heard over the piercing siren.

He pulled the gun out from under his belt. "I don't know."

David peaked over the bank counter and saw five agents with automatic weapons jump out of the copter and head toward the bank. He looked left, and saw another copter landing on the other side of the bank foyer.

He ducked back down and Darlene could see by the look in his eyes, barely discernable in the faint illumination of the exit signs against the wall, that they were not going to be together for long. He set his handgun on the ground.

She reached for him and hugged him tightly. “Oh God! Keep my husband safe,” she said with trembling voice as tears began to stream down their faces. It was a bitter cross to accept the inevitable decision she knew he would have to make between surrender and death.

David began to cry as he pulled his children close. “Dear God. Oh God,” he began to weep. “Oh, I love you all so much. I pray we will see each other again.”

“David Jameson!” the amplified voice of the UN helicopter pilot bellowed throughout the building. “Come out with your hands up or we will fire on you!”

“Stay down!” David urged her before standing with his hands in the air. Immediately, a dozen bright red laser dots were all over his torso and head as he stepped out into the open. “I’m here! I have no weapon! My children are in here! Don’t shoot!”

Just as he spoke those words, large caliber automatic weapon fire could be heard coming from outside the bank to his right. The five agents on that side of the building turned and began to fire at something in the direction of the restaurant. A bullet whizzed past David’s head. “It wasn’t me! Don’t shoot!” he yelled. Another bullet whizzed past him and he ducked. He felt another bullet graze his thigh.

A great boom echoed from the side of the bank where the fighting was breaking out, causing the entire bank to vibrate. The UN Apache helicopter on that side of the building suddenly burst into flames, and most of the agents on that side of the building went down to the ground, either from being shot or to make a smaller target for the heavy caliber gunfire raining down on them from another approaching helicopter.

The four agents that were approaching the bank foyer to David’s left suddenly turned and rushed back to their Cobra.

David crawled back to his family. “It’s the Coalition!”

They heard the UN helicopter take off and fire at a target nearby.

Without warning, the ground began to shake again. The trembling grew exponentially until the walls began to crumble around them and the light of the sun through the broken windows began to grow dark. David and Darlene covered the bodies of their children and cried out to God for deliverance. It sounded like the harsh roar of an approaching train suddenly burst into the room. The whole three-story bank was collapsing on top of them…

* * * * *

The nuclear blast immediately killed 90 percent of all life within a 200 mile radius. Within 15 minutes, the tsunami, brimming with deadly radioactive foam, flooded inland as far as the eastern edge of California, as far north as Oregon, and as far south as Mexico.

The San Andreas fault line, which runs north-south on the eastern edge of California, gaped open 100 yards in the first earthquake. The earthquake was the largest in recorded American history, registering 9.6 on the Richter scale. A second tsunami soon followed the first, and everything west of the Sierra Nevada mountain range remained submerged 20 feet beneath the foul-smelling, foamy black water. With the second quake, the San Andreas fault collapsed together again, with the western edge grinding south 500 yards and dropping ten feet. For two days, the Mississippi River flowed backward as water poured from the river into bottomless pits that opened up in the ground. Not a bridge across that great river or any of its tributaries within 300 miles of Missouri remained intact. In the southern half of California, the eastern edge of the San Andreas fault line became the new border for the United States, whereas in the northern half of the state, the Sierra Nevada mountain range became the country's new border.

The Californians who survived the initial blast and the resulting tsunamis and earthquakes would soon wish they had died already. Faces and hands began to blister and chunks of hair and skin began to fall out as exposed flesh was transformed into an excruciating mush. The radioactive fallout infected everything with misery and death.

The wind blew in a southeastern direction, and so the fallout soon tormented the citizens of Reno and Las Vegas, Nevada; what happened in Vegas definitely stayed in Vegas. The wave of heat transformed Nellis Air Force Base, China Lake Naval Weapons Center, and Fort Irwin National Training Center into huge cemeteries where the dead rotted unburied in the hazy desert sun and the delirious survivors barricaded themselves in rooms without windows, living off insects and toilet water.

Almost 90% of America's most populous state was dead or dying.

26

Washington, D.C.

In the emergency executive bunker in the basement of the U.S. Capitol building, frantic agents and government personnel busied themselves talking on the phone and speaking with intelligence agents online. Others were trying desperately to contact family members in California.

Chief of Staff Dena Halluci and Attorney General Victor Meyers were waiting for the president in the situation room. Dena was yelling at somebody on the phone and Victor was reading important updates on his laptop. Others were present via computer monitors around the room: FBI Director Erdman, Press Secretary Weaver, Homeland Security Chief Davis, and the next in command to the Secretary of Defense, a short masculine woman named General Eve Velasquez.

"Tell me what's going on," the president ordered without even sitting down.

Tom Davis spoke first: "There's been a nuclear strike in the San Francisco area. It's resulted in a large tsunami that has just struck shore, wiping everything out 100 miles inland and – uh, hold on," Davis said as one of the agents behind him handed him a fax and he began to read it.

"Was it the Coalition?"

"I doubt it, Madam President," said General Velasquez in a voice as masculine as her appearance. "The satellite nuclear signature of this blast was not likely to be American. This was a weak bomb."

"A weak bomb?"

"Likely a small nuke stolen or purchased from former Soviet Union nuclear scientists and smuggled in. We've lost all contact with the coast bases in California. General Green, General Urlich, and almost all of the force they were a-massing were well within the blast radius and are presumed dead."

The president angrily slapped her palms against the round, wooden table, and stared at the ground in shock. *200,000 American soldiers, 175,000 UN soldiers – all dead! Trillions of dollars of resources – wasted! Millions and millions of American citizens...*

"It is possible that they made it to a bunker underneath Vandenburg Air Force Base," General Velasquez speculated, "but the Air Force base is underwater at this point, and we don't have radio contact. We've got a rescue team trying to develop a plan to retract them, but there's several feet of radioactive foam covering most of the state west of the Sierra Nevada."

"And it's not receding as we would expect it to," another added.

"And it's not going to!" said Tom Davis, as he looked gravely into the camera on top of the monitor at his Homeland Security office. "I've just been informed that world-record earthquakes just concluded in California and in several midwestern states. A second tsunami also struck again in California."

"Oh, dear goddess!" Brighton exclaimed. "Just when you thought things couldn't get any worse." A few cursed in anger, but most just sat in a state of shock.

"Where does this leave us?" Erdman asked General Velasquez.

"Without about a third of the armed forces we had in the states yesterday. We had transported most of our mobile troops to California in preparation for the final assault on the Coalition. Now, we've lost contact with Ft. Bragg, Camp Pendleton, Ft. Hunter, Chocolate Mountain, Edwards, Ft. Irwin, China Lake—"

"We've got the picture!" the president said, raising a palm.

An aid handed the president a fax, which read, "Speaker of the House, Rich Faulkner, Senators Caldwell and Nolter, Reps Fairview, Franken, and Xander, Secretary of State Randolph, and Supreme Court justice David Sheldon were at a U.N.P.F. fundraiser in Hollywood. Presumed dead."

"Well, at least I'll get to appoint another Supreme Court justice," she mumbled.

"Excuse me?" The comment seemed extremely insensitive to Erdman and he was prepared to reprove the president sternly, but he was distracted with a tap on his shoulder and was handed an urgent memo.

"Nellis Air Force Base in southern Nevada is out of operation," Velasquez said, reading a piece of paper she held out in front of her.

"That far away from the coast?" Erdman wondered.

"With the fallout from a particularly stiff southeastward wind, yes." Velasquez set down the note, glanced at a text on her cell phone, and looked the president in the eye. "Our armed forces intelligence want to meet with you immediately to discuss this further."

"Very well. Set it up next door," Brighton said, nodding at a tech who rushed from the room. When she saw Bill Erdman's eyebrows raise as he read an Email on his laptop, the president called him out: "What do you have, Bill? Do your Coalition insiders have any leads at all?"

"They claim to be as surprised by it as we are, Madam President," he said with a shrug. "There were, uh," – he cleared his throat uneasily – "two Minutemen who've been lecturing at the University of California in Berkeley with a campus invitation. UN intelligence officers were interrogating one of them at the time of the blast. But several of our best agents monitored all the correspondence of the two Minutemen and have twice searched their vehicle and their hotel room without their knowledge, and they didn't have anything besides Christian hate literature. We did discover from one of their fingerprints on a soda can, uh, just this morning actually, that one of them," – he looked up from his laptop – "a Mr. Cal Manning, was wanted for the murder of a police officer in Alabama and was traveling under an alias on a Montana-issued driver's license."

Her eyebrows lifted. "And Berkeley was the place where the bomb detonated?"

"Yes ma'am."

"There you have it. The Coalition's behind it after all."

"It's circumstantial, but it's a lead," said Velasquez, crossing her arms over her lean chest.

"It's more than just a lead," the president said confidently. "

"It's a knockout punch!" Cameron added. "Blame it on the Coalition and watch the tide of national opinion turn drastically against them. Never let a good crisis go to waste."

"It's not them," a new voice proclaimed. Everyone looked up and saw the Director of the CIA, Dick Tralek, on one of the monitors.

"Good to have you with us, Mr. Tralek. How do you know it's not them?"

"We had men on the inside. It's not them. And we have a pretty good idea of who it was."

"Who?"

"This footage was taken just before the blast. You'll see one of the Coalition Minutemen publicly engaging Mitch Paine on the campus of U.C. Berkeley."

"Mitch Paine?"

"This was broadcast live on television at the time of the blast, so this is public information. We've fast-forwarded it to the last five minutes."

The president nodded, impressed. "Go ahead."

The CIA director hit the remote and they watched the whole scenario unfold on his screen, which a technician magnified and projected onto a large screen on the wall.

The president found this absolutely amazing that this was all captured and broadcast live. "This was too rehearsed," she complained when she saw the remorse of the students at the preaching of Cal Manning. "Are you sure that this is authentic?"

"I was watching it live online on CNN when it happened, Madam President," Tralek said, "and I have confirmed it through two different sources."

"It *was* Muslim terrorists!" Erdman moaned as they watched the Muslim thrust a detonator into the air.

"Arabic-appearing terrorists," the president corrected his poor choice of words.

"We knew that there were terrorist cells still on the loose, Madam President," Tralek admitted with a hint of regret in his voice. "Since the '90's, we have given North Korea tens of millions of dollars…"

"Make that hundreds of millions," someone interjected.

"They built a nuke with that money," Tralek added.

"I know. Don't rub it in," the president responded, offended.

"I'm not being critical. I just want you to know that two years ago a North Korean scientist who was on payroll with the CIA as an informant defected and sold a militant in Saudi Arabia a small nuclear weapon. President Fitzgerald had been notified and we were on their trail. It looks like they were able to sneak it across our porous southern border."

"So our foreign aid built the weapon that someone on our payroll detonated on our soil?" The room was silent at the president words. The shame of it all was overwhelming.

“Can you I.D. them?” The president pointed at the screen. “Is that the fellow charged with murder and kidnapping in Alabama?”

“We’ve got men working on it,” the CIA director responded. The video concluded with the screen transforming to static.

“Blame it on the Coalition anyway,” Cameron Weaver urged her. “And do it quick, before there’s evidence you’re wrong.”

“I agree,” said Dena with a nod. “It’s too convenient for them to have this go off on the eve of the annihilation of their Coalition. They had to have had a hand in it in some way. We do know that they sent out ambassadors to the Middle East to drum up support for their independence. Maybe they made some connections. If we blame the Coalition, their citizens would raise such a protest! They’ll have a coup and we’ll win this war before our proof is ever cross-examined.”

“If you’re considering a nuclear retaliation, the bar of evidence would be high for you, Madam President,” Tom Davis, director of the Department of Homeland Security, rebutted. “If your proof didn’t’ hold up under cross-examination, the UN may charge *you* for crimes against humanity, not to mention what Congress would do.”

“We would *not* have to prove it, just announce the possibility,” Weaver disagreed with Davis. “The media will do the rest. First page announcement, last page retraction a week later if we must, when the dust settles. In war, the commander-in-chief must sometimes act quickly on incomplete information. The nation’s forgiving as long as victory is secured.”

President Brighton and Dena Halluci grinned at Cameron Weaver’s subterfuge.

“Is that all you can think about at a time like this!” Victor Meyers snapped critically. “Who gives a hill of beans about politics when tens of millions of Americans have just been extinguished in the greatest act of terrorism in the history of the world!”

“Vengeance for an act of war against us isn’t politics,” the president snapped, motioning to the screen full of static.

“You saw the video!” Meyers raised his voice in an uncharacteristic fashion. “There’s no evidence the Coalition did any of this! Let’s keep our sights set on those who probably did.”

The president thumped the table with both fists. “I saw a Coalition fanatic warning students that they were going to die from a nuclear weapon moments before they did! How do we know that the Christian religious fanatics weren’t in league with the Muslim religious fanatics to destroy the Great Satan?”

"Oh, please," Victor Meyers waved his arms in disbelief. "They were trying to stop the detonation – it looked to me like it was Mitch Paine who was impeding the Minuteman and the police—"

"Mr. Erdman and Mr. Davis," the president said, interrupting Meyers' outburst, "tighten that blockade. Nobody but our soldiers go in or out now, got it?"

In response to the president's predictable disregard of contrary opinion in her cabinet, Victor rolled his eyes and planted his elbows onto the table with a "thump."

"Most of our Coast Guard is dead, Madam President," Erdman said. "We'll have to draw from the heavily-taxed State Guards, but we'll do it. We'll have to take them from the airports…"

Helena, Montana

The Coalition leaders were also having a meeting and spirits were not as high as one would expect after their Coalition had been rescued by an "act of God." Most of the governors were present via satellite.

Ben Boswell was as somber as a funeral director. "The Scripture says that if we rejoice when our enemy is judged, then God might stay His hand and turn it against us instead. Let's stay humble and join our nation in grieving over this terrible tragedy and praying for the survivors."

"Those are words of wisdom, Ben," Governor Reynolds of Utah nodded in agreement.

Governor Boswell's secretary buzzed on the intercom. "I'm sorry, but no one is answering the president's phone lines, sir. The president's press conference is coming on now."

"Thank you, ma'am." Boswell picked up the remote control and turned on the large wall-mounted television.

Washington, D.C.

"Ladies and gentlemen," the president solemnly began. A warm sensation of nausea overcame the governors as they sat quietly in their offices and listened to Margaret Brighton deliver her predictable speech, of course, blaming the Coalition for the deaths of over 20 million Americans and the suffering of so many more. "We are all filled with horror at what has happened to our nation today. It is a day of mourning and weeping for many."

She heralded the loss of so many reps, senators, judges, and bureaucrats in the attack. Apparently, there was a meeting of liberals in Los Angeles, discussing the future of the Democratic Party. The leaders of Planned Parenthood, the Coalition for Reproductive Rights, the A.C.L.U., the Americans United for the Separation of Church and State, Earth First, N.O.W., the National Abortion Rights Action League, and thousands of liberal activists all met their fate in a single moment. And who was to blame for it all?

"The religious totalitarians in the Coalition of Free Christian States!" she exclaimed as the press corps gasped in unison. Many of you saw it on video, as an interaction between a so-called Coalition Minuteman and two Arabic-appearing men was being played live on television when the bomb was apparently detonated. While our intelligence offices are still busy discovering exactly what happened, we do know that Cal Manning, the so-called Coalition Minuteman identified on video, had murdered a police officer in Auburn, Alabama, kidnapped children, and was on the run from the law. Montana's government gave him refuge and a false identity. And there he was on video telling the crowd of college students that a nuclear bomb was in the immediate vicinity!" She paused, looked down, and wagged her head, as if still absorbing the extent of the immense tragedy that had befallen them. "This is just more of the same Coalition terrorism of which we have all been a witness since Day One of their fanatical resistance."

The president promised certain vengeance on the Coalition for the deaths of so many innocent Americans.

Helena, Montana

"This can't be happening!" Littman exclaimed. "She's blaming us? Is it true what she said about the Minuteman? Didn't we send two?"

"We didn't send them," said Boswell. "We just didn't forbid them from going. But we could see only one on the video. And I don't know about her accusation of Cal," he said as he glanced at Dreifuss, who shrugged, "but I know the general character of David's Minutemen and either the accusation is false or I suspect he was justified in doing what he did."

"She's a liar," the Idaho governor responded. "You can't believe anything she says."

"What are we going to do?" Littman asked.

"They have to prove it!" Wilson shouted. "They can't just start attacking us on a hunch."

"They were in the midst of attacking us anyway, and now they have a phenomenal reason to pull out all the stops and destroy us completely," Reynolds rebutted. "They can manufacture evidence if they want to."

Boswell was deep in thought with his forehead in his palms. He looked up and smiled. "I think we should offer man-power and military assistance in the rescue efforts," he said matter-of-factly.

The room was silent at Boswell's proposal. The Coalition leaders were initially stunned at the notion. "What? You're going to commission the Guard to *help them?* Do you remember: it wasn't but a week ago that they were trying to blow us off the map! They were planning on doing it again – with UN forces – when the nuclear blast and tsunami miraculously saved our necks. She just announced publicly that she was planning on bombing us again!"

"Love your enemy. Do good to those who hate you. When your enemy hungers, feed him," said Boswell softly. "When they thirst, give them to drink…"

"…And in so doing, you'll heap coals of fire on their head," said Littman, concluding the verse. He smiled, feeling the presence of God in their midst. "God be praised."

Hobbs, New Mexico

When the rumbling of the third major quake finally slowed, David and Darlene were trembling in each other's arms. They had been trying to protect their children from falling debris, but when the slab of concrete underneath them shifted, they rolled against a wall. They began to cough and gasp as the dust-laden air burned their noses and lungs. The blackness was darker than dark. They could not see anything, and with the burning in their eyes, they both wondered for a moment if they were blind. As the three-story building crumbled to the ground on top of them, they fully expected to perish together.

The siren had been replaced with the cracking, popping, and rumbling of the building's innards.

"We're still alive," Darlene spat out between coughs.

"Mommy!"

"Daddy!" the children cried between hacking coughs.

"It's okay!" Darlene called out and felt around her for her daughters. She clawed at the dust and debris in every direction.

Mary's pitiful screams were punctuated with many seconds of breathlessness, but this was not unusual for Mary in times of duress.

"Are you okay? Are you hurt?"

"I can't stop coughing," Charlotte responded.

"Here," Darlene said, as she pulled Charlotte's skirt up over her mouth and nose and told her to take a deep breath. "Breathe like this, okay honey?"

"Okay Mommy," she responded as Darlene bent down to tend to their three-year-old Mary, who was still screaming. She did not seem to be injured anywhere. "Shhh!" Darlene tried to comfort them. She and David pulled the girls' skirts up over their mouths and urged them to breathe through their dresses, to keep them from sucking the powdered sheetrock and cement that filled the air into their lungs. "It's okay! David! Where's Johanna? She's not here! Johanna!" She hollered her name and began to feel around her in the dark for her youngest.

"Darlene." David spoke with trepidation from three feet away under the bank teller's counter where they hid. The tone of his voice sent chills down her spine. He spoke the name louder this time. "Darlene!"

"What?" She turned to feel for David in the darkness and her elbow banged against a metal rod that was impaled into the cement foundation. "David?"

"Johanna's gone."

"What? David?" David heard the grief in his wife's voice, and he reached for her.

"I'm right here," he said to her, trying to be strong for his wife and pull her close. "She's in heaven now."

"Oh no, no," Darlene began to weep. David hugged her tightly and the two girls hugged their mother from the side. "Are you sure? Maybe she's just unconscious…"

"I'm sure," he responded.

"Where is she?" Darlene pulled away from David and began to crawl in the direction where he found her.

David stopped her, and pulled her upright. He clutched his wife with both arms and began to sob. "I'm sorry, babe. She's dead. I don't think she suffered. She's with Jesus."

A cement piling had crushed little Johanna three feet away from them.

"Oh no, please Jesus," she wept, gripping his shirt tightly in her fists. "Jesus, not my Johanna."

As Darlene pulled her face into David's chest and wept, she noticed that his right shoulder was soaked. "What happened to you? Did you get hurt in the quake?"

David reached with his left hand and touched his right shoulder, noticing the wetness and assuming it was his blood. "I think a bullet hit me. I can't raise it…"

"A bullet?" Darlene squealed.

"My hand hurts more than that, but at least I can feel my fingers now. I think a bullet grazed my thigh too." He felt his leg and noticed the outside of his thigh was numb. His hands felt a warm wetness all the way down to the middle of his calf that concerned him, but he didn't tell his wife about it. He didn't want to worry her. He was so grieved about the loss of Johanna that he didn't care about his own injuries.

"Oh, David, what are we going to do?" Darlene began to hyperventilate between coughs and David sensed that she was losing control of her emotions.

"We are going to do what we've always done, Darlene. We're going to trust in God. He has delivered us through the deepest valleys, and His mercy endures forever."

"We're going to die in here, in this dark hole. What about the children?"

"When the dust settles, we'll try to find our way around some of this debris. Maybe God will provide a way."

"Well? Did you find a way out?"

David ventured back after trying to crawl out through a small area between some pillars.

He reached for his wife and collapsed on his back from exhaustion. "I can't find a way out." He brought his forearm up to his brow as his blood-shot eyes gazed into the pitch-black darkness. "Oh God, help us get out."

Darlene had the girls resting quietly on her lap with her back against the bank teller's counter, but they were getting thirsty. "Did you find any water? There had to have been some water somewhere in this building."

"I can hear water trickling, but only from a distance. I can't get to it."

"There it is again," Darlene said softly.

"What?"

"Hon, I think I'm feeling a draft coming from that direction…"

"What direction? Show me," he said, grabbing her arm. She pointed. "A draft? You're sure?"

"Yeah. I felt it. Wait, there! You feel it?"

David put his face in the direction Darlene pointed, and as he was still, on his hands and knees, he thought he felt it. "I'm trying that way again. I'll be back."

David clawed as far as he could through the debris, trying to move aside chunks of wood and sheetrock, cutting his arms and knees on shards of glass and scraps of metal and wire. He even climbed up a slab of rock and stumbled upon a bed of dollar bills. His girls had woken up, and he could hear them crying for drink in the distance behind him. He was so very thirsty. He knew he must have lost a lot of blood. His muscles spasmed from exhaustion and dehydration. His facial wounds had all re-opened and were filled with dust and debris.

He tried to move a desk that occluded his narrow path, and he cut his hand on a strip of metal that lay on top of it. "Ow!" he cried out. Lying flat, he pushed against the desk with all of his might, but the brick on which his feet were steadied gave way and debris began to fall again all around him. He rolled up in the fetal position to protect himself. The rumbling slowed and he heard Darlene cry out for him.

"David?" The fear in her voice broke his heart. "David! Are you okay? Don't leave us!"

Her words crushed his heart with grief and despair. "Oh God!" he cried out as he bled from a dozen lacerations and gashes onto the dust-covered cement floor. "Save us! Save us! We can't do it on our own strength. Save us!"

All of his attempts at finding a way out ended in failure and accumulated injury upon injury. In the blackness, they were beginning to lose track of time. Their thirst made minutes seem as hours, testing their faith and filling them with dread of the unknown. Ever so often, a snapping sound above them would unleash a torrent of dust and debris that would fall all around them and shake the ground beneath their feet, and they would all begin again to clutch themselves and pray to God for safety. Then the crumbling would gradually subside, leaving only the stillness of the dusty air and the pitiful whimpering of their daughters.

"This is hell," Darlene whispered in David's ear as they held their two girls close. She could sense their lives waning as they wheezed without cessation, their lungs congested from inhaling dust and their little bodies dehydrated from the lack of water. Their three-year-old had broken out in a fever. Her body was chilled and her chest rattled.

"No, Darlene," said David, stroking her cheek with his index finger. "If this is going to be our end, let us rejoice in the mercy of God. We lived a good life, didn't we? When we die, we are going to be with God forever. No pain, no sadness, no more separation." A sob swelled in his chest, trying to get out, but he held it in. He couldn't afford the tears. He felt like one tear drop would drain him of the little moisture left inside his body, and he would lose consciousness. His cracked and dried lips forced a smile. "It's going to be wonderful, dear. After just ten seconds in His presence, and in the presence of our little Johanna, we will not remember the fellowship of His sufferings anymore, but only the joy of His resurrection."

"Yes, yes." Her eyes closed as she focused on the soon-coming comfort.

"Let us worship Him now, my love. We are together. We are in each other's arms. We are in the presence of God. Being with you in the valley of the shadow of death in the presence of our loving Savior isn't hell, my dear. It's heaven."

"Oh David!" she moaned, and fell against his chest. He stroked her sweat-drenched back and her dust-caked hair with his good hand.

He kissed her on the forehead. "Don't despair, my love." The slabs of concrete above them shifted and groaned under their weight, threatening them. "He brought you out of a UN prison, saved you from water-boarding, electrocution, starvation, rape, and humiliation. He saved me out of captivity in a war-zone, beaten and abused, kidnapped and dragged for miles through the woods, shot, separated from my wife and children. Look how far He's brought us! Did you ever think you could suffer so much for your God in the U.S. of A.? Great is our reward in heaven!" he exclaimed with a smile she could hear.

"God is good," she whispered. "I know He is good."

David sang a song to her, out of the depths of his heart. Though his voice was hoarse from the crying and screaming, trying to be heard by those on the outside, she thought it was the most beautiful singing she had ever heard in her life.

"Here my cry, O Lord, attend unto my prayer,
From the ends of the earth, when I cry unto thee.
When my heart is overwhelmed, please lead me to the rock
That is higher than I, higher than I."

A light beam suddenly shone through a crack above him. "David!" came an unexpected voice from above.

David squinted from the bright light. "Hey!" he shouted. "We're here!" David squinted toward the rays of sun that brought hope down to their hellish black hole. God had made a way!

"David! Ha, ha, ha!" Matt shouted and laughed. The gunshot wound in his right shoulder did not prevent him from working around the clock the last 36 hours trying to find David and his family. His right arm was in a sling and he was on top of the pile of rubble with 200 volunteers and guardsmen, hand-picking through the debris with his good arm, searching for signs of life.

"Oh David! God has saved us again!" Darlene cried. "Children! Mary! Char!" she said as she shook them. Char stirred from her uneasy rest, "Mommy?"

"It's okay, honey. We're gonna be rescued."

"Mary!" David said, shaking her gently. "Mary!" Her body was cold, and her breathing was very shallow.

"I'm dropping down some bottled water on a rope," Matt shouted down from about 20 feet above them. "It'll be a couple of hours at least, but I think we can safely spread these beams with this power equipment and bring you up. We're gonna get you out!"

David did not respond. He and Darlene burst into tearless weeping as they knelt over their three-year-old daughter, Mary, and offered their second child in two days into the arms of Jesus.

27

Grand Forks, Minnesota

Jared Keaton walked up to a police station in Grand Forks, just across the Coalition border, with a strapping young fellow in military fatigues following close behind. Jared had a rope tied around the blond fellow's neck with a noose knot, and he had bound his hands tightly behind his back. The young man's gazed was fixed on the ground, his lips pursed in a sour countenance.

Jared walked right up to the front desk with his captive in tow.

The secretary behind the counter just stared at the two of them, unsure of what to do.

"Lemme' speak to the chief," said Jared.

"Who are you?" she asked Jared, "and who is he?"

"I'm a federal agent, and this is Arnie Oswell York. Get a picture of him, upload it online, and you'll be famous in a couple of hours."

"I've been in tight with these right-wing radicals – I couldn't risk them figuring out who I was!" Jared said into the phone, anger filling his voice at the flack he was getting from the FBI's leadership. He paced back and forth in an empty office in the sheriff's department.

Mic Durango, FBI director of the mid-west division in Dallas, protested with machine-gun-like bursts: "We didn't know if you were dead! We didn't know if you'd turned against us! We didn't know anything about you!"

"Turned against you? What? Settle down! This is Chris Chambers talking! How could I ever turn on you?"

"You never updated us!"

"I thought I was onto the biggest take-down in American history! And I was! I'm practically best friends with one of the founders of the Coalition of Free Christian States, David Jameson! I'm a close acquaintance with Elijah Slate, head of the new criminal justice—"

"You went completely against every rule in the book!" Durango interrupted him. "You should have testified against these traitors months ago. You should have stopped them before they ever got that far."

"Oh, we didn't have anything on them but cruddy hate-speech violations. You are high-enough up the totem pole that you know they didn't have anything to do with the Columbus, Ohio bombing, right?"

Durango lowered his voice, as if the walls had ears. "Of course."

"Well, now, we can actually prosecute them for something they have done, something that'll stick before a jury. Now got them for treason! And if the president wants to insist on blaming them for the nuclear blast in California, then I've got her men."

"Did they do it?"

"If she wants to pin it on them, I'll testify to their willingness to do so. They clearly committed treason and were willing to launch nuclear weapons on you the night of the first raid. That nuclear-armed ballistic missile was not fired into space on purpose. It was fired at Washington, D.C., and only re-directed into space after the president called off her air attack."

"What? How do you know that?"

"I told you. I'm close to the top."

"Do you know where those nukes are being stored?"

"I'm not in *that* deep. But I have influence on those who have personal contact with Ben Boswell himself!"

"You are good, Chambers. I've got to hand it to ya'. Think we can get them arrested?"

"No," he blurted out with a shake of his head. "No way. Haven't you had enough failed raids? They're too heavily guarded and too suspicious of people they don't recognize."

"Well, what can you do for me?"

"I said that you couldn't arrest them, but you can kill them."

"Chris Chambers, the assassin," Mic Durango chuckled.

"I'm in position to do it, but it's going to cost you."

"Cost me?"

"You think I'm going to risk losing my own life trying to take down the most notorious traitors to the United States since Benedict Arnold? The Bureau's going to pay."

"How much?"

"Twenty million…"

"Twenty million dollars!?" Durango screamed.

"Tax-free, too. You get that new guy, uh, Erdman on the phone, and he'll get Margaret Brighton on the phone, and they'll approve it. Don't you worry about a thing, Durango. When Brighton finds out your best agent single-handedly annihilated the Coalition's leadership, you'll be director next term."

"Hmmm," thought Durango, licking his lips. "Talk's cheap, Chris. Can you deliver?"

"I'm at the police station in downtown Grand Forks, where I just delivered Arnie Oswald York, the Chicago abortion sniper. That's my down payment on the takedown of the Coalition."

"You've got one of the Army of Yahweh abortion snipers?"

Chris Chambers laughed mischievously. "There's only one, Durango. I heard him boast at a campfire outside of Canyon Ferry that he had sniped 18 abortionists and murdered 793 physicians at Seattle's ACOG convention."

"Ah, man!" Durango laughed heartily. "Great job!"

"You get me some compact explosives in unmarked boxes and I'll get you the Coalition's head on a platter."

Helena, Montana

"Hey Griff!" Jared stuck his head inside the foyer to get the attention of one of the edgy security guards in the capitol in Helena. "Will you give me a hand with something? I've got to carry something up to the governor's office for him."

The guard took a deep breath. "Sure!" He headed for the door. "Uh, hold on," he said to Jared, who held the door open for him. He jogged back to his station, pressed a button on the phone. "Hey Josiah? Watch the monitors. I'm helping Jared carry something into the governor's office. Be right back."

Under his breath, Jared cursed the caution of the 40-year-old veteran security guard.

"Sure you aren't too busy?"

The guard shook his head. "We've beefed up security, so I can afford to help 'ya. Did you hear about David?" the guard asked Jared.

"Jameson? Last thing I heard Matt Wellington rescued him from the bowels of a collapsed bank in New Mexico."

"Two of his daughters died in that collapsed bank."

"Oh no!" The federal agent was close enough to the Jameson family that he couldn't hear such news without an authentic spark of grief in his bosom. "How are David and Darlene handling it?"

"Okay, I think."

"Ah, man. I'll have to call him."

"Dream on. We're back to the dark ages, pal. You'd have to have a military grade sat phone to speak to David. He and his wife will be back up here this week. Well, I need to get back to my station. What do you need, and why on earth are you doing it at this hour?"

"What can I say, Griff? I'm a night owl. I've got some literature I promised David a couple of weeks ago that I would get to the governor's office by tomorrow morning. They're going to be discussing some amendments to the new Constitution pretty soon."

"Oh, that meeting's going to take place quite a ways from here."

"You mean, the Coalition leaders aren't going to meet here this week to discuss the new amendments?"

"It's too risky to have all the Coalition leaders in one well-known government building right now. One satellite-guided smart bomb would be all it'd take to kill all the leaders in one sitting; then there goes our Coalition. Too risky."

"Of course, of course," said Jared, stopping to put his hands on his hips and think. "Well, where do I need to get these?"

"I don't know where they're meeting," Griff said, shrugging his shoulders.

"I guess I don't need your help after all then. Sorry to bother you. I'll ask David when he gets back. We'll figure it out."

"Thank God you made it, David!" Jared exclaimed over the scrambled sat phone from the Minuteman's office in their church's administration building.

"Thank you, my friend." David was in a helicopter that was headed north. He had his left arm over his wife's shoulders. His face was as white as a sheet, and he became short of breath with exertion from all his blood loss, but he felt all right at rest. His right shoulder had been pierced with a bullet and was in a sling and several stitches had been placed in lacerations on his face, arms, and knees. His right hand was tightly bandaged. Darlene had Charlotte in her lap, who drank contentedly from a sippy cup. Beside them in the helicopter was Matt Wellington, two medics, and two small bodybags. "God has seen fit to keep us alive for one more day to serve Him."

"I'm so sorry about Mary and Johanna."

"They made it, Jared!" said David with unusual joy. "They crossed the finish line. They're with Jesus now. We will go to them soon." He spoke with more cheer than Jared anticipated. David glanced at Darlene, who leaned over and kissed him on the cheek, her eyes wet with tears. "Life is so short, Jared. It'll be like going to sleep next to them in bed and then waking up next to them in the morning." Darlene snuggled tightly against him so he could wrap his arm around her and rest it on the side of her abdomen. He patted her, grateful for the new life that God had unexpectedly given them. "We won't have long to miss them."

"No, you won't. When can we meet and talk?"

David pulled away from the phone and asked a guardsman next to him. "You sure this phone's secure?"

The guardsman nodded. "Absolutely."

"There's supposed to be a big meeting in a couple of days in Bighorn Canyon," David told Jared, "on south I-90 along the southern border. I was invited to attend. We're going to have the funeral at the Helena church tomorrow, and then head to the meeting. Maybe you can come, and then we can chat about what God's doing in your life."

"Okay, great!"

"Elijah should be there, too."

"Ah, fantastic!"

"Keep the location of the meeting close to your chest. We're not supposed to tell anyone about it."

Olympia, Washington

General Bryan didn't like the idea of burning up their dwindling fuel supply to transport thousands of his Coalition troops into the radiation-infested swamps that the valleys west of the Sierra Nevadas had become. But he knew that people would die without their help. Besides, Ben Boswell was the boss and he had made up his mind. Bryan sat at a desk in a State Guard storage facility just outside of Olympia, on hold with Ben Boswell's office.

Rod Sanders called out to him. "Hey, General?"

Bryan turned to him. "Yeah?"

Rod Sanders was strapping on his radiation suit with dozens of other guardsmen in their squad. "They're actually going to let us go in?" He found California's acceptance of Coalition aid incredulous. "I thought they were blamin' us for the nuc."

"California doesn't have a government anymore and the feds are without a presence there for the most part. The FBI has granted us permission to go in, which tells us right there that they know we didn't do it. The video proved that," he said, referring to the video of Cal Manning preaching at Berkley's campus at the time of the detonation. "The feds even promised to replenish the fuel we're using for the effort. If the Taliban offered help right now, they'd probably take it. With Congress falling apart and the nation going bankrupt, the president's struggling to get emergency funding for the rescue effort. We're prayin' that our willingness to send troops to help our enemies in their time of crisis will win over the legislature's heart."

Sanders was less optimistic. "Are you sure she won't send another air invasion while our troops are occupied in the rescue efforts?"

"She can't occupy us with two-thirds of her stateside forces suddenly missing. She'll be obsessed with damage control while we win the hearts of the people."

"They've still got bombers, don't they?"

Bryan shrugged. "Like Boswell said, there are ten thousand thirsty Californians withering away in the mountains, and it's our job to get them out and leave the results to God. Do unto others, right?"

"Oh man, what irony." He wagged his head. "We'll be working side by side with the same federal infantry that invaded us and tried to kill us the week before." Sanders strapped on his helmet and opened the door to join the others waiting for him in one of the 50 choppers that were preparing for take-off.

"Get outta' here! And Godspeed ya'," General Bryan said as Sanders shut the door behind him.

General Bryan heard a voice on the phone. "Hello, Governor?"

"This is Governor Boswell."

"This is General Bryan. I just wanted to let you know that we're going in."

"Good."

"Any second thoughts? This is the last chance to call it off."

"Get our boys out there and let's start saving lives."

"Yes sir." He opened a door that led down a hallway to the office where he would help coordinate the rescue efforts. "Our Guard forces will be cooperating with a Marine force from Michigan that is gathering at a mountain base just east of the ridge. They'll be there in about 30 minutes. I'll keep this phone on me."

Sierra Nevada mountain range, California

"Lower. Lower," one of Rod Sanders' privates spoke into his helmet-mounted microphone within his full body radiation suit. The private was in a double-stretcher that was being lowered from a helicopter to a peak of a hill where a family gathered, tattered, burned, and thirsty, on a small ridge northwest of the Sierra Nevada range.

"Lower it down some more!" Sanders ordered the engineer from the rear of the copter. "Sam can't reach them."

"It's too windy!" The pilot turned and shouted back at Sanders. "We've got to get out of here!"

"What is the radiation meter reading?"

"Too high."

Colonel Sanders glanced at the meter affixed to the wall beside him, and watched the needle teeter between the yellow and red zone. "We're fine."

The winds were fierce and the waves of the new coastline tossed frothy poison on the eroding hillsides, dragging soot and debris into the black depths. There was death everywhere. The carcasses of man and animal were strewn erratically across the hellish beach. The stench of rotting burnt flesh and scalded forest seemed to seep through their airtight masks.

"Lower! We've got to get those people!" Sam looked down at the family of five huddled into what appeared to be a shallow hole in the ground that they had dug, with the half burnt material of a tent wrapped about them. The man was the only one standing. He held a cloth of some sort over his face and reached an oozing, scabbed hand up to try to grab the swinging stretcher. When he finally held it fast, and Sam jumped out to check on the family who huddled in the remnants of a purple tent they wrapped about their wet, burned bodies.

"How bad are you?" Sam asked, motioning to those wrapped in the tent linen.

The father removed the towel from off his face to say something to Sam, but his voice was so hoarse that he couldn't understand him. His face was red, his nose and eyelids were blistered, and his lips were bleeding and oozing a yellowish-green drainage. His words were inaudible. Sam's heart skipped a beat when he contemplated the misery this family must have suffered the past two days and nights.

As the father held the stretcher, Sam went to the family, and slowly pulled the tent cloth away to see three children between three and twelve burned severely on their faces and hands. The eldest two were still breathing, but the youngest was only breathing very shallow breaths, and his fingertips had a bluish hue. Their eyes, noses, and mouths were covered with a green slime, and their lips opened and closed in exhausted, gurgled gasps.

"Ma babbies! Take ma babbies." The mother spoke with a swollen tongue through cracked and bleeding lips.

Sam took the tent, wrapped it around the two oldest children, who moaned pitifully with the movement. He lifted them gently into the stretcher as the mother held the youngest. He strapped the children in safely, then took the small child from his mother and cuddled him close to his chest as he sat on the edge of the stretcher. "I'll be back in a minute!" he told the father.

The father nodded, then motioned for them to go.

Sam could not hold back the tears as he held the youngest close to his chest. He despised himself for his inability to bring this suffering toddler inside the state-of-the-art body suit that protected him. As the helicopter began to lift the stretcher up and away from the trees he whispered to the little boy, "Hold on, son. Hold on. It'll be all right."

As Sam told him over the headset of the condition of the children, Sanders sighed heavily. "I think they're dying. They don't look good," Sam said through his helmet mic. Sanders could hear the emotion in his voice. "It reminds me of the Bible verse when God warns of judgment upon Israel for their sin, and He told them that their children would be dashed in pieces upon a stone. Oh, it's a terrible thing to behold." Sam held the boy as close to his chest as he could. "God have mercy on this little one."

Sanders glanced at the three burned and semi-conscious hikers they had picked up an hour earlier. A paramedic was tending to their wounds. Sanders tried to calculate how many more they could fit into the chopper before they had to head back to the medical facility on the other side of the mountains.

"We've got to get more men and more copters out here!" Sanders complained to the pilot. "There are hundreds of people in these hills who are going to die of disease and thirst before we can ever get to them! Get General Bryan on the line."

"Yes sir."

"I know it's bad," General Bryan tried to encourage a choked-up Rod Sanders. "We're flying troops in from the eastern states of the Coalition but they need to work on the western side of these mountains to try and rescue people that are more salvageable. Just help as many of them as you can."

Bighorn Canyon State Park, Montana

The weather was ominous when Jared arrived at the convention center at Bighorn Canyon State Park. The winds were stiff and chilly, the skies gray, and the precipitation was indecisive between sleet, snow, and rain. He donned his mirror sunglasses and zipped up his brown lamb leather jacket as he made his way toward the building. Through the front glass doors, he thought he saw two men in suits speaking with one another. He could barely make out their figures through the fog and the dew-covered glass doors.

Jared saw two cooks at the side of the building under an awning sharing a cigarette, and he thought it appropriate to join them to see what intelligence could be gained.

"'Sup?". Jared coolly pulled a cigarette out of the pocket underneath his jacket. "Got a light?"

One of the cooks flicked his lighter and lit Jared's tobacco without a response.

"What 'ya cooking for the governors?" Jared asked.

The two cooks traded an inquisitive glance and gave no response.

Jared appeared confused. "What?"

"Is the Coalition's leadership meeting here today?" The cooks were surprised that this cigarette-smoker with gelled, blond hair and multiple ear piercings knew something that had been kept secret from them, and they worked there.

"This is just my disguise because I'm a wanted man on the other side of the border. I'm good friends with Minutemen leaders Elijah Slate and David Jameson."

"You know Elijah?" one of them asked with a wide grin.

"Check this out." Jared pulled out his wallet and showed them a picture of Elijah, David, Cal, and him outside of a truck stop in Utah.

"It was a disposable camera, so the quality's not good, but that's David Jameson. He's the—"

"We know who he is," one of the cooks responded with enthusiasm. "Everybody knows who he is."

"Who's that?" asked the other one, pointing to Cal Manning on the photograph. "He looks familiar."

"He's one of the Minutemen. Killed in the blast at Berkeley. He was the one in the video who was rebuking the terrorists when the blast went off." Jared grinned, finding it incredible that he had been able to get so close to the Coalition's heroes.

"You gotta' be kidding me?" the second cook said with a laugh. "Can I hold it?"

Jared put the picture back in his wallet. "Now you're the one that's kidding me. You know how much I can get for that picture on E-bay?"

The cooks laughed. "Wow!"

"One of the reasons I'm here is to give some surprise awards to some of the leaders, and I'd like to get your help on something."

"Sure!"

"I need a place right next to the room where I can store some boxes with gifts and trophies inside – a broom closet, or something like that. It's gotta be a secret place where no one will find it. This *has* to be a surprise."

"My goodness!" one of the two cooks exclaimed as he pulled two of Jared's small boxes in on a dolly. "What in the world is in these boxes?"

"Gifts, I said. Gifts."

"Bowling balls?" he said as he glanced at the other cook.

"Bowling balls made of lead," the other cook added with a grunt as he carried one of the boxes by hand.

The one with the dolly banged a corner of the bottom box into the door as he entered the closet.

"Be careful! They're fragile."

"What kind of fragile gifts?"

"Plaques and stuff. You know, fancy gifts. Hey," Jared reminded them, "you guys promised not to tell anybody."

"What kind of fancy, fragile gifts?"

"I told you," said Jared, as he began to carefully move the boxes off the dolly and into the corner of the closet.

"Lemme' see," said the second cook as he dropped his box six inches onto the floor.

"Hey!" Jared protested the cook's carelessness with outstretched palms and an angry grimace. "Gently, gently."

"What kind of fragile gifts weigh 100 pounds?" The cooks had distrust written all over their faces. "We want to see what's in there."

"Yeah," the other cook responded. "Let us see."

"Let you see? How about after the ceremony?"

"No. Now."

"You wanna see, huh?" Jared lifted the last box and put it safely in the corner of the closet. "Promise you'll keep it secret?"

Jared's two helpers nodded. "Just hurry. Our break's up and we've got to get back."

"Well," said Jared as he reached for a box with the duct tape unraveled at the top, "you two have been a big help to me, it's the least I can do for you."

"Wow!" one of the cooks proclaimed as he gazed with admiration at the large gold plated plaque that Jared held up for them to see.

"Here, hold it," Jared said as he held it out to them.

"Whoa!" the tallest cook said as he held the plaque. "Is it solid gold?"

"No. They're not as expensive as they look."

"You must have 50 of these plaques in there!"

"Ninety-one, to be exact," said Jared. "One for each governor and cabinet member."

"The Coalition of the Free Christian States would like to thank Benjamin Boswell for…" one of the cooks began to read the plaque out loud.

"Do you know the price the FBI has put out for the capture of Benjamin Boswell?" the other cook asked Jared.

"Yeah." He nodded. "It's all over the news. But that's 20 million before taxes. With Marge Brighton's new tax scheme, they won't see a tenth of that money." Jared and the two cooks laughed at his joke.

"Shhh," the first cook blurted out. In the background, the angry voice of the master cook could be heard. "Oh! That's Mr. Goldberg!"

The second cook glanced at his watch and exclaimed, "Five minutes past a 15 minute break. Gotta' go." He handed the plaque back to Jared.

"Thanks for your help, boys. Keep it secret." They rushed down the hallway. He leaned forward, set the half-open box of plaques on top, then reached into his pocket and pulled out a tube of industrial strength super-glue. He thoroughly coated the bolt on the door before shutting it to prevent the door from being opened again.

"General Bryan, it's good to see you." One of the civilian-clothed guardsmen assigned to guard the facility walked up to him and shook his hand vigorously.

"Everything look good?" Bryan inquired as he scanned the premises suspiciously.

"Of course."

"Have you had the dogs sniff it out?"

"Of course," the guardsman responded.

"Looked in the attic? In the woods around the facility? Anything suspicious in your background checks of the workers?"

By the look on the guardsman's face, General Bryan knew that security was taking too much for granted. "Listen to me," Bryan ordered, "most of the Coalition leaders will be here today – there has only been two gatherings like this in the Coalition's history, and this is the first after formal secession and a nuclear detonation on California that has been blamed on us. It is a valuable target for the feds. They're blaming us for what happened in California, and I think at this point, they'd be giddy if they could just kill us all. I want you to get everyone together right now, right here in two minutes, and we're going to scour it room by room, looking for anything suspicious or anyone who looks like they don't belong here."

"Pastor!" Jared was so excited to see David Jameson, though he barely recognized him with his beard shaven and the hair on his head growing back grayer than he expected. He hurriedly walked up to him in the hallway of the conference center. "Oh!" He scrunched up his nose when he got a close-up look at him. "You look like you've been through a blender."

"Hey brother." David pulled him close and gave him as strong of a hug as he could muster. "Oh, easy, easy! It's only been a week and that shoulder hasn't quite healed." David motioned to his right shoulder.

"I'm so sorry about the girls. How's Darlene?"

David sighed at the question. "It's very difficult for her right now, and it was hard to pull away. But she insisted."

"When's Elijah going to be here?"

"He's not."

"What?" Jared was disappointed.

"He said that his priority was going through Washington State's death row cases and doing justice."

"Bummer." Jared was upset at the news, but there wasn't an award for taking down Elijah anyway, only the executive leadership of the Coalition – and David Jameson. So he brushed off his disappointment and feigned a warm smile.

"He was scheduled to give a presentation here on the changes to criminal justice in the state of Washington, but he's going to give it over the net instead."

"I was looking forward to seeing him."

"Stay next to me and remember to keep quiet during the meeting. You're on the roster as my assistant." David followed a few other leaders down the hall toward the conference room.

In the center of the conference room was a large, oval-shaped oak table, with a dozen black leather swivel chairs set up around it. Most of the governors were already seated at their places, designated with placards that read their name and state. A hundred folding chairs were set up in front of narrow tables on elevated platforms circling the governors. The members of the state cabinets wore nametags that revealed their title and their state. They took their places behind their respective governors. The chatter was lively and everyone was shaking hands and congratulating each other on their victories and the founding of their new nation. The rescue outreaches in California seemed such a perfect, picturesque, storybook conclusion to the first chapter of the Coalition's existence.

David sat at the table with the governors. The placard in front of him read, "David Jameson," in bold print, and below that, in italics, "Minuteman." It originally read "Minutemen Director" but David refused the title. He was content to just be a "Minuteman." Jared sat behind David on a folding metal chair. David glanced back at Jared to smile, but Jared was looking at a clock on the wall with a nervous look on his face.

"Are you all right?" David asked him.

"Yeah."

To David's right, General Bob Bryan was to be seated. As the governors took their seats, David noticed that General Bryan's seat was the only seat at the table still empty.

"Tell the chairman that I need five more minutes to have a closer look at the place," General Bryan told one of Boswell's aids in the lobby. General Bryan turned to address the 20 security guards and guardsmen who stood nearby. He saw the chief of security walk through the front door talking on his phone. "Isaiah Knabb!" Bryan called out to him.

Knabb told the person with whom he was speaking, "I'll call you back." He shut the phone. "Yes, General?"

"I am disappointed in security here," General Bryan snarled.

"Well, what else do you want to do?" Knabb responded calmly, trying not to over-react to the general's criticism.

"You should have had two guards at the bottom of the drive, and several all around this place, snipers and mortars on the roof—"

"That's overkill! This is a highly secretive meeting, and a presence like that would alert too many passers-by."

Bryan hesitated and considered the dilemma. "I see. Well, we have five minutes," Bryan addressed Knabb and the security guards that gathered around them. "I want one more thorough look around this place. Look in every closet, every nook and cranny in the basement and in the attic," he said as he motioned behind him toward the conference room. "If you see any suspicious people who don't belong here or any suspicious packages, call me immediately on the radio," he said as he patted the radio on his right hip. "I've got some pilots manning airspace to watch for approaching threats, so keep your radios on." Heads nodded. "Do you understand?"

"Where are those dogs?" General Bryan glanced out the glass doors in the foyer. "Oh, there they are," he said as he saw two guardsmen bringing in four bomb-sniffing dogs on leashes.

"We've already scoured the place with dogs a couple of hours ago," Knabb protested.

"And we're going to do it again."

The clock read five after ten. David was studying the order of events when Jared whispered, "I thought this meeting was supposed to start at ten?"

David chuckled quietly. "They may be men of God, but they're still politicians."

Jared grimaced at David's attempt at humor, and David thought this was unlike him. Jared looked at his own watch, then gazed around the room carefully, taking note of how many were still absent. His gaze stopped at General Bryan's empty seat.

Jared grew troubled when he heard some barking that sounded like it was coming from the area next to the conference room where he had stored the boxes. His eyebrows raised and a cold sweat broke out on his body.

He suddenly jumped up from his chair and briskly began to walk away when David turned and grabbed his jacket. "Where are you going? We're about to start." David was troubled when he saw the beads of sweat on Jared's brow. "What's wrong with you?"

"Chairman?" One of the Guard's generals leaned down and handed Ben Boswell a cell phone.

"Can it wait? We're about to get—"

"It's urgent!"

Boswell took the phone and his countenance lengthened as someone back at military headquarters gave him some bad news.

General Bryan was on the phone with Coalition intelligence at the same time, receiving the same report as he stomped into the room.

"I've got to go to the bathroom." Jared jerked his jacket out of David's grasp and rushed hurriedly toward the exit.

"Can it wait?" Jared ignored David, and walked out the door without looking back.

David glanced at the clock on the wall and then at Chairman Boswell, who looked upset as he spoke on his cell phone and studied something on a laptop that was open in front of him.

Something's wrong, here. David slowly stood and followed Jared out of the room. In the hallway, he looked and saw that Jared's pace had quickened toward the lobby.

"Mr. Knabb, this is Anthony Jay, do you copy?" came the call over the security chief's radio.

Isaiah Knabb had his head and flashlight up the chimney in the foyer's fireplace. He tapped his Bluetooth device: "Yes?"

"Two of the dogs are growling and sniffing at a closet door, scratching at it, and it's locked and no one's got a key. The doorknob won't even—"

"No one's got a key?" he shouted. "Get that door open and you figure out what the heck those dogs are smelling, and do it now!"

"They say that it's just a storage—"

"I said, now!"

General Bryan sat beside Governor Boswell, observing an image on his laptop with a look of horror on his face. The governors who gathered around looking at the computer monitor over Bryan's shoulders were equally disturbed as they watched the electromagnetic imaging of ten stealth bombers drop out of the stratosphere toward the capital cities of each Coalition state. An ominous stillness filled the room like a dark cloud.

"General Bryan!" Knabb rushed into the room.

"What are those dogs barking about?" Boswell inquired anxiously, pointing at the area of the building where the barking seemed to originate.

"Something suspicious in a closet. I think we should evacuate." The sound of wood splintering was heard from the other side of the wall.

Sierra Nevada Mountains, California

"It's been a pleasure working with you." Rod Sanders shook the hand of one of the Marine commanders who was responsible for the military's assistance in the rescue effort in the Sierra Nevada range. Forty of Sanders' men sat in a lounge eating a warm meal of chicken, mashed potatoes, and green beans, at the medical base where they unloaded the surviving victims. Hundreds of guardsmen were taking a much-needed rest wherever they could find a place to recline in and around the drab-green tents of the hastily erected base.

"It has been a pleasure."

"It is my prayer that our nations can be allies again, and in time, you can come to our way of seeing things," said Sanders, hoping that the conversation would turn toward more spiritual matters.

"Who knows, Colonel, who knows," the Marine said as he glanced down at his watch.

"Have you ever given thought to where you will spend eternity?" Sanders' phone rang before the Marine could answer the question. "Hold on." Sanders reached for his phone, but before he could unlatch it from his belt, he saw the Marine commander stand from his seat and pull a handgun on him. The guardsman to Sanders' right saw the draw and reached for his own gun, but not before the sound of the chambered rounds of dozens of M-16's stopped him cold.

"What is this about?" Sanders was stunned as his phone continued to ring unanswered on his hip. "I thought we had agreed to work together in peace to help with the rescue efforts."

"Don't try it!" The Marine commander briefly pointed his gun at a guardsman behind Sanders. "We have orders to shoot you all if just one of you tries to make a move."

"What is going on here?!" Sanders stood to his feet and thrust his fists against the table causing the dishes on it to clash.

The Marine commander did not respond, but motioned for his men to walk to and fro through the crowd of Coalition guardsmen and confiscate side arms.

Bighorn Canyon State Park, Montana

David was gravely concerned when Jared walked past the bathroom and out the front foyer doors. He commenced a slow jog to catch up with him, "Hey Jared!" he shouted just as Jared walked briskly through the front door.

What is he up to and why is he ignoring me? "Jared!"

General Bryan at his chief of security, Isaiah Knabb. Then he slammed his laptop shut and pointed toward the door that led to an exit. "Evacuate this facility immediately!" He told General Bryan. "Notify Guard command! Full alert!" Boswell and Bryan merged into the river of anxious personnel who were trying to press through the double doors to evacuate. General Bryan typed a number into his sat phone when Boswell told him, "Prepare for missile launches!"

"I'm doing it now."

"And get our fighter jets in the—"

"Our jets are already in the air, sir, but two-thirds of our ground forces are in California aiding with the rescue effort!" Bryan had to shout to be heard over the bustle and noise of those evacuating the building.

"Call them back, now!"

Many began to pray out loud with desperation in their voices.

Jared was running full speed away from the building as he pulled a detonator disguised as a cell phone from his jacket pocket. He thought he heard David's voice behind him. Jared looked over his shoulder and saw him leaving the building through the front door.

"Stop!" David ordered Jared as he tried to run to catch up with him. "What's the matter with you?!" He had a familiar déjà vu sensation as he recalled Terry Markison's betrayal of Texas' government, and then the betrayal of Darlene's friend, Janet. "Jared? No!" His mouth went dry. "Jared!"

Jared turned behind his car, flashed an evil grin, and extended his detonator toward the building. David put both of his palms up in the air. "No! Jared! No!"

Jared pushed the button.

The explosion incinerated the building, throwing flames and debris hundreds of feet into the air, killing everybody inside instantly. Even Jared, who stood at the side of his car opposite the building, was knocked backward by the forceful impact of the explosion. Flames of fire and billows of white and then brown smoke darkened the light of day even more than the dreary gray skies. The sleet turned muddy with dust.

"Fire now, Commander Martin!" A Guard sergeant had been given an order to alert the underground bunker where the nuclear weapons were stored. He was on the phone with the commander of the nuclear missile facility in northern Montana. "Fire, now!"

"I need direct authorization from Chairman Boswell," the commander of the nuclear missile facility responded.

"Boswell's not answering, and may already be dead!"

"General Bob Bryan then!"

"I can't get a hold of him either."

"Any governor? Any Guard general? Anybody in charge?"

"Guard communications have been disrupted somehow. Even cell phones aren't functional. I saw the satellite imaging myself, Commander."

"Why can't we pull it up?"

"It's probably been destroyed. Listen to me! We are under attack! Fire!"

"Well, you had better find a governor or General Bryan, or I will *not* fire these nuclear-armed ballistic missiles. This is the protocol agreed upon by Coalition leadership…"

"You just prepare them for firing, put in the coordinates, and I'll try to—" Suddenly, there was static on the other end of the line.

The commander in charge of the nuclear facility tapped on the receiver once. "Anybody there?" The static that answered spoke of only confusion and dread. Commander Martin then ordered the radio commander to try to get Boswell or General Bryan on the line immediately.

"Put in the coordinates," he told one of the engineers, who nodded and immediately began to type in the instructions on the computer. "Prepare them all for launch. Pre-assigned coordinates, grids four and five."

"All right," the radio operator responded.

Engineers began to type hurriedly into their computers, preparing the missiles for launch.

"I don't feel right about this," Commander Martin responded. "We have a chain of command for our protection. I need someone in charge, now!"

"No one's answering," his radio operator responded.

The doors to the underground ballistic missile bunkers opened with a groan and the missiles were raised with precision by the computer-controlled hydraulics. Five dummy ballistic missiles were accompanying six nuclear-armed ballistic missiles, in order to distract their MT-HELs and increase the likelihood that at least one nuclear weapon would reach its primary target. Half of those missiles would target D.C. via different trajectories, and the other half were headed for large military bases.

"Any evidence of an air attack against the Coalition?" the commander inquired.

"Nothing on sonar," one of the technicians informed him. "The monitor where our electromagnetic imaging views were uploaded is blank. Offline. I can't pull it up."

"There's no answer from the base in Seattle that's been sending us the electromagnetic images from our satellite," someone else commented.

"No answer?" Commander Martin shouted. "Did we miss the rapture or what?"

"Hold on! I'm getting a signal." The technician increased the gain and put it on speaker. "Someone's calling in." He pressed the button to put the call on speaker.

"... You... get... air... prepare..."

"Get the static out of that," Commander Martin shouted.

"It's coming from a sat phone," one of the computer technicians responded. "It's coming from General Bryan's sat phone."

"I need those stealth-capturing images now!" Martin ordered.

"I think the feds disrupted that satellite," a subordinate announced worriedly, a phone to his ear. "I can't contact them on the phone or web."

Olympia, Washington

Elijah Slate was trying to peruse computerized files of death row inmates in a large room down the hall from Governor Littman's office. A room full of incorrigible police chiefs and sheriffs constantly interrupted him with snippy, condescending remarks. Big ships turn slowly, and he soon discovered that he could not redeem the entire corrupt criminal justice system of the state in one day. He had to spend all his time teaching from the Scriptures and reproving ungodly attitudes. How do you redeem sewage? Morally, the entire system was in ruins, and it would be easier to gather up the debris into a pile and burn it and rebuild from new materials than to rebuild with the same rotten, rusted, and warped raw materials. He suspected the system was too far gone to fix, so he had urged the governor to dissolve the entire criminal justice system and let the Minutemen take over, but he soon discovered that was a naïve suggestion. To dissolve the criminal justice system, the legislature would have to be dissolved as well. There were 50 thousand prisoners dependent a billion dollar state bureaucracy, and that kind of money speaks volumes to politicians running for re-election. Elijah simply did not have enough men committed to follow God's Word in administrating justice. You just can't trust godless men to administrate justice. *The whole lot of them just need to get saved,* Elijah thought. With all the prison riots and with the blockade of goods coming to the state, choking the prisons of food and basic necessities, the prison officials that most urgently required instruction from God's Word had to spend all their time in crisis management.

The most prominent prison official in the state of Washington was making his case for releasing all drug criminals when Elijah jolted, and then glanced at his watch. He remembered he had to make a presentation to the Coalition's leadership on Washington State's new criminal justice system.

"Oh brother, I'm sorry, I've got to give a lecture in a few minutes." Elijah tapped a few keys on his laptop to pull up his powerpoint presentation. Suddenly, he heard a loud explosion nearby, and felt the building sway slightly. "What in the world?" Elijah looked up from the laptop. "Are they demolishing buildings near here?"

"Not that I know of," one of the justice employees aptly responded, standing to his feet and walking to the window. "That's from the east, the direction of the capitol." Another explosion sounded from just a few blocks away. Elijah turned and looked through the window, and could see the mushroom cloud rise to the sky.

Elijah dropped the file and pushed his chair away from the table, causing the wooden legs to groan against the tile floor. He closed his laptop, jumped to his feet, and walked hurriedly toward the door. He opened it and saw two men in suits with guns pointed at his chest.

"Mr. Elijah Slate, you're under arrest."

Bighorn Canyon State Park, Montana

The back of Jared Keaton's head hit the ground hard. He opened his eyes, unsure of exactly how long he had been unconscious. It couldn't have been that long, because the alarm sirens of dozens of vehicles still resounded through the parking lot. Jared cursed his stupidity as he sat up. He should have ducked behind the car. He didn't realize the explosion would be so powerful. All around him, debris burned and smoked as the sleet turned to light rain and began to fall harder. He touched the back of his head, and then looked at his hand. It was covered in blood.

He stood to his feet and shook the ash and dust off of his body. He gazed in awe at the smoking ruins where the Coalition leadership just tasted the wrath of the federal government. He grinned as he fancied his 20 million dollar reward.

He noticed some movement on the other side of his car and walked to the body of a man who lay burnt on the ground. As he got closer, he realized – this was David Jameson. He was outside the building when the explosion occurred. It threw him across the parking lot, but he was alive.

Jared walked cautiously toward David Jameson. He wasn't sure if David was armed. David moaned and slowly opened his eyes. He was bleeding profusely from a dozen wounds. A piece of wood protruded from his right thigh and glass shards re-opened old wounds from the quake. His face and neck were covered with lacerations and gashes.

"Oh God," David mumbled as he rolled his head back and forth on the ash covered cement. "Have mercy…"

Jared's face developed a contorted smile. "You mean, Jared Keaton, have mercy."

"Jared?" David's eyes fixed on his friend. He squinted and raised his hands to his head. He turned and saw the convention center in flames. Even the brick walls were leveled. He looked like a man who had just spent a year building a skyscraper by hand, and when the last nail was hammered and the last mirror hung, a demolition company had been commissioned to level it to the ground right in front of him. The realization of what just happened began to set in. To his horror, the Coalition's fragile leadership had been entirely destroyed.

Jared put his hands over his face and opened them as if he were playing peek-a-boo with a toddler. "Surprise!" He laughed at his own humor. "Oh, what a great ending to the drama of the past 5 years! Hallelujah!" he mocked, his hands raised as if in praise.

David just groaned in pain so great he was nauseous. He grabbed his stomach, finding his heart-wrenching grief more painful than his physical wounds.

"Ask for mercy from me!" Jared barked. When David didn't respond, Jared delivered a swift right foot into David's ribs.

David gasped, breathless, and rolled away from Jared.

"Oh, this is just perfect." Jared celebrated his exploit. "Beautiful! There is a god after all…"

Momentarily, David turned toward Jared. "What did you do, Jared?"

"I just became 20 million dollars richer and the most celebrated FBI agent in the history of America!"

"Oh God, have mercy," he mumbled.

"Ask *me* for mercy, David." Jared reached down and cruelly twisted the plank of wood that protruded from David's right thigh.

David Jameson replied with a scream of pain and tried in vain to pull away from his tormenter.

Jared stood, looked around him, and then looked down at David Jameson's bloody frame. "Oooh, I could have some fun with you right now, but you know what? I think you'll be pretty valuable to some people on the other side. So, you're coming with me." He bent down to frisk David, and finding him unarmed, he grabbed David's good leg and began to drag him to his car. David bucked and kicked Jared away from him with his good leg. He screamed at him at the top of his voice, his voice echoing in the hills around them, "Murderer! How could you be Judas?" David reached and grabbed the plank of wood in his thigh and pulled it out with a scream and threw it away from him.

Jared stumbled when David kicked him but he quickly regained his balance. He rushed at David in a rage and began to curse as he kicked and beat him without mercy. Even after David lost consciousness from the blows to his head, Jared continued to stomp him in a rage that he had concealed for five years.

Northern Montana

"Fire!" the pilot of the stealth B-52 Halo Fortress bomber ordered. The munitions engineer typed in a command and hit 'enter', sending two air-to-surface missiles toward a suspected Guard facility in the mountains of northern Montana, one that had been missed in the bombing campaign of last week.

"Good job." He banked right, leaving the missiles to find their satellite-guided targets on their own.

"Coalition Boagie at two, nine, seven, bearing one, zero, three…" the co-pilot commented as the feared repetitive chirping sounded in the panel over his head.

"Donna, he's yours."

"I got him," the munitions engineer said as she typed a command in the computer and prepared an air-to-air for engagement.

"No rush. With their satellite destroyed, they're handicapped against stealth."

* * * * *

Commander Martin's computer and radio engineers were working hard to try and get General Bryan's voice back on the line when they stumbled upon another radio message. "Hey! I've got somebody else on the line!" the radio operator told Commander Martin. "Man! Why can't we get a clean signal? It's either radiation from the nuke in California, or our transmissions are being jammed somehow." He continued to twist the dials and magnified the sound over the main speakers.

"Let me put another filter on it," another engineer said as he typed into his computer.

"I think it's from a Coalition fighter."

"We are…" – more static – "…arm your… fire your…"

"Repeat! Say again!" The radio operator practically yelled into the microphone. "We're having a difficult time hearing you!"

"My fighter's been damaged," came the clearer radio signal as the fighter neared, enabling it to overcome the federal government's signal blocking technology with the closer coordinates to the receiver. "The Coalition states are under attack! Stealth bomber headed right for you. Fire everything you've got immediately!"

Everybody gasped in shock as the commander rebutted, "I have direct orders not to fire without the direct command to do so from either Chairman Boswell or General Bryan."

"They're dead."

"Then I must speak to one of the Coalition governors who are next in authority. I need to speak to…"

"Dead, all dead."

"Next in line is Chad Dreifuss, Montana's…"

"Dead. All of them killed by a bomb at Bighorn Canyon. Communications have been jammed. I'm havin' to put a lot of power into the radio to speak to you from a half mile away…"

The commander gasped. He was being forced to place a lot of trust in one Coalition pilot. Commander Martin leaned toward one of the engineers who manned the sonar equipment. "Do you see anything? Anything at all?"

The engineer shook his head. "I wouldn't expect to see a stealth B-52, sir, not with this technology. But I do see the Coalition fighter jet."

"Are you sure he's one of ours?"

"Yes. Signature's definitely ours." Suddenly the engineer's face paled, his eyes fixed upon the screen as if he'd just seen a ghost.

"What is it?" Commander Martin inquired.

"He's gone." He pointed to the monitor. "He was right there."

Commander Martin gulped, finding his mouth quite dry at that moment. "All right, fire away! Fire missiles!" He turned to two helicopter pilots by the door. "Get to Bighorn and find out if there are survivors."

The pilots nodded and rushed for the door. "Stay low to the ground," Martin added, "to keep from being a target for enemy aircraft! I think we're under attack."

The commander turned to his radio operator. "Maybe the imaging's messed up. Find that Coalition pilot and ask how he knows about the deaths of Coalition leadership."

"Yes sir." The radio operator tapped on the computer and tried to communicate with the Coalition fighter pilot, but he only heard static. "He's not there anymore, Commander…"

The sonar engineer turned to the commander. "He's gone."

The radio operator added, "His signal's gone. Line's all static now. Probably taken out by air-to-air."

"Commander!" the sonar engineer blurted out. "I'm picking up an air-to-surface, coming right at us, Mach-4, no, Mach-5…"

"Fire! Fire!"

The engineer typed as fast as he could.

"It's closing!" the sonar operator shouted. "I can't see who fired it. The missile's locked on our position. It's coming right at us!"

"Fire!" the commander shouted.

"Just a moment, just a moment," the engineer mumbled as he typed in the final command as the ballistic missiles were raised to position.

He never hit enter. The satellite-guided air-to-surface missiles hit their target, and completely destroyed the Coalition's nuclear facility. Half of the Coalition's nuclear armament was stored at that facility and completely annihilated with the strike.

"That was a lot easier this time, wasn't it?" the bomber pilot commented. "All right, let's drop our last payload on Helena and get home for pictures and supper." The B-52 Halo Fortress pilot hit a number on the dash in front of him. "Captain Kylar, you may unleash Operation Rat. Have fun!"

Captain Kylar was in the cabin of a transport jet flying at the edge of the stratosphere, just now crossing the Coalition border. In the rear of his jet were 200 paratroopers preparing for their part in the drama.

The Air Force captain updated his paratroopers as they checked each other's belts and fastened their weapons to their person in preparation for their drop on the capital of Montana. His voice was amplified into the large storage cabin. "The capitol building, suspected militia training facilities, and Guard facilities have been destroyed. Our job is to set up a perimeter downtown and secure the entire block between Main, Adams, Jefferson, and Boswell Street for our command center."

"Drop the leaflets!" the B-52 Halo Fortress pilot ordered as he flew low over Helena.

Air Force personnel in the rear cabin motioned to those responsible for dropping tens of thousands of leaflets over downtown Helena. The leaflets informed citizens below that the Coalition leadership and their Guard forces had been destroyed and all would go well with them if they turned in their weapons and submitted to the new government. Otherwise, they would be arrested or shot as enemy combatants.

The bomber circled the town twice as the leaflets were dropped.

“Whoa! What was that?” The pilot felt something strike the cabin of their jet. “Was that from the ground?”

His co-pilot shrugged, and then pointed. “Check it out!” He pointed at the bottom of the windshield and saw a four-inch-long divot in the bullet-proof glass. “Had to be a stray bullet. No one could hit us purposefully this high in the air.”

Jack Handel had taken careful aim with his .50-caliber sniper rifle. He was *en route* from New Mexico to Helena to meet up with Barry Friar. Just outside the city limits he heard the bombs explode and saw the puffs of smoke on the western horizon over the city. He pulled his Jeep over to the side of the road and studied the sky for aerial targets. He had taken several shots at the specks of black when they were seen between puffs of clouds. But now the sky was silent.

He put his weapon into the back seat of the Jeep and sped off toward Helena. He opened his phone and tried to get in touch with his friend, Barry Friar.

He had plenty of fight left.

29

Arlington, Virginia

Dr. Johnny Daffner was a bald Army major of average build and height. He'd have the looks of a magazine model if only he had hair. He had been given the privilege of treating the convicted traitor and hate-speech criminal, James Knight, and with the medication they had forced him to take, Knight was finally beginning to cooperate. Daffner saw a dozen patients a day as an Army psychiatrist, but when Knight wound up on his docket, he'd been freed of his other responsibilities so he could devote himself more fully to rehabilitating the ex-congressman from Wyoming. Johnny was developing an affinity toward the fellow for his fortitude and his old-school patriotism – in spite of all his religious fanaticism. After a few weeks of psychotherapy and hours pouring through the NEA-approved tolerance curriculum with Knight, the psychiatrist came to the place where he didn't believe any of the things he had been told about him.

Finally, after a few of Josh Davis' articles landed in his inbox, his mind began to wander. These questions had driven a fourth of the states all the way to violent secession. Thirteen states! *Just like the last Revolutionary War.* He found it more and more difficult to haphazardly brush their objections to federal rule aside. He began to question his allegiances.

"So, how are you doing today, Jim?" Dr. Daffner asked, taking off his pointy-rimmed, dark-frame reading glasses and setting them on his desk.

Jim's face was pale and dusky today. Drool had dried on the corner of his mouth, and his eyes were dim. His hands were cuffed and his feet shackled to the chair in which he sat.

"Jim?!" Daffner raised his voice. "How are you today?"

Knight cleared his throat. "Hello, Doc." Knight shook his head to try to fight off the lethargy that the medication induced in him. "Where's my attorney?"

"I'm sorry, Jim," Daffner told him. "I've told you this everyday, you should know by now that *habeas corpus* has been suspended and you have been judged by a military tribunal. There'll be no defense attorney for you."

Knight cleared his throat. "I want an attorney. I want a jury trial. I want to see my family."

"I'm sorry, Jim. Tell me more about your association with the Coalition leaders."

"The Coalition?"

"Of Free Christian States, yes."

"Yes, well, uh, I think they're all right," he slurred. "How are they doing?"

"I told you yesterday, Jim. You're forgetting things."

"It's your fault! Take me off these poisonous pills."

Daffner swallowed hard. "I'm sorry I can't do that Jim. The Coalition detonated a nuclear bomb in California three days ago. This morning, their leadership and the remainder of their nuclear arsenal were taken out."

"Huh?"

"Did you hear what I said? The CFC States have killed 25 million Americans with a nuclear weapon! The leadership has been completely destroyed. The capitol buildings in the 13 CFC States are dust." He backed away from his desk, leaned back in his chair, clasped his hands across his torso, and smirked. "What do you think of your Coalition now?"

"You should know that I don't believe a thing you tell me. You're an accessory to my kidnapping. You have violated my constitutional rights." He took a deep breath as he breathed out an imprecatory reproof: "God will grant your enemies victory over you."

"Explain this, then, Jim!" The government psychiatrist extended the front page of a newspaper toward the former congressman. James Knight saw the picture of the Golden Gate Bridge half submerged and the emboldened headline, which read, "Coalition Nukes San Francisco Bay

Area!" In smaller print below, the words were written, "Tsunamis and Earthquakes Destroy Most of California."

Jim stared at it a second and then shook his head. "I don't believe it. Nope."

"It's right here, Jim!" Daffner insisted as he shook the newspaper in James' face.

"Even if they did, they had a good reason to—"

"Twenty-five million people? This is cold-blooded murder!"

Daffner's raised tone helped make Knight more alert. He leaned forward in his chair. "The government you represent has killed twice that many of its own citizens while they slept in their mothers' wombs."

"Oh, brother," mumbled Daffner as he set the newspaper down. "Here we go again."

"If it did happen, you had it comin'. You and your leaders are the enemy of the Constitution and everything that's good and decent!"

"I'll gladly declare myself the enemy of any god who allows this to happen to 25 million innocent people?" Daffner snapped. "That's the angry, bloodthirsty God of the Coalition, not the loving God of the Bible. We're in the New Testament now, Jim, not the Old Testament."

"Jesus Christ, the same yesterday, today, and forever," Knight rebutted, quoting a Bible verse. "God doesn't change. From Genesis all the way to Revelation, Old and New Testament, God judges nations for idolatry and the shedding of innocent blood."

Daffner shook his head, getting frustrated with Knight's stubbornness. Knight sensed his resistance, and reproved him, "Look at that front page, Doc! Look at it!" Daffner picked it up and studied it again. "Except you repent," Knight stated calmly, "you will all likewise perish."

Daffner threw the newspaper back on his desk. "Yeah, yeah, I know Jim, you've told me already. I've got 666 on my forehead and my name's Beelzebub," he mocked.

"I want my mind back, Doc." Knight closed his eyes and shook his head. "Get me off this medicine so I can talk to you better."

Johnny Daffner looked down at James Knight's chart. "You've been diagnosed with paranoid schizophrenia and obsessive compulsive disorder, Jim. We just can't go stopping medicine."

"Please! Lower the dose at least! And let me see my family and, I promise, I'll tell you whatever you want to hear."

"I'm sorry, I can't do that."

Knight rattled his chains. "Just let me speak to them on the phone to see if they're okay. You know, someone made a threat against my daughter, my little girl."

"I'm sorry, Jim."

Jim put his head back and sobbed hard for a long moment. Then he screamed at the top of his lungs, startling Daffner, "Oh God! Oh God! Oh God!" He shook his head back and forth. "God, help me!"

"Calm down, Jim, or I'm gonna have to sedate you."

Jim continued his passionate cries, "Help me, God! Help me, my wife and daughter! My country! Oh God! My enemy's too strong for me…"

This was truly a pitiful sight that tugged at Johnny Daffner's heart strings. He also had two children, about the same age as Knight's, and he couldn't stand the thought of being torn away from them.

He's a religious fanatic, but not a traitor and definitely not a paranoid schizophrenic, Johnny thought, but didn't say. *We **caused** his psychological problems. But what can I do? This is my job…*

The next day, Knight managed to vomit up the medicine they had given him when no one was looking, and he could now speak his thoughts with greater clarity.

"Johnny, please, listen to me." Jim Knight pleaded with his captor.

"No, you listen to me. Your Coalition's dead. It was completely destroyed yesterday. Your precious Ben Boswell's dead. You're being delusional."

"Fine, fine," Knight nodded, "it's dead, I accept that. But I do not accept the execution of my friends. If the president said that we are at war, then the generals of the Coalition Guard and its political leaders should be treated as prisoners of war, not traitors to be executed. A military tribunal has no authority to order United States civilians to be executed!" Knight shook his stainless steel chains for emphasis.

Daffner cursed his own tactical error. He had given James Knight the past two days' newspapers to try to get him to face reality and give up his hope in the Coalition. "Don't waste your time lobbying for the lives of the traitors," Daffner said. "We have a system of checks and balances."

"Exactly!" Knight stretched his right index finger as far as the chains on his wrist would allow. "That's exactly right. A system of checks and balances that has been all but ripped to pieces under Margaret Brighton. How do you think I got here, Dr. Daffner? I'm a democratically elected congressman. It's because I had the audacity to lawfully oppose her—"

"You endorsed state secession on public television!"

"Which is lawful! The states entered the union voluntarily, and they can leave voluntarily if federal tyranny warrants it."

"Jim!" Daffner waved his hands to halt Knight traitorous rhetoric.

"How did the president respond? Wait, listen! How did the president respond? With a cohesive rebuttal? No! Her response was to violate my constitutional right to free speech. She's persecuting political opponents, Doc! She's operating outside of her constitutional authority. Can't you see that she's a tyrant?"

"Maybe she is, Jim, maybe she is. But it's over now. The war's over. We need to try to make the best of this bad—"

"And let my friends be killed with a lethal injection without even a trial by jury?" Knight interrupted with a raised voice. "Come on, Doc! You know those military tribunals are not legal for American citizens! It's unlawful! It's murder!"

"They're not citizens of the United States anymore, Jim."

"Then they can't be traitors, can they? You can't have it both ways! If they're citizens, they deserve a trial where they can defend themselves. If they are not citizens, they should be treated as prisoners of war and under international law they cannot be summarily executed."

"Jim!" Johnny exclaimed, slapping his right hand on his desk. "The Coalition publicly executed two abortionists! Enough!"

"Why is it that Americans are so infatuated with democracy when evil is legalized and socialism expanded, but when the democratic consensus leads to the execution of baby-murderers, they respond with violent objection?"

Johnny Daffner looked down at his desk and began to thump his pencil against it. He toyed with the idea of increasing Knight's medication, but his conscience checked him.

"The Coalition leaders should not be executed!" Knight urged him. "Come on!"

"Well, what do you want me to do about it?" Johnny said with exasperation, accidentally tossing his pencil off his desk in the process. "You want me to sneak you out of here, break you out of prison, become a felon like you?" Johnny was flustered by the prick of his own conscience, and his heretofore well-concealed pity for the Wyoming congressman.

James Knight leaned forward with his elbows on his knees. "You know as well as I do that the average American has had enough of Margaret Brighton. So has the average congressman and congresswoman, Doc. Set me free. Help me save the lives of those fine American Christians who are due to be executed by lethal injection tomorrow!"

"Your dreamin', Jim, dreamin'. You aren't a congressman anymore. Even if you were freed, what could you do?" Daffner hit a button on his desk, setting off a buzz in the hallway.

"Please, Johnny, just think about it." Knight pleaded as the guard walked into the room and began to unlock James Knight's feet shackles. "Time is short!" Johnny looked down, grabbed a pen this time, and began to thump it against his desk. "Look into my eyes, Dr. Daffner, you brave and courageous American! Look at me!" Johnny Daffner raised his gaze to look into the tear-filled eyes of the American congressman from Wyoming. "You can do it, Dr. Daffner. Courage is not beyond you."

The guard jerked James Knight toward the door as Daffner wrote something into James Knight's chart. "I'll see you tomorrow, Jim," the psychiatrist said without looking up. "In the meantime, we're increasing your anti-psychotic dosage to try to get these delusions under control."

"Please, Dr. Daffner, no." Knight protested as the guard slammed the door shut and led Knight back to his eight-by-eight chilly, cement cell. Knight suspected this would be the consequence for vomiting out his medicine; his wits would return and then they would increase the dosage, sedating his intellect and numbing his emotions to keep him under control. Knight wept out a passionate prayer to God as he was led back to the cell.

"Going to be all right, Jim?" his guard asked in a friendly fashion. The guard had come to admire Jim Knight over the past several months.

Knight turned his teary-eyed gaze to the prison guard, and fought off the temptation to despair. "Just pray for Dr. Daffner, Vinny. He's coming around."

Vinny smirked and grunted as he opened the door to Knight's cell. "You've got enough faith to walk on water, Jim. I wish I had your faith."

Knight took a deep breath and sat on his cot. "Jesus said that all things are possible to them that believe."

Chesapeake Beach, Maryland

Josh Davis had accumulated a veritable army of fans and committed assistants in the 37 federally controlled states. Unfortunately, most of the websites that initially printed his articles were forced to withdraw them. The few who posted them anyway were shut down and fined. Every time he would send out articles to his large E-mail list and post them on discussion boards, the feds would pull the plug on his internet service provider. Then he'd have to get another E-mail address under a pseudonym. This kept Josh on the move. He lived on the road and slept in a one-room trailer hooked to the back of his pick up.

Since his last article, he had devoted himself to trying to locate James Knight and the host of other copperheads who were arrested after opposing Brighton's agenda. While perusing the 5,200 E-mails that had gotten past his anti-spam software since his last article, he found one titled, "I guard JK and wanna help." Josh could have slapped himself that he had not seen this E-mail earlier. He had missed it.

He clicked it enthusiastically. It read,

> *Enlightening article! Thank God for you! I work at the VMP in Arlington and am one of the guards who has contact with JK as well as some of the other politicians and pastors who are here because they spoke out in defense of the Coalition. I chat with JK more than the others. They keep him drugged up most of the time.*
>
> *Another closet Christian among the prison guards presides over the block that holds the RW and HA. HA just got here a few days ago, and I haven't seen either of them yet, but my friend tells me that they're both being treated with psychiatric medications.*
>
> *I know it'd get me in trouble if my superiors discovered that I supported you, but I'm taking the chance because I think what you're trying to do is worth the risk. I'll keep you in our prayers. Love to help distribute your articles.*
>
> *V. M.*
> *(921) 55 (Duluth zip)*

He tried to make sense of the abbreviations. *VMP in Arlington? Must be the Virginia Military Prison. JK? Hmm. That's got to be James*

Knight? RW – Randy Woods? Could HA be…? No way! Duluth zip code? Duluth, Minnesota? Maybe that zip is the last five numbers of his phone number…

Goosebumps popped up on his forearms and a chill went up his back. He googled the zip code of Duluth on his cell phone, then grabbed the cordless phone on the small desk in his one room RV. He hit the number "1" and held it three seconds to speed-dial an internet service provider owned by a friend; that connection gave him access to anonymity through telephone software he had designed and uploaded into the ISP's hard drive. He paused until he heard another dial tone, and then dialed VM's number.

Vinny Molder answered it on the first ring. "Hello?"

"Is this VM?"

Arlington, Virginia

"How are ya' doing today, Jim?" Vinny leaned up against the bars of Knight's cell.

Knight, who was sitting at the head of his bed, turned to the friendly guard behind him. "Huh?"

"Here," Vinny whispered as he opened a palm he held out through the bars. Knight slowly reached and took the bottle from Vinny's palm. "Read it behind the bed, out of the view of the cameras," Vinny said before walking briskly away.

James Knight was confused. His mind was in slow motion after the dose of medication he was given that morning. He crawled to the foot of the bed, sat on the ground, and then unwrapped the rubber band that held a small note to the tiny medicine bottle. He slowly unfolded the note, and began to read.

Missoula, Montana

David Jameson opened his eyes, feeling just as much misery as when he had drifted to sleep ten hours earlier. For a moment, the previous week was all a blur. Being reunited with his family, the earthquake, deaths of Mary and Johanna, the bomb that killed Coalition leadership, Jared's betrayal, the hasty military tribunal that lasted ten minutes, and the predictable verdict – he went through it all in his mind. It all seemed like a bad dream, but when he sat up in the jail cell of the maximum-security military prison, he realized it had not been a nightmare at all.

He couldn't see out of his left eye. He put his hand up and felt a bandage over it. His attention immediately went to his ribs and his neck, which were extremely sore after the beating Jared Keaton gave him – or whatever his name was. He sat up slowly on his cot and a sharp pain startled him in his right thigh. He recalled how Jared twisted the protruding log of wood that had lodged into it. A headache crept into his mind as if to distract him from the thoughts of death by lethal injection that he was soon to endure. Of all the things the government could do to him, that was the lightest cross. He would soon be with Jesus, with his daughters Johanna and Mary. His heart would leap for joy if it weren't for the thought of his dear pregnant wife Darlene. Her cross has been so much heavier than his, and his heart broke at the thought of her mourning his death. "Oh my Lord, help her cope…"

"Good to see you're awake."

David turned to see an Episcopal minister with a red priestly collar. "How are you doing?"

"Where am I?"

"A maximum security military prison in Oregon on the morning of the day of your death," he stated coldly. By the tone of his voice, David discerned that this was not a friend.

"Who are you?"

"I was appointed to be your spiritual counselor." David studied the pale, mustached priest who sat in a chair in the corner of his cell. "Is there anything I can do for you? You have about an hour."

"An hour?" David put his hands up to his head to try and stabilize his pounding headache.

"Can I get something for this pain in my head?"

"You had something about an hour ago. You don't remember? They brought you breakfast and medicine. You took the medicine and went back to sleep."

He looked up into the cold, green eyes of the reverend. "What became of Elijah Slate?"

"He was captured and is being held here. He's after you. I hear your wife is here."

"My wife?" David perked up. "My wife is here?"

"She and your daughter are in a half-way house where hate-criminals who've been released from prison are residing, and they're carefully guarded, but they remain together."

That word "daughter" in the singular pained his heart for a moment.

"Your wife requested and was allowed to witness the execution, along with some others who were eyewitnesses to your treason. The government thought it would help her let go and receive the proper re-education."

David chuckled. "Yeah, re-education."

"Yes. Re-education," the priest said calmly. "She needs to learn about the love and acceptance of God. She needs to learn how to accept alternative lifestyle choices and…"

David ignored the priest's counsel and his thoughts went to his family. He missed his wife and children terribly. He dreaded the thought that the last time his wife would see him would be at his execution. He interrupted the priest's sermonizing: "May I speak with Darlene?"

"No," the chaplain blurted out as he turned his gaze away from the condemned traitor. "That's not possible."

David Jameson felt grief well up in his bosom and his eyes became hot with tears. He longed to ask the chaplain to pray with him, but it was clear that this reverend was a fake, a government stooge who would be a dispenser of the "opiate to the masses" but never genuine with his Maker.

"May I pray with you?" the chaplain asked him.

"No. You'd spend your hour better reading the Bible and repenting toward God, than in praying for me."

The minister ignored the rude reproof and thought it best just to try to do his job. "I'd like to pray with you before I leave, Mr. Jameson," he asked him kindly again.

"The Bible says if a man turns his ears away from hearing the law, then God turns his ears away from that man's prayers. Your prayer is an abomination to God, Reverend. He cannot even hear your prayers. You need to turn from your sin."

The chaplain had never been reproved so severely in all of his life. He had read about the audacity and crudeness of the so-called "Minutemen" of whom David was the leader, but now he had been a recipient of their verbal abuse. "Well, Mr. Jameson, I want to give you peace and—"

"You cannot give what you don't have, Reverend. There is no peace, saith my God, to the wicked."

The chaplain stood up and turned to leave. "Very well."

When David was alone with his thoughts again, a heaviness came over him that he had not felt since he had been locked in the police car with Jared outside of the Civic Center in Columbus. The tempter was pulling at him, enticing him to doubt God's deliverance, to even question whether God even cared about him at all. The thought entered his mind like an unwelcomed intruder, yet he did not immediately banish it. Like the invitation of a dark, damp cave to one blistered by a desert sun, the thought of doubting God's goodness was strangely gratifying.

He clenched his fists, quieted his mind, and repented for his doubt. What good was it to start a race and not finish it well? What good was it to start to build a home and then abandon it before it was completed?

He began to call out to God from the depths of his heart, bursting out in a tearful, passionate prayer. "God! Help me!" he cried, the tears filling his eyes. "Spirit of God, be my comforter! You are worthy, oh my Father. I am not." He lifted his good eye to heaven. "Thank you for dying for me, for giving me eternal life. Thank you for my family, and for all of the blessings you have given me. If I never hear another kind word or feel another bit of comfort, if I never kiss my wife or hug my children again," he mumbled softly between sobs, "I am your child and I'm gonna be with you in heaven. And it never gets any better than that. I'm in this for you, God, not for your blessings. I am your servant." He calmed himself and took a deep breath, and felt the Comforter fill him like water would fill a bucket. His Father was embracing him, setting him gently in His lap and whispering peace to him. The Holy Spirit covered him like a blanket would envelop a cold child. Love and joy fell upon him as if it were a waterfall from an unseen source above his head, thick and sweet as honey. He raised his hands toward heaven, and began to worship God as his load lightened.

* * * * *

Darlene sang the hymn to Char that morning before she left, and she couldn't get the tune out of her head. As she walked into the Portland penitentiary, where she would witness her husband's execution, she hummed it still.

Our fathers chained in prisons dark,
Were still in heart and conscience free.
How sweet their children's fate would be,
If we like them could die for Thee.
Faith of our fathers, holy faith, we will be true to Thee till death.

Her preborn child was just beginning to show. She rested her hands on her "baby bump" as she was led into the dark room where dozens of others sat and chatted about the demise of the Coalition. Sabina Manning, who had proudly watched the video footage of her husband sacrificing his life for the Gospel, accompanied her. She had been such a great source of comfort for Darlene through the death of two of her daughters and the capture of her husband.

The room was lit from the bright lights on the other side of the thick glass that made up one wall of the room. A table with straps that would hold the arms and legs of the condemned shone like a glowing cross. She looked into that cold, steel room and was saddened to think that her husband would not be able to look back at her. How she wanted to tell him that she loved him with all her heart, and that Charlotte loved him, and that very soon he would hold and kiss their daughters Mary and Johanna. How she wanted to explain to him that she would keep her faith in God and she would see him again in heaven soon.

Heaven.

She didn't long for heaven as much as she longed for heaven to come to earth. She didn't want to escape the evil around her as much as she wanted to conquer it with love. Heaven seemed so far away, but today she was here, and today she longed so dearly for the unhindered presence of God in her life. She wanted to embrace this lonely, condemned prisoner that would soon be injected with lethal poison and pour her love over him as the broken-hearted harlot wept her tears over the feet of Jesus and dried them with her hair. She so much wanted to show her husband how much she loved and admired him. She was so proud of him!

Her family was her Isaac and there was no ram in the thicket. With the deaths of two of her daughters and her husband within a week, she didn't know if her heart could survive the day. She felt like it would break open and spill out onto the ground as a sacrifice of praise to her Savior. Her grief was so deep, from marrow to skin. She kept her hope in the promise that her Father would not give her more than she could handle. She clung tenaciously to that promise as if it were her only raft in a merciless ocean deep and wide.

Sabina Manning knew how she felt. She wrapped her arms around Darlene's shoulders and tried to whisper comfort to her. All morning they both had sung praise to the Lord and read Scripture to each other, fighting to suppress the sobs that swelled in their throats, but now they could no longer hold it in.

Arlington, Virginia

After his final dose of medication at noon, James Knight developed sudden shortness of breath. He screamed for a guard.

"Guard!" Knight wheezed between hyperventilating breaths. "Guard! I can't breath…"

Vinny Molder rushed to the room to see Knight covered with hives. His black skin began to grow pink splotches right before his eyes. He tapped the radio on his hip. "James Knight's having an allergic reaction! Stretcher! Paramedics! Quick!" He hit a combination on a keypad on the side of Knight's cell, put his eye up to the camera for a retinal scan, then hit another combination to open the door. The door lock clanged open and the guard shoved the door into the recess in the wall. "Hang on, Jim!" He rushed to the side of the former congressman who lay on his back, gasping desperately for air.

The paramedics rushed to the room, lifted him onto the gurney, and gave James Knight an injection of epinephrine and a mask of oxygen as they wheeled him out of the room, through several metal doors toward an elevator. Vinny Molder tried to accompany the prisoner he had grown to appreciate to the clinic, but Molder's superior disallowed him from doing so.

Vinny stood motionless in front of the double doors that led down the hall to the elevator. He stared through the small window in the door as the paramedics pushed the stretcher into the elevator and repeatedly smacked the button to shut the door. "Come on, Jim, hang on."

The prison physician prepared James Knight for intubation even before he listened to his chest with his stethoscope. It was obvious he was going into respiratory failure, an anaphylactic response to a medication. His airway was swelling shut, and he had to intubate him fast.

"What medication was he given?" The physician reached for the intubation tube.

James Knight struggled against the RN who was attempting to insert an I.V. into his antecubital vain.

"I don't know." The guard who accompanied the prisoner to the triage typed into the computer that was in the room, trying to pull up his electronic medical record.

"Come on, get me that EMR!" the physician ordered. "How much epinephrine has he received?"

"One microgram one minute apart times three," an anxious paramedic responded.

The physician sedated, then intubated Knight, and hooked up the tube to the ventilator as he ordered the nurse to give the patient a dose of sedative and an antihistamine intramuscularly. Another nurse prepared an IV bag of steroids to be given as soon as IV access was obtained. The nurse aids were busy stripping his clothes with scissors and inserting a foley catheter into his bladder.

"Stat portable chest film, ECG, CBC, metabolic panel, liver functions, and tox screen," he shouted at the nurse who rushed from the room with three vials of blood. "Give me a CPK/MB and a troponin just in case…"

"B/P's 75 over 35. Pulse 121."

"Another microgram of epinephrine." The doctor had a peak at the EMR that flashed up on the computer screen as nurses and technicians fluttered about the patient, following the doctor's orders. "Get a depakote level too."

"Got it," a nurse announced as she left the room with the tubes of blood.

"Here's the ECG." A nurse handed him a sheet of paper.

The doctor took a deep breath as he studied it, and then announced, "I want everybody out of here!" The physician waved his arm across the room authoritatively as a nurse taped the intubation tube to Knight's face. "This patient's probably going to die. Let's give the former congressman some privacy."

The paramedics and guard who accompanied Knight to the triage center stepped away as one of the nurses pulled the curtain shut around him.

The superior in charge of all the political prisoners on Knight's wing made his way down to the clinic as soon as he heard of his allergic reaction. He wore a beige shirt with a black tie, and smelled of stale cigar smoke.

He stomped up to the guard who sat on a chair outside of where the physician was working on Knight. "What's the matter?" he snapped. "Where's the prisoner?"

"He's there," the seated guard pointed at the curtain with one arm. "They're working on him, but it doesn't look good. His face was so swollen."

"And you took your eyes off him?"

The guard shrugged and the superior charged up to the curtain, rapidly swung it to the right in time to see the physician pull the sheet up over the patient's head.

"Excuse me?" the physician shouted.

"Excuse me!" the superior retorted. "We're not supposed to take our eyes off this traitor. The president's given me that order personally."

"Well, rest content, sir. Unless you want to accompany him to the coffin, you're job's done."

The superior pulled back the sheet to have a look at the face of his most infamous prisoner. His face was swollen and the tape that held the intubation tube to his face contorted his features. Some green slimy substance was protruding from a tube the physician had inserted through the patient's nose into his stomach.

"He's dead?"

"If you'll excuse me, sir, I have other patients to tend to." The physician stomped from the room.

The prison director looked at the wristband on the patient and read it out loud, "James Knight. Allergies: penicillin – anaphylactic."

Meanwhile, on the other side of the curtain, another African American male was being bagged with oxygen as the nurse wheeled him on a gurney into a side elevator and pushed "B" on the elevator panel.

James Knight opened his eyes and reached for the tube that was in his throat. "Hold on," the nurse told him, grabbing his wrists, "hold on, Mr. Knight, I'll take it out." She peeled the tape off his face, retracted the air in the intubation cuff with a syringe, and then pulled the tube out of his throat.

James Knight gagged, sucked in a deep, coarse breath, and tried to sit up.

"You'll be all right," the nurse patted him on the back and smiled as she shoved the intubation tube into a red bag with the other hand. "Your chart said that you were allergic to penicillin, but I've never seen someone that allergic!"

"Oh God!" He coughed. "That almost killed me!"

"With God's help, the guards will think that the prisoner who died of congestive heart failure yesterday is you. Maybe your wife can sue the prison for giving you penicillin and y'all can retire in the Bahamas," the nurse said with a laugh.

"Great plan," James Knight wheezed, "but I have more important things to do than work on my tan. Please, tell me, ma'am, why'd you have to put a catheter in my bladder? I don't think my wife would approve."

The nurse smiled and pushed Knight back down on the cot as the elevator slowed at the appropriate floor.

"Remember, Mr. Knight," she whispered, "you'll have to stay motionless on this gurney until Dr. Patrick gets off duty and Dr. Nottingham comes on in about five minutes."

"And try to hold your breath once you're in the refrigerator," the other nurse added, "or when Dr. Patrick looks at you, he'll see the steam of your breath."

"Well, how am I supposed to know when he's looking at me?"

"And pray Dr. Patrick doesn't get started on an autopsy."

"What?!"

"Shh. Lie down."

"I cannot go into the legislature with this gown on. Do you have some clothes?"

The two nurses looked at each other inquisitively. That little detail had been left out of the plan they carefully contrived with the help of Josh Davis.

Knight coughed involuntarily as the elevator opened, revealing the pathologist, Dr. Patrick, waiting patiently at the door to take the expired patient to the proper refrigerated holding cell where the body would normally remain until delivered for burial, or until they received an order for autopsy. The nurse began to cough vigorously to make Dr. Patrick think it was she who had coughed.

"Coming down with the flu, are we?" Dr. Patrick pulled the gurney into the hall.

Boston, Massachusetts

"Good morning, fellow citizens of the United States of America." Margaret Brighton spoke into the microphone behind her elevated podium in the outdoor amphitheater. Thousands of Americans cheered and applauded her victory over the Coalition. All those held captive in the tight grasp of the religious totalitarians were finally truly free. Behind her was a large banner that read in bold letters, "Free Choice for All Americans."

"We can wave the flag of freedom proudly this beautiful morning!" The president smiled confidently as she held her palms out toward the audience, pretending to try to calm the cheers and vigorous applause. In reality, she lavished it. The war was over and she had won! The greatest American crisis since the Civil War had finally come to a satisfactory conclusion. The devastating terrorist attacks and natural disasters had suddenly become much more manageable, as had her PR image, as a result of the overwhelming victory. The congressmen who had spear-headed impeachment efforts were behind bars. The evidence proving that the Columbus bombing was accidental had been destroyed. The traitorous leaders of the nuclear-armed Coalition were either dead or about to die by lethal injection. The country was unified and her candidacy was thriving. The only Republican who had come near her in the polls had just suffered a carefully organized, media-magnified scandal in the Senate. The nearest third-party candidate, endorsed by the Libertarian and Constitution Parties, was suffering through a politically motivated IRS audit that was threatening prison. No political contestant came anywhere near her in the presidential race. It was five weeks until Election Day, and she was a shoo-in for the next four years.

"Thank you, thank you." She waited a few more moments as the applause slowed to a soft rumble. "Thank you. A great evil sought to tear our nation in two. Their weapon was hate. These fear-mongers hijacked the Christian religion and the Bible – a good book about a loving and tolerant rabbi named Jesus – to promote their terror and deceive millions of Americans into following them down the dead end street of their religious dictatorship. In doing so, they did not follow the example of the Jesus of the Bible, whom they claimed to adore. They threatened and terrorized gays, lesbians, and reproductive health practitioners. They murdered physicians, student protesters, and American soldiers. They played a role in the deaths of over 25 million Californians!" She paused to let the gravity of those numbers sink in before she issued the planned retraction. "We are not confident that the Coalition detonated the nuclear bomb that buried California under death and destruction last week," she said, correcting the misinformation she had propagated at her previous press conference. "That investigation is still ongoing. But we do know this. The Coalition tried to do this very thing, and failed. They would have done it if they could. Their leaders were present when the bomb was detonated, and when it finally happened, they rejoiced. Thank goddess" – Dena had urged her to take that out of the initial draft, but she kept it in – "that the very pit our enemies have dug for us is the very grave into which they have fallen!" Her fans clapped and cheered her poetry.

"The masterminds of the violent revolution that brought such death and destruction to our land have been defeated. The people of the 13 Coalition states have been liberated! Free choice is protected from sea to shining sea. The choices of women in crisis pregnancies will be secured, the sacred choices of gays, lesbians, bisexuals, and transsexuals will be forever solidified in the halls of government," she pronounced victoriously as the applause grew enthusiastic once again. "Tyrants of the world, take note!

"Our deepest gratitude goes to the Senate for its near-unanimous approval of my appointment to the Supreme Court, Vaughn Ben Jacob," she spoke loudly to be heard over the applause. "He is the first Jewish appointment as well as the first openly gay man to be appointed to the high court. He will be a prominent addition who will secure the right to choice for the next generation. I also thank the Senate for its approval of Barack Obama to the high court, the first foreign-born Muslim and first former president to ever make it to the High Court." The crowd began to applaud and the president lavished it. "Thank you, thank you!

"Our heartfelt gratitude also goes to the students, the pastors, priests, and rabbis who opposed the Coalition's perversion of religion, the legislatures of both parties who stood up against the hate, the physicians who refused to be intimidated by the threats and who continued to provide choices to women in crisis pregnancies, our homosexual friends who celebrated their diversity in spite of the terror, the American soldiers who spilled their blood that one nation, indivisible, of the people, for the people, and by the people, would not perish from the earth!" She spoke directly into the microphone to be heard over the uninterrupted applause.

"Thank goddess," she said with all the confidence and enthusiasm she could muster, "that the Coalition of Free Christian States is as dead as their false god. We have beaten them!" She thrust her pale fist into the air as the crowd of ten thousand joined her in a victorious cheer.

In the rear of the massive crowd gathered at the president's campaign stop stood two Secret Service agents. They, too, zealously applauded their president's most famous moment in the limelight.

One of them turned and said to the other, "She's wonderful, isn't she?"

The other stopped clapping and crossed his arms over his chest. "Invincible."

Between the feet of the second agent was a sewer drain, into which dirty water from a light rain two hours earlier trickled. As the drops fell, they struck the iron rung of a makeshift ladder that a construction crew had drilled into the sewer when it was made a century earlier. The drops thudded against the toe of a leather boot, worn by none other than Stein Seibert, still wearing his black beret with the Confederate flag ironed onto it.

For eight hours he held the strategic position, as motionless as possible, covered with black soot and mud, holding his bolt-action .223-caliber varmint rifle over his shoulder with a sling. He clung tightly to the rusty iron rung that stuck out of the moldy, cracked cement. He straightened his arms so he could pull away from the opening of the sewer drain as far as possible, lest the white of his eyes be seen by passers-by. His face was smudged with black. His eyes ceaselessly searched the crowd around the stage for any sign of his ultimate enemy. When the crowds began to grow thick, he quietly cocked his rifle and held it with his left hand.

Stein's muscles began to spasm and his back grew sore during the motionless wait on the iron rungs of the filthy sewer wall, but the memory of his brother being shot by federal agents energized him with hate as he waited and hoped.

He knew it was an unlikely opportunity, but with a decent chance of avoiding capture he had little to lose. The outdoor amphitheater left few clear shots of anyone on the stage from a sniping position this close to the ground. The sewer was the perfect hideout, about 175 yards away from the stage. And even if they saw the flash of the gun, they could not enter the sewer drain from the street. They would have to find the heavy circular iron door and pry it open with a bar, but they would find it firmly stuck, thanks to a tube-full of "Liquid Nails" glue. The feds would have to find another entrance further away and Stein would have time to make his getaway. A stolen motorcycle lay in a culvert covered with branches about three-quarters of a mile away.

The lawn in front of the platform was packed with people and he couldn't even see the stage, let alone, the president of the United States who was speaking behind the podium.

For a moment, he thought one of the S.S. agents who were posted directly in front of his sewer drain had spotted him. But all the agent did was bend down to straighten the cuff on his khakis.

Stein gasped at the stench that emanated from below him. How he hated that smell. *Focus,* he thought to himself. *Focus…*

There! A crack in the crowd of people exposed the podium. For a brief second, he saw the despised face. *There she is,* he thought, as the crowd closed again, concealing his enemy. *Come on, Stein!* he encouraged himself. *If it opens up again, you gotta' hit it...*

He pulled his rifle up to his chest, and was troubled to discover how his arms trembled from maintaining the same position for so many hours. He carefully extended the tip of the black barrel of his weapon between the legs of one of the S.S. agents, and brought the gun up to his shoulder. He gently pressed his cold, wet index finger against the trigger as he searched through the scope for the face of the despised wretch.

He carefully scanned the back of four or five heads, beyond which he knew his target was concluding her speech. *Come on, come on...*

President Margaret Brighton calmed the cheers with her outstretched arms. "I have finally chosen my vice president." She paused as the cheers and applause increased in intensity. "I have picked Terry Markison!"

There! A husband and wife parted about six inches and his target came into view. His held his breath as he tenderly squeezed the damp aluminum trigger.

The kick of the gun was greater than he expected. His fingers slipped on the grimy iron rung and he fell backward down the sewer hole. His head and shoulder hit the back of the four-feet diameter drain and then his upper torso swung forward toward the iron rungs. His head slammed the ladder as he fell, but he managed to get his arm over a rung and hold on tight. He gasped, the breath knocked out of him. He tried to position his feet on top of another rung below him to steady himself. His gun fell below him and struck the last iron rung on the ladder. He cursed his luck and wondered if his bullet had found his target.

The S.S. agents directly in front of the sewer drain jumped when they heard the gun blast. It sounded like it was right beside them! Each of them at first thought that the other agent had discharged his weapon. They unholstered their handguns as the crowds around them scattered. When they heard the clang of Stein's gun against the ladder, they knew that their culprit was directly underneath them.

"Find an entrance!" The senior agent took out his gun and pointed it down the sewer drain.

The younger agent notified their superiors and began to search around him through the rushing bodies of screaming, terrified citizens, for the circular iron door to the sewer system. He glanced at the stage to see the president disappear behind a crowd of Secret Service agents who covered her with their bodies.

The elder agent screamed through the sewer opening: “Freeze!” He pointed his .45-caliber handgun down it and fired three hollow point rounds blindly down the drain, grazing Stein’s shoulder.

Stein let out a scream, released his hold on the grimy ladder and fell 30 more feet. The six inches of sewer filth was not enough to break his fall. He fractured his neck on contact and drowned, his mouth and lungs filling with the putrid filth he so despised.

The S.S. agents who first made it to the president when they heard the gunshot thought she was all right. She stared off in the direction of the shot, and they pushed her to the ground, shielding her from the unseen assassin with their bodies. Moments later, when the assassin had been shot and the situation was under control, they pulled away from her long enough to ask her how she was doing. They saw that her eyes were fixed heavenward and her lips moved as if she were trying to speak.

“Madam President? Madam President?” one of the agents shook her gently. “We need to get her out of here.”

“Do you see any blood?” another agent inquired, concerned about the paleness in her face.

“Maybe she fainted,” another who knelt beside her suggested.

Another commented, “She’s moving, her lips are moving.”

The first agent tried to check her carotid pulse when he saw the bullet hole in the bottom of her throat. The speeding bullet hit the seventh cervical vertebra and shattered it into a dozen fragments, rupturing multiple blood vessels. Her wound did not bleed externally, but internal hemorrhaging rapidly filled her chest cavity with blood, compressing her lungs and hindering her respirations. She moved her lips as if to speak, but not a sound came out. A physician on site began CPR, but Margaret Brighton had already entered eternity.

Arlington, Virginia

“Put these on and follow me.” Dr. Nottingham tossed a janitor’s outfit at the gurney and turned to look out the window of the door of the refrigerated autopsy room to make sure no one was coming. “Hurry!”

Knight pulled the sheet off his face and sat up. There were four dead bodies covered with white sheets in the frigid room. A fifth, in the corner, lay partially covered on a metal table with his chest and scalp cut open.

The doctor turned around and walked quickly to Knight to remove the catheter, and Knight saw that his eyes were full of fear. “Fret not thyself because of evildoers,” he tried to comfort him. “It’s in the hands of God, brother.”

When the physician returned to the window in the door, he saw that the dead man posing as James Knight had just been wheeled in and was left in the hallway by a nurse. The secretary looked at the chart and appeared confused.

“Oh no! I knew this was a weak link in the plan,” Nottingham complained nervously. He looked back at Knight. “That secretary is not on our side.”

“The president’s dead?” Johnny Daffner held the phone tight against his ear, disbelieving the news.

The fellow physician repeated his dramatic announcement. “Yes, shot by a Coalition assassin.”

Daffner quickly tried to recall the constitutional prescription for leadership if a president died without a confirmed V.P. “What happens now?” he wondered aloud.

“All the country’s gone crazy, Johnny. How am I supposed to know?”

Daffner looked at the clock on his desk as he held the phone to his ear. “Where’s James Knight? He was supposed to be here ten minutes ago.”

“Did you not hear about James Knight?”

“No,” he replied. “What?”

“He’s dead.”

“Dead?” Daffner gasped. “James Knight is dead? How? How did he die? When?”

“He died this morning after an anaphylactic reaction to some new medicine you had prescribed. Internal affairs was supposed to interview you about it some time today.”

“What? We didn’t prescribe any new medication.” He stood up beside his desk and wiggled his computer mouse to bring his computer screen to life. “Who said that?”

“I heard it from Sue, who overheard the medical resident telling somebody on the phone.”

Dr. Daffner held the phone to his ear with his shoulder, and typed James Knight's name to find his EMR. "What medicine?"

"I snuck a peak at the chart myself and I couldn't tell. Couldn't read your writing. I saw that you had added something."

"Another pill of the same medicine, *not* another medicine!" He slammed the phone down, put his jacket on and rushed from the room to the end of the hall, around the corner to the elevator, and then down to the basement.

He burst out of the elevator into the basement. "Where is he?"

The pathologist's secretary was startled by the psychiatrist's strange behavior. "Who?"

"James Knight!"

"Uh, room three, there's some confusion on that subject, but Dr. Nottingham's cleared it up. Dr. Nottingham is in there with him now, and asked not to be disturbed."

"Oh, really?" Daffner marched down the hall and reached for the doorknob of room number three. "He asked not to be disturbed with a dead patient?" The secretary shrugged in response to the rhetorical question.

Wham!

The metal door swung open just as he began to pull it toward him, and it connected with Daffner's nose and jaw, and sent him reeling against the wall.

Dr. Nottingham stopped dead in his tracks in the hallway, frightened out of his wits at the sight of the psychiatrist's hemorrhaging nose. Knight peeked past him and saw Dr. Daffner leaning against the wall trying futilely to catch the blood from his nose into his hands. Daffner leaned forward to prevent getting blood on his shirt, then looked up at Nottingham with angry eyes. The psychiatrist looked past Dr. Nottingham and saw James Knight standing just inside the room's entrance, straightening the undersized prison outfit, swollen patches of hives still showing on the dark skin of his face.

Nottingham looked back at Knight. "Now what?"

Daffner took a step forward and pushed the young pathologist out of the way. "You're not going to skip out on our appointment, are you, Jim?" Daffner pulled out a handkerchief and pinched his nose with it. He glanced down the hall at the secretary, who just stepped into the hall to better see what was going on when she heard the collision between Daffner and door number three.

"Call security," Daffner breathed with a nasal tone, pinching his nose.

"No!" Dr. Nottingham turned to the secretary and ordered her. "Don't you dare touch that phone!"

James Knight calmly informed the psychiatrist, "Doc, you can give me a ride to Congress or we can tie you up in this room. The choice is yours."

Dr. Daffner wiped the blood from his chin and glanced down at the secretary, who appeared confused by Dr. Nottingham's outburst. Daffner raised his voice at the secretary, "What do you think you're doing, Janice? You think aiding and abetting traitors will be good for your career?"

"Aiding and abetting what? I have no idea what's going on."

Daffner pointed into the room. "That's James Knight! He's not dead. He's trying to escape."

Nottingham walked over to the secretary as Knight urged Dr. Daffner, "I'm going to Congress, Doc. If it doesn't work, I'll be right back here before dinner. What do you have to lose? You can even tell them I took you at knifepoint if you want. Or I can tie you up in here with the cold corpses. Either way, I'm going."

Nottingham walked back to Knight. "The secretary says she won't sound the alarm or notify anybody, but, to tell you the truth, I don't trust her. She's a progressive."

James Knight sighed and looked down at Daffner. "Ya' can't trust liberals, Dr. Nottingham. They are, by definition, liars. Tie them up together in here."

"Wait, wait," said Daffner. "I'll go with you. He can stay with her."

Knight cocked his head to the side and tried to discern the sincerity of the prison psychiatrist. He was skeptical of the sudden change in his demeanor. "Can I trust you, Doc?"

"Mr. Knight." Daffner paused and took a deep breath in and out of his mouth as he pinched his nose. "The president's been killed."

Knight blinked hard and his whole body jolted. "Killed?" His jaw dropped.

"Shot in the throat by a sniper's bullet. I was told it was a Coalition assassin."

Knight was stunned. What are the chances that she would be killed on the day of his attempt to escape and get into the halls of Congress to save the lives of those Coalition leaders scheduled for execution?

"What a coincidence, huh?" Daffner commented.

"It's no coincidence, Doc. Can you deny the timing is of God? I *have* to speak to Congress now!"

"Don't trust him, Mr. Knight," Dr. Nottingham warned.

"I'll take you right down the aisle." Daffner opened his sports coat and showed him a holstered .45 cal semiautomatic. "If I wasn't sincere, then I'd have already pointed this at you."

James Knight glanced at Nottingham, who protested, "If you were willing to help him anyway, why did you tell the secretary to call for security?"

After a moment of silence, Daffner responded, "Maybe it's because you broke my nose, Dr. Nottingham! I don't know." He shrugged and said, "They know that Jim and the other political prisoners here are innocent of any crime. They know they don't have psychiatric problems. I guess, I'm just tired of being the strong arm with chemical restraints for opponents of Brighton's political agenda. Her abuse of political opponents is, well, it's sickening." He lifted his downcast eyes and looked at Knight: "You weren't delusional or psychotic – I was ordered to do what I did to you, Mr. Knight, and I'm sorry. Now I'm violating those orders, and with Margaret Brighton dead, well, who knows, I may just get away with it. Maybe you'll succeed, and give us our country back."

"Come on," Knight said, reaching for and shaking Johnny Daffner's hand, "let's get out of here."

"You can't leave yet," Nottingham said.

"Why not?"

The elevator dinged and Nottingham shoved Knight and Daffner into the refrigerated room. He rushed toward the elevator, staring coldly at the secretary who studied the EMR of James Knight. There were two James Knights in front of her – one dead and one living – and two frantic physicians who took turns screaming at each other and giving her contradictory orders. Frankly, she was confused by it all. At this point, she just wanted to not offend either physician so she could keep her job.

The elevator opened and a janitor pushed out a covered linen rack, which carried clean towels and sheets. He left it in front of the secretary's desk. "I've got it," Nottingham said. The janitor nodded and stepped back into the elevator.

Enduring the suspicious glare of the secretary, he wheeled the linens past the gurney with the dead James Knight on it, down the hall into room number three. He threw back the nylon cover and they were shocked to see the image of a man curled up under a sheet on the upper rung of the rack.

"Come on out, Governor," said Dr. Nottingham. Henry Adams rolled his chubby frame off the rack and onto the floor with a grunt.

James Knight laughed. "Governor Henry Adams!"

"Shh," Nottingham warned, glancing through the door at the secretary. "Keep it down."

Knight reached down for the governor's forearm and helped him up. "They givin' you those anti-psychotics before bedtime, too?" Knight pinched a roll of fat on his mid-section, which had widened considerably since beginning his meds.

Henry Adams laughed and gave James Knight a bear hug, picking him up off the ground in doing so.

Another grunt came from the bottom level of the towel rack. Somebody sat up, hit their head, then the rack collapsed.

"Who's that?" Knight tried to recall the owner of the course facial features of the skinny man who stood to his feet in front of him. "Is that the sheriff of Bozeman? Is that Randy Woods?"

"And Robert Boniface!" Governor Adams exclaimed when he saw a second man roll off the lower level of the linen rack. "I didn't know you were under me. How'd y'all fit under there?" He laughed as he helped his pastor and press secretary, Robert Boniface, to his feet.

Sheriff Woods shook Representative Knight's hand with a broad, thin smile, while Boniface said, "The worst part of it was squeezing under there under constant threat of death from getting squished by Governor Adams."

Nottingham pointed to a back door in the refrigerated room. "This is our exit."

Daffner flicked on his laser finder for the high-speed race to the United States House of Representatives. On the way, he dialed the phone number Dr. Nottingham had given him.

Someone picked it up halfway through the first ring. "This is Ben. Can I help you?"

"I was told to tell you that we're on our way with four packages."

Josh Davis replied with a conniving grin, "Affirmative."

Washington, D.C.

When Dr. Johnny Daffner pulled into the secure parking garage behind the Capitol building in D.C., he looked in his rearview mirror and noticed a half a dozen vehicles were following him. *The troops,* he thought to himself.

"This is permit only parking, sir." The elderly security guard leaned out of his booth toward the vehicle.

Daffner looked behind him to see if Josh Davis, who he knew was in one of the vehicles behind him, was going to do something to get them past security. "Well, I, uh," mumbled Daffner, "I'm an officer and a psychiatrist in the United States Army."

"Fine," said the guard coldly. "If you can park here, then you must have a permit."

"I think I have a permit back here." Daffner stepped out of the vehicle and went around to the trunk. Daffner saw a redheaded fellow with wire-rimmed spectacles step out of the first vehicle behind him and start to walk toward him.

"You don't understand, sir," the 30-year veteran of Capitol Security sneered. "This parking lot is for congressmen and senators and their staff. Visitors should park a half a mile down there on the right, in the parking garage." The guard pointed down the road.

"There's lots of congressmen and senators back there," Daffner responded, motioning to the dozen cars behind him. "At least they were." Daffner acted as if he were prepared to open the trunk when the fellow with red hair put his hand on Daffner's arm and motioned for him to keep the trunk closed.

That's got to be Josh Davis, Daffner thought. *Hope he's got a plan to get past security.*

"I need a favor, Officer Armstrong," Josh Davis said as he walked up to the security officer and read his nametag. He stretched out his hand as if to shake his, but the skeptical security guard did not reciprocate. Instead, he took one step back toward his booth and reached for the phone.

"Is that Vance Armstrong?" came the muffled cry from inside the trunk. James Knight started banging on the trunk hood, startling the security officer. Even Josh Davis was at a loss of what to do.

"Let me out of here!" Knight shouted as he banged on the hood. "Vance, it's me!"

Dr. Daffner looked at the redheaded man with a shrug as if waiting for instructions.

"Well, let him out," Davis suggested to Daffner. Davis turned to the security guard. "We have an old friend here to see you, Officer Armstrong."

The officer had a natural suspicion of anything that violated routine, and took this strange turn of events as a trap. He stepped back into his booth, unsnapped his holster with his right hand, and punched a number on the phone with his left.

"No, no, no," Davis said with outstretched palm. "Wait!"

The security guard brought the phone to his face with a paranoid frown.

Daffner popped the trunk and offered a hand to James Knight, who stepped out and smiled at the security officer.

"Jim!" the security guard smiled cheerfully.

The officer's superior spoke into the phone, "Yes?"

"Sorry, sir. False alarm." Davis sighed with relief as the security officer hung up the phone and walked toward his old friend to shake his hand. "Oh Jim! I can't believe it's you!" As they exchanged greetings, Daffner and Josh Davis shook hands and made brief introductions.

"What in the world are you doing here?" The security guard's courteous tone relieved those in the cars behind them as they rolled down their windows to listen to their conversation. "Did they drop the charges? Why are you still in prison uniform?" He glanced at the thin line of black skin under the lower edge of the undersize prison shirt on James Knight.

Knight grinned as he tried to pull his shirt a little lower over his love handles. "It's a long story, Vance. Some of my captors have dropped charges," he said, glancing at Daffner, "but not all."

"I recognize that face," Vance said when he caught a glimpse of the second man stepping out of the trunk. "Henry Adams, the Texas hero! Oh my goodness!" The security guard smiled and walked up to Governor Adams to shake his hand as if he were a hero raised from the dead. Woods and Boniface stepped out of the car, and the guard shook his head and blinked hard, as if trying to shake himself out of a strange daydream. "Do you mind telling me what's going on around here?"

"Vance," Knight said, with an earnest look on his face, "I need to get into the floor of the House and I need you to help me do it."

Josh Davis and James Knight looked at each other frightfully for a moment, oblivious of the destiny to which these actions swiftly moved them. All their eggs were in one basket – it was all or nothing today.

* * * * *

Since the death of the Secretary of State Beth Randolph and the Speaker of the House Rich Faulkner in the nuclear explosion in California, all of Congress had been in an uproar. The Constitution designated the Speaker of the House to be sworn in as president if the president died without a confirmed V.P., and if the Speaker was dead, the secretary of state was to assume the presidency. Before the president was assassinated, the debates were already heated over who would be the next Speaker; the interim Speaker, an 85-year-old aging congressman of failing health, refused the honor. With the loss of the president, the secretary of state, and the Speaker all in one week, the contention was completely unmanageable. Since they were without explicit constitutional instructions on what to do and the balance of partisan power depended on the outcome, courtesy had been thrown to the wind in an all-out constitutional and ideological wrestling match about what to do.

The majority Republicans preferred, of course, to vote on the next Speaker, who would then be promoted to president until the elections. The Democrats didn't want to lose the executive branch, so they preferred to first vote on the V.P. nominee Terry Markison, the former economics prodigy for Texas governor Henry Adams who helped the FBI overthrow Texas' leadership and set up martial law. As V.P., Markison would ascend to the presidency until the elections and, if his attorneys succeeded in their plea before the High Court to have an exception to the filing deadline, he could run a strong write-in campaign and still be elected president. The poll numbers of the leading Republican candidate for president, a RINO senator wilting under scandalous fraud allegations, were dismal. The conservative Republicans were fearful of nominating Markison because he was likely to follow the gay agenda's model for executive leadership, which meant one-child-per-family policies, forced abortion of unlicensed children, the legalization of consensual pedophilia, government control over all means of production, full implementation of the Kyoto treaty, longer prison sentences for those convicted of "hate-speech," and more tax-subsidized abortion and sodomy.

The moderates of both parties, appealing to the sentiment of having lost two visionary presidents in six months, insisted that the House exercise its authority under Article 12 of the Constitution to appoint someone as president who could more faithfully fulfill the vision that Fitzgerald and Brighton held, without the extreme nuances of an effeminate gay man like Terry Markison who would alienate the Democratic Party from its grassroots. They argued that if the House appointed a president and the Senate appointed a vice president, then the Democratic Party could then elevate a candidate who would likely be the best choice to win the upcoming election. The Democrats knew that with Markison as president, their chances of keeping a tight grip on the executive branch would shrink considerably.

The top-ranked Republican leader in the House, Lloyd Borders, had no aspirations of anything except retirement. At this point, he didn't even want to be a congressman. The stress of the circumstances and the sleepless nights were combining to make his life absolutely unbearable. First, it was President Fitzgerald's crazy agenda and then his untimely death, which passed that agenda down to a V.P. delusional enough to put wheels on Fitzgerald's hot air. Then came the terrorist attacks to fan the flames of Brighton's disarmament campaign. Then came the secession of Texas and South Carolina and the constant bloody conflict under martial law, which resulted in the deaths of more than 500 civilians and 75 soldiers, plus the disappearance of at least 3,500 Americans presumed to be incarcerated and subjected to torture at dozens of UN-guarded FEMA facilities. Then it was the secession of the Coalition states, the failed federal invasion, the nuclear detonation in California and the subsequent tsunamis and earthquakes that stole away his sleep and made him want to move to Belize. He could sense that the country was under a divine judgment from which he could not flee. When the Speaker of the House died in the California explosion, he was handed a baton he'd rather not have. As if that wasn't enough, the president foolishly chose as her V.P. an openly gay man who helped bring down the popular Texas governor. As fighting words heated up yet again in the House, Floyd Borders put his head in his hands in despair.

Never since the founding of our nation had the Congress and the nation been more in need of morally upright leadership, and never had it been so far out of reach. If they had asked his opinion on the matter, he would have recommended trashing the whole federal government and starting over – he was losing faith in the United States of America. His gut instinct was to try to dissolve Congress, dismantle the federal government, and return 100% of the power back to the states. Absolute power had corrupted absolutely. The federal government was broken beyond repair, and remained the greatest threat to the liberties of the people. The Constitution had been ignored or twisted by the federal government for so long that it simply had no meaning. The system just didn't work anymore. The American experiment failed when its leaders became immoral, when the Creator and the Constitution had been so utterly abandoned.

Maybe James Knight was right...

The gasp throughout the House was audible as Knight, in prison clothing, walked onto the floor from the side door of the House. When Henry Adams followed him into the assembly, one female rep from New York fainted. Behind Governor Adams came Sheriff Randy Woods, Robert Boniface, and a handful of copperhead congressmen from the Coalition states. State leaders from the Coalition followed close behind in more formal attire. James Knight stood behind the microphone in the front of the House while those who followed him stood in two lines behind him, facing their former colleagues.

The ambitious minority whip smelled a rat. "What is the meaning of this?" McGinnis stood and stomped furiously.

"Hello, Representative Borders," Knight greeted the Republican whip who presided over the House debate. "May I address the House?"

Josh Davis held his breath at the back of the room, preparing for a quick get-a-away if things went south or if someone recognized him. He had prayed so hard for enough members of Congress to be sufficiently sympathetic with Knight's cause that they would allow him a minute or two to make his case. *Oh God, make it happen! Help us now...*

Several identified James Knight in spite of the unusual orange prison outfit; they walked up to him to greet him with a handshake or a hug. Two dozen reps stood and approached the congressmen from the Coalition states, fellow reps who had been censored from the assembly when their states seceded.

The elderly Congressman Borders felt dizzy for a moment. He took a deep breath to fight off the sensation of a panic attack. *Could this actually be happening?* He could not trust his senses. How did these men, who were imprisoned for hate crimes and treason the last time he heard, who were in straight jackets on anti-psychotic medication according to a CNN report last week, wind up on the floor of the House the very day of the president's tragic assassination?

At first, the whispering and mumbling of the representatives that filled the House started out as a small roar, and then gradually escalated until there was shouting and bickering. It was chaos! Everyone waited for the new Speaker Lloyd Borders to slam the gavel and bring order to the assembly, but he appeared indecisive. Then it was as if a dam broke.

The elderly democrat and Ethics Committee chairman, Theo Jefferson, stood up on his chair and then his desk and began to clap. The applause encouraged many and was contagious – it spread through the building, shocking the progressives who were furious at Theo Jefferson's public approval of these hate crime outlaws and traitors. Those who did not applaud with Jefferson shouted at the Speaker, Lloyd Borders, insisting on a measure of decorum befitting the House of Representatives.

"Excuse me! Excuse me!" The senior Democrat in the House, Representative McGinnis, screamed in disdain at the conservatives who applauded around him. "This is inappropriate!"

Borders, still in a state of shock, was somewhat impressed with the courtesy James Knight showed him in politely asking for permission to speak. He reluctantly nodded at the former Congressman from Wyoming.

"You're not going to let him speak, are you?" McGinnis stepped into the aisle and pointed critically at Knight. "This is outrageous!" McGinnis uttered a curse word, jolting the new Speaker.

Lloyd Borders pointed the gavel at McGinnis and ordered him, "Your foul tongue is what is outrageous! Silence that potty-mouth! I've given him permission to speak." McGinnis was clearly shocked by Border's tolerance of this disruption, but sufficiently intimidated that he held his peace.

"McGinnis is right," a Rhode Island Republican, who was second in command in the House GOP, commented. "A guest has no right to speak unless he is sponsored by an active member of the House. If you don't want to follow the rules, you shouldn't be Speaker…"

Lloyd Borders dropped his head into his hands, aghast at the cannibalistic vipers in the House, always eating the weak in their lust for power. He was sick of it. He'd drop his gavel and retire right then and there if it weren't for the fact the Rhode Island Republican would pick it up after he left.

"I will represent James Knight!" A rep stood and raised his hand.

"He can talk on my clock!"

Dozens of representatives held their hands aloft and James Knight smiled at their courtesy.

"It must be requested 24 hours in advance," McGinnis announced. "Speaker! If you defy the rules that give this body its order and clout, you will render the legislature's decisions illegitimate. Our actions will not stand in a court of law!"

"His name was placed in the register yesterday!" shouted a rep from Oregon, one of the reps strongly sympathetic with the Coalition who, at the urging of Josh Davis, managed to jot the request into the register the day before without anyone noticing. "Go check it out if you want."

Lloyd Borders glanced at the register beside him, regretting his failing eyesight. "It's here, Mr. McGinnis," he said, lifting the book aloft. "Now, sit down!" Since Faulkner's death, Borders had hated to flex his authority in the House for fear of offending a colleague, but this was one time he enjoyed raising his voice at a fellow congressman.

Knight smiled at the Speaker and turned to the nation's representatives: "I humbly request my former colleagues in the House to do one urgent thing immediately. Grant amnesty to the political and military leaders who were condemned by a military tribunal and are due to die by lethal injection. The Constitution plainly calls Brighton's military tribunals unconstitutional for United States citizens, and international law calls these executions illegal for non-citizens, so either way, it is unlawful to execute these men. Until the new president is sworn in, the House has the power to act for the executive branch. I implore you to pardon them, and all those good people who have—"

"Oh, for heaven's sake! Mr. Speaker!" McGinnis stood up, interrupting Knight's passionate plea. "Please spare us this traitor's sermonizing."

"Be quiet!" a representative beside McGinnis shouted. The verbal boxing matches and partisan wrangling that had characterized communication in the House commenced afresh.

"Order!" Borders shouted as he slammed his gavel down in vain.

As McGinnis began to curse James Knight and the Coalition, Texas Governor Henry Adams stepped out of his line and marched up to McGinnis as if to get physical with the minority whip.

Sheriff Woods rushed between the two and told Adams, "Don't do anything rash, Governor."

"Get this cowardly traitor out of my face!" McGinnis shouted at them before cursing Henry Adams to his face. Henry Adams just glared at McGinnis as if he would punch him.

However, Randy Woods beat him to the draw. Having had enough of McGinnis' vulgarity, he turned and landed a right hook square in the jaw! Half of the House gasped in horror and the other half cheered. McGinnis hit the ground and moaned as he held his bruised face. McGinnis' young female aid rushed to his side to tend to him, showing more affection for him than should be expected.

"Watch your foul language with kids in the room," Woods said while gesturing to the young aid that tended to him. If McGinnis could speak, he would have called for a sergeant at arms, but Sheriff Woods' right hook really rang his bell.

"Don't you see what's happening in our nation?" Henry Adams shouted as he looked around him. "We have forsaken the God of our forefathers! We have shed innocent blood in our land and persecuted God's people! We need to repent!"

"Please," James Knight begged, "hear me out. If we want to save the lives of these American heroes who are being unjustly killed, we must act quickly."

"I make a motion," a bold rep beside James Knight suggested, "that we vote James Knight to be acting Speaker until election-day." Knight turned, and saw Chandler from Montana raising his right hand before repeating the motion. "James Knight is a national hero. He is worthy to be acting Speaker until the election. The Constitution would then declare him acting presid—"

The room erupted with shouts of protest and whispers.

"Are you kidding?!" McGinnis shouted. "You can't make a motion, Mr. Chandler, because you're not even a part of this esteemed body anymore! You have been censored."

"Montana is back in the Union, and I am a representative in good standing."

"Under investigation. Not in good standing!" McGinnis slowly stood to his feet, keeping his aid between him and the wild-eyed Montana Sheriff Randy Woods.

"And innocent until proven guilty!" Chandler shouted back.

"These men are all traitors," McGinnis said, standing to his feet and backing away from the stout governor of Texas and the Bozeman sheriff. "They're barbarians! Section 3 of Amendment 14 says no one who has ever been a traitor to this nation can serve in office ever again. And you want to make him president? Are you mad?"

"But section 3 also says that the House of Representatives can remove this disability with a majority vote," Bo Bennett from Texas rebutted.

This was a turn of events that Knight did not expect. *Me, the acting president of the United States? I'm an escaped convict in a bright orange prison uniform and they want to make me acting president?*

The arguments grew heated again and there was tremendous disorder in the House, so much so that Borders stood at his podium and continued to slam his gavel repeatedly. It appeared that most of the conservatives were willing to give Knight the reigns of the executive branch for one month until Election Day, just out of respect for his courage and integrity. A representative from New York called the police to come arrest the escaped convicts, but when they saw the heated discussion on the floor with Henry Adams and James Knight in the front, the officers waited in the rear of the room out of respect. The chief of security called the military prison to see if the alleged traitors had been reported escaped, but someone who had witnessed the event being played live on television had already notified military prison officials. An elite FBI squad was already descending upon the House.

Knight had to act quick. Lives were on the line and they were about to be returned to prison. He surprised them all by projecting his voice directly into the microphone. "I do **not** accept the nomination to be Speaker!" The room grew silent again. Knight turned and looked back at the elderly interim Speaker of the House, Lloyd Borders. "The only way a transition will be acceptable to the people under these circumstances is if we choose a *Democrat* to be the Speaker." The Republicans gasped, having never guessed that James Knight would dare propose that.

"We must drop our partisan lust for power and do what is best for the country," Knight told his Republican colleagues from the Coalition states, who stood faithfully behind him. They were stunned that he would consider nominating a Democrat for the Speaker when that Speaker would immediately fill the shoes of the executive branch. Knight looked back at Borders, who could not believe his ears. "I nominate Theo Jefferson, Democratic chairman of the Ethics Committee, for Speaker of the House and acting president." Instantly, the House erupted in an uproar of cheers.

The white-haired Theo Jefferson stood up from his seat, shocked. He couldn't believe his ears. Here he was with a ten-point deficit in the polls in his solidly democratic Arkansas district, thanks to his about-face support for James Knight and his impeachment efforts. Now, on the day of the president's assassination and the closing moments of the second revolutionary war, the most prominent religious conservative in the House was supporting *him* – a senior democrat – for president of the United States! His fellow democrats had always admired Jefferson for his virtue in spite of his insane support of Knight's partisan impeachment drive, which they always attributed to the elderly rep's senility. They were as shocked as he was.

Ken McGinnis plopped to his seat, speechless. Here he was in the most precarious political position of his life. How could he protest Knight's sacrificial proposal? Liberals shouted out enthusiastically in favor of the nomination, because they knew he would be the perfect presidential candidate in one week, and with this nomination from James Knight, how could the conservatives object? As a matter of fact, if Knight were restored to favor in the House, Theo Jefferson's candidacy would even be stronger.

"I nominate you on the condition, Theo," said Knight with a hand outstretched toward him, "that you let Americans be judged in civilian courts by independent juries, not with military tribunals. Accept their right to free speech and their right to dissent. Though many in your party might object to our faith now, I pray that you will not silence us with tyrannical force, as has your predecessor. Earn the admiration of the country and govern in the fear of God, who will, sooner or later, hold you accountable."

Theo Jefferson nodded at James Knight, and with trembling voice and tear-filled eyes, exclaimed, "You have my word, James Knight." Many of the Democrats clapped in response, enthusiastic that their chances of keeping a Democratic executive were just resurrected.

Knight turned to the objecting Republicans behind him: "If Christ has free reign in our hearts and the Gospel has free reign in our land, then we *will* win back our freedoms. No earthly ruler can resist God's will if the remnant will be found faithful to speak the truth and pray heaven to earth."

"This is not legal, because you cannot nominate!" a rep from California shouted out. "You're not a member in good standing, Mr. Knight."

Ken McGinnis surprised everybody when he stood and waved his arms to quiet the crowd. His voice bellowed, "I nominate to accept James Knight back into Congress, as a member in good standing." This brought a roar of approval from the entire Congress. Knight smiled broadly, tears of joy filling his eyes, at the Democratic leader's proposal.

The leader of the FBI SWAT squad heard the minority leader's announcement, and ordered his men to hold their positions at every exit from the chamber. Their presence cast an eerie shadow on their proceedings.

Lloyd Borders smiled for the first time since the death of the previous Speaker. "I make a motion for a voice vote," he said.

A dozen reps simultaneously exclaimed, "I second it!"

"All in favor of restoring the reps of the Coalition states as members in good standing, pardoning them for all hate-speech crimes and treason charges, say 'Aye!'" he proposed as the House resounded with their votes. "All opposed?" Very few "nays" were heard at all.

"As a member of this House in good standing," said Knight, "I nominate Theo Jefferson to be the new Speaker, and pray His blessings upon him as our acting president."

"I second!" shouted hundreds of congressmen simultaneously.

The Congress began to clap and cheer the compromise. The elderly Borders turned to James Knight. "I've got to get a roll call vote for this vote."

Missoula, Montana

A clang on the iron door reminded David Jameson of his date with death. He concluded his prayer and turned toward the door, his eyes sensitive to the light, thanks to a throbbing headache that refused to subside. The shuffle at the door of the cell came from five soldiers with somber frowns. They opened his door and stepped dutifully into his room, one with cuffs for his hands and another with shackles for his feet. He embraced those chains without protest. He closed his eyes, recalling how many heroes of the faith throughout the ages had to bear such bonds and endure such shame. He was carrying a cross that the Savior carried. The thought came with a burst of joy in his heart. Blessed, indeed, he was to be counted worthy to walk this path. He couldn't wait to cast his martyr's crown before the feet of the Savior.

They shackled his wrists and hands and then one walked before him, two beside him, and two behind him as they led him down the hall. "Dead man walking," one of them mumbled, prompting the others to break out in muffled cackles. They turned a corner, down a long hall, then around another corner. David's chains danced to the cadence of the guards' footsteps all the way to a hall where several other prisoners were held, their hands dangling through their bars into the hallway. They watched him pass in silence.

"Dead man, comin' through," the soldier in front announced, this time in a somber tone.

Jameson refused to be discouraged by the ominous ritual. "Dead to sin and alive to God. Risen to walk in newness of life." His cheerful declaration prompted 'hoorahs' from the on-looking prisoners.

"Long live the Coalition!" one brave prisoner shouted.

Another began the chant “No King but King Jesus!” and it caught on until the whole prison was bursting with the cheer. “No King but King Jesus!”

He was led away through another large metal door that was opened by a guard unseen to his eyes. He traversed a maze of hallways and doors until he was led into a room with dull steel walls and a guard in each corner. He was turned to face a large mirror on the wall and was pushed backward until his back was tight against a table that was hydraulically raised to meet him. His shackles were removed. His arms and legs were strapped to the vertical table.

From out of the blue, the thought occurred to David that his wife might be on the other side of that mirror. Oh, if he could only see her face again! “Are there witnesses on the other side of that glass?” David asked. One of the guards who inserted the intravenous line into David’s outstretched arm nodded without making eye contact.

Darlene Jameson wept when she saw her bruised and bandaged husband limp to the table and allow himself to be strapped in. He looked so much worse than when she last saw him on the day of their daughters’ funeral. She patted her eyes with tissue in an attempt to conceal her grief from those around her who took pleasure in the execution of the surviving Coalition leaders. She saw David speak with a soldier, and she wondered what they were talking about.

Then, he looked at her! For a moment, she thought he saw her. Then his eyes roamed back and forth along the length and breadth of the glass. He couldn’t see her through the mirrored, inch-thick glass. His face was earnest, as if he searched for her features through the reflection. She studied his bruised, swollen, and lacerated face. His right eye was bandaged, his lip was swollen, and he had many excoriations on his face, neck, and arms – she wondered with dread what kind of attack must have caused those fresh injuries. How she wished she could whisper comforts into his ear and caress his wounds.

Then she saw his lips move, slowly and methodically so as to be understood.

I love you. Darlene, I love you.

It was unmistakable! He spoke to her.

Sabina Manning saw it, too. “Oh, God bless him,” she mumbled as she put her hand on Darlene’s shoulder. Tears welled in her eyes and her voice cracked with emotion, "God is so, so good." She knew David's words were just what Darlene needed.

Darlene's tears flowed freely now. She stood and slowly moved down from the last row of movie-theater-like seats until she was standing directly in front of the glass. She ignored the sneers from those in the shadowy room around her and she knelt down and put her palms on the glass. Through her dainty fingers, she watched a tear flow down her husband's bruised cheek. "I love you, too," she whispered. "I'll see you soon, my love."

Lethal injection occurs in two stages. First, a toxin is injected into the criminal through an intravenous line that causes paralysis of all of the muscles. The criminal appears to fall asleep and stop breathing. Then, a toxin that stops the heart is injected.

"Pray for me," David said out loud as he gazed at the mirror. He hoped beyond hope that one of the soldiers in the room knew the Lord, and could whisper a prayer for him. "Pray for my wife and my little girl."

Darlene read her husband's lips. "Oh God!" she cried out loud. "Give peace to my husband. Accept him with open arms into your kingdom. Bless him, Lord, give him peace." Others in the darkened room grew disturbed by her public proclamations of affection and her loud prayers for this despised terrorist and traitor. She leaned forward and pressed both of her palms against the wall and wept aloud. "Oh God," she began to cry hysterically.

Sabina Manning, with her arm over her shoulders, squeezed her tightly. "Shh. It's all right, Darlene."

"I'm not giving up on him!" she snapped without turning her gaze from David. "Save him, Lord! Let him live! Let not his enemies triumph over him…" She was praying for a miracle. What did she have to lose?

One of the women who were present to witness the executions grew sympathetic with the grieving woman. She pitied this poor woman. She walked over to Darlene and sat beside her. She patted her on the shoulder. "I'm sorry," she whispered.

Darlene wiped the tears off her burning eyes and tried to settle her emotions. She stared into her husband's face as the color drained and his eyes dimmed. David's eyes closed completely as the first injection concluded and the chief executioner gave the order to commence the second.

"No! No!" Darlene screamed now, absolutely terrified at the thought of losing him. "No! You can't kill him! It's wrong!"

She suddenly stood up, pushed Sabina away, and rushed to the door. She flung it open, banked right out the door and ran headlong into two security guards who guarded the entrance to the execution room. Taking them by surprise, she was able to push one of them away and wiggle the locked doorknob to the execution room.

"No!" she screamed. "Stop it! You can't kill my husband! He's innocent!" She sobbed as one of the guards wrapped his arms around her waist and pulled her away from the door and thrust her against the wall.

"Stop, lady!"

"Don't kill him!"

The attention of the executioners around David turned to the commotion outside the door, but David did not move. His breathing had stopped completely.

"Please!" Darlene pleaded with the two guards as they pressed her shoulders against the wall.

Inside the room, the senior guard motioned for another to begin the second injection into the IV line to stop the traitor's heart.

A soldier rushed down the hall with a sat phone and pressed a code into a keypad beside the metal door.

"What is it?" the guard who held Darlene at bay asked him.

"It's the attorney general."

The metal door flung open and the soldier rushed into the room. "Phone call from the attorney general! It's urgent!"

"Attorney general?" He had a confused look on his face as he reached for the cordless satellite phone. "Of the United States?"

The guard nodded. "Why didn't you answer your phone?" the soldier glanced at the phone on the wall.

"It didn't ring," the senior executioner said as he took the sat phone that the subordinate handed him, and he put it to his ear. "This is Captain Peoples." After a pause, he said, "Yes sir. Immediately sir." He handed the phone back to the soldier and announced, "Don't give the second injection!" He raised a hand at the guard who was responsible for giving the injections.

The guard shrugged. "It's done."

"Well, stop it!" Captain Peoples stepped over to the clear plastic IV tubing that led to the needle in Jameson's arm and he pinched it shut.

Through the partially open door, Darlene watched her husband's face transform into a deathly bluish hue. Sabina had stepped out into the hallway to try to comfort Darlene, but the officers pushed her away and told her to go back into the room. She stood in the doorway and watched Darlene's pitiful pleading for them to save her husband.

"What's going on?" the soldier holding Darlene in the hallway asked.

"The Coalition traitors have all been pardoned," Captain Peoples announced.

"Pardoned?" Darlene was ecstatic. "He's been pardoned?" She wiped her tears and turned to the guard that pressed her shoulders against the wall. "Let me go! He's been pardoned."

"Pardoned by the new acting president." Captain Peoples shrugged, flabbergasted with the hastiness of the executive order demanding their immediate execution and the equally perplexing speed with which it had been cancelled.

The guard who grabbed Darlene around the waist was shocked. "That can't be."

"Hurry!" Darlene told the lead executioner, "Resuscitate him!" The guards that held her in the hall released her as the chief executioner checked David Jameson's carotid artery for a pulse. Another guard removed the IV line from David's arm as quickly as possible.

"Call the paramedic team," the captain ordered.

Darlene ran to her husband's side and cried his name. "David! Please! Oh, Jesus, save him!" The others simply stood around the room, wondering what to do. They had never tried to resuscitate a criminal who received a lethal injection, and expected a paramedic team to come rushing into the room to do it for them. Darlene stood and gave her husband two breaths, then began chest compressions on him. "Come on!" she screamed at the dumb-founded soldiers who stood around her. "You heard the Attorney General! Save him! Save him! What are you waiting for?"

"How much of the second injection did he get?" the chief executioner asked.

The guard responsible for giving the injections bent down to check the machine. "All of it, but you pinched the tubing. I don't know."

Darlene brought her fist down hard upon her husband's chest over his heart two times. His eyes were half shut, and his face was cool and pale. "Oh God! You can do this!" She gave him two more breaths and began chest compressions again. "Your wife loves you! Charlotte needs her Daddy! Come on!" His body jolted with her compressions. He was completely unresponsive. She glanced at the man who presided over the execution. “Where are those paramedics?”

“They’re coming, but…” He tenderly stepped over to her and put a palm on her shoulder. “You’re husband’s dead.”

She thumped his chest once more. “No! I’m not giving up! I’m never giving up, God! Come on, David! Your people need you! We need you!”

“Stop for a sec!” he ordered Darlene.

“No!”

“Stop!” he shouted. “I want to check for a pulse.” He pushed her away and felt for a carotid pulse. The room was deathly silent except for Darlene’s rapid breaths. She gazed into his half-closed sullen eyes and saw no life in him. Nothing.

Sabina Manning stepped into the room and walked to Darlene’s side. She put her arm around her. Darlene looked up at her friend, tears streaming down both of their faces.

“I’m sorry,” Sabina whispered.

“No,” Darlene mumbled. “No.” She leaned down and put her ear to David’s chest, listening carefully for any heartbeat. “God, bring him back...”

Bighorn Canyon State Park, Montana

Governor Ben Boswell was led down a deer path to the entrance of a large, well-guarded, drab-green army tent deep in the forest. He was wet, tired, and hungry. He had spent two days hiding in the woods after barely escaping the explosion at the Bighorn Canyon Resort. Three-fourths of the Coalition leaders perished in the explosion. Of those who survived, several of the severely injured expired in the chilly night air as they took refuge in the forest.

After two days of trying to survive in the untempered Rockies, a low-flying Coalition helicopter had caught their attention. With a mirror angled to reflect the sunlight, Boswell managed to attract the pilot’s attention and facilitate their rescue.

The pilot of the helicopter filled them in on all that had happened in the country since the explosion: the assassination of President Brighton, the restoration of James Knight to Congress, and the pardon of the Coalition leaders who had been sentenced to death.

Boswell did not look surprised. Ever since the explosion, he felt like God held a force field around him, protecting him from harm. God was at the steering wheel of the Coalition of Free Christian States, and Ben Boswell was at peace.

At the entrance to the camouflaged Army tent, Jack Handel stood with a pistol holstered at his waist and an M-16 slung over his shoulder. Barry Friar sat in a lawn chair on the other side of the entrance. They saw Ben Boswell approach and hastened to him. "It's so good to see you, Governor Boswell," Jack Handel said as he shook his hand.

The gray-bearded Barry Friar gave his friend a full hug. "Oh Ben! Thank God you made it."

Jack motioned to the entrance of the tent. "Come in. Let me introduce you to some brothers."

Before they entered the tent, Barry Friar's son came sprinting down the path, bypassed Ben Boswell, and threw himself into his father's arms.

"Marion?"

Barry pulled him away and looked into his eyes. "Marion!"

"Oh, Dad!" They hugged and wept for several moments as dozens of liberated political prisoners made their way down the deer path toward the large tent.

"The Coalition freed us when they took over Iowa prison systems!"

"Praise God!" Barry responded, his chin trembling with joy as tears drifted down his cheeks into the maze of his gray beard.

Barry and Marion led Governor Boswell and Jack Handel into the tent, followed by the other surviving Coalition leaders. Boswell was immediately taken aback to see that half of the thirty leaders in the tent looked oriental. There were a dozen Montana state reps, plus several local pastors. Four screens were set up on one end of the room, hooked up to battery-powered laptops where technicians were busy getting other state leaders online for the important meeting with the surviving Coalition leaders.

Barry Friar grabbed the Coalition Chairman's elbow. "Governor, meet the Ambassador from China, Zao Zisheng." Governor Boswell noticed that the ambassador's left hand was shriveled and contracted, with several fingers missing.

The ambassador extended his right hand toward the governor and smiled so widely that his eyes disappeared in narrow slits. "Governor Boswell," he said in perfect English, "I bring word from China's Prime Minister. The resources of our nation are at your service as long as the Coalition of Free Christian States continues to remain free and Christian."

Tears of joy drifted down the unshaven governor's cheeks as he shook the Chinese ambassador's hand. "Oh brother, how else can we be free but through Christ?" The handshake turned into a hug.

"We're going to rule and reign with Christ forever, Brother Boswell," Ambassador Zisheng said, pulling away and looking into the Montana governor's eyes. "But we needn't wait until then. Let His kingdom come, and let His will be done, on earth as it is in heaven."

"Amen," Boswell responded.

"Amen," Barry and Jack simultaneously affirmed the ambassador's comments.

"Amen."

Portland, Oregon

"Hey!" The prison guard startled Elijah, who was reading a Gideon Bible on the floor of his solitary cell.

"Good day, sir," Elijah responded with an unexpected smile.

"You're free." The guard opened the doors and motioned for Elijah to follow him out.

Elijah thought the guard was playing a joke on him. "Don't kid me like that, man. Three hours ago you told me that I was going to meet my Maker by noon."

"For real. You've been pardoned. Someone assassinated President Brighton and the new president has granted you a pardon. Go! Governor Littman's got a limo waiting for you outside."

"Governor Littman?" Elijah's hair stood on end. "He made it?"

"I suppose so."

Elijah Slate followed the guard from his cell, through two locked doors, and into the foyer, where another guard handed him his wallet through a window in an office surrounded by thick glass.

"Did David Jameson get pardoned?"

Without emotion, the guard responded, "Too late, I'm afraid." He glanced at the radio on the counter beside him. "I just heard about it on the radio."

Elijah's heart dropped. He turned to shake the hand of the governor's limo driver, who was waiting for him in the foyer. The guard opened the door for them, and snickered when Elijah passed him. "You won."

"Won?" Elijah hesitated, halfway through the door, as he thought on those words. "You think we won?" He looked into that prison guard's eyes, and was distracted by a teardrop tattoo under his left eye. Behind that artificial bronze tan and that black-dyed hair with the gray roots beginning to show, Elijah saw a life filled with lust and addiction, consumed with his entertainment, apathetic about his children's freedom, and careless about his eternity. At that moment, Elijah's heart broke for that man.

Elijah put a palm on his shoulder and moved a couple of inches closer to him. "Sir, the war for our country is just getting started. Trust in Jesus and get on the right side of the battle line before it's too late for you."

Missoula, Montana

Darlene accompanied the emergency medical technicians in the ambulance on the way to the nearest hospital. At her tireless insistence, they continued chest compressions, administered epinephrine, oxygen, and re-started an IV. To them, this was more about them helping Darlene achieve closure and accept her husband's death. To Darlene, this was her stepping out of the boat and walking on the water.

"Don't stop! Please! He's going to make it. Please, Jesus." Her eyes were red and swollen from weeping, and her voice hoarse from fervent prayers.

"Stop compressions," the senior EMT ordered. All eyes were fastened to the monitor. A squiggly line flattened when they halted compressions. He took a deep breath. "I'm calling it."

"Calling it?" Darlene's tired eyes emanated fear.

He looked over at her. "Ma'am, there's no use pretending until we get to the hospital and let the physician inform you. He's gone."

"You're sure?"

"Positive. We can't work miracles, Mrs. Jameson."

She placed one hand over her gaped-open mouth, and with the other she reached forward and touched her husband's right hand. *Could this be a cross you want me to carry, Lord?* she prayed silently. *Must I lay my husband on the altar? Is that your will? If it is, you know I will accept it.*

"We admire your husband ma'am," the younger EMT added, pitying her as she brought her forehead to his cold hand, weeping. "I wish we could work miracles."

She took a deep breath. "I know someone who can."

"Excuse me?"

She knelt beside the gurney, bowing her body on top of her husband. "Oh God!" she cried out. "*You* are the one who can work miracles. There is nothing too difficult for you! You split the Red Sea, God, sent manna from heaven to feed your people, poured water out of the rock in the desert, and you established this Coalition." She opened her eyes and looked up to heaven. "The Scripture says that since you did not spare your Son from the death on the cross, how will you not freely give us all things? You said that if we ask anything – anything! – and believe that we will receive it, we will have it. You said that if we do those things that are pleasing in your sight, you would answer our prayers and give us our heart's desire. Oh God!" She bowed her head over David's motionless chest, weeping her tears onto his lifeless body. "Oh my Lord! Bring my husband back!" She put her palms on her husband's cold cheeks. "David! Please be the father of my babies – Charlotte and the child in my womb! Please, God!" She raised her fist and slammed it against his chest one more time.

She raised her fist to hit him in the chest again when one of the paramedics squealed, "Ah! Don't! He's opening his eyes!"

Suddenly, David Jameson sat up in the gurney, coughing.

"David!" Darlene threw her arms around her husband as he began to cough.

His coughing spasm eased and he exclaimed, "Oh Darlene!"

The two EMT personnel stood in awe as they watched the flat line on the monitor become a normal heart rhythm.

"David, I love you." She pulled away from him and looked into his eyes. "I love you so much."

"Oh, Darlene." He wept as he kissed her. "I love you." He looked into her wet eyes and patted her gently on her tummy. "Both of you."

Other books by Dr. Johnston:

Johnny and the Mystery of the Rusty Musket

Beating Grim

The Lesser Hills of Kinder County

The Revolt Trilogy Workbook

You can read Dr. Johnston's many booklets and articles on his websites:
www.RightRemedy.org
www.TheRevoltTrilogy.com
www.PersonhoodOhio.com
www.ProLifePhysicians.org

Printed in the USA